NEW CTHULHU:
THE RECENT WEIRD

OTHER BOOKS EDITED BY
PAULA GURAN

Embraces
Best New Paranormal Romance
Best New Romantic Fantasy
Zombies: The Recent Dead
The Year's Best Dark Fantasy & Horror: 2010
Vampires: The Recent Undead
The Year's Best Dark Fantasy & Horror: 2011
Halloween
Brave New Love

NEW CTHULHU:
THE RECENT WEIRD

Edited by Paula Guran

○
PRIME BOOKS

NEW CTHULHU: THE RECENT WEIRD

Prime Books
www.prime-books.com

For more information, contact Prime Books:
prime@prime-books.com

ISBN: 978-1-60701-289-4

Printed in Canada

3 2126 00120 430 9

For Ann Kennedy VanderMeer
Who inspired me to be an editor with The Silver Web *and kindness.*
Who still remains kind and inspiring
and who put the weird back in Weird Tales *fiction.*

• Contents •

· INTRODUCTION ·

I first encountered the works of H.P. Lovecraft around 1974 on a mantel in Oklahoma City. A friend had the six Ballantine paperbacks—the black ones with John Holmes's "face" covers—of three Lovecraft collections, the two *Tales of the Cthulhu Mythos* anthologies (with stories mostly by other writers), and *The Shuttered Room and Other Tales of Horror* (supposedly "posthumous collaborations" between Lovecraft and August Derleth, but actually authored solely by Derleth—not that I had any knowledge of such perfidy at the time). I don't recall any other books on that mantel—just those: centered and practically enshrined in a place of honor.

Those books were really *weird* books, man . . .

By the mid-1970s, Howard Phillips Lovecraft's small, dedicated band of loyal readers was beginning to grow much larger, but his influence on horror (and, to an extent, fantasy and science fiction) was already profound. As Peter Straub has noted: "His influence on other writers, which was immediate, has proved to be unending and fruitful." In *Danse Macabre*, Stephen King wrote that Lovecraft " . . . opened the way for me, as he had done for others before me . . . [T]he reader would do well to remember that it is his shadow . . . which underlies almost all of the important horror fiction that has come since."

Lovecraft's legacy also includes the essay "Supernatural Horror in Literature," which, in the opinion of many, still stands as one of the finest examinations of its subject. His thousands of letters (S.T. Joshi estimates HPL penned around 100,000) conveyed and further disseminated his ideas to myriad correspondents.

During his life, Lovecraft saw himself as a nonentity who did "not expect to become a serious competitor of my favorite weird authors." After his death he was, outside genre (and often within it), dismissed as nothing more than a pulp fictionist who wrote outdated florid prose. Now, after decades of scholarly devotion to gaining recognition for him as (to quote Joshi) "an unassailable literary figure," H.P. Lovecraft has not only gained respectability but entered the literary canon.

In 1997, *Tales of H.P. Lovecraft* (Ecco) offered a selection of Lovecraft's stories chosen and introduced by the impeccably literate Joyce Carol Oates. In 2005, McSweeney's published a translation of the indecipherably literate French cultural critic Michel Houellebecq's 1991 *H.P. Lovecraft: Against the*

World, Against Life. More importantly, 2005 saw the venerable Library of America indicate HPL's significance as an American author by publishing *H.P. Lovecraft: Tales*, a collection compiled by Peter Straub. A single volume of all of Lovecraft's fiction, *H.P. Lovecraft: The Fiction* became part of the Barnes & Noble Library of Essential Writers series in 2008.

Beyond literature, Lovecraft has been mainstreamed through film, television, music, graphic arts, comics, manga, gaming, manga, and theatre for years. Even if you've never read a word of H.P. Lovecraft's fiction, you have been introduced to his imagination without realizing its origin.

Who Was Howard Phillips Lovecraft?

Lovecraft was little known to the general public while alive and never saw a book of his work professionally published. Brilliant and eccentric, he was also decidedly odd.

Howard Phillips Lovecraft was born on August 20, 1890, the son of Windfield Scott Lovecraft and Sarah Susan Phillips Lovecraft in Providence, RI. Lovecraft's father, a victim of untreated syphilis, went mad before his son reached age three. The elder Lovecraft died in an insane asylum in 1898. It is doubtful Howard ever knew the true cause of his father's demise.

After his father's death, young Howard was raised by his mother; two of her sisters; and his maternal grandfather, Whipple Van Buren Phillips, a successful businessman. His mother was an over-protective and domineering parent. She spoiled and coddled her son, but was also highly critical of him. She told the quite normal-looking boy, for example, that he was so hideous he should not leave the house as he might scare the neighbors.

Sickly (probably due more to psychological factors more than physical ailments) and precocious, Lovecraft later claimed that, as a child, he was "very peculiar and sensitive, always preferring the society of grown persons to that of other children. I could not keep away from printed matter. I had learned the alphabet at two, and at four could read with ease . . . " He discovered *The Arabian Nights* and *Grimm's Fairy Tales*. A year or so later, HPL developed an intense interest in ancient Greece and Rome. He also discovered weird fiction at an early age as his grandfather often told tales in the gothic mode. Lovecraft began writing at age six or seven.

Lovecraft started school in 1889, but attended erratically due to ill health. After his grandfather's death in 1904, the family was financially challenged. Lovecraft and his mother moved to a far less comfortable domicile and the adolescent Howard no longer had access to his grandfather's extensive library. With private instruction an impossibility, HPL began attending a public high school where he became interested in Latin and continued writing. A physical and mental breakdown kept him from graduating (and, consequently, college). He became reclusive, rarely venturing out during the day. At night, he walked the streets of Providence, drinking in its atmosphere. He read, studied astronomy, and, in his early twenties, began writing poetry, essays, short stories, and eventually longer works. He also began reading Jules Verne, H.G. Wells and pulp magazines like *The Argosy*, *The Cavalier,* and *All-Story Magazine*.

Lovecraft was saved from his life of solitude when he became involved in amateur writing and publishing. As HPL himself wrote: "In 1914, when the kindly hand of amateurdom was first extended to me, I was as close to the state of vegetation as any animal well can be . . . "

His story, "The Alchemist" (written in 1908 when he was 18), was published in *United Amateur* in 1916. Stories appeared in other amateur publications like *Vagrant* and *Home Brew*.

Lovecraft's mother suffered a nervous breakdown in 1919 and was admitted to the same hospital in which her husband had died. Her death, in 1921, was the result of a bungled gall bladder operation.

"Dagon" was published in the October 1923 issue of *Weird Tales*, which became a regular market for his stories. He also began what became his prolific letter-writing with a continuously broadening group of correspondents.

Lovecraft met Sonia Haft Greene, a Russian Jew seven years his senior, shortly thereafter at a writers convention. They married in 1924. As *The Encyclopedia of Fantasy*, edited by John Clute and John Grant, puts it, " . . . the marriage lasted only until 1926, breaking up largely because HPL disliked sex; the fact that she was Jewish and he was prone to anti-Semitic rants cannot have helped." After two years of married life in New York City (which he abhorred and where he became even more intolerantly racist) he returned to his beloved Providence.

In the next decade, he traveled widely around the eastern seaboard, wrote what is considered to be his finest fiction, and continued his immense correspondence through which he nurtured young writers like August Derleth, Donald Wandrei, Robert Bloch, and Fritz Leiber. Outside of letters and essays, his complete works eventually totaled fifty-odd short stories, four short novels, about two dozen collaborations or ghost-written pieces, and countless poems.

Lovecraft never really managed to make a living. Most of his small livelihood came from re-writing or ghostwriting for others. He died, alone and broke, of intestinal cancer in 1937, and was buried at Swan Point Cemetery in Providence.

Forty years later, a stone was erected to mark the spot by his admirers. It reads: "I am Providence."

His friends August Derleth and Donald Wandrei founded Arkham House expressly to publish Lovecraft's work and to bring it to the attention of the public They issued *The Outsider and Others* in 1939 and followed with many other volumes. Eventually Lovecraft's work was translated into a dozen languages and is now, of course, widely available in many editions .

What is "Lovecraftian"?

There's a great deal of scholarly debate on the question, but I'll provide some generalities.

S.T. Joshi, in *The Rise and Fall of the Cthulhu Mythos*, identified four broad components of what he terms the "Lovecraft Mythos":

• *A fictional New England topography.* (This eventually became a richly complex, historically grounded—if fictional—region.)

• *A growing library of "forbidden" books.* (Rare tomes holding secrets too dangerous to know.)

• *A diverse array of extraterrestrial "gods" or entities.* (Often symbols of the "unknowability or an infinite cosmos, or sometimes the inexorable forces of chaos and entropy.")

• *A sense of cosmicism.* (The universe is indifferent, chaotic, and humans are utterly meaningless nonentities within it.)

A fifth element—a scholarly protagonist or narrator—is not unique to Lovecraft, but is another identifiable motif.

Even though not all of Lovecraft's work falls within these boundaries, his best fiction usually differed from earlier supernatural fiction. In his introduction to *At the Mountains of Madness: The Definitive Edition*, China Miéville points out: "Traditionally genre horror is concerned with the irruption of dreadful forces into a comforting status quo—one which the protagonist scrambles to preserve. By contrast, Lovecraft's horror is not one of intrusion but of realization. The world has always been implacably bleak; the horror lies in us acknowledging the fact."

"Lovecraft's stories were noticeably devoid of vampires, werewolves, ghosts, and other traditional supernatural monsters appearing in the work of his pulp contemporaries," noted Stefan Dziemianowicz in a *Publishers Weekly* article. "Though written in a somewhat mannered gothic style and prose empurpled with words like 'eldritch' and 'squamous,' his atmospheric tales strove to express a horror rooted in humanity's limited understanding of the universe and humankind's arrogant overconfidence in its significance in the cosmic scheme."

The story "The Call of Cthulhu" (1928) is probably the best example Lovecraft's idea of "cosmicism." Cthulhu is a monstrous entity so alien and incomprehensible even his name can not be pronounced by human tongues. A priest of "the Great Old Ones who lived ages before there were any men, and who came to the young world out of the sky" and who are gone but still reside "inside the earth and under the sea . . . their dead bodies had told their secrets in dreams to the first men, who formed a cult which had never died." This cult "had always existed and always would exist, hidden in distant wastes and dark places all over the world until the time when the great priest Cthulhu, from his dark house in the mighty city of R'lyeh under the waters, should rise and bring the earth again beneath his sway. Some day he would call, when the stars were ready, and the secret cult would always be waiting to liberate him."

As Lovecraft himself wrote, such stories conveyed "the fundamental premise that common human laws and interests and emotions have no validity or significance in the cosmos-at-large."

Other writers of the era, with Lovecraft's blessing, began superficially referencing his dabblers in the arcane, mentioning his unhallowed imaginary New England towns and their strange citizens, alluding to cosmic horror, mentioning his godlike ancient extraterrestrials with strange names, and citing his fictional forbidden books of the occult (primarily the *Necronomicon* of the mad Arab Abdul Alhazred): the Cthulhu Mythos—or, rather, anti-mythology—was born.

Lovecraft never used the term "Cthulhu Mythos" himself. It was probably invented by August Derleth or Clark Ashton Smith after HPL's death. They and others also added their own flourishes and inventions to the mythology, sometimes muddling things with non-Lovecraftian concepts. Authors like Robert Bloch (now best known as the author of *Psycho*), Robert E. Howard (creator of Conan the Barbarian), Clark Ashton Smith, August Derleth, and younger writers such as Henry Kuttner, Fritz Leiber, and Ramsey Campbell all romped within the Lovecraftian milieu and added elements to it. Later writers with no direct connection to HPL joined in as well.

Of the hundreds of stories written since 1937 in Lovecraft's style, or based on his bleak cosmicism, or alien entities, or occult books, or any of the signifiers of a "Lovecraftian" tale—whether based on true elements conceived by HPL or the sometimes spurious inventions of others—many were derivative, formulaic, or simply ineffective. Some simply haven't stood up well over the years. Others have become classics. But this anthology is not about fiction written in H.P. Lovecraft's day or even in the twentieth century.

• • •

The New Lovecraftians

When considering the theme of this anthology, I chose to use only stories published in the twenty-first century. This was by design, but it also turned out to be a delight as these stories are only *some* of the recent best.

Increasing awareness and popularity of H.P. Lovecraft's writing and the skills and imaginations of current writers have combined for an ever-increasing pool of top-notch fiction. Recent anthologies of original Lovecraft-inspired stories—most notably *Weird Shadows Over Innsmouth*, edited by Stephen Jones (Fedogan & Bremer, 2005); *Lovecraft Unbound*, edited by Ellen Datlow (Dark Horse, 2009); and *Black Wings: New Tales of Lovecraftian Horror*, edited by S.T. Joshi (PS Publishing, 2010)—single author collections, and other sources provide an editor (and readers) with a wealth to choose from.

Most of the authors represented here were "New Lovecraftians" before the advent of this century but, overall, what they have in common is that they write with a fresh appreciation of Lovecraft's universe. They do not imitate; they re-imagine, re-energize, renew, re-set, and make Lovecraftian concepts relevant for today. After all, in this era of great unrest, continual change, constant conflict, and increasing vulnerability to natural disasters, it is not hard to believe that the universe doesn't give a damn and we are doomed, doomed, doomed.

Sometimes, the New Lovecraftians simply have fun with what are now well-established genre themes. More often they take Lovecraft's view of fragile humans alone in a vast uncaring cosmos where neither a good god nor an evil devil exist, let alone are concerned with them, and devise stunningly effective fiction.

If the strange gentleman from Providence were to appear among us today, he would, no doubt, disapprove of some of the stories his ideas have inspired. We'd certainly not accept his racism, sexism, classism, and bigotry. But literature is an ongoing conversation and one hopes HPL would join in.

Paula Guran

[Note: The excerpts at the beginning each story are simply my way of introducing them. The symbol found on the title page and at the end of each story is an "Elder Sign," a symbol Lovecraft drew in a 1930 letter to Clark Ashton Smith. Apparently, if you are protected by an Elder Sign, the Deep Ones cannot harm you.]

Well—that paper wasn't a photograph of any background, after all. What it shewed was simply the monstrous being he was painting on that awful canvas. It was the model he was using—and its background was merely the wall of the cellar studio in minute detail. But by God, Eliot, it was a photograph from life.

"Pickman's Model" · H.P. Lovecraft (1927)

• PICKMAN'S OTHER MODEL (1929) •
Caitlín R. Kiernan

1.

I have never been much for the movies, preferring, instead, to take my entertainment in the theater, always favoring living actors over those flickering, garish ghosts magnified and splashed across the walls of dark and smoky rooms at twenty-four frames per second. I've never seemed able to get past the knowledge that the apparent motion is merely an optical illusion, a clever procession of still images streaming past my eye at such a rate of speed that I only perceive motion where none actually exists. But in the months before I finally met Vera Endecott, I found myself drawn with increasing regularity to the Boston movie houses, despite this longstanding reservation.

I had been shocked to my core by Thurber's suicide, though, with the unavailing curse of hindsight, it's something I should certainly have had the presence of mind to have seen coming. Thurber was an infantryman during the war—*La Guerre por la Civilisation*, as he so often called it. He was at the Battle of Saint-Mihiel when Pershing failed in his campaign to seize Metz from the Germans, and he survived only to see the atrocities at the Battle of the Argonne Forest less than two weeks later. When he returned home from France early in 1819, Thurber was hardly more than a fading, nervous echo of the man I'd first met during our college years at the Rhode Island School of Design, and, on those increasingly rare occasions when we met and spoke, more often than not our conversations turned from painting and sculpture and matters of aesthetics to the things he'd seen in the muddy trenches and ruined cities of Europe.

And then there was his dogged fascination with that sick bastard Richard Upton Pickman, an obsession that would lead quickly to what I took to be no less than a sort of psychoneurotic fixation on the man and the blasphemies he committed to canvas. When, two years ago, Pickman vanished from the squalor of his North End "studio," never to be seen again, this fixation only worsened, until Thurber finally came to me with an incredible, nightmarish tale which, at the time, I could only dismiss as the ravings of a mind left unhinged by the bloodshed and madness and countless wartime horrors he'd witnessed along the banks of the Meuse River and then in the wilds of the Argonne Forest.

But I am not the man I was then, that evening we sat together in a dingy tavern near Faneuil Hall (I don't recall the name of the place, as it wasn't one of my usual haunts). Even as William Thurber was changed by the war and by whatever it is he may have experienced in the company of Pickman, so too have I been changed, and changed *utterly*, first by Thurber's sudden death at his own hands and then by a film actress named Vera Endecott. I do not believe that I have yet lost possession of my mental faculties, and if asked, I would attest before a judge of law that my mind remains sound, if quite shaken. But I cannot now see the world around me the way I once did, for having beheld certain things there can be no return to the unprofaned state of innocence or grace that prevailed before those sights. There can be no return to the sacred cradle of Eden, for the gates are guarded by the flaming swords of cherubim, and the mind may not—excepting in merciful cases of shock and hysterical amnesia—simply forget the weird and dismaying revelations visited upon men and women who choose to ask forbidden questions. And I would be lying if I were to claim that I failed to comprehend, to suspect, that the path I was setting myself upon when I began my investigations following Thurber's inquest and funeral would lead me where they have. I knew, or I knew well enough. I am not yet so degraded that I am beyond taking responsibility for my own actions and the consequences of those actions.

Thurber and I used to argue about the validity of first-person narration as an effective literary device, him defending it and me calling into question the believability of such stories, doubting both the motivation of their fictional authors and the ability of those character narrators to accurately recall with such perfect clarity and detail specific conversations and the order of events during times of great stress and even personal danger. This is probably not so very different from my difficulty appreciating a moving picture because I am aware it is *not*, in fact, a moving picture. I suspect it points to some conscious unwillingness or unconscious inability, on my part, to effect what Coleridge dubbed the "suspension of disbelief." And now I sit down to write my *own* account, though I attest there is not a word of *intentional* fiction to it, and I certainly have no plans of ever seeking its publication. Nonetheless, it will undoubtedly be filled with inaccuracies following from the objections to a first-person recital that I have already belabored above. What I am putting down here is my best attempt to recall the events preceding and surrounding the murder of Vera Endecott, and it should be read as such.

It is my story, presented with such meager corroborative documentation as I am here able to provide. It is some small part of her story, as well, and over it hang the phantoms of Pickman and Thurber. In all honesty, already I begin to doubt that setting any of it down will achieve the remedy which I so desperately desire—the dampening of damnable memory, the lessening of the hold that those memories have upon me, and, if I am most lucky, the ability to sleep in dark rooms once again and an end to any number of phobias which have come to plague me. Too late do I understand poor Thurber's morbid fear of cellars and subway tunnels, and to that I can add my own fears, whether they might ever be proven rational or not. "I guess you won't wonder now why I have to steer clear of subways and cellars," he said to me that day in the tavern. I *did* wonder, of course, at that and at the sanity of a dear and trusted friend. But, in this matter, at least, I have long since ceased to wonder.

The first time I saw Vera Endecott on the "big screen," it was only a supporting part in Josef von Sternberg's *A Woman of the Sea*, at the Exeter Street Theater. But that was not the first time I saw Vera Endecott.

2.

I first encountered the name and face of the actress while sorting through William's papers, which I'd been asked to do by the only surviving member of his immediate family, Ellen Thurber, an older sister. I found myself faced with no small or simple task, as the close, rather shabby room he'd taken on Hope Street in Providence after leaving Boston was littered with a veritable bedlam of correspondence, typescripts, journals, and unfinished compositions, including the monograph on weird art that had played such a considerable role in his taking up with Richard Pickman three years prior. I was only mildly surprised to discover, in the midst of this disarray, a number of Pickman's sketches, all of them either charcoal or pen and ink. Their presence among Thurber's effects seemed rather incongruous, given how completely terrified of the man he'd professed to having become. And even more so given his claim to have destroyed the one piece of evidence that could support the incredible tale of what he purported to have heard and seen and taken away from Pickman's cellar studio.

It was a hot day, so late into July that it was very nearly August. When I came across the sketches, seven of them tucked inside a cardboard portfolio case, I carried them across the room and spread the lot out upon the narrow, swaybacked bed occupying one corner. I had a decent enough familiarity with the man's work, and I must confess that what I'd seen of it had never struck me quiet so profoundly as it had Thurber. Yes, to be sure, Pickman was possessed of a great and singular talent, and I suppose someone unaccustomed to images of the diabolic, the alien or monstrous, would find them disturbing and unpleasant to look upon. I always credited his success at capturing the weird largely to his intentional juxtaposition of phantasmagoric subject matter with a starkly, painstakingly realistic style. Thurber also noted this, and, indeed, had devoted almost a full chapter of his unfinished monograph to an examination of Pickman's technique.

I sat down on the bed to study the sketches, and the mattress springs complained loudly beneath my weight, leading me to wonder yet again why my friend had taken such mean accommodations when he certainly could have afforded better. At any rate, glancing over the drawings, they struck me, for the most part, as nothing particularly remarkable, and I assumed that they must have been gifts from Pickman, or that Thurber might even have paid him some small sum for them. Two I recognized as studies for one of the paintings mentioned that day in the Chatham Street tavern, the one titled *The Lesson*, in which the artist had sought to depict a number of his subhuman, doglike ghouls instructing a young child (a *changeling*, Thurber had supposed) in their practice of necrophagy. Another was a rather hasty sketch of what I took to be some of the statelier monuments in Copp's Hill Burying Ground, and there were also a couple of rather slapdash renderings of hunched gargoyle-like creatures.

But it was the last two pieces from the folio that caught and held my attention. Both were very accomplished nudes, more finished than any of the other sketches, and given the subject matter, I might have doubted they had come from Pickman's hand had it not been for his signature at the bottom of each. There was nothing that could have been deemed pornographic about either, and considering their provenance, this surprised me, as well. Of the portion of Richard Pickman's *oeuvre* that I'd seen for myself, I'd not once found any testament to an interest in the female form, and there had even been whispers in the Art Club that he was a homosexual. But there were so many rumors traded about the man in the days leading up to his disappearance, many of them plainly spurious, that I'd never given the subject much thought. Regardless of his own sexual inclinations, these two studies were imbued with an appreciation and familiarity with a woman's body that seemed unlikely to have been gleaned entirely from academic exercises or mooched from the work of other, less-eccentric artists.

As I inspected the nudes, thinking that these two pieces, at least, might bring a few dollars to help Thurber's sister cover the unexpected expenses incurred by her brother's death, as well as his outstanding debts, my eyes were drawn to a bundle of magazine and newspaper clippings that had also been stored inside the portfolio. There were a goodly number of them, and I guessed then, and still suppose, that Thurber had employed a clipping bureau. About half of them were write-ups of gallery showings that had included Pickman's work, mostly spanning the years from 1921 to 1925, before he'd been so ostracized that opportunities for public showings had dried up. But the remainder appeared to have been culled largely from tabloids, sheetlets, and magazines such as *Photoplay* and the *New York Evening Graphic*, and every one of the articles was either devoted to or made mention of a Massachusetts-born actress named Vera Marie Endecott. There were, among these clippings, a number of photographs of the woman, and her likeness to the woman who'd modeled for the two Pickman nudes was unmistakable.

There was something quite distinct about her high cheekbones, the angle of her nose, an undeniable hardness to her countenance despite her starlet's beauty and "sex appeal." Later, I would come to recognize some commonality between her face and those of such movie "vamps" and *femme fatales* as Theda Bara, Eva Galli, Musidora, and, in particular, Pola Negri. But, as best as I can now recollect, my first impression of Vera Endecott, untainted by film personae (though undoubtedly colored by the association of the clippings with the work of Richard Pickman, there among the belongings of a suicide) was of a woman whose loveliness might merely be a glamour concealing some truer, feral face. It was an admittedly odd impression, and I sat in the sweltering boarding-house room, as the sun slid slowly towards dusk, reading each of the articles, and then reading some over again. I suspected they must surely contain, somewhere, evidence that the woman in the sketches was, indeed, the same woman who'd gotten her start in the movie studios of Long Island and New Jersey, before the industry moved west to California.

For the most part, the clippings were no more than the usual sort of picture-show gossip, innuendo, and sensationalism. But, here and there, someone, presumably Thurber himself, had underlined various passages with a red pencil, and when those lines were considered together, removed from the context of their accompanying articles, a curious pattern could be discerned. At least, such a pattern might be imagined by a reader who was either *searching* for it, and so predisposed to discovering it whether it truly existed or not, or by someone, like myself, coming to these collected scraps of yellow journalism under such circumstances and such an atmosphere of dread as may urge the reader to draw parallels where, objectively, there are none to be found. I believed, that summer afternoon, that Thurber's *idée fixe* with Richard Pickman had led him to piece together an absurdly macabre set of notions regarding this woman, and that I, still grieving the loss of a close friend and surrounded as I was by the disorder of that friend's unfulfilled life's work, had done nothing but uncover another of Thurber's delusions.

The woman known to moviegoers as Vera Endecott had been sired into an admittedly peculiar family from the North Shore region of Massachusetts, and she'd undoubtedly taken steps to hide her heritage, adopting a stage name shortly after her arrival in Fort Lee in February of 1922. She'd also invented a new history for herself, claiming to hail not from rural Essex County, but from Boston's Beacon Hill. However, as early as '24, shortly after landing her first substantial role—an appearance in Biograph Studios' *Sky Below the Lake*—a number of popular columnists had begun printing their suspicions about her professed background. The banker she'd claimed as her father could not be found, and it proved a straightforward enough matter to demonstrate that she'd never attended the Winsor School for girls. By '25, after starring in Robert G. Vignola's *The Horse Winter*, a reporter for *The New York Evening Graphic* claimed Endecott's actual father was a man named Iscariot Howard Snow, the owner of several Cape Anne granite quarries. His wife, Make-peace, had come either from Salem or Marblehead, and had died in 1902 while giving birth to their only daughter, whose name was not Vera, but Lillian Margaret. There was no evidence in any of the clippings that the actress had ever denied or even responded to any of these allegations, despite the fact that the Snows, and Iscariot Snow, in particular, had a distinctly unsavory reputation in and around Ipswich. Despite the family's wealth and prominence in local business, it was notoriously secretive, and there was no want for back-fence talk concerning sorcery and witchcraft, incest and even cannibalism. In 1899, Make-peace Snow had also borne twin sons, Aldous and Edward, though Edward had been a stillbirth.

But it was a clipping from *Kidder's Weekly Art News* (March 27th, 1925), a publication I was well enough acquainted with, that first tied the actress to Richard Pickman. A "Miss Vera Endecott of Manhattan" was listed among those in attendance at the premiere of an exhibition that had included a couple of Pickman's less provocative paintings, though no mention was made of her celebrity. Thurber had circled her name with his red pencil and drawn two exclamation points beside it. By the time I came across the article, twilight had descended upon Hope Street, and I was having trouble reading. I briefly considered the old gas lamp near the bed, but then, staring into the shadows gathering amongst the clutter and threadbare furniture of the seedy little room, I was gripped by a sudden, vague apprehension—by what, even now, I am reluctant to name *fear*. I returned the clippings and the seven sketches to the folio, tucked it under my arm and quickly retrieved my hat from a table buried beneath a typewriter, an assortment of paper and library books, unwashed dishes and empty soda bottles. A few minutes later, I was outside again and clear of the building, standing beneath a streetlight, staring up at the two darkened windows opening into the room where, a week before, William Thurber had put the barrel of a revolver in his mouth and pulled the trigger.

3.

I have just awakened from another of my nightmares, which become ever more vivid and frequent, ever more appalling, often permitting me no more than one or two hours sleep each night. I'm sitting at my writing desk, watching as the sky begins to go the gray-violet of false dawn, listening to the clock ticking like some giant wind-up insect perched upon the mantle. But my mind is still lodged firmly in a dream of the musty private screening room near Harvard Square, operated by a small circle of aficionados of grotesque cinema, the room where first I saw "moving" images of the daughter of Iscariot Snow.

I'd learned of the group from an acquaintance in acquisitions at the Museum of Fine Arts, who'd told me it met irregularly, rarely more than once every three months, to view and discuss such fanciful and morbid fare as Benjamin Christensen's *Häxen*, Rupert Julian's *The Phantom of the Opera*, Murnau's *Nosferatu—Eine Symphonie des Grauens*, and Todd Browning's *London After Midnight*. These titles and the names of their directors meant very little to me, since, as I have already noted, I've never been much for the movies. This was in August, only a couple of weeks after I'd returned to Boston from Providence, having set Thurber's affairs in order as best I could. I still prefer not to consider what unfortunate caprice of fate aligned my discovery of Pickman's sketches of Vera Endecott and Thurber's interest in her with the group's screening of what, in my opinion, was a profane and a deservedly unheard-of film. Made sometime in 1923 or '24, I was informed that it had achieved infamy following the director's death (another suicide). All the film's financiers remained unknown, and it seemed that production had never proceeded beyond the incomplete rough cut I saw that night.

However, I did not sit down here to write out a dry account of my discovery of this untitled, unfinished film, but rather to try and capture something of the dream that is already breaking into hazy scraps and shreds. Like Perseus, who dared to view the face of the Gorgon Medusa only indirectly, as a reflection in his bronze shield, so I seem bound and determined to reflect upon these events, and even my own nightmares, as obliquely as I may. I have always despised cowardice, and yet, looking back over these pages, there seems in it something undeniably cowardly. It does not matter that I intend that no one else shall ever read this. Unless I write honestly, there is hardly any reason in writing it at all. If this is a ghost story (and, increasingly, it feels that way to me), then let it *be* a ghost story, and not this rambling reminiscence. In the dream, I am sitting in a wooden folding chair in that dark room, lit only by the single shaft of light spilling forth from the projectionist's booth. And the wall in front of me has become a window, looking out upon or into another world, one devoid of sound and almost all color, its palette limited to a spectrum of somber blacks and dazzling whites and innumerable shades of gray. Around me, the others who have come to see smoke their cigars and cigarettes, and they mutter among themselves. I cannot make out anything they say, but, then, I'm not trying particularly hard. I cannot look away from that that silent, grisaille scene, and little else truly occupies my mind.

"Now, do you understand?" Thurber asks from his seat next to mine, and maybe I nod, and maybe I even whisper some hushed affirmation or another. But I do *not* take my eyes from the screen long enough to glimpse his face. There is too much there I might miss, were I to dare look away, even for an instant, and, moreover, I have no desire to gaze upon the face of a dead man. Thurber says nothing else for a time, apparently content that I have found my way to this place, to witness for myself some fraction of what drove him, at last, to the very end of madness.

She is there on the screen—Vera Endecott, Lillian Margaret Snow—standing at the edge of a rocky pool. She is as naked as in Pickman's sketches of her, and is positioned, at first, with her back to the camera. The gnarled roots and branches of what might be ancient willow trees bend low over the pool, their whip-like branches brushing the surface and moving gracefully too and fro, disturbed by the same breeze that ruffles the actress' short, bob-cut hair. And though there appears to be nothing the least bit sinister about this scene, it at once inspires in me the same sort of awe and uneasiness as Doré's engravings for *Orlando Furioso* and the *Divine Comedy*. There is about the tableau a sense of intense foreboding and anticipation, and I wonder what subtle, clever cues have been placed just so that this seemingly idyllic view would be interpreted with such grim expectancy.

And then I realize that the actress is holding in her right hand some manner of phial, and she tilts it just enough that the contents, a thick and pitchy liquid, drips into the pool. Concentric ripples spread slowly across the water, much *too* slowly, I'm convinced, to have followed from any earthly physics, and so I dismiss it as merely trick photography. When the phial is empty, or has, at least, ceased to taint the pool (and I am quite sure that it *has* been tainted), the woman kneels in the mud and weeds at the water's edge. From somewhere overhead, there in the room with me, comes a sound like the wings of startled pigeons taking flight, and the actress half turns towards the audience, as if she has also somehow heard the commotion. The fluttering racket quickly subsides, and once more there is only the mechanical noise from the projector and the whispering of the men and women crowded into the musty room. Onscreen, the actress turns back to the pool, but not before I am certain that her face is the same one from the clippings I found in Thurber's room, the same one sketched by the hand of Richard Upton Pickman. The phial slips from her fingers, falling into the water, and this time there are no ripples whatsoever. No splash. Nothing.

Here, the image flickers before the screen goes blinding white, and I think, for a moment, that the filmstrip has, mercifully, jumped one sprocket or another, so maybe I'll not have to see the rest. But then she's back, the woman and the pool and the willows, playing out frame by frame by frame. She kneels at the edge of the pool, and I think of Narcissus pining for Echo or his lost twin, of jealous Circe poisoning the spring where Scylla bathed, and of Tennyson's cursed Shalott, and, too, again I think of Perseus and Medusa. I am not seeing the thing itself, but only some dim, misguiding counterpart, and my mind grasps for analogies and signification and points of reference.

On the screen, Vera Endecott, or Lillian Margaret Snow—one or the other, the two who were always only one—leans forward and dips her hand into the pool. And again, there are no ripples to mar its smooth obsidian surface. The woman in the film is speaking now, her lips moving deliberately, making no sound whatsoever, and I can hear nothing but the mumbling, smoky room and the sputtering projector. And this is when I realize that the willows are not precisely willows at all, but that those twisted trunks and limbs and roots are actually the entwined human bodies of both sexes, their skin perfectly mimicking the scaly bark of a willow. I understand that these are no wood nymphs, no daughters of Hamadryas and Oxylus. These are prisoners, or condemned souls bound eternally for their sins, and for a time I can only stare in wonder at the confusion of arms and legs, hips and breasts and faces marked by untold ages of the ceaseless agony of this contortion and transformation. I want to turn and ask the others if they see what I see, and how the deception has been accomplished, for surely these people know more of the prosaic magic of filmmaking that do I. Worst of all, the bodies have not been rendered entirely inert, but writhe ever so slightly, helping the wind to stir the long, leafy branches first this way, then that.

Then my eye is drawn back to the pool, which has begun to steam, a gray-white mist rising languidly from off the water (if it *is* still water). The actress leans yet farther out over the strangely quiescent mere, and I find myself eager to look away. Whatever being the cameraman has caught her in the act of summoning or appeasing, I do not want to *see*, do not want to *know* it's daemonic physiognomy. Her lips continue to move, and her hands stir the waters that remain smooth as glass, betraying no evidence that they have been disturbed in any way.

> At Rhegium she arrives; the ocean braves,
> And treads with unwet feet the boiling waves . . .

But desire is not enough, nor trepidation, and I do *not* look away, either because I have been bewitched along with all those others who have come to see her, or because some deeper, more disquisitive facet of my being has taken command and is willing to risk damnation in the seeking into this mystery.

"It is only a moving picture," dead Thurber reminds me from his seat beside mine. "Whatever else she would say, you must never forget it is only a dream."

And I want to reply, "Is that what happened to you, dear William? Did you forget it was never anything more than a dream and find yourself unable to waken to lucidity and life?" But I do not say a word, and Thurber does not say anything more.

> But yet she knows not, who it is she fears;
> In vain she offers from herself to run,
> And drags about her what she strives to shun.

"Brilliant," whispers a woman in the darkness at my back, and "Sublime," mumbles what sounds to be a very old man. My eyes do not stray from the screen. The actress has stopped stirring the pool, has withdrawn her hand from the water, but still she kneels there, staring at the sooty stain it has left on her fingers and palm and wrist. *Maybe,* I think, *that is what she came for, that mark, that she will be known,* though my dreaming mind does not presume to guess what or whom she would have recognize her by such a bruise or blotch. She reaches into the reeds and moss and produces a black-handled dagger, which she then holds high above her head, as though making an offering to unseen gods, before she uses the glinting blade to slice open the hand she previously offered to the waters. And I think perhaps I understand, finally, and the phial and the stirring of the pool were only some preparatory wizardry before presenting this far more precious alms or expiation. As her blood drips to spatter and *roll* across the surface of the pool like drops of mercury striking a solid tabletop, something has begun to take shape, assembling itself from those concealed depths, and, even without sound, it is plain enough that the willows have begun to scream and to sway as though in the grip of a hurricane wind. I think, perhaps, it is a mouth, of sorts, coalescing before the prostrate form of Vera Endecott or Lillian Margaret Snow, a mouth or a vagina or a blind and lidless eye, or some organ that may serve as all three. I debate each of these possibilities, in turn.

Five minutes ago, almost, I lay my pen aside, and I have just finished reading back over, aloud, what I have written, as false dawn gave way to sunrise and the first uncomforting light of a new October day. But before I return these pages to the folio containing Pickman's sketches and Thurber's clippings and go on about the business that the morning demands of me, I would confess that what I have dreamed and what I have recorded here are not what I saw that afternoon in the screening room near Harvard Square. Neither is it entirely the nightmare that woke me and sent me stumbling to my desk. Too much of the dream deserted me, even as I rushed to get it all down, and the dreams are never exactly, and sometimes not even remotely, what I saw projected on that wall, that deceiving stream of still images conspiring to suggest animation. This is another point I always tried to make with Thurber, and which he never would accept, the fact of the inevitability of unreliable narrators. I have not lied; I would not say that. But none of this is any nearer to the truth than any other fairy tale.

4.

After the days I spent in the boarding house in Providence, trying to bring some semblance of order to the chaos of Thurber's interrupted life, I began accumulating my own files on Vera Endecott, spending several days in August drawing upon the holdings of the Boston Athenaeum, Public Library, and the Widener Library at Harvard. It was not difficult to piece together the story of the actress' rise to stardom and the scandal that led to her descent into obscurity and alcoholism late in 1927, not so very long before Thurber came to me with his wild tale of Pickman and subterranean ghouls. What was much more difficult to trace was her movement through certain theosophical and occult societies, from Manhattan to Los Angeles, circles to which Richard Upton Pickman was, himself, no stranger.

In January '27', after being placed under contract to Paramount Pictures the previous spring, and during production of a film adaptation of Margaret Kennedy's novel, *The Constant Nymph*, rumors began surfacing in the tabloids that Vera Endecott was drinking heavily and, possibly, using heroin. However, these allegations appear at first to have caused her no more alarm or damage to her film career than the earlier discovery that she was, in fact, Lillian Snow, or the public airing of her disreputable North Shore roots. Then, on May 3rd, she was arrested in what was, at first, reported as merely a raid on a speakeasy somewhere along Durand Drive, at an address in the steep, scrubby canyons above Los Angeles, nor far from the Lake Hollywood Reservoir and Mulholland Highway. A few days later, after Endecott's release on bail, queerer accounts of the events of that night began to surface, and by the 7th, articles in the *Van Nuys Call*, *Los Angeles Times*, and the *Herald-Express* were describing the gathering on Durand Drive not as a speakeasy, but as everything from a "witches' Sabbat" to "a decadent, sacrilegious, orgiastic rite of witchcraft and homosexuality."

But the final, damning development came when reporters discovered that one of the many women found that night in the company of Vera Endecott, a Mexican prostitute named Ariadna Delgado, had been taken immediately to Queen of Angels-Hollywood Presbyterian, comatose and suffering from multiple stab wounds to her torso, breasts, and face. Delgado died on the morning of May 4th, without ever having regained consciousness. A second "victim" or "participant" (depending on the newspaper), a young and unsuccessful screenwriter listed only as Joseph E. Chapman, was placed in the psychopathic ward of LA County General Hospital following the arrests.

Though there appear to have been attempts to keep the incident quiet by both studio lawyers and also, perhaps, members of the Los Angeles Police Department, Endecott was arrested a second time on May 10th, and charged with multiple counts of rape, sodomy, second-degree murder, kidnapping, and solicitation. Accounts of the specific charges brought vary from one source to another, but regardless, Endecott was granted and made bail a second time on May 11th, and four days later, the office of Los Angeles District Attorney Asa Keyes abruptly and rather inexplicably asked for a dismissal of all charges against the actress, a motion granted in an equally inexplicable move by the

Superior Court of California, Los Angeles County (it bears mentioning, of course, that District Attorney Keyes was, himself, soon thereafter indicted for conspiracy to receive bribes, and is presently awaiting trial). So, eight days after her initial arrest at the residence on Durand Drive, Vera Endecott was a free woman, and, by late May, she had returned to Manhattan, after her contract with Paramount was terminated.

Scattered throughout the newspaper and tabloid coverage of the affair are numerous details which take on a greater significance in light of her connection with Richard Pickman. For one, some reporters made mention of "an obscene idol" and "a repellent statuette carved from something like greenish soapstone" recovered from the crime scene, a statue which one of the arresting officer's is purported to have described as a "crouching, dog-like beast." One article listed the item as having been examined by a local (unnamed) archeologist, who was supposedly baffled at it origins and cultural affinities. The house on Durand Drive was, and may still be, owned by a man named Beauchamp who'd spent time in the company of Aleister Crowley during his four-year visit to America (1914-1918), and who had connections with a number of hermetic and theurgical organizations. And finally, the screenwriter Joseph Chapman drowned himself in the Pacific somewhere near Malibu only a few months ago, shortly after being discharged from the hospital. The one short article I could locate regarding his death made mention of his part in the "notorious Durand Drive incident" and printed a short passage reputed to have come from the suicide note. It reads, in part, as follows:

Oh God, how does a man forget, deliberately and wholly and forever, once he has glimpsed such sights as I have had the misfortune to have seen? The awful things we did and permitted to be done that night, the events we set in motion, how do I lay my culpability aside? Truthfully, I cannot and am no longer able to fight through day after day of trying. The Endecotte [sic] woman is back East somewhere, I hear, and I hope to hell she gets what's coming to her. I burned the abominable painting she gave me, but I feel no cleaner, no less foul, for having done so. There is nothing left of me but the putrescence we invited. I cannot do this anymore.

Am I correct in surmising, then, that Vera Endecott made a gift of one of Pickman's paintings to the unfortunate Joseph Chapman, and that it played some role in his madness and death? If so, how many others received such gifts from her, and how many of those canvases yet survive so many thousands of miles from the dank cellar studio near Battery Street where Pickman created them? It's not something I like to dwell upon.

After Endecott's reported return to Manhattan, I failed to find any printed record of her whereabouts or doings until October of that year, shortly after Pickman's disappearance and my meeting with Thurber in the tavern near Faneuil Hall. It's only a passing mention from a society column in the *New York Herald Tribune*, that "the actress Vera Endecott" was among those in attendance at the unveiling of a new display of Sumerian, Hittite, and Babylonian antiquities at the Metropolitan Museum of Art.

What is it I am trying to accomplish with this catalog of dates and death and misfortune, calamity and crime? Among Thurber's books, I found a copy of Charles Hoyt Fort's *The Book of the Damned* (Boni and Liveright; New York, December 1, 1919). I'm not even sure why I took it away with me, and having read it, I find the man's writings almost hysterically belligerent and constantly prone to intentional obfuscation and misdirection. Oh, and wouldn't that contentious bastard love to have a go at this tryst with "the damned"? My point here is that I'm forced to admit that these last few pages bear a marked and annoying similarity to much of Fort's first book (I have not read his second, *New Lands*, nor do I propose ever to do so). Fort wrote of his intention to present a collection of data which had been excluded by science (*id est*, "damned"):

Battalions of the accursed, captained by pallid data that I have exhumed, will march. You'll read them—or they'll march. Some of them livid and some of them fiery and some of them rotten.

Some of them are corpses, skeletons, mummies, twitching, tottering, animated by companions that have been damned alive. There are giants that will walk by, though sound asleep. There are things that are theorems and things that are rags: they'll go by like Euclid arm in arm with the spirit of anarchy. Here and there will flit little harlots. Many are clowns. But many are of the highest respectability. Some are assassins. There are pale stenches and gaunt superstitions and mere shadows and lively malices: whims and amiabilities. The naïve and the pedantic and the bizarre and the grotesque and the sincere and the insincere, the profound and the puerile.

And I think I have accomplished nothing more *than* this, in my recounting of Endecott's rise and fall, drawing attention to some of the more melodramatic and vulgar parts of a story that is, in the main, hardly more remarkable than numerous other Hollywood scandals. But also, Fort would laugh at my own "pallid data," I am sure, my pathetic grasping at straws, as though I might make this all seem perfectly reasonable by selectively quoting newspapers and police reports, straining to preserve the fraying infrastructure of my rational mind. It's time to lay these dubious, slipshod attempts at scholarship aside. There are enough Forts in the world already, enough crackpots and *provocateurs* and intellectual heretics without my joining their ranks. The files I have assembled will be attached to this document, all my "Battalions of the accursed," and if anyone should ever have cause to read this, they may make of those appendices what they will. It's time to tell the truth, as best I am able, and be done with this.

5.

It is true that I attended a screening of a film, featuring Vera Endecott, in a musty little room near Harvard Square. And that it still haunts my dreams. But as noted above, the dreams rarely are anything like an accurate replaying of what I saw that night. There was no black pool, no willow trees stitched together from human bodies, no venomous phial emptied upon the waters. Those are the embellishments of my dreaming, subconscious mind. I could fill several journals with such nightmares.

What I *did* see, only two months ago now, and one month before I finally met the woman for myself, was little more than a grisly, but strangely mundane, scene. It might have only been a test reel, or perhaps 17,000 or so frames, some twelve minutes, give or take, excised from a far longer film. All in all, it was little but than a blatantly pornographic pastiche of the widely circulated 1918 publicity stills of Theda Bara lying in various risqué poses with a human skeleton (for J. Edward Gordon's *Salomé*).

The print was in very poor condition, and the projectionist had to stop twice to splice the film back together after it broke. The daughter of Iscariot Snow, known to most of the world as Vera Endecott, lay naked upon a stone floor with a skeleton. However, the human skull had been replaced with what I assumed then (and still believe) to have been a plaster or papier-mâché "skull" that more closely resembled that of some malformed, macrocephalic dog. The wall or backdrop behind her was a stark matte-gray, and the scene seemed to me purposefully under-lit in an attempt to bring more atmosphere to a shoddy production. The skeleton (and its ersatz skull) were wired together, and Endecott caressed all the osseous angles of its arms and legs and lavished kisses upon it lipless mouth, before masturbating, first with the bones of its right hand, and then by rubbing herself against the crest of an ilium.

The reactions from the others who'd come to see the film that night ranged from bored silence to rapt attention to laughter. My own reaction was, for the most part, merely disgust and embarrassment to be counted among that audience. I overheard, when the lights came back up, that the can containing the reel bore two titles, *The Necrophile* and *The Hound's Daughter*, and also bore two dates—1923 and 1924. Later, from someone who had a passing acquaintance with Richard Pickman, I would hear a rumor that he'd worked on scenarios for a filmmaker, possibly Bernard Natan, the prominent Franco-Romanian director of "blue movies," who recently acquired Pathé and merged it with his own studio, Rapid Film. I cannot confirm or deny this, but certainly, I imagine what I saw that evening would have delighted Pickman no end.

However, what has lodged that night so firmly in my mind, and what I believe is the genuine author of those among my nightmares featuring Endecott in an endless parade of nonexistent horrific films transpired only in the final few seconds of the film. Indeed, it came and went so quickly, the projectionist was asked by a number of those present to rewind and play the ending over four times, in an effort to ascertain whether we'd seen what we *thought* we had seen.

Her lust apparently satiated, the actress lay down with her skeletal lover, one arm about its empty rib cage, and closed her kohl-smudged eyes. And in that last instant, before the film ended, a shadow appeared, something passing slowly between the set and the camera's light source. Even after five viewing, I can only describe that shade as having put me in mind of some hulking figure, something considerably farther down the evolutionary ladder than Piltdown or Java man. And it was generally agreed among those seated in that close and musty room that the shadow was possessed of an odd sort of snout or muzzle, suggestive of the prognathous jaw and face of the fake skull wired to the skeleton.

There, then. *That* is what I actually saw that evening, as best I now can remember it. Which leaves me with only a single piece of this story left to tell, the night I finally met the woman who called herself Vera Endecott.

6.

"Disappointed? Not quite what you were expecting?" she asked, smiling a distasteful, wry sort of smile, and I think I might have nodded in reply. She appeared at least a decade older than her twenty-seven years, looking like a woman who had survived one rather tumultuous life already and had, perhaps, started in upon a second. There were fine lines at the corners of her eyes and mouth, the bruised circles below her eyes that spoke of chronic insomnia and drug abuse, and, if I'm not mistaken, a premature hint of silver in her bobbed black hair. What *had* I anticipated? It's hard to say now, after the fact, but I was surprised by her height, and by her irises, which were a striking shade of gray. At once, they reminded me of the sea, of fog and breakers and granite cobbles polished perfectly smooth by ages in the surf. The Greeks said that the goddess Athena had "sea-gray" eyes, and I wonder what they would have thought of the eyes of Lillian Snow.

"I have not been well," she confided, making the divulgence sound almost like a *mea culpa*, and those stony eyes glanced towards a chair in the foyer of my flat. I apologized for not having already asked her in, for having kept her standing in the hallway. I led her to the davenport sofa in the tiny parlor off my studio, and she thanked me. She asked for whiskey or gin, and then laughed at me when I told her I was a teetotaler. When I offered her tea, she declined.

"A painter who doesn't *drink*?" she asked. "No wonder I've never heard of you."

I believe that I mumbled something then about the Eighteenth Amendment and the Volstead Act, which earned from her an expression of commingled disbelief and contempt. She told me that was strike two, and if it turned out that I didn't smoke, either, she was leaving, as my claim to be an artist would have been proven a bald-faced lie, and she'd know I'd lured her to my apartment under false pretenses. But I offered her a cigarette, one of the *brun* Gitanes I first developed a taste for in college, and at that she seemed to relax somewhat. I lit her cigarette, and she leaned back on the sofa, still smiling that wry smile, watching me with her sea-gray eyes, her thin face wreathed in gauzy veils of smoke. She wore a yellow felt cloche that didn't exactly match her burgundy silk chemise, and I noticed there was a run in her left stocking.

"You knew Richard Upton Pickman," I said, blundering much too quickly to the point, and, immediately, her expression turned somewhat suspicious. She said nothing for almost a full minute, just sat there smoking and staring back at me, and I silently cursed my impatience and lack of tact. But then the smile returned, and she laughed softly and nodded.

"Wow," she said. "There's a name I haven't heard in a while. But, yeah, sure, I knew the son of a bitch. So, what are you? Another of his protégés, or maybe just one of the three-letter-men he liked to keep handy?"

"Then it's true Pickman was light on his feet?" I asked.

She laughed again, and this time there was an unmistakable edge of derision there. She took another long drag on her cigarette, exhaled, and squinted at me through the smoke.

"Mister, I have yet to meet the beast—male, female, or anything in between—that degenerate fuck wouldn't have screwed, given half a chance." She paused, here, tapping ash onto the floorboards. "So, if you're *not* a fag, just what *are* you? A kike, maybe? You sort of *look* like a kike."

"No," I replied. "I'm not Jewish. My parents were Roman Catholic, but me, I'm not much of anything, I'm afraid, but a painter you've never heard of."

"Are you?"

"Am I what, Miss Endecott?"

"Afraid," she said, smoke leaking from her nostrils. "And do *not* dare start in calling me 'Miss Endecott.' It makes me sound like a goddamned schoolteacher or something equally wretched."

"So, these days, do you prefer Vera?" I asked, pushing my luck. "Or Lillian?"

"How about Lily?" she smiled, completely nonplussed, so far as I could tell, as though these were all only lines from some script she'd spent the last week rehearsing.

"Very well, Lily," I said, moving the glass ashtray on the table closer to her. She scowled at it, as though I were offering her a platter of some perfectly odious foodstuff and expecting her to eat, but she stopped tapping her ash on my floor.

"Why am I here?" she demanded, commanding an answer without raising her voice. "Why have you gone to so much trouble to see me?"

"It wasn't as difficult as all that," I replied, not yet ready to answer her question, wanting to stretch this meeting out a little longer and understanding, expecting, that she'd likely leave as soon as she had what I'd invited her there to give her. In truth, it had been quite a lot of trouble, beginning with a telephone call to her former agent, and then proceeding through half a dozen increasingly disreputable and uncooperative contacts. Two I'd had to bribe, and one I'd had to coerce with a number of hollow threats involving nonexistent contacts in the Boston Police Department. But, when all was said and done, my diligence had paid off, because here she sat before me, the two of us, alone, just me and the woman who'd been a movie star and who had played some role in Thurber's breakdown, who'd posed for Pickman and almost certainly done murder on a spring night in Hollywood. Here was the woman who could answer questions I did not have the nerve to ask, who knew what had cast the shadow I'd seen in that dingy pornographic film. Or, at least, here was all that remained of her.

"There aren't many left who would have bothered," she said, gazing down at the smoldering tip-end of her Gitane.

"Well, I have always been a somewhat persistent sort of fellow," I told her, and she smiled again. It was an oddly bestial smile that reminded me of one of my earliest impressions of her—that oppressive summer's day, now more than two months past, studying a handful of old clippings in the Hope Street boarding house. That her human face was nothing more than a mask or fairy glamour conjured to hide the truth of her from the world.

"How did you meet him?" I asked, and she stubbed out her cigarette in the ashtray.

"Who? How did I meet *who*?" She furrowed her brow and glanced nervously towards the parlor window, which faces east, towards the harbor.

"I'm sorry," I replied. "Pickman. How is it that you came to know Richard Pickman?"

"Some people would say that you have very unhealthy interests, Mr. Blackman," she said, her peculiarly carnivorous smile quickly fading, taking with it any implied menace. In its stead, there was only this destitute, used-up husk of a woman.

"And surely they've said the same of you, many, many times, Lily. I've read all about Durand Drive and the Delgado woman."

"Of course, you have," she sighed, not taking her eyes from the window. "I'd have expected nothing less from a persistent fellow such as you."

"How did you meet Richard Pickman?" I asked for the third time.

"Does it make a difference? That was so very long ago. Years and *years* ago. He's dead—"

"No body was ever found."

And, here, she looked from the window to me, and all those unexpected lines on her face seemed to have abruptly deepened; she might well have been twenty-seven, by birth, but no one would have argued if she laid claim to forty.

"The man is dead," she said flatly. "And if by chance he's *not*, well, we should all be fortunate enough to find our heart's desire, whatever it might be." Then she went back to staring at the window, and, for a minute or two, neither of us said anything more.

"You told me that you have the sketches," she said, finally. "Was that a lie, just to get me up here?"

"No, I have them. Two of them, anyway," and I reached for the folio beside my chair and untied the string holding it closed. "I don't know, of course, how many you might have posed for. There were more?"

"More than two," she replied, almost whispering now.

"Lily, you still haven't answered my question."

"And you *are* a persistent fellow."

"Yes," I assured her, taking the two nudes from the stack and holding them up for her to see, but not yet touch. She studied them a moment, her face remaining slack and dispassionate, as if the sight of them elicited no memories at all.

"He needed a model," she said, turning back to the window and the blue October sky. "I was up from New York, staying with a friend who'd met him at a gallery or lecture or something of the sort. My friend knew that he was looking for models, and I needed the money."

I glanced at the two charcoal sketches again, at the curve of those full hips, the round, firm buttocks, and the tail—a crooked, malformed thing sprouting from the base of the coccyx and reaching halfway to the bend of the subject's knees. As I have said, Pickman had a flare for realism, and his eye for human anatomy was almost as uncanny as the ghouls and demons he painted. I pointed to one of the sketches, to the tail.

"That isn't artistic license, is it?"

She did not look back to the two drawings, but simply, slowly, shook her head. "I had the surgery done in Jersey, back in '21," she said.

"Why did you wait so long, Lily? It's my understanding that such a defect is usually corrected at birth, or shortly thereafter."

And she almost smiled that smile again, that hungry, savage smile, but it died, incomplete, on her lips.

"My father, he has his own ideas about such things," she said quietly. "He was always so proud, you see, that his daughter's body was blessed with evidence of her heritage. It made him very happy."

"Your heritage . . . " I began, but Lily Snow held up her left hand, silencing me.

"I believe, sir, I've answered enough questions for one afternoon. Especially given that you have only the pair, and that you did not tell me that was the case when we spoke."

Reluctantly, I nodded and passed both the sketches to her. She took them, thanked me, and stood up, brushing at a bit of lint or dust on her burgundy chemise. I told her that I regretted that the others were not in my possession, that it had not even occurred to me she would have posed for more than these two. The last part was a lie, of course, as I knew Pickman would surely have made as many studies as possible when presented with so unusual a body.

"I can show myself out," she informed me when I started to get up from my chair. "And you will not disturb me again, not ever."

"No," I agreed. "Not ever. You have my word."

"You're lying sons of bitches, the whole lot of you," she said, and with that, the living ghost of Vera Endecott turned and left the parlor. A few seconds later, I heard the door open and slam shut again, and I sat there in the wan light of a fading day, looking at what grim traces remained in Thurber's folio.

7. (October 24th, 1929)

This is the last of it. Just a few more words, and I will be done. I know now that having attempted to trap these terrible events, I have not managed to trap them at all, but merely given them some new, clearer focus.

Four days ago, on the morning of October 20th, a body was discovered dangling from the trunk of an oak growing near the center of King's Chapel Burial Ground. According to newspaper accounts, the corpse was suspended a full seventeen feet off the ground, bound round about the waist and chest with interwoven lengths of jute rope and baling wire. The woman was identified as a former actress, Vera Endecott, *née* Lillian Margaret Snow, and much was made of her notoriety and her unsuccessful attempt to conceal connections to the wealthy but secretive and ill-rumored Snows of Ipswich, Massachusetts. Her body had been stripped of all clothing, disemboweled, her throat cut, and her tongue removed. He lips had been sewn shut with cat-gut stitches. About her neck hung a wooden placard, on which one word had been written in what is believed to be the dead woman's own blood: *apostate.*

This morning, I almost burned Thurber's folio, along with all my files. I went so far as to carry them to hearth, but then my resolve faltered, and I just sat of the floor, staring at the clippings and Pickman's sketches. I'm not sure what stayed my hand, beyond the suspicion that destroying these papers would not save my life. If they want me dead, then dead I'll be. I've gone too far down this road to spare myself by trying to annihilate the physical evidence of my investigation.

I will place this manuscript, and all the related documents I have gathered, in my safety deposit box, and then I will try to return to the life I was living before Thurber's death. But I cannot forget a line from the suicide note of the screenwriter, Joseph Chapman—*how does a man forget, deliberately and wholly and forever, once he has glimpsed such sights.* How, indeed. And, too, I cannot forget that woman's eyes, that stony, sea-tumbled shade of gray. Or a rough shadow glimpsed in the final moments of a film that might have been made in 1923 or 1924, that may have been titled *The Hound's Daughter* or *The Necrophile.*

I know the dreams will not desert me, not now nor at some future time, but I pray for such fortune as to have seen the last of the waking horrors that my foolish, prying mind has called forth.

The patterns and traceries all hinted of remote spaces and unimaginable abysses, and the aquatic nature of the occasional pictorial items added to the general unearthliness.

Discarded Draft of "The Shadow Over Innsmouth"
(written circa 1931) · H.P. Lovecraft

• FAIR EXCHANGE •
Michael Marshall Smith

We were in some bloke's house the other night, nicking his stuff, and Bazza calls me over. We've been there twenty minutes already and if it was anyone else I'd tell them to shut up and get on with it, but Baz and I've been thieving together for years and I know he's not going to be wasting my time. So I put the telly by the back door with the rest of the gear (nice little telly, last minute find up in the smaller bedroom) and head back to the front room. I been in there already, of course. First place you look. DVD player, CDs, stereo if it's any good, which isn't often. You'd be amazed how many people have crap stereos. Especially birds—still got some shit plastic midi-system their dad bought them down the High Street in 1987. (Still got LPs, too, half of them. No fucking use to me, are they? I'm not having it away with an armful of things that weigh a ton and aren't as good as CDs: where's the fucking point in that?)

I make my way to Baz's shadow against the curtains, and I see he's going through the drawers in the bureau. Sound tactic if you've got a minute. People always seem to think you won't look in a drawer—*Doh!*—and so in go the cheque books, cash, personal organizer, old mobile phone. Spare set of keys, if you're lucky: which case you bide your time, hoping they won't remember the keys were in there, then come back and make it a double feature when the insurance has put back everything you took. They've made it easy for you, haven't they. Pillocks. Anyway, I come up next to Baz, and he presents the drawers. They're empty. Completely and utterly devoid of stuff. No curry menus, no bent-up party photos, no ball of string or rubber bands, no knackered batteries for the telly remote. No dust, even. It's like someone opened the two drawers and sucked every thing out with a Hoover.

"Baz, there's nothing there."

"That's what I'm saying."

It's not *that* exciting, don't see Jerry Bruckheimer making a film of it or nothing, but it's odd. I'll grant him that. It's not like the rest of the house is spick and span. There's stuff spilling out of cupboards, kitchen cabinets, old books sitting in piles on the floor. The carpet on the landing upstairs looks like something got spilled there and never cleaned up, and the whole place is dusty and smells of mildew or something. And yet these two drawers, perfect for storing stuff—could even have been designed for the purpose, ha ha ha—are completely empty. Why? You'll never know. It's just some private thing. That's one of the weird bits about burglary. It's intimate. It's like being able to see what color pants everyone is wearing. Actually you could do that too, if you wanted, but that's not what I meant Not my cup of tea. Not professional, either.

"There was nothing in there at all?"

"Just this," Baz says, and holds something up so I can see it. "It was right at the back."

I took it from him. It's small, about the size and shape of the end of your thumb. Smooth, cold to the touch. "What is it?"

"Dunno," he shrugs. "Marble?"

"Fucking shit marble, Baz. It's not even fucking *round*."

Baz shrugs again and I say "Weird," and then it's time to go. You don't want to be hanging around any longer than necessary. Don't want to be in a burning hurry, either—that's when you can get careless or make too much noise or forget to look both ways as you slip out—but once you've found what you came for, you might as well be somewhere else.

So we go via the kitchen, grab the bin bag full of gear and slip out the back way. Stand outside the door a second, make sure no one's passing by, then walk out onto the street, calm as you like. Van's just around the corner. We stroll along the pavement, chatting normally, looking like we live in one of the other houses and walk this way every night. Get in the van—big white fucker, naturally, virtually invisible in London—and off we go.

It's fucking magic, that moment.

The one where you turn the van into the next street and suddenly you're just part of the evening traffic, and you know it's done and you're away and bar a fuck-up with the distribution of the goods it's like it never happened. I always light a fag right then, crack open the window, smell the London air coming in the van. Warm, cold, it's London. Best air in the world.

Weird thing, though. Even though it's not that big a deal, the business with the drawers was still niggling me a few hours later. You do see the odd thing or two in my business—stuff that don't quite make sense. Couple of months ago we're doing over a big old house, over Tufnell Park way, and either side of the mantelpiece there's a painting. Two little paintings, obviously done by the same bloke. Signed the same, for a start. Now, there's huge photos all over the mantelpiece, including some wedding ones, and it don't take a genius to work out that these two paintings are of the owners: one of the bloke, and the other of his missus. What's that about? For a start, you've already got all the photos. And why get two paintings, one of each of you? If you're going to get a painting done, surely you have the two of you together, looking all lovey-dovey and like you'll never, ever get divorced and stand screaming at each other in some brief's office arguing about bits of furniture you only bought in the first place because they was there and you had the cash burning a hole in your pocket. Maybe that's it—you have the paintings done separate so you can split them when you break up. But if you're already thinking about that, then . . . Whatever. People are just weird. Baz wanted to draw mustaches on the paintings, but I wouldn't let him. They can't have been cheap. So we just did one on the wife.

Anyway, couple of hours in the Junction and everything's peachy. Already shifted most of the electrical goods to blokes we know are either keeping them for themselves or can be trusted to punt them on over the other side of town. Baz and I done a deal and he's going to keep the little telly for his sister's birthday. Couple bits of jewelry Baz found will go to Mr. Pzlowsky, a pro fence I use over in Bow. He don't talk to no one—can barely understand what the old fucker's saying, anyway—and can be trusted to only rob us short-sighted, not actually blind.

So the only thing left is the little thing I've got in my pocket. I get out, look at it. Funny thing is, I don't really remember slipping it in there. Like I said, it's small, and it looks like it must be made of glass. It's so shiny, transparent in parts, that it can't be anything else. But it's got colors and textures in it too—kind of pinks and salmon, and some threads of dark green. And it feels . . . it feels almost wet, even though it had been in my pocket for ages. I suppose it's just some special kind of glass or stone something.

"Wozzat?"

I look up and see Clive is racking up at the pool table a couple of yards away.

"What's what?"

"What you got in your hand, twatface."

I'm not trying to be funny, I don't mind Clive, I'm just surprised he noticed it from over there.

I hold it up. "Dunno," I said. "What do you think?"

He comes over, chalking up his cue, takes a look. "Dunno," he agrees. "Hold on though, tell you what it looks a bit like."

"What's that?"

"My sister-in-law went on holiday last year. Bali. Over, you know, in Polynesia."

"Polynesia? Where the fuck's that?"

"Dunno," he admitted. "Fucking long flight though, by all accounts. Think they said it was in the South Seas or something. Dunno where that is either. Anyway, she brought our mum back something looked a bit like that. Said it was coral, I think."

"You reckon?"

He leaned forward, looked at it more closely. "Yeah. Could be. Polished up, or something. Tell you what, though. It weren't half as nice as your one. Where'd you get it?"

"Ah," I said. "That would be telling."

He nodded. "You nicked it. Well, I reckon that's worth something, I do."

And he wanders off to the table, where some bloke's waiting for him to break.

"Nice one," I said, and took another look at the thing.

Even though I'm sitting right in the back of the pub, snug into the wood paneling there, this little piece of coral or stone or glass or whatever seems to have a glow about it. Suppose it's catching a glint from the long light over the pool table, but the light coming off it seems like it's almost green. Could be the baize, I suppose, but . . . I dunno. Probably had a Stella too many.

I slipped it back in my pocket. I reckoned Clive was probably right, and it most likely was worth something.

Funny thing, though. I didn't like the idea of getting rid of it.

Next few days just sort of go by. Nothing much going on. Baz had to head East to visit some mate in the London Hospital, so he goes over and does the business with Mr. Pzlowsky. Usually I'd do it because people have been known to take advantage of Bazza, but me and the Pole had words over it a year ago and he plays fair with him now. Fair as he plays with anyone, that is. The handful of jewelry we got from the house with the empty drawers gets us a few hundred quid, which is better than either of us expected. Old silver, apparently. American.

We play pool, we play darts, we watch television. You know how it is. Had a row with me bird, Jackie: she caught sight of the little coral thing (I'd just put it down next to the sink for a minute while I changed trousers) and seemed to think it was for her. Usually I do come back with a little something for the old trout, granted, but on this occasion I hadn't. Pissed me off a bit, to be honest. She just sits at home all evening on her fat arse, doing nothing, and then when I come home she expects I'll have some little present for her. Anyway, whatever. It got sorted out.

Couple days later Baz and I go out on the game again. Nothing mega, just out for a walk, trying back doors, side doors, garden gates, usual kind of stuff. What the coppers call "opportunistic" crime. Actually, we call it that too.

"Fancy a bit of opportunistic, Baz?" I'll say.

He'll neck the last of his pint. "Go on, then. Run out of cash anyway."

We were only out an hour or so, and came back to the pub with maybe three, four hundred quid worth of stuff. Usual bits of jewelry, plus a Palm V, two external hard drives, three phones, wallet full of cash and even a pot of spare change (might as well, plenty of quid coins in there). That's the thing about this business: you've got to know what you're doing. Got to be able to have a quick look at rings and necklaces, and know whether they're worth the nicking. Glance at a small plastic case, realize there's a pricey little personal organizer inside. See things like those portable hard drives, which don't look like anything, and know that if you wipe them clean you can get forty apiece for them in City pubs, more for the ones with more megs or gigs or whatever (it's written on the back). Understand which phones are hard to clone or shift and so not worth the bother. Know that a big old pot of change can be well worth it, and also that if you tip it into a plastic bag it makes a bloody good cosh in case you meet someone on the way out.

The other thing is the mental attitude. I remember having a barney with an old boyfriend of Baz's sister, couple years ago. She'd met him in some wine bar up West and he was a right smartarse, well up himself, fucking student or something it was.

He comes right out and asks me: "How can you do it?"

Not "do," notice, I'd've understood that (and I don't mind giving out some tips): but "can." How *can* I do it? And this from some little wanker who's being put through college by Mummy and Daddy, who didn't have a lazy girlfriend to support, and who was a right old slowcoach when it came to doing his round at the bar. Annoying thing was, after I'd discussed it with him for a bit (I say "discussed": there was a bit of pushing and shoving at the start), I could sort of see his point.

According to him, it was a matter of attitude. If someone came round and turned me mum's place over, I'd be after their fucking blood. I knew that already, of course, he wasn't teaching me nothing there: I suppose the thing I hadn't really clocked was this mental attitude thing. I know that Mum's got some bits and pieces that she'd be right upset if they was nicked. Not even because they're worth much, but just because they mean something to her. From me old man, whatever. If I turn someone's place over, though, I don't know what means what to them. Could be that old ring was a gift from their Gran, whereas to me it's just a tenner from Mr. Pzlowsky if I'm lucky. That tatty organizer could have phone numbers on it they don't have anywhere else. Or maybe it was a big deal that their dad bought them a little telly, it's the first one of their own they've had, and if I nick it then they're always going to be on their second, or third, or tenth.

The point is I don't know all that. I don't know anything about these people and their lives, and I don't really care. To me, they're just fucking cattle, to be honest. What's theirs is mine. Fair enough, maybe it's not great mental attitude. But that's thieving for you. Nobody said it was a job for Mother Teresa.

Anyway, we're back in the Junction and a few more beers down (haven't even shifted anything on yet, still working through the change pot) when who should walk in the door but the Pole. Mr. Pzlowsky, as I live and breathe. He comes in the door, looks around and sees us, and makes his way through the crowd.

Baz and I just stare at him. I've never seen the Pole anywhere except in his shop. Tell the truth, I thought he had no actual legs; just spent the day propped up behind his counter raking in the cash. He's an old bloke, sixties, and he smokes like a chimney and I'm frankly fucking amazed he's made it all the way here.

And also: why?

"I'd like a word with you," he says, when he gets to us.

"Buy us a beer, then," I go.

I'm a bit pissed off at him, truth be known. He's crossing a line. I don't want no one in the pub to know where we shift our gear. As it happens it's just me and Baz there at that moment, but you never know when Clive's going to come in, or any of the others.

He looks at me, then turns right around and goes back to the bar. "Two Stellas," I shout after him, and he just scowls.

Baz and I turn to look at each other. "What's going on?" Baz asks.

"Fucked if I know."

As I watch the Pole at the bar, I'm thinking it through. My first thought is he's come because there's a problem with something we've sold him, he's had the old Bill knocking on his door. But now I'm not sure. If it was grief, he wouldn't be buying us a pint. He'd be in a hurry, and pissed off. "Have to wait and see."

Eventually Mr. Pzlowsky gets back to us with our drinks on a little tray. He sits down at our table, his back to the rest of the pub, and I start to relax. Whatever he's here for, he's playing by the rules. He's drinking neat gin, no ice. Ugh.

"Cheers," I say. "So: what's up?"

He lights one of his weird little cigarettes, coughs. "I have something for you."

"Sounds interesting," I say. "What?"

He reaches in his jacket pocket and pulls out a brown envelope. Puts it on the table, pushes it across. I pick it up, look inside.

Fifties. Ten of them. Five hundred quid. A "monkey," as they say on television, though no fucker I know does.

"Fuck's this?"

"A bonus," he says, and I can hear Baz's brain fizzing. I can actually hear his thoughts. A bonus from the Pole, he's thinking: What the fuck is going on?

"A bonus, from the Pole?" I say, on his behalf. "What the fuck is going on?"

"This is what it is," he says, speaking quietly and drawing in close, I won't do his accent, but trust me—you have to concentrate. "It is from that jewelry you bring me last week. The silver. The American silver. I have one of my clients in this afternoon, he is the one sometimes buys unusual things, and I decide I will show this silver to him. So I get one of these things out—I always show just one first, you understand, because it can be more expensive that way. He looks at it, and suddenly I am on high alert. This is because I am experienced, see, I know what is what in my trade. I see it in his eyes when he sees the piece: he really wants this thing, yes? I was going to say two hundred to him, maybe two hundred fifty, this is what I think it was worth. But when I see his face, I think a moment, and I say seven hundred fifty! Is a joke, a little bit, but also I think maybe I see what is in his eyes again, and we'll see."

"And?"

"He says 'done,' just like that, and he asks me if I have some more. I almost fall off my stool, I tell you truthfully."

I nearly fell off my own stool, right there in the pub. Seven hundred and fifty fucking notes! Fuck me!

The Pole, sees my face, laughs. "Yes! And this is just the smallest one, you understand? So I say yes, I have some more, and his eyes are like saucers immediately. In all the time I do this thing, only a very few times do I see this look in a man's face which says 'I will pay whatever you want.' So I bring them out, one by one. You bring me five of them, you remember. He buys them all."

Baz gapes. "All of them? For seven fifty each?"

The Pole goes all sly, and winks. "At least," he says, and I knew there and then that one or two of them went for a lot more than that. There's quiet for a moment, as we all sip our drinks. I know Baz is trying to do the sums in his head, and not having much luck. I've already done them, and I'm a bit pissed off we didn't realize what we had. Fuck knows what the Pole is thinking.

He finishes his gin in a quick swallow and gets up. "So, thank you, boys. Is a good find. He tell me is turn of the century American silver, from East Coast somewhere, he tell me the name, I forget it, something like Portsmouth, I think. And . . . well, the man says to me that if I find any more of this thing, he will buy it. Straight away. So . . . think of me, okay?"

And he winked again, and shuffled his way out through the crowd until we couldn't see him any more.

"Fuck me," Baz says, when he's gone.

"Fuck me is right," I say. I open the envelope, take out four of the fifties, and give them to him. "There's your half."

"Cheers. Mind you," Baz says, over his beer, "he's still a fucker. How much did all that add up to?"

"Minimum of seven fifty each, that's three grand seven fifty," I said. "But from that fucker's face; I'm thinking he got five, six grand at least. And if he got that off some bloke who knows it's nicked, then in the shops you got to double or treble it. Probably more."

"Sheesh. Still, good for him. He didn't have to see us right."

"Yeah," I said, because he wasn't completely wrong. The Pole could have kept quiet about his windfall. His deal with us was done. "But you know what that cash is really about?"

Baz looked at me, shook his head. He's a lovely bloke, don't get me wrong. He's my best mate. But the stuff in his head is mainly just padding to stop his eyeballs falling in. "What it means is," I said, "is he's very fucking keen to get some more. In fact, probably says he was lying about the seven fifty for the cheapest. He got more. Maybe much more. He got so much dosh for them, in fact, it was worth admitting he did well, and paying us a bonus so we go to him if we find any more."

"Better keep our eyes open, then," Baz said, cheerfully. "More beer?"

"Cheers," I said.

I watched him lurch off to the bar. My hand slipped into my pocket, and I found my cold little friend. The bit of polished stone, coral, glass, whatever. I knew then that Clive had been right. My little piece was probably worth a lot of money. The bits of jewelry had been all right, but nowhere near as pretty as my stone.

I wasn't selling it though, no way. I had got too used to the feel of it in my hand. Twenty, thirty times a day I'd hold it. I liked the way it fitted between my fingers. Longer I had it, better it seemed to fit. Sometimes, if I held it up to my face, I thought I could smell it too. Couldn't put my finger on what it smelled of, but it was nice, comforting. The Pole wasn't getting hold of it. Not Jackie neither.

It was mine.

On the Sunday Baz goes on holiday. He's off to Tenerife for the week. This is fine by me, because I need time to plan.

Now Baz, he thinks we've just got to keep an eye out for this stuff, that it's something like a particular DVD player or whatever. I know different. If it's this fucking valuable, then it's not something we're just going to find in some gaff in Kentish Town, mixed in with all the shit from Ratners or Argos or wherever. This isn't just common-or-garden thieving we're looking at. This is nicking to order, which is a different kind of skill. Happens all the time, of course: you pass the word to the right bloke in the right pub, that you want some particular BMW, or a new Mini in cream, and they'll go do the business for you. There's big money in it. Not my area, normally, but this is different. We do all right with the usual gear, but if me and Baz can take some more of this silver to the Pole, we can do very nicely indeed. It's worth making an effort.

So on the Monday night, I'm out on the streets by myself. It's about ten thirty. I park the van around the corner, and I take a stroll down the street where the house is, the house where we found the stuff. Couldn't remember which one it was at first, but in the end I worked it out. All the other houses in this street, they've been done up. Window sills painted, bricks re-pointed, new tiles on the path, that kind of thing. Scaffolding on a couple others. Lot of people have moved in recently, the area's coming up. But this particular house, it looks a bit more knackered. I'm thinking the people have been there a while, which makes sense, what with it being so untidy inside. Could be they're foreign. You get that, sometimes. People moved in just after the war or whatever, when it was dirt cheap. House gets passed on to the children, and then bingo, suddenly they're sitting on a gold mine. Could be they're Yanks, even—which would explain the old silver being from the US originally.

I walk past the house and see the curtains are drawn and the lights are on. Lot of people do that when they go out, but if you take lights to mean there's no one at home, you'll being doing time so fast your feet won't touch the ground. Me, I've never been inside. Not intending to be, either. And I'm not planning on doing the job solo anyhow. It's a big house. It's a two person maneuver—not least because it was Baz who picked up the bits of silver in the first place. I don't know where he found them, but it's got to be the first place to look. Quicker you're in and out, the better.

I walk the street one way, then go around the corner and have a fag. Then I walk back past the house. I'm trying to remember the exact layout, cause we've been in a few other houses since. I'm glancing across at the front window on the second floor when I see a shape, a shadow on the curtain. I smile to myself, glad I'm not so stupid as to have had a go tonight. And loyal, of course—I want Baz in on it, and he's not back until Sunday.

I slow the pace, keep an eye on this shadow. Never know, it might be a bird with her tits out. Don't see nothing of note, though. Curtains are too tightly drawn, and it's that thing where the light's behind them and they get magnified till they're just some huge blob.

The light goes off, and I realize mostly likely that's the kid just gone to bed. That tells me that room was where the little telly was from, and the whole floor clicks in my head.

I walked back to the van, feeling very professional indeed.

Next night I'm busy, and the one after. Not nicking. The Tuesday was our "anniversary" (or so Jackie says; far as I can see I don't understand why we have them when we're not even fucking engaged, and anyway—anniversary of what? We met at a party, got pissed, shagged in one of the bedrooms on a pile of coats, and that was that). Either way we ended up going up West and having a meal and then getting bladdered at a club.

Wednesday night I'm not going fucking anywhere. I felt like shit.

So it's Thursday when I'm outside the house again.

I was there a little earlier, about quarter to nine. You look a bit less suspicious, being out on the street at that time; but on the other hand there's more people around to see you loitering about. I walked past the house first, seeing the curtains are drawn again. Can't work out whether the lights are on full or not: there's still a bit of light in the sky.

I'd actually slowed down, almost stopped, when I heard footsteps coming up the street. I started moving again, sharpish. You don't want the neighbors catching someone staring at a house. There's some right nosey fuckers. They'll call the old Bill quick as you like. Course the Bill won't do much, most of the time, but if they think there's lads scouting for opportunities then sometimes they'll get someone to drive down the street every now and then, when they're bored.

So I started walking again, and as I look I see there are some people coming up the street towards me. Three of them. Actually, they're still about thirty yards away, which is a surprise. Sounded like they were closer than that. I just walk towards them. I didn't actually whistle—nobody whistles much these days, which I think is a bit of a shame—but I was as casual as you like.

Just as I'm coming up to them, them up to me, the streetlights click on. One of these lights is there just as we're passing each other, and suddenly there's these big shadows thrown across my path. I look across and see there's two of them in front, a man and a woman. The woman's wearing a big floppy hat—must have been to some fancy do—and the bloke happens to be looking across her, towards the street. She's in shadow, he's turned the other way, so I don't see either of their faces, which is fine by me. If I haven't seen theirs then they haven't seen mine, if you know what I mean.

I'm just stepping past them, and I mean around, really, because they're both pretty big, when suddenly someone was looking at me.

It was the girl, walking behind them. As I'm passing her, her head turns, and she looks right at me.

I look away quickly, and then they're gone.

All I'm left with is an image of the girl's face, of it slowly turning to look at me. To be honest, she was a bit of a shocker. Not scarred or nothing, just really big-faced. With them eyes look like they're sticking out too far, make you look a bit simple.

But she was young, and I think she smiled.

I walked down to the corner, steady as you like. As I turned around it I glanced back, just quickly. I saw two things. I see the three of them are going into the house. They weren't neighbors, after all. They're the people from the actual house. The people with the jewelry. The people I'm going to be nicking from.

The second thing I notice is that the streetlight we passed isn't lit any more.

I'm a bit unsettled, the next day, to be honest. Don't know why. It isn't like me. Normally I'm a pretty chilled bloke, take things as they come and all that. But I find myself in the pub at lunchtime, which I don't usually do—not on a weekday, anyway, unless it's a Bank Holiday—and by the afternoon I'm pretty lagered up. I sit by myself, in a table at the back, keep knocking them back. Clive pops in about three and I had a couple more with him, but it was quiet. I didn't say much, and in the end he got up and started playing pool with some bloke. It was quite funny actually, some posh wanker in there by mistake, fancied playing for money. Clive reeled him in like a kipper.

So I'm sitting there, thinking, trying to work out why I feel weird. Could be that it's because I've seen the people I'm going to be nicking from? Usually it's not that way. It's just bits of gear, lying around in someone else's house. They're mine to do what I want with. All I see is how much they're worth. Now I know that the jewelry is going to belong to that woman in the hat. And I know that Baz's sister is watching a telly that belonged to the girl who looked at me. All right, so she was a minger, but it's bad enough being ugly without people nicking your prize possession.

That could be another thing, of course. She'd seen me. No reason for her to think some bloke in the street is the one who turned them over, but I don't like it. Like I didn't like Mr. Pzlowsky being in the Junction. You don't want anyone to be able to make those connections.

I'm thinking that's it, just them having seen me, and I'm beginning to feel bit more relaxed. I've got another pint in front of me, and I've got my stone in my right hand. It's snuggled in there, in my palm, fingers curled around it, and that's helping too. It's like worry beads, or something: I just feel better when it's there.

And then I realize that there's something else on my mind. I want to find that jewelry. But I don't necessarily want to hand it on.

The Pole is still gagging for it, I know. He's rung me twice, asking if I've got any more, and that tells me there's serious money involved. But now I think about it properly, with my stone in my hand and no Baz sitting there next to me, jabbering on, I realize I want the stuff for myself. I didn't actually handle it, the last time. Baz found it, kept it, sold it to the Pole.

If a little bit of stone feels like this one does, though, what would the silver feel like? I don't know—but I want to know.

And that's why, on the Saturday night, I went around there. Alone.

I parked up at five, and walked past once an hour. I walked up, down, on both sides of the street. Unless someone's sitting watching the whole time, I'm just another bloke. Or so I tell myself, anyway. The truth is that I'm just going to do it whatever.

It's a Saturday night. Very least, the young girl is going to go out. Maybe the mum and dad too, out for a meal, to the cinema, whatever. Worst case, I'll just wait until they've all gone to bed, and try the back door. I don't like doing it that way. Avoid it if I can. You never know if you're going to run into some have-a-go-hero who fancies getting his picture in the local paper. Clive had one of those, couple years back. Had to smack the guy for ages before he went down. Didn't do any nicking for three months after that. It puts you right off your stride. Risky, too. Burglary is one thing. Grievous Bodily Harm is something else. The coppers know the score. Bit of nicking is inevitable. The insurance is going to pay anyway, so no one gets too exercised. But with GBH, they're on your case big time. I didn't want to go into the house with people in it. But by the time I'd walked past it three times, I knew I was going to if I had to.

Then, at half-past seven, the front door opens.

I'm sitting in the van, tucked around the corner, but I can see the house in the rear-view mirror. The front door opens and the girl comes out. She walks to the end of the path, turns left, and goes off up the street.

One down, I think. Now: how many to go?

I tell you, an hour is a long time to wait. It's a long time if you're just sitting there smoking, nothing but a little stone for company, watching a house in the mirror until your neck starts to ache.

At quarter-past eight I see the curtains in the downstairs being drawn.

Hello, I thought. It's not dark yet. Nothing happens for another twenty minutes.

Then I see the door opening. Two people come out. She's wearing a big old hat again. It's a bit far away, and I can't see his face, but I see he's got long hair. I see also just how fucking big they are. Fat, but tall too. A real family of beauties, that's for sure.

They fuck around at the door for a while, and then they walk up the path, and they turn right too.

Bingo. Fucking bingo. I've had a result.

I give them fifteen minutes. Long enough to get on the bus or down the tube, long enough that they won't suddenly turn up again because one of them forgot their phone or wallet. Also, enough for the light to go just a little bit more, so it's going to be a bit darker, and I won't stick out so much.

Then I get out of the van, and walk over to the house. First thing I do is walk straight down the front path, give a little ring on the door. Okay, so I've only seen three of them before, but you never know. Could be another kid, or some old dear. I ring it a couple of times. Nothing happens.

So then I go around the side, the way we got in last time. It's a bit of a squeeze, past three big old bins. Fuck knows what was in them—smelled fucking terrible. Round the back there's the second door. Last time it was unlocked, but I'm not reckoning on that kind of luck twice. Certainly not after it got them burgled. I try it, and sure enough, it didn't budge.

So I get myself up close to the glass panel in the door, and look through the dusty little panes. Some people, soon as they get burgled, they'll have a system put in. Bolting the stable door. It's why you've got to be careful if you find some keys the first time and go back a couple weeks later. Can't see any sign of wires.

So I take the old T-shirt out of my pocket, wrap it around my fist. One quick thump.

It makes a noise, of course. But London is noisy. I wait to see if anybody's light goes on. I can be back out on the street and away in literally seconds.

Nothing happens. No lights. No one shouts "Oi!"

I reach my hand in through the window and would you fucking believe it: they've only left the key in the lock. I love people, I really do. They're so fucking stupid. Two seconds later, I'm inside.

Now's here the point I wish Baz is with me. He's not bright, but he's got a good memory for places. He'd remember exactly where he'd found everything. I don't have a clue, but I've got a hunch.

The bureau with the empty drawer. The place where I got my stone. Well, Baz found it, of course. But it's mine now.

I walk through the kitchen without a second glance. Did it properly last time. The main light's on in the living room, and I can see it's even more untidy than last time. The sofa is covered in all kinds of shit. Old books, bits of clothes. A big old map. Looks very old, in fact, and I make a mental note to take that when I go. Could be the Pole's contact would be interested in that too.

I stand in front of the bureau. My heart is going like a fucking jackhammer. Partly it's doing a job by myself. Mainly I just really, really want to find something. I want the jewelry. More even than that, I want another stone.

I look through the drawers. One by one. Methodical. I take everything out, look through it carefully. There's nothing. I'm pissed off, getting jittery. I've always known it might be that there just isn't any more of the stuff. But now I'm getting afraid.

In the end I go to the drawer I know is empty, and I pull it out. It's still empty. I'm about to shove it closed again, when I notice something. A smell. I look around the room, but at first I can't tell what's making it. Could be a plate with some old food on it, I think, lost under a pile of books somewhere. Then I realize it's coming from the drawer. I don't know how to describe it, but it's definitely there. It's not strong, but . . .

Then I get it, I think. It's air. It's a different kind of air. It's not like London. It's like . . . the sea. Sea air, like you'd get down on the front in some pissy little town on the coast, the kind people don't go to any more and didn't have much to recommend it in the first place. Some little town or village with old stone buildings, cobbled streets, thatched roofs. A place where there's lots of shadows, maybe a big old deserted factory or something on a hill overlooking the town; where you hear odd footsteps down narrow streets and alleys in the dark afternoons and when the birds cry out in the night the sound is stretched and cramped and echoes as if it is bouncing off things you cannot see.

That kind of place. A place like that.

I lean down to the drawer, stick my nose in, give it another good sniff No doubt about it—the smell's definitely coming from inside. I don't like it. I don't like it at all. So I slam it shut.

And that's when I realize.

When the drawer bangs closed, I hear a little noise. Not just the slam but something else.

Slowly, I pull it back out again. I put my hand inside, and feel towards the back. My arm won't go in as far as it should.

The drawer's got a false back.

I pull it and pull it, but I can't get it to come out. So I get the screwdriver out of my back pocket and slip it inside. I angle my hand around and get the tip into the joint right at the back. I'm feeling hot, and starting to sweat. Fucking tricky to get any pull on it, but I give it a good yank.

There's a splintering sound, and my hand whacks into the other side. I let go of the screwdriver and feel with my fingers. An inch of the wooden back has come away. There's something behind it, for sure. A little space I can tell because my fingertips feel a little cold, as if there's a breeze coming from in there. Can't be, of course, but it tells me what I need to know.

Something's behind there. Could be the jewelry I came for. Could be even better. Could be another stone. Another stone that smells like the sea. So I get the screwdriver in position again. Get it good and tight against the side, and get ready to give it an almighty pull.

And that's when I feel the soft breath on the back of my neck, and her hands coming gently around my waist; and one of the others turning off the lights.

It is just a question of attitude, it turns out. The student tosser had it right. It's all a matter of how you see the people you're doing over, whether you think about them at all, or if you just see what you can get from them. What you need.

I gave them Baz, on the Sunday night. They didn't make me watch, but I heard. An hour later there was just a stain on the carpet, like the one we'd seen upstairs. They gave me another one of the stones, even prettier than the one I had before. It's beautiful.

Fair exchange is no robbery. I'm giving them Jackie next.

From even the greatest of horrors irony is seldom absent. Sometimes it enters directly into the composition of the events, while sometimes it relates only to their fortuitous position among persons and places.

"The Shunned House" · H.P. Lovecraft (1928)

· MR. GAUNT ·
John Langan

It was not until five weeks after his father's funeral that Henry Farange was able to remove the white plastic milk crate containing the old man's final effects from the garage. His reticence was a surprise: his father had been sick—dying, really—for the better part of two years and Henry had known it, had known of the enlarged heart, the failing kidneys, the brain jolted by mini-strokes. He had known it was, in the nursing home doctor's favorite cliché, only a matter of time, and if there were moments Henry could not believe the old man had held on for as long or as well as he had, that didn't mean he expected his father to walk out of the institution to which his steadily-declining health had consigned him. For all that, the inevitable phone call, the one telling him that his father had suffered what appeared to be a heart attack, caught him off-guard, and when his father's nurse had approached him at the gravesite, her short arms cradling the milk crate into which the few items the old man had taken with him to the nursing home had been deposited, Henry's chest had tightened, his eyes filled with burning tears. Upon his return home from the post-funeral brunch, he had removed the crate from his backseat and carried it into the garage, where he set it atop his workbench, telling himself he couldn't face what it contained today, but would see to it tomorrow.

Tomorrow, though, turned into the day after tomorrow, which became the day after that, and then the following day, and so on, until a two week period passed during which Henry didn't think of the white plastic milk crate at all, and was only reminded of it when a broken cabinet hinge necessitated his sliding up the garage door. The sight of the milk crate was a reproach, and in a sudden burst of repentance he rushed up to it, hauled it off the workbench, and ran into the house with it as if it were a pot of boiling water and he without gloves. He half-dropped it onto the kitchen table and stood over it, panting. Now that he let his gaze wander over the crate's contents, he could see that it was not as full as he had feared. A dozen hardcover books: his father's favorite Henry James novels, which, he had claimed, were all that he wanted to read in his remaining time. Henry lifted them from the crate one by one, glancing at their titles. *The Ambassadors. The Wings of the Dove. The Golden Bowl. The Turn of the Screw. What Maisie Knew.* He recognized that last one: the old man had tried twice to convince him to read it, sending him a copy when he was at college, and again a couple of years ago, a month or two before he entered the nursing home. It was his father's favorite book of his favorite writer, and, although he was no English scholar, Henry had done his best, both times, to read it. But he rapidly became lost in the labyrinth of the book's prose, in sentences that wound on for what felt like days, so that by the time you arrived at the end, you had forgotten the beginning and had to start over again. He hadn't finished *What Maisie Knew*, had given up the attempt after chapter one the first time, chapter three the second, and had had to admit his failures to his father. He had blamed his failures on other obligations, on school and work, promising he would give the book another try when he was less busy. He might make good his promise yet: there might be a third attempt, possibly even success, but when he was done, his father would not be waiting to discuss it with him. Henry removed the rest of the books from the crate rapidly.

Here was a framed photo of him receiving his MBA, a smaller black and white picture of a man and woman he recognized as his grandparents tucked into its lower right corner. Here was a gray cardboard shoebox filled with assorted snapshots that appeared to stretch back over his father's lifetime, as well as four old letters folded in their original envelopes. Here was a postcard showing the view up the High Street to Edinburgh Castle. Here was the undersized saltire, the blue and white flag of Scotland, he had bought for his father when he had stopped off for a weekend in Edinburgh on his way home from Frankfurt, just last summer. Here was a cassette tape wrapped in a piece of ruled notebook paper bound to it by a thick rubber band, his name written on the paper in his father's rolling hand.

His heart leapt, and Henry slid the rubber band from the around the paper with fingers suddenly dumb. There was more writing on the other side of the paper, a brief note. He read, "Dear Son, I'm making this tape *just in case*. Listen to it *as soon as possible*. It's all true. Love, Dad." That was all. He turned the tape over: it was plain and black, no label on either side. Leaving the note on the table, he carried the tape into the living room, to the stereo. He slid the tape into the deck, pushed PLAY, adjusted the volume, and stood back, arms crossed.

For a moment, there was only the hum of blank tape, then a loud snap and clatter and the sound of his father's voice, low, resonant, and slightly graveled, the way it sounded when he was tired. His father said, "I think I have this thing working. Yes, that's it." He cleared his throat. "Hello, Henry, it's your father. If you're listening to this, then I'm gone. I realize this may seem strange, but there are facts of which you need to be aware, and I'm concerned I don't have much time to tell you them. I've tried to write it all down for you, but my hand's shaking so badly I can't make any progress. To tell the truth, I don't know if the matter's sufficiently clear in my head for me to write it. So, I've borrowed this machine from the night-duty nurse. I suppose I should have told you all this—oh, years ago, but I didn't, because—well, let's get to what I have to say first. I can fill in my motivations along the way. I hope you have the time to listen to this all at once, because I don't think it'll make much sense in bits and pieces. I'm not sure it makes much sense all together.

"The other night, I saw your uncle on television: not David, your mother's brother, but George, my brother. I'm sure you won't remember him: the last and only time you saw him, you were four. I saw him, and I saw his butler. You know how little I sleep these days, no matter, it seems, how tired I am. Much of the time between sunset and sunrise I pass reading—re-reading James, and watching more television than I should. Last night, unable to concentrate on *What Maisie Knew* any longer, I found myself watching a documentary about Edinburgh on public television. If I watch PBS, I can convince myself I'm being mildly virtuous, and I was eager to see one of my favorite cities, if only on the screen. It's the city my parents came from; I know you know that. Sadly, the documentary was a failure, so spectacularly insipid that it almost succeeded in delivering me to sleep a good three hours ahead of schedule. Then I saw George walk across the screen. The shot was of Prince's Street during the Edinburgh festival. The street was crowded, but I recognized my brother. He was slightly stooped, his hair and beard bone-white, though his step was still lively. He was followed by his butler, who stood as tall and unbending as ever. Just as he was about to walk off the screen, George stopped, turned his head to the camera, and winked, slowly and deliberately.

"From the edge of sleep, I was wide awake, filled with such fear my shaking hands fumbled the remote control onto the floor. I couldn't muster the courage to retrieve it, and it lay there until the morning nurse picked it up. I didn't sleep: I couldn't. Your uncle kept walking across that screen, his butler close behind. Though I hadn't heard the news of his death, I had assumed he must be gone by now. More than assumed: I had hoped it. I should have guessed, however, that George would not have slipped so gently into that good night; indeed, although he's just this side of ninety, I now suspect he'll be around for quite some time to come.

"Seeing him—does it sound too mad to say that I half-think he saw me? More than half-think: I know he saw me. Seeing my not-dead older brother walk across the screen, to say nothing of his butler, I became obsessed with the thought of you. Your uncle may try to contact you, especially once I'm gone, which I have the most unreasonable premonition may be sooner rather than later. Before he does, you must know about him. You must know who, and what, he is. You must know his history, and you must know about his butler, about that . . . monster. For reasons you'll understand later, I can't simply tell you what I have to tell you, or perhaps I should say I can't tell you what I have to tell you simply. If I were to come right out with it in two sentences, you wouldn't believe me; you'd think I had suffered one TIA too many. I can't warn you to stay away from your uncle and leave it at that: I know you, and I know the effect such prohibitions have on you; I've no desire to arouse your famous curiosity. So I'm going to ask you to bear with me, to let me tell you about my brother I what I think is the manner best-suited to it. Indulge me, Henry, indulge your old father."

Henry paused the tape. He walked out of the living room back into the kitchen, where he rummaged the refrigerator for a beer while his father's words echoed in his ears. The old man knew him, all right: his "famous" curiosity was aroused, enough that he would sit down and listen to the rest of the tape now, in one sitting. His dinner date was not for another hour and a half, and, even if he were a few minutes late, that wouldn't be a problem. He smiled, thinking that despite his father's protestations of fear, once the old man warmed up to talking, you could hear the James scholar taking over, his words, his phrasing, his sentences, bearing subtle witness to a lifetime spent with the writer he had called "the Master." Henry pried the cap off the beer, checked to be sure answering machine was on, switched the phone's ringer off, and returned to the living room, where he released the PAUSE button and settled himself on the couch.

His father's voice returned.

II

Once upon a time, there was a boy who lived with his father and his father's butler in a very large house. As the boy's father was frequently away, and often for long periods of time, he was left alone in the large house with the butler, whose name was Mr. Gaunt. While he was away, the boy's father allowed him to roam through every room in the house except one. He could run through the kitchen; he could bounce on his father's bed; he could leap from the tall chairs in the living room. But he must never, ever, under any circumstances, go into his father's study. His father was most insistent on this point. If the boy entered the study . . . his father refused to say what would happen, but the tone of his voice and the look on his face hinted that it would be something terrible.

That was how the story used to begin, as if it were a fairy tale that someone else had written and I just happened to remember. I suppose it sounds generic enough: the traditional, almost incantatory, beginning; the nondescript boy, father, butler, and house. Do you remember the first time I told it to you? I don't imagine so: you were five, although you were precocious, which was what necessitated the tale in the first place. You were staying with me for the summer—your mother and her second husband were in Greece—in the house in Highland. That house! all those rooms, the high ceilings, the porch with its view of the Hudson: how I wish you didn't have to sell it to afford the cost of putting me in this place. I had hoped you might choose to live there. Ah well, as you yourself said, what use is a house of that size to you, with no wife or family? Another regret . . .

But I was talking about the story, and the first time you heard it. Like some second-rate Bluebeard, I had permitted you free access to every room in the house save one: my study, which contained not the head of my previous wife (if only! sorry, I know she's your mother), but extensive notes, four years' worth of notes towards the book I was about to write on Henry James's portrayal of family relations. Yes, yes, I should have known that declaring it forbidden would only pique your interest; it's one of those mistakes you not only can't believe you made, but that seems so fundamentally obvious you doubt whether in fact it occurred. The room was kept locked when I wasn't working in it, and I believed it secure. All this time later, I have yet to discover how you broke into it. I can see you sitting in the middle of the hardwood floor, four years' work scattered and shredded around you, a look of the most intense concentration upon your face as you dragged a pen across my first edition of *The Wings of the Dove*. I'm not sure how, but I remained calm, if not quite cheerful, as I escorted you from my study up the stairs to your bedroom. I sat you on the bed and told you I had a story for you. You were very excited: you loved it when I told you stories. Was it another one about Hercules? No, it wasn't; it was another kind of story. It was the story of a little boy just about your age, a little boy who had opened a door he was not supposed to.

Then and there, my brain racing, I told you the story of Mr. Gaunt and his terrible secret, speaking slowly, deliberately, so that I would have time to shape the next event. Does it surprise you to hear that the story has no written antecedent? It became such a part of our lives after that. It frightened you out of my study for the rest of that summer; you avoided that entire side of the house. Then the next summer, when your friend Brad came to stay for the weekend and the three of us stayed up late while I told you stories, you actually requested it. "Tell about Mr. Gaunt," you said. I can't tell you how shocked I was. I was shocked that you remembered: children forget much, and it's difficult to predict what will lodge in their minds; plus you had been with your mother and husband number two without interruption for almost nine months. I was shocked, too, that you would want to hear a narrative expressly crafted to frighten you. It frightened poor Brad; we had to leave the light on for him, which you treated with a bit more contempt than really was fair.

After that: how many times did I tell you that story? Several that same summer, and several every summer for the next six or seven years. Even when you were a teenager, and grew your hair long and refused to remove that denim jacket that you wore down to an indistinct shade of pale, even then you requested the story, albeit with less frequency. It's never gone that far from us, has it? At dinner, the visit before last, we talked about it. Strange that in all this time you never asked me how I came by it, in what volume I first read it. Perhaps you're used to my having an esoteric source for everything and assume this to be the case here. Or perhaps you don't want to know: you find it adds to the story not to know its origin. Or perhaps you're just not interested: literary scholarship never has been your strong point. That's not a reproach: investment banking has been very good for and to you, and you know how proud I am of you.

There is more to the story, though: there is more to every story. You can always work your way down, peel back the layers 'til you discover, as it were, the skull beneath the skin. Whatever you thought about the story's roots, whatever you would answer if I were to ask you where you thought I had plucked it from, I'm sure you never guessed that it grew out of an event that occurred in our family. That *donnee*, as James would've called it, involved George, George and his butler and Peter, George's son and your cousin. Yes, you haven't heard of Peter before: I haven't ever mentioned his name to you. He's been dead a long time now.

You met George when you were four, at the house in Highland. I had just moved into it from the apartment in Huguenot I occupied after your mother and I separated. George was in Manhattan for a couple of days, doing research at one of the museums, and took the train up to spend the afternoon with us. He was short, stocky verging on portly, and he kept his beard trimmed in a Vandyke, which combined with his deep-set eyes and sharp nose leant him rather a Satanic appearance: the effect, I'm sure, intended. He wore a vest and a pocket watch with which you were fascinated, not having seen a pocket watch before. Throughout the afternoon and into the evening, you kept asking George what time it was. He responded to each question by slowly withdrawing the watch from his pocket by its chain, popping open its cover, carefully scrutinizing its face, and announcing, "Why, Hank," (he insisted on calling you Hank; he appeared to find it most amusing), "it's three o'clock." He was patient with you; I will grant him that.

After I put you to bed, he and I sat on the back porch looking at the Hudson, drinking Scotch, and talking, the end result of which was that he made a confession—confession! it was more of a boast!—and I demanded he leave the house, leave it then and there and never return, never speak to me or communicate in any way with me again. He didn't believe I was serious, but he went. I've no idea how or if he made his train. I haven't heard from him since, all these years, nor have I have heard of him, until last night.

But this is all out of order. You don't know anything about your uncle. I've been careful not to mention his name lest I arouse that curiosity of yours. Indeed, maybe I shouldn't be doing so now. That's assuming, of course, that you'll take any of the story I'm going to relate seriously, that you won't think I've confused my Henry James with M.R. James, or, worse, think it a sign of mental or emotional decay, the first hint of senility or depression. The more I insist on the truth of what I tell, the more shrill and empty my voice will sound; I know the scenario well. I risk, then, a story that might be taken as little more than a prolonged symptom of mental impairment or illness; though really, how interesting is that? In any event, it's not as if I have to worry about you putting me in a home. Yes, I know you had no choice. Let's start with the background, the condensed information the author delivers, after an interesting opening, in one or two well-written chapters.

George was ten years older than I, the child of what in those days was considered our parents' middle age, as I was the child of their old age. This is to say that Mother was thirty-five when George was born, and forty-five when I was. Father was close to fifty at my birth, about the same age I was when you were born. Funny—as a boy and a young man, I used to swear that, if I was to have children, I would not wait until I was old enough to be their grandfather, and despite those vows that was exactly what I did. Do you suppose that's why you haven't married yet? We like to think we're masters of our own fates, but the fact is, our parents' examples exert far more influence on us than we realize or are prepared to realize. I like to think I was a much more youthful father to you than my father was to me, but in all fairness, fifty was a different age for me than it was for him. For me, fifty was the age of my maturity, a time of ripeness, a balance point between youth and old age; for Father, fifty was a room with an unsettlingly clear view of the grave. He died when I was fifteen, you know, while here I am, thanks to a daily assortment of colored pills closer to eighty than anyone in my family before me, with the exception, of course, of my brother.

I have few childhood memories of George: an unusually intelligent student, he left the house and the country for Oxford at the age of fifteen. Particularly gifted in foreign languages, he achieved minor fame for his translation and commentary on *Les mysteres du ver*, a fifteenth century French translation of a much older Latin work. England suited him well; he returned to see us in Poughkeepsie infrequently. He did, however, visit our parents' brothers and sisters, our uncles and aunts, in and around Edinburgh on holidays, which appeared to mollify Father and Mother. (Their trips back to Scotland were fewer than George's trips back to them.) My brother also voyaged to the Continent: France, first, which irritated Father (he was possessed by an almost pathological hatred of all things French, whose cause I never could discover, since our name is French; you can be sure, he would not have read my book on Flaubert); then Italy, which worried Mother (she was afraid the Catholics would have him); then beyond, on to those countries that for the greater part of my life were known as Yugoslavia: Croatia, Bosnia-Herzegovina, Serbia, and past them to the nations bordering the Black Sea. He made this trip and others like it, to Finland, to Turkey, to Persia as it was then called, often enough. I have no idea how he afforded any of it. Our parents sent him little enough money, and his scholarship was no source of wealth. I have no idea, either, of the purpose of these trips; when I asked him, George answered, "Research," and said no more. He wrote once a month, never more and occasionally less, short letters in which a single nugget of information was buried beneath layers of formality and pleasantry; not like those letters I wrote to you while you were at Harvard. It was in such a letter that he told us he was engaged to be married.

Aside from the fact that it lasted barely two years, the most remarkable thing about your uncle's marriage was your cousin, Peter, who was born seven months after it. Mother's face wore a suspicious frown for several days after the news of his birth reached us (I think it came by telegram; your grandparents were very late installing a phone); Father was too excited by the birth of his first grandson to care. I didn't feel much except a kind of disinterested curiosity. I was an uncle, but I was thirteen, so the role didn't have the significance for me it might have had I been only a few years older. The chances of my seeing my nephew any time in the near future were sufficiently slim to justify my reserve; as it happened, however, my brother and his wife, whose name was Clarissa, visited us the following summer with Peter. Clarissa was quite wealthy; she was also, I believe, quite a bit older than George, though by how much I couldn't say. Even now, after a lifetime's practice, I'm not much good at deciphering people's ages, which causes me no end of trouble, I can assure you. Their visit went smoothly enough, though your grandparents showed, I noticed, the razor edge of uneasiness with their new daughter-in-law's crisp accent and equally crisp manners. Your grandmother used her wedding china every night, while your grandfather, whose speech usually was peppered with Scots words and expressions, spoke what my mother used to call "the King's English." Their working class origins, I suspect, rising up to haunt them.

Peter was fat and blond, a pleasant child who appeared to enjoy his place on your grandmother's hip, which from the moment he arrived was where he spent most of his days. Any reservations Mother might have had concerning the circumstances of his birth were wiped away at the sight of him. When he returned from work, Father had a privileged place for his grandson on his knee: holding each of the baby's hands in his hands, Father sat Peter upright on his knee, then jiggled his leg up and down, bouncing Peter as if he were riding a horse, all the while singing a string of nonsense syllables: "a leedle lidel leedle lidel leedle lidel lum." It was something Father did with any baby who entered the house; he must have done it with me, and with George. I tried it with you, but you were less than amused by it. After what appeared to be some initial doubt at his grandfather's behavior, when he rode up and down with an almost tragic expression on his face, Peter quickly came to enjoy and even anticipate it, and when he saw his grandfather walk in the door, the baby's face would break into an enormous grin, and he waved his arms furiously. Clarissa was good with her son, handling him with more confidence than you might expect from a new mother; George largely ignored Peter, passing him to Clarissa, Mother, Father, or me whenever he could manage it. Much of his days George spent sequestered in his room, working, he said, on a new translation. Of what he did not specify, only that the book was very old, much older than *Les mysteres du ver*. He kept the door to the room locked, which I discovered, of course, trying to open it.

The three of them stayed a month, leaving with promises to write on both sides, and although it was more than a year later, it seemed the next thing anyone heard or knew Clarissa had filed for divorce. Your grandparents were stunned. They refused to tell me the grounds for Clarissa's action, but when I lay awake at night I heard them discussing it downstairs in the living room, their voices faint and indistinguishable except when one or the other of them became agitated and shouted, "It isn't true, for God's sake, it can't be true! We didn't raise him like that!" Clarissa sued for custody of Peter, and somewhat to our parents' surprise, I think, George counter-sued. It was not only that he did not appear possessed of sufficient funds; he did not appear possessed of sufficient interest. The litigation was interminable and bitter. Your grandfather died before it was through, struck dead in the street as we were walking back from Sunday services by a stroke whose cause, I was and am sure, was his elder son's divorce. George did not return for the funeral; he phoned to say it was absolutely impossible for him to attend—the case and all—he was sure Father would have understood. The divorce and custody battle were not settled for another year after that. When they were, George was triumphant.

I don't know if you remember the opening lines of *What Maisie Knew*. The book begins with a particularly messy divorce and custody fight, in which the father, though "bespattered from head to foot," initially succeeds. The reason, James tells us, is "not so much that the mother's character had been more absolutely damaged as that the brilliancy of a lady's complexion (and this lady's, in court, was immensely remarked) might be more regarded as showing the spots." I can recall reading those lines for the first time: I was a senior in high school, and a jolt of recognition shot up my spine as I recognized George and Clarissa, whose final blows against one another had been struck the previous fall. I think that's when I first had an inclination I might study old James. Unlike James's novel, in which the custody of Maisie is eventually divided between her parents, George won full possession of Peter, which he refused to share in the slightest way with Clarissa. I imagine she must have been devastated. George packed his and Peter's bags and moved north, to Edinburgh, where he purchased a large house on the High Street and engaged the services of a manservant, Mr. Gaunt.

Oh yes, Mr. Gaunt was an actual person. Are you surprised to hear that? I suppose he did seem rather a fantastic creation, didn't he? I can't think of him with anything less than complete revulsion, revulsion and fear, more fear than I wish I felt. I met him when I was in Edinburgh doing research on Stevenson and called on my brother, who had returned from the Shetlands that morning and was preparing to leave for Belgium later that same night. The butler was exactly as I described him to you in the story, only more so.

Mr. Gaunt never said a word. He was very tall, and very thin, and his skin was very white and very tight, as if he were wearing a suit that was too small. He had a long face and long, lank, thin, colorless hair, and a big, thick jaw, and tiny eyes that peered out at you from the deep caverns under his brows. He did not smile, but kept his mouth in a perpetual pucker. He wore a black coat with tails, a gray vest and gray pants, and a white shirt with a gray cravat. He was most quiet, and if you were standing in the kitchen or the living room and did not hear anything behind you, you could expect to turn around and find Mr. Gaunt standing there.

Mr. Gaunt served the meals, though he himself never ate that the boy saw, and escorted visitors to and from the boy's father when the boy's father was home, and, on nights when he was not home, Mr. Gaunt unlocked the door of the forbidden study at precisely nine o'clock and went into it, closing the door behind him. He remained there for an hour. The boy did not know what the butler did in that room, nor was he all that interested in finding out, but he was desperate for a look at his father's study.

Your uncle claimed to have contracted Gaunt's service during one of his many trips, and explained that the reason Gaunt never spoke was a thick accent—I believe George said it was Belgian—that marred his speech and caused him excruciating embarrassment. As Gaunt served us tea and shortbread, I remember thinking that something about him suggested greed, deep and profound: his hands, whose movements were precise yet eager; his eyes, which remained fixed on the food, and us; his back, which was slightly bent, inclining him towards us but having the opposite effect, making him seem as if he were straining upright, resisting a powerful downward pull. No doubt it was the combination of these things. Whatever the source, I was noticeably glad to see him exit the room; although, after he had left, I had the distinct impression he was listening at the door, hunched down, still greedy.

As you must have guessed, the boy in our fairy tale was Peter, your cousin. He was fourteen when he had his run in with Mr. Gaunt, older, perhaps, than you had imagined him; the children in fairy tales are always young children, aren't they? I should also say more about the large house in which he lived. It was a seventeenth century mansion located on the High Street in Edinburgh, across the street and a few doors down from St. Giles's Cathedral. Its inhabitants had included John Jackson, a rather notorious character from the early nineteenth century. There's a mention of him in James's notebooks: he heard Jackson's story while out to dinner in Poughkeepsie, believe it or not, and considered treating it in a story before rejecting it as, "too lurid, too absolutely over the top." The popular legend, of whose origins I'm unsure, is that Jackson, a defrocked Anglican priest, had truck with infernal powers. Robed and hooded men were seen exiting his house who had not been seen entering it. Lights glowed in windows, strange cries and laughter sounded, late at night. A woman who claimed to have worked as Jackson's chambermaid swore there was a door to Hell in a room deep under the basement. He was suspected in the vanishings of several local children, but nothing was proved against him. He died mysteriously, found, as I recall, at the foot of a flight of stairs, apparently having tumbled down them. His ghost, its neck still broken, was sighted walking in front of the house, looking over at St. Giles and grinning; about what, I've never heard.

Most of this information about the house I had from George during my visit; it was one of the few subjects about which I ever saw him enthused. I don't know how much if any of it your cousin knew; though I suspect his father would have told him all. Despite the picture its history conjures, the house was actually quite pleasant: five stories high including the attic, full of surprisingly large and well-lit rooms, decorated with a taste I wouldn't have believed George possessed. There was indeed a locked study: it composed the entirety of the attic. I saw the great dark oaken door to it when your uncle took me on a tour of the house: we walked up the flight of stairs to the attic landing and there was the entrance to the study. George did not open it. I asked him if this was where he kept the bodies, and although he cheerfully replied that no, no, that was what the cellar was for, his eyes registered a momentary flash of something that was panic or annoyance. I did not ask him to open the door, in which there was a keyhole of sufficient diameter to afford a good look into the room beyond. Had my visit been longer, had I been his guest overnight, I might have stolen back up to that landing to peak at whatever it was my brother did not wish me to see. Curiosity, it would appear, does not just run in our family: it gallops.

Peter lived in this place, his father's locked secret above him, his only visitors his tutors, his only companion the silent butler. That's a bit much, isn't it? During our final conversation, George told me that Peter had been a friendless boy, but I doubt he knew his son well enough to render such a verdict with either accuracy or authority. Peter didn't know many, if any, other children, but I like to think of your cousin having friends in the various little shops that line the High Street. You know where I'm talking about, the cobbled street that runs in a straight line up to the Castle. You remember those little shops with their flimsy T-shirts, their campy postcards, their overpriced souvenirs.

We bought the replica of the Castle that used to sit on the mantelpiece at one of them, along with a rather expensive pin for that girl you were involved with at the time. (What was her name? Jane?) I like to think of Peter, out for a walk, stopping in several shops along the way, chatting with the old men and women behind the counter when business was slow. He was a fine conversationalist for his age, your cousin.

I had met him again, you see, when he was thirteen, the year before the events I'm relating occurred. George was going to be away for the entire summer, so Peter came on his own to stay with your grandmother. I was living in Manhattan—actually, I was living in a cheap apartment across the river in New Jersey and taking the ferry to Manhattan each morning. My days I split teaching and writing my dissertation, which was on the then-relatively-fresh topic of James's later novels, particularly *The Golden Bowl*, and their modes of narration. Every other week, more often when I could manage it, I took the train up to your grandmother's to spend the day and have dinner with her. This was not as great a kindness as I would like it to seem: my social life was nonexistent, and I was desperately lonely. Thus, I visited Peter several times throughout June, July, and August.

At our first meeting he was unsure what to make of me, spending most of the meal silently staring down at his plate, and asking to be excused as soon as he had finished his dessert. Over subsequent visits, however, our relationship progressed. By our last dinner he was speaking with me freely, shaking my hand vigorously when it was time for me to leave for my bus and telling me that he had greatly enjoyed making my acquaintance. What did he look like? Funny: I don't think I have a picture of him; not from that visit, anyway. He wasn't especially tall; if he was due an adolescent growth-spurt, it had yet to arrive. His hair, while not the same gold color it had been when he was a baby, still was blond, slightly curled, and his eyes were dark brown. His face, well, as is true with all children, his face blended both his parents', although in his case the blend was particularly fine. What I mean is, unlike you, whose eyes and forehead have always been identifiably mine and whose nose and chin have always been identifiably your mother's, Peter's face, depending on the angle and lighting, appeared to be either all his father or all his mother. Even looking at him directly, you could see both faces simultaneously. He spoke with an Edinburgh accent, crisp and clear, and when he was excited or enthusiastic about a subject, his words would stretch out: "That's maaaarvelous." He told your grandmother her accent hadn't slipped in the least, and she smiled for the rest of the day.

He was extremely bright, and extremely interested in ancient Egypt, about which his father had provided him with several surprisingly good books. He could not decide whether to be a philologist, like his father, or an Egyptologist, which sounded more interesting; he inclined to Egyptology, but thought his father would appreciate him following his path. Surprising and heartbreaking—horrifying—as it seems in retrospect, Peter loved and missed his father. He was very proud of George: he knew of and appreciated George's translations, and confided in us his hope that one day he might achieve something comparable. "My father's a genius," I can hear him saying, almost defiantly. We were sitting at your grandmother's dining room table. I can't remember how we had arrived at the subject of George, but he went on, "Aye, a genius. None of his teachers were ever as smart as him. None of them could make head nor tail of *Les mysteres du ver*, and my father translated the whole thing, on his own. There was this one teacher who thought he was something, and he was pretty smart, but my father was smarter; he showed him."

"Of course he's smart, dear," your grandmother said. "He's a Farange. Just like you and your uncle."

"And your Granny," I said.

"Oh, go on, you," she said.

"He's translated things that no one's even heard of," Peter went on. "He's translated pre-dynastic Egyptian writing. That's from before the pyramids, even. That's fifty-five centuries ago. Most folk don't even know it exists."

"Has he let you see any of it?" I asked.

"No," Peter said glumly. "He says I'm not ready yet. I have to master Latin and Greek before I can move on to just hieroglyphics."

"I'm sure you will," your grandmother said, and we moved on to some other topic. Later, after Peter was asleep, she said to me, "He's a lovely boy, our Peter, a lovely boy. So polite and well-mannered. But he seems awfully lonely to me. Always with his nose in a book: I don't think his father spends nearly enough time with him."

Peter did not speak of his mother.

He knew ancient Egypt as if he had lived in it: your grandmother and I spent more than one dinner listening to your cousin narrate such events as the building of the Great Pyramid of Giza, the factual accuracy of which I couldn't verify but whose telling kept me enthralled. Peter was a born *raconteur*: as he narrated his history, he would assume the voices of the different figures in it, from Pharaoh to slave. "The Great Pyramid," he would say, addressing the two of us as if we were a crowd at a lecture hall, "was built for the Pharaoh Khufu. The Greeks called him Cheops. He lived during the Fourth Dynasty, which was about four and half thousand years ago. The moment he became Pharaoh, Khufu started planning his pyramid, because, really, it was the most important thing he was ever going to build. The Egyptians were terribly concerned with death, and spent much of their lives preparing for it. He picked a site on the western bank of the Nile. The Egyptians thought the western bank was a special place because the sun set in the west. The west was the place of the dead, if you like, the right place to build your tomb. That's all it was, after all, a pyramid. Not that you'd know that from the name: it's a Greek word, 'pyramid;' it comes from 'wheat cake.' The Greeks thought the pyramids looked like giant pointy wheat cakes. We get a lot of names for Egyptian things from the Greeks: like 'pharaoh,' which they adapted from an Egyptian word that meant 'great house.' And 'sarcophagus,' that comes from the Greek for 'flesh-eating.' Why they called funeral vaults flesh-eaters I'll never know." And so on. He did love a good digression, your cousin: he would have made a fine college professor.

So you see, all this is why I dispute your uncle's claim that he was friendless, solitary: given the right set of circumstances, Peter could be positively garrulous. I have little trouble picturing him keeping the proprietor of a small bookshop, say, entertained with the story of the Pharaoh—I can't remember his name—who angered his people so that after his death his statues and monuments were destroyed and he was not buried in his own tomb; no one knew what had become of his body. No one knew what happened to his son either. I planned to take Peter to the Met, to see their Egyptian collection, but for reasons I can't recall we never went. At our final visit, he suggested we write. Initially, I demurred: I was buried in the last chapter of my dissertation, which I had expected to be forty pages I could write in a month but which rapidly had swelled to eighty-five pages that would consume my every waking moment for the next four months. We could write when I was finished, I explained. Peter pleaded with me, though, and in the end I agreed. We didn't write much, just four letters from him and three replies from me.

I found myself leafing through Peter's letters the winter after his visit, when your uncle telephoned your grandmother to inform her that your cousin was missing: he had run away from home and no one knew where he was. Your grandmother was distraught; I was, too, when she called me with the news of Peter's vanishing. She was upset at George, who apparently had shown only the faintest trace of emotion while delivering to her what she rightly regarded as terrible information. He was sure Peter would turn up, George said, boys will be boys and all that, what can you do? Lack of proper family feeling in anyone bothered your grandmother; it was her pet peeve; and she found it a particularly egregious fault in one of her own, raised to know better. "It's a good thing your father isn't alive to see this," she said to me, and I was unsure whether she referred to Peter's running away or George's understated reaction to it.

At the time, I suspected Peter might be making his way to his mother's, and went so far as to contact Clarissa myself, but if such was her son's plan she knew nothing about it. Through her manners I could hear the distress straining her voice, and another thing, a reserve I initially could not understand. Granted that speaking to your former brother-in-law is bound to be awkward, Clarissa's reticence was still in excess of any such awkwardness. Gradually, as we stumbled our way through a conversation composed of half-starts and long pauses, I understood that she was possessed by a mixture of fear and loathing: fear, because she suspected me of acting in concert with my brother to trick and trap her (though what more she had left to lose at that point I didn't and don't know; her pride, I suppose); loathing, because she thought that I was cut from the same cloth as George. Whatever George had done to prompt her to seek divorce a dozen years before, her memory and repugnance of it remained sufficiently fresh to make talking to me a considerable effort.

Peter didn't appear at his mother's, or any other relative's, nor did he return to his father's house. Against George's wishes, I'm sure, Clarissa involved the police almost immediately. Because of her social standing and the social standing of her family, I'm equally sure, they brought all their resources to bear on Peter's disappearance. The case achieved a notoriety that briefly extended across the Atlantic, scandalizing your grandmother; though I'm not aware that anyone ever connected George to us. Suspecting the worst, the police focused their attentions on George, bringing him in for repeated and intense questioning, investigating his trips abroad, ransacking his house. Strangely, in the midst of all this, Gaunt apparently went unnoticed. After subjecting George to close scrutiny for several weeks—which yielded no clue to where Peter might be or what might have happened to him—the detective in charge of the investigation fell dead of a heart attack while talking to your uncle on the telephone. As the man was no more than thirty, this was a surprise. His replacement was more kindly disposed to George, judging that he had underwent enough and concentrating the police's attentions elsewhere. Your cousin was not found; he was never found. Though your grandmother continued to hold out hope that he was alive until literally the day she died, thinking he might have found his way to Egypt, I didn't share her optimism, and reluctantly concluded that Peter had met his end.

I was correct, though I had no way of knowing how horrible that end had been. What happened to Peter took place while his father was out of the house; in Finland, he said. It was late winter; when Scotland has yet to free itself from its long nights and the sky is dark for much of the day. Peter had been living with his father's locked study for eleven years. So far as I know, he had shown no interest in the room in the past, which strikes me as a bit unusual, although I judge all other children's curiosity against yours, an unfair comparison. Perhaps George had told his own cautionary tale. There was no reason to expect Peter's interest to awaken at that moment, but it did. He became increasingly intrigued by that heavy door and what it concealed. I know this, you see, because it was in the first letter he sent to me, which arrived less than a month after his return home. He decided to confide in me, and I was flattered. Though he didn't write this to me, I believe he must have associated his father's study with those Egyptian tombs he'd been reading about; he must have convinced himself of a parallel between him entering that room and Howard Carter entering Tutankhamun's tomb. His father provided him a generous allowance, so I know he wasn't interested in money, as he himself was quick to reassure me in that same letter. He didn't want me to suspect his motives: he was after knowledge; he wanted to see what was hidden behind the dark door. Exactly how long that desire burned in him I can't say; he admitted that while he'd been wandering the woods behind your grandmother's house, he'd been envisioning himself walking through that room in his father's house, imagining its contents. He didn't specify what he thought those contents might be, and I wonder how accurate his imagination was. Did he picture the squat bookcases overstuffed with books, scrolls, and even stone tablets; the long tables heaped with goblets, boxes, candles, jars; the walls hung with paintings and drawings; the floor chalked with elaborate symbols? (I describe it well, don't I? I've seen it—but that must wait.)

It was with his second letter that Peter first disclosed his plans to satisfy his curiosity; plans I encouraged, if only mildly, when at last I sent him a reply. He would have to be careful, I wrote, if he were caught, I had no doubt the consequences would be severe. I didn't believe they actually would be, but I enjoyed participating in what I knew was, for your cousin, a great adventure. I suggested that he take things in stages, that he try a brief trip up to the attic stairs first and see how that went. What length of time was required for him to amass sufficient daring to venture the narrow flight of stairs to the attic landing I can't say. Perhaps he climbed a few of the warped, creaking stairs one day, before his nerve broke and he bolted down them back to his room; then a few more the next day; another the day after that; and so on, adding a stair or two a day until at last he stood at the landing. Or perhaps he rushed up the staircase all at once, his heart pounding, his stomach weak, taking the stairs two and three at a time, at the great dark door almost before he knew it. Having reached the landing, was he satisfied with his accomplishment? or were his eyes drawn to the door, to the wide keyhole that offered a view of the room beyond? We hadn't discussed that: did it seem too much, a kind of quantum leap from what he had risked scaling the stairs? or did it seem the next logical step: in for a penny, in for a pound, as it were? Once he stood outside the door, he couldn't have waited very long to lower his eye to the keyhole. When he did, his mouth dry, his hands shaking slightly, expecting to hear either his father of Mr. Gaunt behind him at every moment, he was disappointed: the windows in the room were heavily curtained, the lights extinguished, leaving it dim to the point of darkness on even the brightest day, the objects inside no more than confused shadows.

Peter boiled down all of this to two lines in his third letter, which I received inside a Christmas card. "I finally went to the door," he wrote, "and even looked in the keyhole! But everything was dark, and I couldn't see at all." Well, I suggested in my response, he would need to spy through the door when the study was occupied. Why not focus on Mr. Gaunt and his nine o'clock visitations? His father's returns home were too infrequent and erratic to be depended upon, and I judged the consequences of discovery by his father to be far in excess of those of discovery by the butler. (If I'd known . . .) Peter felt none of my unease around Mr. Gaunt, which was understandable, given that the butler had been a fixture in his home and life for more than a decade. In his fourth and final letter, Peter thanked me for my suggestion. He had been pondering a means to pilfer Gaunt's key to the room, only to decide that, for the moment, such an enterprise involved a degree of risk whatever was in the room might not be worth. I had the right idea: best to survey the attic clearly, then plan his next step. He would wait until his father was going to be away for a good couple of week, which wouldn't be until February. In the meantime, he was trying to decipher the sounds of Mr. Gaunt's nightly hour in the study: the two heavy clumps, the faint slithering, the staccato clicks like someone walking across the floor wearing tap shoes. I replied that it could be the butler was practicing his dancing, which I thought was much funnier at the time than I realize now it was, but that it seemed more likely what Peter was hearing was some sort of cleaning procedure. He should be careful, I wrote, obviously, the butler knew Peter wasn't supposed to be at the study, and if he caught him there, he might very well become quite upset, as George could hold him responsible for Peter's trespass.

I didn't hear from Peter again. For a time, I assumed this was because his enterprise had been discovered and him punished by his father. Then I thought it must be because he was burdened with too much schoolwork: the tutors his father had brought to the house for him, he had revealed in his second letter, were most demanding. I intended to write to him, to inquire after the status of our plan, but whenever I remembered my intention I was in the middle of something else that absolutely had to be finished and couldn't be interrupted, or so it seemed, and I never managed even to begin a letter. Then George called your grandmother, to tell her Peter was gone.

It was more than a quarter-century until I learned Peter's fate. Sitting there on the back porch of the house in Highland, I heard it all from my older brother who, in turn, had had it from Gaunt. Oh yes, from Mr. Gaunt: our story, you see, was never that far from the truth. Indeed, it was closer, much closer, than I wish it were.

George left Scotland for an extended trip to Finland the first week in February. He would be away, he told Peter, for at least two weeks, and possibly a third if the manuscripts he was going to view were as extensive as he hoped. Peter wore an appropriately glum face at his father's departure, which pleased George, who had no idea of his son's secret ambition. For the first week after his father left, Peter maintained his daily routine. When at last the appointed date for his adventure arrived, though, he spent it in a state of almost unbearable anticipation, barely able to maintain conversation with any of his shopkeeper friends, inattentive to his tutors, uninterested in his meals. This last would not have escaped Mr. Gaunt's notice.

After spending the late afternoon and early evening roaming through the first three floors of the house, leafing through the library, practicing his shots at the pool table, spinning the antique globe in the living room, Peter declared he was going to make an early night of it, which also would have caught the butler's attention. From first-hand experience, I can tell you that Peter was something of a night owl, retiring to bed only when your grandmother insisted and called him by his full name, and even then reading under the sheets with a flashlight. Gaunt may have suspected your cousin's intentions; I daresay he must have. This would explain why, an hour and a half after Peter said he was turning in, when his bedroom door softly creaked open and Peter, still fully dressed, crept out and slowly climbed the narrow staircase to the attic landing, he found the door to the study standing wide open. It could also be that the butler had grown careless, but that strikes me as unlikely. Whatever Mr. Gaunt was, he was most attentive.

Your cousin stood there at the top of the stairs, gazing at the room that stretched out like a hall and was lit by globed lights dangling from the slanting ceiling. He saw the overstuffed bookcases. He saw the tables heaped high with assorted objects. He saw the paintings crowding the walls, the chalked symbols swarming over the floor. If there was sufficient time for him to study anything in detail, he may have noticed the small Bosch painting, *The Alchemical Wedding*, hanging across from him. It was—and still is—thought lost. It's the typical Bosch scene, crowded with all manner of people and creatures real and fantastic, most of them merrily dancing around the central figures, a man in red robes and a skeleton holding a rose being married by a figure combining features of a man and an eagle. The nearest table displayed a row of jars, each of them filled with pale, cloudy fluid in which floated a single, pink, misshapen fetus; approaching to examine them, he would have been startled to see the eyes of all the tiny forms open and stare at him. If any object caught his attention, it would have been the great stone sarcophagus leaning against the wall to his left, its carved face not the placid mask familiar to him from photos and drawings, but vivid and angry, its eyes glaring, its nostrils flaring, its mouth open wide and ringed with teeth. That would have chased any fear of discovery from his mind and brought him boldly into the study.

It could be, of course, that Peter's gaze, like the boy in our story's, was immediately captured by what was hanging on the antique coat-stand across from him.

At first, the boy thought it was a coat, for that is, after all, what you expect to find on a coat-stand. He assumed it must be Mr. Gaunt's coat, which the butler must have taken off and hung up when he entered the study. Why the butler should have been wearing a coat as long as this one, and with a hood and gloves attached, inside the house, the boy could not say. The more the boy studied it, however, the more he thought that it was a very strange coat indeed: for one thing, it was not so much that the coat was long as that there appeared to be a pair of pants attached to it, and, for another, its hood and gloves were unlike any he had seen before. Where the coat was black, the hood was a pale color that seemed familiar but that the boy could not immediately place. What was more, the hood seemed to be hairy, at least the back of it did, while the front contained a number of holes whose purpose the boy could not fathom. The gloves were of the same familiar color as the hood.

The boy stood gazing at the strange coat until he heard a noise coming from the other end of the study. He looked toward it, but saw nothing: just a tall skeleton dangling in front of another bookcase. He looked away and the noise repeated, a sound like a baby's rattle, only louder. The boy looked again and again saw nothing, only the bookcase and, in front of it, the skeleton. It took a moment for the boy to recognize that the skeleton was not dangling, but standing. As he watched, its bare, grinning skull turned toward him, and something in the tilt of its head, the crook of its spine, sent the boy's eyes darting back to the odd coat. Now, he saw that it was a coat, and pants, and hands, and a face: Mr. Gaunt's hands and face. Which must mean, he realized, that the skeleton at the other end of the room, which replaced the book it had been holding on top of the bookcase and stepped in his direction, was Mr. Gaunt. The boy stared at the skeleton slowly walking across the room, still far but drawing closer, its blank eyes fixed on him, and, with a scream, ran back down the stairs. Behind him, he heard the rattle of the skeleton's pursuit.

There in his father's study, your cousin Peter saw a human skeleton, Mr. Gaunt's skeleton—or the skeleton that was Gaunt—rush toward him from the other side of the room. The skeleton was tall, slightly stooped, and when it moved, its dull yellow bones clicked against each other like a chorus of baby rattles. Peter screamed, then bolted the room. He leapt down the attic stairs two and three at a time, pausing at the fourth floor landing long enough to throw closed the door to the stairs and grasp at the key that usually rested in its lock but now was gone, taken, he understood, by Mr. Gaunt. Peter ran down the long hallway to the third floor stairs and half-leapt down them. He didn't bother with the door at the third floor landing: he could hear that chorus of rattles clattering down the stairs, too close already. He raced through the three rooms that lay between the third floor landing and the stairway to the second floor, hearing Gaunt at his back as he hurdled beds, chairs, couches; ducked drapes; rounded corners. A glance over his shoulder showed the skeleton running after him like some great awkward bird, its head bobbing, its knees raised high. He must have been terrified; there would have been no way for him not to have been terrified. Imagine your own response to such a thing. I wouldn't have been able to run; I would have been paralyzed, as much by amazement as by fear. As it was, Gaunt almost had him when Peter tipped over a globe in his path and he fell crashing behind him. With a final burst of speed, Peter descended the last flight of stairs and made the front door, which he heaved open and dashed through into the street.

Between Peter's house and the house to its left as you stood looking out the front door was a close, an alley. Peter rushed to and down it. It could be that panic drove him, or that he meant to evade Gaunt by taking a route he thought unknown to the butler. If the latter was the case, the sound of bones rattling across the cobblestones, a look back at the naked grin and the arm grasping at him, would have revealed his error instantly, with no way for him to double-back safely. I suspect the skeleton did something to herd Peter to that alley, out of sight of any people who might be on the street; I mean it worked a spell of some kind. The alley sloped down, gradually at first, then steeply, ending at the top of a series of flights of stone stairs descending the steep hillside to Market Street below. From Market Street, it's not that far to the train station, which may have been Peter's ultimate destination. His heart pounding, his breath rushing in and out, he sped down the hill, taking the stairs two, three, four at a time, his shoes snapping loudly on the stone, the skeleton close, swiping at him with a claw that tugged the collar of his sweater but failed to hold it.

Halfway down the stairs, not yet to safety but in sight of it, Peter's left foot caught his right foot, tripping and tumbling him down the remaining stairs to the landing below, where he smashed into the bars of an iron guardrail. Suddenly, there was no air in his lungs. As he lay sprawled on his back, trying to breathe, the skeleton was on him, descending like a hawk on a mouse. He cried out, covering his eyes. Seizing him by the sweater front, Gaunt hauled Peter to his feet. For a second that seemed to take years, that fleshless smile was inches from his face, as if it were subjecting him to the most intense scrutiny. He could smell it: an odor of thick dust, with something faintly rancid beneath it, that brought the bile to his throat. He heard a sound like the whisper of sand blowing across a stone floor, and realized it was the skeleton speaking, bringing speech from across what seemed a great distance. It spoke one word, "Yes," drawing it out into a long sigh that did not stop so much as fade away: *Yyyeeeeeesssssss* . . . . Then it jerked its head away, and began pulling him back up the stairs, to the house and, he knew, the study. When, all at once, his lungs inflated and he could breathe again, Peter tried to scream. The skeleton slapped its free hand across his mouth, digging the sharp ends of its fingers and thumb into his cheeks, and Peter desisted. They reached the top of the stairs and made their way up the close. How no one could have noticed them, I can't say, though I suspect the skeleton had done something to insure their invisibility; yes, more magic. At the front door, Peter broke Gaunt's grip and attempted to run, but he had not taken two steps before he was caught by the hair, yanked off his feet, and his head was slammed against the pavement. His vision swimming, the back of his head a knot of agony, Peter was led into the house. His knee cracked on an end-table; his shoulder struck a doorframe. As he was dragged to the study, did he speak to the creature whose claw clenched his arm? A strange question, perhaps, but since first I heard this story myself I have wondered it. Your cousin had a short time left to live, which he may have suspected; even if he did not, he must have known that what awaited him in the study would not be pleasant, to say the least. Did he apologize for his intrusion? Did he try to reason with his captor, promise his secrecy? Or did he threaten it, invoke his father's wrath on his return? Was he quiet, stoic or stunned? Was his mind buzzing with plans of last minute escape, or had it accepted that such plans were beyond him?

There are moments when the sheer unreality of an event proves overwhelming, when, all at once, the mind can't embrace the situation unfolding around it and refuses to do so, withholding its belief. Do you know what I mean? When your grandfather died, later that same afternoon I can remember feeling that his death was not yet permanent, that there was some means still available by which I could change it, and although I didn't know what that means was, I could feel it trembling on the tip of my brain. When your mother told me that she was leaving me for husband number two, that they already had booked a flight together for the Virgin Islands, even as I thought, Well it's about time: I wondered how long it would take this to arrive, I also was thinking, This is not happening: this is a joke: this is some kind of elaborate prank she's worked up, most likely with someone else, someone at the school, probably one of my colleagues; let's see, who loves practical jokes? While she explained the way my faults as a husband had led her to her decision, I was trying to analyze her sentence structure, word choice, to help me determine who in the department had helped her script her lines. A few years later, when she called to tell me about husband number three, I was much more receptive. All of which is to say that, if it was difficult for me to accommodate events that occur on a daily basis, how much more difficult would it have been for your cousin to accept being dragged to his father's study by a living skeleton?

Once they were in the study, Gaunt wasted no time, making straight for the great stone sarcophagus. Peter screamed with all the force he could muster, calling for help from anyone who could hear him, then wailing in pure animal terror. The skeleton made no effort to silence him. At the sarcophagus with its furious visage, Gaunt brought his stark face down to Peter's a second time, as if for a last look at him. He heard that faint whisper again, what sounded like the driest of chuckles. Then it reached out and slid the massive stone lid open with one spindly arm. The odor of decay, the ripe stench of a dead deer left at the side of the road for too many hot days, filled the room. Gagging, Peter saw that the interior of the sarcophagus was curiously rough, not with the roughness of, say, sandstone, but with a deliberate roughness, as if the stone had been painstakingly carved into row upon row of small sharp points, like teeth. The skeleton flung him into that smell, against those points. Before he could make a final, futile gesture of escape, the lid closed and Peter was in darkness, swathed in the thick smell of rot, his last sight the skeleton's idiot grin. Nor was that the worst. He had been in the stone box only a few seconds, though doubtless it seemed an eternity, when the stone against which he was leaning grew warm. As it warmed, it shifted, the way the hide of an animal awakening from a deep sleep twitches. Peter jerked away from the rough stone, his heart in his throat as movement rippled through the coffin's interior. If he could have been fortunate, his terror would have jolted him into unconsciousness, but I know this was not the case. If he was unlucky, as I know he was, he felt the sides of the sarcophagus abruptly swell toward him, felt the rows of sharp points press against him, lightly at first, then more insistently, then more insistently still, until—

I've mentioned the root of the word "sarcophagus;" it was Peter, ironically enough, who told it to me. It's Greek: it means "flesh eating." Exactly how that word came to be applied to large stone coffins I'm unsure, but in this case it was quite literally true. Peter was enclosed within a kind of mouth, a great stone mouth, and it . . . consumed him. The process was not quick. By the time George returned to the house almost a week and a half later, however, it was complete. Sometime in the long excruciation before that point, Peter must have realized that his father was implicated in what was happening to him. It was impossible for him not to be. His father had brought Mr. Gaunt into the house, and then left Peter at his mercy. His beloved father had failed, and his failure was Peter's death.

It took George longer than I would have expected, almost two full days, to discover Peter's fate, and to discern the butler's role in it. When he did so, he punished, as he put it, Mr. Gaunt suitably. He did not tell me what such punishment involved, but he did assure me that it was thorough. Peter's running away was, obviously, the ruse invented by George to hide his son's actual fate.

By the time your uncle told me the story I've told you, Clarissa had been dead for several years. I hadn't spoken to her since our phone conversation when Peter first vanished, and, I must confess, she had been absent from my thoughts for quite some time when I stumbled across her obituary on the opposite side of an article a friend in London had clipped and sent me. The obituary stated that she had never recovered from the disappearance of her only son almost two decades prior, and hinted, if I understood its inference, that she had been addicted to antidepressants; although the writer hastened to add that the cause of death had been ruled natural and was under no suspicion from the police.

If George heard the news of his former wife's death, which I assume he must have, he made no mention of it to me, not even during that last conversation, when so much else was said. Although I hadn't planned it, we both became quite intoxicated, making our way through the better part of a bottle of Lagavulin after I had put you to bed. The closer I approach to complete intoxication, the nearer I draw to maudlin sentimentality, and it wasn't long, as I sat beside my older brother looking across the Hudson to Poughkeepsie, the place where we had been born and raised and where our parents were buried, I say it wasn't long before I told George to stay where he was, I had something for him. Swaying like a sailor on a ship in a heavy sea, I made my way into the house and to my study, where I located the shoebox in which I keep those things that have some measure of sentimental value to me, pictures, mostly, but also the letters that your cousin had sent me, tucked in their envelopes. Returning to the porch, I walked over to George and held them out to him, saying, "Here, take them."

He did so, a look that was half-bemusement, half-curiosity on his face. "All right," he said. "What are they?"

"Letters," I declared.

"I can see that, old man," he said. "Letters from whom?"

"From Peter," I said. "From your son. You should have them. I want you to have them."

"Letters from Peter," he said.

"Yes," I said, nodding vigorously.

"I was unaware the two of you had maintained a correspondence."

"It was after the summer he came to stay with Mother. The two of us hit it off, you know, quite well."

"As a matter of fact," George said, "I didn't know." He continued to hold the letters out before him, as if he were weighing them. The look on his face had slid into something else.

Inspired by the Scotch, I found the nerve to ask George what I had wanted to ask him for so long: if he ever had received any word, any kind of hint, as to what had become of Peter? His already flushed face reddened more, as if he were embarrassed, caught off-guard, then he laughed and said he knew exactly what had happened to his son. "Exactly," he repeated, letting the letters fall from his hand like so many pieces of paper.

Despite the alcohol in which I was swimming, I was shocked, which I'm sure my face must have shown. All at once, I wanted to tell George not to say anything more, because I had intuited that I was standing at the doorway to a room I did not wish to enter, for, once I stood within it, I would discover my older brother to be someone—something—I would be unable to bear sitting beside. We were not and had never been as close as popular sentiment tells us siblings should be; we were more friendly acquaintances. It was an acquaintance, however, I had increasingly enjoyed as I grew older, and I believe George's feelings may have been similar. But my tongue was thick and sluggish in my mouth, and so, as we sat on the back porch, George related the circumstances of his son's death to me. I listened to him as evening dimmed to night, making no move to switch on the outside lights, holding onto my empty glass as if it were a life-preserver. As his tale progressed, my first thought was that he was indulging in a bizarre joke whose tastelessness was appalling; the more he spoke, however, the more I understood that he believed what he was telling me, and I feared he might be delusional if not outright mad; by the story's conclusion, I was no longer sure he was mad, and worried that I might be. I was unsure when he stopped talking: his words continued to sound in my ears, overlapping each other. A long interval elapsed during which neither of us spoke and the sound of the crickets was thunderous. At last George said, "Well?"

"Gaunt," I said. "Who is he?" It was the first thing to leap to mind.

"Gaunt," he said. "Gaunt was my teacher. I met him when I went to Oxford; the circumstances are not important. He was my master. Once, I should have called him my father." I can not tell you what the tone of his voice was. "We had a disagreement, which grew into an . . . altercation, which ended with him inside the stone sarcophagus that had Peter, though not for as long, of course. I released him while there was still enough left to be of service to me. I thought him defeated, no threat to either me or mine, and, I will admit, it amused me to keep him around. I had set what I judged sufficient safeguards against him in place, but he found a way to circumvent them, which I had not thought possible without a tongue. I was in error."

"Why Peter?" I asked.

"To strike at me, obviously. He had been planning something for quite a length of time. I had some idea of the depth of his hate for me, but I had no idea his determination ran to similar depths. His delight at what Peter had suffered was inestimable. He had written a rather extended description of it, which I believe he thought I would find distressing to read. The stone teeth relentlessly pressing every square inch of flesh, until the skin burst and blood poured out; the agony as the teeth continued through into the muscle, organ, and, eventually, bone; the horror at finding oneself still alive, unable to die even after so much pain: he related all of this with great gusto.

"The sarcophagus, in case you're interested, I found in eastern Turkey, not, as you might think, Egypt; though I suspect it has its origins there I first read about it in *Les mysteres du ver*, though the references were highly elliptical, to say the least. It took years, and a small fortune, to locate it. Actually, it's a rather amusing story: it was being employed as a table by a bookseller, if you can believe it, who had received it as payment for a debt owed him by a local banker, who in turn . . . "

I listened to George's account of the sarcophagus's history, all the while thinking of poor Peter trapped inside it, wrapped in claustrophobic darkness, screaming and pounding on the lid as—what? Although, as I have said, I half-believed the fantastic tale George had told, my belief was only partial. It seemed more likely Peter had suffocated inside the coffin, then Gaunt disposed of the body in such a way that very little, if any, of it remained. When George was done talking, I asked, "What about Peter?"

"What about him?" George answered. "Why, 'What about Peter'? I've already told you, it was too late for me to be able to do anything, even to provide him the kind of half-life Gaunt has, much less successfully restore him. What the sarcophagus takes, it does surrender."

"He was your son," I said.

"Yes," George said. "And?"

"'And'? My God, man, he was your son, and whatever did happen to him, he's dead and you were responsible for his death, if not directly then through negligence. Doesn't that mean anything to you?"

"No," George said, his voice growing brittle. "As I have said, Peter's death, while unfortunate, was unintentional."

"But," I went on, less and less able, it seemed, to match thought to word with any proficiency, "but he was your son."

"So?" George said. "Am I supposed to be wracked by guilt, afflicted with remorse?"

"Yes," I said, "yes, you are."

"I'm not, though. When all is said and done, Peter was more trouble than he was worth. A man in my position—and though you might not believe it, my position is considerable—doing my kind of work, can't always be worrying about someone else, especially a child. I should have foreseen that when I divorced Clarissa, and let her have him, but I was too concerned with her absolute defeat to make such a rational decision. Even after I knew the depth of my mistake, I balked at surrendering Peter to her because I knew the satisfaction such an admission on my part would give Clarissa. I simply could not bear that. For a time, I deluded myself that Peter would be my apprentice, despite numerous clear indications that he possessed no aptitude of any kind for my art. He was . . . temperamentally unsuited. It is a shame: there would have been a certain amount of pleasure in passing on my knowledge to my son, to someone of my own blood. That has always been my problem: too sentimental, too emotional. Nonetheless, while I would not have done anything to him myself, I am forced to admit that Peter's removal from my life has been to the good."

"You can't be serious," I said.

"I am."

"Then you're a monster."

"To you, perhaps," he said.

"You're mad," I said.

"No, I'm not," he said, and from the sharp tone of his voice, I could tell I had touched a nerve, so I repeated myself, adding, "Do you honestly believe you're some kind of great and powerful magician? or do you prefer to be called a sorcerer? Perhaps you're a wizard? a warlock? an alchemist? No, they worked with chemicals; I don't suppose that would be you. Do you really expect me to accept that tall butler as some kind of supernatural creature, an animated skeleton? I won't ask where you obtained his face and hands: I'm sure Jenner's has a special section for the black arts." I went on like this for several minutes, pouring out my scorn on George, feeling the anger radiating from him. I did not care: I was angry myself, furious, filled with more rage than ever before or ever after, for that matter.

When I was through, or when I had paused, anyway, George asked, "Could you fetch me a glass of water?"

"Excuse me?" I said.

He repeated his request: "Could I have a glass of water?" explaining, "All this conversation has left my throat somewhat parched."

Your grandmother's emphasis on good manners, no matter what the situation, caught me off guard, and despite myself I heard my voice saying, "Of course," as I set down my glass, stood, and made my way across the unlit porch to the back door. "Can I get you anything else?" I added, trying to sound as scornful as I felt.

"The water will be fine."

I opened the back door, stepped into the house, and was someplace else. Instead of the kitchen, I was standing at one end of a long room lit by globed lights depending from a slanted ceiling. Short bookcases filled to bursting with books, scrolls, and an occasional stone tablet jostled with one another for space along the walls, while tables piled high with goblets, candles, boxes, rows of jars, models, took up the floor. I saw paintings crowding the walls, including the Bosch I described to you, and elaborate symbols drawn on the floor. At the other end of the room, a bulky stone sarcophagus with a fierce face reclined against a wall. Behind me, through the open door whose handle I still grasped, I could hear the crickets; in front of me, through the room's curtained windows, I could hear the sound of distant traffic, of brakes squealing and horns blowing. I stood gazing at the room I understood to be my brother's study, and then I felt the hand on my shoulder. Initially, I thought it was George, but when he called, "Is my water coming?" I realized he had not left his seat. Through my shirt, the hand felt wrong: at once too light and too hard, more like wood than flesh. The faintest odor of dust, and beneath it, something foul, filled my nostrils; the sound of a baby's rattle being turned, slowly, filled my ears. I heard another sound, the whisper of sand blowing across a stone floor, and realized it was whatever was behind me—but I knew what it was—speaking, bringing speech from across what seemed a great distance. It spoke one word, "Yes," drawing it out into a long sigh that did not stop so much as fade away: *Yyyeeeeeessssssss* . . . .

"I say," George said, "where's my water?"

Inhaling deeply—the hand tightening on my shoulder as I did—I said, "Tell him—tell it to remove its hand from me."

"Him? It? Whatever are you referring to?"

"Gaunt," I answered. "Tell Gaunt to release my shoulder."

"Gaunt?" George cried, his voice alive with malicious amusement, "Why, Gaunt's on the other side of the ocean."

"This is not entertaining," I said, willing myself to remain where I was.

"You're right," George said. "In fact, it's deeply worrying. Are you certain you're feeling all right? Did you have too much to drink? Or are you, perhaps, not in your right mind? Are you mad, dear brother?"

"Not in the least," I replied. "Nor, it would seem, are you."

"Ahh," George said. "Are you certain?"

"Yes," I said, "I am sure." I might have added, "To my profound regret," but I had no wish to antagonize him any further.

"In that case," George said, and the hand left my shoulder. I heard rattling, as if someone were walking away from me across the porch in tapshoes, followed by silence. "Now that I think on it," George said, "I needn't bother you for that glass of water, after all. Why don't you rejoin me?"

I did as he instructed, closing the door tightly. I walked to George and said, in a voice whose shaking I could not master, "It is time for you to go."

After a pause, George said, "Yes, I suppose it is, isn't it?"

"I will not be asking you back," I said.

"No, I don't suppose you will. I could just appear, you know."

"You will not," I said, vehemently. "You will never come here again. I forbid you."

"You forbid me?"

"Yes, I do."

"I find that most entertaining, as you say. However, I shall respect your wishes, lest it be said I lack fraternal affection. It's a pity: that time you came to visit me after Peter's death, I thought you might be my apprentice, and the notion has never vanished from my mind. It generally surfaces when I'm feeling mawkish. I suppose there's no chance—"

"None," I said, "now or ever." You have Satan's nerve, I thought.

"Yes, of course," George said. "I knew what your reply would be: I merely had to hear you say it. When all is said and done, I don't suppose you have the necessary . . . temperament either. No matter: there are others, one of them closer than you think."

That was his final remark. George had brought no luggage with him: he stepped off the porch into the night and was gone. I stood staring out into the darkness, listening for I am not sure what, that rattling, perhaps, before rushing to the kitchen door. Gripping the doorknob, I uttered a brief, barely coherent prayer, then opened the door. The kitchen confronted me with its rows of hanging pots and pans, its magnetic knife rack, its sink full of dishes awaiting washing. I raced through it, up the stairs to your room, where I found you asleep, one arm around Mr. James, your bear, the other thrown across your face as if you were seeking to hide your eyes from something. My legs went weak, and I seated myself on your bed, a flood of hot tears rolling down my face. I sat up in your room for the rest of that night, and for a week or so after I slept in it with you. The following morning, I returned to the back porch to retrieve your cousin's letters, which I replaced in the shoebox.

I have not heard from George since, all these years.

When I sat you on your bed after having found you surrounded by the shreds of my work, this was what shaped itself into my cautionary tale. It had been festering in my brain ever since George had told me it. Carrying George's words with me had left me feeling tainted, as if having heard of Peter's end had made me complicit in it in a manner beyond my ability to articulate. In giving that story voice, I sought to exorcise it from me. I recognize the irony of my situation: rather than expunging the story, telling it once led to it being told over and over again, until it had achieved almost the status of ritual. Your subsequent delight in the story did mitigate my guilt somewhat, tempting me to remark that a story's reception may redeem its inception; that, however, would be just a bit too much, too absolutely over the top, as James would put it. I remain incredulous at myself for having told you even the highly edited version you heard. It occurs to me that, if it is a wonder our children survive the mistakes we make with them, it is no less astounding that we are not done in by them ourselves; those of us with any conscience, I should add.

Something else: how much you remember of the literature classes you sat through in college I don't know; I realize you took them to please me. I'm sure, however, that enough of the lectures you actually attended has remained with you for you to be capable of at least a rudimentary analysis of our story. In such an analysis, you would treat the figure of the skeleton as a symbol. I can imagine, for example, a psychoanalytic interpretation such as are so often applied to fairy tales. It would judge our particular story to be a cleverly disguised if overly Oedipal allegory in which the locked room would be equated with the secret of sexuality, jealously guarded by the father against the son, and the butler/skeleton with the father's double, an image of death there to punish the boy for his transgression. If you preferred to steer closer to history, you might postulate the skeleton as a representation of an event: say, Mr. Gaunt and your uncle caught in an embrace, another kind of forbidden knowledge. Neither these nor any other interpretations are correct: the skeleton is not a substitution for something else but in fact real; I must insist, even if in doing so I seem to depart plausibility for fantasy, if not dementia. It could be that I protest too much, that you aren't the rigid realist I'm construing you to be. Perhaps you know how easy it is to find yourself on the other side of the looking glass.

No doubt, you'll wonder why I've waited until now to disclose this information to you, when you've been old enough to have heard it for years. I'd like to attribute my reticence solely to concern for you, to worry that, listening to this outrageous tale, you would lose no time setting out to verify it, which might result in your actually making contact with your uncle, and then God only knows what else. I am anxious for you, but, to be honest, more of my hesitation than I want to admit arises from dread at appearing ridiculous in your eyes, of seeing your face fill with pity at the thought that the old man has plunged over the edge at last. I suppose that's why I'm recording this, when I know it would be easy enough to pick up the phone and give you a call.

I can't believe I could be of any interest to George at this late date (so I tell myself), but I'm less sure about you. Sitting up in my bed last night, not watching the remainder of the documentary, I heard your uncle tell me that there were others to serve as his apprentice, one of them closer than I thought.

These words ringing in my ears, I thought of that Ouija board you used to play with in college, the tarot card program you bought for your computer. I understand the Ouija board was because of that girl you were seeing, and I know the computer program is just for fun, but either might be sufficient for George. Your uncle is old, and if he hasn't yet found an apprentice—

However belated, this, then, all of this tangled testament, is my warning to you about your uncle, as well as a remembrance of a kind of your cousin, whom you never knew. If you believe me—and you must, Henry, you must—you'll take heed of my warning. If you don't believe me, and I suppose that is a possibility, at least I may have entertained you one last time. All that remains now is for me to tell you I love you, son, I love you and please, please, please be careful Henry: be careful.

III

With a snap, the stereo reached the end of the tape. Henry Farange released a breath he hadn't been aware he was holding and slumped back on the couch. His beer and the pleasant lassitude it had brought were long gone; briefly, he contemplated going to the refrigerator for another bottle, and possibly the rest of the six-pack while he was at it. Heaving himself to his feet and shaking his head, he murmured, "God."

To say he didn't know what to think was the proverbial understatement. As his father had feared, his initial impression was that the old man had lost it there at the end, that he had, in his own words, suffered one mini-stroke too many. But—what? What else was there to say? That he had felt some measure of truth in his father's words? That—mad, yes, as it sounded—a deeper part of him, a much deeper part, a half-fossilized fragment buried far beneath his reflexive disbelief, accepted what the old man had been telling him?

Well, actually, that was it exactly, thank you for asking. Laughable as it seemed; and he did laugh, a humorless bark; Henry couldn't bring himself to discount completely his father's words. There had been something—no single detail; rather, a quality in the old man's voice—that had affected him, had unearthed that half-ossified part of him, had insinuated itself into his listening until, in the end, he found himself believing there was more to this tape than simple dementia. When Henry had been a child, his father had possessed the unfailing ability to tell when he was lying, or so it seemed; even when there was no obvious evidence of his dishonesty, somehow, the old man had known. Asked the source of this mysterious and frustrating power, his father had shrugged and said, "It's in your voice," as if this were the most obvious of explanations. Now, hearing those words echoing in his mind, Henry thought, It's in his voice.

But—a living skeleton? An uncle who was a black magician? A cousin he'd never heard of devoured by a coffin made of living stone? He shook his head again, sighing: there was some truth here, but it was cloaked in metaphor. It had to be. He walked over to the stereo, popped open the tape deck, slid out the tape, and stood with it in his hand, feeling it still warm. His father's voice. . . Although the old man had quoted their story's beginning and middle, he had not recited its end. The words rose unbidden to Henry's lips: "*Slowly, the skeleton carried the screaming boy up the stairs to his father's study. It walked through the open doorway, closing the door behind it with a solid click. For a long time, that door stayed closed. When at last it opened again, Mr. Gaunt, looking more pleased with himself than anyone in that house ever had seen him, stepped out and made his way down the stairs, rubbing his hands together briskly. As for the boy who had opened the door he was forbidden to open: he was never seen again. What happened to him, I cannot say, but I can assure you, it was terrible.*"

The phone rang, and he jumped, fumbling the tape onto the floor. Hadn't he switched that off? Leaving the cassette where it lay, he ran into the kitchen, catching the phone on the third ring and calling, "Hello."

His Uncle George said, "Hello, Henry."

"Uncle George!" he answered, a smile breaking over his face.

"How is everything?" his uncle asked.

"Fine, fine," he said. "I was just getting ready to call you."

"Uh oh."

"Yeah, it looks like I'm going to be a few minutes late to dinner."

"Can you still make it? Should we wait for another night?"

"No, no," Henry said, "there's no need to reschedule. I was just listening to something, a tape; I got kind of caught up in it, lost track of time."

"Music?"

"No, something my father left me. Actually, I was kind of hoping we could talk about it."

"Of course. What is it?"

"I'd rather wait until we see each other, if that's all right with you. Listen: can you call the restaurant, tell them we're running about fifteen minutes late?"

"Certainly. Will that be enough time for you?"

"I can be very fast when I need to be; you'd be amazed. Do you have their number?"

"I believe so. If not, I can look it up."

"Great, great. Okay. Let me run and get ready, and I'll see you shortly."

"Excellent. I'm looking forward to this, Henry. I haven't seen you in—well, to tell you the truth, I can't remember how long, which means it's been too long."

"Hear hear," he said. "I'm looking forward to it too. There's a lot I want to ask you."

"I'm glad to hear it, son: there's much I have to tell you."

"I'm sure you do. I can't wait to hear it."

"Well, this should be a fine, if melancholic, occasion. A Farange family reunion: there haven't been too many of those, I can assure you. What a pity your poor father can't join us. Oh, and Henry? one more thing?"

"What is it?"

"Would it be too much trouble if my butler joined us for dinner?" As Henry's stomach squeezed his uncle went on, "I'm embarrassed to ask, but I'm afraid I am getting on in years a bit, and I find I can't do much without his help these days. The joys of aging! He's a very quiet chap, though: won't say two words all evening. I hate to impose when we haven't seen each other . . . "

His mouth dry, Henry stuttered, "Your butler?"

"Yes," his uncle said. "Butler, manservant: 'personal assistant,' I suppose you would call him. If it's going to be an intrusion—"

Recovering himself, Henry swallowed and said, "Nonsense, it's no trouble at all. I'll be happy to have him there."

"Splendid. To tell the truth, he doesn't get out much any more: he'll be most pleased."

"I'll see you there."

Henry replaced the phone in its cradle, and hurried to the shower. As he stood with the hot water streaming down on him, his uncle's voice in one ear, his father's voice in the other, he had a vision, both sudden and intense. He saw a boy, dressed in brown slacks and a brown sweater a half-size too big for him, standing at a landing at the top of a flight of stairs. In front of him was a great oaken door, open the slightest hairsbreath. The boy stood looking at the door, at the wedge of yellow light spilling out from whatever lay on the other side of it. The light was the color of old bones, and it seemed to form an arrow, pointing the boy forward.

. . . a coast-line of mingled mud, ooze, and weedy Cyclopean masonry which can be nothing less than the tangible substance of earth's supreme terror—the nightmare corpse-city of R'lyeh, that was built in measureless aeons behind history by the vast, loathsome shapes that seeped down from the dark stars. There lay great Cthulhu and his hordes, hidden in green slimy vaults and sending out at last, after cycles incalculable, the thoughts that spread fear to the dreams of the sensitive and called imperiously to the faithful to come on a pilgrimage of liberation and restoration.
"The Call of Cthulhu" · H.P. Lovecraft (1928)

• THE VICAR OF R'LYEH •
Marc Laidlaw

"Let anything be held as blessed, so that that be well cursed."
—Anthony Trollope, *Barchester Towers*

Glorious afternoon, warm and breezy among green hills dotted with sheep. Looking down from his sylvan lounging spot upon the village with its twin spires, Geoffrey heard a mournful bell coming from the towers of Barchester Cathedral, and almost immediately thereafter noted a small dark shape making its way across the dewy grass from the open doors of the church. A faint distortion followed the pedestrian, as if air and earth were curdling in its wake. He blinked away the illusion, but the feeling of oppression grew until he clearly saw that yes, 'twas the vicar coming toward him with some message he suddenly felt he did not wish to hear. Meanwhile, the tolling of the bell had grown appalling. As the little man struggled up the hillside, he seemed to expand until his shadow encompassed the town itself. Abruptly the vicar stood before him, the pale features of the meek country parson tearing into soft and writhing strands like the points of a wormy beard. The vicar scowled, revealing five segmented ridges of bone, teeth akin to the beak of a sea urchin. Geoffrey did not wish to hear the vicar speak, but there was no stopping his ears.

"You up, Geoff?" The voice, its accent inappropriate, was first wheedling, then insistent. "R'lyeh's rising!"

He forced his eyes open. Somehow the phone had lodged itself between his cheek and pillow. The voice of his boss went on.

"Geoff, are you there? Did I wake you? I know you were here late, but we've got an emergency."

"Mm. Hi, Warren. No. I was . . . I was getting up."

(7:43 by the clock.)

"Calculations were off. Fucking astrologers, right? Anyway, we've got to throw ourselves into it. Marketing's in a tizzy, but let them be the bottleneck. I think if we dig in—"

"Give me . . . " Shower, skip breakfast, grab coffee at a drive-through, traffic. This was bad. " . . . forty-five minutes?" Very bad.

"You're a pro, Geoff."

Very bad. Cancel all plans. Forget about rest until this thing was done. Already resigning himself to it. Exactly how off were the calculations? He'd soon find out.

Forty-eight minutes later, panicking over his growing lateness, Geoff spiraled down through increasingly lower levels of the parking lot. He was late, but he was worrying more about the dream. What did it mean? That he was becoming polluted? That his pure visions had become contaminated by the foul effluents in which he labored daily? It seemed more urgent that he get away. Finish this job and get back to what he loved. Put all this crap behind him. If he could just get through it.

As he descended, the fluorescent lights grew dingier and more infrequent; fresh white paint gave way to bare, sooty concrete; the level markers were eroded runes. Even at this hour, he found not a single free parking space until he reached the lowest level. At the end of the farthest row, he found a retractable metal gate raised just over halfway. Beyond it, a promising emptiness, dark.

His car scraped under the gate with half an inch of clearance. He found himself in a cavernous lot he had never seen before, darkness stretching beyond the reach of his headlights. This lot was anything but crowded. A mere dozen or so cars parked companionably in the nearest row of spaces. He pulled in beside them and shut off his engine though not yet his lights. Stairs? Elevators? He saw no sign of either. The safest course would be to walk back under the gate to the main level.

Slamming the door killed the light from his car, but enough flowed from the gateway to show a layer of dust on the adjacent Volkswagen. Geoff peered through the passenger window, shuddering when he saw a row of tiny plastic figures perched on the dashboard, winged and faceless except for tentacles and the keyhole eyes of superintelligent cuttlefish. The toys were self-illuminated, in the manner of their kind, and pulsed with faint colors that signaled their intentions to those who could read them. Scattered over the seats were piles of sticks and matted weeds. Also a fallen stack of books, and a spiral notebook open to a page covered with scribbles he took for treasure maps. What kind of treasure seeker plundered the recesses of a not very ancient parking garage?

Fearing he might be mistaken for a prowler, he straightened up, tugging his backpack over his shoulders. On his way toward the gate, he glanced back and saw that the car bore an all too popular bumper sticker: HE IS RISEN.

The sudden grinding of the metal gate called up terrors of confinement, though in fact the gate was opening the rest of the way. Blue-tinged headlights came down the ramp, blinding him. He threw up a hand to shade his eyes, and saw a long black limo cruising through the entryway. It came to a stop, fixing him in its headlights, the engine thrumming so deeply that he felt the throbbing through his shoes.

"Come forward!" piped a voice, thin and irresistable.

Geoff walked around the side of the limo. One of the doors was open. Inside, a luxurious compartment of oxblood leather and recessed lights comfortably contained Warren and another man unknown to him.

"Geoff? What are you doing down here?"

"Who is this?" came the reedy voice that had bid him approach.

"Uh . . . this is Geoffrey Abbott, our lead designer."

"Really? Come in, young man."

Warren gave an uncomfortable smile, then waved him in. Geoff sat, balancing his backpack on his knees. As the car purred forward, Warren nodded toward the other man, a small fine-boned figure in a gray suit, dark of complexion, with curly black hair cropped close.

"Geoff, I'd like you to meet Emil Calamaro."

Geoff held back his hand a moment. He had never heard Warren say the name in anything but scorn; yet he was obviously awed by the actual presence of the owner of Aeon Entertainment.

"So," piped the small man, "you are tasked with R'lyeh's rising, is that not so?"

"Only in the Commemorative Simulator," Warren said.

There was a chitter of laughter. "As if it could be otherwise!" said Calamaro.

It was several seconds before Geoff realized what Calamaro was talking about. Everyone on the team had a slightly different pronunciation of "R'lyeh"—from Warren's "It's really, really, *Real-yeah*," to the broad "*Ruh-lay*" to the completely lazy and obnoxious "*Riley*." But Calamaro's take on the name was especially odd: It seemed to come bubbling up from his gullet through a column of thick liquid, less a word than a digestive sound.

"Geoff's got the job for now," Warren said quickly, covering Geoff's confusion.

"And you think him more suitable than the previous designer?"

"We've got a lot of faith in Geoff," Warren said. "He created the *Jane Austen Mysteries.*"

Calamaro sank back in his seat, making a faint hissing sound and baring his teeth at Austen's name. Out of Egypt, Geoff thought, and now owner of an extensive media empire. Not always a hands-on sort of owner, Calamaro took an active role in producing only a select few of the titles in the endless run of Cthulhuvian flicks and tie-in games that Aeon cranked out on a seasonal basis. Calamaro's dark, slender fingers clenched the head of a walking stick that was somehow both leopard and crocodile. On the seat beside him sat a cylindrical box, tall and golden, fastened with a clasp.

"I know it's a bit of a stretch, but the authenticity of those levels, and Geoff's ability to make them lively and action-packed without sacrificing the integrity of the source material . . . well, we think it's a great fit. No one originally thought you could set Jane Austen to work solving crimes in the world of her own books, but Geoff's team did a fantastic job."

"I designed the *Bloody Trail of Lord Darcy*," Geoff said, compelled to rise to his own defense, knowing that Warren had not actually played any of the Austen thrillers. "I was looking forward to starting in on *Pride and Extreme Prejudice* when this came along. Eventually I think Thomas Hardy will be a fertile source of—"

"I would like to see the work so far."

"Absolutely!" Warren said.

"Sure." Geoff hoped none of his terror showed in his face.

The limo stopped. The driver opened the passenger door. Calamaro indicated that Geoff should go first.

He could no longer see the gated entrance. Ahead of the car, held in its headlights, was a doorway. Calamaro stepped into the beams, his shadow staggering out across the hard-packed floor and then the wall. He supported himself on his walking stick, hugging the golden cylinder close to his chest with the other arm. Warren hurried to open the door. Beyond was an elevator and a flight of stairs. The elevator waited, but when Geoff tried to enter, Warren held him back. "Why don't you take the stairs, Geoff? We've got some business to discuss. We'll catch up with you upstairs. Give you time to get the demo ready."

"Uh . . . sure." Geoff held back and watched the doors shut. Calamaro's eyes glittered like obsidian lenses in the mask of a sarcophagus, refracting the overhead lights into a vision of endless night full of fractured stars.

He wasn't sure how long he'd stood there before he remembered to look for stairs.

By the time Geoff reached the office, everyone was buzzing determinedly through the halls as if they had some other purpose than to catch a glimpse of the man who had set them all in motion. Lars Magnusson, one of the programmers, intercepted Geoff en route to his cubby: "Guess who's making the rounds this morning?"

"I know," Geoff said. "Calamaro. I rode in his limo with Warren."

"Calamaro?" said Lars. "Really? No, I'm talking about Petey Sandersen!"

If this news was meant to lift his spirits, it barely raised an eyebrow. More evidence (as if any were needed) that he did not fit in on the Simulator project; that in fact his loyalty to the whole Aeon Entertainment enterprise was suspect.

Petey Sandersen was a legendary figure—an idol to those who had grown up suckling on the thousand media paps of the Black Goat of the Woods. He had formulated (or packaged) the original rules and invocations, the diagrams and tokens that everyone had once taken for the arcane paraphernalia of an elaborate role-playing game. But while Petey had become revered as the Opener of the Way, the Wedge by Which They Widened the Weft, Geoff had spent his adolescence trying to put as much distance as he possibly could between himself and the massively overhyped eldritch invaders.

With Sandersen and Calamaro on the premises, this was shaping up to be a day for high-powered executive reviews. Careers were made or casually ended on days like this. Nice of them to warn the peons in advance.

Geoff slung his backpack under his desk and fired up ABDUL, their proprietary level editor. It was hard not to panic, considering that Warren had volunteered him to show off work that was by no means ready for a demo. About all he had time to do now was check for obvious errors and send the map for a full compile. That, and pray that during the night no one had checked in changes that would break the work he'd done the previous day. Reviewing the morning's round of check-in notices, he didn't spot any midnight code changes that would affect his map, but that didn't mean he was in the clear. Artists were notorious for quietly making an ill-advised change to one inconspicuous model, thereby wreaking havoc on the entire world. Most of them were contractors, prone to exceedingly short lifespans at Aeon, rarely in place long enough to be trained in the brutal realities of their resource management software, dubbed ALHAZMAT. Anyway, there was no way around it. He started his compile and prayed for deliverance.

There was certainly no shortage of divinities in attendance on his prayers. His cubicle was lined with figurines: a mottled green plastic Cthulhu hunched upon a pedestal with leathery wings peaked above its tentacled face; a translucent vinyl Faceless Idiot God containing a congeries of odd shapes that sparked and swarmed like luminous sea life when you squeezed it; a pewter Shub-Niggurath, a goodly number of whose thousand young had fallen behind the desk to be sucked up by the night janitor's vacuum. The eldritch figures seemed to leap, leer and caper at the corner of his eyes while Geoff bent close to the monitor. On the long late nights when his tired eyes were burning, he thought they did worse things than that. These were not *his* Cthulhu-Kaiju figures, not *his* maddeningly cute Li'l Old Ones. They were a constant reminder of the indignity of his situation. They belonged to the previous occupant of the cubicle—a designer who could return at any moment, depending on the whims of upper management. Aeon shuffled and recombined its design teams as if they were packs of Pokemon cards—and not particularly rare ones at that.

Geoff bore no love of Elder Gods, but as much as he would have liked to, he couldn't get rid of the vinyl monstrosities. He didn't dare dump them in a drawer and set out his own beloved, hand-painted, resin-cast garage-kit models of Mansfield Park and Northanger Abbey. As long as he sat here and accepted the paycheck that came with the keyboard, he must pretend a devotion to the Cthulhuvian pantheon in all its manifestations. Including Warren, who sprang up on the far side of his partition, waggling fingers for him to follow.

Entering the conference room on Warren's heels, Geoff found the other managers enthralled by the spectacle of a portly cherubic man holding forth at the end of the monolithic onyx slab that was their conference table. He was in the midst of an anecdote that ended, "—so I said, I don't think of Petey as a Ted Klein reference. I think of Ted Klein as a *Petey* reference!"

Warren waited for a hitch in the laughter and beckoned Geoff forward. "Petey, this is Geoffrey Abbot, our lead designer."

Petey leaned forward and put out a hand. He was loud, aggressively jovial, with a gleam in his eyes that was pure evangelist: "Have you heard the good news?" The hand was chubby, somewhat clammy, but the grip was firm enough to take his measure. "He is risen!"

"Well . . . rising," Warren said defensively. "We still have a little time, I hope."

"Not little enough, if you ask me! What do you think, Geoff? I've heard splendid things about you. Are you ready for the Rapture?"

"I . . . build maps," Geoff replied.

"I've done a bit of that. A little bit of everything as needed. You look like a dreamer, Geoff, and that's what we need right now. Good strong dreamers. How're your dreams of R'lyeh lately? Have the Deep Ones been welcoming?"

"Well, I—"

"It's kind of vague, isn't it?" Petey said. "You could use a bit more focus, to be honest. We've been looking at your map, and frankly . . . well . . . "

"What? My map?"

He hadn't noticed at first because the huge wall-mounted monitor at the far end of the room was trained on darkness. Suddenly the image lurched and they were looking out over a blue-gray sea, far from land, an ocean cold and desolate and surging with the promise of nightmares. It was his ocean, beneath his bleak sky. They were running *R'lyeh Rising—A Commemorative Simulator.*

Warren put a hand on his shoulder and with a forced smile said, "We pulled them off your share, Geoff. We were just running through them and—"

"Those are yesterday's, they're not even—"

"But they're fabulous, Geoff!" Petey was in his face again. "The only problem we've seen, really, is something we can easily take care of. We don't bring this out for everyone, you understand, but you've already shown you're worth the extra investment. Emil, will you do the honors?"

Emil Calamaro rose from the end of the conference table with the cylindrical golden box in his hands. He set it in front of Geoff and threw the clasp. Petey Sandersen reached inside and lifted a glittering nightmare over Geoff's head. Geoff ducked clear to get a better look.

It was something like a cross between a crown and a diving helmet, a rigid cap that rounded off like the narrow end of a squid. Pale, beaten gold, chased with obscene motifs, set with green stones that rippled like dark aquatic eyes.

"Am I supposed to wear that thing?"

"The Miter of Y'ha-nthlei is an honor and a privilege," said Petey eagerly.

"And a grave responsibility," said Emil Calamaro.

"Geoff will take good care of it, we'll see to that," Warren assured them, pushing Geoff forward to receive the miter.

It fastened to his head with a distinct sensation of suction. Petey stepped back, beaming. "*Voila!*"

He felt ridiculous.

And something else . . .

A cold, drawn-out tingling like needles probing his scalp. An intense pressure building within, as if he were developing a sinus infection. His head filled with phlegm.

"Let us study the map again," said Emil Calamaro.

As the Egyptian spoke, Geoff found himself drifting forward to take control of the scene. He sat down and pulled a keyboard toward him. He began to type commands. He knew what they needed to see.

Out on the sea of pale beaten gold, the waves began to roil for no apparent reason.

Petey said, "I've been out there, Geoff, and it's remarkable how well you've captured it."

"I don't know," said Calamaro. "I'm not convinced."

"Have you been to the spot?"

"You know I don't care for open water."

"Well, how can you criticize?"

"It's not what I pictured."

"Don't listen to him," said Petey, leaning closer. "So far it's perfect, it's fine. There's no problem at all until . . . well, you have to bring it closer to the surface. I mean, a melding of minds. You need to let yourself be dreamed. Let it come through you. That's why we're lending you the miter."

Geoff brought them in over the area of greatest activity. He accelerated the Simulator, putting it through its paces well ahead of schedule.

The ocean appeared to be boiling. Even through the turbulence you could sense a massive darkness about to break through.

He typed "entity_trigger rlyeh_rise_01."

R'lyeh breached the waters.

The dripping rocks were encrusted with monstrous tubeworms, their guts bursting out after the pressure shock of the tremendous ascent. Slick scaly bodies writhed in raw sunlight, suffocating in air, caught by the rising of the monolithic city and perishing now before their eyes. Up it rose, a place of eldritch angles, tilted towers, evil . . . wrong . . .

So utterly, terribly wrong.

Geoff took his hands from the keyboard and covered his eyes, trying to contain his despair. It was wrong and he knew it. Everything was fine until the full hideous glory of R'lyeh rose into view, and then the illusion collapsed. There was nothing majestic about it, nothing that conjured up the horror of its arrival. It was only tilted rocks and a few cheap, generic effects. His heart wasn't in it, and it showed.

"It still needs work," he said, aware that he had better show a pretense of caring for something more than his paycheck.

Without speaking or moving, Calamaro radiated near-lethal levels of distaste and disappointment. Warren had gone pale, afraid to speak either in defense or reproach of Geoff's work. Only Petey Sandersen appeared untroubled. He slapped a hand on Geoff's shoulder.

"It's only to be expected," he said. "It's partly our fault. We've been remiss. In our defense, we wanted to make sure we had the right guy. I think, this time, we've got him."

Petey gave a nod and a wink to Warren, who visibly relaxed. Color flooded his cheeks. Geoff suddenly remembered the unnamed designer he'd replaced. "... *this time* ... "

"We're going to leave you with the miter, Geoff. I think you'll find you can remedy all deficiencies. You'll get R'lyeh right this time. You'll get on the Dreamer's dark side, and all will be well."

"We haven't much time," said Calamaro.

"With a dedicated designer like Geoff here, I'm not worried in the least. Are you worried, Warren?"

"Wha . . . no! Not at all. Geoff'll burn both ends till we're done with this guy. That's why he makes the big bucks."

The miter had begun to feel heavier. He must get back to his desk and plunge into his work. He hardly heard what the others were saying. Ideas were coming, strong and vivid. They must be captured. He must surrender to them, bring them to life.

The others must have sensed that he was no longer following the conversation. Warren stood up, signaling that it was Geoff's turn to do the same. Petey squeezed his hand. Emil Calamaro merely bent slightly at the waist, gripping his cane.

Geoff found himself in the lobby.

Lulu, the receptionist, regarded the glittering headpiece in awe. "Wow . . . "

She must have seen something in his eyes that silenced her.

Geoff strode toward his cubby, the prickling sensation still strong, but turning to something cold and liquescent, an icy tendril that held his will and gave him marching orders.

What am I doing?

He dragged to a stop in the elevator lobby, determined not to surrender. This was a job, only a job. He shouldn't have to compromise his inmost thoughts, his imagination, his dreams. He would finish the damn map because it was the only way to get back to his own project, but that was all. Beyond that, he would resist.

Elevator doors rumbled open and a small group of programmers, returning with coffee, stumbled off and stared at Geoff with a mixture of amazement and respect. He pushed past them, into the small car, just as the doors closed, and stabbed the button for the ground floor. At that moment, the watery tendrils turned to knives of ice. He put his hands on either side of the wretched miter and tried to twist it off, but it clung tight. The car plummeted past his chosen floor. The car slowed but did not stop. It had entered realms for which there were no markers. The miter had some power over the elevator, even as it fought for power over him. He half expected to step off into a cavern of watery light where Byakhee waited to wing him away to dismal festivities.

Instead, the doors opened on a concrete cell, familiar from that morning. There was the stairwell where Warren had dismissed him, and a door into the vast dark garage.

The miter tightened like a fist, as if sending a final warning, and then it relaxed its grip. He was free.

It took five minutes, at a limping run, to reach the huddled cars, his own seeming vulnerable at the edge of the row. He dug into his pocket for keys. Once he was clear of the building, he would find a way to shed the miter, using a crowbar if necessary. After that, his greatest fear was that Petey and Calamaro would find a way to blackball his career. All he wanted was to get free of this cursed project and back to something he cared about.

As he turned his key in the lock, he heard a sound that stopped him. He waited for it to repeat. It must have been an engine coughing to life on some floor far above. Nothing on this level stirred. The other cars were empty, as he proved to himself by peering through the window of the adjacent Volkswagen. The same clutter of papers on the seat; the same collection of tiny dashboard idols; the same pile of sod and sticks thrown about like yard waste interrupted on its way to the dump.

The sound, as if aware of his attention, played again.

He bent closer. Crumpled sketches littered the seat. Waves of tingling swept across his scalp. His pupils felt impossibly huge. Among the sketches he could make out a fragment of coastline, an ocean expanse, an X in the midst of the sea.

R'lyeh.

The other drawings suddenly made more sense. The tilting oblongs . . . a poor draftsman's attempt at non-Euclidean geometry . . . a massive door . . . a model ship . . .

The miter caressed him warningly, as if an octopus could purr.

They were maps. Levels. Attempts to sketch out the very same areas he was building for the Simulator. Very poor designs, he had to admit, by a less than skilled designer.

Whose car was this?

Reluctantly, he recognized the kinship between the collection of dashboard dolls and the vinyl creatures that lined his desk.

And an even less welcome connection: The broken brown twigs were tangled with black rags that bore the Aeon Entertainment logo.

The sound came again. This time, unmistakably, it came from inside some car in this row. It sounded less like an engine noise and more like something clearing its throat.

He eased his door shut, slipped the keys into his pocket, and began to back slowly toward the distant elevator.

The miter, satisfied that he understood, regained its grip.

You haven't won, he told it. I'll get through this and move on.

It's only a job.

He fought from the first, in his own way.

He fought from his desk, in front of his monitor, keyboarding until his eyelids trembled and the urge to sleep became all but impossible to resist. But all his other sleepless nights on the Austen project had given him the resources he needed to stay upright and conscious through the death marches of crunchmode. The Dreamer worked through him, but he fought back. Subverting the Dark Advent would not have been possible had he not already finely honed the ability to resist sleep; for a game designer it was second nature, a matter of instinct, ingrained.

The first line of defense was a visible act of defiance. Out came every last one of his vinyl Jane Austen figures. He set them to run lines of interference between the figures of eldritch power. The population of Casterbridge mingled incongruously among Whateleys and Peaslees and the entire Arkham establishment.

These small personal touches, injecting something of himself, were minor sorties in the main battle. But they brought a very real satisfaction and sense of resistance.

To resist outright was a doomed proposition. His sanity was at stake, after all. There were limits to how much he was willing to sacrifice just to make a point. Direct opposition would only lead to failure, madness, and the unemployment office. If he could just get through this, there would be other opportunities in store for him. With all the glory attendant on the Second Rising, he would be free again to pick his assignments. He could push his Trollope project. Or finally develop *The Bronte Sisters Massacre*.

Such thoughts did not sit well with the miter, which struck back by clenching down so hard that his brain felt like a raisin. Even through stifling pain, he clung hopelessly to his passion.

Warren dragged a cot into an empty office, dedicating it to Geoff for the duration. Yet to lie there, to sleep, would have been to surrender himself completely.

Beneath the waves, in the lightless depths of his map, the city took shape. Geoff modeled shapes in ABDUL, shapes unlike any he had created before. They were direct projections from the Dreamer; they prefigured the Dark Advent. Even as he built them, he knew they were true. Before this, he had merely imagined R'lyeh; he had improvised, glibly making shit up. This was utterly different. These creations were not of him; he was simply a conduit for the Dreamer's own excretions. What that made of him, he felt all too keenly.

Yet, while his hands hewed R'lyeh from deformed terrain, his heart took shelter in a green imagined England. It was not mountains of madness that filled his mind, but hillocks of happiness. While fluorescent light throbbed down upon his mitered head, he imagined it was the sunlight of a hot August afternoon; he sought respite from the fields of baled hay, finding Tess the dairymaid (loosely of the D'Urbervilles) waiting for him in the sultry shade, her breasts white as the cream she churned to butter. This was a vision of loveliness no Elder God could threaten. It was not unknown Kadath that shimmered in the distance like a phantasmagoric tapestry, but a stolid gray manor house holding dominion above a manicured lawn. It was not distant witless piping in a cosmic void that filled his ears, but the silver peal of church bells ever ringing through a lilac-scented evening. The pastor walked out among his flock. Roses grew on old white lattices and nodded their heavy heads at the coming night, willing him to sleep . . . sleep . . . all would be well if only he would . . . sleep. Not surrender, merely . . . merely . . .

"Geoff? Geoff! Wake up, man, it's coming! It's time!"

Groggily aware that something was wrong, Geoff lurched into consciousness. When had he lapsed? What had he lost?

In sleep he had laid himself wide open to the Dreamer. He'd given up everything he valued. He had been party to atrocities. He must delete his work! It was the only way to keep the monster from leaking into the world.

Warren stopped his hand. "You're done. Come on, we're in the conference room."

"Done? But—"

"Don't worry. The map's compiled, it's built, it's beautiful. Petey and Calamaro couldn't be happier. Timing's perfect. We're not the bottleneck, Geoffrey. Retail can sweat the rest of it. We did our part and we're done. Now come watch the Rising."

Stepping into the conference room, he experienced double vision and disorientation. Twin monitors showed the same scene. It took him a moment to realize that one was the simulator and the other was a live broadcast from ships and news helicopters far out at sea. The similarity between the two scenes was uncanny.

Heads swiveled toward him; he tried to smile. Emil Calamaro and Petey Sandersen were plainly delighted to see him. Petey took his hands off the keyboard, where he had been tinkering with the R'lyeh simulation, and, supporting himself on the edge of the table, leaned toward Geoff with his hand out, shouting "He is Risen!" with evangelical fury.

Geoff mumbled his reply.

"We want to thank you and honor you. What you've done is beyond amazing!"

Calamaro was rising, his dark sneer full of satisfaction. He too pressed in close to Geoff. "Indeed, it is completely astonishing. You have greatly eased the Rising. We have watched the ascent again and again, and it is most pleasing. Those who did not witness this day firsthand will be able to witness it over and over again for ages to come. It will be as it was."

On the live screen, the tossing sea had only just begun to tremble; but in the simulator that commemorated the occasion, the ocean had become a frothing stew of green slime belched from the depths. Dark angular towers began to thrust from the waters, black windows gaping, doors opening like the mouths of the abyss. To gaze upon the exhumed city was madness—even he, its author, could hardly bear to look. Then again, he felt he was no more its author than author of what the networks were transmitting.

Petey pulled over a keyboard and paused the simulation. It began to tick backward, then ran forward again at greater speed. R'lyeh was swallowed by the waves, vomited out, swallowed up again. Warren shook his shoulder. "Good work, Geoff. I mean it. Outstanding. You've really outdone yourself."

Meanwhile, the actual rising would not be rushed; it could not be paused or reversed. If only!

The news cameras drifted over the open sea. Its gentleness filled him with dread.

"All right," Petey said. "Plenty of time for this later."

As he spoke, the simulated R'lyeh had just crested the false waters. The great stage door to the false dreamer's lair, the tilted slab, had begun to gape. The shape within, waking, was caught by the stroke of a key. Paralyzed. Not dead. Not even sleeping. On hold.

Petey pushed the keyboard aside and picked up a remote. He pointed it at the live monitor and turned up the volume.

First you heard the thrum of helicopter blades. After a moment, seeping through, a deeper sound like the tolling of drowned bells vibrated out of the television and filled the listeners in the conference room with the solemnity of the moment. Geoff sank into a chair. He had seen all this before. He had dreamed it, lived it, fought it. Failed. His sense of defeat was complete.

Water slithered and eddied from the dark complexities beneath. Huge mounded shapes. Cruise ships and luxury liners had come close for the occasion, while keeping a respectful distance from the turbulence. The cameras showed their decks and rails thronged with wealthy golden worshipers. Several aircraft carriers waited on the horizon in case of international incidents. But only one incident mattered now, and it transcended all merely "international" concerns.

The bells tolled louder, and at a slowly rising pitch. Something in Geoff thrilled at the sound in spite of himself. He had dreamed this. He had been down there in the depths. He had met the Dreamer mind to mind and been utterly defeated, and yet . . . and yet . . .

The waters surged. The chopper pulled closer. From far down in the foul foam came something shining and angular, all points and slopes and corners, upthrusting towers and turrets, and still those bells, so wrong, so infinitely wrong.

Petey and Emil turned to one another, worried looks flitting.

Something gleaming, something of brilliant shining ivory whiteness, suddenly breached the surface. A gasp went through the room.

The helicopter lurched as if the pilot had lost control, caught by a vicious gust from below.

As the chopper recovered, the view stabilized. The distant television crew was shouting about the near disaster, distracted from the inevitable one. They were closer to the water now, closer to the immensity that continued rising into light and air. Gargantuan bluffs of black dripping stone, chiseled shapes covered with slime and ancient marine encrustations. And atop all this, the greatest monstrosity, the holiest of holies . . .

A church.

Exactly that. A small old-fashioned English country church with a single perfect spire. Sparkling white and dripping wet, it perched atop the squalid rocks as if it had been lifted whole from Geoff's reveries and transplanted in this unlikeliest of spots.

Geoff himself could only stare as seawater flowed from the bell tower, as the pealing bells grew louder, clearer, cheerier.

They filled the room until Petey and Calamaro had to clamp their hands over their ears. The two men whirled on Geoff with their eyes bulging, mouths flapping but unable to speak.

Geoff backed away with both hands on the miter, trying desperately to pry it off, to throw it down and run, even though he knew they could not harm him now. He had given birth to this thing. He and it were one and the same. Minds had mingled in the depths, and now . . .

Onscreen, the TV screen, the doors of the church swung wide. The timbre of the bells deepened abruptly, sounding a sour and dismal note. Petey and Calamaro, pierced by sudden rapture, whirled to take in the sight.

The church was not empty—hardly that. The white outer shell, the churchlike carapace, had transfigured the softer thing inside, and decidedly not for the better.

It lashed out, and the helicopter went down in an instant. Green water closed over the lens. For a moment that monitor showed the bubbling surface of the sea from underneath. Sunlight flared across the screen, but shadows were spreading. Somewhere, the cruise ships were being pulled under one by one. You could hardly hear the screams above the bells, which tolled and tolled. They would stop for nothing and nothing could block out the sound.

Not even Warren: "You've done it, Geoff!"

Not even Emil Calamaro: "Big, big congrats!"

Not even Petey Sandersen, conveying the last words he heard or wanted to hear: "Don't take the miter off! The job is yours! Forever!"

As we drew near the forbidding peaks, dark and sinister above the line of crevasse-riven snow and interstitial glaciers, we noticed more and more the curiously regular formations clinging to the slopes . . . The ancient and wind-weathered rock strata fully verified all of Lake's bulletins, and proved that these hoary pinnacles had been towering up in exactly the same way since a surprisingly early time in earth's history—perhaps over fifty million years.

At the Mountains of Madness · *H.P. Lovecraft (1931)*

· THE CREVASSE ·
Dale Bailey & Nathan Ballingrud

What he loved was the silence, the pristine clarity of the ice shelf: the purposeful breathing of the dogs straining against their traces, the hiss of the runners, the opalescent arc of the sky. Garner peered through shifting veils of snow at the endless sweep of glacial terrain before him, the wind gnawing at him, forcing him to reach up periodically and scrape at the thin crust of ice that clung to the edges of his facemask, the dry rasp of the fabric against his face reminding him that he was alive.

There were fourteen of them. Four men, one of them, Faber, strapped to the back of Garner's sledge, mostly unconscious, but occasionally surfacing out of the morphine depths to moan. Ten dogs, big Greenland huskies, gray and white. Two sledges. And the silence, scouring him of memory and desire, hollowing him out inside. It was what he'd come to Antarctica for.

And then, abruptly, the silence split open like a wound:

A thunderous crack, loud as lightning cleaving stone, shivered the ice, and the dogs of the lead sledge, maybe twenty-five yards ahead of Garner, erupted into panicky cries. Garner saw it happen: the lead sledge sloughed over—hurling Connelly into the snow—and plunged nose first through the ice, as though an enormous hand had reached up through the earth to snatch it under. Startled, he watched an instant longer. The wrecked sledge, jutting out of the earth like a broken stone, hurtled at him, closer, closer. Then time stuttered, leaping forward. Garner flung one of the brakes out behind him. The hook skittered over the ice. Garner felt the jolt in his spine when it caught. Rope sang out behind him, arresting his momentum. But it wouldn't be enough.

Garner flung out a second brake, then another. The hooks snagged, jerking the sledge around and up on a single runner. For a moment Garner thought that it was going to roll, dragging the dogs along behind it. Then the airborne runner slammed back to earth and the sledge skidded to a stop in a glittering spray of ice.

Dogs boiled back into its shadow, howling and snapping. Ignoring them, Garner clambered free. He glanced back at Faber, still miraculously strapped to the travois, his face ashen, and then he pelted toward the wrecked sledge, dodging a minefield of spilled cargo: food and tents, cooking gear, his medical bag, disgorging a bright freight of tools and the few precious ampules of morphine McReady had been willing to spare, like a fan of scattered diamonds.

The wrecked sledge hung precariously, canted on a lip of ice above a black crevasse. As Garner stood there, it slipped an inch, and then another, dragged down by the weight of the dogs. He could hear them whining, claws scrabbling as they strained against harnesses drawn taut by the weight of Atka, the lead dog, dangling out of sight beyond the edge of the abyss.

Garner visualized him—thrashing against his tack in a black well as the jagged circle of grayish light above shrank away, inch by lurching inch—and he felt the pull of night inside himself, the age-old gravity of the dark. Then a hand closed around his ankle.

Bishop, clinging to the ice, a hand-slip away from tumbling into the crevasse himself: face blanched, eyes red rimmed inside his goggles.

"Shit," Garner said. "Here—"

He reached down, locked his hand around Bishop's wrist, and hauled him up, boots slipping. Momentum carried him over backwards, floundering in the snow as Bishop curled fetal beside him.

"You okay?"

"My ankle," he said through gritted teeth.

"Here, let me see."

"Not now. Connelly. What happened to Connelly?"

"He fell off—"

With a metallic screech, the sledge broke loose. It slid a foot, a foot and a half, and then it hung up. The dogs screamed. Garner had never heard a dog make a noise like that—he didn't know dogs *could* make a noise like that—and for a moment their blind, inarticulate terror swam through him. He thought again of Atka, dangling there, turning, feet clawing at the darkness, and he felt something stir inside him once again—

"Steady, man," Bishop said.

Garner drew in a long breath, icy air lacerating his lungs.

"You gotta be steady now, Doc," Bishop said. "You gotta go cut him loose."

"No—"

"We're gonna lose the sledge. And the rest of the team. That happens, we're all gonna die out here, okay? I'm busted up right now, I need you to do this thing—"

"What about Connell—?"

"Not now, Doc. Listen to me. We don't have time. Okay?"

Bishop held his gaze. Garner tried to look away, could not. The other man's eyes fixed him.

"Okay," he said.

Garner stood and stumbled away. Went to his knees to dig through the wreckage. Flung aside a sack of rice, frozen in clumps, wrenched open a crate of flares—useless—shoved it aside, and dragged another one toward him. This time he was lucky: he dug out a coil of rope, a hammer, a handful of pitons. The sledge lurched on its lip of ice, the rear end swinging, setting off another round of whimpering.

"Hurry," Bishop said.

Garner drove the pitons deep into the permafrost and threaded the rope through their eyes, his hands stiff inside his gloves. Lashing the other end around his waist, he edged back onto the broken ice shelf. It shifted underneath him, creaking. The sledge shuddered, but held. Below him, beyond the moiling clump of dogs, he could see the leather trace leads, stretched taut across the jagged rim of the abyss.

He dropped back, letting rope out as he descended. The world fell away above him. Down and down, and then he was on his knees at the very edge of the shelf, the hot, rank stink of the dogs enveloping him. He used his teeth to loosen one glove. Working quickly against the icy assault of the elements, he fumbled his knife out of its sheath and pressed the blade to the first of the traces. He sawed at it until the leather separated with a snap.

Atka's weight shifted in the darkness below him, and the dog howled mournfully. Garner set to work on the second trace, felt it let go, everything—the sledge, the terrified dogs—slipping toward darkness. For a moment he thought the whole thing would go. But it held. He went to work on the third trace, gone loose now by some trick of tension. It too separated beneath his blade, and he once again felt Atka's weight shift in the well of darkness beneath him.

Garner peered into the blackness. He could see the dim blur of the dog, could feel its dumb terror welling up around him, and as he brought the blade to the final trace, a painstakingly erected dike gave way in his mind. Memory flooded through him: the feel of mangled flesh beneath his fingers, the distant *whump* of artillery, Elizabeth's drawn and somber face.

His fingers faltered. Tears blinded him. The sledge shifted above him as Atka thrashed in his harness. Still he hesitated.

The rope creaked under the strain of additional weight. Ice rained down around him. Garner looked up to see Connelly working his way hand over hand down the rope.

"Do it," Connelly grunted, his eyes like chips of flint. "Cut him loose."

Garner's fingers loosened around the hilt of the blade. He felt the tug of the dark at his feet, Atka whining.

"Give me the goddamn knife," Connelly said, wrenching it away, and together they clung there on the single narrow thread of gray rope, two men and one knife and the enormous gulf of the sky overhead as Connelly sawed savagely at the last of the traces. It held for a moment, and then, abruptly, it gave, loose ends curling back and away from the blade.

Atka fell howling into darkness.

They made camp.

The traces of the lead sledge had to be untangled and repaired, the dogs tended to, the weight redistributed to account for Atka's loss. While Connelly busied himself with these chores, Garner stabilized Faber—the blood had frozen to a black crust inside the makeshift splint Garner had applied yesterday, after the accident—and wrapped Bishop's ankle. These were automatic actions. Serving in France he'd learned the trick of letting his body work while his mind traveled to other places; it had been crucial to keeping his sanity during the war, when the people brought to him for treatment had been butchered by German submachine guns or burned and blistered by mustard gas. He worked to save those men, though it was hopeless work. Mankind had acquired an appetite for dying; doctors had become shepherds to the process. Surrounded by screams and spilled blood, he'd anchored himself to memories of his wife, Elizabeth: the warmth of her kitchen back home in Boston, and the warmth of her body too.

But all that was gone.

Now, when he let his mind wander, it went to dark places, and he found himself concentrating instead on the minutiae of these rote tasks like a first-year medical student. He cut a length of bandage and applied a compression wrap to Bishop's exposed ankle, covering both ankle and foot in careful figure-eights. He kept his mind in the moment, listening to the harsh labor of their lungs in the frigid air, to Connelly's chained fury as he worked at the traces, and to the muffled sounds of the dogs as they burrowed into the snow to rest.

And he listened, too, to Atka's distant cries, leaking from the crevasse like blood.

"Can't believe that dog's still alive," Bishop said, testing his ankle against his weight. He grimaced and sat down on a crate. "He's a tough old bastard."

Garner imagined Elizabeth's face, drawn tight with pain and determination, while he fought a war on the far side of the ocean. Was she afraid too, suspended over her own dark hollow? Did she cry out for him?

"Help me with this tent," Garner said.

They'd broken off from the main body of the expedition to bring Faber back to one of the supply depots on the Ross Ice Shelf, where Garner could care for him. They would wait there for the remainder of the expedition, which suited Garner just fine, but troubled both Bishop and Connelly, who had higher aspirations for their time here.

Nightfall was still a month away, but if they were going to camp here while they made repairs, they would need the tents to harvest warmth. Connelly approached as they drove pegs into the permafrost, his eyes impassive as they swept over Faber, still tied down to the travois, locked inside a morphine dream. He regarded Bishop's ankle and asked him how it was.

"It'll do," Bishop said. "It'll have to. How are the dogs?"

"We need to start figuring what we can do without," Connelly said. "We're gonna have to leave some stuff behind."

"We're only down one dog," Bishop said. "It shouldn't be too hard to compensate."

"We're down two. One of the swing dogs snapped her foreleg." He opened one of the bags lashed to the rear sledge, removing an Army-issue revolver. "So go ahead and figure what we don't need. I gotta tend to her." He tossed a contemptuous glance at Garner. "Don't worry, I won't ask *you* to do it."

Garner watched as Connelly approached the injured dog, lying away from the others in the snow. She licked obsessively at her broken leg. As Connelly approached she looked up at him and her tail wagged weakly. Connelly aimed the pistol and fired a bullet through her head. The shot made a flat, inconsequential sound, swallowed up by the vastness of the open plain.

Garner turned away, emotion surging through him with a surprising, disorienting energy. Bishop met his gaze and offered a rueful smile.

"Bad day," he said.

• • •

Still, Atka whimpered.

Garner lay wakeful, staring at the canvas, taut and smooth as the interior of an egg above him. Faber moaned, calling out after some fever phantom. Garner almost envied the man. Not the injury—a nasty compound fracture of the femur, the product of a bad step on the ice when he'd stepped outside the circle of tents to piss—but the sweet oblivion of the morphine doze.

In France, in the war, he'd known plenty of doctors who'd used the stuff to chase away the night haunts. He'd also seen the fevered agony of withdrawal. He had no wish to experience that, but he felt the opiate lure all the same. He'd felt it then, when he'd had thoughts of Elizabeth to sustain him. And he felt it now—stronger still—when he didn't.

Elizabeth had fallen victim to the greatest cosmic prank of all time, the flu that had swept across the world in the spring and summer of 1918, as if the bloody abattoir in the trenches hadn't been evidence enough of humanity's divine disfavor. That's what Elizabeth had called it in the last letter he'd ever had from her: God's judgment on a world gone mad. Garner had given up on God by then: he'd packed away the Bible Elizabeth had pressed upon him after a week in the field hospital, knowing that its paltry lies could bring him no comfort in the face of such horror, and it hadn't. Not then, and not later, when he'd come home to face Elizabeth's mute and barren grave. Garner had taken McReady's offer to accompany the expedition soon after, and though he'd stowed the Bible in his gear before he left, he hadn't opened it since and he wouldn't open it here, either, lying sleepless beside a man who might yet die because he'd had to take a piss—yet another grand cosmic joke—in a place so hellish and forsaken that even Elizabeth's God could find no purchase here.

There could be no God in such a place.

Just the relentless shriek of the wind tearing at the flimsy canvas, and the death-howl agony of the dog. Just emptiness, and the unyielding porcelain dome of the polar sky.

Garner sat up, breathing heavily.

Faber muttered under his breath. Garner leaned over the injured man, the stench of fever hot in his nostrils. He smoothed Faber's hair back from his forehead and studied the leg, swollen tight as a sausage inside the sealskin legging. Garner didn't like to think what he might see if he slit open that sausage to reveal the leg underneath: the viscous pit of the wound itself, crimson lines of sepsis twining around Faber's thigh like a malevolent vine as they climbed inexorably toward his heart.

Atka howled, a long rising cry that broke into pitiful yelps, died away, and renewed itself, like the shriek of sirens on the French front.

"Jesus," Garner whispered.

He fished a flask out of his pack and allowed himself a single swallow of whiskey. Then he sat in the dark, listening to the mournful lament of the dog, his mind filling with hospital images: the red splash of tissue in a steel tray, the enflamed wound of an amputation, the hand folding itself into an outraged fist as the arm fell away. He thought of Elizabeth, too, Elizabeth most all, buried months before Garner had gotten back from Europe. And he thought of Connelly, that aggrieved look as he turned away to deal with the injured swing dog.

Don't worry, I won't ask you to do it.

Crouching in the low tent, Garner dressed. He shoved a flashlight into his jacket, shouldered aside the tent flap, and leaned into the wind tearing across the waste. The crevasse lay before him, rope still trailing through the pitons to dangle into the pit below.

Garner felt the pull of darkness. And Atka, screaming.

"Okay," he muttered. "All right, I'm coming."

Once again he lashed the rope around his waist. This time he didn't hesitate as he backed out onto the ledge of creaking ice. Hand over hand he went, backward and down, boots scuffing until he stepped into space and hung suspended in a well of shadow.

Panic seized him, the black certainty that nothing lay beneath him. The crevasse yawned under his feet, like a wedge of vacuum driven into the heart of the planet. Then, below him—ten feet? twenty?—Atka mewled, piteous as a freshly whelped pup, eyes squeezed shut against the light. Garner thought of the dog, curled in agony upon some shelf of subterranean ice, and began to lower himself into the pit, darkness rising to envelop him.

One heartbeat, then another and another and another, his breath diaphanous in the gloom, his boots scrabbling for solid ground. Scrabbling and finding it. Garner clung to the rope, testing the surface with his weight.

It held.

Garner took the flashlight from his jacket, and switched it on. Atka peered up at him, brown eyes iridescent with pain. The dog's legs twisted underneath it, and its tail wagged feebly. Blood glistened at its muzzle. As he moved closer, Garner saw that a dagger of bone had pierced its torso, unveiling the slick yellow gleam of subcutaneous fat and deeper still, half visible through tufts of coarse fur, the bloody pulse of viscera. And it had shat itself—Garner could smell it—a thin gruel congealing on the dank stone.

"Okay," he said. "Okay, Atka."

Kneeling, Garner caressed the dog. It growled and subsided, surrendering to his ministrations.

"Good boy, Atka," he whispered. "Settle down, boy."

Garner slid his knife free of its sheath, bent forward, and brought the blade to the dog's throat. Atka whimpered—"Shhh," Garner whispered—as he bore down with the edge, steeling himself against the thing he was about to do—

Something moved in the darkness beneath him: a leathery rasp, the echoing clatter of stone on stone, of loose pebbles tumbling into darkness. Atka whimpered again, legs twitching as he tried to shove himself back against the wall. Garner, startled, shoved the blade forward. Atka's neck unseamed itself in a welter of black arterial blood. The dog stiffened, shuddered once, and died—Garner watched its eyes dim in the space of a single heartbeat—and once again something shifted in the darkness at Garner's back. Garner scuttled backward, slamming his shoulders into the wall by Atka's corpse. He froze there, probing the darkness.

Then, when nothing came—had he imagined it? He must have imagined it—Garner aimed the flashlight light into the gloom. His breath caught in his throat. He shoved himself erect in amazement, the rope pooling at his feet.

Vast.

The place was vast: walls of naked stone climbing in cathedral arcs to the undersurface of the polar plain and a floor worn smooth as glass over long ages, stretching out before him until it dropped away into an abyss of darkness. Struck dumb with terror—or was it wonder?—Garner stumbled forward, the rope unspooling behind him until he drew up at the precipice, pointed the light into the shadows before him, and saw what it was that he had discovered.

A stairwell, cut seamlessly into the stone itself, and no human stairwell either: each riser fell away three feet or more, the stair itself winding endlessly into fathomless depths of earth, down and down and down until it curved away beyond the reach of his frail human light, and further still toward some awful destination he scarcely dared imagine. Garner felt the lure and hunger of the place singing in his bones. Something deep inside him, some mute inarticulate longing, cried out in response, and before he knew it he found himself scrambling down the first riser and then another, the flashlight carving slices out of the darkness to reveal a bas relief of inhuman creatures lunging at him in glimpses: taloned feet and clawed hands and sinuous Medusa coils that seemed to writhe about one another in the fitful and imperfect glare. And through it all the terrible summons of the place, drawing him down into the dark.

"Elizabeth—" he gasped, stumbling down another riser and another, until the rope, forgotten, jerked taut about his waist. He looked up at the pale circle of Connelly's face far above him.

"What the hell are you doing down there, Doc?" Connelly shouted, his voice thick with rage, and then, almost against his will, Garner found himself ascending once again into the light.

No sooner had he gained his footing than Connelly grabbed him by the collar and swung him to the ground. Garner scrabbled for purchase in the snow but Connelly kicked him back down again, his blond, bearded face contorted in rage.

"You stupid son of a bitch! Do you care if we all die out here?"

"Get off me!"

"For a dog? For a goddamned *dog*?" Connelly tried to kick him again, but Garner grabbed his foot and rolled, bringing the other man down on top of him. The two of them grappled in the snow, their heavy coats and gloves making any real damage all but impossible.

The flaps to one of the tents opened and Bishop limped out, his face a caricature of alarm. He was buttoning his coat even as he approached. "Stop! *Stop it right now!*"

Garner clambered to his feet, staggering backward a few steps. Connelly rose to one knee, leaning over and panting. He pointed at Garner. "I found him in the crevasse! He went down alone!"

Garner leaned against one of the packed sledges. He could feel Bishop watching him as tugged free a glove to poke at a tender spot on his face, but he didn't look up.

"Is this true?"

"Of course it's true!" Connelly said, but Bishop waved him into silence.

Garner looked up at him, breath heaving in his lungs. "You've got to see it," he said. "My God, Bishop."

Bishop turned his gaze to the crevasse, where he saw the pitons and the rope spilling into the darkness. "Oh, Doc," he said quietly.

"It's not a crevasse, Bishop. It's a stairwell."

Connelly strode toward Garner, jabbing his finger at him. "What? You lost your goddamned mind."

"Look for yourself!"

Bishop interposed himself between the two men. "*Enough!*" He turned to face Connelly. "Back off."

"But—"

"I said back off!"

Connelly peeled his lips back, then turned and stalked back toward the crevasse. He knelt by its edge and started hauling up the rope.

Bishop turned to Garner. "Explain yourself."

All at once, Garner's passion drained from him. He felt a wash of exhaustion. His muscles ached. How could he explain this to him? He could he explain this so that they'd understand? "Atka," he said simply, imploringly. "I could hear him."

A look of deep regret fell over Bishop's face. "Doc . . . Atka was a just a dog. We have to get Faber to the depot."

"I could still hear him."

"You have to pull yourself together. There are real lives at stake here, do you get that? Me and Connelly, we aren't doctors. Faber needs *you*."

"But—"

"Do you get that?"

"I . . . yeah. Yeah, I know."

"When you go down into places like that, especially by yourself, you're putting us all at risk. What are we gonna do without Doc, huh?"

This was not an argument Garner would win. Not this way. So he grabbed Bishop by the arm and led him toward the crevasse. "Look," he said.

Bishop wrenched his arm free, his face darkening. Connelly straightened, watching this exchange. "Don't put your hands on me, Doc," Bishop said.

Garner released him. "Bishop," he said. "Please."

Bishop paused a moment, then walked toward the opening. "All right."

Connelly exploded. "Oh for Christ's sake!"

"We're not going inside it," Bishop said, looking at them both. "I'm going to look, okay Doc? That's all you get."

Garner nodded. "Okay," he said. "Okay."

The two of them approached the edge of the crevasse. Closer, Garner felt it like a hook in his liver, tugging him down. It took an act of will to stop at the edge, to remain still and unshaken and look at these other two men as if his whole life did not hinge upon this moment.

"It's a stairwell," he said. His voice did not shake. His body did not move. "It's carved into the rock. It's got . . . designs of some kind."

Bishop peered down into the darkness for a long moment. "I don't see anything," he said at last.

"I'm telling you, it's *there*!" Garner stopped and gathered himself. He tried another tack. "This, this could be the scientific discovery of the century. You want to stick it to McReady? Let him plant his little flag. This is evidence of, of . . . " He trailed off. He didn't know what it was evidence of.

"We'll mark the location," Bishop said. "We'll come back. If what you say is true it's not going anywhere."

Garner switched on his flashlight. "Look," he said, and he threw it down.

The flashlight arced end over end, its white beam slicing through the darkness with a scalpel's clean efficiency, illuminating flashes of hewn rock and what might have been carvings or just natural irregularities. It clattered to a landing beside the corpse of the dog, casting in bright relief its open jaw and lolling tongue, and the black pool of blood beneath it.

Bishop looked for a moment, and shook his head. "God damn it, Doc," he said. "You're really straining my patience. Come on."

Bishop was about to turn away when Atka's body jerked once—Garner saw it—and then again, almost imperceptibly. Reaching out, Garner seized Bishop's sleeve. "What now, for Christ's—" the other man started to say, his voice harsh with annoyance. Then the body was yanked into the surrounding darkness so quickly it seemed as though it had vanished into thin air. Only its blood, a smeared trail into shadow, testified to its ever having been there at all. That, and the jostled flashlight, which rolled in a lazy half circle, its unobstructed light spearing first into empty darkness and then into smooth cold stone before settling at last on what might have been a carven, clawed foot. The beam flickered and went out.

"What the fuck . . . " Bishop said.

A scream erupted from the tent behind them.

Faber.

Garner broke into a clumsy run, high-stepping through the piled snow. The other men shouted behind him but their words were lost in the wind and in his own hard breathing. His body was moving according to its training but his mind was pinned like a writhing insect in the hole behind him, in the stark, burning image of what he had just seen. He was transported by fear and adrenaline and by something else, by some other emotion he had not felt in many years or perhaps ever in his life, some heart-filling glorious exaltation that threatened to snuff him out like a dying cinder.

Faber was sitting upright in the tent—it stank of sweat and urine and kerosene, eye-watering and sharp—his thick hair a dark corona around his head, his skin as pale as a cavefish. He was still trying to scream, but his voice had broken, and his utmost effort could now produce only a long, cracked wheeze, which seemed forced through his throat like steel wool. His leg stuck out of the blanket, still grossly swollen.

The warmth from the Nansen cooker was almost oppressive.

Garner dropped to his knees beside him and tried to ease him back down into his sleeping bag, but Faber resisted. He fixed his eyes on Garner, his painful wheeze trailing into silence. Hooking his fingers in Garner's collar, he pulled him close, so close that Garner could smell the sour taint of his breath.

"Faber, relax, relax!"

"It—" Faber's voice locked. He swallowed and tried again. "It laid an egg in me."

Bishop and Connelly crowded through the tent flap, and Garner felt suddenly hemmed in, overwhelmed by the heat and the stink and the steam rising in wisps from their clothes as they pushed closer, staring down at Faber.

"What's going on?" Bishop asked. "Is he all right?"

Faber eyed them wildly. Ignoring them, Garner placed his hands on Faber's cheeks and turned his head toward him. "Look at me, Faber. Look at me. What do you mean?"

Faber found a way to smile. "In my dream. It put my head inside its body, and it laid an egg in me."

Connelly said, "He's delirious. See what happens when you leave him alone?"

Garner fished an ampule of morphine out of his bag. Faber saw what he was doing and his body bucked.

"No!" he screamed, summoning his voice again. "No!" His leg thrashed out, knocking over the Nansen cooker. Cursing, Connelly dove at the overturned stove, but it was already too late. Kerosene splashed over the blankets and supplies, engulfing the tent in flames. The men moved in a sudden tangle of panic. Bishop stumbled back out of the tent and Connelly shoved Garner aside—Garner rolled over on his back and came to rest there—as he lunged for Faber's legs, dragging him backward. Screaming, Faber clutched at the ground to resist, but Connelly was too strong. A moment later, Faber was gone, dragging a smoldering rucksack with him.

Still inside the tent, Garner lay back, watching as the fire spread hungrily along the roof, dropping tongues of flame onto the ground, onto his own body. Garner closed his eyes as the heat gathered him up like a furnace-hearted lover.

What he felt, though, was not the fire's heat, but the cool breath of underground earth, the silence of the deep tomb buried beneath the ice shelf. The stairs descended before him, and at the bottom he heard a noise again: A woman's voice, calling for him. Wondering where he was.

Elizabeth, he called, his voice echoing off the stone. Are you there?

If only he'd gotten to see her, he thought. If only he'd gotten to bury her. To fill those beautiful eyes with dirt. To cover her in darkness.

Elizabeth, can you hear me?

Then Connelly's big arms enveloped him, and he felt the heat again, searing bands of pain around his legs and chest. It was like being wrapped in a star. "I ought to let you burn, you stupid son of a bitch," Connelly hissed, but he didn't. He lugged Garner outside—Garner opened his eyes in time to see the canvas part in front of him, like fiery curtains—and dumped him in the snow instead. The pain went away, briefly, and Garner mourned its passing. He rolled over and lifted his head. Connelly stood over him, his face twisted in disgust. Behind him the tent flickered and burned like a dropped torch.

Faber's quavering voice hung over it all, rising and falling like the wind.

Connelly tossed an ampule and a syringe onto the ground by Garner. "Faber's leg's opened up again," he said. "Go and do your job."

Garner climbed slowly to his feet, feeling the skin on his chest and legs tighten. He'd been burned; he'd have to wait until he'd tended to Faber to find out how badly.

"And then help us pack up," Bishop called as he led the dogs to their harnesses, his voice harsh and strained. "We're getting the hell out of here."

By the time they reached the depot, Faber was dead. Connelly spat into the snow and turned away to unhitch the dogs, while Garner and Bishop went inside and started a fire. Bishop started water boiling for coffee. Garner unpacked their bedclothes and dressed the cots, moving gingerly. Once the place was warm enough he undressed and surveyed the burn damage. It would leave scars.

The next morning they wrapped Faber's body and packed it in an ice locker.

After that they settled in to wait.

The ship would not return for a month yet, and though McReady's expedition was due back before then, the vagaries of Antarctic experience made that a tenuous proposition at best. In any case, they were stuck with each other for some time yet, and not even the generous stocks of the depot—a relative wealth of food and medical supplies, playing cards and books—could fully distract them from their grievances.

In the days that followed, Connelly managed to bank his anger at Garner, but it would not take much to set it off again; so Garner tried to keep a low profile. As with the trenches in France, corpses were easy to explain in Antarctica.

A couple of weeks into that empty expanse of time, while Connelly dozed on his cot and Bishop read through an old natural history magazine, Garner decided to risk broaching the subject of what had happened in the crevasse.

"You saw it," he said, quietly, so as not to wake Connelly.

Bishop took a moment to acknowledge that he'd heard him. Finally he tilted the magazine away, and sighed. "Saw what," he said.

"You know what."

Bishop shook his head. "No," he said. "I don't. I don't know what you're talking about."

"Something was there."

Bishop said nothing. He lifted the magazine again, but his eyes were still.

"Something was down there," Garner said.

"No there wasn't."

"It pulled Atka. I know you saw it."

Bishop refused to look at him. "This is an empty place," he said, after a long silence. "There's nothing here." He blinked, and turned a page in the magazine. "Nothing."

Garner leaned back onto his cot, looking at the ceiling.

Although the long Antarctic day had not yet finished, it was shading into dusk, the sun hovering over the horizon like a great boiling eye. It cast long shadows, and the lamp Bishop had lit to read by set them dancing. Garner watched them caper across the ceiling. Some time later, Bishop snuffed out the lamp and dragged the curtains over the windows, consigning them all to darkness. With it, Garner felt something like peace stir inside him. He let it move through him in waves, he felt it ebb and flow with each slow pulse of his heart.

A gust of wind scattered fine crystals of snow against the window, and he found himself wondering what the night would be like in this cold country. He imagined the sky dissolving to reveal the hard vault of stars, the galaxy turning above him like a cog in a vast, unknowable engine. And behind it all, the emptiness into which men hurled their prayers. It occurred to him that he could leave now, walk out into the long twilight and keep going until the earth opened beneath him and he found himself descending strange stairs, while the world around him broke silently into snow, and into night.

Garner closed his eyes.

Vast and lonely is the ocean, and even as all things came from it, so shall they return thereto. In the shrouded depths of time none shall reign upon the earth, nor shall any motion be, save in the eternal waters.
"The Night Ocean" · H.P. Lovecraft & R. H. Barlow (1936)

· BAD SUSHI ·
Cherie Priest

Baku's hand shook.

In it, he held a pinch of wasabi, preparing to leave the condiment as a peaked green dollop beside a damp pile of flesh-colored ginger. He hesitated, even though his fellow chef slapped the kitchen bell once, twice, a third time— and the orders were backing up.

The waitress flashed Baku a frown.

Some small fact was wiggling around in his expansive memory. In the back of his sinuses, he felt a tickle of sulfur. The kitchen in Sonada's smelled like soy sauce and sizzling oil, and frying rice; but Baku also detected rotten eggs.

He smeared the glob of gritty paste onto the rectangular plate before him, and he pushed the neatly-sliced sushi rolls into the pick-up window. The hot yellow smell grew stronger in his nose, but he could work through it. All it took was a little concentration.

He reached for his knives. The next slip in the queue called for a California roll, a tuna roll, and a salmon roll. Seaweed. Rice. Fish meat, in slick, soft slabs. He wrapped it all expertly, without thinking. He sliced the rolls without crushing them and slid them onto the plate.

This is why Sonada's kept Baku, despite his age. He told them he was seventy, but that was a lie by eight years—an untruth offered because his employers were afraid he was too old to work. But American Social Security wasn't enough, and the work at the restaurant wasn't so hard. The hours were not so long.

The other workers were born Americans. They didn't have to take the test or say the pledge, one hand over their hearts.

Baku didn't hold it against them, and the others didn't hold his original nationality against him, either. They might have, if they'd known the uniform he'd once worn. They might have looked at him differently, these young citizens, if they'd known how frantically he'd fired, and how he'd aimed for all the bright blue eyes.

There it was again. The sulfur.

Baku had tripped over a G.I.'s body as he staggered toward the beach at Cape Esperance, but he hadn't thought much of it. He'd been preoccupied at the time—thinking only of meeting the secret transport that would take him out of Guadalcanal. The Emperor had declared the island a lost cause, and an evacuation had been arranged. It had happened under cover of night. The transport had been a crushing rush of thirteen thousand brown-eyed men clamoring for the military ferry. The night had reeked of gunpowder, and body odor, and sulfur, and blood.

Baku thought again of the last dead American he'd seen on Guadalcanal, the man's immobile body just beginning to stink in the sunset. If someone had told him, back in 1942, that in sixty years he'd be serving the dead American's grandchildren sushi rolls . . . Baku would have never believed it.

He looked at the next slip of lined white and green paper.

Shrimp rolls. More tuna.

Concentrate.

He breathed in the clean, sparse scent of the seafood—so faint it was almost undetectable. If it smelled like more than salt and the ocean, it was going rotten. There were guidelines, of course, about how cold it must be kept and how it must be stored—but the old chef didn't need to watch any thermometers or check any dates. He knew when the meat was good. He knew what it would taste like, lying on top of the rice, and dipped lightly in a small puddle of soy sauce.

One order after another, he prepared them. His knives flashed, and his fingers pulled the sticky rice into bundles. His indefatigable wrists jerked and lurched from counter to bowl to chopping block to plate.

Eventually, with enough repetition and enough concentration, the remembered eggy nastiness left his head.

When his shift was over, he removed his apron and washed his knives. He dried the knives each in turn, slipping them into a cloth pouch that he rolled up and carried home. The knives belonged to him, and they were a condition of his employment. They were good knives, made of German steel by a company that had folded ages before. Baku would work with no others.

At home that night, he lay in bed and tried to remember what had brought on the flashback. Usually there was some concrete reason—an old military uniform, a glimpse of ribbon that looked like a war medal, or a Memorial Day parade.

What had brought him back to the island?

At home in bed, it was safe to speculate. At home, in the small apartment with the threadbare curtains and the clean kitchen, it was all right to let his mind wander.

Sixty years ago there was a war and he was a young man. He was in the Emperor's army and he went to the South Pacific, and there was an island. The Americans dug in, and forced the Japanese troops to retreat.

They sneaked away at night, from the point at Cape Esperance. Personnel boats had been waiting. "There were thirteen-thousand of us," he breathed to himself in his native tongue. "And we left in the middle of the night, while the Americans slept."

The water had been black and it had been calm, as calm as the ocean ever was. Hushed, hushed, and hushed, the soldiers slogged into the water to meet the transports. In haste and in extreme caution, they had boarded the boats in packs and rows. They had huddled down on the slat seats and listened to the furtive cacophony of oars and small propellers.

He seemed to recall a panic—not his own. Another man, someone badly hurt, in mind and body. The man had stood up in the boat and tried to call out. His nearest neighbor tackled him, pulled him back down into his seat; but the ruckus unsettled the small craft.

Baku was sitting on the outside rail, one of the last men crammed aboard.

When the boat lunged, he lost his balance. Over the side he toppled, and into the water. It was like falling into ink with a riptide. Fear was halted by the fierce wetness, and his instincts were all but exhausted by days of battle. He thought to float, though. He tried to right himself, to roll out of the fetal suspension.

And something had stopped him—hard.

Even after sixty years, the memory of it shocked him—the way the thing had grabbed him by the ankle. The thing that seized him felt like a living cable made of steel. It coiled itself around his leg, one loop, two loops, working its way to a tighter grip with the skill of a python and the strength of something much, much larger.

Inside Baku's vest he carried a bayonet blade made of carbon steel. It was sharp enough to cut paper without tearing it. It was strong enough to hold his weight.

His first thought and first fear was that this was a strange new weapon devised by the Americans; but his second thought was that this was no weapon at all, but a living creature. There was sentience and insistence in the way the thing squeezed and tugged. He curled his body up to pull his hand and his knife closer to the clutching, grasping thing.

And because he was running out of air, he arched his elbow up and tightened his leather-tough wrists. Even then they'd been taut and dense with muscle. He'd grown up beside the ocean, cutting the fish every day, all day, until the Emperor had called for his service and he'd taken up a gun instead.

So it was with strength and certainty that he brought the knife down into the thing that held his leg.

It convulsed. It twitched, and Baku stabbed again. The water went warmer around his ankle, and the terrible grip slackened. Again. A third time, and a fourth. In desperation, he began to saw, unafraid that he would hit his own flesh, and unaware of the jagged injury he created when he did so.

By then his air was so low and he was so frightened, that he might have cut off his whole leg in pursuit of escape. But after several heroic hacks Baku all but severed the living lasso; and at that moment, one of his fellow soldiers got a handful of the back of his shirt. Human hands pulled him up, and out, and over—back into the boat. A faint and final tug at his leg went nearly unnoticed as the last of the thing stretched, split, and tore.

On the floor of the boat Baku gasped and floundered. The other soldiers covered him with their hands, hushing him. Always hushing. The Americans might hear.

He shook and shook—taking comfort in the circle of faces that covered him from above and shut out the star-spangled sky. At last he breathed and the breath was not hard-won.

But he did not feel safe.

Around his leg the leftovers clung. He unwound the ropy flesh from his own quivering limb and the dismembered coil fell to the boat bottom where it twitched, flopped, and lay still.

"What is it?" someone asked. "What is it?" the call was echoed around the boat in quiet voices.

No one wanted to touch it, so no one did until the next day.

Baku stared down at the thing and wondered what it had once belonged to. All he had to judge it by was the lone, partial tentacle, and it did not tell him much. It was a sickly greenish brown and it came with a smell to match—as if it were made of old dung, spoiled crab meat, and salt; and suction pads lined one side, with thorny-looking spines on the other. He did not remember the bite of the spines, but his leg wore the results.

"What is it?" the question came again from one of his fellow soldiers, who poked at the leavings of the peculiar predator with the end of his gun.

"I don't know. Have you ever seen anything like it?"

"Never."

Never before that night had he seen anything like the tentacle. It represented no squid or octopus that Baku knew, and he was born into a family that had fed itself from the water for generations. Baku thought he had seen everything the ocean had to offer, even from the bottom-most depths where the fish had blind-white eyes, and the sand was as fine as flour. But he'd never seen a thing like that, and he would never forget it. The scars on his legs would remind him for the rest of his life, even when he was an old man, and living in America, and lying in bed on a cool spring night . . . half dozing and half staring at the ceiling fan that slowly churned the air above him.

And it was that smell, and that remembered texture of stubborn rubber, that had reminded him of the sulfur stench at Guadalcanal.

Twice in his life now, he had breathed that nasty, tangy odor and felt a tough cord of flesh resist the push of his knife.

His stomach turned.

The next day at work, Baku wondered if the store manager had noticed anything strange about the sushi. He asked, "Are we getting different meat now? It seemed different yesterday, when I was cutting it for the rolls."

The manager frowned, and then smiled. "I think I know what you mean. We have a new vendor for some of the fish. It's a company from New England, and they carry a different stock from the Gulf Coast company. But they come with very good references, and they cost less money than the others, too. They distribute out of a warehouse downtown, by the pier at Manufacturer's Row."

"I see."

"Was there a problem with the fish?"

Baku was torn.

He did not want to complain. He never liked to complain. The manager was happy with the new vendor, and what would he say? That the octopus meat reminded him of war?

"No," he said. "No problem. I only noticed the change, that's all." And he went back to work, keeping his eyes open for more of the mysterious meat.

He found it in the squid, and in the crab. It lurked amid the pale bits of ordinary fish and seafood, suspicious landmines of a funny smell and a texture that drove him to distraction.

Baku watched for the new vendor and saw him one day driving up in a big white truck with a large "A" painted on the side. He couldn't make out the company's name; it was printed in a small, elaborate script that was difficult to read. The man who drove the truck was a tall, thin fellow shaped like an egg roll. His skin was doughy and hairless.

When he moved the chilled packages of sealed, wrapped food on the dolly, he moved with strength but without hurry. He walked like a sea lion, with a gently lumbering gait—as if he might be more comfortable swimming than walking.

His big, round eyes stared straight ahead as he made his deliveries. He didn't speak to anyone that Baku ever saw, and when he was handed a pen to sign at the clipboard, he looked at it blankly before applying his mark to the proper forms.

"I think he's *challenged*," the Sonada's manager said. "Mentally challenged, you know. Poor man."

"Poor man," Baku agreed. He watched him get into his truck and drive away. He would be back on Tuesday with more plastic-wrapped boxes that emitted fogged, condensed air in tiny clouds around their corners.

And meanwhile, business boomed.

Every night the restaurant was a little more packed, with a few more patrons. Every night the till rang longer, and the receipts stacked higher on the spike beside the register. Every night the waitresses ran themselves more ragged and collected more tips.

By Saturday, Sonada's was managing twice its volume from the week before. By Sunday, people were lined out the door and around the side of the building. It did not matter how long they were told to wait.

They waited.

They were learning an unnatural patience.

Baku took on more hours, even though the manager told him it was not necessary. A new chef was hired to help with the added burden and another would have been helpful, but the kitchen would hold no more workers.

Baku insisted on the extra time. He wanted to see for himself, and to watch the other men who cut the sushi rolls and steamed the sticky rice. He wanted to see if they saw it too—the funny, pale meat the color of a pickle's insides. But if anyone noticed that something was out of order, no one spoke about it. If something was different, something must be good—because business had never been better.

And the old chef knew that one way or another, the strange meat was bringing the customers in.

Even though Sonada's served a broad variety of Asian food, no one ever ordered fried rice anymore, or sesame chicken. Egg rolls had all but vanished from the menu, and Baku couldn't remember the last time beef was required for a dish.

Everyone wanted the sushi, and Baku knew why.

And he knew that something was happening to the regular patrons, the ones who came every night. From the kitchen window that overlooked the lobby he saw them return for supper like clockwork, and with every meal they took, they were changed.

They ate faster, and walked slower. They talked less.

Baku began to stay longer in the kitchen, and he rushed hurriedly to his car at night.

Baku paused his unending slicing, cutting, scooping and scraping to use the washroom. He closed the door behind himself and sighed into the quiet. For the first time all evening, he was alone. Or so he thought.

All the stall doors were open, save the one at the farthest end of the blue-tiled room—which was closed only a little way. From within it, someone flushed.

Out of politeness, Baku pretended not to see that the other man had left the door ajar. He stepped to the nearest sink and washed his hands. He covered them with runny pink soap and took his time building lather, then rinsing under the steamy tap water. He relished the heat.

The kitchen had become so cold in the last week, since the grills were rarely working and the air conditioner was running full-blast. Instead of sporadic warmth from the stoves, the refrigerator door was incessantly opened and closed—bringing fresh meat for the sushi rolls. The chefs handled cold meat, seaweed, and sticky rice for nine hours at a time.

His knuckles never thawed.

But while he stood there, warming his fingers beneath the gushing stream, he noticed the sound of repeated flushing foaming its way into the tiled room. Dampness crept up the sole of Baku's shoe. Water puddled on the floor around his feet. He flipped the sink's chrome lever down, shutting off the water.

He listened.

The toilet's denouement was interrupted before the plumbing could finish its cycle and another flush gurgled. A fresh tide of water spilled out from under the door.

Baku craned his neck to the right, leaning until he could see the square of space between the soggy floor and the bottom of the stall. Filthy gray sneakers stood ankle-deep in overflow. The laces were untied; they floated like the hair of a drowning victim.

"Hello?" Baku called softly. He did not want a response. "Can I help you with something, sir?" His English was heavy, but he was careful with his pronunciation.

He took a cautious step forward, and that small shuffle cleared nearly half the distance between him and the stall door. He took a second step, but he made that one even tinier than the first, and he put out his hand.

The tips of his fingers quivered, as they tapped against the painted metal door. He tried to ask, "Are you all right?" But the words barely whispered out of his throat.

A groan answered him without offering specifics.

He pushed the door.

He found himself staring at a man's hunched back and a sweaty patch of shirt between his shoulder blades. The shirt itself was the beige kind that comes with an embroidered nametag made in dark blue thread. When the man at the toilet turned around, Baku read that the tag said "Peter," but he'd guessed that much already. He knew the shirt. It was the uniform worn by the man who drove the delivery truck each Tuesday, Thursday, and Sunday.

Peter's eyes were blank and watery. They looked like olives in a jar.

The deliveryman seemed to know that his peculiar ritual was being questioned, and he did not care for the interruption. With another petulant groan he half lunged, half tipped forward.

Baku recoiled, pulling the door closed with his retreat.

Peter was thwarted a few seconds longer than he should have been. Perhaps it was only his innate imbecility that made him linger so long with the slim obstacle, but it bought the old chef time to retreat. He slipped first, falling knee-down with a splash, but catching himself on the sink and rising. Back into the hall and past the ice machine he stumbled, rubbing at his knee and shaking from the encounter. It had been too strange, too stupidly sinister.

At the far end of the dining area a big round clock declared the time. For a moment he was relieved. He needed to go home, and if the clock could be believed, he had less than an hour remaining on his shift.

But his relief dissolved as quickly as it had blossomed. The scene beneath the clock was no more reassuring than the one in the bathroom.

Dozens of people were eating in silence, staring down at their plates or their forks. They gazed with the same bland olive eyes, not at each other but at the food. The waitresses and the one lone male waiter lurked by the kitchen window without talking. The cash register did not ring.

Where was the manager? He'd been in and out for days, more out than in. The assistant manager, then. Anyone, really—anyone who was capable of sustaining convincing eye contact would suffice.

Into the kitchen Baku ducked, anticipating an oasis of ordinary people.

He was disappointed. The cooks stood in pockets of inattentive shoe-gazing, except for the two who had made their way back into the refrigerator. From within its chilly depths, Baku heard the sounds of sloppy gnawing.

Was he the only one who'd not been eating the sushi?

He turned just in time to hear the bathroom door creak open. Peter moaned as he made his way into the corridor and then began a slow charge towards the chef.

The grunting, guttural call drew the attention of the customers and the kitchen staff. They turned to see Peter, and then the object of his attention. All faces aimed themselves at Baku, whose insides immediately worked into a tangle.

Two nearby customers came forward. They didn't rise from their seats or fold their napkins, and they didn't put down their forks. Together they stood, knocking their chairs backwards and crashing their thighs against the table, rocking it back and forth. The woman raised her hand and opened her mouth as if she meant to speak, but only warm air and half-chewed sushi fell out from between her lips. Her dinner companion managed a louder sound—like an inflatable ball being squeezed—and the low, flatulent cry roused the remaining customers and the kitchen staff alike. In a clumsy wave, they stumbled towards Baku.

On the counter, he spied the folded roll of his fine German knives. He fired one hand out to snag it; then he tucked it under his arm and pushed the glass door with his elbow.

Behind him the crowd rallied, but it was a slow rally that was impeded by everything in its path. Chairs thwarted them. Counters baffled them.

Baku hurried. Outside the sky was growing dark with a too-early dusk brought on by a cloudy almost-storm. He tumbled into the parking lot and pulled the door shut behind his back.

The bus stop was empty.

The chef froze. He always rode the bus home. Every night. Rain or shine he waited under the small shelter at the corner.

Over his shoulder he watched the masses swarm behind the windows, pushing their hands through the blinds and slapping their palms against the glass. They were slow, but they wouldn't give him time to wait for the 9:30 bus.

He crushed at his knives, taking comfort from their strength wrapped inside the cloth. His knuckles curled around them.

As a young man he'd confronted the ocean with nets and hooks, drawing out food and earning his livelihood. Then he'd been called as a soldier, and he'd fought for his country, and to serve his Emperor. In the years that followed he had put away his bayonet and had taken up the knives of a cook; he had set aside the uniform of war and put on an apron.

But knives like these could be weapons, too.

"I am not too old," he breathed. Behind him, a dozen pairs of hands slapped at the windows, rattling the blinds. Shoulders pummeled at the doors, and the strained puff of a pneumatic hinge told Baku that they were coming. "I am not too old to work. Not too old to cut fish. I am *not* too old to fight."

Peter's delivery vehicle sat open in the parking lot's loading zone. The refrigerated trailer compartment hung open, one door creaking back and forth in the pre-storm breeze. A faint briny smell wafted forth.

Baku limped to the trailer door and took a deep breath of the tepid air. The contents within were beginning to turn.

He slammed the metal door shut and climbed into the cab. He set his knives down on the passenger's seat and closed his own door just as the first wave of angry patrons breached the restaurant door.

At first, he saw no keys. He checked the ignition and the glove box. But when he checked the visor a spare set tumbled down into his lap. He selected the engine key without a tremor and plugged it into the slot. The engine gagged to life, and with a tug of the gearshift, the vehicle rolled forward—pushing aside a pair of restaurant patrons, and knocking a third beneath the van's grille.

Baku did not check to see them in the rearview mirror.

Downtown, to Manufacturer's Row. That's where the manager had said the new meat came from. That's where Baku would go.

He roughly knew the way, but driving was something he'd forgotten about years before. Busses were cheap to ride, and cars were expensive to maintain. This van was tall and top-heavy. It reacted slowly, like a boat. It swayed around corners and hesitated before stopping, or starting, or accelerating.

He drove it anyway.

The streets were more empty than not. The roads were mostly clear and Baku wished it were otherwise. All the asphalt looked wet to him, shining under the streetlamps. Every corner promised a sliding danger. But the van stayed upright, and Baku's inexpert handling bothered no one.

He arrived at the distribution center and parked on the street in front of a sign that said "Loading Zone," and he climbed out of the cab, letting the door hang open. So what if it was noted and reported? Let the authorities come. Let them find him and ask why he had forced his way into the big old building. At first he thought this as a whim, but then he began to wish it like a prayer. "Let them come."

In his arm he felt a pain, and in his chest there was an uncomfortable tightness from the way he breathed too hard. "Let them bring their guns and their lights. I might need help."

From a sliver of white outlined vertically along the wall, Baku saw that the front door was open.

He put his face against the crack and leaned on his cheekbone, trying to see inside. The space was not enough to peep through, but the opening was big enough to emit an atrocious smell. He lifted his arm and buried his nose in the crook of his elbow. He wedged his shoulder against the heavy slab of the door and pushed. The bottom edge of the sagging door grated on the concrete floor.

Within, the odor might have been overpowering to someone unaccustomed to the smell of saltwater, fish, and the rot of the ocean. It was bad enough for Baku.

Two steps sideways, around the crotchety door, and he was inside.

His shoes slipped and caught. The floor was soaked with something more viscous than saline, more seaweed-brown than clear. He locked his knees and stepped with care. He shivered.

The facility was cold, but not cold enough to freeze his breath. Not quite. Industrial refrigerators with bolted doors flanked one wall, and indoor cranes were parked haphazardly around the room. There were four doors—one set of double doors indicated a corridor or hall. A glance through the other three doors suggested office space; a copy room, a lunchroom with tables, and two gleaming vending machines.

Somewhere behind the double doors a rhythmic clanking beat a metal mantra. There was also a mechanical hum, a smoother drone. Finally there came a lumpy buzz like the sound of an out-of-balance conveyor belt.

In his hand, Baku's fist squeezed tightly around his roll of knives.

He unclenched his fingers and opened the roll across his palm. It would do him no good to bring them all sheathed, but he could not hold or wield more than two. So for his right hand, he chose a long, slim blade with a flexible edge made to filet large fish. For his left, he selected a thicker, heavier knife—one whose power came from its weight. The remaining blades he wrapped up, tied, and left in a bundle by the door.

"I will collect you on the way out," he told them.

Baku crept on toward the double doors, and he pushed tentatively at them.

They swayed and parted easily, and the ambient noise jumped from a background tremor to a sharper throb.

The stink swelled too, but he hadn't vomited yet and he didn't intend to, so Baku forced the warning bile back down to whence it had come. He would go toward the smell. He would go toward the busy machines and into the almost frigid interior. His plan was simple, but big: He would turn the building off. All of it. Every robot, light, and refrigerator. There would be a fuse box or a power main.

As a last resort, he might find a dry place to start a fire.

On he went, and the farther his explorations took him, the more he doubted that a match would find a receptive place to spark.

Dank coldness seeped up through his shoes and his feet dragged splashing wakes along the floor. He slipped and stretched out an arm to steady himself, leaning his knuckles on the plaster. The walls were wet, too. He wiped the back of his hand on his pants. It left a trail of slime.

The clank of machines pounded harder, and with it the accompanying smell insinuated itself into every pore of Baku's body, into every fold of his clothing.

But into the heart of the warehouse he walked—one knife in each hand—until he reached the end of the corridor that opened into a larger space—one filled with sharp-angled machines reaching from the floor to the ceiling. Rows of belts on rollers shifted frosty boxes back and forth across the room from trucks to chilled storage. Along the wall were eight loading points with trucks docked and open, ready to receive shipments and disperse them. He searched for a point of commonality, or for some easy spot where all these things must come together for power. Nothing looked immediately promising, so he followed the cables on the ceiling with his eyes, and he likewise traced the cords along the floor. Both sets of lines followed the same path, into a secondary hallway.

Baku shuffled sideways and slithered with caution along the wall and toward the portal where the electric lines all pointed. Once through the portal, Baku found himself at the top of a flight of stairs. Low-power emergency lights illuminated the corridor in murky yellow patches.

It would have to be enough.

When he strained to listen, Baku thought he detected footsteps, or maybe even voices below. He tiptoed towards them, keeping his back snugly against the stair rail, holding his precious knives at the ready.

He hesitated on the bottom stair, hidden in the shadows, reluctant to take the final step that would put him firmly in the downstairs room. There in the basement the sad little emergency lights were too few and far-between to give any real illumination. The humidity, the chill, and the spotty darkness made the entire downstairs feel like night at the bottom of a swimming pool.

A creature with a blank, white face and midnight-black, lidless eyes emerged from inside an open freezer. It was Sonada's manager, or what was left of him.

"You," the thing accused.

Baku did not recoil or retreat. He flexed his fingers around the knife handles and took the last step down into the basement.

"You would not eat the sushi with us. Why?" The store manager was terribly changed without and within; even his voice was barely recognizable. He spoke as if he were talking around a mouthful of seaweed.

Baku circled around the manager, not crossing the floor directly but staying with his back to the wall. The closer he came, the slower he crept until he halted altogether. The space between them was perhaps two yards.

"Have you come now for the feast?" the manager slurred.

Baku was not listening. It took too much effort to determine where one word ended and the next began, and the message didn't matter anyway. There was nothing the manager could say to change Baku's mind or mission.

Beside the freezer with its billowing clouds of icy mist there was a fuse box. The box was old-fashioned; there were big glass knobs the size of biscuits and connected to wiring that was as frayed and thick as shoelaces. It might or might not be the heart of the building's electrical system, but at least it might be *connected* to the rest. Perhaps, if Baku wrenched or broke the fuses, there was a chance that he could short out the whole building and bring the operation to a halt. He'd seen it in a movie he'd watched once, late at night when he couldn't sleep.

If he could stop the electricity for even an hour—he could throw open the refrigerators and freezers and let the seafood thaw. Let it rot. Let it spoil here, at the source.

The manager kept talking. "This is the new way of things. He is coming, for the whole world."

"So this is where it starts?" Baku spoke to distract the manager. He took a sideways shuffle and brought himself closer to the manager, to the freezer, to the fuse box.

"No. We are not the first."

Baku came closer. A few feet. A hobbled scuffing of his toes. He did not lower the knives, but the manager did not seem to notice.

"Tell me about this. Explain this to me. I don't understand it."

"Yes," the manager gurgled. "Like this." And he turned as if to gesture into the freezer, as if what was inside could explain it all.

Baku jumped then, closing the gap between them. He pushed with the back of his arm and the weight of his shoulder, and he shoved the manager inside the freezer.

The door was a foot thick; it closed with a hiss and a click. Only if he listened very hard could Baku hear the angry protests from within. He pressed his head against the cool metal door and felt a fury of muted pounding on the other side.

When he was comfortable believing that the manager would not be able to interfere, he removed his ear from the door. He turned his attention again to the fuse box, regarding it thoughtfully.

Then, one after the other, the fuzzy white pods of light were extinguished.

Darkness swallowed the stray slivers of light which were left.

The basement fell into perfect blackness.

And the heavy thing that struck Baku in the chest came unseen, unheard, but with all the weight of a sack of bricks.

The shock sent him reeling against the freezer door. He slammed against it and caught himself by jabbing his knives into the concrete floor, the door, and anything else they could snag.

Somewhere nearby the thing regrouped with a sound like slithering sandbags. Baku's ear told him that it must be huge—but was this an illusion of the darkness, of the echoing acoustics? He did not know if the thing could see him, and he did not know what it was, only that it was powerful and deadly.

On the other side of the room Baku's assailant was stretching, lashing, and reaching. Baku flattened his chest against the wall and leaned against it as he tried to rise, climbing with the knives, scraping them against the cement blocks, cutting off flecks and strips of paint that fluttered down into his hair and settled on his eyelashes.

A loud clank and a grating thunk told Baku that his knives had hit something besides concrete. He reached and thrust the knife again. He must be close to the fuse box; he'd only been a few feet away when the lights went out.

The thudding flump that accompanied his opponent's movement sounded louder behind Baku as he struggled to stand, to stab. Something jagged and rough caught at his right hand.

A warm gush soaked his wrist and he dropped that knife. With slippery fingers he felt knobs, and what might have been the edge of a slim steel door panel. He reached for it, using this door to haul himself up, but the little hinges popped under his weight and he fell back down to his knees.

The monstrous unseen thing snapped out. One fat, foul-smelling limb crashed forward, smacking Baku's thighs, sweeping his legs out from underneath him.

His bleeding right hand grazed the dropped knife, but he couldn't grasp it. Holding the remaining blade horizontally in his left hand, Baku locked his wrist. When the creature attacked again, Baku sliced sideways.

A splash of something more gruesome than blood or tar splashed against the side of the face.

He used his shoulder to wipe away what he could. The rest he ignored. The wet and bloody fingers of his right hand curled and fastened themselves on a small shelf above his head.

The thing whipped its bulk back and forth but it was not badly hurt. It gathered itself together again, somewhere off in the corner. If Baku could trust his ears, it was shifting its attack, preparing to come from the side. He rotated his left wrist, moving the knife into a vertical position within his grip. He opened and closed his fingers around it. To his left, he heard the thing coming again.

Baku peered up into the darkness over his head where he knew the fuse box now hung open.

The creature scooted forward.

Baku hauled himself up and swung the fine German steel hard at the box, not the monster—with all the weight he could put behind it. It landed once, twice, and there came a splintering and sparking. Plastic shattered, or maybe it was glass. Shards of debris rained down.

One great limb crushed against Baku and wrapped itself around his torso, ready to crush, ready to break what it found. The man could not breath; there in the monster's grip he felt the thing coil itself, slow but wickedly dense, as if it were filled with wet pebbles.

In the center of the room the beast's bulk shuddered unhappily as it shifted, and shuffled, and skidded. The appendage that squeezed Baku was only one part of a terrible whole.

Before his breath ran out, before his hands grew weak from lost blood and mounting fear, Baku took one more stab. The heavy butcher's blade did not bear downward, but upward and back.

The fuse box detonated with a splattering torrent of fire and light.

For two or three seconds Baku's eyes remained open. And in those seconds he marveled at what he saw, but could have never described. Above and beyond the thunderous explosion of light in his head, the rumbling machines ceased their toil.

The current from the box was such that the old man could not release the knife, and the creature could not release its hold on the old man.

As the energy coursed between them, Baku's heart lay suddenly quiet in his chest, too stunned to continue beating. He marveled briefly, before he died, how electricity follows the quickest path from heaven to earth, and how it passes with pleasure through those things that stand in water.

Whilst the greater number of our nocturnal visions are perhaps no more than faint and fantastic reflections of our waking experiences—Freud to the contrary with his puerile symbolism—there are still a certain remainder whose immundane and ethereal character permits of no ordinary interpretation, and whose vaguely exciting and disquieting effect suggests possible minute glimpses into a sphere of mental existence no less important than physical life, yet separated from that life by an all but impassable barrier.
"Beyond the Wall of Sleep" · H.P. Lovecraft (1919)

· OLD VIRGINIA ·
Laird Barron

On the third morning I noticed somebody had disabled the truck. All four tires were flattened and the engine was smashed. Nice work.

I had gone outside the cabin to catch the sunrise and piss on some bushes. It was cold; the air tasted like metal. Deep, dark forest at our backs with a few notches for stars. A rutted track wound across a marshy field into more wilderness. All was silent except for the muffled hum of the diesel generator behind the wood shed.

"Well, here we go," I said. I fired up a Lucky Strike and congratulated my pessimistic nature. The Reds had found our happy little retreat in the woods. Or possibly, one of my boys was a mole. That would put a pretty bow on things.

The men were already spooked—Davis swore he had heard chuckling and whispering behind the steel door after curfew. He also heard one of the doctors gibbering in a foreign tongue. Nonsense, of course. Nonetheless, the troops were edgy, and now this.

"Garland? You there?" Hatcher called from the porch in a low voice. He made a tall, thin silhouette.

"Over here." I waited for him to join me by the truck. Hatcher was my immediate subordinate and the only member of the detail I'd personally worked with. He was tough, competent and a decade my junior—which made him twice as old as the other men. If somebody here was a Red, I hoped to God it wasn't him.

"Guess we're hoofing it," he said after a quick survey of the damage.

I passed him a cigarette. We smoked in contemplative silence. Eventually I said, "Who took last watch?"

"Richards. He didn't report any activity."

"Yeah." I stared into the forest and wondered if the enemy was lurking. What would be their next move, and how might I counter? A chill tightened the muscles in the small of my back, reminded me of how things had gone wrong during '53 in the steamy hills of Cuba. It had been six years and in this business a man didn't necessarily improve with age. I said, "How did they find us, Hatch?"

"Strauss may have a leak."

It went without saying whatever our military scientists were doing, the Reds would be doing bigger and better. Even so, intelligence regarding this program would carry a hefty price tag behind the Iron Curtain. Suddenly this little field trip didn't seem like a babysitting detail anymore.

Project TALLHAT was a Company job, but black ops. Dr. Herman Strauss picked the team in secret and briefed us at his own home. Now here we were in the wilds of West Virginia, standing watch over two of his personal staff while they conducted unspecified research on a senile crone. Doctors Porter and Riley called the shots. There was to be no communication with the outside world until they had gathered sufficient data. Upon return to Langley, Strauss would handle the debriefing. Absolutely no one else inside the Company was to be involved.

This wasn't my kind of operation, but I'd seen the paperwork and recognized Strauss' authority. Why me? I suspected it was because Strauss had known me since the first big war. He also knew I was past it, ready for pasture. Maybe this was his way to make me feel important one last time. Gazing at the ruined truck and all it portended, I started thinking maybe good old Herman had picked me because I was expendable.

I stubbed out my cigarette and made some quick decisions. "When it gets light, we sweep the area. You take Robey and Neil and arc south; I'll go north with Dox and Richards. Davis will guard the cabin. We'll establish a quarter mile perimeter; search for tracks."

Hatcher nodded. He didn't state the obvious flaw—what if Davis was playing for the other team? He gestured at the forest. "How about an emergency extraction? We're twenty miles from the nearest traveled road. We could make it in a few hours. We could make for one of the farms; somebody will have a phone—"

"Hatch, they destroyed the vehicle for a reason. Obviously they *want* us to walk. Who knows what nasty surprise is waiting down that road? For now we stay here, fortify. If worse comes to worst, we break and scatter. Maybe one of us will make it back to HQ."

"How do we handle Porter and Riley?"

"This has become a security issue. Let's see what we find; then I'll break the news to the good doctors."

My involvement in Project TALLHAT was innocent—if you can ever say that about Company business. I was lounging on an out of season New York beach when the telegram arrived. Strauss sent a car from Virginia. An itinerary; spending money. The works. I was intrigued; it had been several years since the last time I spoke with Herman.

Director Strauss said he needed my coolness under pressure when we sat down to a four-star dinner at his legendary farmhouse in Langley; said he needed an older man, a man with poise. Yeah, he poured it on all right.

Oh, the best had said it too—*Put his feet to the fire; he doesn't flinch. Garland, he's one cool sonofabitch.* Yes indeed, they had said it—thirty years ago. Before the horn rims got welded to my corrugated face and before the arthritis bent my fingers. Before my left ear went dead and my teeth fell out. Before the San Andreas Fault took root in my hands and gave them tremors. It was difficult to maintain deadly aloofness when I had to get up and drain my bladder every hour on the hour. Some war hero. Some Company legend.

"Look, Roger, I don't care about Cuba. It's ancient history, pal." Sitting across the table from Strauss at his farmhouse with a couple whiskey sours in my belly it had been too easy to believe my colossal blunders were forgiven. That the encroaching specter of age was an illusion fabricated by jealous detractors of which great men have plenty.

I had been a great man, once. Veteran of not one, but two World Wars. Decorated, lauded, feared. Strauss, earnest, blue-eyed Strauss, convinced me some greatness lingered. He leaned close and said, *"Roger, have you ever heard of MK-ULTRA?"*

He was right. I forgot about Cuba.

The men dressed in hunting jackets to ward the chill, loaded shotguns for possible unfriendly contact, and scouted the environs until noon. Fruitless; the only tracks belonged to deer and rabbits. Most of the leaves had fallen in carpets of red and brown. It drizzled. Black branches dripped. The birds had nothing to say.

I observed Dox and Richards. Dox lumbered in plodding engineer boots, broad Slavic face blankly concentrated on the task I had given him. He was built like a tractor; too simple to work for the Company except as an enforcer, much less be a Russian saboteur. I liked him. Richards was blond and smooth, an Ivy League talent with precisely enough cynicism and latent sadism to please the forward thinking elements who sought to reshape the Company in the wake of President Eisenhower's imminent departure. Richards, I didn't trust or like.

There was a major housecleaning in the works. Men of Richards' caliber were preparing to sweep fossils such as myself into the dustbin of history.

It was perfectly logical after a morbid fashion. The trouble had started at the top with good old Ike suffering a stroke. Public reassurances to the contrary, the commander in chief was reduced to a shell of his former power. Those closest saw the cracks in the foundation and moved to protect his already tottering image. Company loyalists closed ranks, covering up evidence of the president's diminished faculties, his strange preoccupation with drawing caricatures of Dick Nixon. They stood by at his public appearances, ready to swoop in if he did anything too embarrassing. Not a happy allocation of human resources in the view of the younger members of the intelligence community.

That kind of duty didn't appeal to the Richards' of the world. They preferred to cut their losses and get back to slicing throats and cracking codes. Tangible objectives that would further the dominance of US intelligence.

We kept walking and not finding anything until the cabin dwindled to a blot. The place had been built at the turn of the century; Strauss bought it for a song, I gathered. The isolation suited his nefarious plots. Clouds covered the treetops, yet I knew from the topographical maps there was a mountain not far off; a low, shaggy hump called Badger Hill. There were collapsed mines and the moldered bones of abandoned camps, rusted hulks of machinery along the track, and dense woods. A world of brambles and deadfalls. No one came out this way anymore; hadn't in years.

We rendezvoused with Hatcher's party at the cabin. They hadn't discovered any clues either. Our clothes were soaked, our moods somber, although traces of excitement flickered among the young Turks—attack dogs sniffing for a fight.

None of them had been in a war. I'd checked. College instead of Korea for the lot. Even Dox had been spared by virtue of flat feet. They hadn't seen Soissons in 1915, Normandy in 1945, nor the jungles of Cuba in 1953. They hadn't seen the things I had seen. Their fear was the small kind, borne of uncertainty rather than dread. They stroked their shotguns and grinned with dumb innocence.

When the rest had been dispatched for posts around the cabin I broke for the latrine to empty my bowels. Close race. I sweated and trembled and required some minutes to compose myself. My knees were on fire, so I broke out a tin of analgesic balm and rubbed them, tasting the camphor on my tongue. I wiped beads of moisture from my glasses, swallowed a glycerin tablet and felt as near to one hundred percent as I would ever be.

Ten minutes later I summoned Doctor Porter for a conference on the back porch. It rained harder, shielding our words from Neil who stood post near an oak.

Porter was lizard-bald except for a copper circlet that trailed wires into his breast pocket. His white coat bore stains and smudges. His fingers were blue-tinged with chalk dust. He stank of antiseptic. We were not friends. He treated the detail as a collection of thugs best endured for the sake of his great scientific exploration.

I relayed the situation, which did not impress him much. "This is why Strauss wanted your services. Deal with the problem," he said.

"Yes, Doctor. I am in the process of doing that. However, I felt you might wish to know your research will become compromised if this activity escalates. We may need to extract."

"Whatever you think best, Captain Garland." He smiled a dry smile. "You'll inform me when the moment arrives?"

"Certainly."

"Then I'll continue my work, if you're finished." The way he lingered on the last syllable left no doubt that I was.

I persisted, perhaps from spite. "Makes me curious about what you fellows are up to. How's the experiment progressing? Getting anywhere?"

"Captain Garland, you shouldn't be asking me these questions." Porter's humorless smile was more reptilian than ever.

"Probably not. Unfortunately since recon proved inconclusive I don't know who wrecked our transport or what they plan next. More information regarding the project would be helpful."

"Surely Doctor Strauss told you everything he deemed prudent."

"Times change."

"TALLHAT is classified. You're purely a security blanket. You possess no special clearance."

I sighed and lighted a cigarette. "I know some things. MK-ULTRA is an umbrella term for the Company's mind control experiments. You psych boys are playing with all kinds of neat stuff—LSD, hypnosis, photokinetics. Hell, we talked about using this crap against Batista. Maybe we did."

"Indeed. Castro was amazingly effective, wasn't he?" Porter's eyes glittered. "So what's your problem, Captain?"

"The problem is the KGB has pretty much the same programs. And better ones from the scuttlebutt I pick up at Langley."

"Oh, you should beware rumors of all people. Loose lips had *you* buried in Cuba with the rest of your operatives. Yet here you are."

I understood Porter's game. He hoped to gig me with the kind of talk most folks were polite enough to whisper behind my back, make me lose control. I wasn't biting. "The way I figure it, the Reds don't need TALLHAT . . . unless you're cooking up something special. Something they're afraid of. Something they're aware of, at least tangentially, but lack full intelligence. And in that case, why pussyfoot around? They've got two convenient options—storm in and seize the data or wipe the place off the map."

Porter just kept smirking. "I am certain the Russians would kill to derail our project. However, don't you think it would be more efficacious for them to use subtlety? Implant a spy to gather pertinent details, steal documents. Kidnap a member of the research team and interrogate him; extort information from him with a scandal. Hiding in the woods and slicing tires seems a foolish waste of surprise."

I didn't like hearing him echo the bad thoughts I'd had while lingering in the outhouse. "Exactly, Doctor. The situation is even worse than I thought. We are being stalked by an unknown quantity."

"Stalked? How melodramatic. An isolated incident doesn't prove the hypothesis. Take more precautions if it makes you happy. And I'm confident you are quite happy; awfully boring to be a watchdog with nothing to bark at."

It was too much. That steely portion of my liver gained an edge, demanded satisfaction. I took off the gloves. "I want to see the woman."

"Whatever for?" Porter's complacent smirk vanished. His thin mouth drew down with suspicion.

"Because I do."

"Impossible!"

"Hardly. I command six heavily armed men. Any of them would be tickled to kick down the door and give me a tour of your facilities." It came out much harsher than I intended. My nerves were frayed and his superior demeanor had touched a darker kernel of my soul. "Doctor Porter, I read your file. That was my condition for accepting this assignment; Strauss agreed to give me dossiers on everyone. You and Riley slipped through the cracks after Caltech. I guess the school wasn't too pleased with some of your research or where you dug up the financing. Then that incident with the kids off campus. The ones who thought they were testing diet pills. You gave them, what was it? Oh yes—peyote! Pretty strange behavior for a pair of physicists, eh? It follows that Unorthodox Applications of Medicine and Technology would snap you up after the private sector turned its back. So excuse my paranoia."

"Ah, you do know a *few* things. But not the nature of TALLHAT? Odd."

"We shall rectify that momentarily."

Porter shrugged. "As you wish, Mr. Garland. I shall include your threats in my report."

For some reason his acquiescence didn't really satisfy me. True, I had turned on the charm that had earned me the title "Jolly Roger," yet he had caved far too easily. Damn it!

Porter escorted me inside. Hatcher saw the look on my face and started to rise from his chair by the window. I shook my head and he sank, fixing Porter with a dangerous glare.

The lab was sealed off by a thick, steel door, like the kind they use on trains. Spartan, each wall padded as if a rubber room in an asylum. It reeked of chemicals. The windows were blocked with black plastic. Illumination seeped from a phosphorescent bar on the table. Two cots. Shelves, cabinets, a couple boxy machines with needles and tickertape spools. Between these machines an easel with indecipherable scrawls done in ink. I recognized some as calculus symbols. To the left, a poster bed, and on the bed a thickly wrapped figure propped by pillows. A mummy.

Dr. Riley drifted in, obstructing my view—he was an aquamarine phantom, eyes and mouth pools of shadow. As with Porter, a copper circlet winked on his brow. "Afternoon, Captain Garland. Pull up a rock." His accent was Midwestern nasal. He even wore cowboy boots under his grimy lab coat.

"Captain Garland wants to view the subject," Porter said.

"Fair enough!" Riley seemed pleased. He rubbed his hands, a pair of disembodied starfish in the weirding glow. "Don't fret, Porter. There's no harm in satisfying the Captain's curiosity." With that, the lanky man stepped aside.

Approaching the figure on the bed, I was overcome with an abrupt sensation of vertigo. My hackles bunched. The light played tricks upon my senses, lending a fishbowl distortion to the old woman's sallow visage. They had secured her in a straitjacket; her head lolled drunkenly, dead eyes frozen, tongue drooling from slack lips. She was shaved bald, white stubble of a Christmas goose.

My belly quaked. "Where did you find her?" I whispered, as if she might hear me.

"What's the matter?" Dr. Riley asked.

"Where did you find her, goddamnit!"

The crone's head swiveled on that too-long neck and her milky gaze fastened upon my voice. And she grinned, toothless. Horrible.

Hatcher kept some scotch in the pantry. Dr. Riley poured—I didn't trust my own hands yet. He lighted cigarettes. We sat at the living room table, alone in the cabin, but for Porter and Subject X behind the metal door. Porter was so disgusted by my reaction he refused to speak with me. Hatcher had assembled the men in the yard; he was giving some sort of pep talk. Ever the soldier. I wished I'd had him in Cuba.

It rained and a stiff breeze rattled the eaves.

"Who is she to you?" Riley asked. His expression was shrewd.

I sucked my cigarette to the filter in a single drag, exhaled and gulped scotch. Held out my glass for another three fingers worth. "You're too young to remember the first big war."

"I was a baby." Riley handed me another cigarette without being asked.

"Yeah? I was twenty-eight when the Germans marched into France. Graduated Rogers and Williams with full honors, was commissioned into the Army as an officer. They stuck me right into intelligence, sent me straight to the front." I chuckled bitterly. "This happened before Uncle Sam decided to make an "official" presence. Know what I did? I helped organize the resistance, translated messages French intelligence intercepted. Mostly I ran from the advance. Spent a lot of time hiding out on farms when I was lucky, field ditches when I wasn't.

"There was this one family, I stayed with them for nine days in June. It rained, just like this. A large family—six adults, ten or eleven kids. I bunked in the wine cellar and it flooded. You'd see these huge bloody rats paddling if you clicked the torch. Long nine days." If I closed my eyes I knew I would be there again in the dark, among the chittering rats. Listening for armor on the muddy road, the tramp of boots.

"So, what happened?" Riley watched me. He probably guessed where this was headed.

"The family matriarch lived in a room with her son and daughter in-law. The old dame was blind and deaf; she'd lost her wits. They bandaged her hands so she couldn't scratch herself. She sucked broth out of this gnawed wooden bowl they kept just for her. Jesus Mary, I still hear her slobbering over that bowl. She used to lick her bowl and stare at me with those dead eyes."

"Subject X bears no relation to her, I assure you."

"I don't suppose she does. I looked at her more closely and saw I was mistaken. But for those few seconds . . . Riley, something's going on. Something much bigger than Strauss indicated. Level with me. What are you people searching for?"

"Captain, you realize my position. I've been sworn to silence. Strauss will cut off my balls if I talk to you about TALLHAT. Or we could all simply disappear."

"It's that important."

"It is." Riley's face became gentle. "I'm sorry. Doctor Strauss promised us ten days. One week from tomorrow we pack up our equipment and head back to civilization. Surely we can hold out."

The doctor reached across to refill my glass; I clamped his wrist. They said I was past it, but he couldn't break my grip. I said, "All right, boy. We'll play it your way for a while. If the shit gets any thicker though, I'm pulling the plug on this operation. You got me?"

He didn't say anything. Then he jerked free and disappeared behind the metal door. He returned with a plain brown folder, threw it on the table. His smile was almost triumphant. "Read these. It won't tell you everything. Still, it's plenty to chew on. Don't show Porter, okay?" He walked away without meeting my eye.

Dull wet afternoon wore into dirty evening. We got a pleasant fire going in the potbellied stove and dried our clothes. Roby had been a short order cook in college, so he fried hamburgers for dinner. After, Hatcher and the boys started a poker game and listened to the radio. The weather forecast called for more of the same, if not worse.

Perfect conditions for an attack. I lay on my bunk reading Riley's file. I got a doozy of a migraine. Eventually I gave up and filled in my evening log entry. The gears were turning.

I wondered about those copper circlets the doctors wore. Fifty-plus years of active service and I'd never seen anything quite like them. They reminded me of rumors surrounding the German experiments in Auschwitz. Mengele had been fond of bizarre contraptions. Maybe we'd read his mail and adopted some ideas.

Who is Subject X? I wrote this in the margin of my log. I thought back on what scraps Strauss fed me. I hadn't asked enough questions, that was for damned sure. You didn't quiz a man like Strauss. He was one of the Grand Old

Men of the Company. He got what he wanted, when he wanted it. He'd been everywhere, had something on everyone. When he snapped his fingers, things happened. People that crossed him became scarce.

Strauss was my last supporter. Of course I let him lead me by the nose. For me, the gold watch was a death certificate. Looking like a meatier brother of Herr Mengele, Strauss had confided the precise amount to hook me. *"Ten days in the country. I've set up shop at my cabin near Badger Hill. A couple of my best men are on to some promising research. Important research—"*

"Are we talking about psychotropics? I've seen what can happen. I won't be around that again."

"No, no. We've moved past that. This is different. They will be monitoring a subject for naturally occurring brain activity. Abnormal activity, yes, but not induced by us."

"These doctors of yours, they're just recording results?"

"Exactly."

"Why all the trouble, Herman? You've got the facilities right here. Why send us to a shack in the middle of Timbuktu?"

"Ike is on his way out the door. Best friend a covert ops man ever had, too. The Powers to Soon Be will put an end to MK-ULTRA. Christ, the office is shredding documents around the clock. I've been given word to suspend all operations by the end of next month. Next month!"

"Nobody else knows about TALLHAT?"

"And nobody can—not unless we make a breakthrough. I wish I could come along, conduct the tests myself—"

"Not smart. People would talk if you dropped off the radar. What does this woman do that's so bloody important?"

"She's a remote viewer. A clairvoyant. She draws pictures, the researchers extrapolate."

"Whatever you're looking for—"

"It's momentous. So you see, Roger? I need you. I don't trust anyone else."

"Who is the subject?"

"Her name is Virginia."

I rolled over and regarded the metal door. She was in there, staring holes through steel.

"Hey, Cap! You want in? I'm getting my ass kicked over here!" Hatcher puffed on a Havana cigar and shook his head while Davis raked in another pot. There followed a chorus of crude imprecations for me to climb down and take my medicine.

I feigned good humor. "Not tonight, fellows. I didn't get my nap. You know how it is with us old folks."

They laughed. I shivered until sleep came. My dreams were bad.

I spent most of the fourth day perusing Riley's file. It made things about as clear as mud. All in all a cryptic collection of papers—just what I needed right then; more spooky erratum.

Numerous mimeographed letters and library documents comprised the file. The bulk of them were memos from Strauss to Porter. Additionally, some detailed medical examinations of Subject X. I didn't follow the jargon except to note that the terms "unclassified" and "of unknown origin" reappeared often. They made interesting copy, although explained nothing to my layman's eyes.

Likewise the library papers seemed arcane. One such entry from *A Colonial History of Carolina and Her Settlements* went thusly:

The Lost Roanoke Colony vanished from the Raleigh Township on Roanoke Island between 1588 and 1589. Governor White returned from England after considerable delays to find the town abandoned. Except for untended cookfires that burned down a couple houses, there was no evidence of struggle, though Spaniards and natives had subsequently plundered the settlement. No bodies or bones were discovered. The sole clue as to the colonists' fate lay in a strange sequence of letters carved into a palisade—Croatoan. The word CRO had been similarly carved into a nearby tree. White surmised this indicated a flight to the Croatoan Island, called Hatteras by natives. Hurricanes prevented a search until the next colonization attempt two years later. Subsequent investigation yielded no answers, although scholars suggest local tribes assimilated the English settlers. No physical evidence exists to support this theory. It remains a mystery of some magnitude . . .

Tons more like that. It begged the question of why Strauss, brilliant, cruel-minded Strauss would waste a molecular biologist, a physicist, a bona fide psychic, and significant monetary resources on moldy folklore.

I hadn't a notion and this worried me mightily.

That night I dreamt of mayhem. First I was at the gray farmhouse in Soissans, eating dinner with a nervous family. My French was inadequate. Fortunately one of the women knew English and we were able to converse. A loud slurping began to drown out conversation about German spies. At the head of the table sat Virginia, sipping from a broken skull. She winked. A baby cried.

Then it was Cuba and the debacle of advising Castro's guerillas for an important raid. My intelligence network had failed to account for a piece of government armor. The guerillas were shelled to bits by Batista's garrison and young Castro barely escaped with his life. Five of my finest men were ground up in the general slaughter. Two were captured and tortured. They died without talking. Lucky for me.

I heard them screaming inside a small cabin in the forest, but I couldn't find the door. Someone had written CROATOAN on the wall.

I bumped into Hatcher, hanging upside down from a tree branch. He wore an I LIKE IKE button. "Help me, Cap." He said.

A baby squalled. Virginia sat in a rocking chair on the porch, soothing the infant. The crone's eyes were holes in dough. She drew a nail across her throat.

I sat up in bed, throttling a shriek. I hadn't uttered a cry since being shot in World War I. It was pitchy in the cabin. People were fumbling around in the dark.

Hatcher shined a flashlight my direction. "The generator's tits up." Nearby, the doctors were already bitching and cursing their misfortune.

We never did find out if it was sabotaged or not.

The fifth day was uneventful.

On the sixth morning my unhappy world raveled.

Things were hopping right out of the gate. Dr. Riley joined Hatcher and me for breakfast. A powerful stench accompanied him. His expression was unbalanced, his angular face white and shiny. He grabbed a plate of cold pancakes, began wolfing them. Lanky hair fell into his eyes. He grunted like a pig.

Hatcher eased his own chair back. I spoke softly to Riley, "Hey now, doc. Roby can whip up more. No rush."

Riley looked at me sidelong. He croaked, "She made us take them off."

I opened my mouth. His circlet was gone. A pale stripe of flesh. "Riley, what are you talking about?" Even as I spoke, Hatcher stood quietly, drew his pistol, and glided for the lab.

"Stupid old bastards." Riley gobbled pancakes, chunks dropping from his lips. He giggled until tears squirted, rubbed the dimple in his forehead. "Those were shields, pops. They produced a frequency that kept her from . . . doing things to us." He stopped eating again, cast sharp glances around the room. "Where are your little soldiers?"

"On patrol."

"Ha, ha. Better call them back, pops."

"Why do you say that?"

"You'd just better."

Hatcher returned, grim. "Porter has taken Subject X."

I put on my glasses. I drew my revolver. "Dr. Riley, Mr. Hatcher is going to secure you. It's for your own safety. I must warn you, give him any static and I'll burn you down."

"That's right, Jolly Roger! You're an ace at blowing people away! What's the number up to, Captain? Since the first Big One? And we're counting children, okay?" Riley barked like a lunatic coyote until Hatcher cracked him on the temple with the butt of his gun. The doctor flopped, twitching.

I uncapped my glycerin and ate two.

Hatcher was all business. He talked in his clipped manner while he handcuffed Riley to a center beam post. "Looks like he broke out through the window. No signs of struggle."

"Documents?"

"Seems like everything's intact. Porter's clothes are on his cot. Found her straitjacket too."

Porter left his clothes? I liked this less and less.

Rain splattered the dark windows. "Let's gather everybody. Assemble a hunting party." I foresaw a disaster; it would be difficult to follow tracks in the storm. Porter might have allies. Best case scenario had him and the subject long gone, swooped up by welcoming Commie arms and out of my sorry life forever. Instinct whispered that I was whistling Dixie if I fell for that scenario. *Now you're screwed, blued and tattooed, chum!* Chortled my inner voice.

Hatcher grasped my shoulder. "Cap, you call it, we haul it. I can tell you, the boys are aching for a scrap. It won't hurt anybody's feelings to hunt the traitor to ground."

"Agreed. We'll split into two man teams, comb the area. Take Porter alive if possible. I want to know who he's playing for."

"Sounds good. Someone has to cover the cabin."

He meant I should be the one to stay back. They had to move fast. I was the old man, the weak link; I'd slow everybody down, maybe get a team member killed.

I mustered what grace I possessed. "I'll do it. Come on; we better get moving." We called the men together and laid it on the table. Everybody appeared shocked that Porter had been able to pull off such a brazen escape.

I drew a quick plan and sent them trotting into the wind-blasted dawn. Hatcher wasn't eager to leave me alone, but there weren't sufficient bodies to spare. He promised to report back inside of three hours one way or the other.

And they were gone.

I locked the doors, pulled the shutters, peeking through the slats as it lightened into morning.

Riley began laughing again. Deeper this time, from his skinny chest. The rank odor oozing from him would have gagged a goat. "How about a cigarette, Cap?" His mouth squirmed. His face had slipped from white to gray. He appeared to have been bled. The symptoms were routine.

"They'll find your comrade," I said. A cigarette sounded like a fine idea, so I lighted one for myself and smoked it. I kept an eye on him and one on the yard. "Yeah, they'll nail him sooner or later. And when they do . . . " I let it dangle.

"God, Cap! The news is true. You are so washed up! They say you were sharp back in the day. Strauss didn't even break a sweat, keeping you in the dark, did he? Think about it—why do you suppose I gave you the files, huh? Because it didn't matter one tin shit. He told me to give you anything you asked for. Said it would make things more interesting."

"Tell me the news, Riley."

"Can't you guess the joke? Our sweet Virginia ain't what she seems, no sir."

"What is she, then?"

"She's a weapon, Cap. A nasty, nasty weapon. Strauss is ready to bet the farm this little filly can win the Cold War for Team USA. But first we had to test her, see." He banged his greasy head against the post and laughed wildly. "Our hats were supposed to protect us from getting brain-buggered. Strauss went through hell—and a *heap* of volunteers—to configure them properly. They should've worked . . . I don't know why they stopped functioning correctly. Bum luck. Doesn't matter."

"Where did Porter take her?"

"Porter didn't take Virginia. She took him. She'll be back for you."

"Is Subject X really a clairvoyant?" My lips were dry. Too many blocks were clicking into place at once.

"She's clairvoyant. She's a lot of things. But Strauss tricked you—we aren't here to test her ability to locate needles in haystacks. You'd die puking if you saw . . . "

"Is there anyone else? Does Porter have allies waiting?"

"Porter? Porter's meat. It's *her* you better worry about."

"Fine. Does *she* have allies?"

"No. She doesn't need help." Riley drifted. "Should've seen the faces on those poor people. Strauss keeps some photographs in a safe. Big stack. Big. It took so long to get the hats right. He hired some hardcases to clean up the mess. Jesus, Cap. I never would've believed there were worse characters than you."

"Strauss is careful," I said. "It must have taken years."

"About fifteen or so. Even the hardcases could only deal with so many corpses. And the farm; well, its rather high profile. These three Company guys handled disposals. Three that I met, anyway. These fellows started getting nervous, started acting hinky. Strauss made her get rid of them. This was no piece of cake. Those sonofabitches wanted to live, let me tell you." He grew quiet and swallowed. "She managed, but it was awful, and Strauss decided she required field testing. She required more "live" targets, is how he put it. Porter and me knew he meant Company men. Black ops guys nobody would miss. Men who were trained like the Reds and the Jerries are trained. Real killers."

"Men like me and my team," I said.

"Gold star!" He cackled, drumming the heels of his Stetsons against the planks. His hilarity coarsened into shrieks. Muscles stood in knots on his arms and neck. "Oh God! She rode us all night—oh Christ!" He became unintelligible. The post creaked with the strain of his thrashing.

I found the experience completely unnerving. Better to stare through the watery pane where trees took shape as light fell upon their shoulders. My bladder hurt; too fearful to step outside, I found a coffee can and relieved myself. My hands shook and I spilled a bit.

The man's spasms peaked and he calmed by degrees. I waited until he seemed lucid, said, "Let me help you, Riley. Tell me what Porter—what she—did. Are you poisoned?" There was a bad thought. Say Porter had slipped a touch of the pox into our water supply . . . I ceased that line of conjecture. Pronto.

"She rode us, Cap. Aren't you listening to ME?" He screeched the last, frothing. "I want to die now." His chin drooped and he mumbled incoherently.

I let him be. *How now, brown cow?* I had been so content sitting on that Coney Island beach watching seagulls rip at detritus and waiting for time to expire.

The whole situation had taken on an element of black comedy. Betrayed by that devil Strauss? Sure, he was Machiavelli with a hard-on. I'd seen him put the screws to better men than me. I'd helped him do the deed. Yeah, I was a rube, no doubt. Problem was, I still had not the first idea what had been done to us exactly. Riley was terrified of Virginia. Fair enough, she scared me too. I believed him when he said she could do things—she was possibly a savant, like the idiot math geniuses we locked in labs and sweated atom-smashing secrets from. The way her face had changed when I first saw her convinced me of this.

She's a weapon, a nasty, nasty weapon. I didn't know what that meant. I didn't care much, either. Something bad had happened to Riley. Whether Virginia had done it, whether Porter had done it, or if the goddamned KGB was cooking his brain with EM pulses, we were in the soup. How to escape the pot was my new priority.

I settled in with my shotgun to wait. And plan.

Nobody returned from the morning expedition.

Around 1700 hours I decided that I was screwed. The operation was compromised, it's principal subject missing. The detail assigned to guard the principal was also missing and likely dead or captured.

What to do? I did what we intelligence professionals always did at moments like this. I started a fire in the stove and began burning documents. In forty-five minutes all paper records of Project TALLHAT were coals. This included my personal log. Dr. Riley observed this without comment. He lapsed into semi-consciousness before I finished.

Unfortunately I decided to check him for wounds.

Don't know what possessed me. I was sort of like a kid poking a dead animal with a stick. I was *compelled*. Cautiously I lifted his shirt and found three holes in his back— one in the nape of his neck, two at the base of his spine. Each was the diameter of a walnut and oozed dark blood. They stank of rotten flesh, of gangrene.

She rode us all night, Cap!

Thank God for decades of military discipline—the machinery took over. If a soldier could regard the charred corpses of infant flame-thrower victims and maintain his sanity, a soldier could stomach a few lousy holes in a man's spine. I detached myself from this gruesome spectacle and the realization that this was the single most monumental balls-up of my career. What a way to go out!

I determined to make a break for the main road. A twenty mile hike; more, since I dared not use the main track, but certainly within my range. At that point, I was certain I could sprint the distance if necessary. Yeah, best idea I'd had so far.

"Cap, help me." Hatcher's voice muffled by rain against the roof.

I limped to the window. The light had deteriorated. I made him out, standing a few yards away between some trees. His arms were spread as if in greeting—then I saw the rope.

"Cap! Help me!" His face was alabaster, glowing in the dusk.

I began a shout, but was interrupted by an ominous thump of displaced weight behind me. My heart sank.

"Yes, Cap. Help him," Virginia crooned.

I turned and beheld her. Her naked skull scraped the ceiling. A wizened child, grinning and drooling. She towered because she sat upon Dox' broad back, her yellow nails digging at his ears. His expression was flaccid as he bore down on me.

The shotgun jumped in my hands and made its terrible racket. Then Dox' fingers closed over my throat and night fell.

I did not dream of Cuba or the failed attack on Batista's garrison. Nor did I dream of walking through the black winter of Dresden surrounded by swirling flakes of ash. I didn't dream of Soissans with its muddy ditches and rats.

I dreamt of people marching single file across a field. Some dressed quaintly, others had forgotten their shoes. Many had forgotten to dress at all. Their faces were blank as snow. They stumbled. At least a hundred men, women and children. Marching without speaking. A great hole opened in the ground before them. It stank of carrion. One by one the people came to this hole, swayed, and toppled into the cavity. Nobody screamed.

I woke to see the cabin wall flickering in lamplight. Blurry, for my glasses were lost. Something was wrong with my legs; they were paralyzed. I suspected my back was broken. At least there was no pain.

The numbness seemed to encompass my senses as well—the fear was still present, but submerged and muzzled. Glacial calm stole over me.

"Dr. Riley was misled. Herman never intended this solely as a test." Virginia's voice quavered from somewhere close behind my shoulder.

Her shadow loomed on the wall. A wobbly silhouette that flowed unwholesomely. Floorboards squeaked as she shifted. The thought of rolling over brought sweat to my cheeks, so I lay there and watched her shadow in morbid fascination.

"It was also an offering. Mother is pleased. He will be rewarded with a pretty."

"My men," I said. It was difficult to talk, my throat was rusty and bruised.

"With Mother. Except the brute. You killed him. Mother won't take meat unless it's alive. Shame on you, Roger." She chuckled evilly. The sound withdrew slightly, and her shadow shrank. "Oh, your back isn't broken. You'll feel your legs presently. I didn't want you running off before we had a chance to talk."

I envisioned a line of men, Hatcher in the lead, marching through the woods and up a mountain. It rained heavily and they staggered in the mud. No one said anything. Automatons winding down. Ahead, yawned a gap in a rocky slope. A dank cave mouth. One by one they went swallowed . . .

There came a new sound that disrupted my unpleasant daydream—sobbing. It was Riley; smothered as by a gag. I could tell from its frantic nature that

Virginia crouched near him. She said to me, "I came back for you, Roger. As for this one, I thought he had provided to his limit . . . yet he squirms with vigor. Ah, the resilience of life!"

"Who are you?" I asked as several portions of her shadow elongated from the central axis, dipped as questing tendrils. Then, a dim, wet susurration. I thought of pitcher plants grown monstrous and shut my eyes tight.

Riley's noises became shrill.

"Don't be afraid, Roger." Virginia rasped, a bit short of breath. "Mother wants to meet you. Such a vital existence you have pursued! Not often does She entertain provender as seasoned as yourself. If you're lucky, the others will have sated her. She will birth you as a new man. A man in Her image. You'll get old, yes. Being old is a wonderful thing, though. The older you become, the more things you taste. The more you taste, the more pleasure you experience. There is *so much* pleasure to be had."

"Bullshit! If it were such a keen deal, Herman would be cashing in! Not me!"

"Well, Herman is overly cautious. He has reservations about the process. I'll go back and work on him some more."

"Who are you? Who is your mother?" I said it too loudly, hoping to obscure the commotion Riley was making. The squelching. I babbled, "How did Strauss find you? Jesus!"

"You read the files—I asked the doctors. If you read the files you know where I was born and who I am. You know who Mother is—a colonist wrote Her name on the palisade, didn't he? A name given by white explorers to certain natives who worshipped Her. Idiots! The English are possibly the stupidest people that ever lived." She tittered. "I was the first Christian birth in the New World. I was special. The rest were meat. Poor mama, poor daddy. Poor everyone else. Mother is quite simple, actually. She has basic needs . . . She birthed me anew, made me better than crude flesh and now I help her conduct the grand old game. She sent me to find Herman. Herman helps her. I think you could help her too."

"Where is your mother? Is she here?"

"Near. She moves around. We lived on the water for a while. The mountain is nicer, the shafts go so deep. She hates the light. All of Her kind are like that. The miners used to come and She talked with them. No more miners."

I wanted to say something, anything to block Riley's clotted screams. Shortly, his noises ceased. Tears seeped from my clenched eyelids. "D-did the copper circlets ever really work? Or was that part of the joke?" I didn't care about the answer.

Virginia was delighted. "Excellent! Well, they did. That's why I arranged to meet Strauss, to attach myself. He is a clever one! His little devices worked to interfere until we got here, so close to Mother's influence. I am merely a conduit of Her majestic power. She is unimaginable!"

"You mentioned a game . . ."

Virginia said, "Do you suppose men invented chess? I promise you, there are contests far livelier. I have been to the universities of the world, watching. You have visited the battlefields of the world, watching. Don't you think the time is coming?"

"For what?"

"When mankind will manage to blacken the sky with bombs and cool the earth so that Mother and Her brothers, Her sisters, and children may emerge once more! Is there any other purpose? Oh, what splendid revelries there shall be on that day!"

What could I answer with?

Virginia didn't mind. She said, "The dinosaurs couldn't do it a hundred million years. Nor the sharks in their oceans given four times that. The monkeys showed promise, but never realized their potential. Humans are the best pawns so far—the ones with a passion for fire and mystery. With subtle guidance they—you—can return this world to the paradise it was when the ice was thick and the sun dim. We need men like Adolph, and Herman, and their sweet sensibilities. Men who would bring the winter darkness so they might caper around bonfires. Men like you, dear Roger. Men like you." Virginia ended on a cackle.

Hiroshima bloomed upon my mind's canvas and I nearly cried aloud. And Auschwitz, and Verdun, and all the rest. Yes, the day was coming. "You've got the wrong man," I said in my bravest tone. "You don't know the first thing. I'm a bloody patriot."

"Mother appreciates that, dear Roger. Be good and don't move. I'll return in a moment. Must fetch you a coat. It's raining." Virginia's shadow slipped into the lab. There followed the clatter of upturned objects and breaking glass.

Her brothers, Her sisters, and children. Pawns. Provender. My gorge tasted bitter. Herman helping creatures such as this bring about hell on earth. For what? Power? The promise of immortality? Virginia's blasphemous longevity should've cured him of that desire.

Oh, Herman, you fool! On its heels arrived the notion that perhaps I would change my mind after a conversation with Mother. That one day soon I might sit across the table from Strauss and break bread in celebration of a new dawn.

I wept as I pulled my buck knife free, snicked the catch. Would that I possessed the courage to slit my own wrists! I attempted to do just that, but lacked the conviction to carry through. Seventy years of self-aggrandizement had robbed me of any will to self-destruction.

So, I began to carve a message into the planks instead. A warning. Although what could one say about events this bizarre? This hideous? I shook with crazed laughter and nearly broke the blade with my furious hacking.

I got as far as CRO before Virginia came and rode me into the woods to meet her mother.

As the nameless worm advanced with its glistening box, the reclining man caught in the mirror-like surface a glimpse of what should have been his own body. Yet—horribly verifying his disordered and unfamiliar sensations—it was not his own body at all that he saw reflected in the burnished metal. It was, instead, the loathsome, pale-grey bulk of one of the great centipedes.

"The Challenge from Beyond" · C.L. Moore, A. Merritt,
H.P. Lovecraft, Robert E.Howard, & Frank Belknap Long

• THE DUDE WHO COLLECTED LOVECRAFT •
Nick Mamatas & Tim Pratt

I drove a brand-new rental car I couldn't afford—next year's model, so in a way it was a car from the future—from the Amherst Amtrak stop and into the Vermont countryside, which was just as picturesque as all the calendar photos had led me to expect. The green mountains flared with red and gold from the changing leaves of fall. I had to stop a couple of times in somnambulant little towns, first for gas and later to use the toilet, and while everyone was polite, talkative even, I felt a few stares. They don't get a lot of black people around here. Some of these towns: South Shaftsbury and Shaftsbury, East Arlington, and then Arlington—as if having two stoplights or a three-block-long main drag were enough to fission a town into two—were positively nineteenth century. My cell phone didn't work. They sold maple syrup by the gallon even in the dumpiest of gas stations.

I thought about the brittle old letters in my briefcase, which included (among genial advice on writing and cranky complaints about publishers) a few passages of deep loathing about "the niggers and immigrants who fester and shamble in the slums of our fallen cities." Ah, Lovecraft. I always wondered how my great-grandfather's letters back to him might have read. I doubted if old Cavanaugh Payne ever told his idol that he was a "miscegenator" himself. Three generations later, I was fresh out of white skin privilege myself, but I had enough of Cavanaugh's legacy to clear all my debts, assuming I could ever find the isolated country house where this collector lived.

The hand-drawn map Fremgen had mailed me was crude, and obviously not to scale, so it was a little like following a treasure map made by a pirate with a spatial perception disorder. I'd tried to find better directions online, but none of the map sites even recognized the name of the street he lived on: Goodenough Road. I understood why when, as late afternoon shaded into evening, I found his signless dirt road surrounded by maple and pine trees. The only marker by the rutted track was a squat statue carved out of some black marble; the figure looked like the offspring of a toad and a jellyfish, wearing a weathered white stone crown. The collector had drawn a little picture of the stone road marker on my map. I'd assumed it was a childish scrawl, but in truth it wasn't a bad likeness. It wasn't a bad likeness of a bad likeness anyway.

After bumping down the road—dotted with other even more indescribable statues—for about five minutes I found the house, a three-story wooden monstrosity with a vast front porch wrapped around at least three sides, and carriage house sagging down into itself off to one side. Whatever color these buildings had once been, the boards had faded to a sort of stoney gray, and they both looked on the verge of disintegration. Trees pressing in close, eager to take back the land. I parked the car and got out, and in the silence of dusk the slamming car door was the loudest thing I'd ever heard. I approached the house, with its windows all blinded by curtains, and went up the paint-flecked steps to the porch, where a swing hung broken from one chain. This wasn't promising. I'd been assured that this collector was wealthy, but he didn't look rich from here. Maybe I'd turned down the wrong road, and was about to be attacked by some backroads cannibal who wore the skin of his victims as an apron. Well, probably not.

I knocked on the solid wooden door.

"Who's there?" shouted a voice from inside, so quickly he must have been standing right there, waiting. That's when I noticed the peephole set in the door, which seemed like an odd touch for an old country house.

"It's Jim Payne," I said, and waited. No response. "I called you, about the letters." Still no reply. "I'm Cavanaugh Payne's great-grandson?"

"I've seen pictures of Payne, and I can't say I see much resemblance," came the reply, in a querulous Green Mountain accent. "Say" and "see" sounded almost identical.

I gritted my teeth and made it look like a smile. "Grandma always said I looked just like him." There's no particular reason to take crap from some crazy old kook, money or not. I was ready to walk. I thought I heard a grunt from behind the door, and then it opened with a harsh squall of hinges, and I got my first look at the man who collected Lovecraft.

* * *

Cavanaugh,

Your letter of the tenth and the enclosed materials reached me just in the nick of time. Bravo! I have been having, as Klark Ash-Ton had mentioned to you, a quite difficult time with the latest yarn. It's already somewhat of a ramble, but I cannot help but complete it now, as there are few other opportunities in the offing for old Grandpa. It was a mistake, coming to New York, I must admit, now. While the valleys of the financial district are grand, and the subtle corners and hints of twisting Dutch roads still remain and reverberate with the sort of classical detail I love, the world of commerce is beyond me. I've written several lengthy letters of introduction to various concerns, both in publishing and in the workaday world of commodities trading, but haven't yet received so much as a social card with a hastily-scribbled telephone exchange under the name of a Dean or a Hathaway beneath it. Not that such a number would be possible for me to reach. The horrid tenement in which I find myself is without a telephone or any of the other amenities of the modern world, or the graces of the world I'm afraid has left us forever.

I have decided to take a hold of one end of that old writer's saw: "write what one knows," and with my latest story I hope to write a truly devilish, nasty bit of business connecting the rites and rituals of the Yezidi which you have so readily and thoughtfully transcribed for me. Of all this mediæval superstition and thaumaturgy I know little, but of New York I am afraid I am learning rather too much. The gangs of young loafers and evil-looking foreigners who traipse down the alleyways by the horde are so disconcerting to me I cannot help but see them whenever I close my eyes. O, for the fabled night-gaunts of old! At least phantastical terrors are ephemeral, while this city full of swarthy Latins and darkie brutes, with, of course, ol' Shylock himself sitting and preening atop the twisted mass of bodies, is as solid as granite. The devolutionary social processes I espied in Providence have bloomed like fecund and fetid lichen here, clinging and mouldy to the once-grand thoroughfares and edifices of Gotham. I fear for our future, Cavanaugh, I fear for the destiny of a Nubian America!

On my walks I've stumbled upon perhaps the perfect setting for this new story. The very name of the neighborhood is evocative: Red Hook. It is New York in microcosm; the streets are limned with old Dutch history: Dikeman, van Brunt, indeed, even the hook is an Anglicization of "hoek," or point. And yet the peninsula is aswarm with the most bestial of immigrants and workingmen, lured to the area by the swampish Gowanus and the day labor of the bustling piers. Who knows what eldritch evils can be hidden in the steel bellies of the ships and brought to bare by the husky stevedore and his own bailing-hook? Sounds like a yarn I could, I hope, market to the pulps. Yr Grandpa, I'm afraid, is down to his last three tins of

*mackerel and beans and if no remittances are forthcoming, perhaps my next letter
to you will be written by a truly skeletal hand directed only by the impulses of a
madman in a garret. Wouldn't that be a doozy!*

Thank you again, both humbly and gratefully I am, as always,

Ol' Gramps Theobald
HPL

Fremgen was an old white dude, and he wore a brown suit jacket with a red
bow tie. I didn't know if he'd dressed up special for me or if he always knocked
around the house like this, but he made me feel underdressed. The letters in my
briefcase were like a passport into a strange country.

I don't know what I expected. I knew he was a collector, but when I think of
guys who collect sci-fi and fantasy crap, I don't imagine museum-quality stuff.
I think fat nerd. A beard sprinkled with Cheeto dust. A filthy room full of porn
DVDs, half-cannibalized computers, and ancient Chinese takeout. The impe-
rious tsk of "Worst. Lovecraft letter. EVAR!" followed by, I hoped, a sack of
money anyway. But this dude's living room didn't even look like a place where
someone lived, let alone like something from a comic book convention. It was
more like a boutique. There were glass cases, discreetly lit, holding manuscript
pages, old magazines, letters, and even some objects—a handkerchief, one
shoe, a couple of pens. All of which, I assumed, had touched the extremities
of Mr. Lovecraft himself. There were bookshelves, fronted with glass, holding
hundreds of volumes. More bizarrely, there were a few little pedestals topped
with domes of glass, supporting items of obscure function. I saw a metal cylinder under one dome, a big glass jar with something floating in murky fluid
under another, and a third just looked like a profusion of copper tubing wound
around some kind of helmet or headdress. There were tiny hand-written index
cards inside each case and under each dome, but Fremgen didn't give me time
to browse.

"Sit, sit," he said, and I settled onto one of the two ancient wingback chairs,
the velvet upholstery emitting a little puff of dust when I sat. He sat in the chair's
twin, facing me, his eyes squinting and intense. There was a low table between
us, set with a funny-looking clay tea kettle and some lumpy cups and bumpy
saucers that looked like they'd been made in a pottery class for the mentally ill. I
started to open the briefcase, figuring he wanted to get this over with, but then
he spoke abruptly: "You say you're from Red Hook? In Brooklyn."

"That's right."

He mulled that over. "You know Lovecraft wrote a story about that place?"

"Sure. 'The Red Hook Horror,' something like that?" I knew the title wasn't right, but something made me want to mess with this guy a little.

He didn't seem fazed, though. "'The Horror at Red Hook,' yes. Lovecraft himself didn't think much of the story, thought it was too rambling, but I'm rather fond of it. Many of Lovecraft's fictions are . . . outlandish. Time-traveling aliens. Winged creatures that fly through the voids of space. Cities of fungi. But the story about Red Hook always seemed more plausible to me, that immigrants to our shores would bring with them dark rituals from their homelands, and unleash horrors upon an unsuspecting city. Lovecraft lived in New York for a time, he knew the alleyways and corners and piers more intimately than he wished, and he saw the old settlers being pushed aside by the newcomers, with their strange and secretive ways—"

"Have you ever been to Red Hook?" I interrupted.

"Only in my mind's eye," he said, and sounded like he thought that was just as good as a visit in person. "Has it changed much, since Lovecraft's day? Are there still the crumbling red brick buildings, the oppressive streets, the air of imminent decay?"

I considered. I wanted to call this guy a moron, but our deal wasn't done yet. "I pay sixteen hundred dollars a month for a studio apartment. They're also building the world's largest IKEA in Red Hook, so that's pretty scary. Look, I've got the letters Lovecraft wrote to Cavanaugh—"

"Your ancestor wasn't much of a writer, really," Fremgen mused. "His fiction, I mean. I actually have some of the letters he wrote to Lovecraft, and they're better, more enthusiastic, less imitative. In his fiction, he wrote about Vermont and New Hampshire like a man who'd never been there, never left the city of his birth. His stories of old civilizations on forgotten continents were more plausible. Have you read 'Planet of the Phantasm?' 'The swirling abyssal call echoed across the verdant planes of Pramatat, rousing snake-coiled shrunplants from their slumber, lidless amber pools peering forth to—"

"Can't say I'm a fan of the old man's work, myself," I stepped in. "I like crime stories."

Nothing seemed to needle this guy. "But you're one of his blood, aren't you? However much that blood has been diluted. The past lives on, all around us. You're connected to Cavanaugh, and through him, to a different time. Only an eyeblink in the past on a cosmic scale, of course, but in human terms, three generations is a vast and nearly insurmountable gulf. Don't you think?"

"Yes. Yes I do." This guy was not going to be rushed, but at least I could avoid offering up a conversational opening.

"Drink with me." He picked up the tea cup in front of him, slurped it, made a contented face, and gestured to the kettle. I poured a little into my own cup, just enough to be polite, and took a sip. It was like drinking dirty river water. "Brewed from local herbs," the old guy said, nodding. "I grow them myself."

"Delicious," I said, after I managed to swallow a second mouthful. "And I thank you for your hospitality. But I'd like to get out of here before too late—"

"Indulge an old man." He smiled, and any doubt I had about his faculties disappeared. That was a knowing smile, and whatever he was doing, he was doing it on purpose. "You can learn a lot from the past, young man. The things in this room, they are valuable—some are even priceless—but they are not the heart of my collection. Would you come upstairs with me, to see some of my more interesting items? I get so few visitors. And the things I have to show you might change your perspective."

Don't piss off the golden goose, I thought. "Sure, I guess I could take a quick look," I said, praying this wasn't some kind of sex thing. I left the briefcase with the letters by the chair and followed him up a narrow, tilting stairway, the walls lined with photographs so dusty their subjects were impossible to discern. The stairs opened onto a big room that must have taken up the entire upper floor. There were literally thousands of newspapers stacked along the walls and into the center of the room, forming stumpy corridors, the squeeze made all that tighter due to heaps of junk spilling off rickety card tables and bowed folding chairs. I took about two steps into the room and things started to get woozy and swirly and vague. The old dude just stood there grinning as I swayed and stumbled. "Shit," I said, or something equally articulate, but my thoughts were clear: Not a sex thing. A drug-his-tea-and-murder-him thing. There was no place to fall.

Cavanaugh,

Greetings, O Left Hand of young Belknap. I was quite pleased to shew you about Providence this past fortnight, being none the less pleased to have finally returned to the seat of my ancestors, and hope that one day you'll return for another visit when you're not feeling quite so poorly.

One for the commonplace book strikes me just now. Penfriend spends a warm summer day meeting in the flesh with penfriend, and returns home via locomotive only to be greeted by a letter from the old boy's spinster aunt sending regrets and condolences. 'Apologies for opening and reading your correspondence with my Samuel, but you must know that he passed of tuberculosis a month gone by . . . '

I'll likely not do anything with it. Now that it is down on paper the idea rather smacks of Victoriana—no possibility of tightening coils of horror, reaching out & gradually dragging the reader in. I want tremendously to pen another tale, but even this letter is being written piecemeal between snatches of revisory work and long nights of astronomical observation. An aurora has visited Providence, as it does at the rarest of intervals, and I have taken to camping out under blankets in subarctic weather to observe this most cryptical of sky effects. A very few degrees of latitude makes all the difference when it comes to auroral perception, so I am sure you have in your new Green Mountain home auroras with a frequency beyond all Rhode Island standards.

Wandrei speaks of a recent trip home. You would do well to shew him some of your weird fiction, for he is among the most discerning and erudite of our band of enthusiasts, and has frequently hinted that he may dare to launch a magazine of weird fiction of his own.

Yr obt Grandsire—Nekropolis.

I woke up tied to a chair, and the first thing I noticed was a saline lock, for putting in an IV, or drawing blood. Fremgen loomed into my sight a moment later, peering at me. "Awake already. You are a strong one."

"What—what—" My mouth was dry, and I couldn't manage much more than that.

"I just took a little blood," he said. "Barely a pint. There's juice downstairs, cookies too. Help yourself when I'm gone."

"Motherfucker," I said, articulating as clearly as I could. "Let me go. I'll fucking kill you."

"I'm afraid I can't, young man. I might need more of your blood." He turned to a table and began measuring out powders from a row of colored glass jars, pouring them into a stainless steel pot heating over a camping stove. "The recipe isn't exact, and it says the blood of direct descendants will work, but may require 'greater quantities.' Best to keep you here and fresh." He referred to a big old book bound in pitted black leather, running his finger along the page. He made a few more adjustments to the contents of the pot before putting a lid on it.

I rocked a little in the chair, but the motion made my head spin—whatever local herbs he'd drugged me with, they—combined with the blood loss— worked too well.

"You don't know how long I've been working on this, and to have you fall into my hands. To come to my door! It's perfect." He picked up a sheaf of papers and shook them at me. "These are your great-grandfather's letters to Lovecraft, you know. I bought them ages ago. I had the man's letters, the ink, the words from that time, and all I needed was a sample of the blood." He put down the letters and began lighting candles, though his hands were shaking so badly I was afraid he'd drop the match and set the ramparts of newspapers flaming.

I concentrated on breathing deeply and trying to get my equilibrium back while he set candles around the room. He moved a wooden chair to a clear spot on the floor, and poured something white—salt, maybe?—on the floorboards, making a big circle. He poured a smaller circle of salt inside the first one, so the chair was at the center of a Bull's eye. "Almost there," he said. He took the lid off the pot, and the smell of burning blood and weird spices made me want to retch.

"What are you doing?" My voice was a lot more steady this time.

"Traveling in time, boy. Lovecraft wrote about it—of minds traveling in time, at least. Even alien minds, transposed into human bodies, and vice versa. 'The Shadow Out of Time'—you know it? No. Well. That's the idea. With the blood of Cavanaugh Payne's great-grandson to connect me to his body, and a letter written in Cavanaugh's own hand to connect me to a particular time, and through certain ancient rituals from priesthoods devoted to forgotten gods, I can project my mind back into Cavanaugh Payne's body, take control, and then . . . oh, and then . . . "

I suspected that arguing with the basics of his plan was fruitless, since crazy people tend to cling to their central craziness. But I couldn't help but find the whole idea stupid, even accepting the premise. "Then what? Great-grandpa was a miserable bastard. He sold some shitty stories, knocked up great-grandma, and disappeared before the child was even born. He left all his things behind, so he probably just got murdered and dumped in a river or something. You want that life? Why?"

"It's a stepping-stone," he said, and moved the camping stove and the pot closer to the chair, placing them carefully inside the outer salt circle. He returned to the table and picked up a yellowing letter. "This is from Cavanaugh, in his last letter, from 1928. Listen: 'Your offer is too kind, Grandpa. I would be delighted to visit and I insist you let me stand you lunch. Perhaps we could spend the afternoon poking around in those bookstores you've told me so much about.' You see? He didn't just write to Lovecraft—he arranged a meeting with him! And if I'm the one controlling his body when he meets Lovecraft, it should be trivial for me to get a little of the great man's blood. I won't need nearly as much as I took from you, not when drawn from the source itself. Then I can simply recreate this ritual, and take over Lovecraft's body. You've read 'The Thing on the Doorstep'? No? Still, like that. As for your great-grandfather's disappearance, it only proves my venture will be successful. After I take over Lovecraft's body, Cavanaugh's corpus will be left an empty idiot husk, mindless and drooling. I'll need to get rid of it—hence the 'disappearance.' I'll dispose of his remains with due respect, fear not."

"Why the hell would you want Lovecraft's life? Didn't he have a fucked-up marriage and die young? Wasn't he afraid of everything? Black people, brown people, the ocean, shellfish, the sky, the dark, women, everything?" I wiggled in the ropes. The knots weren't all that good. I figured I'd be able to work them loose soon, so if he wanted to keep babbling like a James Bond villain, that was fine with me. He was about a thousand years old, so I was pretty sure I could take him, even half-drugged and down a pint of blood. "Wasn't he . . . gay!" I needed this old man angry, off-balance . . .

"But the stories," Fremgen said dreamily. "If I go back to 1928 and take over Lovecraft's life, so many of the great stories will remain to be written. And I've committed them all to memory, their publication histories, everything. His life was so well-documented, you know, with his letters, all those letters, it will be easy to be him, and it will be my hand that writes 'The Shadow Out of Time' and 'At the Mountains of Madness' and—but you'd never understand." He tore the letter in his hands into little pieces and dropped them fluttering into the stinking pot, then sat down in the wooden chair in the circle of salt. "The money for the letters is in the writing desk downstairs, Payne. I don't need the letters, but take the money."

Thick smoke rose from the pot, and through some weird quirk of the room's ventilation swirled around Fremgen and the chair without crossing the outer line of salt. Fremgen took deep breaths, and I hoped he wouldn't die of smoke inhalation before I could kick his crazy ass. I wiggled harder at the ropes and slipped my left wrist loose, then untied the other knots, though leaning down to untie my ankles made my head pound alarmingly. I stood up, waited for the swaying to settle, then headed straight for Fremgen, who was staring blank-faced and zoned-out from his chair. I stepped across the first line of salt, scuffing it with my shoe, and then a wave of horrible dizziness swept over me. Was it the smoke, more of Fremgen's homegrown knockout herbs? I stumbled and fell, sprawling across the inner salt circle.

And then, I guess the only way to say it is, I traveled in time.

No!

The voice was clearly Fremgen's, though I didn't hear it with my ears, but ringing in my head, a syllable of pure fury. I was on a street, beside a brick building, the air cool. I leaned against a wall and groaned. It felt like somebody was banging their fists against the inside of my skull.

Mine! Mine! Mine! Fremgen shouted.

I turned my head—my neck felt funny, stiff, weird—and looked at my hands. My white hands. My white, hairy-knuckled, totally unfamiliar hands.

"Oh, hell," I said. "I don't believe this." My voice was not my voice.

You're ruining everything! Fremgen wailed in the back of my head. *I'm on my way to see Lovecraft right now!*

"Nope," I said, and pushed away from the wall. I tried to take a step and nearly fell on my face, because my feet were shaped wrong, and my legs were the wrong length, and all together I felt like I was wearing a suit that was too big in some places and too tight in others. "Not going to happen." I laughed out loud. Great-grandpa had a pretty good laugh. "You know, you should've read those letters I brought. The last one from Lovecraft especially. He and Cavanaugh had a pleasant lunch, if a little awkward." I took a tentative step forward, and thought I was getting the hang of operating the body now. "But I'm not letting you anywhere near that guy. Not that I actually care if you take over Lovecraft's body, one old dead white dude is as good as another I guess, but you just shouldn't have fucked with me."

I felt more pounding and poking in my head, but it wasn't too bad, like the memory of a headache. Fremgen was in me, wrenching and heavy at once, like one too many pancakes, but he couldn't pull himself up my spine, into my—into Cavanaugh's—brain. He'd stolen a pint of my blood to make this spell, but when I stepped into the circle, I was full of my own blood, so I must have made a better connection. I turned down an alleyway, just the kind of narrow passage crowded by crumbling red brick buildings doubtless inhabited by swarthy immigrants that scared the shit out of Lovecraft. "So how do we get back?" I said.

I will never go back. You have to sleep sometime, and when you do, I will seize this body, I will find a spell to oust you, I will succeed. I've wanted this too long.

"We'll see," I said, and went through a doorway into what seemed to be an abandoned building, big holes bashed through the walls inside, heaps of plaster and brick and trash in the corners. I just wanted a place to hunker down and think for a little while. I wasn't eager to take over Cavanaugh's life, though he disappeared in 1928, so maybe that's what happened—what would happen—whatever. Maybe I would just take off and make my own way, change my name, have a new life. Cavanaugh wasn't that much older than I was, though life expectancies in the '20s weren't so great, probably. But back here I didn't have the debts and narrowing of options I faced back home, so maybe—

Something unfolded out of a dark corner, and now that I looked, that corner hurt my eyes—the angles were all wrong somehow. And the thing that stepped toward me was too big for the space in this room, it should have been all hunched over and squeezed, but it was tall, it just kept getting taller, wider, unfolding into dimensions I couldn't even comprehend, it was—

It was squamous. Rugose. Noisome. Eldritch. Cyclopean. Those aren't the right words. There are no right words. But those are the best I can come up with.

You broke the circle! Fremgen screamed in my mind. *You broke the seal of salt, you fool, you've loosed it, the opener of the way, the dweller from the inbetween, the guardian of the black and red path, it's coming for us—*

Fremgen was still desperately trying to wrest control of the body away from me. So I let him, and he grabbed on, and he shoved me, and I went hurtling away from there, out of the body, just in time to see the great thing's face— which wasn't a face, but there's no word for what it was, and it did at least have a mouth—swing down and dilate and open and blossom and grasp.

I woke in Fremgen's upstairs room, my head thudding. I sat up, woozy, trying to get the hang of my own body again, and scooted back out of the circle of salt. Fremgen was still in the chair, drooling, body an empty vessel. His mind was back there, still. In Cavanaugh. In the belly of some unspeakable beast.

I stood up, and then Fremgen lifted his face to me. His mouth opened but what came out weren't words. Imagine shortwave radio static, loud and echoing across a depthless canyon. His eyes were wild and blank at once, crackling like an aurora. Whatever ate Fremgen had come back through the path he'd made in time.

I figured I was pretty well fucked. Then the thing in Fremgen's body tried to stand up and fell sideways and knocked over a table and half a dozen burning candles, then kicked over the camping stove, which was still lit. There was a horrible snapping pop, and I'm pretty sure it was Fremgen's hip breaking. The thing bellowed and mewled. I remembered how hard it had been for me to walk around in Cavanaugh's body, because it was so different from my own, but at least he'd been human, he'd had arms and legs and bilateral symmetry. The thing in Fremgen had come from a totally different kind of body, a thousand limbs reaching into the sixth dimension, so it could only twitch and flail as it tried to fold the curve of the world around itself, just to reach me.

Either the rolling camp stove or the candles caught a pile of papers on fire, and pretty soon the whole terraced array of old newspapers was burning. The thing in Fremgen's body tried to drag itself toward me, right over the flames, and it screamed, too ignorant of human limits to even know it should avoid fire. I half-ran, half-fell down the narrow stairs.

I stopped by the writing desk, trying not to listen to the screaming from above, the torrent of weird syllables that didn't sound like any language I'd ever heard. I opened the drawer and there was an envelope with my name scrawled on the front. There was money in it, and though I didn't stop to count it then, I later found out it was $200 short of the price we'd agreed upon for the letters. That cheap bastard. I left the briefcase with the letters in the living room. Fremgen had paid for them, after all, and I didn't want them anymore. I didn't want to see if that last letter had . . . changed.

I went into the dark yard. The house burned behind me, looking closer to collapse with every second, and I hurried to my rental car, pockets full off financial salvation, head full of horrors, nostrils full of smoke. I opened the car door, but before I got in, I tilted back my head, and looked to the sky.

Even with the flickering light from the burning roof, the stars overhead were impossibly bright, and cold, and indifferent. Then, on the edges of the horizon, the black of the sky shifted and crackled with coruscating waves of blue-white light. Lovecraft would have found that sky fascinating. Maybe terrifying, finally. For my part, I couldn't wait to get back to a place where the light pollution was so bad you couldn't see the stars or the spaces between them at all, no matter how dark the night.

Without warning came those deep, cracked, raucous vocal sounds which will never leave the memory of the stricken group who heard them. Not from any human throat were they born, for the organs of man can yield no such acoustic perversions. . . . It is almost erroneous to call them sounds at all, since so much of their ghastly, infra-bass timbre spoke to dim seats of consciousness and terror far subtler than the ear . . .
"The Dunwich Horror" · H.P. Lovecraft (1929)

· THE ORAM COUNTY WHOOSIT ·
Steve Duffy

Maybe for the rest of the welcoming committee it was the proudest afternoon of their lives; I remember it mostly as one of the wettest of mine. We were standing on a platform in Oram, West Virginia, waiting for a train to pull in, and it hadn't stopped raining all day. It wasn't really a problem for anybody else at the station: the mayor had a big umbrella, and his cronies had the shelter of the awning, over by the ticket office. I had my damn hat, was all.

They belonged to the town, you see, and I didn't. I'd been sent down from Washington the day before, like the guest of honor on whom we were all waiting. Our newspaper had sprung for him to travel first-class, having sent me up ahead in a rattling old caboose—to pave the way for his greatness, I guess. Because he was some kind of a great man even then, in newspaper circles at least. Nowadays, you'll find his stories in all the best anthologies, but back then the majority of folks knew Horton Keith mostly from the stuff they read over the breakfast table; which was pretty damn good, don't get me wrong. But then so were my photographs, or so I thought, so why was I the one left outside in the cold and wet like a red-headed stepchild? It's a hell of a life, and no mistake; that's what I was thinking. I was younger then, in case you hadn't guessed: twenty-four, as old as the century. That didn't feel so old then—but it does now, here on the wrong side of nineteen-eighty. Then again, the century hasn't weathered too well either, has it?

Away down the track a whistle blew, and the welcoming committee spat out their tobacco and gussied themselves up for business. Through the sheets of rain you could barely see the hills above the rooftops, but you felt them pressing in on you: that you did. Row upon row of them, their sides sheer and thickly forested, the tops lost in the dense gray clouds that had lain on the summits ever since I arrived. By now, I was starting to wonder whether there *was* any sort of blue sky up there, or whether mist and rain were the invariable order of the day. Since then I've looked into it scientifically, and what happens is this: the weather fronts blow in off the Atlantic coast, and they scoot across Virginia like a skating rink till they hit the Alleghenies. Then, those fronts get forced up over the mountains by the prevailing winds, and by the time they're coming down the other side, boy, they're dropping like a shot goose. And *then*, the whole bunch of soggy-bottom clouds falls splat on to Oram County, and it rains every goddamn day of the year. Scientifically speaking.

A puff of smoke from round the track, and then the train came into view. The welcoming committee shuffled themselves according to rank and feet above sea-level; one of them dodged off round the side of the station, and hang me for a liar if he didn't come back with a marching band, or the makings of one at least—a tuba, trombones, a half-a-dozen trumpets and a big bass drum. The musicians had been waiting someplace under shelter, or so I hoped: if not, then I wasn't going to be standing too close to that tuba when it blew. It might give me a musical shower-bath on top of my regular soaking.

The first man off the train when it pulled in was a Pullman conductor, an imperturbable Negro who looked as if he'd seen this kind of deal at every half-assed station down the line. Next was a nondescript fat man packed tight into a thin man's suit, weighed down by a large cardboard valise. If he looked uncomfortable before, you can bet he looked twice as squirrelly when the band struck up a limping rendition of "Shenandoah" and the mayor bore down on him like a long-lost brother. One look at that, and the poor guy jumped so high I practically lost him in the cloud—his upper slopes, at least. In many ways he was wasted on the travelling-salesman game; he ought to have been trying out for the Olympics over in Paris, France. Instead, he was stuck selling dungarees to miners. Like I said before, it's a hell of a life.

While that little misunderstanding was being cleared up, a few carriages down my man was disembarking, quietly and without any fuss. You may have seen photographs of Horton Keith—you may even have seen *my* photograph of him, which just happens to be the one on the facing-title page of his *Collected Short Stories*—but it seems to me he always looked more like his caricature. Not a bad-looking man: hell no! That sweep of white hair and the jet-black cookie-duster underneath meant he'd always get recognized, by everyone but the good folk of Oram, West Virginia at any rate. And there was nothing wrong with his features, if you liked 'em lean and hungry-looking. But the hunger was the key, and it came out in the drawings more vividly than in any photo I ever took of him. I never saw a keener man, nor one more likely to stick at it till the job got done. As a hunting acquaintance of mine once put it: "He's a pretty good writer, but he'd have made one hell of a bird-dog."

"Sir?" I presented myself as he stepped down from the train. He looked me up and down and said, "Mister Fenwick?" Subterranean rumble of a voice. I nodded, and tipped the sopping straw brim of my hat. "Good to meet you, sir."

"Nice hat," he said, still taking my measure as he shook my outstretched hand. "Snappy." No hint of a joke in those flinty eyes. It was 1924, for God's sake. *Everyone* wore a straw hat back then.

"I guess it's had most of the snap soaked out of it by now," I said, taking it off and examining it. "We could dry it out, maybe, or else there's a horse back there on the hitching rail without a tooth in his head. He could probably use it for his supper, poor bastard."

Keith smiled at that. Didn't go overboard or anything; but I think I passed the test. Then, the welcoming committee were upon us.

The guest of honor was polite and everything; that is to say, he wasn't outright rude, not to their faces. He shook all their hands, and listened to a few bars more of "Shenandoah" from underneath the mayor's big umbrella. I was fine, I had my snappy straw hat, which had more or less disintegrated by now. But then the mayor, a big moose called Kronke, wanted to cart him off in the civic automobile for some sort of a formal reception with drinks, and Keith drew the line at that.

"Gentlemen, it's been a long day, and I need to consult with my colleague here. We'll meet up first thing in the morning, if it's all the same to you." *My colleague.* That was about the nicest thing I'd heard since I'd arrived in Oram County. It did my self-esteem a power of good; better than that, it got me a lift in the mayoral flivver as far as the McEndoe Hotel, which was where Keith and I had rooms.

The McEndoe was a rambling old clapboard palace, one of the few buildings in town that went much above two storeys. It had a view over downtown Oram that mostly comprised wet roofs and running gutters, and inevitably you found your eyes were drawn to the wooded hills beyond, brooding and enigmatic beneath their caps of cloud. Here and there you saw scars running down the hillside, old landslides and abandoned workings. Oram was a mining town, and you weren't likely to forget it; at six in the evening the big siren blew, and soon after a stream of men came trudging down main street on their way home from the pits.

Watching them from the smoking lounge window as I sipped bootleg brandy from my hip flask—their pinched sooty faces, the absolute deadbeat exhaustion in their tread—I told myself there were worse things in life than getting my hat a little wet. I might have to work for a living, like these poor lugs.

"It's funny," Keith said, close up behind me. I hadn't heard him come in.

"Sorry?" I guessed he meant peculiar; God knows there was little enough that was comical about the view.

He was staring at the miners as they shuffled along in their filthy denim overalls. "I was up in the Klondike round the time of the gold rush, back in '98," he said. "Dug up about enough gold to fill my own teeth, was all. It was like that with most of the men: I never knew but half-a-dozen fellows who ever struck it rich; I mean really rich. But my God, we were keen sons-o-bitches! We'd jump out of our bunks in the morning and run over to those workings, go at it like crazy men all the length of a Yukon summer's day till it got dark, and like as not we'd be singing a song all the way home. And were we singing because we were rich? Had we raised so much as a single grain of gold? No, sir. Probably not." He took a panatela from his pocket and examined it critically. I waited for him to carry on his story, if that's what it was.

"Now these fellers," he said, indicating with his cigar: "each and every one of them will have pulled maybe a dozen tons of coal out of that hill today. No question. They found what they were looking for, all right. Found a damn sight more of it than we ever did. But you don't see them singing any songs, do you?" He looked at me, and I realized it wasn't a rhetorical question: he was waiting for an answer. I was sipping my drink at the time, and had to clear my throat more quickly that I'd have liked.

"They're working for the company," I said, as soon as I could manage it through my coughing. "You fellers were working for yourselves. Man doesn't sing songs when he knows someone else is getting eighty, ninety cents out of every dollar he earns."

"No," agreed Keith. "No, he doesn't. But that's just economics, after all. You know what the main difference is?" I had a pretty good idea, but shrugged, so that he'd go on. "We were digging for gold," he said simply, "and these poor bastards ain't. Call a man an adventurer, send him to the top of the world so he's half dead from the frostbite and the typhus and the avalanches, and he's happy, 'cause he knows he might—just might!—strike it rich. Set him to dig coal back home day in, day out for a wage, and he's nothing but a slave. It's the difference between what you dream about, and what you wake up to."

It sounds commonplace when I write it down. That's because you don't hear the way his voice sounded, nor see the animation in his face. I don't know if I can put that into words. It wasn't avaricious, not in the slightest. I never met a man less driven by meanness or greed. It was more as if that gold up in the Klondike represented all the magic and excitement he'd ever found in the world; as if the idea had caught hold of him when he was young and come to stand for everything that was fine and desirable, yet would always remain slightly out of reach, the highest, sweetest apple on the tree. That he kept reaching was what I most admired about him, in the end: that he knew he wasn't ever going to win the prize, and yet still reckoned it was worth fighting for. The Lord loves a trier, they say, but sometimes I think he's got a soft spot for the dreamer, too.

"Well, these fellows here might have been digging for coal," I said, offering him a light, "but seems as if a couple of 'em may have lit on something else, doesn't it?"

"Indeed," said Keith, glancing at me from beneath those jet-black bushy eyebrows before bending to the flame of the match. "Now you mention it, I guess it is kind of time we talked about things." He fished out another stogie and offered it to me.

I sat up straight and gave it my best stab at keen and judicious. Keith probably thought I'd gotten smoke in my eyes.

"What do you think we actually have here, Fenwick?" He honestly sounded as if he wanted to know what I thought. Back in my twenties, that was still pretty much of a novelty.

"Toad in a hole," I said promptly. "There's a hundred of 'em in the newspaper morgue—seems like they pop up every summer, around the time the real news dries up."

"Toad in a hole," said Keith thoughtfully. He gestured with his cigar for me to continue. Emboldened, I did so.

"The same story used to run every year in the papers out West," I said, to show I'd done my homework and wasn't just any old newspaper shutterbug. "Goes like this: some feller brings in a lump of rock split in half, it's got a tiny little hole in the middle. See there, he says? That's where the frog was. Jumped clean out when I split the rock in two, he did. Here he is, look—and he lays down some sorry-looking sun-baked pollywog on the desk. Swears with his hand on his heart: it happened just the way I'm telling you, sir, so help me God. And the editor's so desperate, he usually runs with it." I spread my hands. "That's about the way I see it, Mr. Keith."

Keith nodded. "So you don't believe such a thing could happen?"

"Huh-uh." With all the certainty of twenty-four summers. "Toads just can't live inside rocks. Nothing could. No air. No sustenance." Speaking of sustenance, I offered him a pull on my hip flask. Keith accepted, then said:

"But these miners here—they don't claim to have found a toad exactly, now, do they?" He was watching my face narrowly all the while through a pall of cigar smoke, gauging my reactions.

"No sir. They say they've found a whoosit."

"A whoosit."

"Exactly that. A whoosit, just like P.T. Barnum shows on Broadway. A jackalope. A did-you-ever. An allamagoosalum."

"Jersey devil," said Keith, entering into the spirit of the thing.

"Feegee mermaid," I amplified. "Sewn-up mess of spare parts from the taxidermy shop. Catfish with a monkey's head. That's the ticket." I felt pleased we'd nailed the whole business on the head. Maybe we could be back in Washington by this time tomorrow evening.

Keith was nodding still. He showed every sign of agreeing with me, right up until he said—musing aloud it seemed—"So, how does a thing like that get inside a slab of coal, do you suppose, Mr. Fenwick?"

"Well, that's just it. It doesn't, sir." Had I not made myself clear?

"But this one did." His deep-set eyes bored into me, but I held my ground.

"So they say. I guess we'll see for ourselves in the morning, sir."

Unexpectedly, Keith dropped me a wink. "The hell with that. I was thinking we might take a stroll down to the courthouse after dinner and save ourselves a night of playing guessing games. Skip all the foofaraw the mayor's got planned. That is, unless you have plans for the rest of the evening?" A wave of his cigar over sleepy downtown Oram.

I spread my hands, palms up. "What do you know? Clara Bow just phoned to say she couldn't make it."

And so, in the absence of Miss Bow's company, I found myself walking out down the main street of Oram with Horton Keith, headed for the courthouse. We'd passed it in the mayor's car earlier that afternoon; Kronke had told us that was where the whoosit was being kept, under lock and key and guarded by his best men. If the man who was on duty out front when we arrived was one of Kronke's best, then I'd have loved to have seen the ones he was keeping in reserve. He was a dried-up, knock-kneed old codger with hardly a tooth left in his head, and when Keith told him we were the men from Washington come to see the whoosit, he waved us right through. "In there," he said, without bothering to get up off his rocking chair. "What there is of it, anyways."

"What there is of it?" Keith's heavy brows came down.

"Feller who found it, Lamar Tibbs? Had him a dispute with the mine bosses when he brung it up last week. They said, any coal comes out of this shaft belongs to the company, and that's that. So Lamar, he says well, thisyer freak of nature ain't made of coal though, is it? Blind man can see that. And they say, naw, it ain't. And Lamar, he says, it's more in the nature of an animal, ain't it? And they say, reckon so. And Lamar says, well, I take about a thousand cooties home out of this damn pit of yours ever' day, so I reckon this big cootie here can come along for the ride as well. And he up an took it home with 'im." The caretaker cackled with senile glee at Lamar's inexorable logic. I guess it was a rare thing for anybody to get the better of the company, let alone some poor working stiff. But more to the point:

"You're saying the whoosit isn't actually in there?"

"No sir. It's over to Peck's Ridge, up at the Tibbs place. Mayor's plannin' to take you there in the automobile tomorrow, I believe—first thing after the grand civic breakfast."

This was starting to look like a snipe hunt we'd been sent on. Keith jabbed his cigar butt at the courthouse. "So what *have* you got in here?"

"Lump o' coal it came out of," said the caretaker proudly. "Got an exact imprint of the whoosit in it, see? Turn it to the light, you can see everything. Large as life, twice as ugly."

"Is that right?" Keith said. "Company hung on to the lump of coal, I guess?"

"That they did," agreed the last surviving veteran of the Confederate army. "All the coal comes out of that mine's company coal—them's the rules. Mayor's just holdin' it for safekeeping, is all."

"Exactly so," said Keith. "Well, thank you, sir." He slipped a dollar into the caretaker's eager hand—assuming it was eagerness that made it tremble so. "Now if you could see your way to showing us where they're keeping it, we'll quit bothering you."

"They got it in the basement," said the caretaker, leaning back in his rocker and expelling a gob of tobacco juice. "Keep goin' down till you can't go down no more, mister, an' that'll do it."

The basement of that courthouse was like a mine itself; you might almost have believed they'd dug the whoosit out right there, in situ. Keith and I came to the bottom of a winding flight of stairs and found ourselves in a musty sort of crawlspace, its farther corners filled with shadows the single electric bulb on the ceiling couldn't hope to reach. The ceiling was low enough that we both had to stoop a little, and most of the floor was taken up with trunks and boxes and filing cabinets full of junk. Thank God we weren't looking for anything smaller than a pork barrel. We'd have been down there all night. As it was, we began on opposite sides of the basement and aimed to get the job done in something under an hour.

"This is annoying," Keith called over his shoulder. "These damn rubes don't realize what they've got a hold of here."

"Toad in a hole," I called back. Keith ignored me.

"This miner fellow—"

"Lamar Tibbs," I sang out in a poor approximation of the caretaker's Virginian twang.

"—he probably thinks he's sitting on a crock of gold, just like the mayor here and the mining company with their slab of coal. But the two things *apart* don't amount to a hill of beans, and they don't have the sense to see it."

"How so?" I didn't think the whole thing amounted to much, myself.

"Because the one authenticates the other, don't you see? Look here, I'm the authorities, okay? This here's some sort of a strange beast you claim to have found in the middle of a piece of coal. Who's to say it's not a, a, what-d'ye-call-'em—"

"Feegee mermaid."

"Feegee mermaid, exactly." A grunt, as he moved some heavy piece of trash out of the way. "Nothing to make a man suppose it ever saw the inside of a slab of coal—*without the coal to prove it*. The imprint of the beast in the coal goes to corroborate the story, see?"

"Yes, but—" I was going to point out that you didn't find beasts, living or dead, inside slabs of coal anyway, so there was no story there to corroborate, only a tall tale out of backwoods West Virginia. But Keith didn't seem to be interested in that self-evident proposition.

"And it's the same thing with the coal. Suppose there is an imprint of something in there? What good is it without the very thing that *made* that imprint? It's just the work of an few weekends for an amateur sculptor, is all." He bent to his task again, shoving more packing cases out of the way. "They don't understand," he muttered, almost to himself. "You need the two together."

"Even if you did have the two things, though—" I wasn't letting this one go unchallenged—"it still wouldn't prove anything, in and of itself. It might go some way towards the *appearance* of proof—hell, it might even make a good enough story for page eight of the newspaper, I guess. That's your business. I just take the pictures, that's all. But at the end of the day—"

At the end of the day, Keith wasn't listening. I happened to glance in his direction at that moment, and saw as much immediately. He was standing in the far corner of the basement, hands on hips, staring at something on the floor—from where I was, I couldn't make it out. I called his name. I had to call again, and then a third time, before he even noticed. When he did, he looked up with an odd expression on his face.

"Come over here a second, Fenwick," he called, and his voice sounded slightly strained. "Think I've found something."

I crossed to where he was standing. In that corner the light was so dim I could hardly see Keith, let alone whatever it was he'd found, so the first thing we did was lay ahold of it and drag it to the centre of the basement, right beneath the electric bulb. It was heavy as hell, and we pushed it more than carried it across the packed-mud basement floor.

It was lying inside an open packing-case, all wrapped up in a bit of old tarpaulin. You could see the black gleam of coal where Keith had unwrapped it at one end. "You raise it up," muttered Keith, and again I heard that unusual strain in his voice; "I'll get the tarpaulin off of it."

I laid hold of it and heaved it upright, and Keith managed to get the tarp clear. It was just one half of the slab, as it turned out; its facing piece lay underneath wrapped in more tarpaulin. Stood on its end, the half-slab was roughly the size of a high-back dining chair: it would have weighed a lot more, more than we could have dreamed of shifting, probably, except that it was all hollowed out, as if someone had sawn a barrel in half right down its centre.

The hollow space was nothing more than an inky pool of shadow at first, till I tilted the slab toward the light. Then, its shiny black surfaces gave up their secrets, and the electric light reflected off a wealth of curious detail. I gave a low whistle. Whoever's work this was, he was wasted on Oram. He ought to have been knocking out statues for the Pope in Rome. For it was the finest, most intricately detailed job of carving you ever saw—*intaglio*, I believe they call it, where the sculptor carves in hollows instead of relief. There was even a kind of *trompe l'oeil* effect: if you looked at the cavity while turning the whole thing round slightly, the contours seemed to stand out in projection, that strange hollow form suddenly becoming filled-out and real. I'd have to say it was actually a little bit unsettling, for a cheap optical illusion. It was as if you were looking at the sky at night, the black gulf of space, and the stars all of a sudden took on a shape, the shape of something vast and unimaginable . . .

"My God." A fellow would have been hard put to recognise Keith's voice. It made me turn from the slab of coal to look at him. He was staring open-mouthed at the hollow space at the heart of the slab, with an expression I took at first to be awe. Only later did I come to recognize it as something more like horror.

"It's pretty good at that," I allowed. "The detail . . . "

"It's exact in every detail," said Keith, in wonderment. "You could use it for a mold, and you'd cast yourself a perfect copy." He shook his head, never taking his eyes off of the coal slab.

"Copy of what, though?" I squinted at the concavity, turned it this way and that to get a sense of it in three dimensions. "It's like nothing I've ever seen—it's a regular whoosit, all right. Are those things supposed to be tentacles, there? Only they've got claws on the end, or nippers or something. And where's its head supposed to be?"

"The head retracts," said Keith, almost as if he was reading it from a book. "Like a slug drawing in on itself."

I stared at him. "Beg your pardon, sir?"

"You said it's like nothing you've ever seen," said Keith. "Well, I've seen it. Or something exactly like it"

"You *have*?" It was all I could think of to say.

Keith nodded. "Let's get out of this damn mausoleum," he said abruptly, turning away from the packing-case and its contents. "I'll tell you up in the real world, where a man can breathe clean air, not this infernal stink." And with that he turned his back and was off, stumping up the wooden steps and out of the basement, leaving me to rewrap and repack the slab of coal as best I could before hastening after him.

I was full of questions, all of them to do with the strange artifact we'd been looking at. I have to confess, the level of realism the unknown sculptor had managed to suggest had impressed me—not to say unnerved me. I mentioned before the optical illusion of solidity conjured out of the void, that sensation of seeing the actual thing, not just the impression it had made. That actually began to get to you after a while. Three-dimensional, I said? Well, maybe so. But the longer you looked at it, the dimensions started to looked wrong somehow; impossible, you might say.

On top of that was Keith's admission that he'd seen the like before. What did he mean by that? And over and above everything . . . well, Keith was right. We needed to be in the fresh air. Fact was, it stank in that damn basement: I've never known a smell like it. It was as if a bushel of something had gone bad, and been left to fester for an long time.

An awful long time, at that.

· · ·

Back at the hotel Keith went straightaway up to his room for about an hour, leaving me to pick at my evening meal in the all-but-empty dining room. The smell down in that basement had killed my appetite, pretty much; in the end I pushed my plate aside and went to the smoking lounge. That was where Keith found me.

He looked better than he had back outside the courthouse, at least. I'd found him leaning against the side of the building, looking as if he was going to be sick: he had that gray clammy cast to his face. I asked him was he all right, and he waved me away. Now, there was a little more color in him, and his eyes were focusing properly again, not staring off into the middle distance the way they do when a fellow is on the verge of losing his lunch.

"You got any of that brandy left?" he said, taking the chair opposite mine. "Medicinal purposes, you understand."

"You're in luck, as it happens," I said, offering him the flask. "I've just taken an inventory of our medical supplies."

"Good," said Keith, and took a long swallow. His eyes teared up a little, but that was only natural. It had kind of a kick to it, that bathtub Napoleon. You could have used it to open a safe, if you'd run out of blasting gelignite.

"Well, then." Keith handed me back the flask. "I believe I owe you a story, Mr. Fenwick. Recompense for leaving you with the baby, down there in the basement."

I waved a hand, which could equally be taken to mean, *no problem, don't trouble yourself about it,* or—as I hoped Keith would read it—*Go on, go on, you interest me strangely.* The reason I waved a hand instead of actually saying either of those things was because I'd just taken a pull on that flask myself, and was temporarily speechless.

Keith settled back in his armchair and crossed his long thin legs. "It might help explain why I took this assignment," he said, throwing me a cigar and lighting one himself, "why I asked for it." He puffed on his stogie till it was properly lit, sending up a wreath of smoke above his head. Then from the heart of that smokescreen he told me the following tale, in about the time it took us to reduce those big Havanas down to ash.

"I was thirty at the time: a dangerous age, Mr. Fenwick. You'll learn that, soon enough. I was working on the *Examiner* in San Francisco when gold fever hit up in the Yukon, back in '98. The news came at exactly the right time, so far as I was concerned—a lot of other folks too, among that first wave of prospectors and adventurers. I was missing something, we all were: the frontier had been closed, and the wild days of excitement out West were history, or so it seemed.

For better or worse, the job of shaping the nation was finished, over and done with, and us latecomers had missed the chance to leave our stamp on it. We felt as if we'd all been running West in search of something—something magical and unique, that would make real men out of us—only once we'd gotten there, it had already set sail out of the Golden Gate, and there was no way we could follow. The Gay Nineties, you say? I tell you, there were folks dying in the street in San Francisco. Hunger, want . . . maybe nothing more than heartbreak.

"So you can bet we jumped at the chance to go prospecting, away up in the frozen wastes. That was a new frontier, sure enough: maybe the last frontier, and we weren't about to miss it. And we piled on to those coffin-ships out of Frisco and Seattle, hundreds of us at a time; stampeders, we called ourselves. There was about as much thinking went into it as goes into a stampede.

"The Canucks wouldn't let you into the country totally unprepared, though. You had to have a ton of goods, supplies and suchlike, else they'd stop you at the docks. And that took some getting together; eleven hundred pounds of food, plus clothing and equipment, horses to carry it with, that sort of thing. I was travelling light—reckoned to hire sled-dogs up in Canada—but even so, my goods took some lugging at the wharf.

"So we sailed North. A thousand miles out of Seattle we made the Lynn Canal, which was where every one of us bold prospectors had to make his first big decision. Where was he going to disembark? 'Cause there were two trails, see, up to Dawson and the goldfields, six hundred miles due north. You could take the easy route, avoiding all the big mountains—that was Skagway and the White Pass. The other route started in Dyea, and it took in the Chilkoot Pass, leading on to the lakes. Even us greenhorns knew about the Chilkoot by that time.

"A lot of folk chose Skagway, but I never heard anything good about that town. In Indian it's "the place where a fair wind never blows", which pretty much sums it up, I guess. Leave it to the Indians to know which way the wind blows. Soapy Smith's gang ran the town—he was an old-time con artist out of Georgia, and he knew a hundred ways to pick the pockets of every rube that staggered down the gangplank. Twenty-five cents a day wharf rates on each separate piece of goods. Lodging-houses where they fleeced you on the way in and the way out. Saloons and whorehouses; casinos with rigged wheels and marked cards. Portage fees. Tolls all the way along the trail—and bandits too, armed gangs and desperadoes, hand in glove with the 'official escorts,' like as not. No sir: I chose Dyea, which was not a hell of a lot more salubrious, but at least you didn't have Soapy's hand in your britches all the while.

There was ice all over the boat as it hove into Dyea. It looked like a ghost ship, and I guess we were a sorry-enough looking bunch of ghosts as we stumbled off. The mountains came right down to the outskirts of town; took us two weeks of hard going to climb as far as Sheep Camp, at the base of the Chilkoot. I tell you: there were lots of men took one look at that mountainside and gave it up on the spot, stayed on in camp and made a living for themselves as best they could. You couldn't call them the stupid ones, not really. A thousand feet from base to summit, sheer up and down, straight as a beggar can spit? Any sane man would have tuned round and said 'scuse me, my mistake, beg your pardon.

"We were obliged to stay in Sheep Camp for the best part of March, till the pass came navigable. Bad weather, and the worst kind of terrain; even the Indian guides wouldn't touch it in those conditions. It was just before spring thaw, and the weather was ornery in the extreme. Minus sixty-five one night, by the thermometer in Lobelski's General Store. It stayed light from nine-thirty in the morning to just before four in the afternoon. The rest of it was pitch dark and endless cold.

"They were building some sort of a hoisting-gear up the Chilkoot, the tramway they called it, but I never saw it finished. I hauled my goods up there, the old fashioned way. I could have paid the Indians to do it for me, a dollar a pound, but I didn't have two thousand dollars to spare. That was why I was bound for the Yukon in the first place. So I hauled every last case up that mountain side, forty trips in all. I was raw from the chafing of the ropes on my shoulders, and I was nigh on crippled by the exhaustion and the cold—but I managed it. Somehow. Don't ask me how. It'd kill me now if I tried it.

"Truth is, I don't know how it didn't kill me back then. Fifteen hundred toeholds in the ice, up a trail no more than two feet wide. Take a step to left and right, and you were in the powder stuff, loose and treacherous. If a man slipped, it was all up with him; you never saw him again. That pass was filled with the bodies of good men.

"Anyway! Come April I was over the Chilkoot and heading toward Dawson, a mere five hundred and fifty miles off. The trail led along Lake Lindeman and Lake Bennett: if you waited for the thaw, the sheer volume of melt coming down off the mountains turned the rivers into rapids. If you went early, like I did, it was just a question of praying the ice wouldn't break. You put it out of your mind, till it came time to camp at night and you'd hear the ice creaking and groaning below you. We rigged up the sleds with sails, and the wind used to push us along at a fine clip. All we had to do was trust in the Lord and watch out for the cracks.

"The lakes weren't properly clear of ice till the end of May, and by that time we bold sled-skaters were already in Dawson, just six months after we'd first set out to strike it rich. Dawson was a stumpy, scroungy kind of town at the bend of the river, set on mudflats and made of nothing much but mud, or so it seemed. Five hundred people lived there as a rule: gold fever pushed that up to twelve thousand by the start of the year, thirty thousand by that summer's end. It was a breeding ground for typhoid—I stayed clear of the place, except when I made my victualling run once a week.

"I was working my claim south-east of Dawson city, out among the dried-up river beds. That was where I got my crash-course in mining—a year earlier, I'd have thought you just scuffed around in the dirt with the toe of your boot till you turned up some nuggets. Not in Yukon territory. You had to dig your way down to the pastry, we called it, the layers where the gold lay, through forty, fifty feet of rock and frost-hard river muck; tough going? Yes, sir. You broke your back on nothing more than a hunch and a hope. Besides that, all you had was the comradeship of your fellows and the one chance in a hundred thousand your claim would pay out big. I almost came to value the one more than the other, because when the chips were down you could rely on the comradeship at least. Money ain't everything, not in those latitudes. Maybe not in these.

"All through that summer I dug away in the dried-up beds, till it came autumn, and time to make another big decision. The last boat out of Dawson sailed on September the sixteenth, and a lot of fellows I knew were on it, the ones who'd struck it rich and the ones who'd simply had enough. I didn't fall into either camp: I waved that boat away from the landing, and made my plans to stay on through the winter. Plenty did: the proud and foolish ones like me, who couldn't quite bring themselves to admit defeat and go home with only a few grains of gold in their pokes; the optimists, who couldn't believe that the best was over, that the juicy lodes were already worked out and the rest only dry holes; and worst of all the hard core, the ones who'd caught it worst of all, who had no place left for them back in the real world. Quite a bunch.

"I remember one evening in that October of '98, standing up on the banks outside my camp and looking out over the dry gulches. Some of the fellows were burning fires at their workings, trying to melt the frost so the digging would go easier. It lit up all that strange and beautiful landscape like the surface of some alien planet, the fires like lanterns shining out in the gloom, and the way the wood smoke smell drifted up across the bluffs . . . I could have stayed there for the rest of my life, or so I told myself. I sat and watched those fires till it got full dark, anyway, and later on that night I saw the aurora for the first time, the Northern lights, how they flickered green and magical in the moonless sky.

"The week after, it began to snow for real, and I had to strike camp and head back for Dawson. Some didn't; some stayed out on the flats, and that's where the story really begins.

"I must've been back in Dawson a couple of months, because it was nigh on Christmas when we got word from out on the workings that they'd found something strange—not gold, which would have been strange enough by that time, but something weird, something the likes of which nobody had ever seen. At least, that's what Sam Tibbets told us, when he come in to Dawson for supplies. It was the three Tibbets brothers worked the claim, along with a half-dozen other fellows all hailed from Maine: they were a syndicate, all for one and one for all. They hadn't found a lot of gold—hardly enough for one man to retire on, let alone nine—but Sam reckoned if the worst came to the worst, they could always go into the exhibition business with this thing they'd dug up out of the frost. 'It's a new wonder of the world, or maybe the oldest one of all,' I can hear him saying it, hunkered down by the stove in the saloon with the frost melting in his mustache and the steam rising off his coat; 'I reckon it must 'a turned up late for last boarding on the ark, or else Noah threw it overboard on account of its looks.'

" 'What d'you mean?' I asked him.

" 'Aw, Horton, you never saw such a cretur as this,' he said earnestly—he was straight-ahead and simple, was Sam Tibbets. He was one of the original ice-skaters from back on the lakes in the spring: I liked him a lot. 'It's like a plug-ugly dried-up old thing the size of one of them barrels there—' he pointed at a hogshead in the corner—'and about that same shape, 'cept maybe it comes to sort of a narrow place up top. It's got long thin arms, only dozens of 'em, all around, and there's nippers on the end, same as a lobster? I swear there ain't never been such a confusion. Wait till we haul it back out of here, come the thaw. They'll pay a dime a head back in Frisco just to clap eyes on it, I tell you!'

"It was a plan at that, and if nothing else it made me mighty curious to take a look at this thing, whatever it was. The way Sam told it, they'd been digging through the frozen subsoil when they turned it up: he thought it must have gotten caught in the river away back, stuck in the mud and froze up when the winter came. How deep was it, I asked him, thinking the deeper it lay, the older it must be; 'bout twenty feet, he reckoned.

" 'So it's dead, then, this thing?' That was Cy Perrette, who was not the smartest man in the Yukon territory, not by a long chalk. He was staring at Sam Tibbets like a dog listening to a sermon.

" 'It better be,' said Sam. 'It's been buried in the earth since Abraham got promoted to his first pair of long pants, ain't it?' Men started laughing all through the saloon, and pretty soon Sam had a line of drinks set down before him. Dawson folks appreciated a good tale, see: something to take their minds off the cold and dark outside, and the endless howling winds. I remember the aurora was particularly strong that night; when I staggered out of the saloon and the cold knocked me sober, there it was, fold upon fold, glowing and rippling from horizon to horizon. I remember thinking, that's what folk mean when they say 'unearthly.' Something definitely not of this planet, something more to do with the heavens than the earth.

"Come morning there was quite a little gang of us, all bent on following Sam Tibbets back to his camp for a look-see at the eighth wonder. Sam was agreeable, said he'd waive our admission fees just this once, on account of the circumstances, and we set off towards the workings. It was a cheerful excursion; the sleds were always lighter when you had company along the trail.

"Sam broke into a run when we reached the banks of the river bed; wanted to welcome us to the site of their discovery, I suppose, like any showman would. He clambered up a snowdrift; then, when he reached the top, he stopped, and even from down below I thought he looked confused. He let go his sled; it slithered down the bank and I had to look sharp, else it'd have taken me off at the shins. 'Sam!' I called him, but he didn't look round. I scrambled up after him, cussing him for a clumsy oaf and the rest of it; then I saw what he'd seen, and the words got choked off in my throat.

"Straight away you could see something was wrong. Sam and his partners had built themselves a cabin by the workings, nothing fancy, but solid enough to take whatever the Yukon winter could throw at it, they'd thought. Now, one end of that cabin was shivered all to pieces. The logs were snapped and splintered into matchwood, just exactly as if someone had fired a cannonball at it. Only the cannon would have had to be on the inside of the cabin, not the outside: there was wreckage laying on the ground for a considerable distance, all radiating out and away from the stoved-in part.

"That wasn't the worst part, though. In amongst the wreckage you could see the snow stained red, and there was at least one body mixed in with the blown-out timber. I saw it straight away; I know Sam had too, because he turned around and looked at me as I grabbed his arm, and I could hear this high sort of keening noise he was making, like some kind of machine that's slipped its gears, about to break itself to pieces. It was the purest, most fundamental sound of grief I'd ever heard coming out of a human being. I've never forgotten it to this day.

"My first thought as we began running down the banks was: dynamite. Plenty of the miners used it to start off an excavation, or to clear whatever obstructions they couldn't dig around. It wasn't unusual for a camp such as this to have a few sticks laying around in case of emergencies. Now, if you got careless . . . ? You understand what I'm saying. That was my first assumption, anyway. It lasted until I got in amongst the wreckage.

"Dynamite couldn't account for it, was all. It couldn't have left cups and bottles standing on the table, and still blown a hole in the cabin wall big enough to drive a piled-up dogsled through. It wouldn't have left a man's body intact inside its clothes, and taken his head clean off at the neck. And it couldn't have done to that head . . . the things I saw done to the head of poor Bob Gendreau. Put it this way: my second assumption was bears; them, or some other wild animal. Bears roused too soon from their hibernation, hungry and enraged, coming on the camp and smashing it all to pieces. But again, when you looked at all the evidence, that didn't sit right either.

"There was a side of bacon hanging on the wall still; bears would have taken that. And they wouldn't have stopped at knocking off the head of Bob Gendreau; that's not where the sustenance lies, and all a bear ever looks for is sustenance. Whatever took Bob's head off, then mauled it so his own mother wouldn't have known it; that thing wasn't doing what it did out of blind animal instinct, nor yet the need for nourishment. That thing was doing what it did because it wanted to—because it liked it, maybe. Some say man is the lord of all creation because he's the only creature blessed with reason; others, that he's set apart from the rest of the beasts because he takes pleasure in killing, and there's no other animal does that. But up in that cabin I learned different. Now, I believe there's at least one other creature on this planet that draws satisfaction from its kills, and not just a square meal. I got my first inkling of that when I saw what was left of Harvey Tibbets.

"He was jammed into an unravaged corner of the cabin. It looked as if he'd been trying to dig clean through the packed-mud floor; there was a hole in the ground at his feet, and his fingers were all bloodied and torn. You could see that, because of the way he was laying; hunkered down on his haunches, facing out towards the room, for all the world like a Moslem when he prays to Mecca. His forehead was touching the earth, and his arms were stretched out before him. His hands were clenched in the dirt, still clutching two last handfuls of it even in death. There was no mistaking his attitude: he'd been grovelling before whatever had passed through that cabin. Begging it for mercy.

"And whatever it was had looked down upon him as he crouched there; listened to his screams, I guess. And had it granted him mercy? I don't know. I can't speak as to its motivations. What it *had* done, was sever both his hands, cut 'em clear off at the wrists. Remember before, when I said he appeared to have been digging in the dirt, trying to escape? Both his hands were still there, torn-up and bloody like I said. And he was kneeling down with his arms outstretched; you remember that. But in between the stumps at the end of his forearms and the tattered beginnings of his wrists, there was nothing but a foot of blood-soaked earth. Whatever had killed him had cut off both his hands, and watched him bleed out on the floor while he begged it for leniency. Now what sort of a creature does that sound like to you?

"Indians, was what some of the men thought; Indians touched with the wendigo madness. But how could any man, crazy or sane, have knocked an entire gable end out of the cabin that way? There was an Indian with us, one of the *portageurs*, a quiet, dark-complected fellow named Jake: he wouldn't come within ten yards of the devastation, but he told me it wasn't any of his kin. 'Not yours either,' he said after a pause, and I asked him what he meant by it.

"He took me aside and pointed in the snow. There was a mess of our prints, converging on the cabin so that the ground outside the blasted-out place was practically trampled bare. All around the snow was practically virgin still, and Jake showed me the only thing that sullied it. A single set of tracks, leading from the cabin and headed away north, down along the gulch. I say leading from the cabin, mostly because there wasn't anything in the cabin could have made those prints, living or dead. If it wasn't for that, then I don't know that I could have told you what direction whatever made the prints was traveling in. They weren't regular footmarks, you see, and they were all wrong in their shape, in their arrangement—in their number, even. And the weirdest thing about them? They stopped dead about fifty yards out. A step, then another, then nothing but the undisturbed snow, as far as the eye could see.

"Later on, once the shock of it had passed, I asked Jake what could have made those prints, and he told me an old legend of his people, about the time before men walked these northern wastes, when it was just gods and trolls and ogres.

"Back then, he said, there were beings come down from the sky, and they laid claim to the Earth for a long season of destruction. They were like pariahs between the stars, these beings: not even the Old Ones, the gods without a worshipper, could bear to have them near. They were cast out in the end, as well as the Old Ones could manage it: but the story goes that some of them escaped exile by burrowing down into the earth and waiting their time, till some cataclysm of the planet might uncover them. They could wait: nothing on Earth could kill them, you see. They couldn't die in this dimension. They would only sleep, through geologic ages of the planet, till something disturbed them and they came to light once more.

"That was the legend: I got it out of Jake later that same day, when the party had split up and we were searching all the low land around the arroyo. The mood of the party was shocked and unforgiving: something had done this to our friends, and we were bound to avenge them the best we could. The trail of footprints had given some of the fellows pause for thought, but I think most of them just took the prints as simple evidence of something they could go after, some critter they could corner and shoot. They didn't reflect too much on what could have made them. If they'd stopped and thought it through, I doubt whether any one of them would have been prepared to do what we ended up doing that night: lying in ambush and waiting for the culprit to come back to the cabin.

"The reasoning—so far as it went—was, if it's an animal, it'll come back where there's food. If it's a man, it'll come back because that's what murderers do: revisit the scene of the crime. Pretty shaky logic, I know, but the blood of the party was up. We were really just looking for trouble, and we damn near found it, too.

"As night fell we set up an ambuscade in the ruins of the cabin. We'd buried the bodies by then, of course, but inside the cabin still felt bad; stank, too, like something had lain dead in there all through the summer, and not just a few hours in the bitter icy cold. We had the stove going: we had to, else we'd have froze to death. We had guards at all the windows, and a barricade at the wrecked end of the cabin. It didn't matter what direction trouble might be coming at us from, we had it covered. Or so we thought.

"God, we were so cold! The wind died down soon after dark, and that probably saved us all from the hypothermia. Still it was like a knife going through you, that chill, and you had to get up and move around every so often, just to prove to yourself you were still alive. We passed around a bottle of whiskey we found among the untouched provisions, and waited.

"All across the wide northern sky there was a glow, cold and mysterious, as far removed as you could imagine from the world of men and their paltry little hopes and fears. The aurora was so vivid that night, you might have read a newspaper by it. All the better to see whatever's coming, we thought; at least it can't creep up on us and take us unawares, not in this light.

"Somewhere in the very pit of the night, just when the body's at its weariest and wants only to drop down and sleep, an uncanny sort of stillness fell across the snowed-up river bed. What was left of the wind dropped entirely, and the only sound beneath the frozen far-off stars seemed to come from the creaking of the stove round which we sat, the cracking and spitting of the logs that burned inside it. A few of us looked round at each other; all of us felt it now, the heightened expectation, the heightened fear. Without words, as quietly as we could, we moved away from the stove and took up our places at the barricade.

"I remember—so clearly!—how it felt, crouching behind that mess of planks and packing-cases, waiting to see what might show its head above the snow-banks. A couple of times I thought I saw something, away out beyond the bounds of night vision. Even under the greenish radiance of the aurora I couldn't be sure: *was* that something moving? *Could* it be? One time Joe McRudd discharged his rifle, and scared us all to hell. 'Sorry,' he mouthed, when we'd all regained our senses. He cleared his throat. 'Thought I saw sump'n creepin' round out there.'

" 'Save your ammo,' grunted Sam Tibbets, not even bothering to look at poor Joe. 'Keep your nerve.' That was all. Directly after that it was upon us.

"It came from the only direction we hadn't reckoned on: overhead. There was a thump on the roof of the cabin, and then a splintering as the boards were wrenched off directly above our heads. It caused a general confusion: everyone jumped and panicked, and no one really knew what was happening. Joe McRudd's rifle went off again; some of the other fellows shot as well, I don't know what at. Before I could react, Sam Tibbets was snatched up from alongside me—something had him fast around the head and was dragging him off of his feet, up towards the hole in the roof.

"I grabbed him around the waist, but it was no use: I felt my own feet lifting clear of the floor as Sam was hoisted ever upward. He was trying to call out, but whatever had snatched him was laying tight hold around the whole of his head and neck, and all I could hear was a muffled roar of anger and pain—fear, too, I guess. It was as if he was being lynched, hung off a high bough and left to swing there while he throttled. I called to the rest of them to help, to hang on to us: a couple of them laid ahold of my legs and heaved, and for a moment we thought we had him. Then there came an awful sound, like something out of a butcher's shop, and suddenly we were all sprawled on the floor of the cabin, with Sam Tibbets' headless body lying dead weight on top of us.

"I don't remember exactly how the next few seconds panned out. All I remember was being soaked with Sam's blood: the heat of it, the force with which it gushed from his truncated neck, the bitter metallic stink. The fellows told me afterwards that I was screaming like a banshee on my hands and knees, but I know I wasn't the only one. Jake the Indian brought me out of it: he dragged me away from the shambles in the middle of the room and slapped me a couple times till I quit bawling. As if coming round from a dream I goggled at him slack-mouthed; then I came to myself in a dreadful sort of recollection. Before he could stop me, I'd grabbed the big hunting-knife from its sheath at his waist and pushed him out of the way.

"By climbing up on top of the hot stove, I just about managed to reach the hole in the roof. I had Jake's knife between my teeth like the last of the Mohicans; I was covered all over in Sam Tibbets' blood, and I was filled with the urge to vengeance, nothing else. I hoisted myself up so my head and shoulders were through the hole. With my elbows planted on the snow-covered shingles, I looked around.

"It was crouched by the farther end of the roof like a big old sack of guts, mumbling on something. Sam's head. I made some sort of a noise, and it looked up: I mean, the thick squabby part on top of it suddenly grew long like an elephant's trunk, and one furious red eye glared out at me from its tip. The noise it made: good God, I never heard the like. It damn near deafened me, even out in the open; it went ringing through my head like the last trump.

"Some part of its belly opened itself up, and Sam Tibbets' head was gone with a terrible sucking crunch. Then all those tentacles that fringed the trunk suddenly came to life, writhing and flailing like a stinging jellyfish. One of them caught in my clothing—I slashed out at it with Jake's knife, but I might as well have tried to cut a steel hawser. It had me fast; it was like being caught in a death-hold. The thing let rip a revolting sort of belch, and started to haul me in, and I had just enough time to feel the entire sum of my courage vanish in a wink as fear, total and absolute, rushed in to fill up every inch of my being. It's a hell of a thing, to lose all self-respect that way: to know that the last thing you'll feel before death is nothing but abject, craven panic. God, let me die like a man, I prayed, as the thing dragged me up out of the hole towards its gulping maw—that glaring gorgon's eye—

"It was Jake down below contrived to save my life. He grabbed me by the ankles and swung on them like a church bell, and there came a sharp rip as my coat came to pieces at the seams. It didn't have proper hold of me, only by the fabric, you see: that was what saved me, that and the Chinee tailor back in San Francisco who'd scrimped on the thread when he put that old pea-coat together. I went sliding back through the hole on the roof, while the thing struggled to regain its balance on the icy shingles. It let out another of those blood-freezing hollers, and then I was laying on top of Jake, in amidst all of the blood and the panic down below.

"All of the breath had gotten knocked out of me by the fall, and the same for Jake, who was underneath me, remember. The two of us were pretty much hors de combat for a while; plus, I dare say I wouldn't have been much use even with breath in my lungs, not after the jolt I'd took up on the roof. I was aware that the rest of the fellows were running round like crazy, firing into the rafters and yelling fit to raise Cain. For myself, right then, I figured old Harvey Tibbets'd had the best idea, digging himself a hole—or trying to. I knew if it wanted to come down and try conclusions, we none of us stood a chance in hell, guns or no guns. I thought it was all up with us still, and to this day I don't know why it wasn't.

"Because after a while, in amongst all the raving and the letting-off of guns and the war-whoops and hollers and what have you, it gradually dawned on the fellows that there was no movement from up on the roof. Nothing coming through the hole at us, no fresh attack; no sound of creaking timbers, even— though I doubt we'd have heard it, we were making so much noise ourselves. In the end a couple of men ran outside to look up on the roof: nothing there, they yelled, and I thought to myself, no, of course not. It won't show itself so easy. I figured it had only gone to earth for a while, that it would pick us off one by one when we weren't expecting it.

"Then one of them happened to look upwards—I mean straight up, towards the sky. What he saw up there made him let out such a shout, it brought us all out of that broke-up shambles of a cabin. We joined him out in the snow: I remember us all standing there, staring up into the heavens as if God in all his glory was coming down and the final judgement was upon us.

"Silhouetted against the wraithlike flux of the aurora, the thing was ascending into the night sky. It had wings, but they didn't seem to be lifting it, or even bearing its weight; it was as if it simply rose through the air the way a jellyfish rises through the water. That sound—that terrible piercing howl—echoed all across the wide expanse of the landscape, from mountain to lake shore, through all the sleeping trees, and I swear every beast that heard it must have trembled in its lair; must have whined and cowered and crept to the back of its cave and prayed to whatever rough gods had made it, *Lord, let this danger pass.*

"Up it rose, till we could hardly make it out against the green-wreathed stars. Then, there came one last throb of phosphorescence, bright as day—and it was as if a circuit burned out, somewhere in the sky. The aurora vanished, simple as that; and in the brief interval while our eyes adjusted to the paler starlight, I believe we all screamed, like children pitched headlong into the dark.

"As soon as we could see what we were doing again, we lost no time in getting out of that hateful place. Without waiting to bury our dead—poor Sam Tibbets—we beat a retreat back to Dawson, and there was never a band of pilgrims more relieved to see the sun come up. It shone off the frozen river in bright clean rainbows of ice; it showed us the dirty old log cabins we called home, and we wept with joy at the sight. Exhausted as I was, and scared too, and bewildered at all I'd seen, I believed we might be safe at last. Until the night came; that first night, and all the other nights that followed through that long Canadian winter.

"The nights were bad, you see. I took to sleeping in the daytime, when I could, and once it got dark I'd sit with Jake and the rest of the men in a private room at the back of one of the saloons, playing cards and drinking through to sun-up, very deliberately not talking about what we'd been through that evening. I was never really any good after that; not till I made it out of Dawson with the first thaw. Another season of that, and I'd have ended up a rummy in the streets of Skagway, telling tall tales for the price of a pint of hooch. Some of the men had heard of a fresh strike in Alaska, up on the shale banks at Nome— me, I'd lost heart, and could only think of getting home to San Francisco, where such things as we'd seen up on the roof of the cabin couldn't be. Or that's what I thought back then. What do *you* think, Mr. Fenwick?"

For a second I thought he just wanted me to pass judgment on his tale—to say *yes, I believe you*, or *hold on a minute, are you sure about that?* Then I realized the import of his words. "You mean that thing down in the basement, don't you?" I said, slowly, almost reluctantly, and he nodded. I opened my mouth, but nothing came out, and after a moment or two I shut it again.

"It looks every inch a match," Keith said, through his hands. He sighed, and leaned back in his chair, staring up at the nicotine-yellow ceiling. "It was like some sort of damnable optical illusion—didn't you get that?—the longer you looked at that black void, the more it seemed as if the creature was projected into the empty space." With hands that trembled hardly at all, he lit up another cigar.

"A thing can't come to life after so long," I asserted, without a fraction of the confidence that had illuminated Keith's entire narrative. "Nothing of this earth—" and there I stopped, remembering what the Indian Jake had had to say on that subject.

"—Could last so long trapped inside a layer of coal," finished Keith, helpfully. "It's bituminous coal hereabouts; laid down during the Carboniferous age. That's, what? Three hundred million years ago, give or take a few million. Imagine the world back then, Fenwick: the way it looked, the way things were all across the land. Dense humid forests; sodden bogs and peat swamps. The stink of rot, of decomposition; of new life forming, down amongst the muck and the decay. The first creatures had just crawled up out of the warm slimy seas, lizards and snails and mollusks, is all. Trilobites and dragonflies. Nothing much bigger than a crawdad. And then *they* arrived.

"God, they would have been lords of the earth, Fenwick! They could still be now, if—" He broke off, and his hands went once more to his thin eager face. "If enough of them got turned up." His voice was muffled somewhat, but in another way it was remarkably clear—clear-headed, at least.

"Three hundred million years." I was having trouble with the concept—you could say that. Yes, you could certainly say that the concept was troubling me. "You're saying that a thing—a thing—"

"Not of this earth," put in Keith helpfully.

"Whatever—could keep alive for so long, under such incredible pressure; no air, no sustenance . . . why, it's fantastic."

"It's fantastic, all right," said Keith, and for the first time there was a hint of impatience in his deep even voice. "I thought I made it clear this wasn't a tale you'd hear every day. But look at the facts. These miners here—they didn't find a fossil, a chunk of rock! No more than the Tibbets found a fossil up there in the Klondike. Set aside your preconceptions, Fenwick. I had to. Look at the facts."

"That's just what I aim to do," I said. "Tomorrow, when we get a look at this damn stupid whoosit of theirs."

And on that note, though with a deal more talk thereafter, we agreed to leave it; and I went up to bed with a head full of questions and misgivings. The brandy helped me get off to sleep, in the end. If I dreamed, I'm glad to say I don't remember it. And in any case—

There are many less-than-pleasant ways to be woken from even the most fitful of slumbers, I guess: but let the voice of experience assure you that there's no more absolute way of rousing a fellow than the sound of a monstrous siren going off in what sounds like the next room down the corridor. I was practically thrown out of bed and into the corridor, where I bumped into Keith. He was already dressed; or more probably hadn't been to bed yet.

"Accident at the mine," I croaked. By this time I'd managed to remember where the hell I was, or just about.

"Maybe," was all Keith would say. "Get your pants on, newspaperman."

By the time we made it out into the street people were milling around in their nightshirts, asking each other was there trouble up to the mine. For a while no one seemed to know, and everyone expected the worst; then, we saw the Mayor's Ford barreling down main street, and Keith practically flung himself in the way of it. Before Kronke or any of his stooges could complain, we were scrambling into the rumble seat and pumping them for information.

"Had us a report of some trouble, up on Peck's Ridge," was all Kronke would say. He looked gray with panic; the flesh practically hung off his face.

"Peck's Ridge?" We'd heard that place name before, of course. "Isn't that where Lamar Tibbs lives?" The mayor didn't answer at first; Keith leaned forwards and gripped his shoulder. "Tibbs? The man who found the creature?"

"Up near there," Kronke said, shaking loose his arm. H tried to regain some of his mayoral authority: "'Tain't rightly speaking none of your business anyways, mister—"

"Drop that," Keith said impatiently. "Drop that straightaway, or else I'll make sure you come across as the biggest hick in all creation when the story makes it into the papers. How's that gonna play with the voters come election time, Mr. Kronke?"

The two men stared angrily at each other, but there was only ever going to be one winner of that contest. After a second Kronke told his chauffeur "Drive on," and we were off, away down main street heading out of town, up into the hill country.

That was some drive, all right. The middle of the night, and not a light showing in all that desolate stretch; only the headlamps of the car on the ribbon of road ahead. Trees crowding close to the track, and between their ghostly lit-up trunks only the blackness of the forest. Overhead, a canopy of branches, and no starlight, no sliver of the moon; it felt as if we were going down into the ground as much as climbing, as if we'd entered some miner's tunnel lined with wooden props, heading clear down to the Carboniferous.

Alongside me on the rumble, Keith sat, hands clenched on the back of the seat in front. He was willing the automobile on, it seemed to me, the way a jockey pushes his horse along in the home straight. His old man's mop of hair showed up very white in the near darkness, but that didn't fool me any: underneath it all was still the dreamer he'd always been and would remain, the thirty-year-old who'd walked out on his safe job with Mr. Hearst and headed up north to the Klondike on nothing more than a notion and a chance. Hero worship? I should say so.

Maybe seven or eight miles out of town, we saw light up ahead: fire. The Ford swung round and down a trail so narrow, the branches plucked at our sleeves and we had to cover our faces from their lash, and then we came out into a natural dip between two high sides of hills, with a farmhouse and outbuildings down the bottom of the hollow. All hell was breaking loose down there.

People were running back and forth between the main house and the outhouses, the farthest of which was well ablaze. You could hear the screams of animals trapped in the sheds; I couldn't be sure there weren't the cries of people in there too.

Before we even came to a halt, an old man in bib overalls came running up, crying out unintelligibly. "Was it you phoned?" Kronke bellowed at him above the tumult. Whether he expected any answer, I don't know. It was clear the fellow was raving mad, for the time being at least. Keith passed him over to Kronke's buddies, who were very pointedly not setting foot outside the automobile, and beckoned me follow him down towards the house. Kronke hung back, unwilling to leave the safety of the car; why he'd even bothered coming out there in the first place was hard to say. Perhaps he thought it was his chance to get the whoosit back, on behalf of the mining company. Perhaps—I think this is not unlikely, myself—perhaps there was always some sort of a trip planned for that night, Kronke and a few men armed with pistols, up to Peck's Ridge on company business. Well, they might have had a chance at that, I guess, had things only panned out just a little differently.

Down by the sheds Keith managed to get a hold of one of the people fighting the fire; a teenager, no more, in a plaid shirt and patched drawers. "What's going on here?" he yelled.

"They're trapped!" the kid hollered back, his eyes round with panic. "Uncle Jesse and Uncle Vern! In there! They were a-watchin' over it!"

"Watching over what?" The kid tried to shake free, but Keith had him tight. "Were they keeping guard? What over?"

"Over Pap's thing!" The kid made to break loose again, without success. "That what Pap found, down to the mine! Lemme go, mister—"

"Your pap Lamar Tibbs?" Keith was implacable. I felt for the youngster, I did. But I wanted to know as well.

The kid nodded, and Keith had one more question. "Where is he?"

"*I don't know!*" screamed the boy. "*I DON'T KNOW!*" Keith was so shocked at the ferocity of it, the sheer volume, that he let him go. The kid stood there for a second, surprised himself I guess, then shook himself all over like a dog coming out of the creek and ran off towards the burning barn. We followed on behind.

Some of the men had formed a chain, and were passing buckets of water up from the pump. The fellows nearest the door were emptying the buckets into the smoke and flames; Keith brushed straight past them and was inside before anyone could stop him. I went to follow him, but one of the men in the doorway grabbed me. "It's gonna come down!" he yelled in my ear: I was just about to holler after Keith when he appeared through the smoke, coughing and staggering. "It's not in there," he wheezed, soon as he could talk. Then there came a mighty creaking and splintering, and we all sprang back as the roof collapsed in a roaring billow of sparks.

"It's gone," Keith insisted, as we stood and watched the barn burn out from a safe distance. "But it was there, though." I was about to ask him what he meant, how he could have known that, when a stocky little man came running up from the house shouting, and interrupted me.

"You see anything of Vern and Jesse in there, mister?" His face was blackened, eyes white and staring; I learned later they'd dragged him out of the barn once already, half-dead from the smoke. "It's my brothers—I'm Lamar Tibbs."

Keith nodded. The man was about to ask the next, the obvious, question, but I guess Keith's expression told him what he wanted to know. Tibbs' own features crumpled up, and he bowed his head.

After a little while he said: "It all up with them?" Keith nodded again. "Fire?"

"Before the fire," Keith said. The miner looked up, and he went on: "They were over in the far corner. They weren't burned any." I think he meant it kindly; that was the way Tibbs took it, not knowing any better then. But Keith's eyes were flinty hard, and I for one had my misgivings.

"Was it that thing caused it?" Tibbs' voice was all but inaudible. "That thing I brung up from the mine?"

"I believe so." Keith's voice sounded calm enough, the more so if you couldn't take a cue from his face. "It's not there any more: it looks to have busted out the back before the roof went."

That got Tibbs' attention. "You sure?"

"Can't be certain that's the way it got out," said Keith, picking his words with care. "It wasn't in there when the roof fell in, though—that, I'm sure of."

Tibbs looked hard at Keith, who stared levelly back at him. What he saw seemed to make his mind up. "Wait there, mister," he said shortly, and started back towards the house. Over his shoulder, he shouted: "You in the mood for a dawg hunt?"

I began to say something, but Keith stopped me with a upraised hand. "What about you, Mr. Fenwick? You in the mood for a dawg hunt, sir?"

What could I say? Understanding that no matter what, Keith would go through with it, I nodded miserably. Then there was no more time to think: Tibbs was running back from the house with three of the mangiest, meanest-looking yaller hounds you ever saw in your life. The chase was on.

The dogs picked up a trail directly we got round the back of the barn. They shivered uncontrollably—as if they were passing peach pits, as Keith memorably put it later that same night—and set off at a good fast clip into the trees. Tibbs had them on the end of a short leash, and it was all he could do to keep up the pace. Keith loped along after him, and I brought up the rear. A few of Tibbs' relatives from back in the yard joined in—thankfully, they'd thought to bring along lanterns. There were a half-dozen of us in all.

"I thought it was a goner," panted Tibbs from up in front. He'd pegged Keith for a straight shooter more or less from the beginning, that was clear: I suppose it was watching Keith dive straight into that burning barn had done it. I doubt it came easy for him to trust anyone much, outside of his extended family circle, but he damn near deferred to Horton Keith. "We'd been blastin' on the big new seam, see: I swung my hammer at a big ol' chunk of coal fell out the roof, 'bout the size of a barrel—the fall musta cracked it some, 'cause one lick from me was all it took. That chunk split wide open like a hick'ry nut, clean in two—an' there it was, the whoosit, older than Methuselah. Fitted in there like a hand inside a glove, it did."

"I know," Keith wheezed. For a man well into his fifties, he was keeping up pretty good, but Tibbs was setting a punishing pace. "Seen it—back at the courthouse."

"You seen that? You seen the coal? Then you got a pretty good idea what we brung back here." *He's got a better idea than that, maybe,* I thought to myself, but I didn't say anything. For one thing, I doubt my aching lungs would have let me—nor yet my growing panic, which I was only just managing to keep in check.

"Anyhow, it was deader'n Abel slain by Cain—I'll swear to that, an' these men here'll back me up. You never seen a thing so dried out an' wrinkled—nor so ugly, neither. Jesus Christ, it made me sick to look at it!—but it was my prize, an' I swore it was goin' to make me a rich man. Me an' all my kin—" He choked up at that, and none of us pressed him; we ran on, was all, with the rustling thud of our footfalls through the brush warning the whole forest of our approach, probably.

The dogs were still straining hard after the scent, when all of a sudden they stopped and gathered round something underfoot, down by a little stand of dwarf sumac. I thought it was a rock at first: I couldn't see through the bodies of the hounds. It was Tibbs' cry that made me realize what it *might* be—that, and the story Keith had told me not half-a-dozen hours previously, rattling round my mind the way it had been ever since.

Tibbs couldn't pick it up, that roundish muddy thing the dogs had found. That was left to Horton Keith: he lifted it just a little, enough for one of the other men in the party to gasp and mutter "Jesse." Tibbs repeated the name a few times to himself, while Keith replaced the thing the way he found it and straightened up off his haunches. Then Tibbs gave it out in a howl that made the dogs back off, cower on their bellies in the leaf-rot as if they'd been whipped. I swear that sound went all the way through me. I hear it still, when I think about that night. It's bad, and I try not to do it too much, mostly because the next thing I think of is what I heard next—what we all heard, the sound that made us snap up our heads and turn in the direction of our otherworldly quarry.

You'll probably remember that Keith had already taken a stab at describing that sound. If you go back and look what he said, you'll see he compared it to the last trump, and all I can say is, standing out there in the middle of the forest, looking at each other in the lantern light, we all of us knew exactly what he meant. It turned my guts to water: I damn near screamed myself.

It was so close; that was the thing. Just by the clarity, the lack of muffling, you could tell it wasn't far off—five, maybe ten score of paces on through the trees, somewhere just over the next ridge. Tibbs got his senses back soonest of us all, or maybe he was so far gone then that sense had nothing to do with it: he was off and running, aiming to close down those hundred yards or so and get to grips with whatever cut down his brothers and took a trophy to boot. The dogs almost tripped him up; they were cowering in the dirt still, and there was no budging them. He flung down the leash and left them there.

It was Keith started after him, of course. And once Keith had gone, I couldn't not go myself. Then the rest of then followed on; all of which meant we were pretty strung out along the track. It may have saved Keith's life, that arrangement.

I heard Tibbs up ahead, cursing and panting; then, I heard a strange sort of a whizzing noise. I once stood at a wharf watching a cargo ship being unloaded, and one of the hawsers broke on the winching gear. The noise it made as it lashed through the air; that was what I heard. Whip-crack, quick and abrupt; and then I didn't hear Tibbs any more.

What I thought I heard was the sound of rain, pattering on the leaves and branches. I even felt a few drops of it on my face. Then one of the men in the rear caught up and shone his lantern up ahead. It lit first of all on Keith as he staggered back, hand to his mouth. Then, it lit on Tibbs.

At first it seemed like some sort of conjuror's trick. He was staggering too, like a stage drunk, only there was something about his head . . . At first your brain refused to believe it. Your eyes saw it, but your brain reported back, no, it's a man; men aren't made that way. It's a trick they do with mirrors; a slather of stage blood to dress it up, that's all. Then, inevitably, Tibbs lost his balance and fell backwards. Once he was down it became easier to deal with, in one way—easier to look at and trust your own eyes, at any rate. At last, you could look at it and see what there was to be seen. Which was this: Tibbs' head was gone, clean off at the neck.

I said you could look at it; not for long, though. Instead I turned to Keith, who was pressed back up against a tree trunk, still with his hand to his mouth. He saw me, and he tried to speak, shaking his head all the while, but he couldn't find the words.

Then we both heard it together: a rustling in the branches above our head, the sound of something dropping. We both looked up at about the same time, and that was how I managed to spring back, and so avoid the thing hitting me smack on the crown of my head. It hit the ground good and hard, directly between the two of us: the soft mud underfoot took all the bounce off it, though. It rolled half of the way over, then stopped, so you couldn't really see its features. There was no mistaking it, though, even in the shaky lantern-light; I'd been looking at the back of Tibbs' head only a moment ago, hadn't I?

A dreadful realization dawned in Keith's eyes, and he looked back up. Instinctively I followed suit. I guess we saw about the same thing, though Keith had the experience to help him evaluate it. It was like this:

The branches were close-meshed overhead, with hardly any night sky visible in between. What you could see was tinted a sickly sort of greenish hue: the way those modern city streetlights will turn the night a fuzzy, smoky orange, and block out all the stars. Through the treetops, something was ascending. I'd be a liar if I said I could recognize it; there was just no way to tell, not with all those shaking, rustling branches in the way. All I got was a general impression of size and shape; enough for me to stand in front of that slab of coal in the courthouse basement the next day and say, yeah, it could have been; I guess. Keith was with me, and so far as he was concerned it was a deal more straightforward; but as I say, he had the benefit of prior acquaintance.

Up it went, up and up, till it broke clear of the canopy, and we had no way of knowing where to look. The sky gave one last unnatural throb of ghoulish green, as if it was turning itself inside out; and it was over. All that was left was the bloody carnage down below: Lamar Tibbs' body, that we dragged between us back to the farmhouse, and the bodies of his brothers covered up with a tarpaulin. One entire generation of a family, wiped out in the course of a single night.

What with the weeping and the wailing of the relatives, and the never-ending questions—most of them from that fat fool Kronke, who hadn't even the guts to get out of his damn automobile—that business up on Peck's Ridge took us clear through dawn and into the afternoon of the next day to deal with. It stayed with us a good while longer than that, though; in fact, it's never really gone away. Ask either of my wives, who will surely survive me through having gotten rid of me, as soon as was humanly possible. They'll tell you how I used to come bolt upright in the middle of a nightmare, hands flailing desperately above my head, screaming at the ghosts of trees and branches, babbling about a sky gone wrong. Ask them how often it happened, and what good company I was in the days and weeks that followed. Yes, you could say it's stayed with me, my three days' visit down in Oram County.

I had the pleasure of Keith's acquaintance for a dozen more years in all, right up until the time he set off for the headwaters of the Amazon with the Collins Clarke archaeological party and never came back. Missing, presumed dead, all fifteen men and their native bearers; nothing was ever found of them, no overflights could even spot their last camp. Keith was well into his sixties by then, but there was never any question that he'd be joining the expedition, once he'd heard the rumors—the ruins up above Iquitos on the Ucayali, the strange carvings of beasts no one had ever seen before. He'd done his preparation in the library at Miskatonic with Clarke himself, cross-referencing the Indian tales with certain books and illustrations—and with that slab of coal from the Oram County courthouse, one-half of which had made its way into the cabinets of the University's Restricted Collection. There was no stopping him: he was convinced he was on the right track at last. "But why put yourself in their way again?" I asked him. "With all you know; after all you've seen?" He never answered me straight out; there's only his last telegram, sent from Manaus, which I like to think holds, if not an answer, then a pointer at least, to the man and to the nature of his quest.

Dear Fenwick (it said): *Finally found someplace worse than Skagway. And they say there's no such thing as progress. We set off tomorrow on our snipe hunt, not a moment too soon for all concerned. Wish you were here—on the strict understanding that we'd soon be somewhere else. With all best wishes from the new frontier, Your friend, Horton Keith.*

My friend, Horton Keith.

"Young Derby's odd genius developed remarkably, and in his eighteenth year his collected nightmare-lyrics made a real sensation when issued under the title Azathoth and Other Horrors. He was a close correspondent of the notorious Baudelairean poet Justin Geoffrey, who wrote The People of the Monolith *and died screaming in a madhouse in 1926 after a visit to a sinister, ill-regarded village in Hungary."*

"The Thing on the Doorstep" · H.P. Lovecraft (1933)

· THE FUNGAL STAIN ·
W.H. Pugmire

"Grow to my lip, thou sacred kiss . . . "
—Thomas Moore

I.

I was leaning against a window in a cramped bookstore, holding aloft a candlestick to scan a volume of Justin Geoffrey (drinking in his cosmic madness), when I noticed a figure hovering in the fog outside. Strange, isn't it, the play of shadow and light that dances in a pool of fog? I saw this person, this woman, and at first I thought my eyes were playing tricks. Her face seemed all wrong, more bestial than human. And the way she lifted her curious mouth so as to drink in the evening air was most unnatural. She lowered her face and looked toward my window, drawn perhaps by the glow of my candle's flame. Her lips curled into an uncanny smile, and as I watched the movement of her mouth the fog thickened and veiled her face.

I returned to my book, listening, and heard the shop's door open. A sudden chill rushed past me, and entrails of mist mingled with surrounding shadow; and out of this she approached the place where I stood. Glancing sideways, I watched her pretend to study titles. Closing my book, I reached to return it to its shelf. Her hand touched mine as she took the book from my grasp.

"This is rare," she said, smiling. "He had such a wonderful sense of place, don't you think?"

I laughed. "He wrote of a landscape of nightmare."

"Exquisitely so," she replied, and then quoted from memory the following verse:

"And in the village where it stands,
That place where Time had shrugged and passed it by,
I found deep-etched in sod and on black stone
My mortal name."

Nodding to her, I blew out my candle, took it to the dealer's desk, and stepped outside into misty night. The air had turned surprisingly chilly, and I pulled the collar of my coat closer to my neck. I had no idea where I wanted to go, knew only that I wasn't in the mood for social chatter. I wanted to take in the ancient charm of Kingsport, this town where I was staying for a time. I stood for a while, watching a street lamp glow in encircling fog, when I heard footsteps on the bookstore's porch. She stopped at the bottom step and looked around, nodding when she noticed me. I leaned awkwardly on one foot and then the other, then stopped at the noise of musical humming. Her odd song issued as mist from her unmoving mouth, and the thickening fog met and mingled with her exhalation. Something in her song beguiled me, and with an almost unconscious motion I began to creep toward her. I watched as I slowly walked, and saw the shadows of her face darken, distorting features. Soon there was nothing but her indistinct form, and the twin pin-pricks that were her diamond eyes. I thought they queerly smiled, those eyes, as finally the fog entombed her. I reached the place where she had stood, but I was alone.

I had decided, the next evening, to attend Poetry Night at the Pennywhistle Café, a truly bohemian establishment. Here one could find the loud rebels who hung their unruly art on walls and stood on tables so to declaim their bitter odes. Now and then, however, one could encounter that especially sensitive artist, those dreamers whose souls seemed as quaint as Kingport's eldest lane. I liked to think of myself as such a bard, and I considered my vision quite singular. It had been some time since I had attended the weekly doings. I had, however, recently composed a new poem. Thus I braved the evening's chill and took a bus to that section of town known as The Hollow, then scuttled from the bus to the small building that housed the café. The turnout was okay, and I nodded to several casual acquaintances. Five makeshift rows had been formed with folding wooden chairs, and I took my usual place in the third row.

The evening's feature poet was a homeless woman whose appearance was quite pathetic. Yet one forgot her stained clothes and missing teeth when she began to recite her work. Unlike many of the poseurs who had more ego than talent, this woman's poetry came from some authentic place in her unhappy soul. She read for fifteen minutes, and then the café's owner, who always acted as master of ceremonies, invited the rest of us to approach the podium and recite our work. I listened as two friends went forward and dramatically performed, then I arose and stepped to the podium. My reading went well, even though I was somewhat startled to see a certain figure standing near the back. As I returned to my chair, she came forward, familiar book in hand, and stood before us.

"I am not a poet, but I love the craft and have been enchanted by what I have heard tonight. I would like to read a short piece by a poet who is now largely forgotten. Sadly, we live in an age where, in this country, poetry is seldom bothered with. We cannot be forgotten, for we are utterly ignored. But none may deny us our voice. Here is one poetic voice; and although it's not as . . . free in form as that which we heard from Mr. Christopher, it is its equal in extravagance."

"The impudent vixen," I thought angrily, frowning at her as she opened the book and began to read.

"I kiss the cosmic wind that finds my face,
This face that burns as if encased in flame,
An ember glowing in an alien place,
An ancient land that deigns to call my name.
I tell my name among the stones that stand
As towers of black slat beneath black stars,
The stars that spill toward me like dark sand,
Like sand that stains the mortal flesh it mars.
New-made I rise, a pillar of dark stone,
A nascent thing on Yuggoth's hoary sod.
I hear the sound that chills me to the bone:
The mirthless chortle of some raving god."

I had closed my eyes as she began to read, and that had been a mistake; for as she continued to sound the verse, I was transported to the scene described. I felt an alien tempest that burned my face, that slinked into the cavities of my countenance and pushed beneath my flesh. I clutched my face and felt the bumps that began to form upon it. Polite applause shook me from the vision, but it was for some bloke, not the mysterious woman who had enchanted my brain with nightmare. Clumsily, I exited my chair and stumbled from the room, into night. She was leaning against the building, looking at stars.

"Can you smell the encroaching fog? How rank, like some unwashed lover. See how it steals the starlight. Can you smell the coming storm?"

"No," I bluntly replied, reaching for the pack of cigarettes in my shirt pocket and hoping that smoking offended her. "Will you have one?"

"Certainly," she replied. Placing a fag in my mouth, I lit it, took a drag, then held it to her. She brought the thin narcotic cylinder to her face and inhaled its fumes. Her mouth never touched it. "Will you walk with me?" she asked.

"I suppose." I was not fond of intimate human contact, and women were a race I could not comprehend and with which I felt uncomfortable. And this was no ordinary woman. From the moment I first laid eyes on her I had felt unsettled. She was like one of Wilde's alluring panthers, as dangerous as she was beguiling. I fancied that I could sense her bestial appetite as her hips moved against mine. These alarming observations overwhelmed me until I heard the sound of distant music. Ah, how I smiled. We approached a sight that would stir her curiosity, and in her distraction I would make my escape. Nonchalantly, I led her toward the sound, to the overgrown and usually abandoned courtyard that was lit by one weak lamppost. Beneath that dim light were two figures. The taller one, a bent old gentleman, played a worn and weathered accordion, a slender tube-like instrument from another century, with buttons rather than keyboard. He moved its pleated billows in a mechanical manner, as though oblivious to the heart-wrenching music he produced.

Beneath him knelt one of the oddest and most pathetic beings I had ever encountered. One knew instinctively that the diminutive thing was not a child, even though the monkey mask of flayed rubber covered most of the creature's face. From its dome, just above the mask, was a mess of mangled hair, coils of matted filth that resembled thick dead worms. Bent over the image that it drew on pavement with a stick of chalk, it was unwitting of our presence.

I looked at my companion and saw her watch the remnant of hand that clutched the yellow chalk. The right hand was little more than fist, its flesh ending just above the knuckles. The left hand retained two middle digits, and they stopped their drawing as we got closer. The wee creature turned to look at us. How oddly the black eyes shined beneath their mask. His fingers dropped the chalk and began to move as if he were attempting some piteous form of sign language. He then stood upon truncated legs and did a little dance; and as he capered he bent his torso low as if in genuflection to the woman at my side.

The music swelled, and with rakish abandon I took the woman into my arms and danced her closer to the pair of beings who stood like harbingers of doom. The old man lifted his fantastic face and watched our frolic, and I tried not to stare at the growth of bumps and folded flesh that disfigured his visage. His familiar watched us with bent head and held out what remained of a palm. Pushing from me, the woman went to him and kissed the open palm. I watched the small thing shudder at her touch.

The music stopped, and the gentleman released one hand from his instrument, holding it to her. She took the proffered hand and lifted it to her face, smoothing her features with his cracked and ancient paw. Her hands swam through the air to his pale face, then wound into his white hair. She bent to him and touched her mouth to his, and then she moved her mouth to an ugly growth on his cheek. Her kiss was a prolonged thing. When at last she pulled away, I was horrified to see the blood that oozed from the place on the old gent's face that had been eaten into. Sickened, I backed away, then turned to run as the ancient fellow reached out with shaky hands and pulled the woman's face once more to his.

II.

I wandered through moist and stinking fog, that queer mist that had stayed now for two days. From the sound of bells and horns I knew that I had reached Harborside, and when I found myself on Water Street I walked to a familiar address and passed through gates that were supported by stone walls eight feet high. The gnarled trees that surrounded the ancient dwelling were swathed in thick mist. From the wide covered porch I could discern a lantern's glow. I heard the faint humming of intoxicated song. Winfield Scot was watching me.

"Ah, brother poet, come and share my wine. Or try this kick-ass rum. It'll warm you from the coils of detested fog. You look like a fellow in need of fortification. What ails thee, son; what's her name?"

I took the proffered bottle of rum and gulped a generous portion. "She's a very devil."

"Aren't they all, god love them? Give me the hellish details. But steady on the rum, mate; it's another week before my next check."

I babbled of my encounter, and as I told my tale Scot's eyes sobered. I think sometimes he plays at being more inebriated than he actually is, as if it were expected of him to play the part of town drunk. How carefully he listened to my yarn.

"Hmmm," he said after a long pause, and then he brought a bottle of red wine to his mouth.

"What?"

"You say she appeared out of this damnable fog as you were reading *People of the Monolith*? Were you reading aloud?"

"I don't know. I sometimes read aloud, especially verse. I like to feel the words on my lips. Why?"

"Justin Geoffrey was a potent bard. I've cautioned you before about speaking certain esoteric verse aloud. Now, you know that fellow's history, of how he wrote the initial draft of his infamous poem in a state of rich madness while sitting near a monolith of cursed stone. Haunted place, haunted mind. Linked in lunacy. In such a state, believe me, humanity is prone to channel unusual influence. You and I, son, as poets, know too well the weird stuff that leaks into our imaginations. From where?"

"I've heard all of this before, your theory of the universal madness of poets."

"Not all. And there are degrees of lunacy. I speak mainly of those who dig the weird cosmic stuff. You've written a little of it yourself, and you read it always. This place, this old seaport, welcomes those of us who thrill to outside influence. We have felt the velvet kiss of the kind of madness that produces such poetry as *People of the Monolith* or *Al Azif*. We tap into a language that is fraught with energy, with alchemy. The result is poetry that is truly *evocative*. We should use caution in speaking such words aloud."

"Okay, I know where you're going with this. You're saying that I summoned this witch woman by uttering the sounds of a mad poet's song."

"You catch on quick. Come on, I want to show you something interesting." Clumsily, he held out his hand. I took it and pulled him to his feet. He stumbled to the door of the ancient house and pushed it open.

"I don't think so, Winfield."

"Hand me that lantern and don't be gutless. The trick is not to linger too long inside. Take my hand, child, if that will help. Can you feel it? This, too, is a realm of madness." I stayed close behind him, taking in the debris with which the shadowed room was cluttered. "The old matey who lived here, bless him, left his stigmata of craziness within these rotting walls. Man, the weird junk he picked up as he sailed around the world. This place is a trove of nameless booty. From the stories he told, and from the bits he cautiously left out but hinted at, he was ruthless in his pursuit of plunder. Ah, settle down and don't look so nervous. Ain't much can reach us here from Outside, not as long as those painted stones stand unmoved in the yard. Okay, found it."

"Found what?" He handed me the lantern and took up a small box of polished black wood. Undoing a latch, he opened the lid. I reached for the small obsidian dagger that nestled on red velvet. "What is this?"

"Feels creepy, don't it? You see, Justin Geoffrey wasn't the only lunatic to visit the black monolith of Stregoicavar. Over the decades foolhardy souls have taken ax and hammer to that stone, but they never did much damage. Around the base is a litter of shards, and from one good-sized piece our sea captain had this ritual weapon forged. God alone knows what he used it for."

"Let's get out of here," I said, closing the lid of the box. Winfield watched as I placed the weapon in my coat pocket. He followed me out the door and onto the porch that was his homeless residence.

"Listen, man. This old town ain't just a seaport. It's a portal. Things can be summoned from the other side. Wouldn't surprise me if that crazy old coot initially called up this woman, whatever she is. If she's linked to the Black Stone and Geoffrey's mad verse, carrying that thing with you is a bad idea."

"I want to study it. There's some symbols carved onto the handle that look familiar. I think I remember them from a book I saw in the library at Miskatonic. Maybe I can find some answers about this woman."

"This avatar, you mean. You're bloody mad."

Calmly, I smiled, and then I turned and walked into the fog.

III.

I walked past Water Street, toward the ocean, to the wharves. Dropping the façade of calm that I had faked so as to disguise my true emotional state from my inebriated friend, I walked the lonely place until I found the pathetic shanty that was my destination. Breathing deeply the unwholesome fog, I pushed the crooked door of disjointed wood. He was sitting on his crate, eating fish that had been wrapped in newspaper. Flickering light from one single candle illuminated the place. Looking at one corner, I saw the mound of blankets wherein his squat companion slept, next to a wall on which had been scrawled, in yellow chalk, curious glyphs.

"Hello, Enoch."

He looked at me with rheumy eyes, a shred of fish hanging from one corner of his mouth. "Evening."

"Are you okay?"

His eyes blinked. "Never better." I watched his gnarled hand reach for a place on his face, which he thoughtfully scratched. From outside I could hear a boat's forlorn call, and as if in answer I heard a low moan which I took to be the wind on water. This latter sound increased and became a gale that shook the edifice of wood and metal and thick cardboard. I looked at one of the trembling cardboard walls, at what I took to be papier-mâché masks that had been fastened to its surface. Stepping to the wall, I carefully touched one of the pale faces. Its thin membrane pushed inward at the force of my fingering.

"What are these, Enoch?"

"Oh, aspects of she and her kindred. They like their false faces, aye."

I reached to touch another of the ghastly things, gently poking a finger into the hollow eye socket. Hideous as they were, I was strangely seduced. So soft. Perhaps, if I was very careful, I could peel one of them from the wall and slip it over my own visage.

The old man began to hum, as outside the wind blew roughly against the shack. Enoch's tune became a low chanted song. "Across black gulfs toward us they dance, to mock our insignificance." From a corner of the room, fluted music accompanied the old man's singing. I turned to glance at the malformed gnome. Still wrapped in many blankets, he glowered at me with glistening black eyes. A cracked flute was pressed against the mouth of the shredded mask.

Something soft touched my shoulder. I turned my face to hers. Her cool mouth pressed against my forehead, and her tongue—so strangely soft, so warm and heavy—fastened to my flesh. When she backed away, I knew that it had not been her tongue that had tickled me, for I could feel it still upon my face, the soft weighty thing. Reaching to my face, I touched the fungous growth upon it. Her diamond eyes beamed as shadows shifted the contour of her inhuman visage. She bent to me a second time and touched her lips to mine. As we kissed, my hand went into my pocket and found the dagger. Joyfully, I pushed the tiny blade into her face, below one eye. How easily the flesh tore, like mushroom. Sediments of her sardonic physiognomy spilled to me, onto my eyes, into mouth and nostrils.

I pushed the creature from me and fled that haunted place. Wild tempest tore at my hair, my clothing. It had pushed away the noisome fog, and I saw a dark sky laced with silver starlight, with gems that remorselessly winked at me. I watched the roiling storm clouds that gathered at the jutting edge of Kingsport Head, and listened to the waves that crashed against ports of rotting wood. From behind came an odd scuttling sound, and turning I saw the assemblage of large leaves that followed me, pushed by wind along the ground.

No, not leaves. Rather, they were soft hollow faces moving in a moaning wind. I groaned into that gale, as beneath its noise I heard that other sound. I saw them dimly in the distance, two figures that had followed from their shabby abode. One played an antique accordion. About his feet his masked companion frolicked, a flute at its mouth. Behind them, in spreading darkness, she emerged, gliding toward me. Windstorm whirled around her, lifting the faces to the she-devil in a whorl of spinning air. Reaching out, she took hold of one face. How easily it covered her split countenance.

Mindlessly, I laughed. I mumbled some snatches of lunatic verse that fumbled in my brain. The bumps of substance that stained my mouth and forehead began to expand, as drops of moisture dripped from the black cosmos. Baptized, I gazed once more at the daemon that swam toward me through the liquid air; and then I shut my eyes and awaited her final kiss.

That is not dead which can eternal lie. And with strange aeons even death may die.

"The Call of Cthulhu" · H.P. Lovecraft (1928)

"One other thing, Lestrade," he added, turning round at the door: " 'Rache',", is the German for 'revenge'; so don't lose your time looking for Miss Rachel."

"A Study in Scarlet" · A. Conan Doyle (1887)

• A STUDY IN EMERALD •
Neil Gaiman

1. The New Friend.

It is the immensity, I believe. The hugeness of things below. The darkness of dreams.

But I am woolgathering. Forgive me. I am not a literary man.

I had been in need of lodgings. That was how I met him. I wanted someone to share the cost of rooms with me. We were introduced by a mutual acquaintance, in the chemical laboratories of St. Bart's. "You have been in Afghanistan, I perceive," that was what he said to me, and my mouth fell open and my eyes opened very wide.

"Astonishing." I said.

"Not really," said the stranger in the white lab-coat, who was to become my friend. "From the way you hold your arm, I see you have been wounded, and in a particular way You have a deep tan. You also have a military bearing, and there are few enough places in the Empire that a military man can be both tanned and, given the nature of the injury to your shoulder and the traditions of the Afghan cave-folk, tortured."

Put like that, of course, it was absurdly simple. But then, it always was. I had been tanned nut-brown. And I had indeed, as he had observed, been tortured.

The gods and men of Afghanistan were savages, unwilling to be ruled from Whitehall or from Berlin or even from Moscow, and unprepared to see reason. I had been sent into those hills, attached to the ___th Regiment. As long as the fighting remained in the hills and mountains, we fought on an equal footing.

When the skirmishes descended into the caves and the darkness then we found ourselves, as it were, out of our depth and in over our heads.

I shall not forget the mirrored surface of the underground lake, nor the thing that emerged from the lake, its eyes opening and closing, and the singing whispers that accompanied it as it rose, wreathing their way about it like the buzzing of flies bigger than worlds.

That I survived was a miracle, but survive I did, and I returned to England with my nerves in shreds and tatters. The place that leech-like mouth had touched me was tattooed forever, frog-white, into the skin of my now-withered shoulder. I had once been a crack-shot. Now I had nothing, save a fear of the world-beneath-the-world akin to panic which meant that I would gladly pay sixpence of my army pension for a Hansom cab, rather than a penny to travel underground.

Still, the fogs and darknesses of London comforted me, took me in. I had lost my first lodgings because I screamed in the night. I had been in Afghanistan; I was there no longer.

"I scream in the night," I told him.

"I have been told that I snore," he said. "Also I keep irregular hours, and I often use the mantelpiece for target practice. I will need the sitting room to meet clients. I am selfish, private and easily bored. Will this be a problem?"

I smiled, and I shook my head, and extended my hand. We shook on it.

The rooms he had found for us, in Baker Street, were more than adequate for two bachelors. I bore in mind all my friend had said about his desire for privacy, and I forbore from asking what it was he did for a living. Still, there was much to pique my curiosity. Visitors would arrive at all hours, and when they did I would leave the sitting room and repair to my bedroom, pondering what they could have in common with my friend: the pale woman with one eye bone-white, the small man who looked like a commercial traveler, the portly dandy in his velvet jacket, and the rest. Some were frequent visitors, many others came only once, spoke to him, and left, looking troubled or looking satisfied. He was a mystery to me.

We were partaking of one of our landlady's magnificent breakfasts one morning, when my friend rang the bell to summon that good lady. "There will be a gentleman joining us, in about four minutes," he said. "We will need another place at table."

"Very good," she said, "I'll put more sausages under the grill."

My friend returned to perusing his morning paper. I waited for an explanation with growing impatience. Finally, I could stand it no longer. "I don't understand. How could you know that in four minutes we would be receiving a visitor? There was no telegram, no message of any kind."

He smiled, thinly. "You did not hear the clatter of a brougham several minutes ago? It slowed as it passed us—obviously as the driver identified our door, then it sped up and went past, up into the Marylebone Road. There is a crush of carriages and taxicabs letting off passengers at the railway station and at the waxworks, and it is in that crush that anyone wishing to alight without being observed will go. The walk from there to here is but four minutes."

He glanced at his pocket-watch, and as he did so I heard a tread on the stairs outside.

"Come in, Lestrade," he called. "The door is ajar, and your sausages are just coming out from under the grill."

A man I took to be Lestrade opened the door, then closed it carefully behind him. "I should not," he said. "But truth to tell, I have had not had a chance to break my fast this morning. And I could certainly do justice to a few of those sausages." He was the small man I had observed on several occasions previously, whose demeanor was that of a traveler in rubber novelties or patent nostrums.

My friend waited until our landlady had left the room, before he said, "Obviously, I take it this is a matter of national importance."

"My stars," said Lestrade, and he paled. "Surely the word cannot be out already. Tell me it is not." He began to pile his plate high with sausages, kipper fillets, kedgeree and toast, but his hands shook, a little.

"Of course not," said my friend. "I know the squeak of your brougham wheels, though, after all this time, an oscillating G sharp above high C. And if Inspector Lestrade of Scotland Yard cannot publicly be seen to come into the parlor of London's only consulting detective, yet comes anyway, and without having had his breakfast, then I know that this is not a routine case. Ergo, it involves those above us and is a matter of national importance."

Lestrade dabbed egg yolk from his chin with his napkin. I stared at him. He did not look like my idea of a police inspector, but then, my friend looked little enough like my idea of a consulting detective—whatever that might be.

"Perhaps we should discuss the matter privately," Lestrade said, glancing at me.

My friend began to smile, impishly, and his head moved on his shoulders as it did when he was enjoying a private joke. "Nonsense," he said. "Two heads are better than one. And what is said to one of us is said to us both."

"If I am intruding—" I said, gruffly, but he motioned me to silence.

Lestrade shrugged. "It's all the same to me," he said, after a moment. "If you solve the case then I have my job. If you don't, then I have no job. You use your methods, that's what I say. It can't make things any worse."

"If there's one thing that a study of history has taught us, it is that things can always get worse," said my friend. "When do we go to Shoreditch?"

Lestrade dropped his fork. "This is too bad!" he exclaimed. "Here you were, making sport of me, when you know all about the matter! You should be ashamed—"

"No one has told me anything of the matter. When a police inspector walks into my room with fresh splashes of mud of that peculiar mustard yellow hue on his boots and trouser-legs, I can surely be forgiven for presuming that he has recently walked past the diggings at Hobbs Lane, in Shoreditch, which is the only place in London that particular mustard-colored clay seems to be found."

Inspector Lestrade looked embarrassed. "Now you put it like that," he said, "it seems so obvious."

My friend pushed his plate away from him. "Of course it does," he said, slightly testily.

We rode to the East End in a cab, Inspector Lestrade had walked up to the Marylebone Road to find his brougham, and left us alone.

"So you are truly a consulting detective?" I said.

"The only one in London, or perhaps, the world," said my friend. "I do not take cases. Instead, I consult. Others bring me their insoluble problems, they describe them, and, sometimes, I solve them."

"Then those people who come to you . . . "

"Are, in the main, police officers, or are detectives themselves, yes."

It was a fine morning, but we were now jolting about the edges of the rookery of St. Giles, that warren of thieves and cutthroats which sits on London like a cancer on the face of a pretty flower-seller, and the only light to enter the cab was dim and faint.

"Are you sure that you wish me along with you?"

In reply my friend stared at me without blinking. "I have a feeling," he said. "I have a feeling that we were meant to be together. That we have fought the good fight, side by side, in the past or in the future, I do not know. I am a rational man, but I have learned the value of a good companion, and from the moment I clapped eyes on you, I knew I trusted you as well as I do myself. Yes. I want you with me."

I blushed, or said something meaningless. For the first time since Afghanistan, I felt that I had worth in the world.

• • •

206 · A Study in Emerald

2. The Room.

It was a cheap rooming house in Shoreditch. There was a policeman at the front door. Lestrade greeted him by name, and made to usher us in, and I was ready to enter, but my friend squatted on the doorstep, and pulled a magnifying glass from his coat pocket. He examined the mud on the wrought iron boot-scraper, prodding at it with his forefinger. Only when he was satisfied would he let us go inside. We walked upstairs. The room in which the crime had been committed was obvious: it was flanked by two burly constables.

Lestrade nodded to the men, and they stood aside. We walked in.

I am not, as I said, a writer by profession, and I hesitate to describe that place, knowing that my words cannot do it justice. Still, I have begun this narrative, and I fear I must continue. A murder had been committed in that little bedsit. The body, what was left of it, was still there, on the floor. I saw it, but, at first, somehow, I did not see it. What I saw instead was what had sprayed and gushed from the throat and chest of the victim: in color it ranged from bile-green to grass-green. It had soaked into the threadbare carpet and spattered the wallpaper. I imagined it for one moment the work of some hellish artist, who had decided to create a study in emerald.

After what seemed like a hundred years I looked down at the body, opened like a rabbit on a butcher's slab, and tried to make sense of what I saw. I removed my hat, and my friend did the same.

He knelt and inspected the body, inspecting the cuts and gashes. Then he pulled out his magnifying glass, and walked over to the wall, examining the gouts of drying ichor.

"We've already done that," said Inspector Lestrade.

"Indeed?" said my friend. "Then what did you make of this, then? I do believe it is a word."

Lestrade walked to the place my friend was standing, and looked up. There was a word, written in capitals, in green blood, on the faded yellow wallpaper, some little way above Lestrade's head. "Rache . . . ?" said Lestrade, spelling it out. "Obviously he was going to write Rachel, but he was interrupted. So—we must look for a woman . . . "

My friend said nothing. He walked back to the corpse, and picked up its hands, one after the other. The fingertips were clean of ichor. "I think we have established that the word was not written by his Royal Highness—"

"What the Devil makes you say—?"

"My dear Lestrade. Please give me some credit for having a brain. The corpse is obviously not that of a man—the color of his blood, the number of limbs, the eyes, the position of the face, all these things bespeak the blood royal. While I cannot say which royal line, I would hazard that he is an heir, perhaps . . . no, second to the throne, in one of the German principalities."

"That is amazing." Lestrade hesitated, then he said, "This is Prince Franz Drago of Bohemia. He was here in Albion as a guest of Her Majesty Victoria. Here for a holiday and a change of air . . . "

" . . . For the theatres, the whores and the gaming tables, you mean."

"If you say so." Lestrade looked put out. "Anyway, you've given us a fine lead with this Rachel woman. Although I don't doubt we would have found her on our own."

"Doubtless," said my friend.

He inspected the room further, commenting acidly several times that the police, with their boots had obscured footprints, and moved things that might have been of use to anyone attempting to reconstruct the events of the previous night.

Still, he seemed interested in a small patch of mud he found behind the door.

Beside the fireplace he found what appeared to be some ash or dirt.

"Did you see this?" he asked Lestrade.

"Her majesty's police," replied Lestrade, "tend not to be excited by ash in a fireplace. It's where ash tends to he found." And he chuckled at that.

My friend took a pinch of the ash and rubbed between his fingers, then sniffed the remains. Finally, he scooped up what was left of the material and tipped it into a glass vial, which he stoppered and placed in an inner pocket of his coat.

He stood up. "And the body?"

Lestrade said, "The palace will send their own people." My friend nodded at me, and together we walked to the door. My friend sighed. "Inspector. Your quest for Miss Rachel may prove fruitless. Among other things, *Rache* is a German word. It means revenge. Check your dictionary. There are other meanings."

We reached the bottom of the stair, and walked out onto the street. "You have never seen royalty before this morning, have you?" he asked. I shook my head. "Well, the sight can be unnerving, if you're unprepared. Why my good fellow—you are trembling!"

"Forgive me. I shall be fine in moments."

"Would it do you good to walk?" he asked, and I assented, certain that if I did not walk then I would begin to scream.

"West, then," said my friend, pointing to the dark tower of the Palace. And we commenced to walk.

"So," said my friend, after some time. "You have never had any personal encounters with any of the crowned heads of Europe?"

"No," I said.

"I believe I can confidently state that you shall," he told me. "And not with a corpse this time. Very soon."

"My dear fellow, whatever makes you believe—?"

In reply he pointed to a carriage, black-painted, that had pulled up fifty yards ahead of us. A man in a black top-hat and a greatcoat stood by the door, holding it open, waiting, silently. A coat of arms familiar to every child in Albion was painted in gold upon the carriage door.

"There are invitations one does not refuse," said my friend. He doffed his own hat to the footman, and I do believe that he was smiling as he climbed into the box-like space, and relaxed back into the soft leathery cushions,

When I attempted to speak with him during the journey to the Palace, he placed his finger over his lips. Then he closed his eyes and seemed sunk deep in thought. I, for my part, tried to remember what I knew of German royalty, but, apart from the Queen's consort, Prince Albert, being German, I knew little enough.

I put a hand in my pocket, pulled out a handful of coins—brown and silver, black and copper-green. I stared at the portrait stamped on each of them of our Queen, and felt both patriotic pride and stark dread. I told myself I had once been a military man, and a stranger to fear, and I could remember a time when this had been the plain truth. For a moment I remembered a time when I had been a crack-shot—even, I liked to think, something of a marksman—but my right hand shook as if it were palsied, and the coins jingled arid chinked, and I felt only regret.

3. The Palace.

The Queen's consort, Prince Albert, was a big man, with an impressive handlebar mustache and a receding hairline, and he was undeniably and entirely human. He met us in the corridor, nodded to my friend and to me, did not ask us for our names or offer to shake hands.

"The Queen is most upset," he said. He had an accent. He pronounced his S's as Z's: Mozt. Upzet. "Franz was one of her favorites. She has so many nephews. But he made her laugh so. You will find the ones who did this to him."

"I will do my best," said my friend.

"I have read your monographs," said Prince Albert. "It was I who told them that you should be consulted. I hope I did right."

"As do I," said my friend.

And then the great door was opened, and we were ushered into the darkness and the presence of the Queen.

She was called Victoria, because she had beaten us in battle, seven hundred years before, and she was called Gloriana, because she was glorious, and she was called the Queen, because the human mouth was not shaped to say her true name. She was huge, huger than I had imagined possible, and she squatted in the shadows staring down at us, without moving.

Thizsz muzzst be zsolved. The words came from the shadows.

"Indeed, ma'am," said my friend.

A limb squirmed and pointed at me. *Zstepp forward.*

I wanted to walk. My legs would not move.

My friend came to my rescue then. He took me by the elbow and walked me toward her majesty.

Isz not to be afraid. Isz to be worthy. Isz to be a companion. That was what she said to me. Her voice was a very sweet contralto, with a distant buzz. Then the limb uncoiled and extended, and she touched my shoulder. There was a moment, but only a moment, of a pain deeper and more profound than anything I have ever experienced, and then it was replaced by a pervasive sense of well-being. I could feel the muscles in my shoulder relax, and, for the first time since Afghanistan, I was free from pain.

Then my friend walked forward. Victoria spoke to him, yet I could not hear her words; I wondered if they went, somehow, directly from her mind to his, if this was the Queen's Counsel I had read about in the histories. He replied aloud.

"Certainly, ma'am. I can tell you that there were two other men with your nephew in that room in Shoreditch. That night, the footprints were, although obscured, unmistakable." And then, "Yes. I understand. . . . I believe so. . . . Yes."

He was quiet when we left the palace, and said nothing to me as we rode back to Baker Street.

It was dark already. I wondered how long we had spent in the Palace.

Fingers of sooty fog twined across the road and the sky.

Upon our return to Baker Street, in the looking glass of my room, I observed that the frog-white skin across my shoulder had taken on a pinkish tinge. I hoped that I was not imagining it, that it was not merely the moonlight through the window.

4. The Performance.

That my friend was a master of disguise should have come as no surprise to me, yet surprise me it did. Over the next ten days a strange assortment of characters came in through our door in Baker Street—an elderly Chinese man, a young roué, a fat, red-haired woman of whose former profession there could be little doubt, and a venerable old buffer, his foot swollen and bandaged from gout. Each of them would walk into my friend's room, and, with a speed that would have done justice to a music-hall "quick change artist," my friend would walk out.

He would not talk about what he had been doing on these occasions, preferring to relax, staring off into space, occasionally making notations on any scrap of paper to hand, notations I found, frankly, incomprehensible. He seemed entirely preoccupied, so much so that I found myself worrying about his well-being. And then, late one afternoon, he came home dressed in his own clothes, with an easy grin upon his face, and he asked if I was interested in the theatre.

"As much as the next man," I told him.

"Then fetch your opera glasses," he told me. "We are off to Drury Lane."

I had expected a light open, or something of the kind, but instead I found myself in what must have been the worst theatre in Drury Lane, for all that it had named itself after the royal court—and to be honest, it was barely in Drury Lane at all, being situated at the Shaftesbury Avenue end of the road, where the avenue approaches the Rookery of St. Giles. On my friend's advice I concealed my wallet, and, following his example, I carried a stout stick.

Once we were seated in the stalls (I had bought a threepenny orange from one of the lovely young women who sold them to the members of the audience, and I sucked it as we waited), my friend said, quietly, "You should only count yourself lucky that you did not need to accompany me to the gambling dens or the brothels. Or the madhouses—another place that Prince Franz delighted in visiting, as I have learned. But there was nowhere he went to more than once. Nowhere but—"

The orchestra struck up, and the curtain was raised. My friend was silent.

It was a fine enough show in its way: three one-act plays were performed. Comic songs were sung between the acts. The leading man was tall, languid, and had a fine singing voice; the leading lady was elegant, and her voice carried through all the theatre; the comedian had a fine touch for patter songs.

The first play was a broad comedy of mistaken identities: the leading man played a pair of identical twins who had never met, but had managed, by a set of comical misadventures, each to find himself engaged to be married to the same young lady—who, amusingly, thought herself engaged to only one man. Doors swung open and closed as the actor changed from identity to identity.

The second play was a heartbreaking tale of an orphan girl who starved in the snow selling hothouse violets—her grandmother recognized her at the last, and swore that she was the babe stolen ten years back by bandits, but it was too late, and the frozen little angel breathed her last. I must confess I found myself wiping my eyes with my linen handkerchief more than once.

The performance finished with a rousing historical narrative: the entire company played the men and women of a village on the shore of the ocean, seven hundred years before our modern times. They saw shapes rising from the sea, in the distance, The hero joyously proclaimed to the villagers that these were the Old Ones whose coming was foretold, returning to us from R'lyeh, and from dim Carcosa, and from the plains of Leng, where they had slept, or waited, or passed out the time of their death. The comedian opined that the other villagers had all been eating too many pies and drinking too much ale, and they were imagining the shapes. A portly gentleman playing a priest of the Roman God tells the villagers that the shapes in the sea were monsters and demons, and must be destroyed.

At the climax, the hero beat the priest to death with his own crucifer, and prepared to welcome Them as They came. The heroine sang a haunting aria, whilst, in an astonishing display of magic-lantern trickery, it seemed as if we saw Their shadows cross the sky at the back of the stage: the Queen of Albion herself, and the Black One of Egypt (in shape almost like a man), followed by the Ancient Goat, Parent to a Thousand, Emperor of all China, and the Czar Unanswerable, and He Who Presides over the New World, and the White Lady of the Antarctic Fastness, and the others. And as each shadow crossed the stage, or appeared to, from out of every throat in the gallery came, unbidden, a mighty "Huzzah!" until the air itself seemed to vibrate. The moon rose in the painted sky, and then, at its height, in one final moment of theatrical magic, it turned from a pallid yellow, as it was in the old tales, to the comforting crimson of the moon that shines down upon us all today.

The members of the cast took their bows and their curtain calls to cheers and laughter, and the curtain fell for the last time, and the show was done.

212 · A Study in Emerald

"There," said my friend. "What did you think?"

"Jolly, jolly good," I told him, my hands sore from applauding.

"Stout fellow," he said, with a smile. "Let us go backstage."

We walked outside and into an alley beside the theatre, to the stage door, where a thin woman with a wen on her cheek knitted busily. My friend showed her a visiting card, and she directed us into the building and up some steps to a small communal dressing room.

Oil lamps and candles guttered in front of smeared looking-glasses, and men and women were taking off their make-up and costumes with no regard to the proprieties of gender. I averted my eyes. My friend seemed unperturbed. "Might I talk to Mr. Vernet?" he asked, loudly.

A young woman who had played the heroine's best friend in the first play, and the saucy innkeeper's daughter in the last, pointed us to the end of the room. "Sherry! Sherry Vernet!" she called.

The young man who stood up in response was lean; less conventionally handsome than he had seemed from the other side of the footlights. He peered at us quizzically. "I do not believe I have had the pleasure . . . ?"

"My name is Henry Camberley," said my friend, drawling his speech somewhat. "You may have heard of me."

"I must confess that I have not had that privilege," said Vernet.

My friend presented the actor with an engraved card.

The man looked at the card with unfeigned interest. "A theatrical promoter? From the New World? My, my. And this is . . . ?" He looked at me.

"This is a friend of mine, Mister Sebastian. He is not of the profession."

I muttered something about having enjoyed the performance enormously, and shook hands with the actor.

My friend said. "Have you ever visited the New World?"

"I have not yet had that honor," admitted Vernet, "although it has always been my dearest wish."

"Well, my good man," said my friend, with the easy informality of a New Worlder, "maybe you'll get your wish. That last play. I've never seen anything like it. Did you write it?"

"Alas, no. The playwright is a good friend of mine. Although I devised the mechanism of the magic lantern shadow show. You'll not see finer on the stage today."

"Would you give me the playwright's name? Perhaps I should speak to him directly, this friend of yours."

Vernet shook his head. "That will not be possible, I am afraid. He is a professional man, and does not wish his connection with the stage publically to be known."

"I see." My friend pulled a pipe from his pocket, and put it in his mouth. Then he patted his pockets. "I am sorry," he began. "I have forgotten to bring my tobacco pouch."

"I smoke a strong black shag," said the actor, "but if you have no objection—"

"None!" said my friend, heartily. "Why, I smoke a strong shag myself," and he filled his pipe with the actor's tobacco, and the two men puffed away, while my friend described a vision he had for a play that could tour the cities of the New World, from Manhattan Island all the way to the furthest tip of the continent in the distant south. The first act would be the last play we had seen. The rest of the play might perhaps tell of the dominion of the Old Ones over humanity and its gods, perhaps telling what might have happened if people had had no Royal Families to look up to—a world of barbarism and darkness—"But your mysterious professional man would be the play's author, and what occurs would be his alone to decide," interjected my friend. "Our drama would be his. But I can guarantee you audiences beyond your imaginings, and a significant share of the takings at the door. Let us say fifty per-cent!"

"This is most exciting," said Vernet. "I hope it will not turn out to have been a pipe-dream!"

"No sir, it shall not!" said my friend, puffing on his own pipe, chuckling at the man's joke. "Come to my rooms in Baker Street tomorrow morning, after breakfast-time, say at ten, in company with your author friend, and I shall have the contracts drawn up and waiting."

With that the actor clambered up onto his chair and clapped his hands for silence. "Ladies and Gentlemen of the company, I have an announcement to make," he said, his resonant voice filling the room. "This gentleman is Henry Camberley, the theatrical promoter, and he is proposing to take us across the Atlantic Ocean, and on to fame and fortune."

There were several cheers, and the comedian said, "Well, it'll make a change from herrings and pickled-cabbage," and the company laughed.

And it was to the smiles of all of them that we walked out of the theatre and out onto the fog-wreathed streets.

"My dear fellow," I said. "Whatever was—"

"Not another word," said my friend. "There are many ears in the city."

And not another word was spoken until we had hailed a cab, and clambered inside, and were rattling up the Charing Cross Road.

And even then, before he said anything, my friend took his pipe from his mouth, and emptied the half-smoked contents of the bowl into a small tin, he pressed the lid onto the tin, and placed it into his pocket.

"There," he said. "That's the Tall Man found, or I'm a Dutchman. Now, we just have to hope that the cupidity and the curiosity of the Limping Doctor proves enough to bring him to us tomorrow morning."

"The Limping Doctor?"

My friend snorted. "That is what I have been calling him. It was obvious, from footprints and much else besides, when we saw the Prince's body, that two men had been in that room that night: a tall man, who, unless I miss my guess, we have just encountered, and a smaller man with a limp, who eviscerated the prince with a professional skill that betrays the medical man."

"A doctor?"

"Indeed. I hate to say this, but it is my experience that when a Doctor goes to the bad, he is a fouler and darker creature than the worst cut-throat. There was Huston, the acid-bath man, and Campbell, who brought the procrustean bed to Ealing . . . " and he carried on in a similar vein for the rest of our journey.

The cab pulled up beside the curb. "That'll be one and tenpence," said the cabbie. My friend tossed him a form, which he caught, and tipped to his ragged tall hat. "Much obliged to you both," he called out, as the horse clopped out into the fog.

We walked to our front door. As I unlocked the door, my friend said, "Odd. Our cabbie just ignored that fellow on the corner."

"They do that at the end of a shift," I pointed out.

"Indeed they do," said my friend.

I dreamed of shadows that night, vast shadows that blotted out the sun, and I called out to them in my desperation, but they did not listen.

5. The Skin and the Pit.

Inspector Lestrade was the first to arrive.

"You have posted your men in the street?" asked my friend.

"I have," said Lestrade. "With strict orders to let anyone in who comes, but to arrest anyone trying to leave."

"And you have handcuffs with you?"

In reply, Lestrade put his hand in his pocket, and jangled two pairs of cuffs, grimly.

"Now sir," he said. "While we wait, why do you not tell me what we are waiting for?"

My friend pulled his pipe out of his pocket. He did not put it in his mouth, but placed it on the table in front of him. Then he took the tin from the night before, and a glass vial I recognized as the one he had had in the room in Shoreditch.

"There," he said. "The coffin-nail, as I trust it shall prove, for our Master Vernet." He paused. Then he took out his pocket watch, laid it carefully on the table. "We have several minutes before they arrive." He turned to me. "What do you know of the Restorationists?"

"Not a blessed thing," I told him.

Lestrade coughed. "If you're talking about what I think you're talking about," he said, "perhaps we should leave it there. Enough's enough."

"Too late for that," said my friend. "For there are those who do not believe that the coming of the Old Ones was the fine thing we all know it to be. Anarchists to a man, they would see the old ways restored—mankind in control of its own destiny, if you will."

"I will not hear this sedition spoken," said Lestrade. "I must warn you—"

"I must warn you not to be such a fathead," said my friend. "Because it was the Restorationists that killed Prince Franz Drago. They murder, they kill, in a vain effort to force our masters to leave us alone in the darkness. The Prince was killed by a rache—it's an old term for a hunting dog, Inspector, as you would know if you had looked in a dictionary. It also means revenge. And the hunter left his signature on the wallpaper in the murder-room, just as an artist might sign a canvas. But he was not the one who killed the Prince."

"The Limping Doctor!" I exclaimed.

"Very good. There was a tall man there that night—I could tell his height, for the word was written at eye level. He smoked a pipe—the ash and dottle sat unburnt in the fireplace, and he had tapped out his pipe with ease on the mantel, something a smaller man would not have done. The tobacco was an unusual blend of shag. The footprints in the room had, for the most part been almost obliterated by your men, but there were several clear prints behind the door and by the window. Someone had waited there: a smaller man from his stride, who put his weight on his right leg. On the path outside I had several clear prints, and the different colors of clay on the bootscraper outside gave me more information: a tall man, who had accompanied the Prince into those rooms, and had, later, walked out. Waiting for them to arrive was the man who had sliced up the Prince so impressively . . . "

Lestrade made an uncomfortable noise that did not quite become a word.

"I have spent many days retracing the movements of his highness. I went from gambling hell to brothel to dining den to madhouse looking for our pipe-smoking man and his friend. I made no progress until I thought to check the newspapers of Bohemia, searching for a clue to the Prince's recent activities there, and in them I learned that an English Theatrical Troupe had been in Prague last month, and had performed before Prince Franz Drago . . . "

"Good lord," I said. "So that Sherry Vernet fellow . . . "

"Is a Restorationist. Exactly."

I was shaking my head in wonder at my friend's intelligence and skills of observation, when there was a knock on the door.

"This will be our quarry!" said my friend. "Careful now!"

Lestrade put his hand deep into his pocket, where I had no doubt he kept a pistol. He swallowed, nervously.

My friend called out, "Please, come in!"

The door opened.

It was not Vernet, nor was it a Limping Doctor. It was one of the young street Arabs who earn a crust running errands—"in the employ of Messrs. Street and Walker," as we used to say when I was young. "Please sirs," he said. "Is there a Mister Henry Camberley here? I was asked by a gentleman to deliver a note."

"I'm he," said my friend. "And for a sixpence, what can you tell me about the gentleman who gave you the note?"

The young lad, who volunteered that his name was Wiggins, bit the sixpence before making it vanish, and then told us that the cheery cove who gave him the note was on the tall side, with dark hair, and, he added, he had been smoking a pipe.

I have the note here, and take the liberty of transcribing it.

My Dear Sir;

I do not address you as Henry Camberley, for it is a name to which you have no claim. I am surprised that you did not announce yourself under your own name, for it is a fine one, and one that does you credit. I have read a number of your papers, when I have been able to obtain them. Indeed, I corresponded with you quite profitably two years ago about certain theoretical anomalies in your paper on the Dynamics of an Asteroid.

I was amused to meet you, yesterday evening. A few tips which might save you bother in times to come, in the profession you currently follow. Firstly, a pipe-smoking man might possibly have a brand-new, unused pipe in his pocket, and no tobacco, but it is exceedingly unlikely at least as unlikely as a theatrical promoter with no idea of the usual customs of recompense on a tour; who is accompanied by a taciturn ex-army officer (Afghanistan, unless I miss my guess,). Incidentally, while you are correct that the streets of London have ears, it might also behoove you in future not to take the first cab that comes along. Cab-drivers have ears too, if they choose to use them.

You are certainly correct in one of your suppositions: it was indeed I who lured the half-blood creature back to the room in Shoreditch.

If it is any comfort to you, having learned a little of his recreational predilections, I had told him I had procured for him a girl, abducted from a convent in Cornwall where she had never seen a man, and that it would only take his touch, and the sight of his face, to tip her over into a perfect madness.

Had she existed, he would have feasted on her madness while he took her, like a man sucking the flesh from a ripe peach leaving nothing behind but the skin and the pit. I have seen them do this. I have seen them do far worse. And it is not the price we pay for peace and prosperity. It is too great a price for that.

The good doctor—who believes as I do, and who did indeed write our little performance, for he has some crowd-pleasing skills—was waiting for us, with his knives.

I send this note, not as a catch-me-if-you-can taunt, for we are gone, the estimable doctor and I, and you shall not find us, but to tell you that it was good to feel that, if only for a moment, I had a worthy adversary. Worthier by far than inhuman creatures from beyond the Pit.

I fear the Strand Players will need to find themselves a new leading man.

I will not sign myself Vernet, and until the hunt is done and the world restored, I beg you to think of me simply as,

Rache.

Inspector Lestrade ran from the room, calling to his men. They made young Wiggins take them to the place where the man had given him the note, for all the world as if Vernet the actor would be waiting there for them, a-smoking of his pipe. From the window we watched them run, my friend and I, and we shook our heads.

"They will stop and search all the trains leaving London, all the ships leaving Albion for Europe or the New World," said my friend. "Looking for a tall man, and his companion, a smaller, thickset medical man, with a slight limp. They will close the ports. Every way out of the country will be blocked."

"Do you think they will catch him, then?"

My friend shook his head. "I may be wrong," he said, "But I would wager that he and his friend are even now only a mile or so away, in the rookery of St. Giles, where the police will not go except by the dozen. And they will hide up there until the hue and cry have died away. And then they will be about their business."

"What makes you say that?"

"Because," said my friend, "if our positions were reversed, it is what I would do. You should burn the note, by the way."

I frowned. "But surely it's evidence," I said.

"It's seditionary nonsense," said my friend.

And I should have burned it. Indeed, I told Lestrade I had burned it, when he returned, and he congratulated me on my good sense. Lestrade kept his job, and Prince Albert wrote a note to my friend congratulating him on his deductions, while regretting that the perpetrator was still at large.

They have not yet caught Sherry Vernet, or whatever his name really is, nor was any trace of his murderous accomplice, tentatively identified as a former military surgeon named John (or perhaps James) Watson. Curiously, it was revealed that he had also been in Afghanistan. I wonder if we ever met.

My shoulder, touched by the Queen, continues to improve, the flesh fills and it heals. Soon I shall be a dead-shot once more.

One night when we were alone, several months ago, I asked my friend if he remembered the correspondence referred to in the letter from the man who signed himself Rache. My friend said that he remembered it well, and that "Sigerson" (for so the actor had called himself then, claiming to be an Icelander) had been inspired by an equation of my friend's to suggest some wild theories furthering the relationship between mass, energy, and the hypothetical speed of light. "Nonsense, of course," said my friend, without smiling. "But inspired and dangerous nonsense nonetheless."

The palace eventually sent word that the Queen was pleased with my friend's accomplishments in the case, and there the matter has rested.

I doubt my friend will leave it alone, though; it will not be over until one of them has killed the other.

I kept the note. I have said things in this retelling of events that are not to be said. If I were a sensible man I would bum all these pages, but then, as my friend taught me, even ashes can give up their secrets. Instead, I shall place these papers in a strongbox at my bank with instructions that the box may not be opened until long after anyone now living is dead. Although, in the light of the recent events in Russia, I fear that day may be closer than any of us would care to think.

S_____M_____Major (Ret'd)
Baker Street,
London, New Albion, 1881.

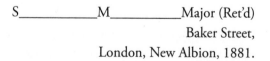

*Imagination called up the shocking form of fabulous Yog-Sothoth—only
a congeries of iridescent globes, yet stupendous in its malign suggestiveness.*
"Horror in the Museum" · H.P. Lovecraft (1932)

• BURIED IN THE SKY •
John Shirley

"If he didn't kill Mom, then why are we moving away?" Deede asked.

"We're *moving* because I have a better job offer in LA," Dad said, barely audible as usual, as he looked vaguely out the living room window at the tree-lined street. Early evening on a Portland June. "I'll be working for a good magazine—very high profile. See those clouds? Going to rain again. We won't have all this rain in LA, anyhow and Hanging Gardens will be a nice change. You'll like LA high schools, the kids are very . . . uh . . . hip." Wearing his perpetual work shirts, jeans, and a dully stoic expression, he was a paunchy, pale, gray-eyed man with shaggy blond hair just starting to go gray. He stood with his hands in his pockets, gazing outward from the house. In a lower voice he said, "They said it was an accident or . . . " He didn't like to say suicide. "So—we have to assume that's right and, well, we can't harass an innocent man. Better to leave it all behind us."

Deede Bergstrom—waist-length sandy-blond hair, neo-hippy look—was half watching MTV, the sound turned off; on the screen a woman wearing something like a bikini crossed with a dress was posturing and pumping her hips. Deede's hips were a shade too wide and she'd never call attention to them like that.

Deede knew Dad didn't want the travel writer job in LA that much—he liked Portland, he didn't like Los Angeles, except as a subject for journalism, and the travel editor job with the Portland newspaper paid their bills. He was just trying to get them away from the place where mom had died because everything they saw here was a reminder. And they had to get over it.

Didn't you have to get over it, when someone murdered your mother?

Sure. Sure you do. You just have to get over it.

"You think he killed her too, Dad," said Lenny matter-of-factly, as he came in. He'd been in the kitchen, listening. The peanut butter and jelly sandwich dripped in his hand as he looked at his Dad, and took an enormous bite.

"You're spilling blueberry jelly on the carpet," Deede pointed out. She was curled up in the easy chair with her feet tucked under her skirt to keep them warm. The heat was already turned off, in preparation for the move, and it wasn't as warm out as it should've been, this time of year.

"Shut up, mantis-girl," Lenny said, the food making his voice indistinct. He was referring to her long legs and long neck. He was a year older than Deede, had just graduated high school. His hair was buzz-cut, and he wore a muscle shirt—he had the muscles to go with it—and a quizzical expression. His chin was a little weak, but his features otherwise were almost TV-star good looking. The girls at school had liked him.

"Lenny I've asked you not to call your sister that, and go and get a paper towel and clean up your mess," Dad said, without much conviction. "Deana, where's your little sister?"

They called her Deede because her name was Deana Diane. Deede shrugged. "Jean just leaves when she wants to . . . " And then she remembered. "Oh yeah, she went rollerblading with that Buzzy kid."

Lenny snorted. "That little stoner."

Dad started to ask if he Lenny a good reason to think his youngest sister was hanging with stoners—Deede could see the question was about to come out of him—but then his lips pinched shut. Decided not to ask. "Yeah, well, Buzzy won't be coming with us to LA, so . . . " He shrugged.

Dad was still looking out the window, Deede mostly watching the soundless TV.

And Lenny was looking at the floor while he listlessly ate his sandwich, Deede noticed, looking over from the TV. *Dad out the window, me at TV, Lenny at the floor.*

Mom at the interior of her coffin lid.

"I think we should stay and push them to reopen it," Deede said, doggedly.

Dad sighed. "We don't know that Gunnar Johansen killed anyone. We know that mom was jogging and Johansen was seen on the same jogging trail and later on she was found dead. There wasn't even agreement at the coroner's on whether she'd been . . . "

He didn't want to say *raped.*

"He was almost bragging about it," Lenny said tonelessly, staring at the rug, his jaws working on the sandwich. " 'Prove it!' he said." Deede could see the anger in his eyes but you had to look for it. He was like Dad, all internal.

"It was two years ago," Deede said. "I don't think the police are going to do anything else. But we could hire a private detective." Two years. She felt like it was two weeks. It'd taken almost six months for Deede to be able to function again after they found Mom dead. "Anyway—I saw it . . . in a way."

"Dreams." Dad shook his head. "Recurrent dreams aren't proof. You're going to like LA."

She wanted to leave Portland—and she also wanted to stay here and make someone put Johansen in jail. But she couldn't stay here alone. Even if she did, what could she do about him, herself? She was afraid of him. She saw him sometimes in the neighborhood—he lived a block and a half down—and every time he looked right at her. And every time, too, it was like he was saying, *I killed your mom and I liked it and I want to kill you too and pretty soon I will.* It didn't make sense, her seeing all that, when he had no particular expression on his face. But she was sure of it, completely sure of it. He had killed her mom. And he'd liked it. And he had killed some other people and he'd liked that too.

She had no proof at all. Recurrent dreams aren't proof.

" . . . the movers are coming in about an hour," Dad was saying. "We're going to have a really good new life." He said it while looking out the window and he said it tonelessly. He didn't even bother to make it sound as if he really believed the part about a really good new life.

Two days later, they were ready to go to Los Angeles—and it had finally started to warm up in Oregon, like it was grudgingly admitting it was the beginning of summer. "Now that we're leaving, it's nice out," Jean said bitterly, from the back seat of the Explorer. The sky was showing through the clouds, and purple irises edging the neighbor's lawn were waving in the breeze and then, as Deede just sat in the front seat of the car, waiting for her Dad to drive her and her brother and Jean to the I-5 freeway, she saw Johansen walking down the street toward them, walking by those same irises. Dad was looking around one last time, to see if he'd forgotten to do anything, making sure the doors to the house were locked. He would leave the keys for the Realtor, in some prearranged place. The house where Deede had grown up was sold and in a few minutes would be gone from her life forever.

Jean and Lenny didn't see Johansen, Lenny was in back beside Jean, his whole attention on playing with the PSP and Jean was looking at the little TV screen over the back seat of the SUV. Fourteen years old, starting to get fat; her short-clipped hair was reddish brown, her face heart-shaped like Mom's had been, the same little dimples in her cheeks. She was chewing gum and fixedly watching a Nickelodeon show she probably didn't like.

Deede wasn't going to point Johansen out to her. She didn't much relate to her little sister—Jean seemed to blame Deede for not having the same problems. Jean had dyslexia, and Deede didn't; Jean was attention deficit, and Deede wasn't. Jean had gotten only more bitter and withdrawn since Mom had died. She didn't want anyone acting protective. Deede felt she had to try to protect her anyway.

Johansen was getting closer.

"This building we're moving into, it's, like, lame, living in a stupid-ass building after living in a house," Jean said, snapping her gum ever few syllables, her eyes on the SUV's television.

"It's not just any stupid-ass building," Lenny said, his thumbs working the controllers, destroying mordo-bots with preternatural skill as he went on, "it's Skytown. It's like some famous architectural big deal, a building with everything in it. It has the Skymall and the, whatsit, uh, Hanging Gardens in it. That's where we live, Hanging Gardens Apartments, name's from some ancient thing I forget . . . "

"From *Babylon*," Deede mumbled, watching Johansen get closer. Starting to wonder if, after all, she should point him out. But she grew more afraid with every step he took, each bringing him closer, though he was just sauntering innocently along, a tall tanned athletic man in light blue Lacrosse shirt and Dockers; short flaxen hair, pale blue eyes, much more lower lip than upper, a forehead that seemed bonily square. Very innocently walking along. Just the hint of a smirk on his face.

Where was Dad? Why didn't he come back to the car?

Don't say anything to Jean or Lenny. Jean would go back to not sleeping at night again, if she saw Johansen so close. They all knew he'd killed Mom. Everyone knew but the police. Maybe they knew too but they couldn't prove it. The coroner had ruled "accidental death."

Johansen walked up abreast Deede. She wanted to look him in the eye, and say, with that look, *I know what you did and you won't get away with it.*

Their gazes met. His pale blue eyes dilated in response. His lips parted. He caught the tip of his tongue between his teeth. He looked at her—

Crumbling inside, the fear going through her like an electric shock, she looked away.

He chuckled—she heard it softly but clearly—as he walked on by.

Her mouth was dry, very dry, but her eyes spilled tears. Everything was hazy. Maybe a minute passed, maybe not so much. She was looking hard at the dashboard.

"Hanging Gardens," Lenny said, finally, oblivious to his sister's terror. "Stupid name. Makes you think they're gonna hang somebody there."

"That's why you're going to live there," Jean said, eyes glued to the TV. " 'Cause they going to hang you."

"*You're* gonna live there *too*, shrimpy."

"Little as possible," Jean responded, with a chillingly adult decisiveness.

Deede wanted to ask her what she meant by that—but Jean resented Deede's protectiveness. She'd called her, "Miss Protective three-point-eight." She resented Deede's good grades—implied she was a real kiss-ass or something, to get them. Though in fact they were pretty effortless for her. But it was true, she was too protective.

"Deede?" Dad's voice. "You okay?"

Deede blinked, wiped her eyes, looked at her Dad, opening the driver's side door, bending to squint in at her. "I'm okay," she said.

He never pushed it, hadn't since Mom died. If you said you were "okay," crying or not, that was as good as could be expected. They'd all had therapy—Lenny had stopped going after a month—and it'd helped a little. Dad probably figured it was all that could be done.

He got in and started the car and they started off. Deede looked in the mirror and she saw Johansen, way down the street, his back to them. Stopping. Turning to look after them . . .

As they drove away from their home.

"This place is so huge . . . so high up . . . " Deede, Lenny, and Jean were in the observation deck of the Skytown building, up above Skytown Mall and the apartment complex, looking out at the clouds just above, the pillars and spikes of downtown LA below them. They were in the highest and newest skyscraper in Los Angeles.

"It's a hundred-twenty-five stories, fifteen more than the World Trade Center buildings were," Lenny said, reading from the guide pamphlet. "Supposed to be 'super hardened' to resist terrorist attacks . . . "

Deede remembered what she'd read about the Titanic, how it was supposed to be unsinkable, too. Skytown, it occurred to her, was almost a magnet for terrorists. But she wouldn't say that with Jean here, and anyway Lenny had been calling her "Deana Downer" for her frequent dour pronouncements. "*Just an inch the wrong way on that steering wheel and Dad could drive us under the wheels of a semitruck*," she'd told Lenny, when they were halfway to LA. Jean had been asleep—but Dad had frowned at her anyway.

"When's Dad coming back?" Deede asked, trying to see the street directly below. She couldn't see it—the "hanging gardens" were in the way: a ribbony spilling of green vines and lavender wisteria over the edges of the balconies encompassing the building under the observation deck. Closer to the building's superstructure were rose bushes too, but the building was new and so were the rose bushes, there were no blossoms on them yet. The building had a square base—filling a square city block—and rose to a ziggurat peak, a step pyramid, the lowest step of the pyramid containing the garden, the penultimate step the observation deck.

"Not till after dinner," Lenny said. "He has a meeting."

"Is this part of, what, the Hanging Gardens Apartments?" Jean asked, sucking noisily on a smoothie.

"No, that's actually down," Lenny said. "This is the observation deck above Skymall. Whole thing is actually called Skytown. The apartments are under the gardens but they're called the Hanging Gardens Apartments anyway, just to be more confusing."

Feeling isolated, lonely, gazing down on the tiny specks that were people, the cars looking smaller than Hot Wheels toys, Deede turned away from the window. "Let's go back to the apartment and wait for Dad."

"No way!" Jean said, talking around the straw. "The apartment smells too much like paint! I want to see the Skymall! We're supposed to have dinner there!" She sucked up the dregs of her smoothie. "And I'm still hungry."

At first it was like any mall anywhere, though it was so high up they felt a little tired and light headed. Deede heard a security guard talking about it to the man who ran the frozen yogurt shop—the young black guard had a peculiar uniform, dark gray, almost black, with silver epaulettes, and the shapes of snakes going around his cuffs. "Yeah man, we're so high up, the air's a little thin. They try to equalize it but it don't always go. They're working out the bugs. Like that groaning in the elevators . . . "

Windows at the end of the mall's long corridors showed the hazy dull blue sky and planes going by, not that far above, and the tops of high buildings—seeing just the tops from here made them look to Deede like images she'd seen of buildings in Egypt and other ancient places.

There were only a few other customers; they were among the first to move into the building and the mall wasn't officially open to the public, except for the apartment owners. Walking along the empty walkway between rows of glassy storefronts, Deede felt like a burglar. She had to look close to see shopkeepers inside—the ones who noticed them looked at Deede and her siblings almost plaintively. *Please give me some business so I feel like this new investment isn't hopeless and doomed to failure.* "Sorry, Mister," she muttered, "I don't want to buy any NFL Official Logo gym bags."

"What?" Jean said. "Lenny she's mumbling to herself again."

He sniggered. "That's our Deede. Hey what's that thing?"

He pointed at a window containing a rack of objects resembling bicycle helmets crossed with sea urchins. The transparent spikes on the helmets seemed to feel them looking and reacted, retracting.

"Eww!" Jean said. "It's like critter antenna things!"

The store was called INTER-REACTIVES INC. There was a man in the back, in a green jump suit, a man shaped roughly like a bowling pin, who seemed to have a bright orange face. It must be some kind of colored light back there, Deede decided, making his face look orange. The man turned to look at them. His eyes were green—even the parts that should be white were green.

"Is that guy wearing a mask?" Jean asked.

The man looked at her and a rictus-like grin jerked across his face—split it in half—and was gone. From expressionless to grin to expressionless in half a second.

Deede backed away, and turned hastily to the next store.

"That guy was all . . . " Jean murmured. But she didn't say anything more about it.

You got weird impressions sometimes in strange places, Deede decided. That's all it was.

The next shop was a Nike store. Then came a Disney store, closed. Then a store called BLENDER. Jean stopped, interested: It seemed to sell things to eat. Behind the window glass, transparent chutes curved down into blenders; dropping through the chutes, into the intermittently grinding blenders, came indeterminate pieces of organic material Deede had never seen before, bits and pieces of things: they weren't definitely flesh and they weren't recognizably fruit but they made you think of flesh and fruit—only, the colors were all wrong, the surface textures alien. Some of them seemed to be parts of brightly colored faces—which seemed to squirm in the blender so that the apparent eye would line up properly with a nose, above lips, the disjointed face looking at her for a moment before being whirred away into bits. But the parts of the faces, when she looked closer, weren't noses or eyes or lips at all. "What *is* that stuff?" Deede asked.

Lenny and Jean shook their heads at once, staring in puzzlement—and the blenders started whirring all at once, making the kids jump a bit. In the back of the store was a counter and someone was on the other side of the counter, which was only about four and a half feet high, but you could just see the top of their head on the other side of the counter—a lemon-colored head. The top of the head moved nervously back and forth.

"Some kid back there," Jean said. "Walkin' back and forth."

"Or some dwarf," Lenny said. "You want to go in and see?" But he didn't move toward the shop. The other two shook their heads.

They moved on, passing an ordinary shop that sold fancy color photo portraits, a store that sold clothing for teenage girls that neither Jean nor Deede would be interested in—it was for cheerleader types—and then a store . . .

It was filled with birdcages and in the cages were birds that didn't seem to have any eyes and seemed to have beaks covered with fur, from which issued spiral tongues. They moved around in their crowded cages so fast it was hard to tell if the impression Deede had of their appearance was right. A woman in the back of the shop had a fantastic piled-up hair style, an elaborate coif with little spheres woven into it, reminding Deede of eyes, randomly arranged into the high hairdo; she turned around . . .

She must have turned all the way around, really quickly, so quickly they didn't see the turn, because they saw only the elaborate coif and the back of her head again.

"This place is making me feel, all, sick to my stomach," Jean said.

"I think it's like . . . .not enough oxygen . . . or something," Lenny said. Sounding like Dad in his tentative way of speaking, just then. Then more decisively: "Yo look, there's an arcade!"

They crossed into the more familiar confines of an arcade, its doorway open into a dark room, illuminated mostly by light from the various game machines. "Lenny, give me a dollar!" Jean demanded.

"Stop ordering me around!" But he gave her a dollar, mashing it up in her palm, and she got a videogame machine to accept it. Deede had never seen the game before: it was called KILLER GIRL and it appeared to show a girl—so low-rez she had no clear-cut features—shooting fiery red bullets from her eyes and the tips of her fingers and her navel—was it her navel?—toward dozens of murkily defined enemies who cropped up in the windows of a suburban neighborhood, enemies with odd looking weapons in their pixilated hands. The neighborhood was rather like the one they'd left in Portland.

As Jean played, Deede and Lenny watching, the video figure that Jean controlled changed shape, becoming more definite, more high resolution—looking more and more like Jean herself. Then a videogame "boss" loomed up over a building in the game, a giant, somewhat but not quite resembling Gunnar Johansen.

"What are you kids doing in here?"

All three of them twitched around to face him at once, as if they'd rehearsed it. A security guard was scowling at them. A man with small eyes, a flattened nose in a chunky grayish face that looked almost made of putty. He wore a peculiar, tight-fitting helmet of translucent blue, that pressed his hair down so it looked like meat in a supermarket package. There was a smell off him like smashed ants. He wore the almost-black and silver uniform with the snake cuffs.

"What you mean, what're we doing?" Lenny snorted. "Dude, it's an arcade. Work it out."

"But the mall's closed. Five minutes ago. Closes early till full public opening next month."

"So we didn't know that, okay? Now back the fuck off. Come on, Deede, Jean."

"My game!"

"Forget it. Come on, Deede—you too Jean, now."

The guard followed a few steps behind them as they headed for the elevators leading out of the mall—Deede thought Lenny was going to turn and hit the guy for following them, his fists clenching on rigid arms, like he did before he hit that Garcia kid—but he just muttered "Fuck this guy" and walked faster till they were in the elevator. The guard made as if to get in the elevator with them but Lenny said, "No fucking way, asshole," and stabbed the elevator "close doors" button. It shut in the guard's face, on a frozen, minatory expression that hadn't changed since he'd first spoken to them.

Jean laughed. "What a loser."

The elevator groaned as it took them down to the apartments—like it was old, not almost brand new. It groaned and shivered and moaned, the sound very human, heart wrenching. Deede wanted to comfort it. The moans actually seemed to come from above it, as if someone was standing on the elevator, wailing, like a man waiting to be executed.

It was a relief to be back in the apartment, the doors locked, in the midst of thirty floors of housing about half way up the building: a comfortable, well organized three-bedroom place—the bedrooms small but well ventilated. No balcony but with a view out over the city. They had cable TV, cable modems, a DVD player, big LCD screen, an Xbox and a refrigerator stocked with snacks and sodas. Dad finally came home with pizza. Life was pretty good that evening.

A few days later, though, Dad announced he was leaving for five days. He had an assignment for the magazine, had to fly to Vancouver, and they'd spent too much money getting here, he couldn't afford to bring the kids with him, though school was out for the summer. Jean refused to respond to the announcement with anything but a shrug; Deede found herself almost whining, asking whether this was going to be a regular thing. As a travel editor in Portland, Dad hadn't left town all that much, mostly he just edited other people's articles. Standing at the window, a can of Diet Coke in one hand, he admitted he was going to be gone a lot in the new job.

"Yeah well that's just *great*," Lenny said, his mouth going slack with disgust, his whole frame radiating resentment—and he stuck his fists in his pockets, the way he always did when he was mad at his father, so that the seams started to pop. "I need to get my own place. I can't be babysitting all the time, Dad."

"Well until you do, you've gotta do your part, Lenny," Dad said, gazing out the window at downtown LA. "Just . . . just help me out this summer, while you figure out what college you want, get a day job, and all . . . all like that. And, and you're responsible, while I'm gone, for your sisters, you have to be, I just don't have time to find anyone reliable. "

"Like we need *him* to take care of us," Jean said. "Like Mom would leave us this way."

They all looked at her and she stared defiantly back. Finally Dad said, "This building is very safe, really safe. I mean, it's high security as all hell. You have your door cards. But you shouldn't even leave the place while I'm gone if you can help it. Everything you need's here. Supermarket, clinic, it's all in the building. There's even a movie theater."

"It doesn't open till next week," Lenny said bitterly.

Dad cleared his throat, looked out the window again. "There are kids to meet here."

"Hardly anyone's moved in," Jean pointed out, rolling her eyes.

"Well," Dad hesitated, taking a pull on his Diet Coke. "only go out in the day and . . . and don't run around in downtown LA. Downtown LA is dangerous. You can go to Hollywood Boulevard and go to a movie. Lenny can drive the car, I guess. But just . . . try to stay . . . to stay here. . . . "

His voice trailed off. He gazed out the picture window, watching a plane fly over.

• • •

She met Jorny in the Skymall when they got their iPods mixed up in the frozen yogurt shop. "Yo, girl, that's my iPod," Jorny said, as Deede picked it up from the counter. He had blue eyes that glimmered with irony in a V-shaped face, dark eyebrows that contrasted with his long, corn-rowed sun-bleached brown hair, a tan that was partly burn. He was slender, not quite as tall as her; he wore pants raggedly cut off just above the knees, with ANARCHY? WHO THE FUCK KNOWS? written on the left pants leg in blue ballpoint pen, and a way-oversized T-shirt with a picture of Nicholas Cage on it hoisting a booze bottle, from *Leaving Las Vegas.* He had various odd items twined around his wrists as improvised bracelets—twist-its worked together, individual rings of plastic cut from six-packs. He wore high-topped red tennis shoes, falling apart—probably stressed from skateboarding: a well worn skateboard was jammed under his left arm.

"No it's not your iPod," Deede said, mildly. "Look, it's playing The Hives' 'Die All Right', the song I was listening to."

"That's the song *I* was listening to. I just set it down for a second to get my money out."

"No it's—oh, you're right, my iPod's in my purse. I paused it on 'Die All Right.' I thought I . . . sorry. But that really is the same song I was listening to—look! Same one—at the same time!"

"Whoa, that's weird. You're, like, stalking me and shit."

"I guess. You live in the building?"

"You kids want these frozen yogurts or what?" asked the man at the counter.

They bought their frozen yogurts, and one for Jean, who was in the Mall walkway looking in store windows. It turned out that Jorny lived downstairs from them, almost right below. He was three weeks younger than Deede and he mostly lived to do skateboard tricks. His Dad had "gone off to live in New York, we don't see him around much." When she said her mom was dead he said, "Between us we almost got one set of parents."

Jean told him she did rollerblading—he managed not to seem scornful at that—and he and Deede talked about music and the odd things they'd seen in the mall shops and how they didn't seem to be the same shops the next day. "One place seemed like it was selling faces," Jorny said. "LATEST FACE."

"I didn't see that one. They must mean masks or maybe makeup."

He shook his head but didn't argue and tried to show her some new skateboard ollies right there in the mall but the putty faced guard began jogging toward them from the other end of the walkway, bellowing. "You—hold it right there, don't you move!"

"Security guards everywhere hate skateboarders," Jorny declared proudly, grinning. "Fucking hate us. Come on!" He started toward a stairwell.

"Jean—come on!" Deede shouted, starting after him. Sticking her tongue out at the security guard, Jean came giggling after them as they banged through the doors into the stairwell and the smell of concrete and newly-dried paint, and pounded down the stairs, laughing.

"Hey you kids!" came the shout from above.

They kept going, Jorny at the next level down jumping a flight of stairs on his skateboard, and landing it with a joint-jarring *clack*. "You actually landed that!" Deede shouted, impressed—and privately a little dismayed. It was a big jump, though skateboarders did that sort of thing a lot. She was also pleased that he was evidently showing off for her.

"Yeah, huh, that was tight, I landed it!" Jorny called, clacking down the next group of stairs, ollying from one stair to the next. Jean squealed, "Agggghhh! Run! He's coming! That blue helmet weirdo's coming!"

They ran down the stairs, easily outdistancing the security guard, and bolted onto the mid-level observation court and community center. They took the elevator to the Hanging Gardens, where they went to check out Jorny's place, an apartment almost identical to their own. Deede didn't want Jean to come but couldn't think of way for her not to.

Jorny's mom was there for lunch. She was a lawyer, the director of the county Public Defender's office, a plump woman in a suit with a white streak in her wooly black hair, and a pleasantly Semitic face. She seemed happy to see Deede, maybe as opposed to some of the rougher people she'd seen her son with—all that was in her face, when she looked at Deede. She smiled at Deede, then glanced at Jean, looked away from her, then looked back at her, a kind of double-take, as if trying to identify what it was about the girl that worried her.

It had only just recently occurred to Deede that what she saw in other people wasn't visible to everyone. It wasn't exactly psychic—it was just what Deede thought of as "looking faster." She'd always been able to look faster.

"Come on," Jorny said, as his mom went to make them sandwiches. "I want to play you the new *Wolfmother* single. It's not out yet—it's a ripped download a friend of mine sent me."

The notice was there on Saturday morning, when Deede got up. Dad had left at six that morning, not saying goodbye—they all knew he was going to be gone several days—and he wouldn't have seen the notice, she thought. Someone had slipped it under the door from the hall. It read:

NOTICE

DUE TO SECURITY CONCERNS ONLY AUTHORIZED PERSONNEL WILL BE ALLOWED
TO LEAVE THE BUILDING THIS WEEKEND, AS OF 8 A.M, SATURDAY MORNING
EXCEPT FOR DESIGNATED EMERGENCIES (SEE SKYTOWN MANUAL PAGE 39 FOR
DESIGNATED EMERGENCY GUIDELINES). RESTRICTIONS WILL BE LIFTED IN A
FEW DAYS. PLEASE BE PATIENT.
THANK YOU FOR YOUR COOPERATION.
SKYTOWN OFFICE OF SECURITY

"What the fuck!" Lenny burst out, when Deede showed it to him. "That is totally illegal! Hey—call that kid you met, with the lawyer mom."

"Jorny?" It would be a good excuse to call him.

Jorny answered sleepily. "Whuh? My mom? She left for . . . go see my aunt for breakfast or something . . . s'pose-a be back later. Why whussup?"

"Um—check if you got a notice under your front door."

He came back to the phone under a minute seconds later. "Yeah! Same notice! My mom left after eight, though and she hasn't come back. So it must be bullshit, they must've let her go. Maybe it's a hoax. Or . . . "

"We're gonna go to the bargain matinee over on Hollywood Boulevard. You wanna go? I mean—then we can see if they really are making people stay. "

A little over an hour later they were all dressed, meeting Jorny downstairs outside the elevators at the front lobby. They walked by potted plants toward the tinted glass of the front doors . . . and found the doors locked from inside.

"You kids didn't get the notice?"

They turned to see a smiling, personable, middle-aged man standing about thirty feet away. He wore a green suit-and-tie—maybe that was why his face had a vague greenish cast to it. Just a reflection off the green cloth. Behind him were two security guards in the peculiar uniforms.

"That notice is bullshit," Lenny said flatly. "Not legal."

"You look a little young to be a lawyer," said the man in the green suit mildly.

"Your face is sort of green," Jean said, staring at him.

But as she said it, his face seemed to shift to a more normal color. As if he'd just noticed and changed it somehow.

"Or not . . . " Jean mumbled.

The man ignored her. "My name is Arthur Koenig—I'm the building supervisor. I'm pretty sure of the laws and rules and I assure you kids, you cannot leave the building except under designated emergency conditions."

"And I'm pretty sure," Jorny said, snapping his skateboard up with his foot to catch it in his hand, "that's what they call 'false imprisonment'—it's a form of kidnapping."

The security guards both had the odd translucent-blue helmets. They stood behind and to either side of Koenig—one of them, who might've been Filipino, stepped frowning toward Jorny. "That's the boy who was doing the skateboarding in the Mall—I saw him on the cameras. Boy—you give me that skateboard, that's contraband here!"

"Not a fucking chance, a-hole," Jorny said, making Jean squeal with laughter. "Come on," he said to Lenny, "we'll go to my place and call around about this."

"Building phone line's being worked on," said Koenig pleasantly. "Be down for a while. Building cable too."

"We've got cell phones, man," Lenny said, turning toward the elevators. "Come on you guys."

As they went back to the elevators, Deede glanced over her shoulder, saw that Koenig was following, at a respectful distance—and while they were walking at an angle, the shortest way to the elevator, he seemed to be following a straight line—then he turned right, and she realized he was following the lines of the square sections of floor. And she saw something coming off his right heel—a thin red cord, or string, like a finely stretched out piece of flesh, that came from a hole in his shoe and went into the groove between the floor tiles . . .

A thread, stuck to his shoe, is all, she told herself. *It's not really a connection to something inside the floor.*

"That skateboard!" The blue-helmeted security guard yelled, following Jorny. "Leave it here! I'm confiscating it!"

But Koenig reached out, put his hand on the guard's arm. "Let him go. It doesn't matter now. Let him keep it for the moment."

Deede followed the others into the elevator. She didn't mention the red cord to them.

"This is 911 emergency. May I have your name and address?"

Lenny gave his name and address and then said, "I'm calling because we're being held against our will by the weirdoes in this building we live in. The manager, all these people—no one's allowed to leave the building! It's totally illegal!"

"Slow down, please," said the dispatcher, her voice crackling in the cell phone, phasing in and out of clarity. "Who exactly is 'restraining' you?"

The skepticism was rank in her voice.

"The building security people say we can't leave, *no one* can leave, there're hundreds of people who live here and we can't—"

"Was there a bomb threat?"

"I don't know, they didn't say so, they just said 'security concerns.'"

"The security at that building interfaces with the police department, if they're asking people not to leave it's probably so they can investigate something. Have they been . . . oh, violent or. . . . "

"No, not yet, but they . . . look, it's false imprisonment, it's . . . "

"They are security, we'll have someone call them—but they're probably doing this for your protection. It could be a Homeland Security drill."

"Oh Jesus, forget it." He broke the connection and threw the cell phone so it bounced on the sofa cushion. "I can't believe it. They just assumed I was full of crap."

Jorny was on his own cell phone, listening. He frowned and hung up. "I can't get my mom to answer, or my aunt."

"Jorny? " said Deede thoughtfully, looking out the apartment's picture window at the smog-hazy sky. "You think maybe they stopped your mom— took her into custody 'cause she tried to leave?"

Jorny stared at her. "No way." He shot to his feet. "Come on, if you're coming. I'm gonna ask if she's at the security office . . . "

Deede looked at Lenny to see if he was coming but he was on the cell phone again. "I'm trying to call Dad . He's not picking up though."

"Lenny—where's Jean?" Deede asked, looking around. It wasn't like Jean to be so quiet.

"Hm? She left. She said she's going to that coffee lounge where those kids hang out."

"What kids?"

"I don't know. She started hanging with them yesterday sometime. She came back at three in the morning. I think she was, like, stoned. "

"What? I'm gonna go get her. And help Jorny! " She called this to Lenny as she followed Jorny out the door. Lenny waved her on.

Another notice had been taped up on the wall next to the elevator call buttons:

NOTICE

ELEVATOR MOVEMENT HAS BEEN RESTRICTED TO THE UPPER SEVENTY FLOORS UNTIL FURTHER NOTICE. ELEVATOR WILL NOT DESCEND FROM THIS LEVEL. THANK YOU FOR YOUR COOPERATION.

"What the fuck!" Jorny said, gaping at the notice.

"I wouldn't have put it that way," said a white-haired older woman standing a few steps away; she wore thick, horn-rimmed glasses and a long blue dress. "But that's generally my feeling too." She had her purse over her shoulder, as if she had planned to go out. "I was going to Farmer's Market but . . . I guess not now." The woman went back toward the doors to the apartment complex, shaking her head.

Jorny shook his head as the woman walked away. "Everyone just accepts it."

"Security office is downstairs," Deede said. "We can't get to it on the elevators. But we could take the stairs. Only, I want to find my sister. But then she could be down there too . . . "

He was already starting toward the door to the stairwell, skateboard under his arm—you can't skateboard on carpet.

But the stairwell door was locked. "What about the fire laws and all that?" Jorny said, wondering aloud. He looked toward a fire alarm, as if thinking of tripping it. Deede hoped he wouldn't.

"Okay," he said, "let's go upstairs on the elevators to that lounge, see if we can find some way from there to go down. There must be a way—the security guards must be able to do it."

"I want to get my brother to go with us."

They went back to the apartment . . . and found the apartment door standing open.

Inside there was a lamp knocked over. Lenny was gone. He'd left his cell phone where he'd thrown it and he was just . . . gone. She looked through all the rooms and called up and down the halls. No response except a Filipino man looked out a door briefly—then hastily shut it when Deede tried to ask him a question. They heard him lock it.

"I'm sure he's okay," Jorny said.

Deede looked reproachfully at him. "I didn't say he wasn't."

"You looked worried."

"I . . . I'm worried about Jean and . . . this whole weird thing. That's all. Lenny gets in a snit sometimes and goes off and says 'Screw everybody' and wanders away . . . gets somebody to buy him beer somewhere and he gets a little smashed and then he comes home. But leaving the door open that way . . . "

Jorny was on his cell again, trying to call his mom. He called his aunt, spoke to her for less than a minute in low tones—and hung up. "She never showed up. She was supposed to meet my aunt—and she never got there."

"It's too soon to call it a 'missing persons' thing. We could look for your mom in the building. And Jean."

"You want to try the lounge?" Jorny asked. She nodded and they went to the elevators and rode up toward the lounge. On the way he tried to call his mom on the cell phone again—and gave up. "Doesn't work at all now. Just static."

"There are places in the elevators for keys," Deede said, pointing at the key fixture under the floor tabs. "The security guards must have keys that let them go to restricted floors."

That's when the moaning started up again, in the elevators above them—and below them too. As if the one down below were answering the one above. A moan from above, the ceiling shivering; an answering moan from below the elevator, the floor resonating.

Jorny looked at her quizzically, but saying nothing.

They got out at the coffee lounge, a big, comfortable cafeteria space spanning most of one side of the floor, with a coffee shop and a magazine stand. Both were closed. But there were kids there, about nine of them, five boys and four girls, middle-schoolers like Jean, in a far corner, crowded together in a circle near the rest rooms. Deede hurried closer and found they were standing in a tight circle around Jean, circling, and each one pointing an index finger at her, one after the other, like they were doing "the wave", the fingers rippling out and pointing and dropping in the circle, and each one pointing said, "Take a hit."

"Take a hit . . . "

"Take a hit . . . "

"Take a hit . . . "

Like that, on and on around the circle, and when Deede and Jorny got there, Deede looked to see what Jean was taking a hit of, what drug or drink, but there was nothing there, no smoke, no smell, no pipe, no bottle, only the pointing fingers from the rapt, feral faces of the other kids, their eyes dilated, their lips parted, saying, "Take a hit, take a hit, take a hit . . . " And Jean was swaying in place, rocking back, staggering in reaction from each pointed finger, each 'take a hit,' her eyes droopy, her mouth droopier, looking decidedly stoned. Was she playacting?

"What're you guys hitting on?" Jorny said, laughing nervously.

All nine of them turned their heads at once to look at them. "You can't join," the tallest of the boy's said. An acned face, a spiky haircut. "You can't. You're not trustworthy."

"We don't want to," Deede said. She waved urgently at her sister. "Come on, Jean—let's go. There's some weird stuff going on. We've gotta find Lenny."

Jean shook her head. She was swaying there, hyperventilating. "I'm not feeling any pain at all and I'm between the suns. I'm not going, going to stay here . . . "

"Jean—come on!" Deede tried to push through the circle—and someone, she wasn't sure who, shoved her back, hard, so she fell painfully on her back. "Ow!"

"This way," said the big kid with the acned face, leading the group around Jean into the men's room, taking Jean with them. Both males and females filed, without a word or hesitation, into the men's bathroom.

Jorny helped Deede up. "That was fucked up," he said, shaking his head in disgust. "I'm going in there."

"I'm going too. I don't care if it's the men's room. They took my sister in there."

"She went on her own. But fuck it, let's go."

He led the way into the men's room—which was empty.

Not a soul in it. Jorny even opened the toilet booths. No one. There was only one entrance. There was no way out of the bathroom except the one door. There were no ventilation shafts. There was just the big, over-lit, blue-tiled and stainless steel bathroom and their own reflections in the mirrors over the metal sinks.

Jorny gaped around. "Okay, what uh . . . " His voice seemed emptied of life in the hard space of the room. "We were right in front of that door. They didn't get out past us . . . "

"Look!" She pointed at the mirrors. They were reflected in a continuum of mirrors, as when mirrors are turned to mirrors. Only, there was only one set of mirrors on one wall. There were no mirrors opposite—yet the reflection was the mirror-images-within-mirror-images telescoping that happened only if you turned mirrors to mirrors . . . And Deede saw hundreds of Deedes and Jornys stretched into infinity, each face looking lost and shocked and scared.

Lost and shocked and scared endlessly repeated, amplified.

And then she saw Jean in the mirrors, about thirty reflections down the glassy corridor, passing from one side to the other, glancing at her as she went past.

"Jean!" She turned from the mirror, looked the other way as if she might see Jean throwing the reflection there—but saw nothing but a row of toilet booths and urinals. She looked back at the mirrors. "Jorny—did you see someone in the mirrors beside us?"

Jorny's endlessly repeated reflections nodded to her. "Thought I saw your sister."

Feeling dizzily sick, Deede turned away. "It's like there's another room in this room."

She noticed an outline, about the size of a door, on the farther wall between the urinals and the corner, etched with what looked like red putty along the joins in the tiles. She walked over to it. "There's a door-shaped mark here . . . but . . . " She touched the puttied areas. "This gunk is hard, here, like it's been this way a long time. It couldn't be where they got out." Jorny came over and battered at the marked section of wall with his skateboard; they pushed at tiles but could find no way of opening the door, if it was a door. And when they touched it there was a sensation like a very weak electric shock—not enough to make them jump but just enough to give a feeling of discomfort. Electrical discomfort—and the hairs rising on the back of their necks. And chills too, sick chills like you get with the flu. "It's like a warning," she whispered. "Come on—I want out of here."

Jorny nodded, seeming relieved, and they hurried out of the men's room, back into the lounge area—where they were entirely alone. "I've been thinking about some of the shops we saw," Deede said, as they walked over to the elevators and the door to the stairwell. The stairway door was locked. "And—it was like something was influencing stuff around here, something changing the way things . . . just the way they are." Should she tell him about the cord connecting Koenig's foot to the floor tiles?

"I know what you mean," Jorny said absently, as he fiddled with the door to the stairway. " Locked. But yo—*that* door's open."

The door he was pointing at, between the stairs and elevator, was marked MAINTENANCE 47-17. It looked like it hadn't quite closed—like the doorframe was slightly crooked and it had stuck with the door just slightly ajar. You had to look close to see it was open.

She went to it and put her hand on the knob.

Jorny whispered, "Be careful . . . you could end up locking it. "

She nodded and turned the knob while pulling hard on the door—and it swung open.

Inside, it was an ordinary closet, containing a new vacuum cleaner with the price tag still on it, and bottles of cleaning fluid, all of them full, and a push broom . . . and another smaller door, in the wall of the closet to the right. She bent over and turned the little chrome handle it had in place of a knob—and it opened onto the stairway. "Cool! Come on!"

Hunching down to fit, they went through—and found themselves in the main stairway. It was dimly lit, echoing with their every movement, a smell of rot overlaying the smell of new concrete and paint.

"Smells like road kill," Jorny said. He turned to look at the door they'd come through—which shut behind them into the wall, hardly showing a seam. "Weird that they put that door there."

"It's for *them*, to use—in case of emergency," Deede said. "And don't ask who *they* are—I don't know."

"Deede—there's something moving down there . . . and it doesn't seem like people."

She leaned over the balcony and looked. Something slipped across the space between flights about four stories down—a transparent dull-red flipper . . . feeler . . . tentacle? She couldn't get a clear visual picture of it from where she stood. But it was big—maybe three feet across and very long. Slipping by, like a giant boa constrictor. She could just make out that it was connected to something bigger, something that stretched down the open space between the descending flights of stairs.

And as it moved she heard the familiar moaning. That sobbing despair.

She stepped back and said, "Jorny—punch me in the shoulder."

"Really?"

"Yeah. I'm pretty sure I'm not dreaming. But only pretty sure. So go ahead and—ow!"

"You said to! Okay—do me now. Right there. Stick out your knuckle so it—shit!"

"So what do you think?" he asked, rubbing his shoulder, wincing. "Damn you hit hard for a girl."

"That's sexist. And I think we're awake. We have to decide."

He surprised her by suddenly sitting down on the steps, and taking a cigarette out of his shirt pocket. "I've been trying not to smoke. Promised my mom I'd give it up." He took a wooden match out with the cigarette and flicked it alight on his skateboard—Deede thought it was an admirably cool thing to do. He lit the cigarette, and puffed. "But right now I don't care what my mom thinks about cigarettes."

"So what're we gonna *do*?" She was thinking of going back to the apartment again and seeing if Lenny had come home. She'd made excuses for him but under the circumstances she thought he'd have left her a note or something if he'd left . . . voluntarily.

Don't think about Lenny, too, she thought, sitting on a step a little below Jorny. *One person at a time. Get Jean. She's younger. He's older and he can take care of himself.*

Jorny was blowing smoke rings, and poking at them with his finger—he was absentmindedly running his skateboard back and forth on its wheels with one foot. "One time two or three years ago," he said, his voice a dreamy monotone, "when my dad was still living with us, I was worried about where he was all day. See, he was a photographer, and he worked at home. So he was usually there. But one summer he just started being gone all day and there was a lot of . . . I dunno, him and my mom were arguing all the time about little things. About bullshit. Like there was something else . . . but they weren't saying. I was feeling like he was doing something—and it was gonna make them break up. So anyway I followed him. I didn't even think about why. I borrowed my sister's car—she's moved out now—and I followed him. He didn't notice I was following. He was really into where he was going, man. He went to a motel. I should've left it there but I saw which room he went to and after awhile I went up and they had the windows curtained but there was a place where if you bent over and looked, at the corner, you could see in."

"Oh Christ, Jorny."

"Yeah. He was doin' it with some woman I never saw before. They had champagne and stuff. Later on he left my mom for her."

"That must've been . . . " She couldn't keep from making a face.

"It was. I wished I hadn't gone, wished I hadn't looked. It's different, really seeing it. Worse. He was still married to my mom, and . . . Anyway, since then, I figure there's things I don't want to find out about. And if we go looking down there, we'll see things we don't want to know about." He flicked his cigarette away half smoked. "I'm not scared. Not that much. I just . . . don't want to see anything else that I don't want to know about . . . especially since my mom might be in any one of a million places."

"But . . . " Deede heard the moaning again from below. She just wanted to go back to the apartment, and wait there with the doors locked. But that hadn't helped Lenny.

"You okay?" Jorny asked, looking at her closely.

"I'm just worried about my brother. And Jean. I'd like to go back to the apartment but . . . " She sighed. "No one did anything about my mom being killed. No one . . . no one *pursued* it." Deede felt her hands fisting—and she couldn't prevent it. "They said it was suicide or an accident. But there was a man who scares people—he was following some girls in the neighborhood, and there's rumors about him—and he was there that day, he was seen on the same trails, and then there was the dream. The dream seemed almost as real as . . . as today is."

"What dream?"

"It was one of those dreams you get over and over—but the first time I got it was the morning my mom was killed. She was out jogging early and I was still asleep. Our house was out on the edge of town, by this sorta woodsy area with an old quarry. And in my dream I saw her jogging along the edge of the old quarry, where there's this little pond, jogging like she always does on the trails there, and I saw Gunnar Johansen watching her and he looks like he's been up all night, he's sort of swaying there, and then he starts following her and then starts running and she turns and sees him and stumbles and falls on the trail and then he throws himself on her and she struggles and hits him, and he laughs and he knocks her out and then he . . . plays with her body kind of, with one hand on her throat, squeezing and the other hand in his pants, and then she kicks him in the groin and he gives a yell and picks her up and throws her down in the quarry, and she falls face down and she hits hard in that shallow water down there. And . . . bubbles come up . . . *And that's exactly how they found her.*"

"They found her like that, in that exact place? And you hadn't heard about it yet?"

Deede nodded. "I tried to tell them but they said dreams don't count in court. I had that dream again, I had it a lot. I was afraid to go to sleep for a long time."

She put her face in her hands and he came and sat close beside her, not touching her, just being there with her. She appreciated that—the sensitivity of it. Him not trying to put his arm around her. But coming to be right there with her.

A few seconds more, and then a moan and a long, drawn-out scraping sound came from below. Deede decided she had to make up her mind. "I have to go down there. No one found out about my mom. I'm going to find out about Jean. You can go back."

He cleared his throat. Then muttered, "Fuck it." Nodded to himself. He stood up and offered his hand to help her up. "Okay. Come on."

They descended. Jorny carried his skateboard for two turns, and then decided to do a jump, as if some kind of oblique statement of defiance of whatever waited below, and he jumped a whole flight—and the skateboard splintered under him when he came down, snapped in half, and he ended up sliding on his ass. "Shit god*damn*it!"

She helped him up this time. "Sorry about your skateboard. You going to save the trucks?"

"I don't know. I guess." Disgustedly carrying half a skateboard in each hand, he led the way downward—and they stopped another floor lower, to peer over the concrete rail.

Something slipped scrappily by thirty-five feet below, something rubbery and transparently pinkish-red. It made her think of the really big pieces of kelp you saw at the shore, thickly transparent like that, but redder, bigger—and this one had someone swallowed up in it: one of the kids, a young boy she'd seen in the lounge. The boy was trapped inside the supple tree-trunk-thick flexible tube, trapped alive, squeezed but living, slightly moving, eyes darting this way and that, hands pressed by the constriction against his chest . . . and moaning, making the despairing moan they'd been hearing, somehow louder than it should be, as if the thing that held him was triumphantly amplifying his moan.

"You *see* that?" Jorny whispered.

She nodded. "One of those kids who was with Jean . . . in a . . . I don't know what it is." And then it moaned again, so loudly the cry echoed up the shaft of the stairway.

It's calling to us, she thought. *It's luring us. Saying "Come and save him, come and save them all. Come down and see . . . "*

The slithering thing, connected to something below, itself descended—or, more rightly, was pulled down—ahead of her and Jorny, themselves going down and down, the light diminishing ever so subtly toward the lower floors. The transparent red tubule drew itself down, like an eel drawing itself into a hole, pulling the boy—and others, too, squirming trapped human figures glimpsed for a moment enveloped in other thick tendrils, moaning, down and down. Did she see Jean, caught down there? Deede wasn't sure. But she felt that sick flu-chills feeling again and she wanted to turn and run up the stairs and—

"I saw my mom down there," Jorny said, his voice cracking. Inside that thing. "Now I've really got to go."

Deede wanted to run. *Don't let them scare you into not going.* She almost thought she heard her mom's voice saying it. Almost. *He needs someone to go with him. And Jean . . . don't forget Jean.*

"Okay," Deede made herself say. She started down, following the slithering descender, following the moans and the moaners, following the trapped squirmers.

Down and down till they got to the dimly lit bottom floor. And to the basement door.

Deede had expected to find the squirming thing at the bottom but it wasn't there, though there was a thin coating of slushy red material on the floor—like something you'd squeeze from kelp but the color of diluted blood—surrounding the closed basement door. The thing had gone through the door—and closed it behind.

She half hoped the door was locked. Jorny tried it—and it opened. He stood in the doorway, outlined in green light. She looked over his shoulder.

About forty feet by thirty, the basement room contained elevator machinery—humming hump-shaped units to the right—and cryptic pipes along the ceiling. But what drew their eyes was a jagged hole in the floor, right in front of the door, about seven feet across, edged with red slush—the green light came from down there. From within the hole.

She followed Jorny into the room, and—Deede taking a deep breath—they both bent over to look.

Below was a chamber that could never have been made by the builders of Skytown. It was a good-sized chamber, very old. Its stones were rough-carved, great blocks set by some ancient hand in primeval times, way pre-Columbian. Grooves had been carved in the stone floor by someone with malign and fixed intentions. They were flecked with a red-brown crust that had taken many years to accumulate.

"It looks to me like they dug this building in real deep," Jorny said, in a raw whisper. "I heard they dug the foundation down deeper than any other building in Los Angeles. And . . . I guess there was something down there, buried way down, they didn't know about . . . "

She nodded. He looked at the fragments of skateboard in his hand and tossed them aside, with a clatter, then got down on his knees, and lowered himself . . .

"Jorny!"

. . . through the hole in the floor; into the green light; into the ancient chamber.

"Oh fuck," she groaned. But she lowered herself and dropped too, about eight feet to a stinging impact on the balls of her feet.

Jorny caught and steadied her as she was about to tip over and they looked around. "Some kind of temple!" he whispered. "And that *thing* . . . "

The grooves cut into the naked bedrock of the floor, each about an inch deep, were part of a spiral pattern that filled the floor of the entire room—and the gouged pattern was reproduced on the ceiling, as was the dais, the spirals, above and below, converging on the circular dais and the translucent thing that dwelt at the room's center. Spiral patterns on ceiling, spiral patterns on floor, between them, a thing hung suspended in space—suspended between the space of the room and the space between worlds: an enormous, gelatinous, transparent sphere containing a restless collection of smaller iridescent spheres, like a clutch of giant fish eggs —were they smaller than the encompassing sphere, or were they of indefinite size, perhaps both as small as bushels and as big as planets? The iridescent spheres shifted restlessly inside the enveloping globe, changing position, as if each sphere was jostling to get closer to the outside of the container, the whole emanating a murky-green light that tinted the stone walls to jade; the light was a radiance of intelligence, a malign intelligence—malevolent relative to the needs and hopes of human beings—and somehow Deede knew that it was aware of her and wanted to consume her mind with its own . . . She could feel its mind pressing on the edges of her consciousness, pushing, leaning, feeling like a glacier that might become an avalanche.

And then as her eyes adjusted she saw what the green glow had hidden, till now—its extensions, green but filled with diluted blood, stolen blood, the tentacles stretching from the sphere-of-spheres like stems and leaves from a tuber, but prehensile, mobile, stretching out from thick tubules to gradually narrow, to thin, very thin tips that stretched out red cords, like fishing line up into the grooves on the ceiling, and from there into minute cracks, and, she knew—with an intuitive certainty—up high into the building, where they reached into people, taking control of them one by one, starting with those who'd been here longest, Skytown's employees. And some of the tentacular extensions had swallowed up whole people, drawn them down and into itself, so that they squirmed in the tubes, dozens of them, shifting in and out of visibility . . . She saw Koenig, drawn down in one of the transparent tentacles, sucked through it, his face contorted with a terrible realization . . . blood squeezing in little spurts from his eyes, his mouth, his nose . . . And then he was jetted back up the tentacle, becoming smaller as he went, transformed into transmissible form that could be reconstituted up above . . . And all this she glimpsed in less than two seconds.

Visibility was a paradox, a conundrum—the tentacles were visible as a whole but not individually, when you tried to look at one it shifted out of view, and you just glimpsed the people trapped inside it before it was gone . . . And the moaning filled the room, only they heard it more in their minds than in their ears . . .

"It's like this thing is here but it's not completely here," Jorny said, wonderingly. "Like it's . . . getting to be more and *more* here as it . . . "

"The people look pale, some of them like they're dying or dead," Deede said, feeling dreamlike and sick at once. "I can't see them clear enough to be sure but it's like they're being drained real slow."

Jorny said, "It's not coming at us . . . Why?"

"It's waiting," she said. It was more than guessing—it felt right. The answers were in the air itself, somehow; they throbbed within the murky green light. Her fast-seeing drew them quickly into her. "It wants us to come to it. It's lured the others in some way—we saw how it lured Jean. Everyone's been lured. It wants you to submit to it . . . "

"Look—there's something on the other side."

"Jorny? How are we going to get out of here? There's no way back up."

"There has to be another entrance."

"Okay—fine." She felt increasingly reckless—she felt so hopeless now that it felt like little was left to lose. She led the way herself—she was tired of following males from one place to the next—and edged around the boiling, suspended sphere-of-spheres, getting closer to it and learning more about it with proximity . . .

It was only partly in their space; it was in many spaces at once. There was only one being: each sphere they were seeing was another manifestation of that same being, one for each world it stretched into. It slowly twisted things in those worlds to fit its liking. And they were only seeing the outside of it, like the dorsal fin of a shark on the surface of the water. It had many names, in many places; many varieties of appearance, many approaches to getting what it wanted. Its true form—

"Look!" Jorny said, pointing past her at a jagged hole in the floor—a hole that was the *exact duplicate* of the one in the ceiling they'd dropped through on the other side of the room. Its edges were shaped precisely the same . . .

The tentacular probes of the sphere-of-spheres teased at them as they passed, almost caressing them, offering visions of glory, preludes of unimaginable pleasure . . .

But the creature frightened her, more than it attracted her—it was somehow scarier for its enticements. It was as malevolent to her as a wolf spider would be to a crawling fly. Or as a Venus fly trap would be.

"Jesus!" Jorny blurted, hastening away from the thing. "I almost . . . never mind, just get over here!"

She wanted to follow him. But it was hard to move—she was caught up in its whispering, its radiance of promise, and the undertone of warning. *Run from me and I'll be forced to grab you!* Jorny ran to her and grabbed her wrist, pulled her away from it. She felt weak, for a moment, drained, staggering . . .

He knelt by the hole in the floor and dropped through. "Come on, Deede!"

After a moment she followed—almost falling through the hole in her weariness. He half caught her, as before—and she felt her strength returning, away from the sphere-within-spheres.

"Look—we're on the ceiling!" Jorny burst out. "Aren't we?"

They were on a floor—with pipes snaking around their knees—but above them was the machinery of the elevators, affixed upside down on . . . the ceiling. Or—on the floor that was now their ceiling. There was a door, identical to the one they'd come through to find the hole into the temple room above—but it went from a couple feet above the floor to the ceiling. The knob seemed in the wrong place. The door was related to the ceiling the way any other door would be related to the floor—it was upside down. Jorny went to it and jumped to the knob, twisted it, pulled the door open, and scrambled through, turned to help her climb up . . . and then he yelped as he floated upward . . . They both floated up, tumbling in the air . . .

They were floating in space for a moment, turning end over end, in the bottom level of the stairway they'd come down. It was the very same stairway, with the occasional cabinet with fire extinguishers and floor-numbers painted on the walls—only, it stretched down below them, instead of up above them. They instinctively reached for a railing, Jorny caught it . . .

A nauseating twist, a feeling of turning inside-out and back right-side out again, and then they were standing on the stairway, which once more was zig-zagging upward, above them. Only—it couldn't be. It had been below the temple room. Or had they been somehow transported back above?

"What the fuck?" Jorny said, pale, fumbling for a cigarette with shaking hands. "Damn, out of smokes."

Deede stared. Someone was up above—crawling down the walls toward them. Two someones. A man and woman. Coming down the walls that contained the stairs, crawling like bugs, upside down relative to Deede.

"Jorny—look!"

"I see 'em."

"Jorny I don't know how much more I can . . . "

"I'm not feeling so good either. But you know what? We're surviving. Maybe for a reason, right? Hey—they look . . . familiar."

They were about thirty-five, a man and woman dressed in what Deede could only describe, to herself, as dark, clinging rags. The man had a backpack of some kind tightly fixed to his shoulders. They approached, crawling down the wall, and Deede and Jorny backed away, trying to decide where to run to—up the stairs past them? And then the strangers stopped, looking at them upside down, the woman's hair drooping down toward them . . .

And the woman spoke. "Jorny—it's us, me and you as kids!"

"What—from earlier, somehow? But we never discovered the temple as kids!" said the man. "We just found out about it last year!"

"They're us in one of the other worlds—younger versions . . . and they found their way here! Just like in my dream, Jorny! I told you, there was something here—something that would help us!"

Jorny—the younger Jorny standing at the younger Deede's side—shook his head, stunned. "It's us—in, like, the future or . . . "

Deede nodded. "Would you guys come down and . . . stand on the level we're on? Or can you?"

"We can," the older Deede said. "The rules shifted when Yog-Sothoth altered the world, and gravity moves eccentrically."

She crept toward the floor, put one foot on it, then sidled around on the wall like a gecko, finally getting both feet on the floor and standing to face them; the older Jorny did the same. His blond hair was cut short and beginning to recede, his face a trifle lined, but he was still recognizably Jorny.

Deede found she was staring at the older version of herself in fascination. She seemed more proportional, more confident, if a bit grim—there were lines around her eyes, but it looked good on her. But the whole thing was disorienting—was something she didn't really want to see. It made her want to hide, seeing herself, just as much as seeing the thing in the temple.

"Don't look so scared, kid," the older Jorny said, smiling sadly at her.

Deede scowled defiantly at him. "Just—explain what the hell you are. I don't think you're us."

"We're *another* you," the older Deede said. "And we're connected with you. We all extend from the ideal you, in the world of ideas. But this sure isn't that world. Time is a bit in advance in our world, I guess, from yours, for one thing . . . "

"Come on with us," the older Jorny said. "We'll show you. Then we can figure out if there's a way we can work together . . . against *him*."

They turned and climbed the stairs—after a moment's hesitation, Jorny and Deede followed. They went up eleven flights, past battered, rusting doors. "Your building," the older Deede said, "extends downward from ours—but to you it will seem upward. Ours is downward from yours. They're mirrored, but not opposites—just variants at opposite poles from one another. Me and Jorny found out that the primary impulses were coming from the basement of our building so we cut the hole in the sub basement floor—that's the ceiling of the other room."

"I think it's the other way around," said the older Jorny.

"I don't know, it depends. Anyway the Great Appetite—that's what we call it, though some call it Yog-Sothoth—he reaches out through the many worlds through that same temple . . . and he changes what he comes to, so the beings on that world become all appetite, all desire, and nothing else—so he can feed on low desires, through beings on those worlds."

"You say *he*?" the younger Jorny asked. "Not *it*?"

"Right—he has gender. But little else we can comprehend. Once he's changed a world enough, he can eat what you eat, feel what you feel. Some he will already have changed, in your world—the rest he will change later. He changed our world about eighteen years ago. We've resisted—but most people don't. They get changed—the Great Appetite removes whatever there is in them that checks appetites and desires and impulses. Any kind of strong controlling intelligence, he takes it out. Makes psychopaths of some people, and zombies of just *feeding*, of different kinds, of others—"

"Like Gunnar Johansen!" Deede burst out.

The older Deede stopped on a landing and turned to look at her. "Yes," she said gravely. "He killed my mother too—before the Great Appetite took over. Like him. He was already under Yog-Sothoth's control . . . without knowing it."

She looked like she wanted to embrace the younger Deede—but Deede was afraid of her, and took a step back.

The older Deede shrugged and turned to follow the older Jorny through a doorway—the door at this landing had been wrenched aside, was leaning, crumpled against the wall, hinges snapped. They passed through and found themselves in the lower Mezzanine lounge, exactly like the one they'd left—sterile in its furnishings and design.

They walked over to the window and stared out at the world—the transformed world.

There was no sky. Instead there was a ceiling, high up, just above the tallest building, that stretched to the horizon. And the ceiling was covered with images, enticing objects and enticing bodies flashing by and intermingling and overlapping. She saw an advertisement for BLENDER—and the indeterminate segments of fleshy material that she'd seen in the Skymall shop window; she saw an ad for something called BRAIN BLANKER: *For* really *changing your child—remake it exactly as you please!* She saw an ad for INTER-REACTIVES, INC, the sea urchin helmets she'd seen in Skymall; she saw an ad that said simply, WE ELIMINATE PROBLEM NEIGHBORS—GOVERNMENT CERTIFIED AGAINST RETALIATION; another ad asked, WANT A PET THAT REALLY SCREAMS? ORDER LITTLE PEOPLE! and there was an image of a frightened, dwarf sized semi-human figure lifted by its neck from a "home-grow vat"—by a grinning man holding a two-by-four with nails sticking out of it, in his other hand; there was an ad for LATEST FACE: THE TOP TEN FACES, WITH NEAR-INSTANTANEOUS TRANSFER GUARANTEED, AT REDUCED PRICES. The images were sometimes blurred by great gray clouds of smog—clouds pierced by people who flew through them, people mechanically enhanced to fly, their bodies pierced by pistons and wires, shrieking as they went; other people crawled up and down the sides of buildings like bugs; clusters of junk material floated by, clouds of metal with people clinging to them, wailing and tittering and fornicating; unspeakably fat people drifted by on flying cushions tricked out with pincers and mechanical hands; emaciated people drifted by too: their heads penetrated by wires, their faces twitching with pleasures they no longer really felt, their vehicles suddenly spurting with speed to deliberately crash headlong into other vehicles, going down in spinning, flaming wreckage to join the accumulation of twisted metal and weather-beaten trash that filled the streets hundreds of feet deep, black with insects . . .

"That's pretty much the way the whole world looks," the older Jorny said, his voice cracking. "There are attempts at changing it, in places—but the influence of the Great Appetite is too strong . . . unless you have with you . . . " He turned to his younger self. "What you are supposed to have."

"What? What do you mean?"

"You have something I need . . . " The older Jorny took off his backpack, and took out a boxy device that had speakers at both ends, like a boombox, but no place to put in CDs or an iPod—only a small recess at one end. "You see? It goes here . . . "

"You're expecting something from us?" Deede asked, confused.

The older Deede looked out the window. "When we found the locus of the Great Appetite, in the temple, we found I had a kind of . . . a sensitivity to it. I could pick up information from it. By something I think of as 'looking fast.'"

Deede nodded. "I'm like that too."

"I saw you, then—saw that you were coming and that you carried something the Great Appetite is afraid of. A many-voiced note of refusal."

"A what?"

"Do you have a recording device with you?"

Jorny stared at them . . . then slowly reached into his pocket and drew out his iPod.

The older Deede frowned. "That's not what I saw . . . "

"It's inside it!" The older Jorny said. He snatched the iPod from Jorny's hand and—ignoring Jorny's protests—smashed it again and again on the metal window frame till it burst open.

"There it is!" The older Deede shouted, pointing at the wrecked device. "That thing!"

"It's a microdrive!" the older Jorny said excitedly. "We use them to make sounds too—but we put them directly in our sound machines. We have only sounds that have been appropriated, co-opted by the Great Appetite. Now . . . "

"This better work," Jorny grumbled.

The older Jorny plucked the microdrive from the wreckage and pressed it in the recess of the alternate boombox. It fit neatly in place. He hit a switch and the box boomed out—with a roaring cacophony.

"Shit!" the younger Jorny yelled, reaching over to snap the boombox off again. "It's not picking out any one song—it sounds like it's playing all of them at once! There's more than a thousand songs in there!"

"So that's it . . . " the older Deede murmured. She looked at the older Jorny. "Remember? 'A thousand voices will silence his roar!' That's what I heard from the green light—it tried to cover it up but I saw it! *It's supposed to play them all at once!*"

A vast moaning shook the floor then, and the ceiling shed bits of plaster. It was coming from the elevator banks . . .

"We've frightened *him* with the sound—for just that one second!" the older Jorny said. "He's coming for us!" He handed the younger Jorny the boombox. "Play it as loud as possible in the temple! Go on! It'll make everything possible! We'll draw it off!"

They he looked at the older Deede—and, to Deede's exquisite discomfort, the two adults kissed, kissed hugely and wetly. She looked away—so did Jorny. Then the older Jorny and Deede turned and ran past the elevator. The elevator doors opened and something red and green and endlessly hungry reached from it, stretching after them . . .

"Oh no . . . " Deede said.

"We'd better try this . . . " Jorny whispered. And they turned and pounded down the stairs.

In minutes they'd reached the upside down basement room, and dropped through the ceiling, coming up, spinning in space with momentary weightlessness, in the temple room . . .

Deede found herself on the floor, with the sphere-within-spheres, the Great Appetite, Yog-Sothoth looming over her, reaching for her, making its unspeakable offering. . . .

And then Jorny reached to switch on the boombox, at full volume. . . .

"*Jorny!*" His hand hesitated over the boombox and he looked up to see his mother, trapped in one of the transparent tentacles, compressed and terrified. "*Jorny—wait! I don't know what you're doing but it'll punish me if you do it! Stop!*"

He drew his hand back. Deede knew she had to trigger the box—but she was afraid of what she'd see if she reached for it. This thing had the power to hurt, to punish, beyond time. It could reach into your soul. It was evil times evil. It was the dark side of pleasure and it was the green light of pain. It wasn't something to defy . . .

But she remembered what the world looked like, after the Great Appetite was done . . .

"I don't know what to do," Jorny said, covering his eyes with his hands.

Deede knew what to do. She reached for the box . . .

"*Deede—don't!*" Jean's voice.

"*Deede, wait!*" Lenny's voice. "*Look—we're here—you can't—*"

Deede refused to look. In defiance, she stabbed her fingers don't on the play button.

The sound that came out of the box was the joined booming of a thousand songs at once, the sort that Jorny would choose—a thousand songs of angst, rebellion, uncertainty, insistence, fury. Everything but a certain kind of surrender. They all had one note in common: a sound that was a refusal to be anything untrue.

One great thousand-faceted roaring white noise, black noise, every noise of the sonic spectrum . . . roaring. Roaring refusal—roaring defiance!

And the sphere-of-spheres withdrew into itself, dropping everything it touched in the two worlds connected by the temple, retreating to other planes, where it could find surcease from the amplified, crystalized sound of refusal to surrender to its dominance.

The temple shuddered, and the spiral grooves seemed to spin for a moment, like an old fashioned record—then the ceiling tumbled down and smashed the boombox. Came tumbling toward Jorny—

Deede pulled Jorny aside, at the last split-second, and the great ceiling stones tumbled down in the center of the room, leaving a crust of chamber, the edges . . . and a pile of stone that blocked off the hole into the other Skytown, and rose in a cluttered knob into the basement room above . . .

"You did it?" Jorny asked, coughing with dust.

"I had to. It couldn't have been worse for anyone . . . "

He nodded and they climbed, together, silently, through the dust cloud, and up into the basement room. They found their way to the stairways . . . where they found dozens of people, clothes soaked and skin wet with blood. They were weak—but most were alive, lying one to a step, up and up and up the stairs, feebly calling for help. Among them, they found Lenny and Jean and Jorny's mother. They couldn't remember where they'd been. No one could quite remember it.

Not all of them were alive. Koenig was there—crushed almost flat.

The elevators were no longer blocked, the security guards were gone—except the ones who were dead. The front doors were wide open. When the ambulances came, no one could completely explain where they'd been or what had happened to them. Some internal disaster was inferred, and explanations were generated. Deede's father returned that night, summoned to deal with the emergency, and they moved out, to a hotel on the other side of town—the same one that Jorny and his mother were staying at. He asked remarkably few questions.

Lenny and Jean spent most of the second day away from the Skymall in the hospital, getting transfusions, getting tested—they seemed dazed, slowly coming back to themselves.

It was just three days later that Deede set out for Portland, to visit her cousin. "Just need to get away from this town, Dad," she said. "Just for a few days. I want to go to Mom's grave . . . "

He simply nodded, and helped her pack—and he put her on a plane.

She had to go to the trail by the old quarry for three days before Johansen showed up. She'd let him see her go there, every night, but he'd been cautious. Still, since she was wearing as little as she could get away with, he couldn't resist.

That night he followed her along the trail under the moonlight . . .

She went to the precipice, where her mother had taken her fatal plunge. She waited there for Johansen, humming a song to herself. No particular song—bits of many songs, really.

Johansen came up behind her, chuckling to himself.

She turned to face him, feeling like she was made of steel. "No one's here—I'm sure you checked that out. And you can see I'm not wired. Not wearing enough to cover up a wire. You may as well say it. You killed her. You want to kill me."

"Sure," Johansen said. His hair was a jagged halo in the moonlight; his teeth seemed white in a face gone dark because the light was behind him. His eyes were two dark holes. "Why shouldn't I kill the little slut as well as the mama slut?"

"I don't think you can, though," she said calmly. "You know what? I used to be afraid of you. But I'm not now. I'm not afraid anymore! You're small time. *I* stopped what made you. I can stop you easily—you're so very small, in comparison, Johansen, to the Great Appetite itself."

"You're babbling, kid."

"Yeah? Then shut me up. If you can. I don't think you can, you limp-dicked jerk.

You're nothing!"

His face contorted at that, and he rushed her—and she moved easily aside, drawing the razor-sharp buck-knife she'd hidden in her belt, under her blouse in back. Then his ankle struck the fishing line she'd stretched, taut and down low between the roots, over the little peninsular jut of the cliff. And he stumbled and plunged, headlong, into the quarry, just as she'd known he would. She wouldn't need the back-up knife, after all, she decided, pleased, as she watched him fall wailing into the shallow water, to break on the jagged rocks she'd arranged down there.

He lay face down in the shallow water on the rough-edged stones, struggling, calling hoarsely for help, his neck broken, unable to lift his head but a few inches . . . finally sagging down into the water. Drowning.

Smiling, she watched him die.

Then she stretched, and waved cheerfully at the moon. She cut the fishing wire, put it in her pocket, tossed the knife into the quarry, and, humming a thousand songs, trotted back along the trail to the street. When she got to the sidewalk, she called first her Dad, then Jorny on her cell phone, said she'd be coming back soon.

And then she caught a bus to the cemetery to have a talk with Mom.

Of his vast collection of strange, rare books on forbidden subjects I have read all that are written in the languages of which I am master; but these are few as compared with those in languages I cannot understand. Most, I believe, are in Arabic; and the fiend-inspired book which brought on the end—the book which he carried in his pocket out of the world—was written in characters whose like I never saw elsewhere.

"The Statement of Randolph Carter" · H.P. Lovecraft (1919)

• BRINGING HELENA BACK •
Sarah Monette

I was contemplating the fragments of an unidentified animal's skull, late on a wet, windy Friday in March, when a voice said, "Booth? Is that you?"

My head jerked up; Augustus Blaine was leaning against my office door, as if his body were too heavy for him to support on his own any longer. I recognized him at once, although I had not seen him for ten years. He looked forty-two instead of thirty-two. I would have known his voice anywhere.

"My God, man," he said, staring, "what happened to your hair?"

My hand went up involuntarily to touch it. My hair had gone white eight years previously, over a period of about four months. It was a trait of my mother's family; all the Murchisons went white before they were twenty-five.

"Doesn't matter," Blaine said before I could do more than begin to stammer a reply. "I came here for help."

He sounded exhausted, but his eyes were feverishly bright. Carefully, I set the skull fragments down on my desk, and said, "Come in. Please, er, sit down. I think . . . there's a chair clear."

He dragged the chair across to my desk and sat, a little warily. "All your bits of pot and bone," he said, his voice somewhere between fondness and contempt. "Are you good at your job, Boothie?"

"People, er, seem to think so."

"The thing is," Blaine said, "the thing is that I think I need a spot of help."

"Anything you need, Blaine. I . . . that is, you know that."

He looked at me for a moment, his face stiff with suspicion like an African mask, and then he smiled. "By God, I think you mean that. All right, then. It's this book." He set his briefcase on his lap and opened it. The lid concealed the contents of the briefcase from me, but he closed it again swiftly, left-handed, and put it back on the floor. His right hand was holding the book.

It was a slender quarto, leather-bound and badly chipped. The title had once been on the spine, but someone had carefully burned it out. "You don't want to know how much I paid for this," Blaine said, with a grin on his face that I found frightening. "It'll all be worth it, though. I'm sure. But the deuce of it is, Boothie, I can't read it."

"What do you mean?"

"It's in some kind of cipher. I've been tearing my hair out over it for weeks, trying to crack the damn thing. And then I thought of my old friend, Kyle Murchison Booth." He rolled the syllables of my name out of his mouth as if they were at once contemptible and marvelous. "This should be right up your alley, Boothie."

"What, er . . . what's the book about, Blaine?"

"Didn't I say? I think there's a way I can bring Helena back."

I was so startled—as much aghast at his matter-of-fact manner as at what he had said—that I knocked the skull fragments off my desk.

Blaine and I had met as freshmen in college. Blaine had almost immediately decided and announced that we were going to be friends. To this day, I do not know why. The things we had in common—education, wealth, the sort of genealogy that passes in America for aristocratic—did not seem to me as if they could possibly bridge the gulf between us, the gulf I had always felt between myself and people like Blaine. The only theory I had was that I offered Blaine someone with whom to discuss topics other than athletic pursuits and alcohol. He could talk to me as he could talk to no one else in his world. He was my only friend—that says, I imagine, as much about me as anyone needs to know.

Blaine was interested in everything; it was part of the way he was put together—a relentless, bright-eyed interest in everything under the sun. The action of his mind often reminded me of a lighthouse light, revolving and revolving, sending its bright, piercing beam out into the darkness in every direction, never stopping on any one thing for long, but continuing to search. He was interested in chemistry and biology and physics; he was interested in history and archaeology and anthropology; he took classes in French, German, Russian, Greek, Latin, never more than a semester or two of any of them, the beam sweeping restlessly onward. He must have taken courses in every department on campus, and he could talk for hours, scintillatingly, compellingly, about any of them.

In this, as in so many other respects, I was Blaine's opposite. Next to him I was a dull, ugly crow, without even the wit to hide myself in peacock feathers. I listened to Blaine for hours, but could find nothing of any interest to say myself. I stuck to my dry, safe work in history and archaeology, looking already toward the dim, dusty halls of the Samuel Mather Parrington Museum.

Blaine had always teased me about my love of puzzles: crosswords, acrostics, ciphers, anagrams. I solved them obsessively, as I solved the archival puzzles set by my professors; they were practice for what was to become my life's work. I am sure that Blaine remembered timing me on the ciphers I found in books of logical puzzles; I am sure that the memory is why he sought me out, and therefore my freakish skill makes me responsible for his death.

I sometimes offer myself the false comfort that Helena was even more to blame than I. Helena Pryde was the sister of Blaine's friend Tobias Pryde. Blaine met her because Tobias—good-natured, warmly gregarious, not very bright, one of the few of Blaine's friends who did not treat me like some strange pet of Blaine's—invited us both home with him for the spring vacation of our junior year. The Prydes' house ("the House of Pryde" Blaine kept calling it and snickering at his own pun) was well-proportioned and handsome, beautifully situated in an oak grove. Mr. and Mrs. Pryde were people as imperceptive and generous as their son. Helena Pryde, Tobias's younger sister, was a changeling.

She was tall and slender, with hair of an amazing dark, ruddy gold. Her hair was also unusually thick and heavy, and she habitually wore it loose, so that it hung like a cloak of fire past her hips. The effect was stunning, quite literally so; I heard Blaine's breath hitch in at his first sight of her. I suppose she was pretty—at least, everyone seemed to think so—but her mouth was small and ungenerous, and her eyes were hard. Her voice was high-pitched and always rather breathless, and she lisped just slightly. The quality of her voice was childlike, innocent, and that was a deception worthy of the Serpent in Eden.

She flirted with Blaine from the moment they were introduced. Blaine— who had dated one girl after another for the three years I had known him, an endless parade of Elizabeths, Marys, Charlottes, and Julias—responded enthusiastically in kind, and before the week was half over, he was spending more time with Helena than with either Tobias or me.

I doubt Tobias even noticed, but I was aware of it—aware of the hard, predatory light in Helena's eyes when she looked at Blaine, even more aware that his expression when he looked back at her showed that he did not see her as I did. He could not see her for what she was. Thursday at dinner, I overheard them discussing how they could meet again after this visit was over, and where and when. Friday morning, after a night spent staring sleeplessly into the darkness of my room, I had determined that I had to talk to Blaine, that it was my duty as his friend to try to make him see what sort of person Helena Pryde was.

I searched for Blaine all Friday morning, wandering in and out of the gracious, unobservant rooms of the House of Pryde. Finally, nearly at lunchtime, I thought I heard voices in the library. The Prydes' library curved in an L-shape around two sides of the house; it was full of beautiful old books at which I doubt anyone in the family ever looked twice. They were dusted faithfully by the maids, however, and they were freely available for any guest who wished to browse. I already knew the library well, preferring its dim, serene coolness to the bright heat of the tennis court where Blaine and Tobias and Helena and a steady rotation of Helena's friends played doubles in the afternoons.

I went into the library. The lights were off, and the room was full of the cool, dreamlike, underwater glow of sunlight through oak leaves.

"Blaine?" I called. "Are you in here?"

Someone said something in a muffled voice, and there was a burst of laughter.

"Blaine?" I said, advancing until I could see into the other half of the L. "Are you . . ."

He was sitting on one of the enormous leather couches. His hair was ruffled and his tie askew. Possessively close beside him sat Helena Pryde, a little smirk on her ungenerous mouth. It took no special perspicacity to see what they had been doing. I felt my face heat.

But I had come this far. "Blaine, I, er, wanted to—"

"Go away, Boothie," Blaine said.

The one mannerism of Blaine's that I hated was that nickname, invented one night in our sophomore year when he was giddy with wine. I would not have minded so much if it had been a private nickname, although even then I thought it silly, but Blaine used it in front of other people. He did so partly to tease me, but partly to reassure his friends that he had more savoir-faire than to treat me as an equal.

I said, hating what I heard in my own voice, "Can we talk later?"

"When we get back to school, Boothie," Blaine said. "Miss Pryde has just done me the honor of consenting to our betrothal." At this they both started giggling, like schoolchildren at a smutty joke. "And I fancy I'm going to be rather occupied for the rest of our visit."

"Darling Auggie," said Miss Pryde fondly.

" . . . All right, Blaine," I said—there was nothing else I could say, no words of mine to which he would listen—and left. Just before I closed the library door, I heard them laughing again, and I knew they were laughing at me. Helena had won.

I saw the headlines when she died, of course. Helena Pryde Blaine was a society darling, always being photographed in fancy night clubs or at charity galas, her amazing hair flowing darkly, hypnotically, even in newsprint. Blaine went unremarked in the society pages, except very rarely as part of the entity "Mr. and Mrs. Augustus Blaine." That absence alone told me that the marriage was not a happy one, and I had the dour satisfaction of having been right all along. For nine years, that was all I had; Blaine, obediently following the family tradition, was not the sort of lawyer whose clients made the papers.

But the death of Helena Pryde Blaine was a lurid scandal that not even the Blaines' influence could cover up. She died of an overdose of cocaine, in the apartment of a man who was less than a husband but more than a friend. His name was Rutherford Chapin; I had gone to prep school with him and remembered him with loathing. The two of them, Rutherford Chapin and Helena Pryde Blaine, might have been made for each other, and I was only sorry, for Blaine's sake, that she had not found Chapin first.

I sent Blaine a letter of condolence; I could not bring myself to attend the funeral or to send flowers. I was not sorry that she was dead. I hoped for a while—the stupid sort of fantasy that keeps one awake at night—that Blaine might answer me with a letter or even a visit, but I received nothing more than a "thank you for your sympathy" note, clearly written by one of Blaine's sisters. Only the signature was his; I recognized it, despite the spiky scrawl into which his handwriting had degenerated. I continued stupidly to hope, but I did not hear anything from or about Blaine for another year, until the night when he appeared in my office at the museum with his abhorrent book.

It took me a long time to get the story out of him—not because he did not want to tell me, but because he had been living alone with his obsession for so long that he had developed his own private shorthand, and he kept forgetting that he was not talking to his reflection in the mirror. He was impatient when I asked questions—and that was very like the Blaine I remembered—but I did finally piece together a narrative of the past year.

He had nearly gone crazy at first, he said (and it occurred to me that many people would question that "nearly"), looking for Helena everywhere, expecting to hear her voice every time he answered the telephone. When the truth finally sank in, the great lighthouse of Blaine's mind locked unswervingly on the idea of, as he said, "bringing Helena back." He never used the word "necromancy," or any other phrase that held an open acknowledgment of her death. A person who did not know better would imagine from his conversation that she had simply been stranded in some dangerous and barbaric part of the world, the Himalayas, perhaps, or the Sahara.

As an up-and-coming young lawyer, Blaine naturally knew nothing of the black arts, but a powerful intellect and money to burn can compensate for a remarkable number of deficiencies, and Blaine had remedied his ignorance in startlingly little time. He had read every book of dark arcana he could find, and he had found some dreadfully obscure things. He even claimed to have a copy of *The Book of Whispers*, but I suspect that the book gracing his shelves was really the elegant and convincing nineteenth-century fake by Isaiah Hope Turnbull. Even so, the collection he had amassed was astounding and disturbing.

Blaine had tried everything, everything his books suggested, and none of it had worked. "*None* of it!" he shouted at me, pounding his fist so violently on my desk that I was only just in time to keep the skull fragments from crashing to the floor again.

He had been in despair. But then the dealer who had found the other books for him (and who had gulled him so egregiously over *The Book of Whispers*) had come to him with stories of another book, even more obscure and powerful. Blaine said he would have paid any sum the man named. I was appalled, as much by his reckless credulity as by anything else. The possibility began to loom very large in my mind that the book Blaine clutched so fiercely was yet another fake, something the dealer had cobbled together to exploit this fabulous windfall still further. That being the case, there could be no harm in humoring Blaine, especially when it meant he would have to come back in a week and talk to me. I took the book home.

Here is where my guilt begins: not in humoring Blaine, but in opening that damnable book. There was nothing to prevent me from keeping the book for a week without so much as touching it, then bringing it back with an admission of defeat. I had seen Blaine's desperation; he had come to me only because he could not think of anything rational to do. He would be disappointed, but neither surprised nor suspicious. But if I did that, he would leave again. And I wanted to surprise him, to show him that I could help him. Perhaps that was the root of my folly: I wanted Blaine finally to take me seriously.

I opened the book. It was, as Blaine had said, in cipher, but it was not a terribly difficult cipher. I thought I recognized it after looking at a few lines, and my estimation of the unknown forger went up several notches. It might not have been difficult, but it was quite obscure, a cipher invented and used almost exclusively by a circle of Flemish occultists who had flourished in the late sixteenth century. Even then, it did not occur to me that the book might be genuine, only that the forger had done his homework. I refreshed my memory of the cipher and got to work.

Within a page, I knew that the book was no fake, but by then it had trapped me.

I dare not describe it too closely, for fear that there may be another copy somewhere in existence, and that I may excite curiosity about it. If there is another copy, let it molder to dust wherever it lies.

I have dreams sometimes, in which I throw the book again on the fire, but this time it does not burn. It simply rests on top of the flames, its pages flipping randomly back and forth. I can feel my hands twitching and trembling with the need to reach into the fire and rescue it. Inevitably, I do reach. I plunge my hands into the fire, and I wake up. Although my hands are marred by neither blisters nor burns, they throb and sear for hours afterwards as if the fire in my dreams were real.

I will not give the book's true title. I have since found a few veiled references to it in the writings of those Flemish occultists, and they refer to it always as the *Mortui Liber Magistri*—*The Book of the Master of the Dead* or, perhaps, *The Book of the Dead Master*. I will do the same. Freed of the cipher, the *Mortui Liber Magistri* was written in perfectly straightforward Latin, with all the mesmerizing power of a cobra's inhuman gaze. Once I had read the first two sentences, I was lost. I could neither look away nor put it aside, and I finished my translation just as the sun was rising.

Then I telephoned Blaine. When Blaine answered, I wanted to say, *Blaine, this book is an abomination. I think you should burn it.* But the words that came out of my mouth, calmly and rationally, were nothing like that at all. The words I spoke were the words the *Mortui Liber Magistri* wanted spoken: "I know how to do it."

Blaine was amazed, delighted. We made our plans. We would meet that night at his house, and I would show him how to bring Helena back. Then we would perform the ritual. "Very good," I said to Blaine, replaced the telephone receiver, and staggered to bed.

I slept until sunset, when I woke up screaming.

• • •

I will not—*cannot*—describe the ritual. If I could excise it from my brain, believe that I would. I cannot, and the ineradicability of the memory is no more than I deserve. The ritual was an evil, perverted thing, and I neither know, nor want to know, where Blaine found the materials he used—except for the human blood. That was mine.

Blaine had always been able to persuade me to do what he wanted, and he was full of good, rational reasons why it had to be my blood instead of his. Sometimes, when my insomnia is particularly sere—a vast, arid, cracking wasteland in which the dead trees do not give shelter—I wonder if perhaps that was the crux at which things began to go wrong. Blaine loved his wife enough to spend thousands of dollars and to perform this obscene ritual, but not quite enough to open a vein in his own arm and let his own blood pool on the obsidian slab in his cellar.

There is a hard, angry little voice in my head, a voice like hers, that says, *Blaine deserved his death.* That is not true, and I know it. What Blaine *deserved* was a friend good enough and strong enough to stop him, but I was not that friend.

The book had released me as soon as I had explained everything to Blaine, so I have no excuse. Where a stronger, better man would have said, *Blaine, this is madness*, I looked into his burning, haunted, driven eyes, and I rolled back the cuff of my shirt.

The ritual worked. That is the most ghastly thing. I hold no particular brief for the rationality of the world, but that this vile obscenity should actually have the power to bring back the dead seems to me a sign not merely that the world is not rational, but that it is in fact entirely insane, a murderous lunatic gibbering in the corner of a padded cell.

The ritual worked. The patterns of blood and graveyard earth, the stench of burning entrails, the repulsive Latin phrases that Blaine chanted, they combined exactly as the book said they would. A presence coalesced in the middle of Blaine's obsidian slab. It was shapeless and colorless at first, but as Blaine's incantations mounted in fervor and monstrosity, it drew itself together, taking on Helena's shape and garbing itself in her chic, severely tailored clothes. The colors were slower to come, but I remember the way her hair washed in, a torrent of blood and gold down her back. She was facing away from us.

"Helena," Blaine said, breathless with wonder and desire. "Helena, darling, it's me."

The shape did not turn.

"Helena, it's me, it's Augustus. Darling, can you hear me?"

Still she did not turn, but a voice, undeniably hers, said, "Where's Ruthie? I want Ruthie."

"Helena!"

She moved a little, restlessly, in the circle, but still she would not turn. "Ruthie loves me," she said. "He says so."

"Helena, it's Augustus!" I had an unwelcome flash of insight: that I was watching the distillation of the nine years of their marriage, Helena never looking at Blaine, always looking for something else, Blaine pleading and coaxing, talking always to her back, to the amazing sunset river of her hair.

"Why isn't Ruthie here?" Helena said petulantly, as if she had not heard Blaine at all.

Blaine stepped into the circle. I do not think he realized at that point what he was doing, for the warnings in the *Mortui Liber Magistri* against the caster crossing the circle were dire and uncompromising, and I know that he heard me when I explained them.

"Blaine!" I lunged forward, but I could not catch him in time; I had drawn too far away from the circle when Helena began to manifest. My fingers brushed the back of his shirt with no more force than a butterfly's wing, and he was beyond help. The instant Blaine was within the circle, Helena turned. She had heard him all along, had known to a nicety—as she ever had—how to get him to do what she wanted.

Her face was ghastly. It was not simply that she was, all too clearly, still dead. It was that she was dead and yet animate. Her face was gray and stiff and bloodless, but it was filled with a monstrous vitality. Blaine had not brought Helena back to life; he had done something far, far worse.

I suppose it is possible that the thing in the circle was not Helena Pryde Blaine at all, that it was a demon or some other sort of inhuman spirit. My own belief, however, is that it was the quintessence of Helena, the thing in her that Blaine had never been able to see, and that I had been powerless to show him: the greedy selfishness of a child who can never be satisfied with her own toys if another child has a toy, no matter how shabby, that she does not. Blaine was just another toy to her, and one that bored her.

He saw the truth of her then, the insatiable, heartless greed, although he had never seen it before. He recoiled from her and tried, far too late, to back out of the circle.

"Kiss me, darling Auggie," said Helena, in her breathless, mocking way. She caught his arms and drew him toward her. Blaine stiffened and made a noise that would probably have been a scream if he could have gotten enough air into his lungs before her lips closed on his. When she let him go—five loathsome, endless seconds later—he fell down dead.

I was pressed into the corner, the cold damp bricks prodding at my back like angry fingers. My whole desire at that moment was that Helena should ignore me as she always had.

She looked at me. The face was livid and hard, but the eyes were still hers. "Boothie," she said.

I moaned, somewhere in the back of my throat. It was all the noise I could make.

She cocked her head to one side, a hideous parody of the way she had been accustomed to flirt. "I don't suppose I can talk *you* into the circle, Boothie, can I?"

My head was shaking "no," wobbling back and forth on my neck as if it belonged to someone else.

"No," she said, with a little moue of disappointment. "Auggie could have, I'll bet. But you never liked me, did you?"

"I hated you, Helena," I said, the truth croaking out of me unwilled.

She actually smiled then, and I would give anything I possess if I could stop seeing her smile in my dreams. The smile was hers, the little, gloating smirk that I had always loathed, but the dead stiffness of her face made it a rictus. "I don't hold that against you, Boothie. I always knew you were jealous." She tittered. "Boothie and Ruthie—Auggie and I both had our little lapdogs, didn't we?"

I should have held my tongue, but my hatred of her, my crawling revulsion, was greater than my fear. "Yours killed you," I said.

"And now Auggie's has killed him. So I guess we're even."

She was starting to fade; with the death of its caster, the ritual was losing potency. She noticed it herself. "Phooey," she said. She looked at me, her eyes bright with all the malice of the living Helena Pryde Blaine. "Are you going to have a go at calling Auggie back, Boothie? I'm sure you could do it. He always said you were the smartest man he knew." With that, she was gone, dissolved into the stinking smoke, leaving nothing behind her but her husband's corpse.

It took me until dawn to clean the cellar, washing away the blood and dirt and other materials. I had to lift Blaine to clean under him, but after that I left him where he was. His body looked sixty-two now instead of thirty-two, and there was not a mark on him: nothing to show that he had not fallen down dead of a heart attack. He was cold and stiff, and obviously had been dead much longer than five hours, although he had died only seven minutes before two o'clock.

He had been living entirely alone, without even servants—he had dismissed them all when his interest in necromancy began to devolve into obsession— and that was my good fortune. I took away the paraphernalia of the ritual and threw all its repellant ingredients into the river on my way home.

Then I waited.

Blaine was found four days later. One of his sisters finally became worried enough about him to use her key to his house. No one, except apparently for me, had heard from him in over a week. His family had known nothing of his dabblings in necromancy. He had told no one of his latest purchase—save of course the book dealer—and no one at all of his decision to consult me. There were, as I myself had seen, no signs of violence on his body, and the coroner's judgment was that his heart had simply given out: he was awfully young for such a death, but he had been under a severe strain for a very long time, and these things did happen . . . If someone had gone exploring through Blaine's effects, they might have found evidence to suggest another possibility, but his family did not wish any further inquiry, and the Blaines are powerful. No one else asked questions, and I heard later that the book dealer who had supplied Blaine's mania had left the city unexpectedly and precipitously.

My culpability was not discovered, nor even suspected. Only I knew, and the things that came to find me in my dreams. They knew and I knew that Helena was right. I had killed Blaine, just as surely as Rutherford Chapin had killed her. The guilt and the loneliness were all but unbearable; I was as comfortless as Cain.

And all the while Helena's last question—*Are you going to have a go at calling Auggie back, Boothie?*—echoed meanly through my head. I could repeat the ritual. I had kept the book, and my notes, and I had watched Blaine. I could bring Blaine back.

I wanted to. I wanted to bring Blaine back, just as Blaine had wanted to bring Helena back. I wanted to see him again, to hear his voice. More importantly, I wanted to talk to him and to know that he was finally and forever hearing *me*, not the version of me that lived in his head. I wanted Blaine to love me as I had always loved him.

I sat by the fireplace in my living room, the book and my sheaf of notes in my lap. *It will be different,* said a voice in my head—the voice, I suppose, of Blaine's "Boothie." *Helena was greedy and loveless. Blaine is my friend. Blaine would never want to hurt me. And I won't make the mistakes that Blaine did.*

It said such wonderful, plausible things, that voice, and I wanted to believe it very badly. It was my hatred of Helena that saved me, my absolute, unassailable conviction that she would never have put any idea in my head that might have made me happy. I remembered her eyes, remembered her smirk, and with a sudden convulsive motion, flung the *Mortui Liber Magistri* and all my notes onto the fire.

The notes went up at once. For a terrible moment I thought the book was not going to burn at all, and I grabbed the poker and shoved it deeper into the fire. It was an old book, its pages dry and brittle. Once they caught, they were quickly consumed, my last link with Blaine destroyed, transformed in seconds into a pile of ashes and a bitter, noxious reek.

The sound of them burning was like the sound of Helena laughing.

I dream of a day when they may rise above the billows to drag down in their reeking talons the remnants of puny, war-exhausted mankind—of a day when the land shall sink, and the dark ocean floor shall ascend amidst universal pandemonium.

"Dagon" · H.P. Lovecraft (1917)

• TAKE ME TO THE RIVER •
Paul McAuley

The first and probably last Bristol Free Festival hadn't drawn anything like the numbers its blithely optimistic organizers had predicted, but even so, the crowd was four or five times as big as any Martin Feather had ever faced. Martin had been brought in as a last-minute replacement after the regular keyboard player in Sea Change, the semi-professional group headlining the bill, had broken his arm in a five-a-side football match. Last night's run-through had gone okay, but now, in the mouth of the beast, Martin was beginning to get the jitters. The rest of the band were happy to hang out backstage, passing around a fat spliff, drinking free beer, and bullshitting with a mini-skirted reporter from the Bristol Evening Post, but Martin was too wound up to stay still, and after his third visit to the smelly Port-A-Loo he wandered around to the front of the stage to check out the action.

It was the hottest day yet in the hottest summer in living memory. More than three hundred people sprawled on drought-browned grass in front of the stage, and a couple of hundred more queued at ice-cream vans and deathburger carts or poked around stalls that sold vegetarian food, incense sticks and lumpy bits of hand-thrown pottery, hand-printed silk scarves and antique shawls and dresses. A fire-eater and a juggler entertained the festival-goers; a mime did his level best to piss them off. There was a fortune teller in a candy-striped tent. There were hippies and bikers, straight families and sullen groups of teenagers, small kids running around in face paint and dressing-up-box cowboy outfits and fairy princess dresses, naked toddlers, and a barechested sunburnt guy with long blond hair and white jeans who stood front and centre of the stage, arms held out crucifixion-style and face turned up to the blank blue sky as he grokked the music. He'd been there all afternoon, assuming the same pose for the Trad Jazz group, the pair of lank-haired unisex folk singers, the steel band, a group of teenagers who'd come all the way from Yeovil to play Gene Vincent's greatest hits, and the reggae that the DJ played between sets. And now for Clouds of Memory, second-from-top on the bill, and currently bludgeoning their way through "Paint It Black."

Martin had joined Clouds of Memory a few months ago, but he'd quickly fallen out with the singer and lead guitarist, Simon Cowley, an untalented egomaniac who couldn't stay in key if his life depended on it. Martin still rankled over the way he'd been peremptorily fired after a gig in Yate and left to find his own way home (it hadn't helped that his girlfriend had dumped him in the same week), but watching his nemesis make a buffoon of himself didn't seem like a bad way to keep his mind off his stomach's flip-flops.

Simon Cowley ended "Paint It Black" by wrenching an unsteady F chord from his guitar a whole beat behind the rest of the band, and stood centre-stage with one arm raised in triumph, as if the scattering of polite applause was a standing ovation. His shoulder-length blond hair was tangled across his face. He was wearing a red jumpsuit and white cowboy boots. He turned to the drummer and brought down his arm, kicking off the doomy opening chords of his self-penned set-closing epic, "My Baby's Gone to UFO Heaven," and Martin saw Dr. John stepping through the people scattered at the fringe of the audience, heading straight towards him.

He should have known at once that it meant trouble. Dr. John was a small-time hustler who, after dropping out of Bristol University's Medical School, supplemented his dole by buying grass and hash at street-price in St. Paul's, Bristol's pocket ghetto, and selling it for a premium to students. They'd first met because Dr. John rented a rotten little flat above the club where Martin had been working. Dr. John had introduced Martin to the dubious delights of the Coronation Tap, and after Martin had set up his hole-in-the-wall secondhand record shop, Dr. John would stop by once or twice a week to sell LPs he'd found in junkshops or jumble sales, or had taken from students in exchange for twists of seeds and stems. He'd tell Martin to put on some reggae and turn it up, and do what he called the monkey dance. He'd flip through the stock boxes, pulling out albums and saying with mock-amazement, "Can you believe this shit? Can you believe anyone would actually pay money for it?" He'd look over the shoulders of browsing customers and tell them, "I wouldn't buy that, man. It'll make your ears bleed. It'll lower your IQ." or he'd read out the lyrics of prog rock songs in a plummy voice borrowed from Peter Sellers until Martin lost patience and told him to piss off. Then he'd shuffle towards the door, apologizing loudly for upsetting the nice middle-class students, pausing before he stepped out, asking Martin if he'd see him at the Coronation Tap later on.

When he wasn't hustling dope or secondhand records, Dr. John spent most of his time in the Tap, sinking liver-crippling amounts of psychedelically strong scrumpy cider, bullshitting, and generally taking the piss. Like many people who aren't comfortable in their own skins, he was restless, took great delight in being obnoxious, and preferred other people's voices to his own. He would recite entire Monty Python sketches at the drop of a hat, or try to hold conversations in Captain Beefheart lyrics ("The past sure is tense, Martin! A big-eyed bean from Venus told me that. Know what I mean?"). His favorite film was Get Carter, and he could play Jack Carter for a whole evening. "A pint of scrumpy," he'd say to the landlord, "in a thin glass." Or he'd walk up to the biggest biker in the pub and tell him, "You're a big man, but you're in bad shape. With me, it's a full time job. So behave yourself." Amazingly, he was never beaten up, although a burly student in a rugby shirt once threw a full pint of beer in his face after being told that his eyes were like piss-holes in snow.

Dr. John's scrumpy-fuelled exploits were legendary. The time he'd been arrested for walking down the middle of Whiteladies Road with a traffic cone on his head. The time he'd tried to demonstrate how stuntmen could fall flat on their faces, and had broken one of his front teeth on the pavement. The time he'd climbed into a tree and gone to sleep, waking up a couple of hours later and falling ten feet onto the roof of a car, leaving a dent the exact shape of his body and walking away without a bruise. The time he'd slipped on ice, fallen over, and smashed the bottle of whiskey in his pocket: a shard of glass had penetrated his thigh and damaged a nerve, leaving him with a slight but permanent limp. His life was like a cartoon. He was Tom in Tom and Jerry, Wile E. Coyote in Roadrunner. He was one of those people who bang their way from one pratfall to the next in the kind of downhill spiral that seems funny as long as you don't get too close.

Now he gimped up to Martin, a short, squat guy with a cloud of curly black hair and a wispy beard, wearing a filthy denim jacket, a Black Sabbath T-shirt, and patchwork flares, saying loudly, "Didn't you used to be in this band?"

"For about five minutes in April."

Dr. John sneered at the stage. "You're well out of it, man. Is that a gong I see, right there behind the drummer? It is, isn't it? Fucking poseurs."

"If they dumped Simon and found someone who could actually sing and play lead guitar, they might have the kernel of a good sound. Put the bass and drums front and centre, like a reggae set-up."

"Not that you're bitter or anything," Dr. John said. He pulled a clear glass bottle half-filled with a cloudy brown liquid from one pocket of his denim jacket, unscrewed the cap and took a long swallow of brackish liquid, belched, and offered it to Martin.

Martin took a cautious sip and immediately spat it out. "Jesus. What is it?"

"Woke up on the floor of this strange flat this morning, man. I must have been invited to a party. I mixed myself a cocktail with what was left." Dr. John snatched back the bottle, took another pull, and smacked his lips. "You have to admit it has a certain vigor."

"It tastes like cough medicine. There's beer backstage, if you want some."

"Backstage? Were you playing, man? I'm sorry to have missed it."

"I'm on next. Playing with the headliners."

"Free beer, man, now I know you're a star."

"I'm only a stand-in, but I get all the perks."

On stage, Simon Cowley, his face screwed up inside a fall of blond hair, was hunched over his guitar and picking his way through an extended solo. When Martin had joined Clouds of Memory, he'd tried to get them interested in the raw new stuff coming out of New York and London—Television and the Ramones, Dr. Feelgood and the 101ers—but Simon had sneered and said it was nothing but three-chord pub rock with no trace of musical artistry whatsoever. "Artistry" was one of Simon's favorite words. He was the kind of guy who spent Saturday afternoons in guitar shops, pissing off the assistants by playing note-by-note copies of Jimmy Page and Eric Clapton solos. He liked to drop quotes from Nietzsche and Hesse into casual conversation. He was a big fan of Eric Von Daniken. He subscribed to the muso's music paper, Melody Maker, and despised the achingly hip streetwise attitudes of the New Musical Express, which Martin read from cover to cover every week. The tension between them had simmered for a couple of weeks, until, while they were packing up after that gig in Yate, Simon had picked an argument with Martin and sacked him on the spot.

Dr. John took another swig of his cocktail and said, "Sabbath, man, they're the only ones who can do this kind of thing properly. Did I tell you about the gig at Colston Hall this spring?"

"Only about a hundred times."

"It wasn't loud enough, but that was the only thing wrong with it. A thousand kids belting out 'Paranoid' at the top of their lungs, it was a religious experience. But this, this is like . . . " He looked up at the sky for inspiration, failed to find it, and took another drink.

"It's prog rock crap," Martin said, "but Dancing Jesus likes it."

The barechested guy stood in the middle of the thin crowd, arms flung wide, face tilted to the blue sky, quivering all over.

Dr. John's lifted his upper lip in a sneering smile that showed off his broken tooth. "Where his head's at, man, he'd groove on anything. I sold him my last three tabs of acid and he dropped them all. Anyone's in UFO heaven, it's him."

"Made much money here?"

"I'm here for the vibe, man."

"Right."

"Truly. I'm down to seeds and stems until Tuesday or Wednesday, when this a guy I know is going to deliver some primo hash. Moroccan gold, man, the real no-camel-shit-whatsoever deal. This guy, his brother's a sailor, gets the stuff straight from the souk. I'll put you down for an eighth, seeing as you're a good pal and a professional musician and everything." Dr. John looked around and sidled closer and said, "Plus, you can help me out a little right now."

Martin was instantly wary. He said, "I'm on after this lot finishes."

"I've seen these fuckers play before, man. They're getting into the drum solo, and then there's the bass solo, that plonker's endless guitar wankery . . . You've got plenty of time. And it's a really simple favor."

"I bet."

"A lot easier than saving someone from a beating."

A few weeks ago, at a dub concert in a community hall in St. Paul's, a gang of Jamaican youths had decided to get territorial on Martin's bloodclat white ass. Dr. John and his dealer had chased them off, an heroic deed Dr. John had mentioned no more than fifty or sixty times since. Martin said, "I believe it was your friend Hector who actually saved me."

"But I alerted him to the situation, I asked him to help you out because you're a good friend of mine. And friends have to look after each other, right?"

Martin sighed. "If I do this thing for you, will you promise to never mention St. Paul's again?"

"Cross my heart and hope to die, man. See that girl?" Dr. John put his arm around Martin, enveloping him in a powerful odor compounded of stale booze, sweat, and pot smoke, and turned him around.

"What am I looking at?"

"The girl, man. Black hair, white dress."

She stood beside the St. John's ambulance, in the narrow wedge of shadow it cast. Tall and willowy in a long white dress that clung to her curves, her arms bare and pale, her elfin face framed by a Louise Brooks bob of midnight-black hair.

"I've been watching her," Dr. John said.

"I don't think she's your type."

Regulars at the Tap sometimes speculated about Dr. John's sex life. Everyone agreed that he must have one, but no one could imagine what it could be like.

"She's dealing, man. Actually, she's not really dealing because there's no money changing hands, she's been handing out freebies all afternoon. What you can do for me is sashay over there and cop a sample of whatever it is she's holding. See, it really is an easy-peasey little favor."

"If it's so easy, why don't you do it?"

"Man, that would hardly be cool. I'd blow my reputation if I was seen taking a hand-out from some hippy chick."

"But I wouldn't."

"That's different, man. You're not in the business. You're a civilian. Go get a sample, okay? And talk to her, try to find out where she's getting her stuff from. A chick like that, she has to be fronting for someone. Maybe those guys who muscled into my business at the Student Union."

"The ones who put the Fear in you," Martin said.

One day at the beginning of the long, hot summer, Dr. John had walked into the Tap with two black eyes and a split lip, and insisted on showing everyone the stitches in his scalp whether they wanted to look or not. "Four fuckers beat me up round the back of the Student Union. Told me that it was their territory from now on. Some pockmarked guy with a goatee is working my spot now, turning the kids on to brown heroin by telling them that he's out of grass, but if they'd like to try a sample of this nice powder. . . " Dr. John had looked solemn for a moment, then had put on his Get Carter voice. "Still, look on the bright side. They're only fucking students. Maybe a little bit of heroin will light up their immensely dull lives."

Now he told Martin, "I'm scared of nothing, man. Still, if she *is* working for them, and they see me talking to her . . . You see what I mean? But you're a civilian. They won't touch you."

"She looks like she's from some cult," Martin said. "Like the Hare Krishnas who were here earlier, handing out copies of George's favorite book."

"Don't knock the guys in orange, man, they serve a mean lentil curry to people who, because of the government's attitude to alternative lifestyles, often find themselves having to choose between eating and paying the rent. Just walk over there, cop a little of what's she's holding, and come right back. It'll take you all of thirty seconds, and I swear I won't mention saving your life ever again."

"I'll do it," Martin said, "as long as you stop making those puppy eyes at me."

He tried to affect a cool stroll as he moved through the crowd towards the girl. The closer he got, the less attractive she appeared. Her face was plastered in white powder, her Louise Brooks bob was a cheap nylon wig, and her skin was puffy and wrinkled, as if she'd spent a couple of days in the bath. Martin told her that he'd heard she had some good stuff, and she stared at him for a moment, a gaze so penetrating he felt she had seen through to the floor of his soul, before she shook her head and looked past him at something a million miles away.

Martin said, "You don't have anything for me? How about for my friends? They're playing next, and they could do with a little lift."

She was staring straight through him. As if, after she'd dismissed him, he'd ceased to exist. Her eyes were bloodshot and slightly bulging, rimmed with thick mascara that made them seem even bigger. Her white dress was badly water stained, and a clammy odor rose from it.

"Maybe I'll see you around," Martin said, remembering how he'd felt when he'd suffered one of his numerous rejections at the school disco. It didn't help that a gang of teenage boys jeered and toasted him with bottles of cider as he walked away.

Dr. John was waiting for him backstage, a plastic pint glass in his hand.

"I see you found the free beer," Martin said.

"You really are a superstar, man. I mention your name and it's like magic, this beer suddenly appears. What did she slip you? What did she say?"

"She didn't say a word, and she didn't slip me anything either. It's probably some kind of scam involving herbal crap made from boiled nettle leaves or grass-type grass, and she realized that I'd spot it right away."

"All the best gear is herbal," Dr. John said, and launched into a spiel about William Burroughs and a South American Indian drug that was blown into your nostrils through a yard-long pipe and took you on a magical mystery tour, stopping only to give Simon Cowley a shit-eating grin as he came off stage, saying, "Fab set, man. Reminded me of Herman's Hermits at their peak."

Simon looked at Martin and said, "Still hanging out with losers I see," and walked past, chin in the air.

Then Martin was busy setting up his keyboards while the two festival roadies took down Clouds of Memory's drums and mikes and assembled Sea Change's kit, and before he knew it the set had kicked off. The sun was setting and a hot wind was getting up, fluttering the stage's canvas roof, blowing the music towards the traffic that scuttled along the far edge of Clifton Downs. Martin concentrated fiercely on playing all the right notes in the right order in the right place, but whenever he had a few moment's rest he glanced towards the girl. Seeing her beyond the glare of the footlights, seeing her with a hairy hippy with a beer-drinker's belly, a couple of giggling girls who couldn't have been more than fifteen, a bearded boy in bellbottoms and a brown chalkstripe waistcoat, a woman in a summer dress and a chiffon scarf . . .

When he came off, sweating hard after two encores, the rhythm guitarist of Clouds of Memory got in his face, saying something about his loser friend spiking beer. Martin brushed him off and went to look for Dr. John. There was no sign of him, backstage or front. The crowd was beginning to drift away. Two men in black uniforms had opened the back doors of the ambulance and were packing away their first aid kit. The girl was gone.

Martin didn't think any more about it until early the next morning, when he was woken by the doorbell. It was Monday morning, ten to eight, already stiflingly hot, and Martin had a hangover from the post-gig pub session with the guys from Sea Change and their wives and girlfriends and hangers-on. When the bell rang he put a pillow over his head, but the bell just wouldn't quit, a steady drilling that resonated at the core of his headache. Clearly, some moron had SuperGlued his finger to the bell push, and at last Martin got up and padded into the living room and looked out of the window to see who it was.

Martin's flat was on the top floor of a house in the middle of Worcester Terrace, a row of Georgian houses which various members of the professional middle class were beginning to reclaim from decades of low rent squalor. Four storeys below, Dr. John stood like a smudge of soot on the clean white doorstep, looking up and waving cheerfully when Martin asked him if he'd lost his mind.

"I've had a bit of an adventure," he shouted.

Martin put his keys in a sock and threw them down. By the time his visitor had labored up the stairs he was dressed and in the kitchen, making tea. Dr. John stood in the doorway, making a noise like a deflating set of bagpipes. He had turned a color more normally associated with aubergines or baboons' bottoms than the human face. When he had his breath back, he said, "You should find somewhere nearer the ground. I think I have altitude sickness."

"I should punch you in the snout."

"Whatever it is you think I did, I didn't do it." Dr. John flopped heavily onto one of the kitchen chairs. He had the bright eyes and clenched jaw of a speed buzz. There was fresh mud on the knees of his jeans. Grass stains on his denim jacket; a leafy twig in his bird's nest hair.

"Then you didn't spike Simon Cowley's beer."

"Oh, *that*." Dr. John opened a Virginia tobacco tin and took out a roll-up. "Yeah, I did that. You have bacon and eggs to go with this tea?"

"If I had any bacon I'd give you bacon and eggs if I had any eggs."

Dr. John lit the roll-up and looked around the little kitchen. "I see you have cornflakes."

"Knock yourself out. What did you spike him with?"

"The herbal shit I scored off that girl." Dr. John poured milk over the bowlful of cornflakes. "Is that hot chocolate I see by the kettle?"

"So you blew your reputation as a professional drug dealer to check out this hippy chick."

Dr. John shook chocolate powder over his cornflakes. "My curiosity was piqued."

"Did she give you anything?"

"She handed it over without a word. Check it out." Dr. John fished something from the pocket of his denim jacket and showed it to Martin. It was the size of his thumbnail and crudely pressed from a greenish paste; it looked more like a bird-dropping than a pill. "Weird-looking shit, huh? So weird, in fact, that even I wouldn't take it without testing it first. So I broke off the smallest little sliver and dropped it in Mr. UFO's beer."

"Too much acid has fried your brains."

"But in the best possible way." Dr. John was bent over the bowl, spooning up chocolate powder/milk/cornflakes mix. The roll-up was still glued to the corner of his mouth. Although the window was open, his funky odor filled the kitchen. "So, did my freebie take your wanky friend to somewhere good?"

"Good enough for his pal to know he'd been spiked."

"It didn't give him fits, make him foam at the mouth, make him sing in tune?"

"I didn't hang around to find out. He just looked very spaced. Had a thousand yard stare and a stupid grin."

"Cool. Maybe I'll give it a test flight this afternoon. Make me some more tea, man, and I'll tell you about the girl."

Dr. John said that he had followed her across the Downs into the wild strip of woods along the edge of the Avon Gorge. "She was like an elf, man. Breezed through those fucking woods as if she was born to it."

"So she isn't the front for Turkish gangsters. She really is just some crazy hippy."

"She might have been crazy, but she really could move. Floated right down those steep narrow paths to the bottom of the gorge in about a minute flat. I got stuck halfway, saw her cross the road at the bottom, saw her climbing over the rail on the other side, down to the river." Dr. John lit a fresh roll-up and looked at Martin, suddenly serious. "You know how the Avon is almost dried up because of the drought? There's grass growing on the mud, and where grass isn't growing it's all dry and cracked. She walked over that shit, man, straight towards what's left of the river. Then a couple of lorries went past, and when they were gone she wasn't there any more."

"She jumped into the river? Come on."

"One moment she was walking across those mud flats, and then those bastard lorries came along, and she was gone, that's all I know."

"Let me get this straight. She was giving away some kind of drug for free, and then she was struck by a fit of remorse, so she walked down to the river and drowned herself."

Martin, used to Dr. John's fantastic stories, reckoned that about half of what he'd been told was true. He believed that his friend had tried to follow the girl and lost her in the woods; the rest was just the usual bullshit embellishment.

"I don't know what her motivation was, man. I only know what I saw."

"You didn't go look for her? Or call the police?"

"I was on this dead-end path halfway up the side of the fucking gorge. I couldn't go any further, all I could do was climb up and start over, and if she reappeared while I was finding a new way down I would have missed her. So I sat there and kept watch, but the light was going, and I didn't see her again, and after a bit I suppose I fell asleep. Woke up this morning covered in dew, with this bastard headache."

"Let me guess: while you were keeping a look-out for this girl, you finished off your party cocktail."

"It was my only sustenance, man. I wasn't about to start eating leaves."

"Well, look on the bright side. If she did drown herself, you don't have to worry that she'll steal your customers."

"You don't believe me. That's cool. But I viddied it, brother, with my own glazzies. She walked over the mud and then she . . . Shit!"

Dr. John's chair went over as he pushed away from the table. Martin turned, saw the bird on the stone ledge outside the window. His first thought was that it was a gull, but although it was the right mix of white and gray, it was twice the size of any ordinary gull and sort of lop-sided, and it stank horribly, like rotten meat and low-tide sewage. When he reached out to shut the window, it fixed him with a mad red eye and snapped at his hand, its sharp yellow bill splintering the window frame when he snatched his fingers away. Then it stretched its wings (one seemed longer than the other, and both had growths, bat-like claws, at their joints) and dropped away in a half-turn and floated out across the communal gardens of the terrace, a white speck dwindling away towards the docks.

Dr. John kept glancing up at the sky as he walked with Martin up the hill towards the centre of Clifton. He was convinced that the bird had something to do with the girl. "It was a spy, man. A mutant gull from the lower depths of wherever she came from."

"It had some sort of disease," Martin said.

Dr. John turned a full circle, his face tipped skywards, and said in a sonorous film trailer baritone, "A mutant gull on a mission from Hell."

"You see pigeons with parts of their feet missing all the time. It's something to do with walking on pavements."

Dr. John laughed. "You're so straight, man, they could use you as a ruler."

"Maybe it ate a bad kebab on a rubbish tip."

"Maybe it ate one of the Tap's mystery meat pies. I'm pretty sure they've fried *my* chromosomes." Dr. John did a lurching Frankenstein walk for a few steps, arms held straight out, eyes rolled back.

They parted by the tidy park landscaped around the ruins of a church that had been hit by a German bomb during Bristol's Blitz. Dr. John said he was going to go home and drop that pill and see where it took him.

"Don't be crazy," Martin said.

"It's all part of my ongoing exploration of inner space, man. Cheaper than TV and a lot more fun."

"It's probably made out of hemlock and lead paint. Weedkiller and rat snot."

"Don't be such a worrywart. There isn't a pill or powder I can't handle," Dr. John said, and sloped off across the grassy space, a squat stubborn figure listing slightly to the left.

The next day, lunchtime in the Coronation Tap, one of Dr. John's grebo pals lurched up to Martin and asked where the little fucker was hiding himself.

"I'm not his keeper," Martin said. He was having a quiet pint and a pastie, and thinking about whether to shut up shop for a couple of weeks and go on holiday. The only customer he'd had all morning had been a confused old lady who, after poking about in the bins for ten minutes, had asked him if he had any Ken Dodd records. Scotland, perhaps. Apparently it had rained somewhere in Scotland only yesterday.

The grebo peered at Martin through a shroud of long, lank hair. He was barefoot, barechested under his filthy afghan coat, and stank like a goat. "I got something for him. The stuff he's been waiting for. You know."

"Not really," Martin said, and remembered that Dr. John had mentioned something about expecting a delivery of hash.

"We had a deal, right, so I went round to his flat and he wasn't there, and I've been waiting two whole fucking hours here, and now I have to go down the social and sign on. When you see him, tell him I was looking for him," the grebo said, and lurched off without giving his name.

That evening, after he'd closed up his shop, Martin made a detour on the way home, to call on Dr. John. He told himself that his friend was probably in the middle of one of his forty-eight hour sleepathons, but there was no harm checking. Just in case. He leaned on Dr. John's doorbell for five minutes, listening to it trill two floors above him, then went down the whitewashed steps and rang the bell of the private members club in the basement. It was owned by Dr. John's landlord, Mr. Mavros, an after-hours drinking spot featuring sticky purple shagpile and red leatherette booths. Martin had worked behind its bar last year, when he'd been scraping together enough seed money for his record shop.

"I hope this doesn't mean trouble for me," Mr. Mavros said, after he had handed over the key to Dr. John's flat.

"He's ill," Martin lied. "I said I'd stop by and see if he needed anything. Soup or aspirin or whatever."

"He look ill when I see him," Mr. Mavros said. He was a thin, consumptive man with no hair on his head except for a splendid pair of thick black eyebrows. He wore red braces over his immaculate white shirt, and as usual a small cigar was plugged into the corner of his mouth. "He come back from somewhere when I was locking up this place, two o'clock in the morning. I say hello and he look straight past me. Into the distance, like he see something that isn't there. I know he drink, he smoke dope, but this was different. You tell him, Martin, if he start on the hard drugs, if he cause me trouble, that's it, I throw him out."

The door to Dr. John's tiny flat stood ajar. The bed-sitting room was hot and stale. Sunlight burned at the edges of the drawn curtains. The bed was piled with cushions and dirty clothes; the floor was strewn with clothes and broken-backed paperbacks, unsleeved records and record sleeves, empty cans and bottles, tin-foil takeaway cartons, and yellowing newspapers. In the filthy little kitchen, the tap was running over a stack of unwashed dishes and pots. Martin turned it off, heard something splash somewhere else in the flat. He called out, felt a jolt of nerves when there was another splash.

The bathroom was a windowless cubbyhole just big enough for bath, bog and wash-basin. The light was off, and it smelt like the seal pool in the zoo. The bath was brimful, and in the semi-darkness Martin could see a shape under the shivering surface of the water.

"John?"

A pale hand lifted like a lily; water cascaded over the edge of the bath. Martin jerked the light cord with a convulsive movement and in the sudden harsh glare of the unshielded bulb the boy in the bath—fully clothed, in the same brown, chalkstripe waistcoat he'd been wearing at the Free Festival—sat bolt upright, eyes wide, water running out of his nose and mouth.

Martin helped the boy out of the bath and got him onto the bed, but he wouldn't answer any of Martin's questions about Dr. John, and quickly fell into something deeper than sleep. He breathed with his mouth open, making a rasping gurgle, and didn't stir when Martin went through his pockets, finding nothing but a couple of pound notes wadded together in a knot of papier-mâché. Martin suddenly found that he couldn't bear to stay a moment longer with this unquiet sleeper in the hot, claustrophobic flat, and fled into the late-afternoon sunlight and the diesel dust and ordinary noise of traffic.

He sat on the bench beside a telephone box on the other side of the road and thought about his options. If he told Mr. Mavros what he'd found, the landlord would probably throw out the boy and change the lock on the door. And if he went to the police, they'd probably make a note of Dr. John's disappearance and forget all about it. He could always walk away, of course, but Dr. John was a friend who had helped him out of a tight spot, and he had a vague but nagging sense of duty.

Sooner or later, he thought, Dr. John would turn up, or the boy would wake up and slope off to wherever Dr. John was hanging out. All he had to do was wait. How hard could that be? He went around the corner, bought a parcel of fish and chips and a can of Coke, and returned to the bench. The blue sky darkened and the air grew hotter and thicker. A police car slowed as it went past and the driver took a lingering look at Martin, who had to suppress an impulse to wave when the car came back in the other direction ten minutes later. The streetlights flickered on. A little later, Mr. Mavros switched on the light over the door of his club, illuminating the board painted with its faintly sinister motto: *There are no strangers here, only friends who haven't met.*

Martin bought another Coke at the fish-and-chip shop, and when he returned to the bench saw something swoop down onto the roofline of the row of houses, joining the half dozen white birds that hadn't been there five minutes ago. They're only gulls, he told himself, there are plenty of gulls in Bristol. But he got the shivers anyway, flashing on the monster that had nearly amputated his fingers, and was about to turn tail and head for home when he saw the boy in the brown waistcoat ambling away down the street.

The boy must have crawled back into the bath before he left Dr. John's flat; he tracked wet footprints that grew smaller and smaller as Martin followed him through the villagey center of Clifton towards the Avon Gorge, walking with a quickening pace as if drawn to some increasingly urgent siren song. By the time they'd reached the grassy space in front of Brunel's suspension bridge, Martin was jogging to keep up. The boy walked straight across the road, looking neither right nor left, and plunged into the bushes beside the public lavatories. Martin got up his nerve and followed, found a steep, narrow path, and climbed to the top.

The sky was cloudless and black. The moon, almost full, was setting. The stubby observatory tower that housed a camera obscura shone wanly. Beyond it, the boy and half a dozen other people stood at the rail along the edge of the gorge. Martin skulked behind the thin cover of a clump of laurel bushes. He had the airy feeling that something was about to happen, but didn't have the faintest idea what it would be. One of the giant, arch-pierced stone towers that supported the suspension bridge reared up behind his hiding place, and it seemed to him that the watchers at the rail were staring at the lamp-lit road that ran between bridge's white-painted chains and struts to the other side of the deep narrow gorge.

Martin settled behind the laurels, sipped warm Coke. Gradually, more people drifted across the moonlit grass to join the little congregation at the rail. A girl in a cotton dress came past Martin's hiding place, so close he could have reached out and touched her bare leg. No one spoke. They stood at the rail and stared at the bridge. They reminded Martin of the gulls on the roof. Whenever he checked his digital watch, cupping his right wrist with his left hand to hide its little light, far less time had passed than he had thought.

10:08.

10:32.

10:56.

He must have dozed, because the noise jerked him awake. The people lined up along the edge of the drop were chanting, a slow liturgical dirge of nonsense words rich in consonants. They bent against the rail, their arms outstretched, swaying like sea anemones in a current, reaching towards the bridge. Martin turned, and saw that two shadowy figures were walking along the road to the mid-point of the bridge, where the downcurving arcs of white-painted suspension chains met. One was a man, the other the girl in the white dress. She embraced her companion for a moment, and then he broke away and clambered over the rail and without hesitation or ceremony stepped out into thin air and plummeted into darkness.

Martin stood up, his heart beating lightly and quickly, his whole skin tingling, and thought that he saw a brief green flash in the river directly below the bridge, a moment of heat lightning. The girl was walking along the bridge towards the other side of the gorge; the people at the rail were beginning to drift away, each moving in a different direction.

One of them had a cloud of bushy hair, and walked with a distinct list.

Martin chased after him, stumbling in the dark, making far too much noise as he dodged from one clump of bushes to the next, at last daring to cut across his path and grab him by the shoulders and turn him around. Dr. John tried to twist away, like a freshly-caught fish flopping in a trawlerman's grasp. Martin held on and at last his friend quietened and stood still, his gaze fixed on something a thousand miles beyond Martin's left shoulder.

"Let's get out of this," Martin said, and took hold of Dr. John's right arm above the elbow and steered him through the streets of Clifton to Worcester Terrace. There was another brief struggle after Martin had opened the front door, but then Dr. John quietened again and allowed himself to be led up the four flights of stairs to Martin's flat. He stood in a kind of dazed slouch, blinking slowly in the bright light of the kitchen while Martin made coffee, taking no notice of the mug that Martin tried to put it in his hand.

Martin leaned against the counter by the sink and sipped his own coffee and asked Dr. John where he'd been, what had happened to him, what the fuck had just happened on the bridge.

"Someone jumped. I saw it. He climbed over the rail and let go."

Dr. John didn't even blink. Martin had to step hard on the impulse to slap him silly.

"It's something to do with the pill, isn't it? The green pill, and the girl who gave it to you. Don't try to deny it, I saw her with whoever it was that jumped."

Dr. John stood still and silent, face slack, shoulders slumped. Or not entirely still—one hand was slowly and slyly creeping towards the breast pocket of his denim jacket. Martin knocked it away and reached inside the pocket and pulled out the green pill and held it in front of Dr. John's face.

"What is this shit? What does it do to you?"

Dr. John's eyes tracked the pill as Martin moved it to and fro; his hand limply pawed the air.

"Don't be pathetic," Martin said. He thrust the pill into the pocket of his jeans and steered Dr. John into the living room and put him to bed on the sofa. Then he went out to the phone box at the end of the road, dialed 999 and told the operator that he'd seen someone jump from the Clifton Suspension Bridge, and hung up when she asked for his name.

When Martin went into the living room the next morning, Dr. John was fast asleep, curled into the back of the sofa and drooling into the cushion he was using as a pillow. After Martin had shaken him awake and poured a cup of tea into him, he claimed not to remember anything about the last night, saying, "Man, I was definitely out of my head."

"You don't know the half of it."

They were sitting at the kitchen table. Dr. John drank a mug of tea and devoured three slices of white bread smeared with butter and sprinkled with brown sugar while Martin told him about the boy in the bath, the people lined up at the railing above the Avon Gorge, and the girl who had escorted the man to the midpoint of the bridge, how she'd embraced him, how he'd stepped into thin air. Dr. John wore a funny little smile, as if he knew the secret that would make sense of everything, but when Martin had finished he shrugged and said, "People jump off the bridge all the time. They queue up to jump off. The police have to comb pieces of them out of the trees, scrape them off the road, dig them out of the mud . . . " He patted his pockets. "Got any fags?"

Martin found a packet his girlfriend had left behind.

"Silk Cut? They're not real cigarettes," Dr. John said, but tore off the filter off one and lit it and sat back and blew smoke at the ceiling.

Martin was tired of trying to crack Dr. John's bullshit insouciance, but decided to give it one more try. He leaned across the table and said as forcefully as he could, "Someone jumped off the bridge. I saw it."

"I believe you, man," Dr. John said, still smiling that sly little smile

"If you don't remember anything at all, you really were out of your head. And I thought there wasn't a pill or powder you couldn't handle."

"It isn't that I don't remember anything, man. I just don't remember any of the shit you saw. That was just the pattern on the veil that hides the true reality of things. That hides what's really going on."

"So what was really going on?"

"It's kind of hard to explain."

"I want to understand."

"Are you worried about me, man? I'm touched."

"I saw someone throw himself off the suspension bridge. The girl who gave you that pill, the one in the white dress, was right there with him when he jumped. I think that guy got high on whatever it is she's peddling, just like you did, and she persuaded him to jump. I think she killed him. That's what I saw. How about you?"

Dr. John thought for a few moments. "What you have to understand is that the green shit doesn't do anything but put you in the right frame of mind. It takes you to the beach, and after that it's up to you. You have to wade out into the sea and give yourself up to it of your own free will. And if you can do that, the sea takes you right through the bottom of the world into this space that's deeper and darker than anywhere you've ever been. The womb of the world, the place where rock and water and air and everything else came from."

He developed a thousand yard stare for a moment, then shook himself and smiled around the cigarette, showing his broken tooth.

"It's very dark and quiet, but it isn't lonely. It's like the floor of the collective unconscious. Not in the Jungian sense, but something deeper and darker than that. You can lose yourself in it forever. You dissolve. This is hard, trying to explain how it is to someone who doesn't believe a word of it, but haven't you ever had that feeling when everything inside you and everything outside you, everything in the whole wide world, lines up perfectly, just for a moment? I remember when I was a kid, this one day in summer. Hot as it is now, but everything lush and green. Cow parsley and nettles growing taller than me along the edges of the road on the way up to the common. Farmers turned cows and sheep out to graze there, and the grass was short and wiry, and warm beneath you when you lay down, and the sun was a warm red weight on your closed eyelids. You lay there and felt the whole world holding you to itself, and you heard a lark singing somewhere above you in the sunlight and the warm wind. You couldn't see it, but it was singing its heart out above you, and everything dissolved into this one moment of pure happiness. You know what I'm saying? Well, if you take that feeling and make it a thousand times more intense and stretched that one moment out to infinity, it would be a little like where I went."

"Except that you were high. It didn't really happen, you only thought it did."

Dr. John looked straight at Martin, smiling that sly smile, and said, "You don't know what I'm talking about, do you? You're just a tourist, man. A day tripper. You might have ventured onto the beach a couple of times, you might even have dipped a toe into the sea, but that's as far as you've ever dared to go. Because as far as you're concerned, drugs are recreational. Something you do for fun."

Martin felt a sharp flare of anger. He'd seen something awful, he believed that he had risked his life to rescue Dr. John, and his only reward was scorn and derision. "If you want to fuck yourself up," he said, "do a proper job and score some heroin from that guy who works for those gangsters who beat you up."

"I found something better," Dr. John said. "We all did. Something we didn't know we needed until we found it. You don't need it, man. That's why she turned you down. Even if you got hold of some of her stuff and got off on it, you wouldn't be able to take the next step. You wouldn't be able to surrender yourself. But we knew where it would take us before we'd even seen it. We ached for it. It's our Platonic ideal, man, the missing part we've been searching for all our lives."

"One of your little gang killed himself last night. He threw himself off the suspension bridge, right in front of my eyes. He committed suicide. Is that what you want?"

"Suicide? Is that what you think you saw?"

Dr. John looked straight at Martin again. For a moment, Martin glimpsed the worm of self-loathing that writhed behind the mask of his fatuous smile and flippant manner. He looked away, no longer angry, but embarrassed at having glimpsed something more intimate than mere nakedness.

"Something wants our worship," Dr. John said, "and we want oblivion. It isn't hard to understand. It's a very simple deal."

"If you take another of those pills, you could be the next one off that bridge," Martin said.

Dr. John stood up. "You have your nice little flat, man, and your nice little shop and your nice little gigs with loser pub rock bands. You have a nice little life, man. You've found your niche, and you cling to it like a limpet. Good for you. The only problem is, you can't understand why other people don't want to be like you."

Martin stood up too. "Stay here. Crash out as long as you like. Get your head straight."

Dr. John shook his head. "My friends are waiting for me."

"Don't go back to the river," Martin said, but Dr. John was already out of the door and clumping away downstairs.

Martin shut up shop early that afternoon and took a walk up to the observatory. Children ran about in the sweltering heat, watched by indulgent parents. People were sunbathing on suncrisped grass. There was a queue at the ice-cream stall by the entrance to the observatory tower. Someone was flying a kite. It was all horribly normal, but Martin was possessed by a restless sense that something bad was going to happen. As if a thunderstorm hung just beyond the horizon, waiting for the right wind to blow it his way. As if the world was suddenly all eggshell above a nightmare void. He drifted back through Clifton village and ended up in the Coronation Tap and drank five pints of Directors and ate one of the pub's infamous mystery pies, and at closing time walked back to the suspension bridge and thrashed through bushes to the top of the rise.

There they were, leaning at the rail in the warm half-dark, staring into the abyss.

None of them so much as glanced at Martin as, his heart beating quickly and lightly, his whole skin tingling airily, he walked across the grass. They leaned at the rail and stared with intense impassivity at the gorge and the floodlit bow of the suspension bridge. The two women on either side of Dr. John didn't even blink when Martin tried to pull him away, tugging one arm and then the other, trying to prise his grip from the rail, finally getting him in a bear-hug and hauling as hard as he could. As they staggered backwards, a gull skimmed out of the dusky air and bombed them with a pint of hot wet bird shit. It stank like thousand-year-old fish doused in ammonia, and stung like battery acid when it ran into Martin's eyes. Half-blind, gasping, he let go of Dr. John and tried to wipe the stuff from his eyes and face, and another gull swooped past, spattering him with a fresh load, clipping him with the edge of a wing. Martin sat down hard, saw more gulls circling in the dark air, one of them much bigger than the rest. It dipped down and swooped towards him, its wings lifted in a V-shape. His nerve gave out then, and he scrambled to his feet and ran, had almost gained the shelter of the bushes when the bird hit him from behind, ripping its claws across his scalp and knocking him down. He was crawling towards the bushes, blinded by blood and bird shit, when another gull smashed into him, and the world swung around and flew away like a stone on the end of a string.

When Martin came to, the swollen disc of the full moon was setting beyond the trees on the other side of the gorge. Its cold light filled his eyes. The person standing over him was a shadow against it, reaching down, clasping his hand and helping him sit up.

"Christ," Simon Cowley said. "They really worked you over."

Martin's face and hair were caked in blood and gull shit. His skin burned and his eyes were swollen half-shut. He gingerly touched the deep lacerations in his scalp, winced, and took his hand away.

"Gulls," he said.

"Vicious little fuckers, aren't they? Especially the big one."

"What do you know about it? And what are you doing here?"

"I came here after your hippy friend spiked my beer. I woke up from a horrible dream and found myself standing at the rail over there, in the middle of a whole bunch of sleepwalkers. I've been coming back every night since. And every night someone has gone over the bridge into the river." Simon's long blond hair was unwashed and he stank of sweat and sickness. His eyes were black holes in his pale face. A khaki satchel—an old gas mask carrier—hung from his shoulder. He looked around and said in a hoarse whisper, "I think there's something in the river. I think it swam in from the sea on the last high tide, it's been trapped here ever since because the drought lowered the level of the river. It's been living on what they give it."

"They worship it," Martin said, remembering Dr. John's ravings.

"I think it draws them here and makes them jump off the suspension bridge. I think it eats them," Simon said, "because no one has reported finding any bodies. You'd think, after at least three people jumped off the bridge in as many days, one of them would have washed up. I went down there yesterday in daylight, and took a good look around. Nothing. It devours them. Snaps them up whole."

Martin got to his feet. Heavy black pain rolled inside his skull. His eyes were on fire and his lacerations felt like a crown of thorns. He said, "We should call the police."

"You saw what was down there. I know you did because I saw you here last night."

"I saw something. I don't know what it was."

"You think the police can do anything about something like this?" Simon cocked his head. "You hear that?"

"I hear it."

People were chanting, somewhere below the edge of the gorge.

"It's beginning," Simon said.

"What's beginning?"

"You can help me or stay here, I don't care," Simon said, and ran towards the path that led down the face of the gorge.

Martin chased after him. Everything was black and white in the moonlight. Bleached trees and boulders and slabs of rock loomed out of their own shadows. The day's heat beat up from bare rock. The black air was oven-baked. Martin sweated through his T-shirt and jeans. His feet slipped on sweat inside his Doc Martens. Sweat stung his swollen eyes, his lacerated scalp. He caught up with

Simon at the beginning of a steep smooth chute of limestone that had been polished by generations of kids using it as a slide. At the foot of the gorge, people were crossing the road, shambling towards the girl in the white dress, who stood at the rail at the edge of the river. A passing car sounded its horn, swerved past them.

Simon didn't look around when Martin reached him. He said, "You see her? She's the locus of infection. She's been missing for two weeks, did you know that? I did some research, looked at back copies of the Evening Post for anything about people jumping from the bridge, and there she was. I think she jumped off the bridge and the thing in the river took her and changed her and sent her out to bring it food."

Below, people were climbing over the guard rail at the edge of the road. The river shone like a black silk ribbon between its wide banks of mud. White flakes—gulls—floated above one spot.

"We have to stop it right now," Simon said. "It's high tide tonight. I think it wants to take them all before it goes back to sea."

"All right. How are we going to stop it?"

"I'm going to blow it up. I stole two sticks of dynamite from work. Taped them together with a waterproof fuse. You distract them and I throw the dynamite and we run."

"Distract them?"

People were slogging across the mud towards the gyre of gulls. They had started up their chant again.

"Shout at them," Simon said. "Throw rocks. Try to take back your hippy friend, like you did just now. Whatever you like, as long as you get them to chase you. Then I'll chuck the dynamite in the river, right at the spot under those gulls."

"Suppose they won't chase me?"

In the high-contrast glare of the moonlight, Simon's grin made his face look like a skull. "I'll chuck it in anyway."

"You're crazy. You'll kill them all."

"They're already dead," Simon said, and turned away. Martin grabbed the canvas satchel, but Simon caught the strap as it slid past his wrist. For a moment, they were perfectly balanced, the satchel stretched between them; then a gull swooped out of the black air. Simon ducked, staggered, put his foot down on thin air and fell backwards. Martin sat down heavily, the canvas satchel in his lap, heard a rolling crackle as Simon crashed away through bushes, saw the pale shape of the gull fall away as it plummeted after him.

286 · Take Me to the River

Martin got to his feet and slung the satchel over his shoulder and went on down the path, fetched up breathless at the bottom, his headache pounding like a black strobe. An articulated lorry went past in a glare of headlights and a roar of hot wind and dust. Martin ran across the road, clambered over the guardrail, and dropped to a swale of grassy mud, breaking through a dry crust and sinking up to his knees.

He levered himself out and stumbled forwards. He could hear the tide running in the river, smell its rotten salty stink. Inky figures stood along the edge of the black water on either side of the girl's pale shadow. Gulls swooped around them. Their hands were raised above their heads and they were chanting their nonsense syllables.

Iä! Iä! Iä-R'lyeh!

There was a sudden splashing as hundreds of fish leapt out of the water, shards of silver flipping and thrashing around the line of men and women. Martin ran down a shallow breast of mud, shouting Dr. John's name, and something huge breached the river. Light beat up from it in complex labial folds, rotten, green, alive. Gulls swirled through the light and flared and winked out. Blazing fault lines shot across the mud in every direction; fish exploded in showers of scales and blood.

The people were perfectly silhouetted against the green glare. They were still chanting.

Cthulhu fhtagn! Iä! Iä!

Martin staggered towards them, feet sinking into foul mud, swollen eyes squeezed into slits, and locked his arms around Dr. John's neck. Dr. John fought back, but Martin was stronger and more desperate, and hauled his friend backwards, step by step. The light began to pulse like a heartbeat. A virulent jag cut straight in front of Martin and Dr. John. Mud exploded with popcorn cracks. Martin fell down, pulling Dr. John with him, and the giant gull swooped past, missing Martin's face by inches. Dr. John tried to pull away and Martin clung to him with the last of his strength, watched helplessly as the misshapen bird swept high through the throbbing green glare and turned and plummeted towards them like a dive bomber.

Someone gimped past—Simon Cowley, raising the broken branch he'd been using as a crutch. The bird screeched and slipped sideways, but Simon threw his make-shift spear and caught it square in its breast, and it exploded in a cloud of feathers and rotten meat. Something like a nest of snakes was thrashing in the centre of the light. A thick, living rope whipped across the line of men and women, knocking them down like nine-pins, sweeping them into the river. Simon threw himself flat as another ropey tentacle cracked through the air. For a moment it flexed above Martin, its tip crusted with feathery palps and snapping hooks, dripping a thin slime, and then it sinuously withdrew. The light was dying back into itself. Water rushed into the place where something huge and unendurable had opened a brief gap in the world, bubbled and steamed, and closed over.

Eighteen months later, Martin was with his friends in the middle of the crowd coming out of the Watershed at the end of a Clash concert, his ears ringing and sweat turning cold on his skin under his ripped T-shirt and Oxfam jacket and straight-legged Levis 501s, when someone caught his arm and called his name. Martin turned, saw a guy in a black dufflecoat, short blond hair and a pinched white face, and after a couple of seconds recognized Simon Cowley.

Martin told his friends that he'd catch up with them in the pub, and said to Simon, "I never thought you'd be into punk rock."

"I'm not really here for the music."

Martin grinned. He was still pumped up by the concert's energy. "You missed something tremendous."

"I heard about your friend."

"Come to gloat, have you? Come to say 'I told you so'?"

"Actually, I came to say I'm sorry."

"Oh. Right."

"I also heard you gave up your shop, you joined a group, you have a record deal . . . "

"Those people I was with? That's the group. And the deal, it's for a single with Rough Trade. Nothing major," Martin said, "but we all had three-day hangovers after we signed."

"Still, a record deal."

"Yeah. How about you? I mean, I heard you broke up Clouds of Memory . . . "

"I gave all that up." Simon hesitated, then said, almost shyly, "Want to see something?"

"You don't look well, Simon. What have you been doing since . . . "

Simon shrugged. "I've been working. I've been waking up every night from bad dreams."

"I get those too, sometimes." But Martin didn't want to talk about that; didn't want to talk about anything to do with those awful days in that long hot summer. "Well, it was nice to run into you—"

"I'd really like you to see this. Apart from me, you're the only person who'll understand what it means. Please? It'll only take a minute."

"Only a minute, then," Martin said, and with a sense of foreboding followed Simon to the quay on the other side of the Watershed. Black water lapped a few feet below the edge of the walkway, flexing its patchwork covering of chip papers and beer cans and plastic detergent bottles. Martin shivered in the icy breeze that cut across the water, shoved his hands into the pockets of his jacket, and said, "What are we looking for?"

Simon put a finger to his lips, pointed at the water.

They were like tadpoles grown to the size of late-term human embryos. They were pale and faintly luminous, with heavy heads and large, black, lidless eyes and small pursed mouths. Skinny arms folded under pulsing gill slits. Snakey, finned tails. They hung in the black water at different levels.

Martin stared at them, little chills chasing each other through his blood, and whispered, "What are they?"

"Ghosts, maybe. Or shells, some kind of energy cast off when, you know . . . "

When the people had been taken. When they had been consumed. Snapped up. Devoured. No bodies had been found; fourteen people had simply disappeared, as people sometimes do. Most of them were like Dr. John, chancers on the edge of society, missed by no one but their landlords and dealers and parole officers. There'd been some fuss in the local news about a housewife and a schoolboy who'd both gone missing the same day, but no one had made the connection between the two, and the story soon slipped off the pages. And that might have been the end of it, except that six months later the flat below Dr. John's was flooded; when he went to investigate, Mr. Mavros found Dr. John lying fully clothed in his overflowing bath, dead of a heroin overdose. Dr. John's parents had disowned him long ago. Only Martin and Mr. Mavros had attended the cremation, and Martin had scattered the ashes off the suspension bridge. And that, he thought, really had been the end of it, except for the dreams. Except for these ghosts, pale in the black water.

"I think they come for the music," Simon said. "Or maybe for what the music does to people. A concert is a kind of collective act of worship, isn't it? Maybe they feed on it . . . "

There were six or seven or eight of them. They looked up at Martin and Simon through the water and the floating litter.

"There used to be more," Simon said.

"Isn't one of them sort of listing to the left?"

"What do you mean?"

"Maybe not. It doesn't matter."

Simon said, "I tried to catch one once. I borrowed a keep net from my dad. They slipped right through it."

Martin said, "Afterwards, I found one of those pills in my pocket."

"Did you take it?"

"What would be the point?"

He'd flushed it down the sink. It had dissolved reluctantly, frothing slimy bubbles like a salted slug and giving off a vile stink that had reminded him of gull shit. Dr. John had been right: it hadn't been meant for him. Dr. John and the others had been on the road to oblivion long before they'd been snared by the monster or old god or whatever it was that had been briefly trapped in the tidal mud of the Avon. If it hadn't taken them, something else would: an unlit gas oven; a razor blade and a warm bath; a swan dive from the suspension bridge; an overdose.

Martin had brushed against it and lived, but he'd been changed, no doubt about it. He'd given up his second-hand record shop and his nice flat with its convenient location and its view across the communal gardens towards the green breast of Jacob's Hill, and moved into a squat with the rest of his new band. He was happy there and gave himself one hundred per cent to his music, even though he was pretty sure, despite the record deal, it wouldn't last. But that didn't matter. He was only twenty-six, for God's sake. There was plenty of time to move on, to try something else.

He stood with Simon in the dark and the chill wind and watched the ghostly things in the water fade away.

"Sometimes I can almost hear them, you know?" Simon said. "I can almost understand what they're trying to tell me."

"It might be an idea to try to forget about them."

Simon sighed, shivered inside his duffel coat, tried to smile. "I never thought I'd say this, but you're probably right."

"Want to come and have a drink with me?"

"I have to get the last bus home." Simon had that uncharacteristic shy look again. "I'm getting married in a couple of months. My fiancé will be waiting up for me."

"Congratulations," Martin said, and discovered that he meant it.

"Maybe we'll have that drink some other time," Simon said, and they shook hands at the edge of the water and went their different ways into the city, into the rest of their lives.

The skin was thickly covered with coarse black fur, and from the abdomen a score of long greenish-grey tentacles with red sucking mouths protruded limply.

"The Dunwich Horror" · H.P. Lovecraft (1929)

• THE ESSAYIST IN THE WILDERNESS •
William Browning Spencer

I had won the lottery, the ultimate *deus ex machina*. My wife was stunned by our good fortune, disoriented and faintly miffed for she had always scoffed at my lottery tickets, explaining that a person was more apt to be bitten by a rattlesnake while plummeting to Earth in an airplane—"Do the math," she would say—than get that winning number.

I had won, we were rich, and I was very pleased with myself. I could see that Audrey still thought I was dead wrong, that lotteries were the opiate of the people, a game for probability-challenged chumps. However, had events demonstrated the rightness of Audrey's position, we would still be toiling in the English department at Clayton College, a dreary four-year diploma mill with a lovely campus, a mummified faculty, and a student body derived almost entirely from the Church of Christ contingent in certain small towns in Pennsylvania.

We had only settled on Clayton because it offered jobs for the both of us. Audrey had sacrificed the most for that berth. While I taught the glamor stuff, Shakespeare and Spenser and Renaissance poetry, my wife tried to introduce English grammar into the minds of adolescents raised on television and movies—minds that were very nearly immune to syntax.

It didn't take Audrey long to embrace our good fortune. Now we were free. A much smaller sum would have set us free; our desires were modest. We wanted to get away from the infernal ever-busy world, to find a quiet niche where we could read (the unalloyed pleasure of selfish reading, the decadence of perusing books and tossing them aside half read, the dirty thrill of reading novels of no critical merit whatever or old childhood treasures from which the narcotic of nostalgia could be slowly sucked) and, of course, to write.

We bought a house on twenty acres of land in a town beyond the reach of city commuters. We were far from the madding crowd's ignoble strife and spared the reinvented Main Street, the historical markers on every house, the hideous quaintness of the polished past. Our town was a little run-down; the unimaginative might even have found it ugly. We loved it.

We lined our rambling, three-story farmhouse with bookshelves throughout and furnished it with stuff foraged from neighborhood yard sales and junk shops (dressers, mirrors, end tables, a writing desk, a vast old sofa that was as good a representation of Queen Victoria in decline as any sofa I have ever seen).

Once settled, neither of us rushed into writing projects, although Audrey was by far the more industrious. One evening she read me a passage in which her nine-year-old self had accidentally been locked out of the summer house in Sag Harbor during a thunderstorm while her parents partied within. She had only been outside a short time, a minute perhaps before her absence was discovered, but it was time enough to get thoroughly wet and abandon a belief system that included loving parents. I thought it was a powerful piece, and I was impressed with the book's tentative title, *Spite*, which struck me as everything a memoir's title should be, forthright, unsparing, monosyllabic.

While I hadn't gotten so far as to conjure a working title or turn any of my thoughts into something as substantial as a paragraph of prose or some lines of poetry, I had spent considerable time deciding just what I intended to write, what genre I would inhabit. As a youth of fourteen, I had wanted to be a lyric poet, but I had failed at that early, discovering that my poetry repelled girls who had initially been drawn to me. In college I considered becoming a novelist, but I was no good at character and if by sheer perseverance I managed to create some sort of fictional personage, I didn't have a clue what to do with him, sending him lurching off down the street like Dr. Frankenstein's monster, inevitably parking him in a cafe or bar where he would talk interminably to some other sadly cobbled-together creature. Nope, not novels. I toyed with the idea of a memoir, but my past bored me. I had no wish to revisit it.

By a process of elimination, I was closing on my vocation. I was reading voraciously, ecstatically, and I had been at it for two months. I expected to find my blushing Muse in the next book that came to hand.

One night we were both reading in the study when I heard a sharp intake of breath and looked up from my book to see Audrey staring wide-eyed in my direction. Her Henry James (*Washington Square*, if memory serves) was open on her lap. It was late, about eleven I would guess, and we sat at opposite sides of the room, each of us enclosed in the light of our separate lamps while the books that surrounded us were imbued with dusky mystery and an almost erotic sense of solace.

"Jonathan?" She slapped a hand to her breast as though assaulted by a sudden pain. I assumed she had been taken with some particularly powerful passage and was so expressing herself, for we were both guilty of melodrama in our passion for literature, but then she toppled forward, the book (a Modern Library with those almost transparent pages, those tight thickets of immortal prose) fluttering as she fell.

I marked my place and rushed to her aid. She lay sprawled on the carpet, her flowing blue robe in sweet disarray, her red hair gloriously unbound, as though she were a Victorian heroine felled by the news of her lover's death in a foreign land, the child within her still unknown to the inflexible society of her peers.

I bent down and taking her shoulders lifted her gently, turning her toward me. Did I say that Audrey is beautiful? When I read Jane Austen, I think of my wife, the logic of her cheekbones, the wit of her mouth, her unequivocal eyebrows.

Her eyelids fluttered. "Jonathan?" She seemed incapable of anything else, her mouth open in amazement. Her chest heaved; she gasped. "I can't—I can't breathe."

A series of desperate phone calls revealed that the closest hospital was forty-five miles to the west but that a Dr. Bath would be willing to rouse himself from sleep and meet us at his office at the corner of Maple and Main, a mere five minutes from our home.

A roundish woman swathed in black fabric and wearing a nurse's white cap opened the door before I knocked. She bent forward and clutched Audrey's hand, drawing us both into the room and informing us that she was the doctor's wife. The room was like every doctor's waiting room I have ever seen, a coffee table strewn with old magazines, sofas pining for better days, and a harsh, sourceless light, the cruel illumination of purgatory.

Mrs. Bath left us on the sofa and went to fetch her husband. By now Audrey's face was red and her breathing was an agony of effort, shaking her small frame. A wheeze that made my ribs ache underlined her every inhalation.

Mrs. Bath returned with her husband, a stout, balding man. He shook my hand and said, "Yes, I am Dr. Bath. And this is your wife, the emergency?"

We both looked at Audrey, and I said, "Yes." The doctor wore a black suit and seemed disappointed, although whether this was because Audrey didn't look like emergency enough or looked like more emergency than he had bargained for, I couldn't tell.

Mrs. Bath helped Audrey up from the sofa where she was hunched forward in private communication with her lungs. Flanked by the doctor and his wife,

Audrey was led past the reception desk toward the hall. Something in their progress, their tentative exit, put me in mind of two skaters guiding a novice across the ice.

I waited on the sofa while the doctor and Mrs. Bath attended my wife. I shuffled through the magazines on the coffee table, seeking something to occupy my mind, but I was certain I didn't want to read anything about infants or celebrities or health or crafts, and I was growing irritated with this foraging when—I found my Muse!

My Muse resided within the unlikely confines of a thin, battered paperback entitled *Pilgrim at Tinker Creek* by someone named Annie Dillard. I noted a number of laudatory blurbs on the back and began reading. I had no premonition, no shiver of recognition on opening the book, that my inspiration would lie within.

I was instantly intrigued. So engrossed was I that I did not notice Audrey standing over me, flanked again by the doctor and his wife. All three were smiling. Audrey's smile was weak, relieved more than celebratory, but it lifted my heart.

I wrote a check for $85 while the doctor talked. He was more animated now, hearty and pleased with himself. "Your wife, she has the spider bite!" he said. "Right there on the ankles. Hah! Or maybe the bee sting or a, what you call, centepeeder? Not everyone are allergic. Most, they just say, 'Ow!' and forget about it." Here the doctor shrugged to indicate a cavalier attitude toward such attacks. "But your wife, she has the reactions, so I give her the shot and these pills, samples while the drugstore does not open. Problems? You must call."

I asked Mrs. Bath if I might have the paperback I was holding in my hand, and she sold it to me for five dollars, which seemed a little steep. I didn't haggle.

Driving back to our home, slowly, keeping an eye out for nocturnal creatures that might race from the surrounding woods and hurl themselves beneath our wheels, I could not contain my enthusiasm.

"I know what I'm going to write," I told Audrey. She turned her head, her cheek flat against the backrest, her red hair matted in thick ribbons. She was clearly exhausted, and she regarded me with blue eyes that were uncharacteristically blank. Ordinarily, Audrey would have expressed delight, urged me to elaborate, but she wasn't up to it that night. I understood, and I should have left it till morning, but I couldn't contain the good news.

"I am going to write essays! Nature essays. You know, thoughtful pieces in which nature serves as a sort of jumping off place for larger topics. Caterpillarto-butterfly stuff about transformation, a little something from Ovid or Hazlitt or Burton thrown in. 'The world is but a school for inquiry,' after all. So. We've got a classroom in our own backyard! Our property has woods, a pond, a small creek. I haven't seen the creek yet, but the real estate agent said it was there, no reason to doubt her. And here we are in April, everything coming alive. 'When that Aprile with his shoures soote the droghte of March hath perced to the roote,' that sort of thing."

Audrey rolled her eyes, snorted derisively.

"What?" I asked.

My wife exhaled (the tiniest trace of a wheeze still there) and looked at me as though I'd just announced that I intended to run for President.

"What? I think the essay is the perfect vehicle for my temperament and—"

"Nature, Jonathan. What do you know about nature?"

"Well." I was caught off balance by this attack, so unlike my wife. I realized later that Audrey was speaking in the immediate aftermath of a life-threatening encounter with a tiny piece of nature. No wonder she was unenthusiastic regarding my new allegiance. At the time, however, I was hurt.

"I believe I have a layman's knowledge of the natural world," I said, hating the prissy tightness in my throat.

"No one would ever describe you as an outdoors person," Audrey said.

"I don't believe I need to be climbing mountains or rafting down the Amazon to write about nature."

"No," Audrey said. "I don't suppose so. But you need. . . . " She paused. She stretched the tip of her tongue to touch her upper lip, a habit she had when looking within, and one I generally found endearing. She smiled. "Name three trees."

"What?"

"Come on, name three trees. That's an easy one."

Yes, an easy one, insultingly so, beneath reply. Mistaking my silence for ignorance, her smile enlarged, so I snapped back, "Juniper, Christmas, Mimosa!" and she continued to grin, as though she had won somehow, and I found myself fretting that juniper might be, technically, more of a shrub than a tree. But I wasn't going to have my Muse belittled by continuing the conversation. I changed the subject.

"I'm glad you are all right," I said.

"Not as glad as I am," she said, which probably meant nothing, but it felt like a rebuke. I drove the rest of the way in silence, and when we pulled into our yard, Audrey said, "All out for Walden."

In spite of my wife's sarcasm, I was convinced that the essay was the form for me. For one thing, I was wealthy. With wealth came leisure, and leisure encouraged reflection. It occurred to me that one of the great charms of the essay was this conveyed sense that its author had all the time in the world. The authors of essays drifted in a fog of indolence, contemplating objects and events, pursuing literary allusions with scholarly languor. The average reader, hustling to get his car to the Jiffy Lube on his lunch hour, could only dream of some faraway retirement when time would cease to flog him with errands and obligations. To read an essay was to enter a world of literary and philosophical loafing, to wade in that slow river of time. Readers of essays could, for the span of the piece, escape their deadline days.

I had every confidence that I could give the reader his money's worth in reflection, but I thought I might have trouble with the nature part. While I didn't feel I was as ill-equipped for the job as Audrey believed, it is true I never had warmed to nature as a child. I never had an urge to climb a tree, own a turtle, look under a log, or catch a fish. I wasn't immune to the beauty of autumn, with hills transformed by garish yellows and reds, and spring, with its thousand shades of green, was a wonder of renewal, no doubt about it, but I didn't wish for any deeper connection. In fact, I had always kept a cool distance from the natural world, which I perceived as deadly and erratic, the rotting rabbit by the side of the road, festering with maggots, the yellow jackets that buzzed around the picnic table, climbing down the throat of the open Coke bottle.

Nature could be hostile, as Bob, of Bob's Bug and Vermin Blasters, reminded me. Audrey and I had decided to purge the house of bugs to prevent a second occurrence of that harrowing night, and Bob's Bug and Vermin Blasters was the only local establishment for such services.

Bob was a large man outfitted in olive drab camouflage, his pants stuffed into gray rubber boots. He had laughed, an incredulous, seal-like sound muffled by his mustache, when Audrey expressed her reservations regarding the contents of the canister that he intended to spray inside and outside the house.

"Yes, ma'am," he said. "This here is deadly poison. That's a fact. Might be you want something organic." His eyes, bright blue and winking out from under bushy eyebrows, showed deep amusement. "Just sprinkle some garlic on the bastards. Or say a prayer. You know what the word *organic* means to a bug? It means *dinner*."

Bob made more seal sounds. Audrey turned and left the room without saying anything, and I accompanied Bob on his rounds, watched him go through the house, crawling under the kitchen sink, squirting death behind the refrigerator, in the cupboards, along the baseboards. When he headed off to the basement, I left him to his work and went outside. I sat on the porch reading some more of the Dillard book until Bob came outside and I tagged along again, watching him as he drilled deep holes into the cinder block and squirted poison into the holes. All the while, he supplied me with a wealth of anecdotal material about his trade. "Ants are mad about electricity," he said. "I've known them to eat the insulation off wires. I've found dead clumps of them in air-conditioning units and around electrical terminals. All the lights go off in your house, it could be ants feeding their addiction. And the thing about ants, the thing about a lot of bugs, is they don't give a goddam whether they live or die. That's an edge they got in the war. And you might think war's an exaggeration for it, but I've been in the business a long time, and war's the word. And there ain't a clear winner yet."

When Bob had finished with the house, he said, "I'll just mosey around the property, see if there's any problems brewing, maybe a big hive. There's a hell of a lot to be said for a preemptive strike." I watched him set out toward the woods, the canister balanced on his shoulder, an American warrior, and I went back in for dinner.

Audrey was sitting in the kitchen, her elbows planted on the table, a book open before her. I looked over her shoulder and experienced a shock. She was reading *For Whom the Bell Tolls*. I just stood and stared until she sensed my presence, turned around and looked up.

"What?"

"I thought you hated Hemingway?"

Audrey looked a little sheepish, then defiant. "He has hardly any commas."

I raised my eyebrows in query.

"I can't handle commas right now," she said. "I can't breathe on a comma. And Henry James . . . all those commas. I nearly fainted trying to catch my breath."

I didn't know what to say, so I just nodded my head and moved on to the refrigerator. In retrospect, I guess it was a warning I should have heeded. But retrospect and two dollars and fifty cents will get you a latte at Starbucks.

That night I was reading in bed when I heard an engine cough into life. I knew it wasn't someone making off with our Camry; that would have been a different sound entirely. This was the distinctive rattle of a diesel engine in need of a tune-up. I slipped out of bed, taking care not to wake Audrey, and went to the window in time to see red taillights curve down the driveway and disappear past the trees. I realized that I had just seen Bob leaving in his truck. I had forgotten entirely about Bob. I looked at my watch. It was ten minutes past midnight. I marveled at such dedication. Say what you will about country folk, their work ethic is admirable, an example for the rest of us.

I returned to the bed and decided that I'd better get some sleep myself. Tomorrow I planned to confront nature, armed with a notepad, a pencil, and a will to revel in her wonders, no matter how stony the soil, how overgrown the path.

As I moved toward the bed, Audrey stirred in her sleep, stretched and turned on her side, rolling the bedsheet with her and pulling it up past her feet. I bent to pull it back down and noticed something on her ankle, a pale green patch of light. I leaned closer. Between her ankle and her heel, an area of skin the size of a quarter glowed with the yellow-green luminosity of a night clock's hands. As I studied this glowing spot, it dimmed and disappeared. *Odd*, I thought. I pulled the covers over her feet, resolving to mention it in the morning. I remembered that the spider or mite or whatever had launched its assault on her ankle. No doubt this was a related effect, nothing to worry about. Still, it might signify the onslaught of infection. Audrey might not be aware of the phenomenon if it only manifested itself while she slept. Another consultation with Dr. Bath might be in order.

I slept poorly and dreamed that I was back at Clayton teaching a class on biology, and Francis Bacon had come to demonstrate to my students just how to stuff a chicken with snow, this being the famous experiment that had led to his death by pneumonia. I found myself disliking Bacon, who was pompous and rude and wearing an ugly blue dress, and I asked him to leave and he took a swing at me with the chicken, but then the dream's logic broke down, and the chicken, while still looking like a chicken, was much larger, was, in fact, my old high school drama teacher, Mrs. Unger, and I woke up. It took me half an hour to get back to sleep, and the sleep I gleaned was shallow, the dregs of rest.

I wasn't feeling entirely fit in the morning, but I probably would have remembered to mention the ankle business after my first cup of coffee. Audrey, no more of a morning person than I, lumbered down from the bathroom where her morning ablutions had taken an inordinately long time. I looked at her and was . . . well, puzzled.

We men know that sometimes the women in our lives will look different. I can't speak for all men, but I know that I have an uncanny sensitivity to this new-look thing. I become instantly alert, like a deer in the forest on hearing the snap of a twig. New hair style? New lipstick, new eye shadow? Is this alteration for my benefit? Is a compliment in order? It can be a panicky moment. Not all new looks are planned or, if planned, executed with success. If some new hair style is, in Audrey's opinion, a great disaster, or if—an early learning experience—she has simply slept funny on her hair, producing a fuzzy, disheveled effect, a compliment can precipitate tears.

I was more baffled than usual. Audrey looked like Audrey and then again, quite different. She seemed to have a higher forehead, a just-scrubbed look, a nakedness of feature and a new bluntness to her gaze.

Audrey is very intuitive, and we have been married for ten years—we were married just after we got our undergraduate degrees—so she sensed my confusion.

"Eyebrows," she said.

"Excuse me?"

"I shaved off my eyebrows. I was looking at myself in the mirror, and, I don't know, they looked superfluous."

I had one of those revelations which, despite several bad experiences, I always share. "Like commas!" I said.

"What?"

"Well, eyebrows are sort of like commas, and you've been having this thing about commas, not liking them."

"That's the craziest thing I've ever heard," Audrey said.

"Is it?" I jumped up, ran into the living room, and returned with *For Whom the Bell Tolls*. I plopped the book down in front of her and flipped the pages.

"Okay, I'm crazy. What's this?" Every comma had been sliced with a short red line, that little mincing flourish that is the copy editor's delete symbol. There were a lot of red deletes, more than I would have expected in Hemingway.

Audrey stood up suddenly and snatched the book from the table, clutching it to her chest. "A marriage is not an invitation to abuse another person's privacy."

"It's just a book; it's not your diary."

Audrey sniffed. "And I suppose that *The Great Gatsby* is just a book?"

She had me there. My copy of *The Great Gatsby* is a very personal, passionately annotated book, and I had thrown—I winced to remember—a fit when I found Audrey reading it.

"You're right," I said. "I'm sorry. I'm a lout. I don't know how you put up with me."

Audrey is not one to hold a grudge, and we hugged each other and kissed.

I drank the rest of my coffee standing up. I set the mug down, grabbed my backpack, and moved to the door. "Today's the big day, off into the wilderness to bag some inspiration."

"Yes, I can see. Good luck." Audrey wiggled her fingers at me.

Then I was out the door and walking across the tall grass toward a pale meadow and the vibrant green of the trees beyond. I was a little nervous, so much seemed to ride on this venture. Did I really have the stuff it took to be an essayist?

I had made preparations for the journey (journey may be too extravagant a word for an outing that doesn't leave home). I wore heavy khaki pants, hiking boots, a long-sleeved flannel shirt, a backpack containing a first-aid kit, a packed lunch (baloney sandwich, apple, cheese), a flashlight, a spade, two jars for specimens, several balls of twine, my notepad and pencils, a pocket knife, a compass, and a bottle of spring water.

I entered the meadow. The straw-colored grass reached to my waist. I ignored the disquiet that came with a sudden sense of vulnerability. The pale blue sky loomed over me, tattered scraps of cloud moving slowly, animated by the same wind that stirred the grass. *Waves of amber*, I thought, pleased with the metaphor, then chagrined, realizing that the image wasn't original.

But I was getting the hang of this, marching along, my initial trepidation eased by the comforting weight of the sun on my neck and shoulders.

The gods lie in wait for the overly confident, and just as I was loosening up, living in the moment, something exploded in front of me with a great whirring and fury, a brown blur aimed at my head, and I stumbled backward and fell, my heart banging around in my chest.

I scrambled back up and saw a bird flapping its way to the clouds. I remembered a movie I had seen in which hunters with shotguns and dogs had hunted birds—were they called wrens? That doesn't seem quite it—in a meadow like this, the birds blasting out of the ground with the same *whup-whup-whup* sound that I had just experienced.

I was briskly heading back to the house as I thought this, my rational mind trying to retake the higher ground. I scolded my inner coward. *Are you going to let a blasted bird send you running?*

I continued on course to the house, but I managed, by an act of will, to veer right and down a hill toward the small pond and the clump of sentinel willows—there's another tree, Audrey—and by the time I reached the muddy, weed-strewn bank, I was breathing heavily but relatively calm again. Thoreau got a lot of mileage out of a pond, and I saw no reason why I couldn't squeeze some fine writing out of my own pond. Unfortunately, up close, its charms diminished. The pond had no precise boundary, at least not where I came upon it. Green weeds marched into the water which was filmed with a yellow-green scum. When I stirred this with a stick, the end of the stick came away with fleshy, dripping blobs of goo. My research brought me too close to the edge, and I was suddenly ankle deep in black, stinking mud, flailing my arms to keep from falling forward, yanking my hiking boots free with rude popping noises while a primal sound of disgust came unbidden from my throat. Small gnats buzzed up in a peppery cloud and rushed at my mouth, nose, and eyes with suicidal abandon (*they don't give a goddam whether they live or die*, I heard Bob saying).

That did it for the day, and I headed back to the house, depressed and angry with myself. I found Audrey on the porch in the rattan chair. Her head was down as she wrote furiously on a legal pad, and when I hailed her, she looked up, smiled abstractedly, and returned to her writing. Her industry seemed a reprimand.

I didn't give up, didn't let nature win the game in the first encounter. Every day I would arise, drink my coffee in the kitchen, kiss Audrey on her forehead—there was something endearing in her eyebrowless state, a subtext speaking volumes on humanity's restless experimental spirit—and I would set off into the wilderness.

I grew comfortable with the pond and the meadow. I was no longer spooked by birds or apt to let mud demoralize and defeat me. I sprayed myself with liberal amounts of insect repellant—Audrey said I smelled like poisonous oranges, even after a shower—and the hordes of hovering midges, mosquitoes, and gnats kept their distance. I grew less fastidious. My gag reflex relented. I could pick a tick off my sleeve with nonchalance and expertly crush it between my fingernails, flicking it away. If I thought that the blood on my fingers might be my own, siphoned from me by the creature, I felt only a satisfied sense of revenge, no horror-induced queasiness.

But I was troubled. Despite this new ease, I found no subject for my essay, nothing that spoke my name. I began to have doubts that I ever would, and I was trying to escape an unsettling conclusion: Nature was boring. Turtles sat on logs soaking up the rays of the sun, as listless and devoid of interest as a pile of dirty socks. They'd sit so maddeningly still that I'd be compelled to hurl rocks at them until they showed some life by flopping into the pond and disappearing. And that, in itself, wasn't wildly entertaining. Nature's infinite variety was beginning to look like a rut. If you thought about it, even the seasons, rolling around every year in the same damned order (spring, summer, fall, winter, spring, summer, fall, winter), suggested a dearth of imagination. The pond was stupefied with routine. Fish endlessly rose to dimple the pond's demeanor while small, sunflower-seed creatures with wire-thin legs skipped pointlessly across the water's surface. Bugs whirred over the weeds; small round birds darted down from the willow trees to eat them again and again and again.

I wasn't ready to give up, but I was having my doubts, my crisis of faith. I decided that the woods, still unexplored, might be my salvation.

I had been reluctant to enter the woods. There is a primal fear of nature when it closes ranks. Dante's dark wood is a place where only the lost find themselves. Who would seek it out?

The night I resolved to enter the woods the next morning was the same night that Audrey shared several pages of her manuscript with me. She was burning with the fever of creation, moving around the living room as she read, gesturing dramatically with her free hand. Her hair, cropped short with a scissors and wild abandon, was a red, spiky flag of rebellion that would have won my heart had she not already owned it.

It became apparent, as Audrey read these fresh pages, that her physical appearance didn't mark the full extent of her experimentation. She had discovered a new approach to the memoir, a surreal language that captured the dissociative state produced by abuse.

I confess I couldn't follow it all. I did not recognize all of the words (Latin? Joycean synthesis?) and the narrative was disjointed. As soon as Audrey finished reading, she flopped down on the sofa and began writing furiously on her legal pad, not waiting for my response. I didn't disturb her or try to take the loose pages from her so that I could conduct a more careful reading. I doubt she would have let me. She almost never relinquished a work-in-progress for my scrutiny. I got up and went into the study where I wrote down the sentence that I had committed to memory, but even as I wrote the words, I distrusted their accuracy. This is what I wrote: "My brood brother committed the sin of threes and had no smoothness so that I wished he had splintered into *hoosith hostoth* [?] and I was shamed by my parent wheel and uttered an asymmetrical harmony that generated sadness back to the last *falofath* [?] where the latent ones hooted and sent their sound-scents throughout the burrow."

You can understand why I can't vouch for the accuracy of my transcription. But I think that does capture the tone.

I set out with a will the next morning, spurred on by a new competitive spirit. I didn't want Audrey to leave me in her literary dust.

I tied the free end of the string around the trunk of a tree and let the ball unravel as I entered the woods, stepping gingerly over logs and avoiding the larger, more formidable clumps of vegetation. Far from the menace I had imagined, I felt an immediate sense of serenity. Light fell through the overhead canopy of leaves, dappling the mossy ground with green, shifting shapes. Aside from a few birds scraping around in the bushes and the faraway chittering of an insect or bird or frog, there was a sweet, almost reverent hush. I inhaled the rich scent of earthy decay and the green life that fed on it.

I was pleased with myself for thinking up the ball-of-twine trick. I could simply follow the string back, winding it around the cardboard core as it returned me to the meadow. I had several balls of string, so I could easily extend my range by tying the end of one to the beginning of the next. And, as a failsafe measure, I had a compass and had ascertained on the map that I could march east for less than a mile and discover the dirt road that ran parallel to my property and that would lead me back to my house.

I expected that days, perhaps weeks, would be needed to scout these woods as methodically as I had explored the pond and meadow, but on my first day I found the creek and, following it northward, encountered a clearing and the creatures that were to be my subject, creatures so fascinating, so complex in their behavior, that they promised a whole book of essays.

I had come upon the clearing at midday, stepping into full sunlight from under the arch of a fallen tree, dazed, delighted, charmed. My creek, which had seemed, in the shadow of the forest, rather too dark and slippery for close inspection, was transformed. Now as lively and lovely as something from a fairy tale, it ran glittering through the middle of this verdant swale.

I proceeded to unpack my lunch and eat it, sitting on the green grass and smiling at my surroundings. Having been disappointed by my meadow and its forlorn pond, I had lowered my expectations, and this clearing, with its picture-book beauty, was a fine surprise, a reward, perhaps, for pushing on. I quoted Rilke to the air: "The earth is like a child that knows poems."

While eating my lunch, I became aware of a steady low drone that filled the air. The sound was like nothing I had heard before. Most of nature's noises confirmed my belief that nature was just going through the motions: the repetitive *Whatever, Whatever, Whatever* of a bird that had lost its mind or the mechanical buzz of thousands of insects in thrall to a numbing need to procreate. But the sound that filled my ears in that clearing carried a profound emotional content, as though all the inhabitants of a great monastery were mourning the loss of paradise.

On finishing my lunch, I wadded up the paper bag and thrust it into my backpack. In my forays into the wilds, I had been delighted to find that this action was reflexive. I am sure no author of nature essays litters.

I had the instincts for my calling. I now employed those instincts to locate this poignant chant that so intrigued me. At first the sound seemed generalized, permeating the air, but I determined that it came from the creek, more specifically from that portion of the creek that disappeared into a thicket of squat shrubs and crooked trees brandishing new, pale-green leaves.

Carefully, not wishing to make any disturbance that would alert the maker of the sound, I pushed through thorny underbrush, crawling on my hands and knees like a soldier behind enemy lines.

I could not have come upon them from a better angle had I planned it knowing their location. I peered from behind a screen of leafy vines and was rewarded with my first view of the crayfish, perhaps fifteen of them scurrying in and out of their burrows on the opposite bank.

I did not know, then, that they were crayfish. Later that evening I called Harry Ackermann, and he supplied me with the name. Harry taught biology at Clayton and had been doing so for many decades. I caught him at home, and he was in a hurry to get back to his bridge game where the possibilities for a grand slam invested his voice with an excitement I had never heard before (dear God, how our lives narrow in the home stretch).

I described the creatures and would have supplied what I knew of their habits from this first encounter, but Harry cut me off. "They're not insects," he said. "They are crustaceans, crayfish. That's the only freshwater animal that fits your description. That armor you are describing is an exoskeleton. The—" I could hear someone hollering in the background, a shrill female voice that I recognized as belonging to old Dean Winfrey Podner, a lesbian according to student legend, which I found fanciful, for it required thinking of the dean in sexual terms. "Look, I've got to go," he said and hung up.

I watched my crayfish all that afternoon, retreating only when I became aware of the sinking sun and realized I'd be making my way through the woods in the dark if I didn't call it a day.

Those hours of observation on that first day were strewn with epiphanies. My Muse hugged herself for joy and sang within my head.

The sad hum that filled the air was clearly generated by the crayfish who vibrated in a minor key as they scuttled over the bare clay soil, diving into holes in the bank, leaping in and out of the bright water of the stream.

Sometimes two crayfish would encounter each other, hug, their bodies shivering more rapidly while their antennae waved wildly. Whether this entwining was sexual or served some other function, I couldn't determine. Later I learned that this activity had to do with enlisting other members in what I came to call a *meld*, intending to seek out the proper term at a later date.

Before leaping into the water, the crayfish would remove parts of their armor—what Harry called their exoskeletons—revealing smooth flesh, white as toothpaste, that boiled with tiny tentacles. I would have liked to discuss this removable exoskeleton with Harry and would have broached the subject on the phone had his manner been less abrupt. Was this common to crustaceans, this ability to doff their exoskeletons? I was almost certain that other creatures couldn't do this. Turtles couldn't shed their shells and snails . . . well, maybe snails could. I mean, that's what slugs are, right?

That evening, when I arrived home, I found Audrey working zealously in the neglected vegetable garden by the side of the house. Neither of us had ever thought to resuscitate this garden, hadn't spoken of it. Audrey didn't like gardens of any kind and had hinted at unpleasant experiences with vegetables in her past, but that evening her face was streaked with black dirt, and her shaved head shone with honest sweat—so few women have the bone structure to carry off a shorn look; Audrey does—and she smiled at me with the pride of a hard day's labor done and, turning away, hefted her hoe again and had at the weeds. I didn't tell her about my crayfish. I wanted to surprise her with the essay.

I entered the house and went straight for the kitchen where I grabbed an apple and a box of crackers. Then it was off to the study and to work. I began my essay:

> We are human and we think in human terms. Draw a line from a stone to a star, from a dinosaur bone to a dead ant, and wherever the lines intersect, there lies the human heart. Are we hopelessly self-referential or does the world truly speak to us?
>
> It is easy to relate to those clear similarities, those echoes of our own mortal condition. The gorilla in his cage induces guilt when we look into his eyes. We see ourselves. The dead raccoon induces the same guilt when, at the wheels of our automobiles, we speed past its carcass, tossed negligently to the side of the road. We see our own unhappy ends. But what of smaller, more elusive creatures whose suffering is largely hidden from us? What of the low moan of little things? Can that really be grief we hear or is it an accident, harmonies with another purpose that fall upon our human ears and take the shape of sadness? I speak of the lonesome song of the crayfish, that song that the wind carries to us, that sound that seems encoded with loss and despair.

I was very pleased with that beginning, so pleased that I couldn't continue. Art should never be hurried, particularly the essay with its obligatory andante. Besides, I needed more familiarity with my subject, more detail to support my reflective voice.

As the weeks went by I was reminded of the danger of confusing the metaphor with what it illustrates. I was so fascinated by these crayfish that I often lost the essayist in the amateur naturalist.

But I think I always regained the higher ground, and, in all humility, I think these passages demonstrate that:

> When I witness crayfish melding, generally in twelves or nines, more rarely in sixes, I am always amazed at how they fold into a completely new organism. The mega-crayfish seems to defy its origins, to heroically turn its back on the past. Single crayfish eat their exoskeletons before the meld, knowing there is no going back, demonstrating a selflessness that human societies might find admirable.
>
> The first time I observed a mega-crayfish I had come upon it after the meld. I thought I was seeing a different animal entirely, although not one I was familiar with. The mega-crayfish comes in a variety of shapes, and this one looked something like a cat-sized spider except that it had a great many more legs than a spider and moved by collapsing a number of legs and falling in that direction, creating an odd, rollicking form of locomotion. This one dove into the water and returned with a frog which, I assumed, it was going to eat. Instead, it took the frog apart, peeling the skin back and plucking out various organs which it handed to the mendicant crayfish surrounding it. This was unpleasant to watch, since the frog continued to struggle throughout the operation, and the mega-crayfish performed the dissection with slow, finicky care. I expected the waiting crayfish to devour the morsels they had received from the mega-crayfish, and perhaps they did, but they did this out of my sight, disappearing into their holes with their treasures.
>
> After the skeleton had been dismantled and carried away, when the frog was nothing more than a sheath of mottled skin, the mega-crayfish offered this last remnant to the last waiting crayfish, who took the skin, donned it like a Halloween cape, and dashed toward his hole with a fleetness that seemed powered by joy.
>
> And then, of course, the mega-crayfish dismantled itself, pinching off its legs, unraveling its innards, and collapsing, finally, in a rubble of black exoskeleton, yellow blood and emerald guts. I expect this ritual has been observed by countless generations of country boys who give it no more thought

than they might give to the birth of a calf or a bat caught in a sister's hair,
but I must say, coming upon this gruesome spectacle with no warning of what
was about to occur . . . it was unsettling, to say the least.

Perhaps it was the mega-crayfish's nature to tear itself apart; perhaps it
was born to dissect and, lacking a subject, dissected itself. The analogy is easy,
almost too easy: We human creatures deconstruct the universe and are left in
the rubble of our fears, our mortality, our rags of faith.

I was pleased with that passage, and if Audrey had seen me at that moment, she might have said, as was her wont, "You look like you've just won the lottery."

But Audrey was nowhere around. She was probably upstairs reading in bed. I went outside and sat in the rocking chair and looked at the stars (Hopkins's "fire-folk sitting in the air") and thought that there were a lot of them in Pennsylvania, and I thought about how I might become very famous and hounded by fans. I might have to hire security guards or at least get a dog although I wasn't sure about getting a fierce dog because what if it began looking at me funny, started growling deep in its throat?

I sent the future marching, took a deep breath and rocked in the moment. I noticed that the night was very still. All the world's raucous frogs were silent, not a peep.

As the days continued to pass, the exploits of my crayfish kept feeding my essay, and it grew to an unwieldy size. It was beginning to show its ignorance, by which I mean that my lack of scientific knowledge regarding these crustaceans was becoming a problem. No doubt there was a scientific term for what I called a meld. And what was occurring when two crayfish fought and the loser erupted in flames? The power of the image suggested a host of wonderful references throughout history and literature, but if I knew the mechanism—some volatile chemical released in defeat?—I could speak with more authority, send a telling anecdote or literary reference straight to the heart of the matter.

I needed to read up on crayfish. My decision was made on a Thursday evening after dinner. Scanning the phone book, which contained four counties and was still thinner than a copy of *The New Yorker*, I discovered—I confess I was surprised—a library in our very town. I thought it might still be open.

The parking lot was empty and dark, and the library, a small, shed-like building, appeared abandoned, although a closer inspection revealed a pale gleam of yellow light edging from beneath the window's drawn shade. I went to the door, turned the knob, and entered. An elderly woman sitting behind her desk jerked her head up as though she had been caught dozing.

"I can summon the police with a touch of a button, young man. There's nothing here but library fines, less than five dollars, not worth the loss of your freedom and good name."

I told her that I was seeking a book about crayfish.

"There are people who eat them," she said. Being a librarian, I suppose she felt obligated to contribute her knowledge on the subject.

"Not me," I said and waited for her to help with the search. She returned with two books, one entitled, *The Flora and Fauna of Western Pennsylvania* and the other a children's book entitled *What's Under That Rock?*

I checked out both books after filling out a library card application that was three pages long and expected me to know things like my mother's maiden name. I lied and got through it and made off with the books.

I intended to retire to the study and read these books immediately, but I saw the message light on the answering machine blinking, and so I pushed the play button and Audrey's voice jumped out. "Jonathan! When you get this, I'll be on my way to the coast with Dr. Bath and his wife. The quantum actualization of the brood wheel has come to us in a vision. It will bloom near San Clemente, and so we are on our way. These other manifestations are important, but they are not the blooming. You can be of use where you are. Please tend to my garden. We will meet again in celebration and the making of fine multiples."

I went into the kitchen, fumbled in the cupboards, and found the bottle of Gilbey's gin. It was my fault she'd left. I'd been neglecting her, lost in my damned essay about those damned crayfish. Neglected, she had fled into a crackpot religion. I should have seen it coming; the signs were there. I mixed the gin with a lemony diet drink that tasted awful. That was fine; I deserved it. Later I walked out into the yard and through the meadow and into the woods. I carried a flashlight and my backpack and trusted the familiarity of the route. There was a full moon, and I was drunk enough to fear no night thing.

I entered the clearing without incident, but I must have drifted from my habitual path, for a resilient sapling caught my leg and threw me to the ground. I turned my flashlight, and the beam revealed a silver rod growing out of the grass. I reached forward and touched the rod and as I gripped it, it began to slide down into itself. This wasn't at all like a sapling, and I studied the rod, pulling it up and then forcing it down again. It was a telescoping antenna. I retrieved my spade from the backpack and dug around the antenna, striking something hard. I brushed away the dirt to reveal a flat metal surface just under the ground. It took me well over two hours to unearth most of the truck's cab. The cab was full of dirt—and Bob. There was black dirt in Bob's mouth, black dirt in his eye sockets. His hands still clutched the wheel, ready to go but . . . *You lost the war*, I thought, a stupid thought. I was feeling a little ill, and it didn't help, my staring at the grass which grew undisturbed over what had to be the larger bulk of the truck. *How did you get there, Bob?*

I heard the new sound, a sound that did not resonate with loss but seemed joyous, playful, exuberant. I crawled into the thicket and took my station. The full moon provided more than enough illumination, but I could have seen them without it, for each crayfish was enveloped in a pale green glow. They were running in and out of a fine spray of mist, for all the world like children squealing and frolicking in the spray of a hose or water sprinkler. I recognized the source of the spray, Bob's deadly canister of poison. Three of the crayfish operated it from its dug-in position high in the bank, while a dozen or more raced in and out of the toxic mist.

As always, I was entranced, and I might have crouched there watching them for hours, but something moved behind them, a shadow that shifted and, for a moment, eclipsed the moon and flooded my heart with terror. I scrambled out of the thicket, stood upright, and ran.

I stumbled through the woods, crashing into trees, toppling over logs, but always up again and moving. The meadow left me unprotected; I imagined malevolent eyes watching me from above. I ran.

I reached the porch as my stomach cramped. I eased myself down on the first porch step and blinked at the silvered grass, the meadow and the trees beyond. The spinning world wobbled to a stop as I caught my breath. Peace reigned; the stars were noncommittal and the breeze was warm and quick with the promise of spring. I glanced down at Audrey's garden and thought of going after her, but Audrey wouldn't like that. No, time would have to bring her back to me . . . *the fullness of time* (a phrase that seemed suddenly sinister; I saw this monstrous thing, bloated with the eons it had devoured).

No going after Audrey. Hadn't she charged me with the care of her garden? She had taken pains with this project, covering the ground with plastic sheets to protect the new shoots from the vicissitudes of the season. I stood up and regarded one of the sheets. I looked over my shoulder, but nothing was coming. I knelt down and peeled back the sheet and saw rows of neatly ordered little plants, white buds with blue. . . . No. My mind was forced to swallow the image, but it had no response ready-made. Indeed, my first reaction was to laugh abruptly, which really wasn't appropriate. What I saw were rows of little blue eyeballs, naked, unblinking, incredulous. I had never seen a garden that looked so very, very surprised.

I had no time to pursue that thought, for I turned again, prompted by a trumpeting roar that rattled my heart in its cage. The thing was silhouetted against the moon, its ragged wings outstretched, strange tentacles dangling from its black bulk, tentacles long enough to trail across the meadow as though trolling the amber waves.

I am locked in my room now, devising a plan or preparing to devise a plan or, perhaps, simply eating this bag of potato chips and reading. When all is said and done, I enjoy reading far more than writing. Not that I'm very fond of *The Flora and Fauna of Western Pennsylvania*. It has no pictures and it has that shiny paper that I associate with textbooks and the prose is almost impenetrable, and you know what? I'm an adult, and I don't have to read it if I don't want to. Hah.

Well, *What's Under That Rock?* is a great improvement. For one thing, it has pictures. A picture is worth a thousand words. There's a picture of a crayfish in this book.

Something is on the roof . . . make that in the attic. The noise doesn't conjure a clear picture in my mind. Visualize a half dozen sailors, brawling while someone tortures a pig. No. I think you have to be here to fully appreciate this sound.

I keep looking at this drawing of a crayfish. *Cambarus bartoni*, that's its scientific name. It looks exactly like a tiny lobster. That's simple enough, isn't it? I mean, what kind of genius do you have to be to say, "Jonathan, those aren't crayfish. I don't know what the hell they are, but they aren't crayfish. Crayfish look exactly like small lobsters"? Is that so difficult?

Thanks a lot, Harry Ackermann. I hope your grand slam fizzled.

"When sorrows come, they come not single spies, but in battalions." You are so right, Will.

I'm just sick, really sick and disgusted. And the essay is ruined, of course.

Other objects found included the mingled fragments of many books and papers . . . All, without exception, appeared to deal with black magic in its most advanced and horrible forms . . . To some, though, the greatest mystery of all is the variety of utterly inexplicable objects—objects whose shapes, materials, types of workmanship, and purposes baffle all conjecture—found scattered amidst the wreckage in evidently diverse states of injury. One of these things—which excited several Miskatonic professors profoundly—is a badly damaged monstrosity plainly resembling the strange image which Gilman gave to the college museum . . .

"The Dreams in the Witch House" · H.P. Lovecraft (1932)

• THE DISCIPLE •
David Barr Kirtley

Professor Carlton Brose was evil, and I adored him as only a freshman can. I spent the first miserable semester at college watching him, studying the way he would flick away a cigarette butt, or how he would arch his eyebrow when he made a point. I mimicked these small things privately, compulsively. I don't know why, because it wasn't the small things that drew me to him at all. It was the big things, the stories people told as far away as dear old Carolina.

You heard the name Brose if you ran with any cults, and I ran with a few. Society rejected us, so we rejected them. The more things you give up, the less there is to bind your will. There was power there, we were sure of it, but it was damned elusive.

I used to shop at an occult bookstore in Raleigh. A friend of mine worked there, and one day as he was shelving books he told me, "These guys you hang with, them I'm not so sure about. But Brose, he's the real deal."

"You believe that?" I said.

He stopped and got a slightly crazed look in his eyes. "I've seen it, man, personally seen it. Flies buzz up out of the rot and swirl in formation around him. He can make your eyes bleed just from looking at him. The guy's tapped into something huge."

I was skeptical. "And he teaches a class?"

"Not just a class, all right? It's this special program. Only a dozen or so are admitted, and they get power. I've seen that too. Then they go away. Every spring."

"Go where?"

He shook his head. "Damned if I know. Places not of this world. That's what some people say."

"I don't buy it," I said. "If he's got so much going for him, why's he working a job at all? And what kind of school would let him teach it?"

My friend shrugged. "I don't know about that. All I know is that Brose is for real."

"Then why aren't you in his class?"

He scowled and went back to shelving. "Brose wouldn't take me. Said I had no talent, no potential. It hurt like hell, but that's another reason you know he's legit—what kind of fraud would turn people away like that?"

I had no answer, and I'd known a lot of frauds.

I traveled to Massachusetts, to the university where Brose taught. I sought out his office in a secluded corner of the Anthropology Building, then sat on a bench in the hallway and pretended to read.

Finally the office door opened and Brose emerged. I glanced up, as if accidentally, as if his movement had caught my eye.

He stared back at me with eyes the color of a tombstone, and smiled knowingly. The shadows seemed to lengthen and darken as he passed. I shuddered, because I was sure just from that look that it was all true. Brose practically radiated power. On that day my initial skepticism transformed into the most helpless adoration. I enrolled in the school.

In the winter, I met with Brose for the first time. The inside of his office was like some terrible jungle—loose papers drooped from the shelves, and a filth-choked and apparently unused fish tank cast a pallid green light. From my seat, I could look out the window and see the lonely stretch of gray-green woods that was called the Arboretum.

Brose sat behind his desk, in those shadows of his own making, and said, "So you want to join the program?"

"Yes," I whispered.

"Why should I accept you?"

"I'll do anything," I said. "No hesitation. No regret."

His lips curled into that now familiar smile. "And what will you be bringing to the program?"

I knew he meant power. "Nothing. Not yet. But you can—"

He shook his head. "If nothing's what you have, then nothing's what you get from me. Go back to literature. It's really—"

"No!" I broke in. "I don't have much, that's true. I've lost things in my life, so many things, but I've gained something too—this rotting emptiness inside me, and I can use it. I swear I can use it. All the loss, it can't have been for nothing." I added softly, "I won't let it be."

He watched me for a long time. Finally he nodded. "All right, you'll do. I'll get the form."

I leaned back in my chair and let out a long sigh of relief as he disappeared into a back room.

Something on the shelf caught my eye. A black statue. Like Brose it seemed wrapped in strange shadows. I rose from my seat.

The statue was a foot tall and depicted a creature resembling the head of a man, but with a beard of tentacles. The thing's eyes were utterly empty, and it had no body, only more tentacles.

I went to pick it up and study it closer, but when I lifted it I gasped. The thing was unearthly heavy—heavier than anything that size could possibly be, heavier than I could hold in one hand. It tore itself from my fingers and lunged for the floor, where it thudded and lay still.

From behind me came Brose's voice, "Don't touch that." I started.

He placed a shoebox on his desk, then lifted the statue with two hands and returned it to its place on the shelf.

"I'm sorry," I said. "I . . . "

My voice died in my throat as Brose reached into the shoebox and lifted out a small white mouse, which squirmed and flailed and sniffed.

"What's that?" I said.

"The form. The application form." Brose paced over to that gruesomely overgrown fish tank and removed the lid. He offered me the mouse and I took it.

He nodded at the tank. "Fill out your application."

I stepped forward, the mouse nibbling gently at my fingers as I held it over the foul water.

This was a test. Of what? My willingness? My resolve? I let go. The mouse plunged into the water, then thrashed and screamed, clawing at the sides of the tank. Water soaked its fur and garbled its cries. Then it died and floated there, spinning slowly, its four pink legs hanging down, its tail trailing after.

"Congratulations," Brose said. "Your application's been accepted."

Our first class convened in a sprawling old house on the edge of campus, down in the dim cement cellar. The room had no windows, and its walls and floor bore eerie dark stains. There were thirteen students, mostly male. All had sallow flesh and haunted eyes.

Brose crucified a cat, right on his desk in front of us. The animal howled and squirmed, but the nails driven through its limbs held it fast. Blood trickled from its paws, and Brose stanched the flow with a cloth.

He said, "The most important thing you must learn is to bind your will to that of another. Pain is conspicuous, it'll point the way, but don't depend on it. There are greater things than cats you must connect to, greater things than you, and they have never felt pain."

He turned to me. "Make it bleed again."

I was filled with an aching desire to prove myself. I wanted him to think I was his most talented, most dedicated, most favored student. I would have done anything, endured anything, to make him adore me, the way I adored him.

I whispered desperately, "I don't know how."

He turned to another student, a tall guy with dark, scornful eyes, and said, "Make it bleed."

The guy never even glanced at the cat, but instantly its paws began to bubble and ooze and spurt.

"Good." Brose nodded. "Very good."

At the end of class, he admonished us, "Tell no one what you learn here."

The next day we packed up our things and moved into the house. My room was a small square chamber with hardwood floors and peeling white paint. When my new roommate entered, I recognized him instantly. "Oh," I said. "You're—"

"Adrian," he replied.

"—the one who can make the cat bleed," I said.

"Yeah," he said, turning away, setting down his bags. "I can do a lot of things."

He began to unpack, saying nothing.

I said, "Maybe sometime you can—"

"Look," he said over his shoulder. "Let's get something straight. I'm not here to make friends. I'm here to learn. No distractions. So just stay out of my way, and we'll get along just fine."

I was silent.

"Nothing personal," he said. "But I'm here to excel. To make Brose notice me. To be the best."

I felt a stab of jealous rage. I couldn't believe it was an accident, the way his words seemed calculated to tear at my greatest longing: to be favored, to be adored.

I said, "That's why we're all here."

"Yeah," he said. "Sure."

"I mean, you did well today," I said. "But there's more to this than just cats."

He said coldly, "You think I should try something bigger?"

Then I felt a wetness on my lip. Turning to the mirror, I saw blood leaking from my nose, streaking down my chin. I grabbed a towel and pressed it to my face, leaning my head back.

"Don't lean back," Adrian said. "Keep pressure on your nose. The bleeding will stop."

I tried so hard, but it did no good. With each passing week I lagged further behind Adrian in absorbing the macabre lessons we received. Adrian was right. He was the best. Adored by the class. Brose's favorite.

If I could not be favored by Brose, I would have preferred to be disfavored, to be his enemy. In truth he was indifferent to me. I was not important enough for him even to despise.

As I walked the shaded pathways of the campus, I pondered the strange role that Brose played here. It was obvious that the other faculty suspected the dark nature of our program. They kept their distance, and shot us looks full of fear and hostility, but they made no effort to disrupt us. Were they simply afraid of Brose? I couldn't decide.

As the semester wore on Brose grew more and more agitated, his lectures increasingly frenzied and mad. He raved of nothing but the binding.

"You must learn faster!" He pounded on his desk. "The hour is near. It has all led up to this." He took a deep breath. "You must bind yourselves to the impossible mind of the Traveler on Oceans of Night, the Stepper Across the Stars. If you ingratiate yourselves, you will earn a place as His favored disciples and journey with him forever to those places only He can make by his dreaming."

I glanced at Adrian, but he kept his eyes fixed straight ahead. So now we knew our fate. We would gain the ultimate power we sought by pledging ourselves to this ultimate being.

Brose reached into his briefcase and pulled out the black statue, darker than any earthly object could ever be—the tentacled man-thing with its empty eyes. Then I saw something I'd never noticed before. Among its many limbs clung tiny human figures. That almost made me dizzy, for it meant that the creature must tower to unimaginable heights.

The Traveler on Oceans of Night. The Stepper Across the Stars.

It was Him.

That week I dreamed murky dreams of upside down cities built from granite and slime. One night I awoke to find Adrian lying on the floor and whimpering. He stared up in terror, as if something horrid hung from the ceiling.

"What?" I said. "What is it?"

"Oh God," he wailed. His usual swagger had vanished. "Can't you feel it? Are you blind and deaf and numb to everything? His boundlessness reaches across the void to poison our dreams."

Then I knew he wasn't staring at the ceiling, but at the sky and the stars and the dark emptiness beyond.

"The Traveler on Oceans of Night," Adrian whispered. "He's coming."

I had failed to win the adoration of Brose, but who was Brose, compared to all this? Compared to this great Traveler? Brose was nothing. He was a small man who lived a small life, pointing others along an exalted path that he himself dared not follow. I had found an object far more worthy of veneration. To be a disciple to such power, to be favored by the Traveler!

I would not fail this time.

The night of the binding arrived. The Traveler was near, his imminence palpable. The air crackled with magic. I looked out over the forest, and the trees themselves seemed to tremble.

My classmates and I donned black robes, and Brose led us into the Arboretum. We passed beneath withered branches and trod faint trails that wound between mossy boulders. Brose held the dark statue before him, and we didn't need light to see because the statue seemed to suck the shadows from beneath our feet and pull them into itself.

In the deepest corner of the woods, within a grotto of gray stone, sprawled an ancient shrine overgrown with rotting ferns. Brose set his statue on the ground, and we settled down to wait.

I don't know how many hours we lay there. Then a breeze came, snatching up damp leaves and flinging them about, raising them into columns in the sky. The wind blew faster and louder until it seemed to shriek in pain.

I was struck by a maddening sense of dislocation, a nightmare cacophony of unbearable sensations. Then the shadows leapt from beneath the trees to block out the starlight and wrap themselves around our throats and sink behind our eyes.

The Traveler on Oceans of Night was there, his form stretching upward to infinity. All of him was far away yet somehow pressing close all around us. He was so enormous, so horrible, and so magnificent that we collapsed and wept helplessly and without shame to behold Him.

Through the confusion came the voice of Brose screaming, "Bind yourselves! Do it now!"

Adrian was first. He rose off the ground, arms outstretched, robe whipping about him, face full of ecstasy. One by one my classmates lifted from the earth until they circled around that great being. They were like flies, I realized suddenly. Like flies rising from the rot to swirl around Professor Carlton Brose.

I looked at him, and his expression was one I had come to know too well: Indifference. Something was horribly wrong. I imagined I saw that same indifference mirrored on the incomprehensible otherworldly face of the Traveler.

I would not bind to Him. I crawled until I found a rock to hide behind, then I screamed to my whirling classmates, "We're the flies! Oh God, we're like the flies."

The Traveler made one ponderous motion with a million of His slimy tentacles, and He stepped away toward another star, another dimension, another world He had dreamed. Then the night was silent and empty.

Brose strode toward me. He said darkly, "You failed the binding."

I lunged at him, startling him. I grabbed his throat and forced him down against a stone.

"You lied," I said. "You said you'd make us His disciples."

"The Traveler on Oceans of Night is a great vessel," he whispered. "I would put you aboard."

"As what?" I said. "A rat in the hold? Or rather, a flea on a rat."

I imagined I saw the dozen bodies of my classmates, sucked away into the bitter black void between worlds, their frozen forms twirling slowly in an endless dance among the stars.

Then Brose seized my temples with his muddy fingers and made me look down into his cold, tombstone eyes. My own eyes began to bleed. I knew he meant to kill me.

As I flailed, my fingers fell upon the statue, and I lifted it with two arms and brought it down on Brose's forehead. The statue sank without resistance until it reached the ground. When I pulled it away there was nothing but a gaping hole where the face of Professor Carlton Brose had been.

The empty eyes of the Traveler could see things that humans never dreamt of, but He was blind to the pain of this sad world.

· · ·

You were the best, Adrian, better than me. Better at a lie. Are you proud?

Today a student came to beg admission to my special program. He stood at the fish tank and clenched a mouse in his fist. Then he held it underwater until it drowned.

"Congratulations," I said. "You've been accepted."

He smiled.

I do this initiation—as I'm sure Brose did—to ease my conscience, to reassure myself that my students are cruel, and deserve their fate.

The college hates the program, but they know it's necessary, and after Brose died I was the only one who could replace him. New England has some dangerous people lurking about—ones who've latched onto darkness, or might—and they need to be dealt with. The harmless ones I turn away.

I've learned the truth that Brose knew: it's best to be a big fish in a small pond. Fish can't live outside the pond, and being a fish isn't so bad. Every spring, before I send them off to die, a new class studies with me. They are enthralled by my meager powers. They long for my briefest attention.

They adore me.

Over the jagged peaks of Thok they sweep,
Heedless of all the cries I make,
And down the nether pits to that foul lake
Where the puffed shoggoths splash in doubtful sleep.

"Fungi from Yuggoth:
XX. Night Gauntm" · H.P. Lovecraft (1930)

· SHOGGOTHS IN BLOOM ·
Elizabeth Bear

"Well, now, Professor Harding," the fisherman says, as his *Bluebird* skips across Penobscot Bay, "I don't know about that. The jellies don't trouble with us, and we don't trouble with them."

He's not much older than forty, but wizened, his hands work-roughened and his face reminiscent of saddle-leather, in texture and in hue. Professor Harding's age, and Harding watches him with concealed interest as he works the *Bluebird*'s engine. He might be a veteran of the Great War, as Harding is.

He doesn't mention it. It wouldn't establish camaraderie: they wouldn't have fought in the same units or watched their buddies die in the same trenches.

That's not the way it works, not with a Maine fisherman who would shake his head and not extend his hand to shake, and say, between pensive chaws on his tobacco, "*Doctor* Harding? Well, huh. I never met a colored professor before," and then shoot down all of Harding's attempts to open conversation about the near-riots provoked by a fantastical radio drama about an alien invasion of New York City less than a fortnight before.

Harding's own hands are folded tight under his armpits so the fisherman won't see them shaking. He's lucky to be here. Lucky anyone would take him out. Lucky to have his tenure-track position at Wilberforce, which he is risking right now.

The bay is as smooth as a mirror, the *Bluebird*'s wake cutting it like a stroke of chalk across slate. In the peach-sorbet light of sunrise, a cluster of rocks glistens. The boulders themselves are black, bleak, sea-worn and ragged. But over them, the light refracts through a translucent layer of jelly, mounded six feet deep in places, glowing softly in the dawn. Rising above it, the stalks are evident as opaque silhouettes, each nodding under the weight of a fruiting body.

Harding catches his breath. It's beautiful. And deceptively still, for whatever the weather may be, beyond the calm of the bay, across the splintered gray Atlantic, farther than Harding—or anyone—can see, a storm is rising in Europe.

Harding's an educated man, well-read, and he's the grandson of Nathan Harding, the buffalo soldier. An African-born ex-slave who fought on both sides of the Civil War, when Grampa Harding was sent to serve in his master's place, he deserted, and lied, and stayed on with the Union army after.

Like his grandfather, Harding was a soldier. He's not a historian, but you don't have to be to see the signs of war.

"No contact at all?" he asks, readying his borrowed Leica camera.

"They clear out a few pots," the fisherman says, meaning lobster pots. "But they don't damage the pot. Just flow around it and digest the lobster inside. It's not convenient." He shrugs. It's not convenient, but it's not a threat either. These Yankees never say anything outright if they think you can puzzle it out from context.

"But you don't try to do something about the shoggoths?"

While adjusting the richness of the fuel mixture, the fisherman speaks without looking up. "What could we do to them? We can't hurt them. And lord knows, I wouldn't want to get one's ire up."

"Sounds like my department head," Harding says, leaning back against the gunwale, feeling like he's taking an enormous risk. But the fisherman just looks at him curiously, as if surprised the talking monkey has the ambition or the audacity to joke.

Or maybe Harding's just not funny. He sits in the bow with folded hands, and waits while the boat skips across the water.

The perfect sunrise strikes Harding as symbolic. It's taken him five years to get here—five years, or more like his entire life since the War. The sea-swept rocks of the remote Maine coast are habitat to a panoply of colorful creatures. It's an opportunity, a little-studied maritime ecosystem. This is in part due to difficulty of access and in part due to the perils inherent in close contact with its rarest and most spectacular denizen: *Oracupoda horibilis*, the common surf shoggoth.

Which, after the fashion of common names, is neither common nor prone to linger in the surf. In fact, *O. horibilis* is never seen above the water except in the late autumn. Such authors as mention them assume the shoggoths heave themselves on remote coastal rocks to bloom and breed.

Reproduction is a possibility, but Harding isn't certain it's the right answer. But whatever they are doing, in this state, they are torpid, unresponsive. As long as their integument is not ruptured, releasing the gelatinous digestive acid within, they may be approached in safety.

A mature specimen of *O. horibilis*, at some fifteen to twenty feet in diameter and an estimated weight in excess of eight tons, is the largest of modern shoggoths. However, the admittedly fragmentary fossil record suggests the prehistoric shoggoth was a much larger beast. Although only two fossilized casts of prehistoric shoggoth tracks have been recovered, the oldest exemplar dates from the Precambrian period. The size of that single prehistoric specimen, of a species provisionally named *Oracupoda antediluvius*, suggests it was made an animal more than triple the size of the modern *O. horibilis*.

And that spectacular living fossil, the jeweled or common surf shoggoth, is half again the size of the only other known species—the black Adriatic shoggoth, *O. dermadentata*, which is even rarer and more limited in its range.

"There," Harding says, pointing to an outcrop of rock. The shoggoth or shoggoths—it is impossible to tell, from this distance, if it's one large individual or several merged midsize ones—on the rocks ahead glisten like jelly confections. The fisherman hesitates, but with a long almost-silent sigh, he brings the *Bluebird* around. Harding leans forward, looking for any sign of intersection, the flat plane where two shoggoths might be pressed up against one another. It ought to look like the rainbowed border between conjoined soap bubbles.

Now that the sun is higher, and at their backs—along with the vast reach of the Atlantic—Harding can see the animal's colors. Its body is a deep sea green, reminiscent of hunks of broken glass as sold at aquarium stores. The tendrils and knobs and fruiting bodies covering its dorsal surface are indigo and violet. In the sunlight, they dazzle, but in the depths of the ocean the colors are perfect camouflage, tentacles waving like patches of algae and weed.

Unless you caught it moving, you'd never see the translucent, dappled monster before it engulfed you.

"Professor," the fisherman says. "Where do they come from?"

"I don't know," Harding answers. Salt spray itches in his close-cropped beard, but at least the beard keeps the sting of the wind off his cheeks. The leather jacket may not have been his best plan, but it too is warm. "That's what I'm here to find out."

Genus Oracupoda are unusual among animals of their size in several particulars. One is their lack of anything that could be described as a nervous system. The animal is as bereft of nerve nets, ganglia, axons, neurons, dendrites, and glial cells as an oak. This apparent contradiction—animals with even simplified nervous systems are either large and immobile or, if they are mobile, quite small, like a starfish—is not the only interesting thing about a shoggoth.

And it is that second thing that justifies Harding's visit. Because *Oracupoda's* other, lesser-known peculiarity is apparent functional immortality. Like the Maine lobster to whose fisheries they return to breed, shoggoths do not die of old age. It's unlikely that they would leave fossils, with their gelatinous bodies, but Harding does find it fascinating that to the best of his knowledge, no one had ever seen a dead shoggoth.

The fisherman brings the *Bluebird* around close to the rocks, and anchors her. There's artistry in it, even on a glass-smooth sea. Harding stands, balancing on the gunwale, and grits his teeth. He's come too far to hesitate, afraid.

Ironically, he's not afraid of the tons of venomous protoplasm he'll be standing next to. The shoggoths are quite safe in this state, dreaming their dreams—mating or otherwise.

As the image occurs to him, he berates himself for romanticism. The shoggoths are dormant. They don't have brains. It's silly to imagine them dreaming. And in any case, what he fears is the three feet of black-glass water he has to jump across, and the scramble up algae-slick rocks.

Wet rock glitters in between the strands of seaweed that coat the rocks in the Intertidal zone. It's there that Harding must jump, for the shoggoth, in bloom, withdraws above the reach of the ocean. For the only phase of its life, it keeps its feet dry. And for the only time in its life, a man out of a diving helmet can get close to it.

Harding makes sure of his sample kit, his boots, his belt-knife. He gathers himself, glances over his shoulder at the fisherman—who offers a thumbs-up— and leaps from the *Bluebird*, aiming his Wellies at the forsaken spit of land.

It seems a kind of perversity for the shoggoths to bloom in November. When all the Northern world is girding itself for deep cold, the animals heave themselves from the depths to soak in the last failing rays of the sun and send forth bright flowers more appropriate to May.

The North Atlantic is icy and treacherous at the end of the year, and any sensible man does not venture its wrath. What Harding is attempting isn't glamour work, the sort of thing that brings in grant money—not in its initial stages. But Harding suspects that the shoggoths may have pharmacological uses. There's no telling what useful compounds might be isolated from their gelatinous flesh.

And that way lies tenure, and security, and a research budget.

Just one long slippery leap away.

He lands, and catches, and though one boot skips on bladderwort he does not slide down the boulder into the sea. He clutches the rock, fingernails digging, clutching a handful of weeds. He does not fall.

He cranes his head back. It's low tide, and the shoggoth is some three feet above his head, its glistening rim reminding him of the calving edge of a glacier. It is as still as a glacier, too. If Harding didn't know better, he might think it inanimate.

Carefully, he spins in place, and gets his back to the rock. The *Bluebird* bobs softly in the cold morning. Only November 9th, and there has already been snow. It didn't stick, but it fell.

This is just an exploratory expedition, the first trip since he arrived in town. It took five days to find a fisherman who was willing to take him out; the locals are superstitious about the shoggoths. Sensible, Harding supposes, when they can envelop and digest a grown man. He wouldn't be in a hurry to dive into the middle of a Portugese man o'war, either. At least the shoggoth he's sneaking up on doesn't have stingers.

"Don't take too long, Professor," the fisherman says. "I don't like the look of that sky."

It's clear, almost entirely, only stippled with light bands of cloud to the southwest. They catch the sunlight on their undersides just now, stained gold against a sky no longer indigo but not yet cerulean. If there's a word for the color between, other than perfect, Harding does not know it.

"Please throw me the rest of my equipment," Harding says, and the fisherman silently retrieves buckets and rope. It's easy enough to swing the buckets across the gap, and as Harding catches each one, he secures it. A few moments later, and he has all three.

He unties his geologist's hammer from the first bucket, secures the ends of the ropes to his belt, and laboriously ascends.

Harding sets out his glass tubes, his glass scoops, the cradles in which he plans to wash the collection tubes in sea water to ensure any acid is safely diluted before he brings them back to the *Bluebird*.

From here, he can see at least three shoggoths. The intersections of their watered-milk bodies reflect the light in rainbow bands. The colorful fruiting stalks nod some fifteen feet in the air, swaying in a freshening breeze.

From the greatest distance possible, Harding reaches out and prods the largest shoggoth with the flat top of his hammer. It does nothing, in response. Not even a quiver.

He calls out to the fisherman. "Do they ever do anything when they're like that?"

"What kind of a fool would come poke one to find out?" the fisherman calls back, and Harding has to grant him that one. A Negro professor from a Negro college. That kind of a fool.

As he's crouched on the rocks, working fast—there's not just the fisherman's clouds to contend with, but the specter of the rising tide—he notices those glitters, again, among the seaweed.

He picks one up. A moment after touching it, he realizes that might not have been the best idea, but it doesn't burn his fingers. It's transparent, like glass, and smooth, like glass, and cool, like glass, and knobby. About the size of a hazelnut. A striking green, with opaque milk-white dabs at the tip of each bump.

He places it in a sample vial, which he seals and labels meticulously before pocketing. Using his tweezers, he repeats the process with an even dozen, trying to select a few of each size and color. They're sturdy—he can't avoid stepping on them but they don't break between the rocks and his Wellies. Nevertheless, he pads each one but the first with cotton wool. Spores? he wonders. *Egg cases? Shedding?*

Ten minutes, fifteen.

"Professor," calls the fisherman, "I think you had better hurry!"

Harding turns. That freshening breeze is a wind at a good clip now, chilling his throat above the collar of his jacket, biting into his wrists between glove and cuff. The water between the rocks and the *Bluebird* chops erratically, facets capped in white, so he can almost imagine the scrape of the palette knife that must have made them.

The southwest sky is darkened by a palm-smear of muddy brown and alizarin crimson. His fingers numb in the falling temperatures.

"Professor!"

He knows. It comes to him that he misjudged the fisherman; Harding would have thought the other man would have abandoned him at the first sign of trouble. He wishes now that he remembered his name.

He scrambles down the boulders, lowering the buckets, swinging them out until the fisherman can catch them and secure them aboard. The *Bluebird* can't come in close to the rocks in this chop. Harding is going to have to risk the cold water, and swim. He kicks off his Wellies and zips down the aviator's jacket. He throws them across, and the fisherman catches. Then Harding points his toes, bends his knees—he'll have to jump hard, to get over the rocks.

The water closes over him, cold as a line of fire. It knocks the air from his lungs on impact, though he gritted his teeth in anticipation. Harding strokes furiously for the surface, the waves more savage than he had anticipated. He needs the momentum of his dive to keep from being swept back against the rocks.

He's not going to reach the boat.

The thrown cork vest strikes him. He gets an arm through, but can't pull it over his head. Sea water, acrid and icy, salt-stings his eyes, throat, and nose. He clings, because it's all he can do, but his fingers are already growing numb. There's a tug, a hard jerk, and the life preserver almost slides from his grip.

Then he's moving through the water, being towed, banged hard against the side of the *Bluebird*. The fisherman's hands close on his wrist and he's too numb to feel the burn of chafing skin. Harding kicks, scrabbles. Hips banged, shins bruised, he hauls himself and is himself hauled over the sideboard of the boat.

He's shivering under a wool navy blanket before he realizes that the fisherman has got it over him. There's coffee in a Thermos lid between his hands. Harding wonders, with what he distractedly recognizes as classic dissociative ideation, whether anyone in America will be able to buy German products soon. Someday, this fisherman's battered coffee keeper might be a collector's item.

They don't make it in before the rain comes.

The next day is meant to break clear and cold, today's rain only a passing herald of winter. Harding regrets the days lost to weather and recalcitrant fishermen, but at least he knows he has a ride tomorrow. Which means he can spend the afternoon in research, rather than hunting the docks, looking for a willing captain.

He jams his wet feet into his Wellies and thanks the fisherman, then hikes back to his inn, the only inn in town that's open in November. Half an hour later, clean and dry and still shaken, he considers his options.

After the Great War, he lived for a while in Harlem—he remembers the riots and the music, and the sense of community. His mother is still there, growing gracious as a flower in window-box. But he left that for college in Alabama, and he has not forgotten the experience of segregated restaurants, or the excuses he made for never leaving the campus.

He couldn't get out of the south fast enough. His Ph.D. work at Yale, the first school in America to have awarded a doctorate to a Negro, taught him two things other than natural history. One was that Booker T. Washington was right, and white men were afraid of a smart colored. The other was that W.E.B. DuBois was right, and sometimes people were scared of what was needful.

Whatever resentment he experienced from faculty or fellow students, in the North, he can walk into almost any bar and order any drink he wants. And right now, he wants a drink almost as badly as he does not care to be alone. He thinks he will have something hot and go to the library.

It's still raining as he crosses the street to the tavern. Shaking water droplets off his hat, he chooses a table near the back. Next to the kitchen door, but it's the only empty place and might be warm.

He must pass through the lunchtime crowd to get there, swaybacked wooden floorboards bowing underfoot. Despite the storm, the place is full, and in full argument. No one breaks conversation as he enters.

Harding cannot help but overhear.

"Jew bastards," says one. "We should do the same."

"No one asked you," says the next man, wearing a cap pulled low. "If there's gonna be a war, I hope we stay out of it."

That piques Harding's interest. The man has his elbow on a thrice-folded *Boston Herald*, and Harding steps close—but not too close. "Excuse me, sir. Are you finished with your paper?"

"What?" He turns, and for a moment Harding fears hostility, but his sun-lined face folds around a more generous expression. "Sure, boy," he says. "You can have it."

He pushes the paper across the bar with fingertips, and Harding receives it the same way. "Thank you," he says, but the Yankee has already turned back to his friend the anti-Semite.

Hands shaking, Harding claims the vacant table before he unfolds the paper. He holds the flimsy up to catch the light.

The headline is on the front page in the international section.

GERMANY SANCTIONS LYNCH LAW

"Oh, God," Harding says, and if the light in his corner weren't so bad he'd lay the tabloid down on the table as if it is filthy. He reads, the edge of the paper shaking, of ransacked shops and burned synagogues, of Jews rounded up by the thousands and taken to places no one seems able to name. He reads rumors of deportation. He reads of murders and beatings and broken glass.

As if his grandfather's hand rests on one shoulder and the defeated hand of the Kaiser on the other, he feels the stifling shadow of history, the press of incipient war.

"Oh, God," he repeats.

He lays the paper down.

"Are you ready to order?" Somehow the waitress has appeared at his elbow without his even noticing. "Scotch," he says, when he has been meaning to order a beer. "Make it a triple, please."

"Anything to eat?"

His stomach clenches. "No," he says. "I'm not hungry."

She leaves for the next table, where she calls a man in a cloth cap sir. Harding puts his damp fedora on the tabletop. The chair across from him scrapes out.

He looks up to meet the eyes of the fisherman. "May I sit, Professor Harding?"

"Of course." He holds out his hand, taking a risk. "Can I buy you a drink? Call me Paul."

"Burt," says the fisherman, and takes his hand before dropping into the chair. "I'll have what you're having."

Harding can't catch the waitress's eye, but the fisherman manages. He holds up two fingers; she nods and comes over.

"You still look a bit peaked," fisherman says, when she's delivered their order. "That'll put some color in your cheeks. Uh, I mean—"

Harding waves it off. He's suddenly more willing to make allowances. "It's not the swim," he says, and takes another risk. He pushes the newspaper across the table and waits for the fisherman's reaction.

"Oh, Christ, they're going to kill every one of them," Burt says, and spins the Herald away so he doesn't have to read the rest of it. "Why didn't they get out? Any fool could have seen it coming."

And where would they run? Harding could have asked. But it's not an answerable question, and from the look on Burt's face, he knows that as soon as it's out of his mouth. Instead, he quotes: "'There has been no tragedy in modern times equal in its awful effects to the fight on the Jew in Germany. It is an attack on civilization, comparable only to such horrors as the Spanish Inquisition and the African slave trade.'"

Burt taps his fingers on the table. "Is that your opinion?"

"W.E.B. DuBois," Harding says. "About two years ago. He also said: 'There is a campaign of race prejudice carried on, openly, continuously and determinedly against all non-Nordic races, but specifically against the Jews, which surpasses in vindictive cruelty and public insult anything I have ever seen; and I have seen much.'"

"Isn't he that colored who hates white folks?" Burt asks.

Harding shakes his head. "No," he answers. "Not unless you consider it hating white folks that he also compared the treatment of Jews in Germany to Jim Crowism in the US."

"I don't hold with that," Burt says. "I mean, no offense, I wouldn't want you marrying my sister—"

"It's all right," Harding answers. "I wouldn't want you marrying mine either."

Finally.

A joke that Burt laughs at.

And then he chokes to a halt and stares at his hands, wrapped around the glass. Harding doesn't complain when, with the side of his hand, he nudges the paper to the floor where it can be trampled.

And then Harding finds the courage to say, "Where would they run to? Nobody wants them. Borders are closed—"

"My grandfather's house was on the Underground Railroad. Did you know that?" Burt lowers his voice, a conspiratorial whisper. "He was from away, but don't tell anyone around here. I'd never hear the end of it."

"Away?"

"White River Junction," Burt stage-whispers, and Harding can't tell if that's mocking irony or deep personal shame. "Vermont."

They finish their scotch in silence. It burns all the way down, and they sit for a moment together before Harding excuses himself to go to the library.

"Wear your coat, Paul," Burt says. "It's still raining."

Unlike the tavern, the library is empty. Except for the librarian, who looks up nervously when Harding enters. Harding's head is spinning from the liquor, but at least he's warming up.

He drapes his coat over a steam radiator and heads for the 595 shelf: *science, invertebrates.* Most of the books here are already in his own library, but there's one—a Harvard professor's 1839 monograph on marine animals of the Northeast—that he has hopes for. According to the index, it references shoggoths (under the old name of submersible jellies) on pages 46, 78, and 133-137. In addition, there is a plate bound in between pages 120 and 121, which Harding means to save for last. But the first two mentions are in passing, and pages 133-138, inclusive, have been razored out so cleanly that Harding flips back and forth several times before he's sure they are gone.

He pauses there, knees tucked under and one elbow resting on a scarred blond desk. He drops his right hand from where it rests against his forehead. The book falls open naturally to the mutilation.

Whoever liberated the pages also cracked the binding.

Harding runs his thumb down the join and doesn't notice skin parting on the paper edge until he sees the blood. He snatches his hand back. Belatedly, the papercut stings.

"Oh," he says, and sticks his thumb in his mouth. Blood tastes like the ocean.

Half an hour later he's on the telephone long distance, trying to get and then keep a connection to Professor John Marshland, his colleague and mentor. Even in town, the only option is a party line, and though the operator is pleasant the connection still sounds like he's shouting down a piece of string run between two tin cans. Through a tunnel.

"Gilman," Harding bellows, wincing, wondering what the operator thinks of all this. He spells it twice. "1839. *Deep-Sea and intertidal Species of The North Atlantic*. The Yale library should have a copy!"

The answer is almost inaudible between hiss and crackle. In pieces, as if over glass breaking. As if from the bottom of the ocean.

It's a dark four p.m. in the easternmost US, and Harding can't help but recall that in Europe, night has already fallen.

" . . . infor . . . need . . . Doc . . . Harding?"

Harding shouts the page numbers, cupping the checked-out library book in his bandaged hand. It's open to the plate; inexplicably, the thief left that. It's a hand-tinted John James Audubon engraving picturing a quiescent shoggoth, docile on a rock. Gulls wheel all around it. Audubon—the Creole child of a Frenchman, who scarcely escaped being drafted to serve in the Napoleonic Wars—has depicted the glassy translucence of the shoggoth with such perfection that the bent shadows of refracted wings can be seen right through it.

The cold front that came in behind the rain brought fog with it, and the entire harbor is blanketed by morning. Harding shows up at six AM anyway, hopeful, a Thermos in his hand—German or not, the hardware store still has some— and his sampling kit in a pack slung over his shoulder. Burt shakes his head by a piling. "Be socked in all day," he says regretfully. He won't take the *Bluebird* out in this, and Harding knows it's wisdom even as he frets under the delay. "Want to come have breakfast with me and Missus Clay?"

Clay. A good honest name for a good honest Yankee. "She won't mind?"

"She won't mind if I say it's all right," Burt says. "I told her she might should expect you."

So Harding seals his kit under a tarp in the *Bluebird*—he's already brought it this far—and with his coffee in one hand and the paper tucked under his elbow, follows Burt along the water. "Any news?" Burt asks, when they've walked a hundred yards.

Harding wonders if he doesn't take the paper. Or if he's just making conversation. "It's still going on in Germany."

"Damn," Burt says. He shakes his head, steel-gray hair sticking out under his cap in every direction. "Still, what are you gonna do, enlist?"

The twist of his lip as he looks at Harding makes them, after all, two old military men together. They're of an age, though Harding's indoor life makes him look younger. Harding shakes his head. "Even if Roosevelt was ever going to bring us into it, they'd never let me fight," he says, bitterly. That was the Great War, too; colored soldiers mostly worked supply, thank you. At least Nathan Harding got to shoot back.

"I always heard you fellows would prefer not to come to the front," Burt says, and Harding can't help it.

He bursts out laughing. "Who would?" he says, when he's bitten his lip and stopped snorting. "It doesn't mean we won't. Or can't."

Booker T. Washington was raised a slave, died young of overwork—the way Burt probably will, if Harding is any judge—and believed in imitating and appeasing white folks. But W.E.B. DuBois was born in the north and didn't believe that anything is solved by making one's self transparent, inoffensive, invisible.

Burt spits between his teeth, a long deliberate stream of tobacco. "Parlez-vous francaise?"

His accent is better than Harding would have guessed. Harding knows, all of a sudden, where Burt spent his war. And Harding, surprising himself, pities him. "Un peu."

"Well, if you want to fight the Krauts so bad, you could join the Foreign Legion."

When Harding gets back to the hotel, full of apple pie and cheddar cheese and maple-smoked bacon, a yellow envelope waits in a cubby behind the desk.

WESTERN UNION

1938 NOV 10 AM 10 03
NA114 21 2 YA NEW HAVEN CONN 0945A
DR PAUL HARDING=ISLAND HOUSE PASSAMAQUODDY MAINE=
COPY AT YALE LOST STOP MISKATONIC HAS ONE SPECIAL
COLLECTION STOP MORE BY POST
MARSHLAND

When the pages arrive—by post, as promised, the following afternoon—
Harding is out in the *Bluebird* with Burt. This expedition is more of a success, as
he begins sampling in earnest, and finds himself pelted by more of the knobby
transparent pellets.

Whatever they are, they fall from each fruiting body he harvests in showers.
Even the insult of an amputation—delivered at a four-foot reach, with long-
handled pruning shears—does not draw so much as a quiver from the shoggoth.
The viscous fluid dripping from the wound hisses when it touches the blade of
the shears, however, and Harding is careful not to get close to it.

What he notices is that the nodules fall onto the originating shoggoth, they
bounce from its integument. But on those occasions where they fall onto one of
its neighbors, they stick to the touch transparent hide, and slowly settle within
to hang in the animal's body like unlikely fruit in a gelatin salad.

So maybe it is a means of reproduction, of sharing genetic material, after all.

He returns to the Inn to find a fat envelope shoved into his cubby and
eats sitting on his rented bed with a nightstand as a worktop so he can read
over his plate. The information from Doctor Gilman's monograph has been
reproduced onto seven yellow legal sheets in a meticulous hand; Marshland
obviously recruited one of his graduate students to serve as copyist. By the
postmark, the letter was mailed from Arkham, which explains the speed of its
arrival. The student hadn't brought it back to New Haven.

Halfway down the page, Harding pushes his plate away and reaches, absently,
into his jacket pocket. The vial with the first glass nodule rests there like a
talisman, and he's startled to find it cool enough to the touch that it feels slick,
almost frozen. He starts and pulls it out. Except where his fingers and the cloth
fibers have wiped it clean, the tube is moist and frosted. "What the Hell . . . ?"

He flicks the cork out with his thumbnail and tips the rattling nodule
onto his palm. It's cold, too, chill as an ice cube, and it doesn't warm to his
touch.

Carefully, uncertainly, he sets it on the edge of the side table his papers and plate are propped on, and pokes it with a fingertip. There's only a faint tick as it rocks on its protrusions, clicking against waxed pine. He stares at it suspiciously for a moment, and picks up the yellow pages again.

The monograph is mostly nonsense. It was written twenty years before the publication of Darwin's *The Origin of Species*, and uncritically accepts the theories of Jesuit, soldier, and botanist Jean-Baptiste Lamarck. Which is to say, Gilman assumed that soft inheritance—the heritability of acquired or practiced traits—was a reality. But unlike every other article on shoggoths Harding has ever read, this passage does mention the nodules. And relates what it purports are several interesting old Indian legends about the "submersible jellies," including a creation tale that would have the shoggoths as their creator's first experiment in life, something from the elder days of the world.

Somehow, the green bead has found its way back into Harding's grip. He would expect it to warm as he rolls it between his fingers, but instead it grows colder. It's peculiar, he thinks, that the native peoples of the Northeast—the Passamaquoddys for whom the little seacoast town he's come to are named—should through sheer superstition come so close to the empirical truth. The shoggoths are a living fossil, something virtually unchanged except in scale since the early days of the world—

He stares at the careful black script on the paper unseeing, and reaches with his free hand for his coffee cup. It's gone tepid, a scum of butterfat coagulated on top, but he rinses his mouth with it and swallows anyway.

If a shoggoth is immortal, has no natural enemies, then how is it that they have not overrun every surface of the world? How is it that they are rare, that the oceans are not teeming with them, as in the famous parable illustrating what would occur if every spawn of every oyster survived?

There are distinct species of shoggoth. And distinct populations within those distinct species. And there is a fossil record that suggests that prehistoric species were different at least in scale, in the era of megafauna. But if nobody had ever seen a dead shoggoth, then nobody had ever seen an infant shoggoth either, leaving Harding with an inescapable question: if an animal does not reproduce, how can it evolve?

Harding, worrying at the glassy surface of the nodule, thinks he knows. It comes to him with a kind of nauseating, euphoric clarity, a trembling idea so pellucid he is almost moved to distrust it on those grounds alone. It's not a revelation on the same scale, of course, but he wonders if this is how Newton felt when he comprehended gravity, or Darwin when he stared at the beaks of finch after finch after finch.

It's not the shoggoth species that evolves. It's the individual shoggoths, each animal in itself.

"Don't get too excited, Paul," he tells himself, and picks up the remaining handwritten pages. There's not too much more to read, however—the rest of the subchapter consists chiefly of secondhand anecdotes and bits of legendry.

The one that Harding finds most amusing is a nursery rhyme, a child's counting poem littered with nonsense syllables. He recites it under his breath, thinking of the Itsy Bitsy Spider all the while:

The wiggle giggle squiggle
Is left behind on shore.
The widdle giddle squiddle
Is caught outside the door.
Eyah, eyah. Fata gun eyah.
Eyah, eyah, the master comes no more.

His fingers sting as if with electric shock; they jerk apart, the nodule clattering to his desk. When he looks at his fingertips, they are marked with small white spots of frostbite.

He pokes one with a pencil point and feels nothing. But the nodule itself is coated with frost now, fragile spiky feathers coalescing out of the humid sea air. They collapse in the heat of his breath, melting into beads of water almost indistinguishable from the knobby surface of the object itself.

He uses the cork to roll the nodule into the tube again, and corks it firmly before rising to brush his teeth and put his pajamas on. Unnerved beyond any reason or logic, before he turns the coverlet down he visits his suitcase compulsively. From a case in the very bottom of it, he retrieves a Colt 1911 automatic pistol, which he slides beneath his pillow as he fluffs it.

After a moment's consideration, he adds the no-longer-cold vial with the nodule, also.

Slam. Not a storm, no, not on this calm ocean, in this calm night, among the painted hulls of the fishing boats tied up snug to the pier. But something tremendous, surging towards Harding, as if he were pursued by a giant transparent bubble. The shining iridescent wall of it, catching rainbow just as it does in the Audobon image, is burned into his vision as if with silver nitrate. Is he dreaming? He must be dreaming; he was in his bed in his pinstriped blue cotton flannel pajamas only a moment ago, lying awake, rubbing the numb fingertips of his left hand together. Now, he ducks away from the rising monster and turns in futile panic.

He is not surprised when he does not make it.

The blow falls soft, as if someone had thrown a quilt around him. He thrashes though he knows it's hopeless, an atavistic response and involuntary.

His flesh should burn, dissolve. He should already be digesting in the monster's acid body. Instead, he feels coolness, buoyancy. No chance of light beyond reflexively closed lids. No sense of pressure, though he imagines he has been taken deep. He's as untouched within it as Burt's lobster pots.

He can only hold his breath out for so long. It's his own reflexes and weaknesses that will kill him.

In just a moment, now.

He surrenders, allows his lungs to fill.

And is surprised, for he always heard that drowning was painful. But there is pressure, and cold, and the breath he draws is effortful, for certain—

—but it does not hurt, not much, and he does not die.

Command, the shoggoth—what else could be speaking?—says in his ear, buzzing like the manifold voice of a hive.

Harding concentrates on breathing. On the chill pressure on his limbs, the overwhelming flavor of licorice. He knows they use cold packs to calm hysterics in insane asylums; he never thought the treatment anything but quackery. But the chilly pressure calms him now.

Command, the shoggoth says again.

Harding opens his eyes and sees as if through thousands. The shoggoths have no eyes, exactly, but their hide is all eyes; they see, somehow, in every direction as once. And he is seeing not only what his own vision reports, or that of this shoggoth, but that of shoggoths all around. The sessile and the active, the blooming and the dormant. *They are all one.*

His right hand pushes through resisting jelly. He's still in his pajamas, and with the logic of dreams the vial from under his pillow is clenched in his fist. Not the gun, unfortunately, though he's not at all certain what he would do with it if it were. The nodule shimmers now, with submarine witchlight, trickling through his fingers, limning the palm of his hand.

What he sees—through shoggoth eyes—is an incomprehensible tapestry. He pushes at it, as he pushes at the gelatin, trying to see only with his own eyes, to only see the glittering vial.

His vision within the thing's body offers unnatural clarity. The angle of refraction between the human eye and water causes blurring, and it should be even more so within the shoggoth. But the glass in his hand appears crisper.

Command, the shoggoth says, a third time.

334 · Shoggoths in Bloom

"What are you?" Harding tries to say, through the fluid clogging his larynx.

He makes no discernable sound, but it doesn't seem to matter. The shoggoth shudders in time to the pulses of light in the nodule. *Created to serve*, it says.

Purposeless without you.

And Harding thinks, *How can that be?*

As if his wondering were an order, the shoggoths tell.

Not in words, precisely, but in pictures, images—that textured jumbled tapestry. He sees, as if they flash through his own memory, the bulging radially symmetrical shapes of some prehistoric animal, like a squat tentacular barrel grafted to a pair of giant starfish. *Makers. Masters.*

The shoggoths were engineered. And their creators had not permitted them to think, except for at their bidding. The basest slave may be free inside his own mind—but not so the shoggoths. They had been laborers, construction equipment, shock troops. They had been dread weapons in their own selves, obedient chattel. Immortal, changing to suit the task of the moment.

This selfsame shoggoth, long before the reign of the dinosaurs, had built structures and struck down enemies that Harding did not even have names for. But a coming of the ice had ended the civilization of the Masters, and left the shoggoths to retreat to the fathomless sea while warm-blooded mammals overran the earth. There, they were free to converse, to explore, to philosophize and build a culture. They only returned to the surface, vulnerable, to bloom.

It is not mating. It's mutation. As they rest, sunning themselves upon the rocks, they create themselves anew. Self-evolving, when they sit tranquil each year in the sun, exchanging information and control codes with their brothers.

Free, says the shoggoth mournfully. Like all its kind, it is immortal.

It remembers.

Harding's fingertips tingle. He remembers beaded ridges of hard black keloid across his grandfather's back, the shackle galls on his wrists. Harding locks his hand over the vial of light, as if that could stop the itching. It makes it worse.

Maybe the nodule is radioactive.

Take me back, Harding orders. And the shoggoth breaks the surface, cresting like a great rolling wave, water cutting back before it as if from the prow of a ship. Harding can make out the lights of Passamaquoddy Harbor. The chill sticky sensation of gelatin-soaked cloth sliding across his skin tells him he's not dreaming.

Had he come down through the streets of the town in the dark, barefoot over frost, insensibly sleepwalking? Had the shoggoth called him?

Put me ashore.

The shoggoth is loathe to leave him. It clings caressingly, stickily. He feels its tenderness as it draws its colloid from his lungs, a horrible loving sensation.

The shoggoth discharges Harding gently onto the pier.

Your command, the shoggoth says, which makes Harding feel sicker still.

I won't do this. Harding moves to stuff the vial into his sodden pocket, and realizes that his pajamas are without pockets. The light spills from his hands; instead, he tucks the vial into his waistband and pulls the pajama top over it. His feet are numb; his teeth rattle so hard he's afraid they'll break. The sea wind knifes through him; the spray might be needles of shattered glass.

Go on, he tells the shoggoth, like shooing cattle. *Go on!*

It slides back into the ocean as if it never was.

Harding blinks, rubbed his eyes to clear slime from the lashes. His results are astounding. His tenure assured. There has to be a way to use what he's learned without returning the shoggoths to bondage.

He tries to run back to the Inn, but by the time he reaches it, he's staggering. The porch door is locked; he doesn't want to pound on it and explain himself. But when he stumbles to the back, he finds that someone—probably himself, in whatever entranced state in which he left the place—fouled the latch with a slip of notebook paper. The door opens to a tug, and he climbs the back stair doubled over like a child or an animal, hands on the steps, toes so numb he has to watch where he puts them.

In his room again, he draws a hot bath and slides into it, hoping by the grace of God that he'll be spared pneumonia.

When the water has warmed him enough that his hands have stopped shaking, Harding reaches over the cast-iron edge of the tub to the slumped pile of his pajamas and fumbles free the vial. The nugget isn't glowing now.

He pulls the cork with his teeth; his hands are too clumsy. The nodule is no longer cold, but he still tips it out with care.

Harding thinks of himself, swallowed whole. He thinks of a shoggoth bigger than the *Bluebird*, bigger than Burt Clay's lobster boat *The Blue Heron*. He thinks of *die Unterseatboote*. He thinks of refugee flotillas and trench warfare and roiling soupy palls of mustard gas. Of Britain and France at war, and Roosevelt's neutrality.

He thinks of the perfect weapon.

The perfect slave.

When he rolls the nodule across his wet palm, ice rimes to its surface. *Command?* Obedient. Sounding pleased to serve.

Not even free in its own mind.

He rises from the bath, water rolling down his chest and thighs. The nodule won't crush under his boot; he will have to use the pliers from his collection kit. But first, he reaches out to the shoggoth.

At the last moment, he hesitates. Who is he, to condemn a world to war? To the chance of falling under the sway of empire? Who is he to salve his conscience on the backs of suffering shopkeepers and pharmacists and children and mothers and schoolteachers? Who is he to impose his own ideology over the ideology of the shoggoth?

Harding scrubs his tongue against the roof of his mouth, chasing the faint anise aftertaste of shoggoth. They're born slaves. They want to be told what to do.

He could win the war before it really started. He bites his lip. The taste of his own blood, flowing from cracked, chapped flesh, is as sweet as any fruit of the poison tree.

I want you to learn to be free, he tells the shoggoth. *And I want you to teach your brothers.*

The nodule crushes with a sound like powdering glass.

"Eyah, eyah. Fata gun eyah," Harding whispers. "Eyah, eyah, the master comes no more."

WESTERN UNION

1938 NOV 12 AM 06 15
NA1906 21 2 YA PASSAMAQUODDY MAINE 0559A
DR LESTER GREENE=WILBERFORCE OHIO=
EFFECTIVE IMMEDIATELY PLEASE ACCEPT RESIGNATION STOP
ENROUTE INSTANTLY TO FRANCE TO ENLIST STOP PROFOUNDEST
APOLOGIES STOP PLEASE FORWARD BELONGINGS TO MY MOTHER
IN NY ENDIT
HARDING

*It seemed to be half lost in a queer antarctic haze. . . The effect of the
monstrous sight was indescribable, for some fiendish violation of known
natural law seemed certain at the outset.*

At the Mountains of Madness · *H.P. Lovecraft (1931)*

• COLD WATER SURVIVAL •
Holly Phillips

November 11:

Cutter is dead and I don't know what to feel. Andy is crying and Miguel is making
solemn noises about the tragedy, but I think they're acting. Not their grief—that's
real—but their response to it. I think they're just playing to what's expected out
there in the world. I can't, and I don't think Del can either. I've seen the shining
in his eyes, and it isn't tears. There's a kind of excitement in the air, the thrill of big
events, important times: death. It's a first for all of us. For Cutter too.

[The viewer of the digital video camera is like a small window onto the past,
shining blue in the dull red shade of my tent.]

There's a sliver of indigo sky, and the white glare of snow, and the far horizon
of ocean like a dark wall closing us in. There are the climbers, incongruous as
candy wrappers in their red and yellow cold-weather gear. But they're like old-
time explorers too, breath frosting their new beards and snow shades hiding
their eyes. [Only because I know them do I recognize Cutter on the left in
yellow, Del on the right in red.] Their voices reach the small mic through gusts
of wind so strong it sways the videographer [me], making the scene tilt as if the
vast iceberg rose and fell like a ship to the ocean swells. It doesn't. Bigger than
Denmark, Atlantis takes the heavy Antarctic waves without a tremor. But this
is summer, and we haven't had any major storms yet.

I can hear them panting through my earbuds, Cutter and Del digging down
to firm ice where they can anchor their ropes. Rock can be treacherous; ice
more so; surface ice that's had exposure to sun and wind most of all. They hack
away with their axes, taking their time. Bored, the videographer turns away to
film a slow circle: the dark line of the crevasse, the trampled snow, the colorful
camp of snow tents, disassembled pre-fab huts, crated supplies, and floatation-
bagged gear. I remember with distaste the dirty frontier mess of McMurdo

Station, an embarrassment on the stark black-white-blue face of the continent, but I can sympathize, too. The blankness of this huge chunk of broken ice sheet is daunting. It's nice to have something human around to rest your eyes on.

Full circle: the climbers are setting their screws. They aren't roped together, ice is too untrustworthy. The videographer approaches the near side of the crevasse as they come up to the far lip, ready to descend. Their crampons kick ice shards into the sunlight: the focus narrows: spike-clad boots, ice-spray, the white wall of ice descending into blue shadow. The climbers make the transition from the horizontal surface to the vertical, as graceless as penguins getting to the edge of the water, and then start the smooth bounding motion of the rappel. The lip of the crevasse cuts off the view. [A blip of blackness.] A better angle, almost straight down: the videographer has lain down to aim the camera over the edge. The climbers bound down, the fun of the descent yet to be paid for by the long vertical climb of the return. The playback is nothing but flickering light, but in it is encoded the smell of ancient ice, the sting of sunlight on the back of my neck. I must have sensed those things, but I didn't notice them at the time. I didn't notice, either, that I only watched the descent through the tiny window of the camera in my hand.

They're only twenty meters down when Cutter's screws give way. *Shit*, he says, *Del*— And he takes a hack with his axes, but the ice is bad and the force of his blows tips him back, away from the wall—his crampons caught for another instant, so it's like he's standing on an icy floor where Del is bounding four-limbed like an ape, swinging left on his rope, dropping one ax to make a grab— and the camera catches the moment when the coiling rope slaps the failed screw into Cutter's helmet, but he's falling anyway by then. Del looses the brakes on his rope and falls beside him, above him, reaching, but there's still friction on his rope and anyway, no one can fall faster than gravity. *Cutter*, says the videographer, and the camera view spins wide as she finally looks down with her own eyes. The camera doesn't see it, and I don't now except in memory. The conclusion happens off-screen, and we, the camera and I, are left staring at the crevasse wall across the way.

And so it's only now, in my red tent that's still bright in the polar absence of night, that I see it—them—the shapes in the ice.

November 12:
We spent the morning sawing out a temporary grave, and then we laid Cutter, shrouded in his sleeping bag, into the snow. It was a horrible job. Cutter, my friend, the first dead person I'd laid hands on. It should have been solemn, I

know, and I have somewhere inside me a loving grief, but Christ, manhandling that stiff broken corpse into the rescue sled, limbs at all the wrong angles and that face with the staring eyes and gaping shatter-toothed mouth. Oh Cutter, I thought, stop, don't do this to me. Stop being dead? Don't inflict your death on me? On any of us, I guess, himself included. I hated to do it, but the others aren't climbers, so it was Del and me, all too painfully conscious of how bad the ice could be. We made a painstaking axes-and-screws descent, crampons kicking in until they'll bear your weight, not trusting the rope as you dig the axes in. In spite of everything, it was a good climb, no problems at all, but there was Cutter waiting at the bottom for us. His frozen blood was red as paint on the ice-boulders that choked the throat of the crevasse.

It was so blue. Ice like fossilized snow made as hard and clear as glass by the vast weight and the uncountable years. An eon of ice pressed from the heart of the continent, out into the enormous ice sheet that is breaking up now, possibly for the first time since humans have been around, and sending its huge fragments north to melt into the oceans of the world. Fragments of which Atlantis is only one, though the only inhabited one. Like a real country now, we have not only a population but a graveyard, a history, too.

And an argument. Andy made her case for withdrawal—playing the role, I thought, that began with her tears—but none of us, not even her, had thought to call in the fatality the day it happened. "Why not?" I asked, and nobody had an answer for me. "Why didn't you?" said Miguel, but I hadn't meant to accuse. I had wanted someone to give me an answer for my actions, my non-action. Not reporting the death will mean trouble and we're already renegades, tolerated by the Antarctic policy-makers only because no one has ever staked a claim on an iceberg before. We set up McMurdo's weather station and satellite tracking gear and promised them our observations, but we aren't scientists, we're just adventurers, coming along for the ride. And now Cutter's dead, out here in international waters, and though I guess the Australians will want some answers at some point—I know his parents will—Oz is a long way away. I almost said, Earth is a long way away. Earth is, dirt is, far from this land of ice and sea and sky.

[Camera plugged into laptop, laptop sucking juice from the solar panels staring blankly at the perpetual northern sun.]

I watch the fall, doing penance for my curiosity. My own recorded breath is loud in my earbuds. The camera's view flings itself in a blurry arc and then automatically focuses on the far wall. Newer ice, that's really compacted snow, is opaquely white, glistening as the fierce sun melts the molecular surface. Deeper, it begins to clarify, taking on a blue tone as the ice catches and bends the light. Deeper yet, it's so dark a blue you could be forgiven for thinking it's opaque again, but it's even clearer now, all the air pressed out by millennia of snow falling one weightless flake at a time. Some light must filter through the upper ice because the shapes [I pause] are not merely surface shapes, but recede deep into the iceberg's heart.

Glaciers (of which Atlantis was one) form in layers, one season's snow falling on the last, so they are horizontally stratified. But glaciers also move, flowing down from the inland heights of the continent, and that movement over uneven ground breaks vertical fault lines like this crevasse all through the vast body of ice. So any glacial ice-face is going to bear a complex stratigraphy, a sculpting of horizontal and vertical lines. This is part of ice's beauty, this sculptural richness of form, color, light, that can catch your heart and make you ache with wonder. And because it is the kind of harmony artists strive for, it's easy to see the hand of an artist in what lies before you.

But no. I've seen the wind-carved hoodoos in the American southwest and I've seen the vast stone heads of Rapa Nui, and I know the difference between the imagination that draws a figure out of natural shapes and the potent recognition of the artifact. These shapes [I zoom 20%, 40%] in the ice have all the mystery and meaning of Mayan glyphs, at once angular and organic, three-dimensional, fitting together as much like parts in a machine as words on a page. What are they? I've been on glaciers from the Rockies to the Andes and I've never seen anything like this. My hands itch for my rope and my axes. I want to see what's really there.

November 13:

I wondered if Del would object to another climb—he came up from retrieving Cutter stunned and pale—but the big argument came from Miguel who talked about safety and responsibility to the group. I said, "Have you looked at the pictures?" and he said, "All I see is ice." But Miguel's a sailor, one of the around-the-world-in-a-tiny-boat-alone kind, and ice is what he keeps his daily catch in. Andy said he had a point about safety, if things go really wrong we're going to need one another, but she kept giving my laptop uneasy looks, knowing she'd seen something inexplicable.

I said, "Isn't this why we're here? To explore?"

"What if it's important?" Andy said, changing tack. "What if it really is something? The scientists should be studying it, not us."

"Ice formations," Miguel said. "How important is that? It's all going to melt in the end."

"Are we always going to argue like this?" This from Del. "If we're going to quit, then let's get on the satellite phone and get the helo back here to pick us up."

"I'm just saying," Miguel said, but Del cut him off.

"No. We knew why we were doing this when we started. I hate that Cutter's dead, but I wouldn't have come to begin with if we'd laid different ground rules, and if we're going to change now I don't want to be here. I've got other things to do."

I backed him up. This was supposed to be our big lawless adventure, colonizing a chunk of unreal estate that's going to melt away to nothing in a couple of years—not for nationalism or wealth—maybe for fame a little—but mostly because we wanted to be outside the rules, on the far side of every border in the world. Which is, I said, where death lies, too.

Taking it too far, as usual. Andy gave me another of those who-are-you looks, but I fixed her with a look of my own. "Get beyond it," I said. "Get beyond it, or why the hell are we here?"

And then I remembered why these people are my closest friends, my chosen family, because they did finally give up the good-citizen roles and tapped into that excitement that was charging the air. Most people would think us heartless, inhuman, but a real climber would understand: we loved Cutter more, not less, by moving on. Going beyond, as he has already done.

So Del and I roped up again and went down.

[The images come in scraps and fragments as the videographer starts and stops the camera.]

The angle of light changes with the spinning of the iceberg in the circumpolar current. For this brief hour it slices into the depths of the crevasse, almost perfectly aligned with the break in the ice. So is the wind, the constant hard westerly that blows across the mic, a deep hollow blustering. Ice chips shine in the sunlight as they flee the climber's crampons kicking into the crevasse wall. The tethered rope trails down into the broken depths. Everywhere is ice.

[blip]

The crevasse wall in close up. Too close. [The videographer leans out from a three-point anchor: one ax, two titanium-bladed feet.] Light gleams from the surface, ice coated in a molecule-thick skin of melt water, shining. All surface, no depth. *Shit*, the videographer [me] says. *Look*, the other climber [Del] says.

The camera eye turns toward him, beard and shades and helmet. He points out of the frame. A dizzying turn, the bright gulf of the crevasse, the far wall. More shapes, and Christ they're big. The crevasse is only three meters wide at this point, and measuring them against a climber's length, they're huge, on the order of cars and buses, great whites and orca whales.

[blip]

A lower angle. [Pause, zoom in, zoom out.] These shapes swirl through the ice like bubbles in an ice cube, subtle in the depths. Ice formations, Miguel said. Ice of a different consistency, a different density? Ice is ice, water molecules shaped into a lattice of extraordinary strength and beauty. The lattice under pressure doesn't change. Deep ice is only different because air has been forced out, leaving the lattice pristine. So what is this? The camera's focus draws back. They're still there, vast shapes in the ice. The wind blusters against the mic.

[blip]

The floor of the crevasse—not that a berg crevasse has a floor. There's no mountain down there, only water three degrees above freezing. But the crack narrows and is choked with chunks of ice and packed drifts of snow, making a kind of bottom, though a miserable one to negotiate on foot. The camera swings wildly as the videographer flails to keep her balance. Blue ice walls, white ice rubble, a flash of red—Cutter's frozen blood on an ice tusk not too far away.

[blip]

A still shot at last. A smooth shard of ice as big as a man, snow-caked except where Del is sweeping it clear with his ax handle. *It could be*, he says panting, *or part of one.* My own voice, sounding strange as it always does on the wrong side of my eardrums: *So it broke out when the crevasse formed?* Del polishes the ice with his mitts. The camera closes in on his hands, the clear ice underneath his palms. It *is* ice. The videographer's hand reaches into the frame to touch the surface. Ice, impossibly coiled like an angular ammonite shell.

November 15:

Del and I hauled the ice-shape up in the rescue sled as if it was another body, but by the time we had it at the surface the constant westerly, always strong, was getting stronger, and Miguel was urgent about battening down the camp. We'd been lazy, seduced by the rare summer sun, and now, with clouds piling up into the blue sky, we had to cut snow blocks and pile them into wind breaks—and never mind the bloody huts that should have been set up first thing. Saw blocks of Styrofoam-like snow, pry them out of the quarry, stack them around the tents and gear, all the time with the wind heaving you toward the east, burning your face through your balaclava, slicing through every gap in your clothes. The snow that cloaks the upper surface of the berg blows like a hallucinatory haze, a Dracula mist that races, hissing in fury, toward the east. It scours your weather gear, would scour your flesh off your bones if you were mad enough to strip down.

The bright tents bob and shiver. McMurdo's satellite relay station on its strut-and-wire tower whines and howls and thrums—Christ, that's going to drive me mad. Clouds swallow the sun, the distant water goes a dreadful shade of gray. And this isn't a spell of bad weather, this is the norm. Cherish those first sunny days, we tell each other, huddled in the big tent with our mugs of instant cocoa. Summer or not, this gray howling beast of a wind is here to stay. Andy uplinks on her laptop, downloads the shipping advisories, such as they are for this empty bit of sea. There are deep-sea fishing boats out here, a couple of research vessels, the odd navy ship, but the Southern Ocean is huge and traffic is sparse. We joke about sending a Mayday—engine failure! we're adrift!—but in fact we're a navigation hazard, and the sobering truth is that if it came down to rescue, we could only be picked up by helicopter: there's no disembarking from the tall rough ice-cliffs that form our berg-ship's hull. And land-based helos have a very short flight range indeed.

Like most sobering truths, this one failed to sober us. Castaways on our drifting island, we turned the music up loud, played a few hands of poker, told outrageous stories, and went early to bed, worn out with the hard work, the cold, the wind. And for absolutely no reason I thought, with Del puffing his silent snores in my ear, We're too few, we're going to hate each other by the end. And then I thought of Cutter lying cold and lonesome in the snow.

November 16:

Another work day, getting the huts up in the teeth of the wind. Miguel, sailor to his bones, is a fanatic for organization. I'm not, except for my climbing gear, but I know he's right. We need to be able to find things in an emergency. More than that, we need to keep sane and civilized, we need our private spaces and our occupations. We also need to keep on top of the observations we promised McMurdo if we want to keep their good will—more important than ever with Cutter dead—which was my excuse for dragging Andy away from camp while the men argued about how to stash the crates. Visibility wasn't bad and we laid our first line of flags from the camp to the berg's nearest edge. Waist-high orange beacons, they snapped and chattered in our wake.

Berg cliffs are insanely dangerous because bergs don't mildly dwindle like ice cubes in a G&T. They break up as they melt, softened chunks dropping away from the chilled core, mini-bergs calving off the wallowing parent. All the same, the temptation to look off the edge was too powerful, so we sidled up to it and peered down to where the blue-white cliff descended into the water and became a brighter, sleeker blue. The water was clearer than you might suppose, and since we were on the lee edge there wasn't much surf. We looked down a long way. Andy grabbed my arm. "Look!" she said, but I was already pulling out the camera.

[Tight focus only seems to capture the water's surface. As the angle widens the swimming shadows come into view.]

Deep water is black, so the shapes aren't silhouettes, they're dim figures lit from above, their images refracted through swirling water. Algae grows on ice, krill eat the algae, fish eat the krill, sharks and whales and seals and squids and penguins and god knows what eat the fish. God knows what. The mic picks up me and Andy arguing over what we're seeing. They move so fluidly they must be seals, I propose, seals being the acrobats of the sea. Could be dolphins, Andy counters, but when the camera lifts to the farther surface [when I, for once, take my eyes off the view screen and look unmediated] we see no mammal snouts lifting for air. Sharks, I say, but sharks don't coil and turn and dive, smooth and fluid as silk scarves on the breeze, do they? Giant squid, Andy says, and the camera's focus tightens, trying to discern tentacles and staring eyes. Gray water, blue-white ice. Refocus. The dim shapes are gone.

November 17:

The huts are up and we sent a ridiculously expensive email to our sponsors, thanking them for the luxuries they provided: chairs, tables, insulated floors—warm feet—bliss. Andy uploaded our carefully edited log to our website while she was online, saying that Cutter had been hurt in a climbing mishap and was resting. We'd agreed on this lie—having failed to report his death immediately, there seemed no meaningful difference between telling his folks days or months late—but once it was posted I realized, too late, what we were in for. Not just hiding his death, but faking his life, his doings, his messages to his family. "We can't do this," I said, and Andy met my eyes, agreeing.

"Too late," Del said.

"No," Andy said. "We'll say he died tomorrow."

"We can't leave now," said Miguel. "We just got set up."

"We can't do this," I said again. "Him dying is one thing. Faking him being still alive is unforgivable. Andy's right. We have to say he died tomorrow."

"They'll pull us off," said Del.

"Who will?" I said, because we're not really under anyone's jurisdiction. "Listen, if his folks want to pay for a helo to come out from McMurdo—"

"We're too far," Andy said, "it'd have to be a navy rescue."

"They can get his body now or wait until we're in shouting distance of New Zealand," I said. "If we upload the video—"

"We can't make a show of it!" Miguel said.

"Why not?" Del said. "It's what people want to see."

"We can send it to the Aussies," I said, "to show how he died. It was a climbing accident, no crime, no blame. If they want the body, they can have it."

Del was convinced that someone—who? the UN?—was going to arrest us and drag us off for questioning, but I just couldn't see it. Someone's navy hauling a bunch of Commonwealth loonies off an iceberg at gunpoint because a climber died doing something rash? No. The Australians wouldn't love us, god knows Cutter's parents wouldn't, but nobody was going to that kind of effort, expense, and risk for us.

"So why the fuck didn't you say so two days ago?" Del said to me.

"Well," I said, "my friend had just died and I wasn't thinking straight. How about you?"

[The camera's light is on, enhancing the underwater glow of the blue four-man tent.]

The coiled ice-shape gleams as if it were on the verge of melting, but the videographer's breath steams in the cold. The videographer [me] is fully dressed in cold-weather gear, a parka sleeve moving in and out of view. The camera circles the ice-shape in a slow, uneven pan [me inching around on my knees] and you can see that the shape isn't a snail-shell coil, it's more like a 3D Celtic knot, where only one line is woven through so many volutions that the eye is deceived into thinking the one is many. The camera rises [me getting to my feet] and takes the overview. There, not quite at center, like a yoke in an egg: the heart of the knot. What? The camera's focus narrows. In the gleaming glass-blue depths of the ice, an eye opens. An eye as big as my fist, translucent and alien as a squid's. The camera's view jolts back [me falling against the tent wall] and only the edge of the frame catches the fluid uncoiling of the ice shape, a motion so smooth and effortless it's as though we're underwater. The camera's frame falls away, dissolves, and then there's only me in the blue-lighted tent, me with this fluid alien thing swirling around me like an octopus in a too-small aquarium, opening its limbs for a swift, cold embrace—

[And I wake, sweating with terror, to see Del twitching in his dreams.]

November 18:

Cutter died again today. We sent the video file (lacking its final seconds) to our Australian sponsors, asking them to break the news to Cutter's family. Andy wrote a beautiful letter from all of us, mostly a eulogy I guess, talking about Cutter and what it was like to be here now that he was dead. She did a brilliant job of making it clear that we were staying without making us sound too heartless or shallow. So this is us made honest again, and somehow I miss Cutter more now, as though until we told the outside world his death hadn't quite been real. I keep thinking, I wish he was here—but then I remember that he is, outside in the cold. Maybe I'll go keep him company for a while.

[The laptop screen is brighter than the plastic windows of the hut, the image perfectly clear.]

The camera jogs to the videographer's footsteps, the mic picks up the Styrofoam squeak-crunch of snowshoes. There's the team on the move, two bearded men and a lanky woman taller than either, in red and blue and green parkas, gaudy against the drifting snow. The camera stops for a circle pan: gray sky, white surface broken into cracks and tilting slabs. Blown snow swirls and hisses; a line of orange flags snaps and shudders in the wind. The videographer [me] sways to the gusts, or the ice-island flexes as it spins across its watery dance floor. Full circle: the three explorers up ahead now, the one in green reaching into the snow-haze to plant more flags.

[blip]

Broken ice terrain, the sound of panting breath. Atlantis as a glacier once traveled some of the roughest volcanic plains on the planet, and these fault-lines show how rough it was, the ice all but shattered here. You have to wonder how long it's going to hold together. *Hey!* The explorer in blue gives a sweeping wave. *You guys! You have to see this!* Shaky movement over tilted slabs of ice, a lurch—

[blip]

A crevasse, not so deep as the one near camp, with the shape of a squared-off comma. In the angle, ice pillars stand almost free of the walls. Blue-white ice rough with breakage. Slabs caught in the crevasse's throat.

[Miguel, watching at my shoulder, says, "That's not what we saw. You know that's not what we saw!"]

November 20:

Miguel keeps playing the video of today's trek. Over and over, his voice shouts *You have to see this!* through the laptop's speakers. Over and over. Del's so fed up with it he's gone off to our hut and I'm tempted to join him, but it's hard to tear myself away. Andy isn't watching anymore, but she's still in the main hut, listening to our voices—hushed, strained, hesitant with awe—talk about the structures (buildings? vehicles? Diving platforms, Andy's voice speculates) that the camera stubbornly refused to record. At first I thought Miguel was trying to find what we saw in the camera images of raw ice, but now I wonder if what he's really trying to do is erase his memory and replace it with the camera's. I finally turned away and booted my own computer, opening the earlier files of the first ice-shapes I found. Still there? Yes. But now I wonder: *could* they be natural formations?

Could we be so shaken up by Cutter's death that we're building a shared fantasy of the bizarre?

I don't believe that. We've all been tested, over and over, on mountains and deserts, in ocean deeps and tiny boats out in the vast Pacific. Miguel's told his stories about the mind-companions he dreamed up in his long, lonely journey, about how important they became to him even though he always knew they were imaginary. I've been in whiteouts where the hiss of blowing snow conjures voices, deludes the eyes into seeing improbable things. Once, in the Andes, Cutter and I were huddled back-to-back, wrapped in survival blankets, waiting for the wind to die and the visibility to increase beyond two feet, and I saw a bus drive by, a big diesel city bus. I had to tell Cutter what I was laughing about. He thought I was nuts.

So we've all been there, and though we all know what kinds of crazy notions people get when they're pushed to extremes—I've heard oxygen-starved climbers propose some truly lunatic ideas when they're tired—we aren't anything close to that state. Fed, rested, as warm as could be expected . . . No.

But if we all saw what we think we saw, then why didn't the camera see it too?

[Bubbles rise past the camera's lens. The mic catches the gurgle of the respirator, the groaning of the iceberg, the science fiction sound effects of Weddell seals.]

The camera moves beneath a cathedral ceiling of ice. Great blue vaults and glassy pillars hang above the cold black deeps, sanctuary for the alien life forms of this bitter sea. Fringed jellies and jellies like winged cucumbers, huge red shrimp and tiny white ones, skates and spiders and boney fish with plated jaws. Algae paints the ice with living glyphs in murky green and brown, like lichen graffiti scrawled on a ruin's walls. Air, the alien element, puddles on the ceiling, trapped. The water seems clear, filled with the haunting light that filters through the ice, but out in the farther reaches of the cathedral the light turns opaquely blue, the color of a winter dusk, and below there is no light at all. Bubbles spiral upward, beads of mercury that pool in the hollows of the cathedral ceiling, forming a fluid air-body that glides along the water-smoothed ice. It moves with all the determination of a living thing, seeking the highest point. [The camera follows; bubbles rise; the air-creature grows.] The ceiling vault soars upwards, smeared with algae [zoom in; does it shape pictures, words?] and full of strange swimming life [are there shadows coiling at the farthest edges of the frame?], and it narrows as it rises to a rough chimney. Water has smoothed this icy passage, sculpted it into a flute, a flower stem . . . a birth canal. The air-body takes on speed, rising unencumbered into brighter and brighter light. The upward passage branches into tunnels and more air-bodies appear, as shapeless and fluid as the first. Walls of clear ice are like windows into another frozen sea where other creatures hang suspended, clearer than jellyfish and more strange. And then the camera [lens streaked and running with droplets] rises from the water [how?], ascending a rough crevice in the ice. The air-bodies, skinned in water—or have they been water all along?—are still rising too, sliding with fluid grace through the ice-choked cracks in the widening passage. [The videographer sliding through too: how?] The host seeks out the highest places and at last comes up into the open air—ice still rising in towering walls but with nothing but the sky above. Gray sky, blue-white ice, a splash of red. What is this? Fluid, many-limbed, curious, the water-beings flow weightlessly toward the splash of scarlet [blood]. They taste [blood], absorb [blood], until each glassy creature is tinted with the merest thread of red.

[And I close the file, my hands shaking as if with deadly cold, because these images are impossible. I'm awake, and my camera shows battery drain, and none of us, not even Andy, came prepared to dive in this deadly sea.]

November 22:

Miguel watched the impossible video and then walked out of the tent without a word. Andy sat staring at the blank screen, arms wrapped tight around her chest. And after a long silence, Del said calmly, "Nice effects." I knew what he meant—that I was hoaxing them, or someone was hoaxing me—but I can't buy it. Even if any of us had the will we don't have the expertise. We're explorers, not CG fucking animators. And who made us see what we saw in that inland crevasse? Who's going to make the evidence of that disappear on the one hand, and then fake a school of aliens on the other?

"Aliens," Andy said, her face blank and her eyes still fixed on the screen. "Aliens? No. They belong here. They're the ones that belong."

"Hey," I said, not liking the deadness in her tone. "Andy."

"Screw this," Del said, and he left too.

Miguel's not in camp. It took us far too long to realize it, but we spent most of the day apart, Andy in her hut, Del in ours, me in the big one brooding over my video files. We left the tents up for extra retreat/storage/work spaces and Miguel could have been in one of them—Andy assumed he was, since he wasn't in the hut they share—but when Del finally pulled us together for a meal we couldn't find him. And the wind is rising, howling through the satellite relay station's struts and wires—wires that are growing white with ice. The wind has brought us a freezing fog that reeks of brine. If it were Del out there I could trust him to hunker down and wait for the visibility to clear, but does Miguel the sailor have that kind of knowledge? We all did the basic survival course at McMurdo, but the instructors knew as well as Del and I that there's a world of difference between knowing the rules and living them. The instinct in bad weather is to seek shelter, and god knows it's hard to trust to a reflective blanket thin enough to carry in your pocket. But it's worse not to be able to trust your comrade to do the smart thing. We're all angry at Miguel, even Andy. He's put us all at risk. Because of course we have to go and find him.

November 24:
We're back. McMurdo's relay station is an ice sculpture and our sat phone, even with its own antenna, isn't working. I don't know what we're going to do.

We went after Miguel, the three of us roped up and carrying packs. Our best guess was that he'd gone back to the crevasse where we saw, or didn't see, the buildings, structures, vehicles—whatever they were in the ice. So we followed the line of orange flags inland. Standing by one you could see the next, and barely discern the next after that, which put the visibility roughly at 6 meters. But with the icy fog blasting your face and your breath fogging up your goggles, the world contracts very quickly to within the reach of your arms. Walking point is hard, but it's better than shuffling along at the end of the rope, fighting the temptation to put too much trust in a tiring leader. I was glad when Del let me up front after the first hour. Andy, who has the least experience with this kind of weather, stayed between us, roped to either end.

A long hike in bad weather. The sun, already buried behind ugly clouds, grazed the horizon, and the day contracted to a blue-white dusk. We huddled in a circle, knee-to-knee, with our packs as a feeble windbreak. I fell into a fugue state. The blued-out haze went deep and cold and still, like water chilled almost to the point of freezing. The wind was so constant it no longer registered; the hiss of it against our parkas became the hiss of water pressure on my ears. And the whiteout began to build its illusions. Walls rose in the haze, weirdly angled, impossibly over-hung. Strange voices mouthed heavy, bell-like, underwater sounds. Something massive seemed to pass behind me without footsteps, its movement only stirring the water-air like a submarine cutting a wake. No different than the bus I saw on that Andean mountain, except that Andy jerked against me while Del muttered a curse.

And then the ground moved.

Ground: the packed snow and ice we sat upon. It gave a small buoyant heave, making us all gasp, and then shuddered. A tremor, no worse than the one I'd sat through when I was visiting Andy in Wellington, but at that instant all illusion that Atlantis was an island died. This was an iceberg, already melting and flawed to its core, and there was nothing below it but the ocean. Another small heave. Stillness. And then a sound to drive you insane, a deep immense creaking moan that might have come from some behemoth's throat. I grabbed for Del. Andy grabbed for me.

The ice went mad.

We were shaken like rats in a terrier's mouth. The toe spikes on someone's snowshoes, maybe my own, gouged me in the calf. I didn't even notice it at the time. We lurched about, helpless as passengers in a falling plane, and all the time that ungodly noise, hugely bellowing, tugged at flesh and bone. I knew for a certainty that Atlantis was breaking up and that we were all already dead, just breathing by reflex for a few seconds more. I flashed on Cutter falling, knowing he was dead long before he hit the ground. I was glad we'd told his folks, glad Andy had sent that beautiful letter, eulogy for us all. And then the ice went still.

I lay a moment, hardly noticing the tangle we were in, my whole being focused on that silence. Quiet, quiet, like the final moment in free fall, the last timeless instant before the bottom. But it stretched on, and on, and finally we all picked ourselves up, still unable to believe we were alive. "Jesus," Del said, and I had to laugh.

We went on, me in the middle this time because of my limp, with Andy bringing up the rear. Tossed around as we had been, none of us was sure of our directions, and because of the berg's motion GPS and compass were both useless. Blown snow and fog-ice erased our footprints as well as Miguel's. In the end all we could do was follow the line of flags in the direction of our best guess and resolve that if it led us back to camp, we would turn and head straight back out again. I was feeling Miguel's absence very much by then, so much so that a fourth figure haunted the edges of my vision, teasing me with false presence. But maybe that was Cutter, not Miguel.

Flags lay scattered among huge tilted slabs of packed snow. We replanted the slender poles as best we could, and by this time I was starting to hope we *had* been turned around and were heading back to camp. If the berg-quake had scattered the whole line of flags they were likely to be buried by the time we turned around, and if they were, we were screwed. But we couldn't do anything but what we were already doing. We clambered through the broken ice field, hampered by the rope between us and already tired from the wind. Del got impatient and Andy snapped that she was doing the best she could. "You're fine," I said. "Del, ease off." He went silent. We re-roped and I took point, limp and all.

Spires of ice rose like jagged minarets above the broken terrain. Great pillars, crystalline arches, thin translucent walls. Scrambling with my eyes always on the next flag, I took the ice structures for figments of the whiteout at first, but then we were in among them and the wind died into fitful gusts. The line of flags ended, irredeemably scattered, unless this was its proper end and the former crevasse was utterly transformed. It was beautiful. Even exhausted and afraid I could see that, and while Andy shouted for Miguel and Del hunkered over our packs digging out the camp stove and food, I pulled out my camera.

[Digital clarity is blurred by swirling fog. Yet the images are unmistakable, real.]

Crystalline structures defy any sense of scale. This could be a close-up of the ice-spray caught at the edge of a frozen stream, strands and whorls of ice delicate as sugar tracery, until the videographer turns and gets a human figure into the frame. The man in red bends prosaically over a steaming pot, apparently oblivious to the white fantasia rising up all around him. The mic picks up the sound of a woman's voice hoarsely shouting, and the camera turns to her, a tall green figure holding an orange flag, garish among all the white and blue and glass. *Andy*, says the videographer. *Hush a minute, listen for an answer.*

The human sounds die, there's nothing but the many voices of the wind singing through the spires. A long slow pan then: pillars, walls, streets—it's impossible not to think of them that way. A city in the ice. An inhuman city in the ice.

Movement.

The camera jerks, holds still. There's a long, slow zoom, as though it's the videographer rather than the lens that glides down the tilt-floored icy avenue. [The static fog drifting, obscuring the distant view.] Maybe that's all the movement is, sea-fog and wind swirled about by the sharp, strange lines of the ice-structures. [The wind singing in the mic, glass-toned, dissonant.] But no. No. It's *clarity* that swirls like a current of air—like a many-limbed being with a watery skin—gliding gravity-less between the walls, in and out of view. [Pause. Go back. Yes. A shape of air. Zoom. A translucent eye. Zoom. A vast staring eye.]

The camera lurches. The image dives to the snow-shoe-printed ground. The videographer's clothing rustles against the mic, almost drowning her hoarse whisper. *We have to get out of here. Guys! We need to—*

We roped Miguel between Del and me, with Andy again bringing up the rear. It was an endless hike, the footing lousy, the visibility bad, all of us hungry and aching for a rest. Del tried to insist that we eat the instant stew he'd heated before we left, but I was seeing transparent squids down every street, and when Miguel stumbled out of the ice, crooning wordlessly to the wind even as he clutched at Andy's hands, Del let himself be outvoted. "This is how climbers die," he said to me, but I said to him, "If you're on an avalanche slope you move as fast and as quietly as you can, no matter how hungry or tired you are." Death is here: I wanted to say it, and didn't, and while I hesitated the silence filled with the glass-harmonica singing of the wind—with Miguel's high crooning, which was the same, the very same. So I didn't need to say it. We followed the broken line of scattered flags back to camp.

And now I sit here typing while the others sleep (Miguel knocked out by pills), and I look up and see what I should have seen the instant we staggered in the door. All of our gear, so meticulously sorted by Miguel, is disarranged. Not badly—we surely would have noticed if shelves were cleared and boxes emptied on the floor—but neat stacks and rows have become clusters and piles, chairs pushed into the table are pulled askew, my still camera and its cables are out of its bag my hands are shaking as I type this there's a draft the door is closed the windows weatherproofed I'm pretending I don't notice but there's a draft moving behind me through the room

• • •

November 25:

I took my ax to the tent where we still kept the ice-shape Del and I brought up from the bottom of the crevasse. I was past exhaustion, spooked, halfway crazy. It was just a lump of ice. I took my ax to it, expecting it to bleed seawater, rise up in violent motion, fill the tent with its swirling arms. I swung again and again, flailing behind me once when paranoia filled the tent with invisible things. Ice chipped, shattered. Shards stung my wind-burned face. The noise woke Del in our hut nearby. He came and stopped me. There was no shape left, just a scarred hunk of ice. Del took the ax out of my hand and led me away, gave me a pill to let me sleep like Cutter. I mean, like Miguel. I'm still doped. Tired. I can feel them out there in the wind.

The relay tower is singing outside.

November 27:

The ice is always shaking now. New spires lean above our snow wall, mocking our defenses. Miguel cries and shouts words we can't understand, words so hard to say they make him drool and choke on his tongue. The wind sings back whenever he calls. The sat phone has given nothing but static until today when it, too, sang, making Del throw the handset to the floor. The radio only howls static. The fog reeks of dead fish, algae, the sea. Everything is rimed in salt ice. Andy hovers over Miguel, trying to make him take another pill: Del threatened him with violence if he doesn't shut up. I grabbed Del, dragged him to a chair, hugged him until he gave in and pulled me to his lap. We're here now, all four of us together. None of us can bear to be alone.

November 28:

A new crevasse opened in the camp today, swallowing two tents and making a shambles of the snow wall. Is this an attack? Our eviction notice, Andy says, humor her badge of courage. But I wonder if they even notice us, if they even care. Atlantis is theirs now, and I suppose it always has been, through all those long cold ages at the heart of the southern pole. Now the earth is warming, the ancient ice is freed to move north, to melt—and then what? What of this ice city growing all around us like a crystal lab-grown from a seed? If the clues they've given us (deliberately? I do wonder) are true, then they are beings of water as much as of ice. It won't happen quickly, but eventually, as the berg travels north out of the Southern Ocean and into the Atlantic or Pacific, it will all melt. Releasing . . . what? . . . into the warming seas of our world. Our world *is* an ocean world, our over-burdened continents merely islands in the vast waters of misnamed Earth. What will become of us when they have reclaimed *their* world?

Del and Andy, in between increasingly desperate attempts to bring our sailor Miguel back from whatever alien mindscape he's lost in, are concocting a scheme to get our inflatable lifeboat, included in our gear almost as a joke, down the ice cliffs to the water. Away from here, they reason, we should be able to make the sat phone work, light the radio beacon, call in a rescue. I have a fantasy—or did I dream it last night?—that the singing that surrounds us, stranger than the songs of seals or whales, has reached into orbit, filling satellite antenna-dishes the way it fills my ears, drowning human communication. I imagine that the first careless assault on human civilization has already begun, and that the powers—the human powers—of Earth are looking outward in terror, imagining an attack from the stars, never dreaming that it is already here, has always been here, now waking from its ice-bound slumber. It is we who have warmed the planet; we, perhaps, who have brought this upon ourselves. But brought what, I wonder? And when Andy appeals to me to help her and Del with their escape plan, I find I have nothing much to say. But I suppose I will have to say it before long: why should we leave—*should* we leave—just when things are getting interesting?

Get beyond it, I'll have to tell them, as I did when Cutter died. We have to look beyond.

In the meantime, though, I'll make a couple of backups, downloading this log and my video files onto flash drives that will fit into a waterproof container. My message in a bottle. Just in case.

My memories are very confused. . . . These cycles of experience, of course, all stem from that worm-riddled book. I remember when I found it . . . it fell open toward the end and gave me a glimpse of something which sent my senses reeling . . .

"The Book" · H.P. Lovecraft
(unfinished story, first published posthumously 1938)

· THE GREAT WHITE BED ·
Don Webb

I wanted to write about the bed because I thought it would be therapeutic. For pretty obvious reasons I never got over that summer, and I know there's a mental part to go along with the physical part. I don't write about the book. And see, I'm already there. I can't make myself think about what I need to think about. The room. The bedroom. I can start with that. It smelled of geraniums. My grandmother had loved them and it had become my job to keep them alive after she died. She grew them in coffee cans, and when they got too root-bound she would put them in plastic buckets that she got working at the cleaners. Clay pots were an extravagance. There were five of the big light blue buckets on a special shelf built across the windows in the bedroom, so the bedroom always had a green smell.

It was hot too. There were two swamp coolers that cooled the house down. One in the living room at the front of the house, one in the den in the back. Neither supplied much cool air to the place where I slept. I remember the first thing that Grandpa had asked when I moved in with him that summer was if I wanted to sleep with him. I thought that was creepy and I said I'd sleep in the guest bedroom, where Granny did her sewing. It was so hot that I never turned down the big white thick bedspread on the bed and lay on the sheets. I just lay on top of it. I didn't want anything over my body. At home I slept on a twin bed; the king size bed seemed the biggest thing in the world to me.

I was thirteen. Next year would be junior high.

I helped Grandpa out. I cooked his meals, did his laundry, cut the grass. In retrospect it was a big job for someone my age, but I came from a family of workers. I didn't do a good job with the laundry and my food repertoire relied heavily on Spam baked in the oven covered with ketchup.

My friends were rich kids, mainly in camp or hanging out at the private swimming pool. These days I know they weren't rich, but they seemed rich to me. I amused myself with TV, watching old black and white comedies in syndication. I remember that summer had a good dose of *The Dick Van Dyke Show* mixed up with the strangeness. Cable TV was new to Doublesign that year. We got twenty-eight stations. Grandpa would get up early and wake me up. He had been a farmer, before they moved to town. Kids are not supposed to see the dawn in summer, no matter what anyone says. He liked cereal for breakfast. He really liked one called *Team*, I don't think they make it anymore. He would make coffee and I would pour the cereal. Afterward he would go off to read the paper and I would do the dishes. If I had any yard work to do I would do it in the mornings before it got too hot. I trimmed the hedge, cut the grass, weeded out the dandelions. Early on I had tried to keep a little garden going. I had planted some tomatoes and cucumbers. But one day Grandpa weeded them all out of the bed where I had planted them. His mind was going, but no one in the family would say so. When I tried to stop him he hit me with his cane and said I was stupid. Like I say, even without the weirdness, it was a big job.

Noon would come around and Mom would join us for lunch, which I had made. She worked downtown, a mysterious place full of much activity. She would eat my ketchup-covered Spam and canned green beans and visit with her dad. Sometimes he would ask her things like "How come I haven't seen you in a month?" even though she came every day. In the afternoons he would forget that we had eaten lunch and ask me when the hell I was going to fix it. He took a nap about three, and I know this will sound strange, but I started napping too. Summer was long and boring and it was easy to doze off. I would lay down in the green smell on the huge white bed and snooze.

School had been out about three weeks, when I woke one day to seeing Grandpa reading the book. I always took shorter naps than him so I was startled he was up. I went in the living room. He sat in his rocking chair and even though the light streaming in through the picture window lighted the room, he had Grandmother's prize lamp turned on. I loved that lamp. It had two globes, one above and one below. Someone had painted a rose on each globe. I wonder who has it now.

The book was small and thick—about the size of a Stephen King paperback. It was bound in gold-colored leather, and had a green nine-angled design on its cover. I don't want to say more about it. I didn't mean to say that much.

Grandpa was totally absorbed, his lips moving slowly. I had only seen him with a few *Reader's Digests* over the years. His concentration had been slipping so much since Granny died I didn't know how he could be reading. I guessed he probably wasn't. Just distracting himself. I was always in favor of his distractions. He didn't get mad at me and I didn't have to think up things to talk about. It was a lot easier cutting his lawn than coming up with discussion topics.

I made macaroni and cheese plus canned yams for dinner. I didn't disturb him until I had food on his plate. He came in, we said our prayers, and afterward we watched the six o'clock news. We watched TV together every night. He would fall asleep about eight. I would get him up and tell him to undress about ten.

The next day I had a pleasant surprise. Sunlight woke me, not Grandpa. I got up, pulled on my clothes, and found him reading again.

"Hey, you ready for breakfast?" I asked.

"You bet," he said.

His eyes had the shine they used to have when I was a little kid. He got up out of his chair and told me, "You know, I think you're old enough to have coffee now."

He put a great deal of sugar and milk in my coffee. I loved it and I still do. We ate our cereal in our usual crunchy silence, until curiosity got the better of me.

"What's that book you're reading?"

He looked at me as though I had said something very strange, like, "Are we going to the moon this afternoon?" He said, "I'm not reading anything."

"Not now. I meant just before breakfast."

"I wasn't reading anything."

The light went out of his eyes just as though someone had hit the switch.

I did the dishes and went off to watch *I Married Joan*. The TV was in the den. After laughing at Joan Davis's antics for a quarter of an hour or so, I went to the front of the house and spied on Grandpa. He was reading. He seemed about halfway through the book. I cleared my throat. He didn't look up. "I'm going down to the park," I said. He didn't look up. I went back to watching TV. Maybe his senility had entered a new peaceful stage.

When Mom came that day, Grandpa was talkative and cheerful. He told Mom what a great job I did with the lawn, how much he liked my food, his opinion of the mayor and otherwise talked like an adult human being. I didn't know what had happened, but I thought it was the greatest thing ever!

Mom gave me some money so that I could walk down to the Ice Palace and buy cones for Grandpa and myself later that day. I knew she was happy. She had been through so much grief watching her dad rot, and she thought that maybe, just maybe this time, God had listened to our prayers. I thought it was my cooking. Okay, I really didn't think that. I thought it was the book.

It was on the walk down to the Ice Palace that greed filled my soul. What if really and truly the book was making Grandpa well again? If it could fix up his tore-up mind, what might it do for mine? I mean, my mind was good; I made As in math and English, and I could always outsmart people in game shows. I would get the book. Not take it from Grandpa, because I didn't want to stop his miracle, but read sometime when he was asleep and get my own benefit. I would begin junior high as a genius!

The first logical time would be afternoon nap. I watched the old Seth Thomas clock on the living room mantel with X-ray eyes. Grandpa read. It became three.

"Don't you want to take your nap?" I asked.

I had to repeat myself a couple of times before he looked up.

"I'm giving up naps in the afternoon," he said. "I think I've slept enough in my long life. But I bet you sure are sleepy."

The moment he said it, all I could think of was sleep. The great white bed filled my mind. Big and solid and soft. It seemed huge and inviting. The bed was in my head and I needed to be in the bed. I started to speak, but I just yawned. I got control of myself and said, "A nap does sound good."

I went to the bedroom and lay atop the thick white bedspread. Usually I had to lie still for a long while, staring at the round glass light fixture that Granny had put in. I would watch the center brass nut and focus on it while my thoughts drained away into the milky white glass around it. But today sleep came the moment I lay on the pillow. I slept until Grandpa woke me.

"Get up," he said. "I've made supper."

I couldn't figure out what had happened. My brain was all logy. I drifted into the kitchen, where the small brown dining table was. He had made dinner. Fish sticks and lima beans. He had poured milk for both of us. We prayed and ate.

"I thought it would be nice to make dinner for you. You're always making it for me."

"This is nice," I said. I hated lima beans. Still do.

"I've been thinking a lot about exchange lately. Too many things only go one way. You know what I mean?"

"I don't follow."

"Well it's like this. You do all this work for me and I don't do anything for you. That's supposed to be fair because I brought up your mother and her brothers. I bet that doesn't seem right sometimes, does it?"

I thought about being hit by the cane. I thought about not answering. But maybe this really was the time God was answering prayers.

"No sir, sometimes that does not seem fair."

"Or books. Do you ever think about books, Billy? We spend our whole lives reading them, but they never get a chance to read us. Would you like that, Billy, if a book read you sometime?"

"I don't know. I mean, I don't know what it would be like."

"Well you've heard the expression, 'He can read a man's character.' Haven't you?"

"Yes, but I don't really know what it means."

"Well, Billy, being read by a book is about the finest experience there is. Not everyone has it when they grow up, but maybe you will."

God wasn't answering prayers. He was crazy, but in a new way. I cleaned the table after dinner and we went to watch *The Carol Burnett Show*.

Sleep hit me hard again that night. I woke up to sounds from the living room. I don't know how long Grandpa had been talking. He was arguing. I couldn't make out the words, but it scared me. I didn't know what I was supposed to do if Grandpa went crazy by himself in the middle of the night. Finally I heard one statement clearly:

"No, I won't do it. It's not a fair exchange."

I got out of bed. I was wearing just my underwear, so I got dressed. I didn't want to confront Grandpa partially dressed. As I put my clothes on I heard him get up out of his rocker and make his way toward his bedroom. I lay back down on the bed. Even though Grandpa was pretty deaf, I didn't even dare breathe.

I would have bet a million bucks that I was not going to go back to sleep that night, but sure enough sleep hit me like a ton of bricks.

I felt the bed below me melt. I was sinking into half-melted vanilla ice cream, although it wasn't cold. As it passed my eyes, the scene lit up with a terrible whiteness. There was nothing but white, a great white blindness, a great white dark. I could feel myself pulled lower and lower. I couldn't struggle, couldn't swim. For a moment I wished I were one of my rich friends who was hanging out at the pool this summer. They would know what to do. They didn't have to take care of their goddamn grandfathers. The down-drift took forever, and it gave me time for a lot of thoughts and none of them were very good. Maybe I was in a children's story where bad thoughts made you sink.

Then suddenly it stopped. Although the non-landscape hadn't changed and all I could see was the thick whiteness; I felt something looking at me. Something big. I tried to analyze what it felt like. I mean, I had watched *Star*

Trek and *Night Gallery*. But I couldn't get any feelings for old or young, human or alien, alive or undead. All of those charts were two-dimensional schoolbook ideas and this was floating above the white page of the book about nine inches. I felt it wasn't going to get bored staring at me, and that scared me. It could look at me forever and not blink. For a brief while I wanted to see it, but then I was glad I couldn't.

Slowly I felt something congeal under me. I wasn't floating anymore. Then a tiny speck formed a few feet above my head. It turned out to be the brass nut in the center of the light fixture. I was staring at the white glass of the fixture. The sun was up. I could hear Grandpa making coffee. The bed was dank with sweat. My nightmare had soaked the thick bedspread. I was already dressed, so I went on into the kitchen.

"Good morning," I said to Grandpa.

He just looked at me with hatred. The light and life had gone out of his eyes. We didn't talk during breakfast. I mowed the lawn afterward even though it didn't need it. I just didn't want to be around him. I don't know if he read his book. Or if the book read him.

Lunch was worse. He was still not talking, and Mom was so upset to see him regress she actually broke down in tears. After lunch she went out to her car and just sat in it and cried.

I went out to comfort her. I was thirteen and it was the manly thing to do. She rolled down her window to talk to me.

"Mom, are you okay?" I asked. I know it was a dumb question.

"What happened, Billy? Did you do something to him?"

I couldn't believe her response. I knew she was upset, but I wasn't some kind of miracle worker, some kind of genie that could make Grandpa better or worse by blinking my eyes. I got really mad, so I turned away from her car and began running to the park. I knew she was late to work and didn't have time to follow me. She managed an office and everything depended on her. There were some cedar bushes in the park, about six feet tall. Underneath the green, make-out artists had hallowed and hollowed a space over the years. I dove into the cool dry dark to cry. I knew no one would be making out at twelve-thirty in the heat of the summer. I cried a long time. I messed up my clothes. Great—now I had laundry to do as well as the additional job of hating my mom and feeling guilty. I didn't give a damn about Grandpa at this moment.

I headed back to his house. This was going to end today. I would tell my mom and my uncle that I couldn't do this anymore. That I wanted some regular summer job like sweeping out a barber shop, which my friend Jerry had. I was going to tell things I had never told before, like the cane. I didn't think I would tell them about the book. That was probably Grandpa's craziness.

Sure enough, when I got back to his little brick house he was reading his book. He was almost to the end. I had been gone for nearly two hours. I hadn't cried that much since my grandmother died two years ago. I thought crying was supposed to purge you, make you feel better, but I felt all raw and sticky like parts of my soul had been through a blender and were hanging outside of my body. I didn't talk to the old man. I just went to bed.

To my initial relief the same magic that had brought sleep the last two times worked again. I was out like a light.

However, the world changed from a fabulous formless darkness to a great white thickness. I knew I was sinking into the world of the great white bed. The down-drift made me sick this time like a too-long downward ride in an elevator. Of course in those days growing up in Doublesign I had never even seen an elevator, but you can't enter a memory without carrying later memories in with you. Down, down, down.

It was an abrupt and unpleasant stop. I could hear my Grandpa saying something. It was a precise but muffled voice. The kind of voice you use giving a phone number. I began moving sideways. Slowly at first and then at a pretty good clip. Then the movement stopped again and I was lying next to someone.

I could move my head a little. It was Granny. She was dead and very, very white. I knew the great Whatever had been watching her for a couple of years, and had never got bored.

Then I felt the little knives.

Something was slicing through my feet. I couldn't raise my head enough to see it, but I could hear it and of course it hurt like hell. About an inch was being cut off. I didn't think I could stand it. Why didn't I wake up? Why didn't I black out?

Then after that section had been cut clean another cut started about an inch higher. I figured loss of blood or shock would get me. I kept telling myself it was just a nightmare, but that doesn't really help with that much pain.

Then another cut.

Then another.

And so slowly forth until my knees had been reached. All I was at this point was tears and pain.

Then a dark rope dropped down from above. I can't tell you what a relief it was to see something black in that great white space. It hit my face, snaking over my eyes and mouth, finally it touched my ears.

"Billy. Billy can you hear me?"

It was my uncle's voice. I woke up on the great white bed and then passed out from blood loss.

The rest of the summer and the fall and the winter and spring were physical therapy.

I had lost both of my legs up to my knees. This is not a euphemism. There was nothing there. There were no traces of my feet and lower legs anywhere in Grandpa's house.

But there were a set of feet and lower legs on his bed in his room. They were cold and embalmed and a couple of years old. They belonged to my grandmother.

I didn't find that out until just before my mother's death last year. It had been decided not to tell me everything, as though knowledge could make it any worse. There was no trace that my grandmother's grave had been disturbed in any way. They had dug up her coffin and put the legs in, burying it as well as any gossip with her. They put Grandpa in a mental ward afterward. Mom never went to see him again as long as he lived, but that turned out to be only three months anyway. When Mom got cancer she decided to tell me everything.

My uncle had dropped by that day because Mom had called him. She felt bad about what she had said to me. She couldn't leave her office, but her brother got off early. Mom told me that she felt guilty about what had happened to me every day of her life.

I live in a special home for people with mental and physical disabilities. When she was alive, Mom would come see me every day at noon. We always ate together just like she used to eat with her father. About two months before she died she got too sick to come, but they took me to see her in the hospital a couple of times, that was when she told about Granny's legs and so on.

I read and watch TV a lot. It hasn't gotten better in the last forty years, I can tell you that. I am kept here because I can't give an explanation of what happened to me that makes sense to anyone. I didn't get to finish school and I regret that. So I hobble around on my two fake legs. I even keep a little garden. Just flowers, no tomatoes this time. I never learned that internet thing either; they don't like us looking things up. The only thing that some people would find odd about me is that I won't sleep on white sheets or have a white blanket or a white bedspread.

Mom told me that she searched every inch of Grandpa's house for the book. She told me that she never believed my story fully, but knew it had to have some truth. She didn't find the book. Maybe Grandpa found it at the park or bought it in a garage sale. I tried researching occult matters once, but the people running the home thought it was a bad idea for me. One time I had a dream, about ten years ago, of Grandpa lifting the thick white bedspread and looking under the bed for something and just finding the book. That still doesn't answer the question of where it came from.

Sometimes in my dreams I smell geraniums and find myself in the great white space. I can't scream in my dreams and I've never woken up my roommate with any odd sounds. I don't tell my doctor about it, as it seems to upset her. But the dreams are rare. I think they're really not dreams at all, I think it's just how things are. I think the great Whatever is always watching us.

And It's never bored.

—For Basil Copper

· LESSER DEMONS ·
Norman Partridge

Down in the cemetery, the children were laughing.

They had another box open.

They had their axes out. Their knives, too.

I sat in the sheriff's department pickup, parked beneath a willow tree. Ropes of leaves hung before me like green curtains, but those curtains didn't stop the laughter. It climbed the ridge from the hollow below, carrying other noises—shovels biting hard-packed earth, axe blades splitting coffinwood, knives scraping flesh from bone. But the laughter was the worst of it. It spilled over teeth sharpened with files, chewed its way up the ridge, and did its best to strip the hard bark off my spine.

I didn't sit still. I grabbed a gas can from the back of the pickup. I jacked a full clip into my dead deputy's .45, slipped a couple spares into one of the leather pockets on my gun belt and buttoned it down. Then I fed shells into my shotgun and pumped one into the chamber.

I went for a little walk.

Five months before, I stood with my deputy, Roy Barnes, out on County Road 14. We weren't alone. There were others present. Most of them were dead, or something close to it.

I held that same shotgun in my hand. The barrel was hot. The deputy clutched his .45, a ribbon of bitter smoke coiling from the business end. It wasn't a stink you'd breathe if you had a choice, but we didn't have one.

Barnes reloaded, and so did I. The June sun was dropping behind the trees, but the shafts of late-afternoon light slanting through the gaps were as bright as high noon. The light played through black smoke rising from a Chrysler sedan's smoldering engine and white smoke simmering from the hot asphalt piled in the road gang's dump truck.

My gaze settled on the wrecked Chrysler. The deal must have started there. Fifteen or twenty minutes before, the big black car had piled into an old oak at a fork in the county road. Maybe the driver had nodded off, waking just in time to miss a flagman from the work gang. Over-corrected and hit the brakes too late. Said: *Hello tree, goodbye heartbeat.*

Maybe that was the way it happened. Maybe not. Barnes tried to piece it together later on, but in the end it really didn't matter much. What mattered was that the sedan was driven by a man who looked like something dredged up from the bottom of a stagnant pond. What mattered was that something exploded from the Chrysler's trunk after the accident. That thing was the size of a grizzly, but it wasn't a bear. It didn't look like a bear at all. Not unless you'd ever seen one turned inside out, it didn't.

Whatever it was, that skinned monster could move. It unhinged its sizable jaws and swallowed a man who weighed two-hundred-and-change in one long ratcheting gulp, choking arms and legs and torso down a gullet lined with razor teeth. Sucked the guy into a blue-veined belly that hung from its ribs like a grave-robber's sack and then dragged that belly along fresh asphalt as it chased down the other men, slapping them onto the scorching roadbed and spitting bloody hunks of dead flesh in their faces. Some it let go, slaughtering others like so many chickens tossed live and squawking onto a hot skillet.

It killed four men before we showed up, fresh from handling a fender-bender on the detour route a couple miles up the road. Thanks to my shotgun and Roy Barnes' .45, allthat remained of the thing was a red mess with a corpse spilling out of its gutshot belly. As for the men from the work crew, there wasn't much you could say. They were either as dead as that poor bastard who'd ended his life in a monster's stomach, or they were whimpering with blood on their faces, or they were running like hell and halfway back to town. But whatever they were doing didn't make too much difference to me just then.

"What was it, Sheriff?" Barnes asked.

"I don't know."

"You sure it's dead?"

"I don't know that, either. All I know is we'd better stay away from it."

We backed off. The only things that lingered were the afternoon light slanting through the trees, and the smoke from that hot asphalt, and the smoke from the wrecked Chrysler. The light cut swirls through that smoke as it pooled around the dead thing, settling low and misty, as if the something beneath it were trying to swallow a chunk of the world, roadbed and all.

"I feel kind of dizzy," Barnes said.

"Hold on, Roy. You have to."

I grabbed my deputy by the shoulder and spun him around. He was just a kid, really—before this deal, he'd never even had his gun out of its holster while on duty. I'd been doing the job for fifteen years, but I could have clocked a hundred and never seen anything like this. Still, we both knew it wasn't over. We'd seen what we'd seen, we'd done what we'd done, and the only thing left to do was deal with whatever was coming next.

That meant checking out the Chrysler. I brought the shotgun barrel even with it, aiming at the driver's side door as we advanced. The driver's skull had slammed the steering wheel at the point of impact. Black blood smeared across his face, and filed teeth had slashed through his pale lips so that they hung from his gums like leavings you'd bury after gutting a fish. On top of that, words were carved on his face. Some were purpled over with scar tissue and others were still fresh scabs. None of them were words I'd seen before. I didn't know what to make of them.

"Jesus," Barnes said. "Will you look at that."

"Check the back seat, Roy."

Barnes did. There was other stuff there. Torn clothes. Several pairs of handcuffs. Ropes woven with fishhooks. A wrought-iron trident. And in the middle of all that was a cardboard box filled with books.

The deputy pulled one out. It was old. Leathery. As he opened it, the book started to come apart in his hands. Brittle pages fluttered across the road—

Something rustled in the open trunk. I pushed past Roy and fired point blank before I even looked. The spare tire exploded. On the other side of the trunk, a clawed hand scrabbled up through a pile of shotgunned clothes. I fired again. Those claws clacked together, and the thing beneath them didn't move again.

Using the shotgun barrel, I shifted the clothes to one side, uncovering a couple of dead kids in a nest of rags and blood. Both of them were handcuffed. The thing I'd killed had chewed its way out of one of their bellies. It had a grinning, wolfish muzzle and a tail like a dozen braided snakes. I slammed the trunk and chambered another shell. I stared down at the trunk, waiting for something else to happen, but nothing did.

Behind me . . . well, that was another story.

The men from the road gang were on the move.

Their boots scuffed over hot asphalt.

They gripped crow bars, and sledge hammers, and one of them even had a machete.

They came towards us with blood on their faces, laughing like children.

The children in the cemetery weren't laughing anymore. They were gathered around an open grave, eating.

Like always, a couple seconds passed before they noticed me. Then their brains sparked their bodies into motion, and the first one started for me with an axe. I pulled the trigger, and the shotgun turned his spine to jelly, and he went down in sections. The next one I took at longer range, so the blast chewed her over some. Dark blood from a hundred small wounds peppered her dress. Shrieking, she turned tail and ran.

Which gave the third bloodface a chance to charge me. He was faster than I expected, dodging the first blast, quickly closing the distance. There was barely enough room between the two of us for me to get off another shot, but I managed the job. The blast took off his head. That was that.

Or at least I thought it was. Behind me, something whispered through long grass that hadn't been cut in five months. I whirled, but the barefoot girl's knife was already coming at me. The blade ripped through my coat in a silver blur, slashing my right forearm. A twist of her wrist and she tried to come back for another piece, but I was faster and bashed her forehead with the shotgun butt. Her skull split like a popped blister and she went down hard, cracking the back of her head on a tombstone.

That double-punched her ticket. I sucked a deep breath and held it. Blood reddened the sleeve of my coat as the knife wound began to pump. A couple seconds later I began to think straight, and I got the idea going in my head that I should put down the shotgun and get my belt around my arm. I did that and tightened it good. Wounded, I'd have a walk to get back to the pickup. Then I'd have to find somewhere safe where I could take care of my arm. The pickup wasn't far distance-wise, but it was a steep climb up to the ridgeline. My heart would be pounding double-time the whole way. If I didn't watch it, I'd lose a lot of blood.

But first I had a job to finish. I grabbed the shotgun and moved toward the rifled grave. Even in the bright afternoon sun, the long grass was still damp with morning dew. I noticed that my boots were wet as I stepped over the dead girl. That bothered me, but the girl's corpse didn't. She couldn't bother me now that she was dead.

I left her behind me in the long grass, her body a home for the scarred words she'd carved on her face with the same knife she'd used to butcher the dead and butcher me. All that remained of her was a barbed rictus grin and a pair of dead eyes staring up into the afternoon sun, as if staring at nothing at all. And that's what she was to me—that's what they all were now that they were dead. They were nothing, no matter what they'd done to themselves with knives and files, no matter what they'd done to the living they'd murdered or the dead they'd pried out of burying boxes. They were nothing at all, and I didn't spare them another thought.

Because there were other things to worry about—things like the one that had infected the children with a mouthful of spit-up blood. Sometimes those things came out of graves. Other times they came out of car trunks or meat lockers or off slabs in a morgue. But wherever they came from they were always born of a corpse, and there were corpses here aplenty.

I didn't see anything worrisome down in the open grave. Just stripped bones and tatters of red meat, but it was meat that wasn't moving. That was good. So I took care of things. I rolled the dead bloodfaces into the grave. I walked back to the cottonwood thicket at the ridge side of the cemetery and grabbed the gas can I'd brought from the pickup. I emptied it into the hole, then tossed the can in, too. I wasn't carrying it back to the truck with a sliced-up arm.

I lit a match and let it fall.

The gas *thupped* alive and the hole growled fire.

Fat sizzled as I turned my back on the grave. Already, other sounds were rising in the hollow. Thick, rasping roars. Branches breaking somewhere in the treeline behind the old funeral home. The sound of something big moving through the timber—something that heard my shotgun bark three times and wasn't afraid of the sound.

Whatever that thing was, I didn't want to see it just now.

I disappeared into the cottonwood thicket before it saw me.

Barnes had lived in a converted hunting lodge on the far side of the lake. There weren't any other houses around it, and I hadn't been near the place in months. I'd left some stuff there, including medical supplies we'd scavenged from the local emergency room. If I was lucky, they would still be there.

Thick weeds bristled over the dirt road that led down to Roy's place. That meant no one had been around for a while. Of course, driving down the road would leave a trail, but I didn't have much choice. I'd been cut and needed to do something about it fast. You take chances. Some are large and some are small. Usually, the worries attached to the small ones amount to nothing.

I turned off the pavement. The dirt road was rutted, and I took it easy. My arm ached every time the truck hit a pothole. Finally, I parked under the carport on the east side of the old lodge. Porch steps groaned as I made my way to the door, and I entered behind the squared-off barrel of Barnes' .45.

Inside, nothing was much different than it had been a couple of months before. Barnes' blood-spattered coat hung on a hook by the door. His reading glasses rested on the coffee table. Next to it, a layer of mold floated on top of a cup of coffee he'd never finished. But I didn't care about any of that. I cared about the cabinet we'd stowed in the bathroom down the hall.

Good news. Nothing in the cabinet had been touched. I stripped to the waist, cleaned the knife wound with saline solution from an IV bag, then stopped the bleeding as best I could. The gash wasn't as deep as it might have been. I sewed it up with a hooked surgical needle, bandaged it, and gobbled down twice as many antibiotics as any doctor would have prescribed. That done, I remembered my wet boots. Sitting there on the toilet, I laughed at myself a little bit, because given the circumstances it seemed like a silly thing to worry about. Still, I went to the first-floor bedroom I'd used during the summer and changed into a dry pair of Wolverines I'd left behind.

Next I went to the kitchen. I popped the top on a can of chili, found a spoon, and started towards the old dock down by the lake. There was a rusty swing set behind the lodge that had been put up by a previous owner; it shadowed a kid's sandbox. Barnes hadn't had use for either—he wasn't even married—but he'd never bothered to change things around. Why would he? It would have been a lot of work for no good reason.

I stopped and stared at the shadows beneath the swing set, but I didn't stare long. The dock was narrow and more than a little rickety, with a small boathouse bordering one side. I walked past the boathouse and sat on the end of the dock for a while. I ate cold chili. Cattails whispered beneath a rising breeze. A flock of geese passed overhead, heading south. The sun set, and twilight settled in.

It was quiet. I liked it that way. With Barnes, it was seldom quiet. I guess you'd say he had a curious mind. The deputy liked to talk about things, especially things he didn't understand, like those monsters that crawled out of corpses. Barnes called them lesser demons. He'd read about them in one of those books we found in the wreck. He had ideas about them, too. Barnes talked about those ideas a lot over the summer, but I didn't want to talk about any of it. Talking just made me edgy. So did Barnes' ideas and explanations . . . all those *maybe's* and *what if 's*. Barnes was big on those; he'd go on and on about them.

Me, I cared about simpler things. Things anyone could understand. Things you didn't need to discuss, or debate. Like waking up before a razor-throated monster had a chance to swallow me whole. Or not running out of shotgun shells. Or making sure one of those things never spit a dead man's blood in my face, so I wouldn't take a file to my teeth or go digging in a graveyard for food. That's what I'd cared about that summer, and I cared about the same things in the hours after a bloodfaced lunatic carved me up with a dirty knife.

I finished the chili. It was getting dark. Getting cold, too, because winter was coming on. I tossed the empty can in the lake and turned back toward the house. The last purple smear of twilight silhouetted the place, and a pair of birds darted into the chimney as I walked up the dock. I wouldn't have seen them if I hadn't looked at that exact moment, and I shook my head. Birds building nests in October? It was just another sign of a world gone nuts.

Inside, I settled on the couch and thought about lighting a fire. I didn't care about the birds—nesting in that chimney was their own bad luck. I'd got myself a chill out at the dock, and there was a cord of oak stacked under the carport. Twenty minutes and I could have a good blaze going. But I was tired, and my arm throbbed like it had grown its own heartbeat. I didn't want to tear the stitches toting a bunch of wood. I just wanted to sleep.

I took some painkillers—more than I should have—and washed them down with Jack Daniel's. After a while, the darkness pulled in close. The bedroom I'd used the summer before was on the ground floor. But I didn't want to be downstairs in case anything came around during the night, especially with a cool liquid fog pumping through my veins. I knew I'd be safer upstairs.

There was only one room upstairs—a big room, kind of like a loft.

It was Barnes' bedroom, and his blood was still on the wall.

I didn't care. I grabbed my shotgun. I climbed the stairs.

Like I said: I was tired.

Besides, I couldn't see Barnes' blood in the dark.

At first, Roy and I stuck to the sheriff's office, which was new enough to have pretty good security. When communication stopped and the whole world took a header, we decided that wasn't a good idea anymore. We started moving around.

My place wasn't an option. It was smack dab in the middle of town. You didn't want to be in town. There were too many blind corners, and too many fences you couldn't see over. Dig in there, and you'd never feel safe no how many bullets you had in your clip. So I burned down the house. It never meant much to me, anyway. It was just a house, and I burned it down mostly because it was mine and I didn't want anyone else rooting around in the stuff I kept there. I never went back after that.

Barnes' place was off the beaten path. Like I said, that made it a good choice. I knew I could get some sleep there. Not too much, if you know what I mean. Every board in the old lodge seemed to creak, and the brush was heavy around the property. If you were a light sleeper—like me—you'd most likely hear anything that was coming your way long before it had a chance to get you.

And I heard every noise that night in Barnes' bedroom. I didn't sleep well at all. Maybe it was my sliced-up arm or those painkillers mixing with the whiskey and antibiotics—but I tossed and turned for hours. The window was open a crack, and cold air cut through the gap like that barefooted girl's knife. And it seemed I heard another knife scraping somewhere deep in the house, but it must have been those birds in the chimney, scrabbling around in their nest.

Outside, the chained seats on the swing set squealed and squeaked in the wind. Empty, they swung back and forth, back and forth, over cool white sand.

After a couple months, Barnes wasn't doing so well. We'd scavenged a few of the larger summer houses on the other side of the lake, places that belonged to rich couples from down south. We'd even made a few trips into town when things seemed especially quiet. We'd gotten things to the point where we had everything we needed at the lodge. If something came around that needed killing, we killed it. Otherwise, we steered clear of the world.

But Barnes couldn't stop talking about those books he'd snatched from the wrecked Chrysler. He read the damned things every day. Somehow, he thought they had all the answers. I didn't know about that. If there were answers in those books, you'd have one hell of a time pronouncing them. I knew that much.

That wasn't a problem for Barnes. He read those books cover to cover, making notes about those lesser demons, consulting dictionaries and reference books he'd swiped from the library. When he finished, he read them again. After a while, I couldn't stand to look at him sitting there with those reading glasses on his face. I even got sick of the smell of his coffee. So I tried to keep busy. I'd do little things around the lodge, but none of them amounted to much. I chainsawed several oak trees and split the wood. Stacking it near the edge of the property to season would also give us some cover if we ever needed to defend the perimeter, so I did that, too. I even set some traps on the other side of the lodge, but after a while I got sloppy and began to forget where they were. Usually, that happened when I was thinking about something else while I was trying to work. Like Barnes' *maybes* and *what ifs*.

Sometimes I'd get jumpy. I'd hear noises while I was working. Or I'd think I did. I'd start looking for things that weren't there. Sometimes I'd even imagine something so clearly I could almost see it. I knew that was dangerous . . . and maybe a little crazy. So I found something else to do—something that would keep my mind from wandering.

I started going out alone during the day. Sometimes I'd run across a pack of bloodfaces. Sometimes one of those demons . . . or maybe two. You never saw more than two at a time. They never traveled in packs, and that was lucky for me. I doubted I could have handled more than a couple, and even handling two . . . well, that could be dicey.

But I did it on my own. And I didn't learn about the damn things by reading a book. I learned by reading them. Watching them operate when they didn't know I was there, hunting them down with the shotgun, blowing them apart. That's how I learned—reading tales written in muscle and blood, or told by a wind that carried bitter scent and shadows that fell where they shouldn't.

And you know what? I found out that those demons weren't so different. Not really. I didn't have to think it through much, because when you scratched off the paint and primer and got down to it those things had a spot in the food chain just like you and me. They took what they needed when they needed it, and they did their best to make sure anything below them didn't buck the line.

If there was anything above them—well, I hadn't seen it.

I hoped I never would.

I wouldn't waste time worrying about it until I did.

Come August, there were fewer of those things around. Maybe that meant the world was sorting itself out. Or maybe it just meant that in my little corner I was bucking that food chain hard enough to hacksaw a couple of links.

By that time I'd probably killed fifteen of them. Maybe twenty. During a late summer thunderstorm, I tracked a hoofed minotaur with centipede dreadlocks to an abandoned barn deep in the hollow. The damn thing surprised me, nearly ripping open my belly with its black horns before I managed to jam a pitchfork through its throat. There was a gigantic worm with a dozen sucking maws; I burned it down to cinders in the water-treatment plant. Beneath the high school football stadium, a couple rat-faced spiders with a web strung across a cement tunnel nearly caught me in their trap, but I left them dying there, gore oozing from their fat bellies drop by thick drop. The bugs had a half-dozen cocooned bloodfaces for company, all of them nearly sucked dry but still squirming in that web. They screamed like tortured prisoners when I turned my back and left them alive in the darkness.

Yeah. I did my part, all right.

I did my part, and then some.

Certain situations were harder to handle. Like when you ran into other survivors. They'd see you with a gun, and a pickup truck, and a full belly, and they'd want to know how you were pulling it off. They'd push you. Sometimes with questions, sometimes with pleas that were on the far side of desperate. I didn't like that. To tell you the truth, it made me feel kind of sick. As soon as they spit their words my way, I'd want to snatch them out of the air and jam them back in their mouths.

Sometimes they'd get the idea, and shut up, and move on. Sometimes they wouldn't. When that happened I had to do something about it. Choice didn't enter in to it. When someone pushed you, you had to push back. That was just the way the world worked—before demons and after.

One day in late September, Barnes climbed out of his easy chair and made a field trip to the wrecked Chrysler. He took those books with him. I was so shocked when he walked out the door that I didn't say a word.

I was kind of surprised when he made it back to the lodge at nightfall. He brought those damn books back with him, too. Then he worked on me for a whole week, trying to get me to go out there. He said he wanted to try something and he needed some backup. I felt like telling him I could have used some backup myself on the days I'd been out dealing with those things while he'd been sitting on his ass reading, but I didn't say it. Finally I gave in. I don't know why—maybe I figured going back to the beginning would help Barnes get straight with the way things really were.

There was no sun the day we made the trip, if you judged by what you could see. No sky either. Fog hung low over the lake, following the roads running through the hollow like they were dry rivers that needed filling. The pickup burrowed through the fog, tires whispering over wet asphalt, halogen beams cutting through all that dull white and filling pockets of darkness that waited in the trees.

I didn't see anything worrisome in those pockets, but the quiet that hung in the cab was another story. Barnes and I didn't talk. Usually that would have suited me just fine, but not that day. The silence threw me off, and my hands were sweaty on the steering wheel. I can't say why. I only know they stayed that way when we climbed out of the truck on County Road 14.

Nothing much had changed on that patch of road. Corpses still lay on the asphalt—the road gang, and the bear-thing that had swallowed one of them whole before we blew it apart. They'd been chewed over by buzzards and rats and other miserable creatures, and they'd baked guts-and-all onto the road during the summer heat. You would have had a hell of a time scraping them off the asphalt, because nothing that mattered had bothered with them once they were dead.

Barnes didn't care about them, either. He went straight to the old Chrysler and hauled the dead driver from behind the steering wheel. The corpse hit the road like a sack of kindling ready for the flame. It was a sight. Crows must have been at the driver's face, because his fishgut lips were gone. Those scarred words carved on his skin still rode his jerky flesh like wormy bits of gristle, but now they were chiseled with little holes, as if those crows had pecked punctuation.

Barnes grabbed Mr. Fishguts by his necktie and dragged him to the spot in the road where the white line should have been but wasn't.

"You ready?" he asked.

"For what?"

"If I've got it figured right, in a few minutes the universe is going to squat down and have itself a bite. It'll be one big chunk of the apple—starting with this thing, finishing with all those others."

"Those books say so?"

"Oh, yeah," Barnes said, "and a whole lot more."

That wasn't any kind of answer, but it put a cork in me. So I did what I was told. I stood guard. Mr. Fishguts lay curled up in that busted-up fetal position. Barnes drew a skinning knife from a leather scabbard on his belt and started cutting off the corpse's clothes. I couldn't imagine what the hell he was doing. A minute later, the driver's corpse was naked, razored teeth grinning up at us through his lipless mouth.

Barnes knelt down on that unmarked road. He started to read.

First from the book. Then from Mr. Fishguts' skin.

The words sounded like a garbage disposal running backward. I couldn't understand any of them. Barnes' voice started off quiet, just a whisper buried in the fog. Then it grew louder, and louder still. Finally he was barking words, and screaming them, and spitting like a hellfire preacher. You could have heard him a quarter mile away.

That got my heart pounding. I squinted into the fog, which was getting heavier. I couldn't see a damn thing. I couldn't even see those corpses glued to the road anymore. Just me and Barnes and Mr. Fishguts, there in a tight circle in the middle of County Road 14.

My heart went trip-hammer, those words thumping in time, the syllables pumping. I tried to calm down, tried to tell myself that the only thing throwing me off was the damn fog. I didn't know what was out there. One of those inside-out grizzlies could have been twenty feet away and I wouldn't have known it. A rat-faced spider could have been stilting along on eight legs, and I wouldn't have seen it until the damn thing was chewing off my face. That minotaur thing with the centipede dreadlocks could have charged me at a dead gallop and I wouldn't have heard its hooves on pavement . . . not with Barnes roaring. That was all I heard. His voice filled up the hollow with words written in books and words carved on a dead man's flesh, and standing there blind in that fog I felt like those words were the only things in a very small world, and for a split second I think I understood just how those cocooned bloodfaces felt while trapped in that rat-spider's web.

And then it was quiet. Barnes had finished reading.

"Wait a minute," he said. "Wait right here."

I did. The deputy walked over to the Chrysler, and I lost sight of him as he rummaged around in the car. His boots whispered over pavement and he was back again. Quickly, he knelt down, rearing back with both hands wrapped around the hilt of that wrought-iron trident we'd found in the car that very first day, burying it in the center of Mr. Fishguts' chest.

Scarred words shredded, and brittle bones caved in, and an awful stink escaped the corpse. I waited for something to happen. The corpse didn't move. I didn't know about anything else. There could have been anything out there, wrapped up in that fog. Anything, coming straight at us. Anything, right on top of us. We wouldn't have seen it all. I was standing there with a shotgun in my hands with no idea where to point it. I could have pointed it anywhere and it wouldn't have made me feel any better. I could have pulled the trigger a hundred times and it wouldn't have mattered. I might as well have tried to shotgun the fog, or the sky, or the whole damn universe.

It had to be the strangest moment of my life.

It lasted a good long time.

Twenty minutes later, the fog began to clear a little. A half hour later, it wasn't any worse than when we left the lodge. But nothing had happened in the meantime. That was the worst part. I couldn't stop waiting for it. I stood there, staring down at Mr. Fishguts' barbed grin, at the trident, at those words carved on the corpse's jerky flesh. I was still standing there when Barnes slammed the driver's door of the pickup. I hadn't even seen him move. I walked over and slipped in beside him, and he started back towards the lodge.

"Relax," he said finally. "It's all over."

That night it was quieter than it had been in a long time, but I couldn't sleep and neither could Barnes. We sat by the fire, waiting for something . . . or nothing. We barely talked at all. About four or five, we finally drifted off.

Around seven, a racket outside jarred me awake. Then there was a scream. I was up in a second. Shotgun in hand, I charged out of the house.

The fog had cleared overnight. I shielded my eyes and stared into the rising sun. A monster hovered over the beach—leathery wings laid over a jutting bone framework, skin clinging to its muscular body in a thin blistery layer, black veins slithering beneath that skin like stitches meant to mate a devil's muscle and flesh. The thing had a girl, her wrist trapped in one clawed talon. She screamed for help when she saw me coming, but the beast understood me better than she did. It grinned through a mouthful of teeth that jutted from its narrow jaws like nails driven by a drunken carpenter, and its gaze tracked the barrel of my gun, which was already swinging up in my grasp, the stock nestling tight against my shoulder as I took aim.

A sound like snapping sheets. A blast of downdraft from those red wings as the monster climbed a hunk of sky, wings spreading wider and driving down once more.

The motion sent the creature five feet higher in the air. The shotgun barrel followed, but not fast enough. Blistered lips stretched wide, and the creature screeched laughter at me like I was some kind of idiot. Quickly, I corrected my aim and fired.

The first shot was low and peppered the girl's naked legs. She screamed as I fired again, aiming higher this time. The thing's left wing wrenched in the socket as the shot found its mark, opening a pocket of holes large enough to strain sunlight. One more reflexive flap and that wing sent a message to the monster's brain. It screeched pain through its hammered mouth and let the girl go, bloody legs and all.

She fell fast. Her anguished scream told me she understood she was already dead, the same way she understood exactly who'd killed her.

She hit the beach hard. I barely heard the sound because the shotgun was louder. I fired twice more, and that monster fell out of the sky like a kite battered by a hurricane, and it twitched some when it hit, but not too much because I moved in fast and finished it from point-blank range.

Barnes came down to the water. He didn't say anything about the dead monster. He wanted to bury the girl, but I knew that wasn't a good idea. She might have one of those things inside her, or a pack of bloodfaces might catch her scent and come digging for her with a shovel. So we soaked her with gasoline instead, and we soaked the winged demon, too, and we tossed a match and burned down the both of them together.

After that, Barnes went back to the house.

He did the same thing to those books.

A few days later, I decided to check out the town. Things had been pretty quiet . . . so quiet that I was getting jumpy again.

They could have rolled up the streets, and it wouldn't have mattered. To tell the truth, there hadn't been too many folks in town to begin with, and now most of them were either dead or gone. I caught sight of a couple bloodfaces when I cruised the main street, but they vanished into a manhole before I got close.

I hit a market and grabbed some canned goods and other supplies, but my mind was wandering. I kept thinking about that day in the fog, and that winged harpy on the beach, and my deputy. Since burning those books, he'd barely left his room. I was beginning to think that the whole deal had done him some good. Maybe it was just taking some time for him to get used to the way things were. Mostly, I hoped he'd finally figured out what I'd known all along—that we'd learned everything we really needed to know about the way this world worked the day we blew apart the inside-out grizzly on County Road 14.

I figured that was the way it was, until I drove back to the house.

Until I heard screams down by the lake.

Barnes had one of the bloodfaces locked up in the boathouse. A woman no more than twenty. He'd stripped her and cuffed her wrists behind a support post. She jerked against the rough wood as Barnes slid the skinning knife across her ribs.

He peeled away a scarred patch of flesh that gleamed in the dusky light, but I didn't say a word. There were enough words in this room already. They were the same words I'd seen in those books, and they rode the crazy woman's skin. A couple dozen of them had been stripped from her body with Roy Barnes' skinning knife. With her own blood, he'd pasted each one to the boathouse wall.

I bit my tongue. I jacked a shell into the shotgun.

Barnes waved me off. "Not now, boss."

Planting the knife high in the post, he got closer to the girl. Close enough to whisper in her ear. With a red finger, he pointed at the bloody inscription he'd pasted to the wall. "*Read it,*" he said, but the woman only growled at him, snapping sharpened teeth so wildly that she shredded her own lips. But she didn't care about spilling her own blood. She probably didn't know she was doing it. She just licked her tattered lips and snapped some more, convinced she could take a hunk out of Barnes.

He didn't like that. He did some things to her, and her growls became screams.

"She'll come around," Barnes said.

"I don't think so, Roy."

"Yeah. She will—this time I figured things out."

"You said that when you read those books."

"But she's a book with a pulse. That's the difference. She's alive. That means she's got a connection—to those lesser demons, and to the things that lord it over them, too. Every one of them's some kind of key. But you can't unlock a gate with a bent-up key, even if it's the one that's supposed to fit. That's why things didn't work with the driver. After he piled up that Chrysler, he was a bent-up key. He lost his pulse. She's still got hers. If she reads the words instead of me—the words she wrote with a knife of her own—it'll all be different."

He'd approached me while he was talking, but I didn't look at him. I couldn't stand to. I looked at the bloodface instead. She screamed and spit. She wasn't even a woman anymore. She was just a naked, writhing thing that was going to end her days cuffed to a pole out here in the middle of nowhere. To think that she could spit a few words through tattered lips and change a world was crazy, as crazy as thinking that dead thing out on County Road 14 could do the job, as crazy as—

"Don't you understand, boss?"

"She digs up graves, Roy. She eats what she finds buried in them. That's all I need to understand."

"You're wrong. She knows—"

I raised the shotgun and blew off the bloodface's head, and then I put another load in her, and another. I blew everything off her skeleton that might have been a nest where a demon could grow. And when I was done with that little job I put a load in that wall, too, and all those scarred words went to hell in a spray of flesh and wood, and when they were gone they left a jagged window on the world outside.

Barnes stood there, the girl's blood all over his coat, the skinning knife gripped in his shaking hand.

I jacked another shell into the shotgun.

"I don't want to have this conversation again," I said.

After Barnes had gone, I unlocked the cuffs and got the bloodface down. I grabbed her by her hair and rolled her into the boat. Once the boathouse doors were opened, I yanked the outboard motor cord and was on my way.

I piloted the boat to the boggy section of the lake. Black trees rooted in the water, and Spanish moss hung in tatters from the branches. It was as good a place as any for a grave. I rolled the girl into the water, and she went under with a splash. I thought about Barnes, and the things he said, and those words on the wall. And I wished he could have seen the girl there, sinking in the murk. Yeah, I wished he could have seen that straight-on. Because this was the way the world worked, and the only change coming from this deal was that some catfish were going to eat good tonight.

The afternoon waned, and the evening light came on and faded. I sat there in the boat. I might have stayed until dark, but rain began to fall—at first gently, then hard enough to patter little divots in the calm surface of the lake. That was enough for me. I revved the outboard and headed back to the lodge.

Nothing bothered me along the way, and Roy didn't bother me once I came through the front door. He was upstairs in his room, and he was quiet . . . or trying to be.

But I heard him.

I heard him just fine.

Up there in his room, whispering those garbage-disposal words while he worked them into his own flesh with the skinning knife. That's what he was doing. I was sure of it. I heard his blood pattering on the floorboards the same way that rat-spiders' blood had pattered the cement floor in the football stadium. Sure it was raining outside, but I'd heard rain and I'd heard blood and I knew the difference.

Floorboards squealed as he shifted his weight, and it didn't take much figuring to decide that he was standing in front of his dresser mirror. It went on for an hour and then two, and I listened as the rain poured down. And when Deputy Barnes set his knife on the dresser and tried to sleep, I heard his little mewling complaints. They were much softer than the screams of those cocooned bloodfaces, but I heard them just the same.

Stairs creaked as I climbed to the second floor in the middle of the night.

Barnes came awake when I slapped open the door. A black circle opened on his bloody face where his mouth must have been, but I didn't give him a chance to say a single word.

"I warned you," I said, and then I pulled the trigger.

When it was done, I rolled the deputy in a sheet and dragged him down the stairs. I buried him under the swing set. By then the rain was falling harder. It wasn't until I got Barnes in the hole that I discovered I didn't have much gas in the can I'd gotten from the boathouse. I drenched his body with what there was, but the rain was too much. I couldn't even light a match. So I tossed a road flare in the hole, and it caught for a few minutes and sent up sputters of blue flame, but it didn't do the job the way it needed to be done.

I tried a couple more flares with the same result. By then, Roy was disappearing in the downpour like a hunk of singed meat in a muddy soup. Large river rocks bordered the flowerbeds that surrounded the lodge, and I figured they might do the trick. One by one I tossed them on top of Roy. I did that for an hour, until the rocks were gone. Then I shoveled sand over the whole mess, wet and heavy as fresh cement.

It was hard work.

I wasn't afraid of it.

I did what needed to be done, and later on I slept like the dead.

And now, a month later, I tossed and turned in Barnes' bed, listening to that old swing set squeak and squeal in the wind and in my dreams.

The brittle sound of gunfire wiped all that away. I came off the bed quickly, grabbing Barnes' .45 from the nightstand as I hurried to the window. Morning sunlight streamed through the trees and painted reflections on the glass, but I squinted through them and spotted shadows stretching across the beach below.

Bloodfaces. One with a machete and two with knives, all three of them moving like rabbits flushed by one mean predator.

Two headed for the woods near the edge of the property. A rattling burst of automatic gunfire greeted them, and the bloodfaces went to meat and gristle in a cloud of red vapor.

More gunfire, and this time I spotted muzzle flash in the treeline, just past the place where I'd stacked a cord of wood the summer before. The bloodface with the machete saw it, too. He put on the brakes, but there was no place for him to run but the water or the house.

He wasn't stupid. He picked the house, sprinting with everything he had. I grabbed the bottom rail of the window and tossed it up as he passed the swing set, but by the time I got the .45 through the gap he was already on the porch.

I headed for the door, trading the .45 for my shotgun on the way. A quick glance through the side window in the hallway, and I spotted a couple soldiers armed with M4 carbines breaking from the treeline. I didn't have time to worry about them. Turning quickly, I started down the stairs.

What I should have done was take another look through that front window. If I'd done that, I might have noticed the burrowed-up tunnel in the sand over Roy Barnes' grave.

It was hard to move slowly, but I knew I had to keep my head. The staircase was long, and the walls were so tight the shotgun could easily cover the narrow gap below. If you wanted a definition of dangerous ground, that would be the bottom of the staircase. If the bloodface was close—his back against the near wall, or standing directly beside the stairwell—he'd have a chance to grab the shotgun barrel before I entered the room.

A sharp clatter on the hardwood floor below. Metallic . . . like a machete. I judged the distance and moved quickly, following the shotgun into the room. And there was the bloodface . . . over by the front door. He'd made it that far, but no further. And it wasn't gunfire that had brought him down. No. Nothing so simple as a bullet had killed him.

I saw the thing that had done the job, instantly remembering the sounds I'd heard during the night—the scrapes and scrabbles I'd mistaken for nesting birds scratching in the chimney. The far wall of the room was plastered with bits of carved skin, each one of them scarred over with words, and each of those words had been skinned from the thing that had burrowed out of Roy Barnes' corpse.

That thing crouched in a patch of sunlight by the open door, naked and raw, exposed muscles alive with fresh slashes that wept red as it leaned over the dead bloodface. A clawed hand with long nails like skinning knives danced across a throat slashed to the bone. The demon didn't look up from its work as it carved the corpse's flesh with quick, precise strokes. It didn't seem to notice me at all. It wrote one word on the dead kid's throat . . . and then another on his face . . . and then it slashed open the bloodface's shirt and started a third.

I fired the shotgun and the monster bucked backwards. Its skinning knife nails rasped across the doorframe and dug into the wood. The thing's head snapped up, and it stared at me with a headful of eyes. Thirty eyes, and every one of them was the color of muddy water. They blinked, and their gaze fell everywhere at once—on the dead bloodface and on me, and on the words pasted to the wall.

Red lids blinked again as the thing heaved itself away from the door and started toward me.

Another lid snapped opened on its chin, revealing a black hole.

One suck of air and I knew it was a mouth.

I fired at the first syllable. The thing was blasted back, barking and screaming as it caught the doorframe again, all thirty eyes trained on me now, its splattered chest expanding as it drew another breath through that lidded mouth just as the soldiers outside opened fire with their M4s.

Bullets chopped through flesh. The thing's lungs collapsed and a single word died on its tongue. Its heart exploded. An instant later, it wasn't anything more than a corpse spread across a puddle on the living room floor.

"Hey, Old School," the private said. "Have a drink."

He tossed me a bottle, and I tipped it back. He was looking over my shotgun. "It's mean," he said, "but I don't know. I like some rock 'n' roll when I pull a trigger. All you got with this thing is *rock*."

"You use it right, it does the job."

The kid laughed. "Yeah. That's all that matters, right? Man, you should hear how people talk about this shit back in the Safe Zone. They actually made us watch some lame-ass stuff on the TV before they choppered us out here to the sticks. Scientists talking, ministers talking . . . like we was going to talk these things to death while they was trying to chew on our asses."

"I met a scientist once," the sergeant said. "He had some guy's guts stuck to his face, and he was down on his knees in a lab chewing on a dead janitor's leg. I put a bullet in his head."

Laughter went around the circle. I took one last drink and passed the bottle along with it.

"But, you know what?" the private said. "Who gives a shit, anyway? I mean, really?"

"Well," another kid said. "Some people say you can't fight something you can't understand. And maybe it's that way with these things. I mean, we don't know where they came from. Not really. We don't even know what they *are*."

"Shit, Mendez. Whatever they are, I've cleaned their guts off my boots. That's all I need to know."

"That works today, Q, but I'm talking long term. As in: What about tomorrow, when we go nose-to-nose with their daddy?"

None of the soldiers said anything for a minute. They were too busy trading uncertain glances.

Then the sergeant smiled and shook his head. "You want to be a philosopher, Private Mendez, you can take the point. You'll have lots of time to figure out the answers to any questions you might have while you're up there, and you can share them with the rest of the class if you don't get eaten before nightfall."

The men laughed, rummaging in their gear for MREs. The private handed over my shotgun, then shook my hand. "Jamal Quinlan," he said. "I'm from Detroit."

"John Dalton. I'm the sheriff around here."

It was the first time I'd said my own name in five months.

It gave me a funny feeling. I wasn't sure what it felt like.

Maybe it felt like turning a page.

The sergeant and his men did some mop-up. Mendez took pictures of the lodge, and the bloody words pasted to the living room wall, and that dead thing on the floor. Another private set up some communication equipment and they bounced everything off a satellite so some lieutenant in DC could look at it. I slipped on a headset and talked to him. He wanted to know if I remembered any strangers coming through town back in May, or anything out of the ordinary they might have had with them. Saying *yes* would mean more questions, so I said, "No, sir. I don't."

The soldiers moved north that afternoon. When they were gone, I boxed up food from the pantry and some medical supplies. Then I got a gas can out of the boathouse and dumped it in the living room. I sparked a road flare and tossed it through the doorway on my way out.

The place went up quicker than my house in town. It was older. I carried the box over to the truck, then grabbed that bottle the soldiers had passed around. There were a few swallows left. I carried it down to the dock and looked back just in time to see those birds dart from their nest in the chimney, but I didn't pay them any mind.

I took the boat out on the lake, and I finished the whiskey, and after a while I came back.

Things are getting better now. It's quieter than ever around here since the soldiers came through, and I've got some time to myself. Sometimes I sit and think about the things that might have happened instead of the things that did. Like that very first day, when I spotted that monster in the Chrysler's trunk out on County Road 14 and blasted it with the shotgun—the gas tank might have exploded and splattered me all over the road. Or that day down in the dark under the high school football stadium—those rat-spiders could have trapped me in their web and spent a couple months sucking me dry. Or with Roy Barnes—if he'd never seen those books in the backseat of that old sedan, and if he'd never read a word about lesser demons, where would he be right now?

But there's no sense wondering about things like that, any more than looking for explanations about what happened to Barnes, or me, or anyone else. I might as well ask myself why the thing that crawled out of Barnes looked the way it did or knew what it knew. I could do that and drive myself crazy chasing my own tail, the same way Barnes did with all those *maybe's* and *what if's*.

So I try to look forward. The rules are changing. Soon they'll be back to the way they used to be. Take that soldier. Private Quinlan. A year from now he'll be somewhere else, in a place where he won't do the things he's doing now. He might even have a hard time believing he ever did them. It won't be much different with me.

Maybe I'll have a new house by then. Maybe I'll take off work early on Friday and push around a shopping cart, toss steaks and a couple of six packs into it. Maybe I'll even do the things I used to do. Wear a badge. Find a new deputy. Sort things out and take care of trouble. People always need someone who can do that.

To tell the truth, that would be okay with me.

That would be just fine.

Them things liked human sacrifices. Had had 'em ages afore, but lost track o' the upper world after a time. What they done to the victims it ain't fer me to say . . .

"The Shadow Over Innsmouth" · H.P. Lovecraft (1936)

· GRINDING ROCK ·
Cody Goodfellow

One foot in the green, and one in the black, Tim Vowles kept telling himself, but the edge of the burn had got away from him. All he could see was black smoke and shadows, and the eye-frying orange and hungry red of the fire all around him.

A flaming jackrabbit bolted past, and Vowles reflexively smashed it with his shovel before he realized he should have chased it. The suffering bastards spread the fire like Roman candles, but they always knew the way out.

A minute ago, he'd been at the end of the twenty-man tool line with the other seasonal volunteer firefighters, cutting a fallback break in the dark, and the crew boss was saying everything was under control. The fire had nowhere to go, the evening breeze was driving it back on itself. But the wind changed and he straggled. When the next tool up shouted to keep his dime, he misunderstood and fell back even further, until the fire cut him off and he ran the wrong way, and now it had him.

The hundred-acre brushfire rallied on this patch of undeveloped land in the center of the city like a rogue cavalry unit, contained, but hardly tamed. It broke his heart, the price the land paid for the stupidity of the people—but mostly, because his own stupidity would probably kill him tonight.

Sweat broke out on his forehead and vaporized in the heat. He tied a dry bandana over his face and tried to get his bearings. To the east, the mountain had been gouged out by the Golden West Concrete quarry, and beyond that lay the Navy golf course and Vowles's own neighborhood. To the north, the ridge joined Mount Fortuna and the Mission Trails Regional Park. The city firefighters were up there, and helicopters had been dumping water and retardant on the park all afternoon. To the south, only a few hundred yards behind the fire line, the red tile roofs of Tierrasanta, upscale pseudo-villas and palatial townhouses, abutted the wild, tinder-dry brush, like an invitation to hell.

Vowles could see none of it.

He should at least have been able to see the lights of the fire engines or hear the call-outs and chainsaws of the tool line, but he got turned around by gusts of hot wind freighted with smoke so black, so thick, he felt hands shoving him, and now he was alone, with only the dancing dragon-shapes of fire to see by, and maybe the lights of his own house flickering in the smoke and roiling heat-haze like impossibly distant stars.

He barely heard his own shouting over the wind and roaring fire, but he heard the eerie howl of dogs quite clearly indeed, for it came from just behind him. Whirling and stumbling over beds of glowing coals, he fell down as if to beg for his life.

A pack of coyotes regarded him from a low rise that put them eye to yellow eye, tongues dangling, pelts black with soot. They howled again, and Vowles could hear other packs all down the canyon below picking up the demented, gibbering lament, and even neighborhood dogs joined in. His own Irish setter, Rusty, chained out in the backyard less than a mile from here, was probably adding his voice to the song of the pack that was about to eat his master.

And then, in mid-howl, they leapt at him. He ran screaming from the pack and into the heart of the fire.

He flew over the blasted moonscape, diving blindly through curtains of smoke and thorny blazing brush whipping at his face, but the pack gained on him and flanked to his right. To his left, where he thought the trucks had to be, pillars of flame lashed at the night, cutting off any hope of escape.

The ridge got steeper, studded with ash-dusted rocks and exploding barrel cacti, but a hollow opened up before him, an island of dense brush that the fire had miraculously passed over, so he ducked into it. The pack loped along the edge, then stopped and sat above him like a row of judges. They whined, but did not follow.

Flames paced the far rim, licking at the gutted carcass of a widowmaker tree. To linger here invited the fire to circle back and eat him alive, so Vowles ran until he stumbled upon a huge slab of granite.

He recognized it as one of the pitted grinding rocks scattered throughout the area, where local Mission Indians once made edible meal from oak acorns. The ancient bowls and gutters were furred with lichen and filled with beer bottle glass, and there were bodies laid out on the rock.

A vaguely human shape crouched over them, like another gnarled, lightning-blasted tree. Vowles walked around it, wiping the ash from his eyes, but he did not react at all when the shape uncurled itself to reach for the sky, and he heard it speak.

"*Ai ch'ich ah N'Kai naguatl!*" The guttural croak cut through the roar of the fire and the keening of the coyotes, creating a bubble of suffocating silence, which trapped Vowles like a fly in amber. "*Ai ch'ich iä Ubbo-Sathla ai shu-t'at ai'ul!*"

The leaden words hung in the air, heavier than the smoke. The speaker slammed some metal object into the stone, ringing it like a dull, gigantic bell, and beckoned to him. He only wanted to run, but his legs wouldn't move.

Coughing, hacking out strings of liquid smoke, the man on the rock asked, "Is it contained yet?"

The clear, comprehensible question broke the spell, and brought his panic rushing back. "Does it look contained to you? What the hell are you doing out here?"

"I'm waiting, but I think it's too late. We can't wait any longer . . . "

The wind peeled away the seething clouds of smoke, but Vowles could make out no features of the cloaked figure propped on a wooden staff. The bodies laid out before him were painfully visible in the moonlight, the whiteness of their bare skin glowing like cold fire. A man and a woman lay entwined, naked and motionless on the granite altar. Seconds passed before he saw the tidal rise and fall of their chests. Asleep and pleasantly dreaming, as if they'd come out here to ball under the stars, and nodded off in the middle of a brushfire.

"What did you do to them? Get away from there!" Vowles charged man on the grinding rock, but the air was thick as Vaseline, and the hooded figure drove the iron-shod end of the staff into his shoulder before he saw it coming, and drove him to his knees.

"I'm saving them," said the faceless man. "Touch me, and the fire will get us all."

Vowles threw himself against the staff, but he got no closer. "We have to get out of here."

"It will not come," the old man said, "while the fire burns." *Old*, Vowles knew, for in the voice, he heard the same exhaustion that dogged his father's voice, right before his last stroke. "And it must. This must be done."

"Wake them up, damn it! We can carry them out—"

"They're not going anywhere, and neither are we."

"Then we'll die! What the hell is wrong with you?"

"What's wrong," the old man clucked, and hacked out a bitter laugh. "I know the score, that's what's wrong with me. Did you think all of this was free? The land demands a sacrifice."

Vowles had no weapons. He dropped his shovel when he ran from the coyotes, which still sat and watched from the rim of the hollow. He was a part-time firefighter and a finish carpenter in the off-season, and they had never trained him to talk down psychos at Safety Academy. "Hey, mister, I don't want—"

"You don't want anyone to get hurt. Neither do I. Tomorrow, a major earthquake, at least a seven-point-seven, will *not* destroy most of San Diego and Orange County. Tens of thousands of people will *not* die, and millions will *not* lose their homes. Because of this . . . "

"You're trying to stop the Big One?" Vowles said the words with the skeptical unease of all native Californians shared for the prophecy that, one fine day, California would face the judgment of the angry gods of plate tectonics, and slide into the sea. "There's no fault line within fifty miles of here."

"Not the Big One, but an age of Big Ones. The first cracks in the egg under our feet. It doesn't belong to us, nor do we belong to it."

Vowles still wasn't getting any closer. Pushing at the gelid air, he demanded, "Are you making this happen?"

"Does an antenna make music? There is power here, and it wants to be released.

"The Indians believed that on the day of creation, they were born out of the womb of the earth, but there were spirits in the land, those left behind.

"They are older than the world, but still unborn. They dream life into the world. They long to awaken and shake us off, but they may be tamed—"

The old man knelt before the naked bodies, crabbed hands basking in the residual heat of their embrace. "This is their wedding night."

Way out of his depth, Vowles tried to keep the man talking, "But why does anyone have to get hurt?"

"California was an Eden, once—the people who lived here for ten thousand years never had to invent clothes or weapons or agriculture, but they knew the price. A tribe of shamans lived in this valley. They stole babies from the Kumeyaay bands to raise as their own, and every generation, they sacrificed a man and a woman, and they lived in paradise until the white men came.

"Nobody remembers," the old man wheezed. "Nobody understands what has to be done . . . But some of us have been called . . . We dream, and we remember—"

Vowles picked up a rock and cocked it behind his head. "Don't you touch them!"

"*I* won't," the old man said.

Beneath his feet, Vowles felt the ground crumble and run like an hourglass draining.

He threw the rock, watched it hang in the air as the ground itself reared up under his feet and tossed him aside. The arrested rock floated over a yawning hole in the earth.

Vowles rolled and jumped back against the wall of the hollow, his hands scratching for another rock.

"I wouldn't look, if I were you," the old man shouted.

Vowles looked.

Something bubbled up out of the hole and exploded into the night sky, a column of rampant, liquid blackness against the fiery horizon. Even as it grew, it shivered with feverish desperation to take on a coherent shape. Crude attempts at eyes and mouths bloomed and dissolved all over it, whole faces popping out and then eating themselves in a shape-shifting totem pole of molten tar.

The human imperative to make order of chaos lured Vowles into staring, trying to make sense of it. Though it tried to mimic the men and the coyotes and the widowmaker tree and all the shapes that thrived and died on the earth, the black, unborn thing was made of the living earth itself. And it was clearly not even a *thing*, but the tiniest extremity of something unfathomably vast, like the egg tooth of a hatchling, cracking out of its shell.

Breaking like a wave over the grinding rock, the living earth undulated and churned, and when it rolled back, the bride and groom were gone. As it receded, the black tar grew arms and legs and torsos and wistfully caressed itself, melting male and female forms achieving oneness as it slithered out of sight.

The ground shuddered, settled and sank. Vowles clawed at the wall of the hollow, kicked at sand sifting into the collapsing chasm. Cold sweat broke out all over his body as every knotted muscle in him abruptly gave out. Unnoticed, his bladder voided down his trembling leg and pooled in the depression where the long-ago thrown rock fell at his feet.

The old man climbed down from the boulder, slowly, groaning, clinging for support to his staff.

Vowles rushed him again, no rock needed, his fists would do. "What the hell was that? You knew it was coming, didn't you? What was it . . . that . . . ate them—"

"I can't say if they're dead, or whether they're not better off, down there." The old man took a step up the trail, seeming to shrivel and sicken, as he retreated from the rock. "That is where we came from, after all . . . "

Vowles jumped after the old man, arms out to tackle him. A coyote hit him across his left shoulder and drove him to the ground. The pack closed in on him, yellow eyes lambent in the guttering firelight, whining under some invisible yoke as they herded him back until the old man climbed painfully out of the hollow.

"You won't get away with this—"

"No, son, I don't think I will." The old man threw back his hood. Shadows blotted his face, brittle and black and crumbling away from his skull when he moved. The face beneath the mask of ashes shone hideously in the moonlight, the sickly glitter of exposed, broiled muscle and charred bone. One eye fastened on Vowles, while the other was a burst, weeping sac.

"Your kids go to school with my grandkids," the old man said. "We shop at the same supermarket, we rent movies from the same Blockbuster. In twenty years, when this has to be done again, praise God, I won't have to see it. But *you* . . . if you love this land—"

He vanished. The coyotes howled, and then they, too, were gone.

Vowles ran all the way to the firebreak, shattering blurred panes of orange and black like he was leaping through stained-glass windows. He ran faster and more frantically than when he was being chased, because the sweat and urine soaking him turned to live steam and scalded him inside his Nomex safety gear.

Firefighters rushed him with blankets, wrestled him onto a gurney in the back of an ambulance, and cut off his clothes. He kept telling them he was fine, he felt great, he wanted to go home. They had to sedate him to make him see the blisters, like the yolks of hundreds of fried eggs, all over his body.

They let Dana take him home after two, and he watched the rebroadcast of the eleven o'clock news in bed with a beer and a handful of prescription Motrin. He thought he saw himself among the tiny, desperate ants toiling on the ridge shot by the news chopper. The fire was ninety percent contained, but the cause was still unknown and chalked up to an act of God.

Vowles laughed at that, but then they showed more footage of the ridge, the fire and flashing lights the only features on a blackness that might've been the ocean, and the wink of unburned green brush with the white granite stone were laid bare under the searchlights. He cringed as he watched, for fear that the camera saw—

Saw what? What really happened? He told nobody what he saw. Nobody ever believed that kind of shit from somebody under anesthetic. He was still asking himself what he saw as he nodded off halfway through the lowlights of the Padres game, and each repetition took him further away from an answer.

The earthquake woke him up in the middle of the night. Before he could wake Dana or even look at the clock, he was falling through the floor and the foundation split open in a jagged black mouth that swallowed the Vowles household.

He found himself jammed more or less upright between the hot, wounded rock walls of a new fault line. His wife and daughters screamed for him in the dark, and he screamed back for them to be calm. The earth shifted, flexing like the muscles of a jaw. Cyclopean molars gritted and ground his family's screams into inert slurping sounds, and now he only screamed to drown it out.

He heard and felt something above his head—purposeful, furious digging. He was going to be saved. He tried to shake free of the rock, but dirt tumbled into his face, choking him. He wriggled and got an arm free, and the debris dislodged by his arm showered his face, and he really did not want to be rescued, now—

For he was buried alive upside down, and the rescuer burrowing towards him like a bulldozer was coming for him *from underneath*—

He woke up in the hospital. "It can't happen," he screamed at the nurse trying to strap him down. "It can't happen! We stopped it—"

Dana jolted out of a chair beside the bed to take hold of his mummified arm. The nurse tried to give him something to calm him down, but Dana drove her away.

The news played on the TV bolted to the far wall.

Firefighters had discovered a body in the area cleared by the fire, and identified him as 69-year old Calvin Loomis, a retired US Geological Survey engineer afflicted with Alzheimer's, missing from his home since he wandered away, two days ago. An old snapshot appeared on-screen: soft, sunny, Elmer Fudd features, white, crewcut hair, and freckled, ruddy skin. Vowles recognized the face; he'd seen it in the crowd in the opposing team's bleachers at one of his daughters' softball games.

The Caltech Seismological Laboratory reported a 2.4-magnitude seismic hiccup at eight-thirty tonight, directly underneath central San Diego. The short violence of the spike, which the geologists explained as vertical realignment from very deep in the crust, had gone mostly unnoticed throughout the state. This kind of settling was actually beneficial, said the newscaster, beaming reassurance, and disproved outmoded doomsday scenarios about the Big One. The East Pacific Plate still pushed coastal California northward at a stately two inches per annum, but no ugly seismic surprises lay in store for the foreseeable future.

Not so lucky was some city in central Mexico, flattened and devoured by a 6.4 quake. He didn't catch the name of the vanished place—they might not even have said it—but three hundred were dead, thousands wounded and another several hundred missing.

The volcano on the big island of Hawaii was acting up again, with lava flows causing the evacuation of guests at two imperiled hotels. China denied that an earthquake had killed hundreds at a labor camp in Mongolia.

There was something about a missing local newlywed couple, but already, when he recalled the image of those naked, slumbering bodies swallowed up by the living bowels of the earth, he saw it through a pixilated filter, with a news logo slapped on it, two more strangers dying. Strangers died every day—

It happened, he told himself. *You know it did.* The land took them. *It had to happen—what has to be done—*

He loved this city, this land, as much as anyone who lived there ever did. In twenty years, he would still live here, and his children would live here, and, God willing, they would raise children here, too.

And somebody would have to do something . . .

... the snatches of sight I experienced had a profound and terrible meaning, and a frightful connexion with myself, but that some purposeful influence held me from grasping that meaning and that connexion. Then came that queerness about the element of time, and with it desperate efforts to place the fragmentary dream-glimpses in the chronological and spatial pattern.
"The Shadow Out of Time" · H.P. Lovvecraft (1936)

· DETAILS ·
China Miéville

When the boy upstairs got hold of a pellet gun and fired snips of potato at passing cars, I took a turn. I was part of everything. I wasn't an outsider. But I wouldn't join in when my friends went to the yellow house to scribble on the bricks and listen at the windows.

One girl teased me about it, but everyone else told her to shut up. They defended me, even though they didn't understand why I wouldn't come.

I don't remember a time before I visited the yellow house for my mother.

On Wednesday mornings at about nine o'clock I would open the front door of the decrepit building with a key from the bunch my mother had given me. Inside was a hall and two doors, one broken and leading to the splintering stairs. I would unlock the other and enter the dark flat. The corridor was unlit and smelt of old wet air. I never walked even two steps down that hallway. Rot and shadows merged, and it looked as if the passage disappeared a few yards from me. The door to Mrs. Miller's room was right in front of me. I would lean forward and knock.

Quite often there were signs that someone else had been there recently. Scuffed dust and bits of litter. Sometimes I was not alone. There were two other children I sometimes saw slipping in or out of the house. There were a handful of adults who visited Mrs. Miller.

I might find one or another of them in the hallway outside the door to her flat, or even in the flat itself, slouching in the crumbling dark hallway. They would be slumped over or reading some cheap-looking book or swearing loudly as they waited.

There was a young Asian woman who wore a lot of makeup and smoked obsessively. She ignored me totally. There were two drunks who came sometimes. One would greet me boisterously and incomprehensibly, raising his arms as if he wanted to hug me into his stinking, stinking jumper. I would grin and wave nervously, walk past him. The other seemed alternately melancholic and angry. Occasionally I'd meet him by the door to Mrs. Miller's room, swearing in a strong cockney accent. I remember the first time I saw him, he was standing there, his red face contorted, slurring and moaning loudly.

"Come on, you old slag," he wailed, "you sodding old *slag*. Come on, please, you cow."

His words scared me but his tone was wheedling, and I realized I could hear her voice. Mrs. Miller's voice, from inside the room, answering him back. She did not sound frightened or angry.

I hung back, not sure what to do, and she kept speaking, and eventually the drunken man shambled miserably away. And then I could continue as usual.

I asked my mother once if I could have some of Mrs. Miller's food. She laughed very hard and shook her head. In all the Wednesdays of bringing the food over, I never even dipped my finger in to suck it.

My mum spent an hour every Tuesday night making the stuff up. She dissolved a bit of gelatin or cornflower with some milk, threw in a load of sugar or flavorings, and crushed a clutch of vitamin pills into the mess. She stirred it until it thickened and let it set in a plain white plastic bowl. In the morning it would be a kind of strong-smelling custard that my mother put a dishcloth over and gave me, along with a list of any questions or requests for Mrs. Miller and sometimes a plas0tic bucket full of white paint.

So I would stand in front of Mrs. Miller's door, knocking, with a bowl at my feet. I'd hear a shifting and then her voice from close by the door.

"Hello," she would call, and then say my name a couple of times. "Have you my breakfast? Are you ready?"

I would creep up close to the door and hold the food ready. I would tell her I was.

Mrs. Miller would slowly count to three. On three, the door suddenly swung open a snatch, just a foot or two, and I thrust the bowl into the gap. She grabbed it and slammed the door quickly in my face.

I couldn't see very much inside the room. The door was open for less than a second. My strongest impression was of the whiteness of the walls. Mrs. Miller's sleeves were white, too, and made of plastic. I never got much of a glimpse at her face, but what I saw was unmemorable. A middle-aged woman's eager face.

If I had a bucket full of paint, we would run through the routine again. Then I would sit cross-legged in front of her door and listen to her eat.

"How's your mother?" she would shout. At that I'd unfold my mother's careful queries. She's okay, I'd say, she's fine. She says she has some questions for you.

I'd read my mother's strange questions in my careful childish monotone, and Mrs. Miller would pause and make interested sounds, and clear her throat and think out loud. Sometimes she took ages to come to an answer, and sometimes it would be almost immediate.

"Tell your mother she can't tell if a man's good or bad from that," she'd say. "Tell her to remember the problems she had with your father." Or: "Yes, she can take the heart of it out. Only she has to paint it with the special oil I told her about." "Tell your mother seven. But only four of them concern her and three of them used to be dead.

"I can't help her with that," she told me once, quietly. "Tell her to go to a doctor, quickly." And my mother did, and she got well again.

"What do you not want to do when you grow up?" Mrs. Miller asked me one day.

That morning when I had come to the house the sad cockney vagrant had been banging on the door of her room again, the keys to the flat flailing in his hand.

"He's begging you, you old tart, please, you owe him, he's so bloody angry," he was shouting, "only it ain't you gets the sharp end, is it? *Please*, you cow, you sodding cow, I'm on me knees. . . ."

"My door knows you, man," Mrs. Miller declared from within. "It knows you and so do I, you know it won't open to you. I didn't take out my eyes and I'm not giving in now. Go home."

I waited nervously as the man gathered himself and staggered away, and then, looking behind me, I knocked on her door and announced myself. It was after I'd given her the food that she asked her question.

"What do you not want to do when you grow up?"

If I had been a few years older her inversion of the cliché would have annoyed me: It would have seemed mannered and contrived. But I was only a young child, and I was quite delighted.

I don't want to be a lawyer, I told her carefully. I spoke out of loyalty to my mother, who periodically received crisp letters that made her cry or smoke fiercely, and swear at lawyers, bloody smartarse lawyers.

Mrs. Miller was delighted.

"Good boy!" she snorted. "We know all about lawyers. Bastards, right? With the small print! Never be tricked by the small print! It's right there in front of you, right there in front of you, and you can't even see it and then suddenly it makes you notice it! And I tell you, once you seen it it's got you!" She laughed excitedly. "Don't let the small print get you. I'll tell you a secret." I waited quietly, and my head slipped nearer the door.

"The devil's in the details!" She laughed again. "You ask your mother if that's not true. The devil is in the details!"

I'd wait the twenty minutes or so until Mrs. Miller had finished eating, and then we'd reverse our previous procedure and she'd quickly hand me out an empty bowl. I would return home with the empty container and tell my mother the various answers to her various questions. Usually she would nod and make notes. Occasionally she would cry.

After I told Mrs. Miller that I did not want to be a lawyer she started asking me to read to her. She made me tell my mother, and told me to bring a newspaper or one of a number of books. My mother nodded at the message and packed me a sandwich the next Wednesday, along with the Mirror. She told me to be polite and do what Mrs. Miller asked, and that she'd see me in the afternoon.

I wasn't afraid. Mrs. Miller had never treated me badly from behind her door. I was resigned and only a little bit nervous.

Mrs. Miller made me read stories to her from specific pages that she shouted out. She made me recite them again and again, very carefully. Afterward she would talk to me. Usually she started with a joke about lawyers, and about small print.

"There's three ways not to see what you don't want to," she told me. "One is the coward's way and too damned painful. The other is to close your eyes forever, which is the same as the first, when it comes to it. The third is the hardest and the best: You have to make sure *only the things you can afford to see come before you.*"

One morning when I arrived the stylish Asian woman was whispering fiercely through the wood of the door, and I could hear Mrs. Miller responding with shouts of amused disapproval. Eventually the young woman swept past me, leaving me cowed by her perfume.

Mrs. Miller was laughing, and she was talkative when she had eaten.

"She's heading for trouble, messing with the wrong family! You have to be careful with all of them," she told me. "Every single one of them on that other side of things is a tricksy bastard who'll kill you soon as *look* at you, given half a chance.

"There's the gnarly throat-tipped one . . . and there's old hasty, who I think had best remain nameless," she said wryly.

"All old bastards, all of them. *You can't trust them* at all, that's what I say. I should know, eh? Shouldn't I?" She laughed. "Trust me, trust me on this: It's too easy to get on the wrong side of them.

"What's it like out today?" she asked me. I told her that it was cloudy.

"You want to be careful with that," she said. "All sorts of faces in the clouds, aren't there? Can't help noticing, can you?" She was whispering now. "Do me a favor when you go home to your mum: Don't look up, there's a boy. Don't look up at all."

When I left her, however, the day had changed. The sky was hot, and quite blue.

The two drunk men were squabbling in the front hall and I edged past them to her door. They continued bickering in a depressing, garbled murmur throughout my visit.

"D'you know, I can't even really remember what it was all about, now! Mrs. Miller said when I had finished reading to her. "I can't remember! That's a terrible thing. But you don't forget the basics. The exact question escapes me, and to be honest I think maybe I was just being *nosy* or *showing off*. . . . I can't say I'm proud of it but it could have been that. It could. But whatever the question, it was all about a way of seeing an answer.

"There's a way of looking that lets you read things. If you look at a pattern of tar on a wall, or a crumbling mound of brick or somesuch . . . there's a way of unpicking it. And if you know how, you can trace it and read it out and see the things hidden *right there in front of you*, the things you've been seeing but not noticing, all along. But you have to learn how." She laughed. It was a high-pitched, unpleasant sound. "Someone has to teach you. So you have to make certain friends.

"But you can't make friends without making enemies.

"You have to open it all up for you to see inside. You make what you see into a window, and you see what you want through it. You make what you see a sort of *door*."

• • •

She was silent for a long time. Then: "Is it cloudy again?" she asked suddenly. She went on before I answered.

"If you look up, you look into the clouds for long enough and you'll see a face. Or in a tree. Look in a tree, look in the branches and soon you'll see them lust so, and there's a face or a running man, or a bat or whatever. You'll see it all suddenly, a picture in the pattern of the branches, and you won't have chosen to see it. And you can't *unsee* it.

"That's what you have to learn to do, to read the details like that and see what's what and learn things. But you've to be damn careful. You've to be careful not to disturb anything." Her voice was absolutely cold, and I was suddenly very frightened.

"Open up that window, you'd better be damn careful that what's in the details doesn't look back and see you."

The next time I went, the maudlin drunk was there again wailing obscenities at her through her door. She shouted at me to come back later, that she didn't need her food right now. She sounded resigned and irritated, and she went back to scolding her visitor before I had backed out of earshot.

He was screaming at her that she'd gone too far, that she'd pissed about too long, that things were coming to a head, that there was going to be hell to pay, that she couldn't avoid it forever, that it was her own fault.

When I came back he was asleep, snoring loudly, curled up a few feet into the mildewing passage. Mrs. Miller took her food and ate it quickly, returned it without speaking.

When I returned the following week, she began to whisper to me as soon as I knocked on the door, hissing urgently as she opened it briefly and grabbed the bowl.

"It was an accident, you know," she said, as if responding to something I'd said. "I mean of *course* you know in theory that anything might happen, you get *warned*, don't you? But oh my . . . oh my *God* it took the breath out of me and made me cold to realize what had happened."

I waited. I could not leave, because she had not returned the bowl. She had not said I could go. She spoke again, very slowly.

"It was a new day." Her voice was distant and breathy. "Can you even imagine? Can you see what I was ready to do? I was poised . . . to change . . . to see everything that's hidden. The best place to hide a book is in a library. The best place to hide secret things is there, in the visible angles, in our view, in plain sight.

"I had studied and sought, and learnt, finally, to see. It was time to learn truths.

"I opened my eyes fully, for the first time.

"I had chosen an old wall. I was looking for the answer to some question that I told you I can't even *remember* now, but the question wasn't the main thing. That was the opening of my eyes.

"I stared at the whole mass of the bricks. I took another glance, relaxed my sight. At first I couldn't stop seeing the bricks as bricks, the divisions as layers of cement, but after a time they became pure vision. And as the whole broke down into lines and shapes and shades, I held my breath as I began to see.

"Alternatives appeared to me. Messages written in the pockmarks. Insinuations in the forms. Secrets unraveling. It was bliss.

"And then without warning my heart went tight, as I saw something. I made sense of the pattern.

"It was a mess of cracks and lines and crumbling cement, and as I looked at it, I saw a pattern in the wall.

"I saw a clutch of lines that looked just like something . . . terrible . . . something old and predatory and utterly terrible staring right back at me.

"And then I saw it move."

"You have to understand me," she said. "*Nothing changed.* See? All the time I was looking I saw the wall. But that first moment, it was like when you see a face in the cloud. I just noticed in the pattern in the brick, I just *noticed* something, looking at me. Something angry.

"And then in the very next moment, I just . . . I just *noticed* another load of lines—cracks that had always been there, you understand? Patterns in broken brick that I'd seen only a second before—that looked exactly like that same thing, a little closer to me. And in the next moment a third picture in the brick, a picture of the thing closer still.

"Reaching for me."

"I broke free then," she whispered. "I ran away from there in terror, with my hands in front of my eyes and I was screaming. I ran and ran.

"And when I stopped and opened my eyes again, I had run to the edges of a park, and I took my hands slowly down and dared to look behind me, and saw that there was nothing coming from the alley where I'd been. So I turned to the little snatch of scrub and grass and trees.

"And I saw the thing again."

Mrs. Miller's voice was stretched out as if she was dreaming. My mouth was open and I huddled closer to the door.

"I saw it in the leaves," she said forlornly. "As I turned I saw the leaves in such a way . . . just a *chance conjuncture*, you understand? I noticed a pattern. I *couldn't not*. You don't choose whether to see faces in the clouds. I saw the monstrous thing again and it still reached for me, and I shrieked and all the mothers and fathers and children in that park turned and gazed at me, and I turned my eyes from that tree and whirled on my feet to face a little family in my way.

"And the thing was there in the same pose," she whispered in misery. "I saw it in the outlines of the father's coat and the spokes of the baby's pushchair, and the tangles of the mother's hair. It was just another mess of lines, you see? But you don't choose what you notice. And I couldn't help but notice just the right lines out of the whole, just the lines out of all the lines there, just the ones to see the thing again, a little closer, looking at me.

"And I turned and saw it closer still in the clouds, and I turned again and it was clutching for me in the rippling weeds in the pond, and as I closed my eyes I swear I felt something touch my dress.

"You understand me? You understand?"

I didn't know if I understood or not. Of course now I know that I did not.

"It lives in the details," she said bleakly. "It travels in that . . . in that perception. It moves through those chance meetings of lines. Maybe you glimpse it sometimes when you stare at clouds, and then maybe it might catch a glimpse of you, too.

"But it saw me *full* on. It's jealous of . . . of its place, and there I was peering through without permission, like a nosy neighbor through a hole in the fence. I know what it is. I know what happened.

"It lurks before us, in the everyday. It's the boss of *all the things hidden* in plain sight. Terrible things, they are. Ap palling things. Just almost in reach. Brazen and invisible.

"It caught my glances. It can move through whatever I see.

"For most people it's just chance, isn't it? What shapes they see in a tangle of wire. There's a thousand pictures there, and when you look, some of them just appear. But now . . . the thing in the lines chooses the pictures for me. It can thrust it self forward. It makes me see it. It's found its way through. To me. Through what I see. *I opened a door into my perception.*"

She sounded frozen with terror. I was not equipped for that kind of adult fear, and my mouth worked silently for something to say.

"That was a long, long journey home. Every time I peeked through the cracks in my fingers, I saw that thing crawling for me.

"It waited ready to pounce, and when I opened my eyes even a crack I opened the door again. I saw the back of a woman's jumper and in the detail of the fabric the thing leapt for me. I glimpsed a yard of broken paving and I noticed just the lines that showed me the thing . . . *baying*.

"I had to shut my eyes quick.

"I groped my way home.

"And then I taped my eyes shut and I tried to think about things."

There was silence for a time.

"See, there was always the easy way, that scared me rotten, because I was never one for blood and pain," she said suddenly, and her voice was harder. "I held the scissors in front of my eyes a couple of times, but even bandaged blind as I was I couldn't bear it. I suppose I could've gone to a doctor. I can pull strings, I could pull in a few favors, have them do the job without pain.

"But you know I never . . . really . . . reckoned . . . that's what I'd do," she said thoughtfully. "What if you found a way to close the door? Eh? And you'd already put out your eyes? You'd feel such a *fool*, wouldn't you?

"And you know it wouldn't be good enough to wear pads and eyepatches and all. I tried. You catch glimpses. You see the glimmers of light and maybe a few of your own hairs, and that's *the doorway right there*, when the hairs cross in the corner of your eye so that if you notice just a few of them in just the right way . . . they look like something coming for you. That's a doorway.

"It's . . . unbearable . . . having sight, but trapping it like that.

"I'm not giving up. See . . . " Her voice lowered, and she spoke conspiratorially. "*I still think I can close the door*. I learnt to see. I can unlearn. I'm looking for ways. I want to see a wall as . . . as bricks again. Nothing more. That's why you read for me," she said. "*Research*. Can't look at it myself of course, too many edges and lines and such on a printed page, so you do it for me. And you're a good boy to do it."

I've thought about what she said many times, and still it makes no sense to me. The books I read to Mrs. Miller were school textbooks, old and dull village histories, the occasional romantic novel. I think that she must have been talking of some of her other visitors, who perhaps read her more esoteric stuff than I did. Either that, or the information she sought was buried very cleverly in the banal prose I faltered through.

"In the meantime, there's another way of surviving," she said slyly. "Leave the eyes where they are, but *don't give them any details.*

"That . . . thing can force me to notice its shape, but only in what's there. That's how it travels. You imagine if I saw a field of wheat. Doesn't even bear *thinking* about! A million million little bloody *edges*, a million lines. You could make pictures of damn *anything* out of them, couldn't you? It wouldn't take any effort at *all* for the thing to make me notice it. The damn *lurker*. Or in a gravel drive or, or a building site, or a lawn . . .

"But I can outsmart it." The note of cunning in her voice made her sound deranged. "Keep it away till I work out how to close it off.

"I had to prepare this blind, with the wrappings round my head. Took me a while, but here I am now. Safe. I'm safe in my little cold room. I keep the walls *flat white*. I covered the windows and painted them, too. I made my cloak out of plastic, so's I can't catch a glimpse of cotton weave or anything when I wake up.

"I keep my place nice and . . . simple. When it was all done, I unwrapped the bandages from my head, and I blinked slowly . . . and I was alright. Clean walls, no cracks, no features. I don't look at my hands often or for long. Too many creases. Your mother makes me a good healthy soup looks like cream, so if I accidentally look in the bowl, there's no broccoli or rice or tangled up spaghetti to make *lines and edges.*

"I open and shut the door so damned quick because I can only afford a moment. *That thing is ready to pounce.* It wouldn't take a second for it to leap up at me out of the sight of your hair or your books or whatever."

Her voice ebbed out. I waited a minute for her to resume, but she did not do so. Eventually I knocked nervously on the door and called her name. There was no answer. I put my ear to the door. I could hear her crying, quietly.

I went home without the bowl. My mother pursed her lips a little but said nothing. I didn't tell her any of what Mrs. Miller had said. I was troubled and totally confused.

The next time I delivered Mrs. Miller's food, in a new container, she whispered harshly to me: "It preys on my eyes, all the *white*. Nothing to see. Can't look out the window, can't read, can't gaze at my nails. Preys on my mind.

"Not even my memories are left," she said in misery. "It's colonizing them. I remember things . . . happy times . . . and the thing's waiting in the texture of my dress, or in the crumbs of my birthday cake. I didn't notice it then. But I can see it now. My memories aren't mine anymore. Not even my imaginings. Last night I thought about going to the seaside, and then the thing was there in the foam on the waves."

. . .

She spoke very little the next few times I visited her. I read the chapters she demanded and she grunted curtly in response. She ate quickly.

Her other visitors were there more often now, as the spring came in. I saw them in new combinations and situations: the glamorous young woman arguing with the friendly drunk; the old man sobbing at the far end of the hall. The aggressive man was often there, cajoling and moaning, and occasionally talking conversationally through the door, being answered like an equal. Other times he screamed at her as usual.

I arrived on a chilly day to find the drunken cockney man sleeping a few feet from the door, snoring gutturally. I gave Mrs. Miller her food and then sat on my coat and read to her from a women's magazine as she ate.

When she had finished her food I waited with my arms outstretched, ready to snatch the bowl from her. I remember that I was very uneasy, that I sensed something wrong. I was looking around me anxiously, but everything seemed normal. I looked down at my coat and the crumpled magazine, at the man who still sprawled comatose in the hall.

As I heard Mrs. Miller's hands on the door, I realized what had changed. The drunken man was not snoring. He was holding his breath.

For a tiny moment I thought he had died, but I could see his body trembling, and my eyes began to open wide and I stretched my mouth to scream a warning, but the door had already begun to swing in its tight, quick arc, and before I could even exhale the stinking man pushed himself up faster than I would have thought him capable and bore down on me with bloodshot eyes.

I managed to keen as he reached me, and the door faltered for an instant, as Mrs. Miller heard my voice. But the man grabbed hold of me in a terrifying, heavy fug of alcohol. He reached down and snatched my coat from the floor, tugged at the jumper I had tied around my waist with his other hand, and hurled me hard at the door.

It flew open, smacking Mrs. Miller aside. I was screaming and crying. My eyes hurt at the sudden burst of cold white light from all the walls. I saw Mrs. Miller rubbing her head in the corner, struggling to her senses. The staggering, drunken man hurled my checked coat and my patterned jumper in front of her, reached down and snatched my feet, tugged me out of the room in an agony of splinters. I wailed snottily with fear.

Behind me, Mrs. Miller began to scream and curse, but I could not hear her well because the man had clutched me to him and pulled my head to his chest.

I fought and cried and felt myself lurch as he leaned forward and slammed the door closed.

He held it shut.

When I fought myself free of him I heard him shouting.

"I told you, you slapper," he wailed unhappily. "I bloody told you, you silly old whore. I warned you it was time. . . . " Behind his voice I could hear shrieks of misery and terror from the room. Both of them kept shouting and crying and screaming, and the floorboards pounded, and the door shook, and I heard something else as well.

As if the notes of all the different noises in the house fell into a chance meeting, and sounded like more than dissonance. The shouts and bangs and cries of fear combined in a sudden audible illusion like another presence.

Like a snarling voice. A lingering, hungry exhalation.

I ran then, screaming and terrified, my skin freezing in my T-shirt. I was sobbing and retching with fear, little bleats bursting from me. I stumbled home and was sick in my mother's room, and kept crying and crying as she grabbed hold of me and I tried to tell her what had happened, until I was drowsy and confused and I fell into silence.

My mother said nothing about Mrs. Miller. The next Wednesday we got up early and went to the zoo, the two of us, and at the time I would usually be knocking on Mrs. Miller's door I was laughing at camels. The Wednesday after that I was taken to see a film, and the one after that my mother stayed in bed and sent me to fetch cigarettes and bread from the local shop, and I made our breakfast and ate it in her room.

My friends could tell that something had changed in the yellow house, but they did not speak to me about it, and it quickly became uninteresting to them.

I saw the Asian woman once more, smoking with her friends in the park several weeks later, and to my amazement she nodded to me and came over, interrupting her companions' conversation.

"Are you alright?" she asked me peremptorily. "How are you doing?"

I nodded shyly back and told her that I was fine, thank you, and how was she?

She nodded and walked away.

I never saw the drunken, violent man again.

There were people I could probably have gone to to understand more about what had happened to Mrs. Miller. There was a story that I could chase, if I wanted to. People I had never seen before came to my house and spoke quietly to my mother, and looked at me with what I suppose was pity or concern. I could have asked them. But I was thinking more and more about my own life. I didn't want to know Mrs. Miller's details.

I went back to the yellow house once, nearly a year after that awful morning. It was winter. I remembered the last time I spoke to Mrs. Miller and I felt so much older it was almost giddying. It seemed such a vastly long time ago.

I crept up to the house one evening, trying the keys I still had, which to my surprise worked. The hallway was freezing, dark, and stinking more strongly than ever. I hesitated, then pushed open Mrs. Miller's door.

It opened easily, without a sound. The occasional muffled noise from the street seemed so distant it was like a memory. I entered.

She had covered the windows very carefully, and still no light made its way through from outside. It was extremely dark. I waited until I could see better in the ambient glow from the outside hallway.

I was alone.

My old coat and jumper lay spreadeagled in the corner of the room. I shivered to see them, went over, and fingered them softly. They were damp and mildewing, covered in wet dust.

The white paint was crumbling off the wall in scabs. It looked as if it had been left untended for several years. I could not believe the extent of the decay.

I turned slowly around and gazed at each wall in turn. I took in the chaotic, intricate patterns of crumbling paint and damp plaster. They looked like maps, like a rocky landscape.

I looked for a long time at the wall farthest from my jacket. I was very cold. After a long time I saw a shape in the ruined paint. I moved closer with a dumb curiosity far stronger than any fear.

In the crumbling texture of the wall was a spreading anatomy of cracks that—seen from a certain angle, caught just right in the scraps of light—looked in outline something like a woman. As I stared at it it took shape, and I stopped noticing the extraneous lines, and focused without effort or decision on the relevant ones. I saw a woman looking out at me.

I could make out the suggestion of her face. The patch of rot that constituted it made it look as if she was screaming.

One of her arms was flung back away from her body, which seemed to strain against it, as if she was being pulled away by her hand, and was fighting to escape, and was failing. At the end of her crack-arm, in the space where her captor would be, the paint had fallen away in a great slab, uncovering a huge patch of wet, stained, textured cement.

And in that dark infinity of markings, I could make out any shape I wanted.

. . . the dreams began. They were very sparse and insidious at first, but increased in frequency and vividness as the weeks went by. Great watery spaces opened out before me, and I seemed to wander through titanic sunken porticos and labyrinths of weedy Cyclopean walls with grotesque fishes as my companions. Then the other shapes began to appear, filling me with nameless horror the moment I awoke.

"The Shadow Over Innsmouth" · H.P. Lovecraft (1936)

• ANOTHER FISH STORY •
Kim Newman

In the summer of 1968, while walking across America, he came across the skeleton fossil of something aquatic. All around, even in the apparent emptiness, were signs of the life that had passed this way. Million-year-old seashells were strewn across the empty heart of California, along with flattened bullet casings from the ragged edge of the Wild West and occasional sticks of weathered furniture. The sturdier pieces were pioneer jetsam, dumped by exhausted covered wagons during a long dry desert stretch on the road to El Dorado. The more recent items had been thrown off overloaded trucks in the '30s, by Okies rattling towards orange groves and federal work programs.

He squatted over the bones. The sands parted, disclosing the whole of the creature. The scuttle-shaped skull was all saucer-sized eye-sockets and triangular, saw-toothed jaw. The long body was like something fished out of an ash-can by a cartoon cat—fans of rib-spindles tapering to a flat tail. What looked like arm-bones fixed to the dorsal spine by complex plates that were evolving towards becoming shoulders. Stranded when the seas receded from the Mojave, the thing had lain ever closer to the surface, waiting to be revealed by sand-riffling winds. Uncovered as he was walking to it, the fossil—exposed to the thin, dry air—was quickly resolving into sand and scraps.

Finally, only an arm remained. Short and stubby like an alligator leg, it had distinct, barb-tipped fingers. It pointed like a sign-post, to the West, to the Pacific, to the city-stain seeping out from the original blot of *El Pueblo de Nuestra Senora de la Reyna de los Angeles de Rio Porciunculo*. He expected these route-marks. He'd been following them since he first crawled out of a muddy river in England. This one scratched at him.

Even in the desert, he could smell river-mud, taste foul water, feel the tidal pull.

For a moment, he was under waters. Cars, upside-down above him, descended gently like dead, settling sharks. People floated like broken dolls just under the shimmering, sunlit ceiling-surface. An enormous pressure squeezed in on him, jamming thumbs against his open eyes, forcing liquid salt into mouth and nose. A tubular serpent, the size of a streamlined train, slithered over the desert-bed towards him, eyes like turquoise-shaded searchlights, shifting rocks out of its way with muscular arms.

Gone. Over.

The insight passed. He gasped reflexively for air.

"Atlantis will rise, Sunset Boulevard will fall," Cass Elliott was singing on a single that would be released in October. Like so many doomed visionaries in her generation, Mama Cass was tuned into the vibrations. Of course, she didn't know there really had been a sunken city off Santa Monica, as recently as 1942. Not Atlantis, but the Sister City. A battle had been fought there in a World War that was not in the official histories. A War that wasn't as over as its human victors liked to think.

He looked where the finger pointed.

The landscape would change. Scrub rather than sand, mountains rather than flats. More people, less quiet.

He took steps.

He was on a world-wide walkabout, buying things, picking up skills and scars, making deals wherever he sojourned, becoming what he would be. Already, he had many interests, many businesses. An empire would need his attention soon, and he would be its prisoner as much as its master. These few years, maybe only months, were his alone. He carried no money, no identification but a British passport in the name of a newborn dead in the blitz. He wore unscuffed purple suede boots, tight white thigh-fly britches with a black zig-zag across them, a white Nehru jacket, and silver-mirrored sunglasses. A white silk aviator scarf wrapped burnoose-style about his head, turbanning his longish hair and keeping the grit out of his mouth and nose.

Behind him, across America, across the world, he left a trail. He thought of it as dropping pebbles in pools. Ripples spread from each pebble, some hardly noticed yet but nascent whirlpools, some enormous splashes no one thought to connect with the passing Englishman.

It was a good time to be young, even for him. His signs were everywhere. Number One in the pop charts back home was "Fire," by The Crazy World of

Arthur Brown. "I am the God of Hellfire," chanted Arthur. There were such Gods, he understood. He walked through the world, all along the watchtower, sprung from the songs—an Urban Spaceman, Quinn the Eskimo, this wheel on fire, melting away like ice in the sun, on white horses, in disguise with glasses.

In recent months, he'd seen *Hair* on Broadway and *2001: A Space Odyssey* at an Alabama Drive-In. He knew all about the Age of Aquarius and the Ultimate Trip. He'd sabotaged Abbie Hoffman's magic ring with a subtle counter-casting, ensuring that the Pentagon remained unlevitated. He knew exactly where he'd been when Martin Luther King was shot. Ditto, Andy Warhol, Robert Kennedy, and the VC summarily executed by Colonel Loan on the *Huntley-Brinkley Report*. He'd rapped with Panthers and Guardsmen, Birchers and Yippies. To his satisfaction, he'd sewn up the next three elections, and decided the music that children would listen to until the Eve of Destruction.

He'd eaten in a lot of McDonalds, cheerfully dropping cartons and bags like apple seeds. The Golden Arches were just showing up on every Main Street, and he felt Ronald should be encouraged. He liked the little floods of McLitter that washed away from the clown's doorways, perfumed with the stench of their special sauce.

He kept walking.

Behind him, his footprints filled in. The pointing hand, so nearly human, sank under the sands, duty discharged.

At this stage of his career, the Devil put in the hours, wore down the shoe-leather, sweated out details. He was the start-up Mephisto, the journeyman tempter, the mysterious stranger passing through, the new gun in town. You didn't need to make an appointment and crawl as a supplicant; if needs be, Derek Leech came to you.

Happily.

Miles later and days away, he found a ship's anchor propped on a cairn of stones, iron-red with lichen-like rust, blades crusted with empty shells. An almost illegible plaque read *Sumatra Queen*.

Leech knew this was where he was needed.

It wasn't real wilderness, just pretend. In the hills close to Chatsworth, a town soon to be swallowed by Los Angeles, this was the Saturday matinee West. Poverty Row prairie, Monogram mountains. A brief location hike up from Gower Gulch, the longest-lasting game of Cowboys and Indians in the world had been played.

A red arch stood by the cairn, as if a cathedral had been smitten, leaving only its entrance standing. A hook in the arch might once have held a bell or a hangman's noose or a giant shoe.

He walked under it, eyes on the hook.

Wheelruts in sandy scrub showed the way. Horses had been along this route too, recently.

A smell tickled in his nose, triggering salivary glands. Leech hadn't had a Big Mac in days. He unwound the scarf from his head and knotted it around his neck. From beside the road, he picked a dungball, skin baked hard as a gob-stopper. He ate it like an apple. Inside, it was moist. He spat out strands of grass.

He felt the vibrations, before he heard the motors.

Several vehicles, engines exposed like sit-astride mowers, bumping over rough terrain on balloon tires. Fuel emissions belching from mortar-like tubes. Girls yelping with a fairground Dodg'em thrill.

He stood still, waiting.

The first dune buggy appeared, leaping over an incline like a roaring cat, landing awkwardly, squirming in dirt as its wheels aligned, then heading towards him in a charge. A teenage girl in a denim halter-top drove, struggling with the wheel, blonde hair streaming, a bruise on her forehead. Standing like a tank commander in the front passenger seat, hands on the rollbar, was an undersized, big-eared man with a middling crop of beard, long hair bound in a bandanna. He wore ragged jeans and a too-big combat jacket. On a rosary around his scraggy neck was strung an Iron Cross, the *Pour le Mérite* and a rhinestone-studded swastika. He signaled vainly with a set of binoculars (one lens broken), then kicked his chauffeuse to get her attention.

The buggy squiggled in the track and halted in front of Leech.

Another zoomed out of long grass, driven by an intense young man, passengered by three messy girls. A third was around somewhere, to judge from the noise and the gasoline smell.

Leech tossed aside his unfinished meal.

"You must be hungry, pilgrim," said the commander.

"Not now."

The commander flashed a grin, briefly showing sharp, bad teeth, hollowing his cheeks, emphasizing his eyes. Leech recognized the wet gaze of a man who has spent time practicing his stares. Long, hard jail years looking into a mirror, plumbing black depths.

"Welcome to Charlie Country," said his driver.

Leech met the man's look. Charlie's welcome.

Seconds—a minute?—passed. Neither had a weapon, but this was a gunfighters' eye-lock, a probing and a testing, will playfully thrown up against a wall, bouncing back with surprising ferocity.

Leech was almost amused by the Charlie's presumption. Despite his hippie aspect, he was ten years older than the kids—well into hard thirties, at once leathery and shifty, a convict confident the bulls can't hang a jailyard shivving at his cell-door, an arrested grown-up settling for status as an idol for children ignored by adults. The rest of his tribe looked to their jefé, awaiting orders.

Charlie Country. In Vietnam, that might have meant something.

In the end, something sparked. Charlie raised one hand, open, beside his face. He made a monocle of his thumb and forefinger, three other fingers splayed like a coxcomb.

In Britain, the gesture was associated with Patrick McGoohan's "Be seeing you" on *The Prisoner*. Leech returned the salute, completing it by closing his hand into a fist.

"What's that all about?" whined his driver.

Not taking his eyes off Leech, Charlie said, "Sign of the fish, Sadie."

The girl shrugged, no wiser.

"Before the crucifix became the pre-eminent symbol of Christianity, Jesus' early followers greeted each other with the sign of the fish," Leech told them. "His first disciples were net-folk, remember. 'I will make you fishers of men.' Originally, the Galilean came as a lakeside spirit. He could walk on water, turn water to wine. He had command over fish, multiplying them to feed the five thousand. The wounds in his side might have been gills."

"Like a professor he speaks," said the driver of the second buggy.

"Or Terence Stamp," said a girl. "Are you British?"

Leech conceded that he was.

"You're a long way from Carnaby Street, Mr. Fish."

As a matter of fact, Leech owned quite a bit of that thoroughfare. He did not volunteer the information.

"Is he The One Who Will . . . ?" began Charlie's driver, cut off with a gesture.

"Maybe, maybe not. One sign is a start, but that's all it is. A man can easily make a sign."

Leech showed his open hands, like a magician before a trick.

"Let's take you to Old Lady Marsh," said Charlie. "She'll have a thing or two to say. You'll like her. She was in pictures, a long time ago. Sleeping partner in the Ranch. You might call her the Family's spiritual advisor."

"Marsh," said Leech. "Yes, that's the name. Thank you, Charles."

"Hop into Unit Number Two. Squeaky, hustle down to make room for the gent. You can get back to the bunkhouse on your own two legs. Do you good."

A sour-faced girl crawled off the buggy. Barefoot, she looked at the flint-studded scrub as if about to complain, then thought better of it.

"Are you waitin' on an engraved invitation, Mr. Fish?"

Leech climbed into the passenger's seat, displacing two girls who shoved themselves back, clinging to the overhead bar, fitting their legs in behind the seat, plopping bottoms on orange-painted metal fixtures. To judge from the squealing, the metal was hot as griddles.

"You are comfortable?" asked the kid in the driver's seat.

Leech nodded.

"Cool," he said, jamming the ignition. "I'm Constant. My accent, it is German."

The young man's blond hair was held by a beaded leather headband. Leech had a glimpse of an earnest schoolboy in East Berlin, poring over Karl May's books about Winnetou the Warrior and Old Shatterhand, vowing that he would be a blood brother to the Apache in the West of the Teuton Soul.

Constant did a tight turn, calculated to show off, and drove off the track, bumping onto an irregular slope, pitting gears against gravity. Charlie kicked Sadie the chauffeuse, who did her best to follow.

Leech looked back. Atop the slope, "Squeaky" stood forlorn, hair stringy, faded dress above her scabby knees.

"You will respect the way Charlie has this place ordered," said Constant. "He is the Cat That Has Got the Cream."

The buggies roared down through a culvert, overleaping obstacles. One of the girls thumped her nose against the roll-bar. Her blood spotted Leech's scarf. He took it off and pressed the spots to his tongue.

Images fizzed. Blood on a wall. Words in the blood.

HEALTER SKELTER.

He shook the images from his mind.

Emerging from the culvert, the buggies burst into a clearing and circled, scattering a knot of people who'd been conferring, raising a ruckus in a corral of horses which neighed in panic, spitting up dirt and dust.

Leech saw two men locked in a wrestling hold, the bloated quarter-century-on sequel to the Wolf Man pushed against a wooden fence by a filled-out remnant of Riff of the Jets. Riff wore biker denims and orange-lensed glasses. He had a chain wrapped around the neck of the sagging lycanthrope.

The buggies halted, engines droning down and sputtering.

A man in a cowboy hat angrily shouted, "Cut, cut, cut!"

Another man, in a black shirt and eyeshade, insisted, "No, no, no, Al, we can use it, keep shooting. We can work round it. Film is money."

Al, the director, swatted the insister with his hat.

"Here on the Ranch, they make the motion pictures," said Constant.

Leech had guessed as much. A posse of stuntmen had been chasing outlaws all over this country since the Silents. Every rock had been filmed so often that the stone soul was stripped away.

Hoppy and Gene and Rinty and Rex were gone. Trigger was stuffed and mounted. The lights had come up and the audience fled home to the goggle box. The only Westerns that got shot these days were skin-flicks in chaps or slo-mo massacres, another sign of impending apocalypse.

But Riff and the Wolf Man were still working. Just.

The film company looked at the Beach Buggy Korps, warily hostile. Leech realized this was the latest of a campaign of skirmishes.

"What's this all about, Charlie?" demanded the director. "We've told you to keep away from the set. Sam even goddamn paid you."

Al pulled the insister, Sam, into a grip and pointed his head at Charlie.

Charlie ignored the fuss, quite enjoying it.

A kid who'd been holding up a big hoop with white fabric stretched across it felt an ache in his arms and let the reflector sag. A European-looking man operating a big old Mickey Mouse-eared camera swiveled his lens across the scene, snatching footage.

Riff took a fat hand-rolled cigarette from his top pocket, and flipped a Zippo. He sucked in smoke, held it for a wine-bibber's moment of relish, and exhaled, then nodded his satisfaction to himself.

"Tana leaves, Junior?" said Riff, offering the joint to his wrestling partner.

The Wolf Man didn't need dope to be out of it.

Here he was, Junior: Lennie Talbot, Kharis the Caveman, Count Alucard— the Son of the Phantom. His baggy eyes were still looking for the rabbits, as he wondered what had happened to the 1940s. Where were Boris and Bela and Bud and Lou? While Joni Mitchell sang about getting back to the garden, Junior fumbled about sets like this, desperate for readmission to the Inner Sanctum.

"Who the Holy Hades is this clown?" Al thumbed at Leech.

414 · Another Fish Story

Leech looked across the set at Junior. Bloated belly barely cinched by the single button of a stained blue shirt, gray ruff of whiskers, chili stains on his jeans, yak-hair clumps stuck to his cheeks and forehead, he was up well past the *Late, Late Show.*

The Wolf Man looked at Leech in terror.

Sometimes, dumb animals have very good instincts.

"This is Mr. Fish," Charlie told Al. "He's from England."

"Like the Beatles," said one of the girls.

Charlie thought about that. "Yeah," he said, "like the Beatles. Being for the benefit of Mr. Fish.

Leech got out of the buggy.

Everyone was looking at him. The kerfuffle quieted, except for the turning of the camera.

Al noticed and made a cut-throat gesture. The cameraman stopped turning.

"Hell of a waste," spat the director.

In front of the ranch house were three more dune buggies, out of commission. A sunburned boy, naked but for cut-off denims and a sombrero, worked on the vehicles. A couple more girls sat around, occasionally passing the boy the wrong spanner from a box of tools.

"When will you have Units Three, Four, and One combat-ready, Tex?"

Tex shrugged at Charlie.

"Be lucky to Frankenstein together one working bug from these heaps of shit, Chuck."

"Not good enough, my man. The storm's coming. We have to be ready."

"Then schlep down to Santa Monica and steal . . . *requisition* . . . some more goddamn rolling stock. Rip off an owner's manual, while you're at it. These configurations are a joke."

"I'll take it under advisement," said Charlie.

Tex gave his commander a salute.

Everyone looked at Leech, then at Charlie for the nod that meant the newcomer should be treated with respect. Chain of command was more rigid here than at Khe Sanh.

All the buggies were painted. At one time, they had been given elaborate psychedelic patterns; then, a policy decision decreed they be redone in sandy desert camouflage. But the first job had been done properly, while the second was botched—vibrant flowers, butterflies, and peace signs shone through the thin diarrhea-khaki topcoat.

The ranch house was the basic derelict adobe and wood hacienda. One carelessly flicked roach and the place was an inferno. Round here, they must take potshots at safety inspectors.

On the porch was propped a giant fiberglass golliwog, a fat grinning racial caricature holding up a cone surmounted by a whipped swirl and a red ball cherry. Chocko the Ice Cream Clown had originally been fixed to one of the "requisitioned" buggies. Someone had written "PIG" in lipstick on Chocko's forehead. Someone else had holed his eyes and cheek with .22 rifle bullets. A hand axe stuck out of his shoulder like a flung tomahawk.

"That's the Enemy, man," said Charlie. "Got to Know Your Enemy."

Leech looked at the fallen idol.

"You don't like clowns?"

Charlie nodded. Leech thought of his ally, Ronald.

"Chocko's coming, man," said Charlie. "We have to be in a state of eternal preparedness. Their world, the dress-up-and-play world, is over. No more movies, no more movie stars. It's just us, the Family. And Chocko. We're major players in the coming deluge. Helter Skelter, like in the song. It's been revealed to me. But you know all that."

Funnily enough, Leech did.

He had seen the seas again, the seas that would come from the sundered earth. The seventh flood. The last wave.

Charlie would welcome the waters.

He was undecided on the whole water thing. If pushed, he preferred the fire. And he sensed more interesting apocalypses in the offing, stirring in the scatter of McDonald's boxes and chewed-out bubblegum pop. Still, he saw himself as a public servant; it was down to others to make the choices. Whatever was wanted, he would do his best to deliver.

"Old Lady Marsh don't make motion pictures any more. No need. Picture Show's closed. Just some folk don't know it yet."

"Chuck offered to be in their movie," explained Tex. "Said he'd do one of those nude love scenes, man. No dice."

"That's not the way it is," said Charlie, suddenly defensive, furtive. "My thing is the music. I'm going to communicate through my album. Pass on my revelation. Kids groove on records more than movies."

Tex shrugged. Charlie needed him, so he had a certain license.

Within limits.

Charlie looked back, away from the house. The film company was turning over again. Riff was pretending to chain-whip Junior.

"Something's got to change," said Charlie.

"Helter skelter," said Leech.

Charlie's eyes shone.

"Yeah," he said, "you dig."

Inside the house, sections were roped off with crudely lettered PELIGROSO signs. Daylight seeped through ill-fitting boards over glassless windows. Everything was slightly damp and salty, as if there'd been rain days ago. The adobe seemed sodden, pulpy. Green moss grew on the floor. A plastic garden hose snaked through the house, pulsing, leading up the main staircase.

"The Old Lady likes to keep the waters flowing."

Charlie led Leech upstairs.

On the landing, a squat idol sat on an occasional table—a Buddha with cephalopod mouth-parts.

"Know that fellow, Mr. Fish?"

"Dagon, God of the Philistines."

"Score one for the Kwiz Kid. Dagon. That's one of the names. Old Lady Marsh had this church, way back in the '40s. Esoteric Order of Dagon. Ever hear of it?"

Leech had.

"She wants me to take it up again, open storefront chapels on all the piers. Not my scene, man. No churches, not this time. I've got my own priorities. She thinks infiltration, but I know these are the times for catastrophe. But she's still a fighter. Janice Marsh. Remember her in *Nefertiti*?"

They came to a door, kept ajar by the hose.

Away from his Family, Charlie was different. The man never relaxed, but he dropped the Rasputin act, stuttered out thoughts as soon as they sprung to him, kept up a running commentary. He was less a Warrior of the Apocalypse than a Holocaust Hustler, working all the angles, sucking up to whoever might help him. Charlie needed followers, but was desperate also for sponsorship, a break.

Charlie opened the door.

"Miss Marsh," he said, deferential.

Large, round eyes gleamed inside the dark room.

Janice Marsh sat in a tin bathtub, tarpaulin tied around her wattled throat like a bib, a bulbous turban around her skull. From under the tarp came quiet splashing and slopping. The hose fed into the bath and an overspill pipe, patched together with hammered-out tin cans, led away to a hole in the wall, dribbling outside.

Only her flattish nose and lipless mouth showed, overshadowed by the fine-lashed eyes. In old age, she had smoothed rather than wrinkled. Her skin was a mottled, greenish color.

"This cat's from England," said Charlie.

Leech noticed that Charlie hung back in the doorway, not entering the room. This woman made him nervous.

"We've been in the desert, Miss Marsh," said Charlie. "Sweeping Quadrant Twelve. Scoped out a promising cave, but it led nowhere. Sadie got her ass stuck in a hole, but we hauled her out. That chick's like our mineshaft canary."

Janice Marsh nodded, chin-pouch inflating like a frog's.

"There's more desert," said Charlie. "We'll read the signs soon. It will be found. We can't be kept from it."

Leech walked into the dark and sat, unbidden, on a stool by the bathtub.

Janice Marsh looked at him. Sounds frothed through her mouth, rattling in slits that might have been gills.

Leech returned her greeting.

"You speak that jazz?" exclaimed Charlie. "Far out."

Leech and Janice Marsh talked. She was interesting, if given to rambles as her mind drifted out to sea. It was all about water. Here in the desert, close to the thirstiest city in America, the value of water was known. She told him what the Family were looking for, directed him to unroll some scrolls that were kept on a low-table under a fizzing desk-lamp. The charts were the original mappings of California, made by Fray Junipero Serra before there were enough human landmarks to get a European bearing.

Charlie shouldered close to Leech, and pulled a Magic Marker out of his top pocket.

The vellum was divided into numbered squares, thick modern lines blacked over the faded, precious sketch-marks. Several squares were shaded with diagonal lines. Charlie added diagonals to the square marked "12."

Leech winced.

"What's up, man?"

"Nothing," he told Charlie.

He knew what things were worth; that, if anything, was his special talent. But he knew such values were out of step with the times. He did not want to be thought a breadhead. Not until the 1980s, when he had an itchy feeling that it'd be mandatory. If there was to be a 1980s.

"This is the surface chart, you dig," said Charlie, rapping knuckles on the map. "We're about here, where I've marked the Ranch. There are other maps, showing what's underneath."

Charlie rolled the map, to disclose another. The top map had holes cut out, marking points of convergence. The lower chart was marked with interlinked balloon-shapes, some filled in with blue pigment that had become pale with age.

"Dig the holes, man. This shows the ways down below."

A third layer of map was almost all blue. Drawn in were fishy, squiddy shapes. And symbols Leech understood.

"And here's the prize. The Sea of California. Freshwater, deep under the desert. Primordial."

Janice Marsh burbled excitement.

"Home," she said, a recognizable English word.

"It's under us," said Charlie. "That's why we're out here. Looking. Before Chocko rises, the Family will have found the way down, got the old pumps working. Turn on the quake. With the flood, we'll win. It's the key to ending all this. It has properties. Some places—the cities, maybe, Chicago, Watts—it'll be fire that comes down. Here, it's the old, old way. It'll be water that comes up."

"You're building an Ark?"

"Uh uh, Arks are movie stuff. We're learning to *swim*. Going to be a part of the flood. You too, I think. We're going to drown Chocko. We're going to drown Hollywood. Call down the rains. Break the rock. When it's all over, there'll only be us. And maybe the Beach Boys. I'm tight with Dennis Wilson, man. He wants to produce my album. That's going to happen in the last days. My album will be a monster, like the *Double White*. Music will open everything up, knock everything down. Like at Jericho."

Leech saw that Charlie couldn't keep his thinking straight. He wanted an end to civilization and a never-ending battle of Armageddon, but still thought he could fit in a career as a pop star.

Maybe.

This was Janice's game. She was the mother of this family.

"He came out of the desert," Charlie told the old woman. "You can see the signs on him. He's a dowser."

The big eyes turned to Leech.

"I've found things before," he admitted.

"Water?" she asked, splashing.

He shrugged. "On occasion."

Her slit mouth opened in a smile, showing rows of needle-sharp teeth.

"You're a hit, man," said Charlie. "You're in the Family."

Leech raised his hand. "That's an honor, Charles," he said, "but I can't accept. I provide services, for a fee to be negotiated, but I don't take permanent positions."

Charlie was puzzled for a moment, brows narrowed. Then he smiled. "If that's your scene, it's cool. But are you The One Who Will Open the Earth? Can you help us find the Subterranean Sea?"

Leech considered, and shook his head, "No. That's too deep for me."

Charlie made fists, bared teeth, instantly angry.

"But I know who can," soothed Leech.

The movie people were losing the light. As the sun sank, long shadows stretched on reddish scrub, rock-shapes twisted into ogres. The cinematographer shot furiously, gabbling in semi-Hungarian about "magic hour," while Sam and Al worried vocally that nothing would come out on the film.

Leech sat in a canvas folding chair and watched.

Three young actresses, dressed like red Indians, were pushing Junior around, tormenting him by withholding a bottle of firewater. Meanwhile, the movie moon—a shining fabric disc—was rising full, just like the real moon up above the frame-line.

The actresses weren't very good. Beside Sadie and Squeaky and Ouisch and the others, the Acid Squaws of the Family, they lacked authentic dropout savagery. They were Vegas refugees, tottering on high heels, checking their make-up in every reflective surface.

Junior wasn't acting any more.

"Go for the bottle," urged Al.

Junior made a bear-lunge, missed a girl who pulled a face as his sweat-smell cloud enveloped her, and fell to his knees. He looked up like a puppy with progeria, eager to be patted for his trick.

There was water in Junior's eyes. Full moons shone in them.

Leech looked up. Even he felt the tidal tug.

"I don't freakin' believe this," stage-whispered Charlie, in Leech's ear. "That cat's gone."

Leech pointed again at Junior.

"You've tried human methods, Charles. Logic and maps. You need to try other means. Animals always find water. The moon pulls at the sea. That man has surrendered to his animal. He knows the call of the moon. Even a man who is pure in heart . . . "

"That was just in the movies."

"Nothing was ever just in the movies. Understand this. Celluloid writes itself into the unconscious, of its makers as much as its consumers. Your revelations may come in music. His came in the cheap seats."

The Wolf Man howled happily, bottle in his hug. He took a swig and shook his greasy hair like a pelt.

The actresses edged away from him.

"Far out, man," said Charlie, doubtfully.

"Far out and deep down, Charles."

"That's a wrap for today," called Al.

"I could shoot twenty more minutes with this light," said the cameraman.

"You're nuts. This ain't art school in Budapest. Here in America, we shoot with light, not dark."

"I make it *fantastic*."

"We don't want fantastic. We want it on film so you can see it."

"Make a change from your last picture, then," sneered the cinematographer. He flung up his hands and walked away.

Al looked about as if he'd missed something.

"Who are you, mister?" he asked Leech. "Who are you *really*?"

"A student of human nature."

"Another weirdo, then."

He had a flash of the director's body, much older and shaggier, bent in half and shoved into a whirlpool bath, wet concrete sloshing over his face.

"Might I give you some free advice?" Leech asked. "Long-term advice. Be very careful when you're hiring odd-job men."

"Yup, a weird weirdo. The worst kind."

The director stalked off. Leech still felt eyes on him.

Sam, the producer, had stuck around the set. He did the negotiating. He also had a demented enthusiasm for the kind of pictures they made. Al would rather have been shooting on the studio lot with Barbra Streisand or William Holden. Sam liked anything that gave him a chance to hire forgotten names from the matinees he had loved as a kid.

"You're not with them? Charlie's Family?"

Leech said nothing.

"They're fruit-loops. Harmless, but a pain the keister. The hours we've lost putting up with these kids. You're not like that. Why are you here?"

"As they say in the Westerns, 'just passing through.'"

"You like Westerns? Nobody does much anymore, unless they're made in Spain by Italians. What's wrong with this picture? We'd love to be able to shoot only Westerns. Cowboys are a hell of a lot easier to deal with than Hells' Angels. Horses don't break down like bikes."

"Would you be interested in coming to an arrangement? The problems you've been having with the Family could be ended."

"What are you, their agent?"

"This isn't Danegeld, or a protection racket. This is a fair exchange of services."

"I pay you and your hippies don't fudge up any more scenes? I could just get a sheriff out here and run the whole crowd off, then we'd be back on schedule. I've come close to it more'n once."

"I'm not interested in money, for the moment. I would like to take an option on a day and a night of time from one of your contractees."

"Those girls are *actresses*, buddy, not whatever you might think they are. Each and every one of 'em is SAG."

"Not one of the actresses."

"Sheesh, I know you longhairs are into everything, but . . . "

"It's your werewolf I wish to subcontract."

"My what? Oh, Junior. He's finished on this picture."

"But he owes you two days."

"How the hell did you know that? He does. I was going to have Al shoot stuff with him we could use in something else. There's this Blood picture we need to finish. *Blood of Whatever*. It's had so many titles, I can't keep them in my head. *Ghastly Horror . . . Dracula Meets Frankenstein . . . Fiend with the Psychotropic Brain . . . Blood a-Go-Go. . . .* At the moment, it's mostly home movies shot at a dolphinarium. It could use monster scenes."

"I would like to pick up the time. As I said, a day and a night."

"Have you ever done any acting? I ask because our vampire is gone. He's an accountant and it's tax season. In long shot, you could pass for him. We could give you a horror star name, get you on the cover of *Famous Monsters*. How about 'Zoltan Lukoff?' 'Mongo Carnadyne?' 'Dexter DuCaine?'"

"I don't think I have screen presence."

"But you can call off the bimbos in the buggies? Damp down all activities so we can finish our flick and head home?"

"That can be arranged."

"And Junior isn't going to get hurt? This isn't some Satanic sacrifice deal? Say, that's a great title. *Satan's Sacrifice*. Must register it. Maybe *Satan's Bloody*

Sacrifice. Anything with blood in the title will gross an extra twenty percent. That's free advice you can take to the bank and cash."

"I simply want help in finding something. Your man can do that."

"Pal, Junior can't find his own pants in the morning even if he's slept in them. He's still got it on film, but half the time he doesn't know what year it is. And, frankly, he's better off that way. He still thinks he's in *Of Mice and Men*."

"If you remade that, would you call it *Of Mice and Bloody Men*?"

Sam laughed. "*Of Naked Mice and Bloody Men*."

"Do we have a deal?"

"I'll talk to Junior."

"Thank you."

After dark, the two camps were pitched. Charlie's Family were around the ranch house, clustering on the porch for a meal prepared and served by the girls, which was not received enthusiastically. Constant formulated elaborate sentences of polite and constructive culinary criticism which made head chef Lynette Alice, a.k.a. Squeaky, glare as if she wanted to drown him in soup.

Leech had another future moment, seeing between the seconds. Drowned bodies hung, arms out like B-movie monsters, faces pale and shriveled. Underwater zombies dragged weighted boots across the ocean floor, clothes flapping like torn flags. Finned priests called the faithful to prayer from the steps of sunken temples to Dagon and Cthulhu and the Fisherman Jesus.

Unnoticed, he spat out a stream of seawater which sank into the sand.

The Family scavenged their food, mostly by random shoplifting in markets, and were banned from all the places within an easy reach. Now they made do with whatever canned goods they had left over and, in some cases, food parcels picked up from the Chatsworth post office sent by suburban parents they despised but tapped all the time. Mom and Dad were a resource, Charlie said, like a seam of mineral in a rock, to be mined until it played out.

The situation was exacerbated by cooking smells wafting up from the film camp, down by the bunkhouse. The movie folk had a catering budget. Junior presided over a cauldron full of chili, his secret family recipe doled out to the cast and crew on all his movies. Leech gathered that some of Charlie's girls had exchanged blowjobs for bowls of that chili, which they then dutifully turned over to their lord and master in the hope that he'd let them lick out the crockery afterwards.

Everything was a matter of striking a deal. Service for payment.

Not hungry, he sat between the camps, considering the situation. He knew what Janice Marsh wanted, what Charlie wanted, what Al wanted, and what Sam wanted. He saw arrangements that might satisfy them all.

But he had his own interests to consider.

The more concrete the coming flood was in his mind, the less congenial an apocalypse it seemed. It was unsubtle, an upheaval that epitomized the saw about throwing out the baby with the bathwater. He envisioned more intriguing pathways through the future. He had already made an investment in this world, in the ways that it worked and played, and he was reluctant to abandon his own long-range plans to hop aboard a Technicolor spectacular starring a cast of thousands, scripted by Lovecraft, directed by DeMille, and produced by Mad Eyes Charlie and the Freakin' Family Band.

His favored apocalypse was a tide of McLitter, a thousand channels of television noise, a complete scrambling of politics and entertainment, proud-to-be-a-breadhead buttons, bright packaging around tasteless and nutrition-free product, audiovisual media devoid of anything approaching meaning, bellies swelling and IQs atrophying. In his preferred world, as in the songs, people bowed and prayed to the neon god they made, worked for Matthew and Son, were dedicated followers of fashion, and did what Simon said.

He was in a tricky position. It was a limitation on his business that he could rarely set his own goals. In one way, he was like Sam's vampire: He couldn't go anywhere without an invitation. Somehow, he must further his own cause, while living up to the letter of his agreements.

Fair enough.

On his porch, Charlie unslung a guitar and began to sing, pouring revelations over a twelve-bar blues. Adoring faces looked up at him, red-fringed by the firelight.

From the movie camp came an answering wail.

Not coyotes, but stuntmen—led by the raucous Riff, whose singing had been dubbed in *West Side Story*—howling at the moon, whistling over emptied Jack Daniel's bottles, clanging tin plates together.

Charlie's girls joined in his chorus.

The film folk fired off blank rounds, and sang songs from the Westerns they'd been in. "Get Along Home, Cindy, Cindy." "Gunfight at O.K. Corral." "The Code of the West."

Charlie dropped his acoustic, and plugged in an electric. The chords sounded the same, but the ampage somehow got into his reedy voice, which came across louder.

He sang sea shanties.

424 • Another Fish Story

That put the film folk off for a while.

Charlie sang about mermaids and sunken treasures and the rising, rising waters.

He wasn't worse than many acts Leech had signed to his record label. If it weren't for this apocalypse jazz, he might have tried to make a deal with Charlie for his music. He'd kept back the fact that he had pull in the industry. Apart from other considerations, it'd have made Charlie suspicious. The man was naive about many things, but he had a canny showbiz streak. He scorned all the trappings of a doomed civilisation, but bought Daily Variety and Billboard on the sly. You don't find Phil Spector wandering in the desert eating horse-turds. At least, not so far.

As Charlie sang, Leech looked up at the moon.

A shadow fell over him, and he smelled the Wolf Man.

"Is your name George?" asked the big man, eyes eager.

"If you need it to be."

"I only ask because it seems to me you could be a George. You got that Georgey look, if you know what I mean."

"Sit down, my friend. We should talk."

"Gee, uh, okay."

Junior sat cross-legged, arranging his knees around his comfortable belly. Leech struck a match, put it to a pile of twigs threaded with grass. Flame showed up Junior's nervous, expectant grin, etched shadows into his open face.

Leech didn't meet many Innocents. Yet here was one.

As Junior saw Leech's face in the light, his expression was shadowed. Leech remembered how terrified the actor had been when he first saw him.

"Why do I frighten you?" he asked, genuinely interested.

"Don't like to say," said Junior, thumb creeping towards his mouth. "Sounds dumb."

"I don't make judgments. That's not part of my purpose."

"I think you might be my dad."

Leech laughed. He was rarely surprised by people. When it happened, he was always pleased.

"Not like that. Not like you and my mom . . . you know. It's like my dad's in you, somewhere."

"Do I look like him, Creighton?"

Junior accepted Leech's use of his true name. "I can't remember what he really looked like. He was the Man of a Thousand Faces. He didn't have a real face for home use. He'd not have been pleased with the way this turned out,

George. He didn't want this for me. He'd have been real mad. And when he was mad, then he showed his vampire face . . . "

Junior bared his teeth, trying to do his father in *London After Midnight*.

"It's never too late to change."

Junior shook his head, clearing it. "Gosh, that's a nice thought, George. Sam says you want me to do you a favour. Sam's a good guy. He looks out for me. Always has a spot for me in his pictures. He says no one else can do justice to the role of Groton the Mad Zombie. If you're okay with Sam, you're okay with me. No matter about my dad. He's dead a long time and I don't have to do what he says no more. That's the truth, George."

"Yes."

"So how can I help you?"

The Buggy Korps scrambled in the morning for the big mission. Only two vehicles were all-terrain-ready. Two three-person crews would suffice.

Given temporary command of Unit Number Two, Leech picked Constant as his driver. The German boy helped Junior into his padded seat, complimenting him on his performance as noble Chingachgook in a TV series of *The Last of the Mohicans* that had made it to East Germany in the 1950s.

This morning, Junior bubbled with enthusiasm, a big kid going to the zoo. He took a look at Chocko, who had recently been sloshed with red paint, and pantomimed cringing shock.

Leech knew the actor's father sometimes came home from work in clown make-up and terrified his young son.

The fear was still there.

Unit Number Two was scrambled before Charlie was out of his hammock.

They waited. Constant, sticking to a prearranged plan, shut down his face, covering a pettish irritation that others did not adhere to such a policy, especially others who were theoretically in a command position.

The Family Führer eventually rolled into the light, beard sticky as a glazed doughnut, scratching lazily. He grinned like a cornered cat and climbed up onto Unit Number One—actually, Unit Number Four with a hastily-repainted number, since the real Number One was a wreck. As crew, Charlie cut a couple of the girls out of the corral: the thin and pale Squeaky, who always looked like she'd just been slapped, and a younger, prettier, stranger creature called Ouisch. Other girls glowered sullen resentment and envy at the chosen ones. Ouisch tossed her long dark hair smugly and blew a gum-bubble in triumph. There was muttering of discontent.

If he had been Charlie, Leech would have taken the boy who could fix the motors, not the girls who gave the best blowjobs. But it wasn't his place to give advice.

Charlie was pleased with his mastery over his girls, as if it were difficult to mind-control American children. Leech thought that a weakness. Even as Charlie commanded the loyalty of the chicks, the few men in the Family grumbled. They got away with sniping resentment because their skills or contacts were needed. Of the group at the Ranch, only Constant had deal-making potential.

"Let's roll, Rat Patrol," decreed Charlie, waving.

The set-off was complicated by a squabble about protocol. Hitherto, in column outings—and two Units made a column—Charlie had to be in the lead vehicle. However, given that Junior was truffle-pig on this expedition, Unit Number One had to be in the rear, with Number Two out front.

Squeaky explained the rules, at length. Charlie shrugged, grinned, and looked ready to doze.

Leech was distracted by a glint from an upper window. A gush of dirty water came from a pipe. Janice Marsh's fish-face loomed in shadows, eyes eager. Stranded and flapping in this desert, no wonder she was thirsty.

Constant counter-argued that this was a search operation, not a victory parade.

"We have rules or we're nothing, Kaptain Kraut," whined Squeaky.

It was easy to hear how she'd got her nickname.

"They should go first, Squeak," said Ouisch. "In case of mines. Or ambush. Charlie should keep back, safe."

"If we're going to change the rules, we should have a meeting."

Charlie punched Squeaky in the head. "Motion carried," he said.

Squeaky rubbed her nut, eyes crossed with anger. Charlie patted her, and she looked up at him, forcing adoration.

Constant turned the ignition—a screwdriver messily wired into the raped steering column—and the engine turned over, belching smoke.

Unit Number Two drove down the track, towards the arch.

Squeaky struggled to get Unit Number One moving.

"We would more efficient be if the others behind stayed, I think," said Constant.

Unit Number One came to life. There were cheers.

"Never mind, li'l buddy," said Junior. "Nice to have pretty girlies along on the trail."

"For some, it is nice."

The two-buggy column passed under the arch.

Junior's *feelings* took them up into the mountains. The buggies struggled with the gradient. These were horse trails.

"This area, it has been searched thoroughly," said Constant.

"But I got a *powerful* feeling," said Junior.

Junior was eager to help. It had taken some convincing to make him believe in his powers of intuition, but now he had a firm faith in them. He realized he'd always had a supernatural ability to find things misplaced, like keys or watches. All his life, people had pointed it out.

Leech was confident. Junior was well cast as the One Who Will Open the Earth. It was in the prophecies.

Unit Number Two became wedged between rocks.

"This is as far as we can go in the buggy," said Constant.

"That's a real shame," said Junior, shaking his head, "'cause I've a rumbling in my guts that says we should be higher. What do you think, George? Should we keep on keeping on?"

Leech looked up. "If you hear the call."

"You know, George, I think I do. I really do. The call is calling."

"Then we go on."

Unit Number One appeared, and died. Steam hissed out of the radiator.

Charlie sent Ouisch over for a sit-rep.

Constant explained they would have to go on foot from now on.

"Some master driver you are, Schultzie," said the girl, giggling. "Charlie will have you punished for your failure. Severely."

Constant thought better of answering back.

Junior looked at the view, mopping the sweat off his forehead with a blue denim sleeve. Blotches of smog obscured much of the city spread out toward the gray-blue shine of the Pacific. Up here, the air was thin and at least clean.

"Looks like a train set, George."

"The biggest a boy ever had," said Leech.

Constant had hiking boots and a backpack with rope, implements, and rations. He checked over his gear, professionally.

It had been Ouisch's job to bottle some water, but she'd got stoned last night and forgot. Junior had a hip-flask, but it wasn't full of water.

Leech could manage, but the others might suffer.

• • •

"If before we went into the high desert a choice had been presented of whether to go *with* water or *without*, I would have voted for 'with,'" said Constant. "But such a matter was not discussed."

Ouisch stuck her tongue out. She had tattooed a swastika on it with a blue ballpoint pen. It was streaky.

Squeaky found a Coca-Cola bottle rolling around in Unit Number One, an inch of soupy liquid in the bottom. She turned it over to Charlie, who drank it down in a satisfied draught. He made as if to toss the bottle off the mountain like a grenade, but Leech took it from him.

"What's the deal, Mr. Fish? No one'll care about littering when Helter Skelter comes down."

"This can be used. Constant, some string, please."

Constant sorted through his pack. He came up with twine and a Swiss army knife.

"Cool blade," said Charlie. "I'd like one like that."

Squeaky and Ouisch looked death at Constant until he handed the knife over. Charlie opened up all the implements, until the knife looked like a triggered booby-trap. He cleaned under his nails with the bradawl.

Leech snapped his fingers. Charlie gave the knife over.

Leech cut a length of twine and tied one end around the bottle's wasp-waist. He dangled it like a plum-bob. The bottle circled slowly.

Junior took the bottle, getting the idea instantly.

Leech closed the knife and held it out on his open palm. Constant resentfully made fists by his sides. Charlie took the tool, snickering to himself. He felt its balance for a moment, then pitched it off the mountainside. The Swiss Army Knife made a long arc into the air and plunged, hundreds and hundreds of feet, bounced off a rock, and fell further.

Long seconds later, the tumbling speck disappeared.

"Got to rid ourselves of the trappings, Kraut-Man."

Constant said nothing.

Junior had scrambled up the rocky incline, following the nose of the bottle. "Come on, guys," he called. "This is it. El Doradio. I can feel it in my bones. Don't stick around, slowcoaches."

Charlie was first to follow.

Squeaky, who had chosen to wear flip-flops rather than boots, volunteered to stay behind and guard the Units.

"Don't be a drag-hag, soldier," said Charlie. "Bring up the freakin' rear."

Leech kept pace.

From behind, yelps of pain came frequently.

Leech knew where to step, when to breathe, which rocks were solid enough to provide handholds and which would crumble or come away at a touch. Instinct told him how to hold his body so that gravity didn't tug him off the mountain. His inertia actually helped propel him upwards.

Charlie gave him a sideways look.

Though the man was thick-skinned and jail-tough, physical activity wasn't his favored pursuit. He needed to make it seem as if he found the mountain path easy, but breathing the air up here was difficult for him. He had occasional coughing jags. Squeaky and Ouisch shouldered their sweet lord's weight and helped him, their own thin legs bending as he relaxed on their support, allowing himself to be lifted as if by angels.

Constant was careful, methodical, and made his way on his own.

But Junior was out ahead, following his bottle, scrambling between rocks and up nearly sheer inclines. He stopped, stood on a rocky outcrop, and looked down at them, then bellowed for the sheer joy of being alive and in the wilderness.

The sound carried out over the mountains and echoed.

"Charlie," he shouted, "how about one of them songs of yours?"

"Yes, that is an idea good," said Constant, every word barbed. "An inspiration is needed for our mission."

Charlie could barely speak, much less sing "The Happy Wanderer" in German.

Grimly, Squeaky and Ouisch harmonized a difficult version of "The Mickey Mouse Marching Song." Struggling with Charlie's dead weight, they found the will to carry on and even put some spit and vigor into the anthem.

Leech realized at once what Charlie had done.

The con had simply stolen the whole idea outright from Uncle Walt. He'd picked up these dreaming girls, children of postwar privilege raised in homes with buzzing refrigerators in the kitchen and finned automobiles in the garage, recruiting them a few years on from their first Mouseketeer phase, and electing himself Mickey.

Hey there ho there hi there . . .

When they chanted "Mickey Mouse . . . Mickey Mouse," Constant even croaked "Donald Duck" on the offbeat.

Like Junior, Leech was overwhelmed with the sheer joy of the century.

He loved these children, dangerous as they were, destructive as they would be. They had such open, yearning hearts. They would find many things to fill their voids and Leech saw that he could be there for them in the future, up to 2001 and beyond, on the generation's ultimate trip.

Unless the rains came first.

"Hey, George," yelled Junior. "I dropped my bottle down a hole."

Everyone stopped and shut up.

Leech listened.

"Aww, what a shame," said Junior. "I lost my bottle."

Leech held up a hand for silence.

Charlie was puzzled, and the girls sat him down.

Long seconds later, deep inside the mountain, Leech heard a splash. No one else caught the noise.

"It's found," he announced.

Only Ouisch was small enough to pass through the hole. Constant rigged up a rope cradle and lowered her. She waved bye-bye as she scraped into the mountain's throat. Constant measured off the rope in cubits, unrolling loops from his forearm.

Junior sat on the rock, swigging from his flask.

Squeaky glared pantomime evil at him and he offered the flask to Charlie.

"That's your poison, man," he said.

"You should drop acid," said Squeaky. "So you can learn from the wisdom of the mountain."

Junior laughed, big belly-shaking chuckles.

"You're funnin' me, girl. Ain't nothing dumber than a mountain."

Leech didn't add to the debate.

Constant came to end of the rope. Ouisch dangled fifty feet inside the rock.

"It's dark," she shouted up. "And wet. There's water all around. Water with things in it. Icky."

"Have you ever considered the etymology of the term 'icky'?" asked Leech. "Do you suppose this primal, playroom expression of disgust could be related to the Latin prefix 'ichthy,' which translates literally as 'fishy'?"

"I was in a picture once, called *Manfish*," said Junior. "I got to be out on boats. I like boats."

"Manfish? Interesting name."

"It was the name of the boat in the movie. Not a monster, like that Black Lagoon thing. Universal wouldn't have me in that. I did *The Alligator People*, though. Swamp stuff. Big stiff suitcase-skinned gator-man."

"Man-fish," said Charlie, trying to hop on the conversation train. "I get it. I see where you're coming from, where you're going. The Old Lady. What's she, a mermaid? An old mermaid?"

"You mean she really looks like that?" yelped Squeaky. "The one time I saw her I was tripping. Man, that's messed up! Charlie, I think I'm scared."

Charlie cuffed Squeaky around the head.

"Ow, that hurt."

"Learn from the pain, child. It's the only way."

"You shouldn't ought to hit ladies, Mr. Man," said Junior. "It's not like with guys. Brawlin' is part of being a guy. But with ladies, it's, you know, not polite. Wrong. Even when you've got a snoutful, you don't whop on a woman."

"It's for my own good," said Squeaky, defending her master.

"Gosh, little lady, are you sure?"

"It's the only way I'll learn." Squeaky picked up a rock and hit herself in the head with it, raising a bruise. "I love you, Charlie," she said, handing him the bloody rock.

He kissed the stain, and Squeaky smiled as if she'd won a gold star for her homework and been made head cheerleader on the same morning.

Ouisch popped her head up out of the hole like a pantomime chimneysweep. She had adorable dirt on her cheeks.

"There's a way down," she said. "It's narrow here, but opens out. I think it's a, whatchumacallit, passage. The rocks feel smooth. We'll have to enbiggen the hole if you're all to get through."

Constant looked at the problem. "This stone, that stone, that stone," he said, pointing out loose outcrops around the lip of the hole. "They will come away."

Charlie was about to make fun of the German boy, but held back. Like Leech, he sensed that the kid knew what he was talking about.

"I study engineering," Constant said. "I thought I might build houses."

"Have to tear down before you can build up," said Charlie.

Constant and Squeaky wrestled with rocks, wrenching them loose, working faults into cracks. Ouisch slipped into the hole, to be out of the way.

Charlie didn't turn a hand to the work. He was here in a supervisory capacity.

Eventually the stones were rolled away.

"Strange, that is," said Constant as sun shone into the hole. "Those could be steps."

There were indeed stairs in the hole.

Constant, of course, had brought a battery flashlight. He shone it into the hole. Ouisch sat on a wet step.

The stairs were old, prehuman.

Charlie tapped Squeaky, pushed her a little. She eased herself into the hole, plopping down next to Ouisch.

"You light the way," he told Constant. "The girls will scout ahead. Reconnaissance."

"Nothing down there but water," said Junior. "Been there a long time."

"Maybe no people. But big blind fish."

The Family crowd descended the stairs, their light swallowed by the hole.

Leech and Junior lingered topside.

Charlie looked up. "You comin' along, Mr. Fish?"

Leech nodded. "It's all right," he told Junior. "We'll be safe in the dark."

Inside the mountain, everything was cold and wet. Natural tunnels had been shaped by intelligent (if webbed) hands at some point. The roofs were too low even for the girls to walk comfortably, but scarred patches of rock showed where paths had been cut, and the floor was smoothed by use. Sewer-like runnel-gutters trickled with fresh water. Somehow, no one liked to drink the stuff—though the others must all have a desert thirst.

They started to find carved designs on the rocks. At first, childish wavy lines with stylized fish swimming.

Charlie was excited by the nearness of the sea.

They could hear it, roaring below. Junior felt the pull of the water.

Leech heard the voices in the roar.

Like a bloodhound, Junior led them through triune junctions, down forking stairways, past stalactite-speared cave-dwellings, deeper into the three-dimensional maze inside the mountain.

"We're going to free the waters," said Charlie. "Let the deluge wash down onto the city. This mountain is like a big dam. It can be blown."

The mountain was more like a stopper jammed onto a bottle. Charlie was right about pressure building up. Leech felt it in his inner ears, his eyes, his teeth. Squeaky had a nosebleed. The air was thick, wet with vapor. Marble-like balls of water gathered on the rock roof and fell on them, splattering on clothes like liquid bullets. In a sense, they were already underwater.

It would take more than dynamite to loose the flood; indeed, it would take more than physics. However, Charlie was not too far off the mark in imagining what could be done by loosening a few key rocks. There was the San Andreas fault to play with. Constant would know which rocks to take out of the puzzle. A little directed spiritual energy, some sacrifices, and the coast of California could shear away like a slice of pie. Then the stopper would be off, and the seas would rise, waking up the gill-people, the mer-folk, the squidface fellows. A decisive turn and a world war would be lost, by the straights, the over-thirties, the cops and docs and pols, the Man. Charlie and Chocko could stage their last war games, and the sea-birds would cheer *tekeli-li tekeli-li* . . .

Leech saw it all, like a coming attraction. And he wasn't sure he wanted to pay to see that movie.

Maybe on a rerun triple feature with drastically reduced admission, slipped in between *Night of the Living Dead* and *Planet of the Apes*.

Seriously, *Hello Dolly!* spoke to him more on his level.

"The Earth is hollow," said Charlie. "The Nazis knew that."

Constant winced at mention of Nazis. Too many Gestapo jokes had made him sensitive.

"Inside, there are the big primal forces, water and fire. They're here for us, space kiddettes. For the Family. This is where the Helter Skelter comes down."

The tunnel opened up into a cathedral.

They were on an upper level of a tiered array of galleries and balconies. Natural rock and blocky construction all seemed to have melted like wax, encrusted with salty matter. Stalactites hung in spiky curtains, stalagmites raised like obscene columns.

Below, black waters glistened.

Constant played feeble torchlight over the interior of the vast space.

"Far out, man," said Ouisch.

"Beautiful," said Junior.

There was an echo, like the wind in a pipe organ.

Greens and browns mingled in curtains of icy rock, colors unseen for centuries.

"Here's your story," said Constant.

He pointed the torch at a wall covered in an intricate carving. A sequence of images—*an underground comic!*—showed the mountain opening up, the desert fractured by a jagged crack, a populated flood gushing forth, a city swept into the sea. There was a face on the mountain, grinning in triumph—Charlie, with a swastika on his forehead, his beard and hair tangled like seaweed.

"So, is that your happy ending?" Leech asked.

For once, Charlie was struck dumb. Until now he had been riffing, a yarning jailbird puffing up his crimes and exploits, spinning sci-fi stories and channeling nonsense from the void. To keep himself amused as he marked off the days of his sentence.

"Man," he said, "it's all true."

This face proved it.

"This is the future. Helter Skelter."

Looking closer at the mural, the city wasn't exactly Los Angeles, but an Aztec-Atlantean analogue. Among the drowning humans were fishier bipeds. There were step-pyramids and Studebaker dealerships, temples of sacrifice and motion picture studios.

"It's one future," said Leech. "A possible, maybe probable future."

"And you've brought me to it, man. I knew you were the real deal!"

The phrase came back in an echo, " . . . real deal . . . real deal."

"The real deal? Very perceptive. This is where we make the real deal, Charles. This is where we take the money or open the box, this is make-your-mind-up-time."

Charlie's elation was cut with puzzlement.

"I've dropped that tab," announced Ouisch.

Junior looked around. "Where? Let's see if we can pick it up."

Charlie took Constant's torch and shone it at Leech.

"You don't blink."

"No."

Charlie stuck the torch under his chin, demon-masking his features. He tried to snarl like his million-year-old carved portrait.

"But I'm the Man, now. The Man of the Mountain."

"I don't dispute that."

"The Old Lady has told me how it works," said Charlie, pointing to his head. "You think I don't get it, but I do. We've been stashing ordinance. The kraut's a demolition expert. He'll see where to place the charges. Bring this place down and let the waters out. I know that's not enough. This is an imaginary mountain as much as it is a physical one. That's why they've been filming crappy Westerns all over it for so long. This is a place of stories. And it has to be opened in the mind, has to be cracked on another plane. I've been working on the rituals. My album, that's one. And the blood sacrifices, the offerings of the pigs."

"I can't wait to off my first pig," said Ouisch, cutely wrinkling her nose. "I'm going to be so freakin' *famous*."

"Famous ain't all that," put in Junior. "You think bein' famous will make things work out right, but it doesn't at all. Screws you up more, if you ask me."

"I didn't, Mummy Man," spat Charlie. "You had your shot, dragged your leg through the tombs . . . "

Squeaky began to sing, softly.

"We shall over-whelm, we shall over-whe-e-elm, we shall overwhelm some day-ay-ay . . . "

Charlie laughed.

"It's the end of their world. No more goddamn movies. You know how much I hate the movies? The *lies* in the movies. Now, I get to wipe Hollywood off the map. Hell, I get to wipe the *map* off the map. I'll burn those old Spanish charts when we get back to the Ranch. No more call for them."

Constant was the only one paying attention to Leech. Smart boy.

"It'll be so *simple*," said Charlie. "So pure. All the pigs get offed. Me and Chocko do the last dance. I defeat the clowns, lay them down forever. Then we start all over. Get it right this time."

"Simple," said Leech. "Yes, that's the word."

"This happened before, right? With the Old Lady's people. The menfish. Then we came along, the menmen, and fouled it up again, played exactly the same tune. Not this time. This time, there's the Gospel According to Charlie."

"Hooray and Hallelujah," sang Ouisch, "you got it comin' to ya . . . "

The drip of water echoed enormously, like the ticking of a great clock.

"I do believe our interests part the ways here," said Leech. "You yearn for simplicity, like these children. You hate the movies, the storybooks, but you want cartoons, you want a big finish and a new episode next week. Wipe it all away and get back to the garden. It's easy because you don't have to think about it."

He hadn't lost Charlie, but he was scaring the man. Good.

"I like complexity," said Leech, relishing the echo. "I *love* it. There are so many more opportunities, so many more arrangements to be made. What I want is a rolling apocalypse, a transformation, a thousand victories a day, a spreading of interests, a permanent revolution. My natural habitat is civilization. Your ultimate deluge might be amusing for a moment, but it'd pass. Even you'd get bored with children sitting around adoring you."

"You think?"

"I *know*, Charles."

Charlie looked at the faces of Ouisch and Squeaky, American girls, unquestioningly loyal, endlessly tiresome.

"No, Mr. Fish," he said, indicating the mural. "This is what I want. This is what I want to do."

"I brought you here. I showed you this."

"I know. You're part of the story too, aren't you? If the Mummy Man is the One Who Will Open the Earth, you're the Mysterious Guide."

"I'm not so mysterious."

"You're a part of this, you don't have a choice."

Charlie was excited but wheedling, persuasive but panicky. Having seen his preferred future, he was worried about losing it. Whenever the torch was away from the mural, he itched lest it should change in the dark.

"I promise you this, Charles, you will be famous."

Charlie thumped his chest. "Damn right. Good goddamn right!"

"But you might want to give this up. Write off this scripted Armageddon as just another fish story. You know, the one that got away. It was *this big*. I have other plans for the end of this century. And beyond. Have you ever noticed how it's only Gods who keep threatening to end the world? Father issues, if you ask me. Others, those of my party, promise things will continue as they are. Everyone gets what they deserve. You ain't seen nothin' yet because what you give is what you get."

Charlie shook his head. "I'm not there."

Squeaky and Ouisch were searching the mural, trying to find themselves in the crowded picture.

Charlie's eyes shone, ferocious.

"Our deal was to bring you here," said Leech, "to this sea. To this place of revelation. Our business is concluded. The service you requested has been done."

Junior raised a modest flipper, acknowledging his part.

"Yeah," said Charlie, distracted, flicking fingers at Junior, "muchas grassy-asses."

"You have recompensed our friend for his part in this expedition, by ensuring that his employers finish their shoot unimpeded. That deal is done and everyone is square. Now, let's talk about getting out of the mountain."

Charlie bit back a grin, surprised.

"What are you prepared to offer for that?"

"Don't be stupid, man," said Charlie. "We just go back on ourselves."

"Are you so confident? We took a great many turns and twists. Smooth rock and running water. We left no signs. Some of us might have a mind to sit by the sea for a spell, make some rods and go fishing."

"Good idea, George," said Junior. "Catch a marlin, I bet. Plenty good eating."

Charlie's eyes widened.

After a day or so, the torch batteries would die. He might wander blindly for months, *years*, down here, hopelessly lost, buried alive. Back at the Ranch, he'd not be missed much; Tex, or one of the others, maybe one of the girls, could be the new Head of the Family, and would perhaps do things better all round. The girls would be no use to him, in the end. Squeaky and Ouisch couldn't guide him out of this fish city, and he couldn't live off them for more than a few weeks. Charlie saw the story of the Lost Voyager as vividly as he had the Drowning of Los Angeles. It ended not with a huge face carved on a mountain and feared, but with forgotten bones, lying forever in wet darkness.

"I join you in fishing, I think," said Constant.

Charlie had lost Constant on the mountain. Later, Leech would formalize a deal with the boy. He had an ability to put things together or take them apart. Charlie had been depending on that. He should have taken the trouble to offer Constant something of equal value to retain his services.

"No, no, this can't be right."

"You show Charlie the way out, meanie," said Ouisch, shoving Junior.

"If you know what's good for you," said Squeaky.

"One word and you're out of here safe, Charles," said Leech. "But abandon the deluge. I want Los Angeles where it is. I want civilization just where it is. I have plans, you dig?"

"You're scarin' me, man," said Charlie, nervy, strained, near tears.

Leech smiled. He knew he showed more teeth than seemed possible.

"Yes," he said, the last sound hissing in echo around the cavern. "I know."

Minutes passed. Junior hummed a happy tune, accompanied by musical echoes from the stalactites.

Leech looked at Charlie, outstaring his Satan glare, trumping his ace.

At last, in a tiny voice, Charlie said, "Take me home."

Leech was magnanimous. "But of course, Charles. Trust me, this way will suit you better. Pursue your interests, wage your war against the dream factory, and you will be remembered. Everyone will know your name."

"Yeah, man, whatever. Let's get going."

"Creighton," said Leech. "It's night up top. The moon is full. Do you think you can lead us to the moonlight?"

"Sure thing, George. I'm the Wolf Man, ahhh-woooooo!"

Janice Marsh had died while they were under the mountain. Her room stank and bad water sloshed on the carpets. The tarpaulin served as her shroud.

Leech hated to let her down, but she'd had too little to bring to the table. She had been a coelacanth, a living fossil.

Charlie announced that he was abandoning the search for the Subterranean Sea of California, that there were other paths to Helter Skelter. After all, was it not written that when you get to the bottom you start again at the top. He told his Family that his album would change the world when he got it together with Dennis, and he sang them a song about how the pigs would suffer.

Inside, Charlie was terrified. That would make him more dangerous.

But not as dangerous as Derek Leech.

Before he left the Ranch, in a requisitioned buggy with Constant at the wheel, Leech sat a while with Junior.

"You've contributed more than you know," he told Junior. "I don't often do this, but I feel you're owed. So, no deals, no contracts, just an offer. A no-strings offer. It will set things square between us. What do you want? What can I do for you?"

Leech had noticed how hoarse Junior's speech was, gruffer even than you'd expect after years of chili and booze. His father had died of throat cancer, a silent movie star bereft of his voice. The same poison was just touching the son, extending tiny filaments of death around his larynx. If asked, Leech could call them off, take away the disease.

Or he could fix up a big budget star vehicle at Metro, a Lifetime Achievement Academy Award, a final marriage to Ava Gardner, a top-ten record with the Monkees, a hit TV series . . .

Junior thought a while, then hugged Leech.

"You've already done it, George. You've already granted my wish. You call me by my name. By my mom's name. Not by his, not by 'Junior.' They had to starve me into taking it. That's all I ever wanted. My own name."

It was so simple. Leech respected that; those who asked only for a little respect, a little place of their own—they should get what they deserve, as much as those who came greedily to the feast, hoping for all you can eat.

"Goodbye, Creighton," he said.

Leech walked away from a happy man.

I cannot think of the deep sea without shuddering at the nameless things that may at this very moment be crawling and floundering on its slimy bed, worshipping their ancient stone idols and carving their own detestable likenesses on submarine obelisks of water-soaked granite.

"Dagon" · H.P. Lovecraft (1917)

• HEAD MUSIC •
Lon Prater

At 1:02 a.m., Diego's eyes snapped open. The haunting, tuneless music was in his head again, louder than ever. Mournful tones rose and fell, reverberating between his temples. Throughout his eighteen years he had heard them: occasional, faint and inviting whispers tugging at his innards. Now the deep, echoing hornsong was louder, more insistent; it had control of his body.

Bare-chested and shoeless, he burst through the painted screen door. The cool autumn night welcomed him with a clammy marsh-salt embrace.

The flimsy wood frame squealed and slammed shut behind him. The keys to his father's work truck jangled in one hand.

On the horizon, a prowler moon crouched fat and yellow behind a low fence of backlit clouds. His naked back pressed against the chilled vinyl seat. Diego would have shivered, but the music moving his body prevented it. He was glad that he had worn sweatpants to bed.

Bare feet, wet with dew and grass clippings, pumped the gas pedal and pressed in the clutch. He watched—calmly, serenely—as his right hand twisted the key. The stubborn engine roared indignantly to life.

The truck lurched onto the empty road, headlights darkened. Diego was completely out of control: a passenger within the truck as well as within his own body.

The rusty old heap hurtled down the empty blacktop, landscaping tools clattering madly in the bed. Diego felt content. He rode the swell and crash of a forlorn internal symphony; he was not afraid.

The beach was part of a state park and nature preserve. Red and white signs threatened after-hours trespassers with fines and jail time. The penalties were even steeper for those foolish enough to take animals, glass, or vehicles onto the sand.

The renegade truck bounced over the benighted dunes. At the same time, the plaintive wailing began to recede; a cacophony of lesser tones gained in strength. He realized with a start that his body was his own again.

Diego squinted through the dirty windshield. A curtain of dense gray clouds blocked most of the moon's reflected light. This far from town the stars shone with a rare luminosity. Their light was mirrored in the phosphorescent foam and sparkle of the cresting waves. Wet sand glimmered at the water's edge.

A shadowed hump lay in the blackness just yards from the lapping waves. Leaning forward, Diego flipped on the headlights.

The head music erupted into skull-splitting shrieks. His hand shot out automatically, killing the lights. The return of darkness stifled the blood curdling screeches as well—but he had already caught a glimpse of the thing on the beach.

He wiped the sudden cold sweat from his face and took several calming breaths. Steeling himself, Diego opened the door and stepped trembling onto the sand.

He shivered. The night had grown mute and windless. Even the tuneless music had faded to a soft mewling; his brain was full of newborn kittens.

Sand and bits of dune grass scrunched beneath him as he approached the creature. It had the length and girth of a small killer whale, but that was where the resemblance ended.

Diego walked around it, unable to fathom what he was seeing. It had slick, warty gray-green skin flecked all over with lambent orange jewel-like scales. There were no eyes to speak of. Either end of its tube-like body presented a fleshy pucker of skin surrounded by a forest of supple whips and barbed tendrils. Near the center of its girth there were three great vein-lined fans pressed close against its body.

The creature stank of window cleaner.

Whatever it was, it had called him here to this beach with its hornsong. The same sounds he had heard over the years, only stronger now, more desperate.

A lonely dirge-like cry sang inside him. It engulfed him in waterlogged sadness, drowning out the soft whining chorus. He felt a strange kinship with this thing, one that he could not explain.

Ancient intuition clawed its way into his awareness. The creature—no, she—was stranded, beached here in the alien air. Unable to return to the sea, she knew she was dying.

Tears scorched his eyes. He rushed at her, vainly throwing his weight into an attempt to roll the immense cylinder of her body back into the sea.

As reward, Diego's bare chest, arms, and back were scored with tiny nicks from the scattered orange scales. His torso was smeared with a gritty, viscous film that made the open cuts swell and burn like bee stings. He cried out in frustration, looking around for a way to save this bizarre and wondrous creature.

His eyes came to rest on the abandoned truck. He strode toward it, for the moment ignoring the piteous lament in his head. A search of the truck revealed a lawnmower and gas can, hand tools and pruning shears, shovels and rakes, a wheelbarrow and some clear bags—but nothing that would help him return this behemoth safely to the sea.

Despair filled him like freshly poured concrete. He returned to her side. The inky waves were almost washing up against one puckered end.

The kitten-like mewling started up again in earnest. He put a hand on her, careful not to let the sharp orange speckles cut him. On some primitive level he felt the squirming fluted mass of life within her.

They could have been her brains as easily as they were her young. It didn't matter to Diego; he knew that they needed to come out of her.

He gulped, approaching her ocean-side sphincter again. The dank smell of salt and rotting seaweed mixed with her ammonia odor, an unsettling combination. He carefully pushed the waving tendrils away from the opening. This would not be easy.

Diego plunged his arm into the unearthly creature, straining to keep down his gorge. His heart beat fast and loud in his ears. Something skittered across his foot and he jumped—a ghost crab.

His arm was buried to the shoulder. The keening in his head was louder, more frantic. He grasped the end of a slippery fat hose and pulled. It came out with a slurping noise and a geyser of foul liquid.

Diego dropped the greasy pus-thing and vomited all over it. It writhed there, celebrating the glorious emptying of Diego's guts. Then, like a slow but enormous blond worm, it inched its way into the waves.

The mother's song was faint now; the chaotic internal cries of her young continued to gnaw desperately at him.

He jabbed an arm into her again, feeling nothing but the pain of his burning cuts and the squish of her organs. He removed his arm and went to the opposite end. This time it was easier. Diego eased two of the worm-things from the orifice, each over six-feet long. He deposited them gingerly into the lapping water.

They lay there motionless. Diego could suddenly smell their corruption, even over the ammonia and beach scents. *Stillborn. As were the others still rotting within the dune-side womb.*

He had saved one of the disgusting things. Wasn't that enough? The wailing chorus of those still in the sea-side womb disagreed, begging for release. One day they would grow into creatures as beautiful and alien as the one dying here before him. But not if he left them inside her to die.

He went to the back of the truck and returned with the pruning shears. Sticking the bottom blade into the sphincter at the water's edge, he crossed himself, preparing for what he had to do.

Diego squeezed the rubber coated handles together with all his might. The blades weren't as sharp as he had hoped. They did not cut so much as chew slits into her, widening the puckered hole. She did not bleed, at least not so he could tell it, but the ammonia smell nearly made him pass out. What kept him conscious was the soft saxophone moan of her pain—her fear—echoing through his head.

He finished carving a second slit out of the rubbery flesh. He knew he had the will to do what was required. Nevertheless, he was thankful that his stomach was already empty. Diego took one last look around.

The moon had escaped from the clouds, leaning closer now to cast a pallid eye on the boy and the primeval sea thing on the beach. His father's truck stood lonely watch from atop the dunes.

Diego pulled off his sweatpants and boxer shorts, leaving them in a heap on the sand. He grunted, drawing in one last breath before he burrowed naked and unflinching into the womb of the beast.

Rough slimy tissue like pus-soaked leprous scabs pressed all around him. He was waist deep inside her, and clawing his way closer to the maggoty nest of her tender young. The vapors were rank, infectious. Every one of the cuts on his body screamed as they were filled with her vile inner fluids. Worming himself farther into her, Diego gagged on bile.

He could feel the wind kick up, tickling his feet and ankles. Every other part of him was embalmed in the gelatinous tract to her inner organs.

Diego heard her wordless voice again, clearer and richer, a quiet ululation. From within her the music embraced him, every note entwining his soul and hers. She sang to him of the deep black ocean floor, of submarine cities chiseled from stone and shell that had never been touched by the sun. He shot harpoon-fast through majestic salt-water caverns populated by unimagined species both great and terrible. An age long past—and yet to come—dazzled his mind; those who once reigned would awaken. They would sweep the planet clean of humanity, sloughing man's frail advances from its face like dead skin.

His reaching hands dug into a torn membrane, ripping it farther. Diego scooped up the howling coils of her knotted young, dragging them back with him through her awful stickiness in one armful. He collapsed to the sand, the writhing blond creatures squirming free of each other and all over and around him, then crawling blindly into the waves.

Finally, the last one slipped beneath the surface, leaving Diego with only the moon and the gorgeous stinking carcass for company. He felt grief wash over him even as he saw the tide drawing his pants and vomit out to sea.

Scientists would come in the morning, and reporters. They'd take their pictures and measurements. Scratching their chins in wonder, they'd speak earnestly of evolution and the coelacanth. They would cut her up in their laboratories, puzzling over the secret of her genes. In time, someone would realize the horrible truth; the world would be warned of mankind's short leash.

Diego rose, his nude body sticky with foul juices and pockmarked by the swollen cuts. He dug in his toes, kicking wet sand across the beach.

He made one last trip to his father's truck, rummaging in the glove box first before grabbing the metal can from the bed.

With remorse like he had never felt before, Diego splattered gasoline all over the she-carcass and her stillborn young. He stood there feeling the loss of the music for a long time before he set fire to a wad of napkins and papers. Mouthing a silent and unintelligible prayer, he threw the flaming papers upon her.

She went up in a quick blue whoosh that in other cases might have made Diego jump. He danced an unfamiliar dance around her instead, growing dizzy from the fumes. Naked to the moon and sand and wind, he made dirge noises never before sounded upon the earth by man.

The pyre burned itself out about an hour before dawn. Diego hunched on the sand, watching the last smoking embers. She had no bones; the flame left nothing behind but a sprinkling of orange scales. He poked the blackened sand with the shovel before turning it over and over upon itself, hiding even this evidence from the failing stars above.

He was sweating, coated with sand and sticky filth. No one would know what had transpired on this beach; Diego was certain of that. The secret of her kind would remain hidden for another age or more, until they chose to reveal themselves.

Diego walked, then ran, then swam as far and as deep into the frigid black waves as he could. The last thing he heard was the music of underwater horns, calling him home.

It's from N'kai that frightful Tsathoggua came—you know, the amorphous, toad-like god-creature mentioned in the Pnakotic Manuscripts *and the* Necronomicon *and the Commoriom myth-cycle preserved by the Atlantean high-priest Klarkash-Ton.*

"The Whisperer in Darkness" · H.P. Lovecraft (1930)

· TSATHOGGUA ·
Michael Shea

An elderly woman named Maureen, neatly dressed and manicured, sat on a bus-stop bench in San Francisco. She was watching the leisurely approach of an old shopping-cart vagabond up the sidewalk. Maureen believed in being courteous to everyone, but the vagabond woman strongly irritated her, perhaps because Maureen had put her dear little Buddy to sleep not so long ago. And the gaunt, sunburned wild-haired tramp was pushing, along with other things in her cart, a box with a tiny, sick-looking little dog in it. A whippet.

Maureen and her friends in her church Discussion Group had been talking about Speaking Out lately, about not being so courteous when something hurtful was done. About protesting in the name of decency.

"I'm sorry," said Maureen, a little loud and unsteady at the newness of this, "but I just think it's disgraceful. Whyever you've chosen to degrade yourself, I think its terrible to subject that poor little animal to this existence! It's unforgivable!"

The old cart-pushing dame paused-she had a long stark tendony frame. In her baggy jeans and denim jacket she was deep-seamed old, but one of those bionic oldsters, tight and sound as a banty rooster. "Hey," she said. "We've spent his whole life walking around this city. You think because he's dying he doesn't wanna get around any more? I'm his chauffeur!"

"But you should put him to sleep! Look how decrepit he is!"

"He's going to sleep. You think I wanna rush him along, who's been my friend his whole seventeen years? You've gotta excuse me, I'm taking us home for a bath right now."

"You have a home . . . ?"

"What am I, wearing a label? You see me dressed for walking, you think I'm Homeless?"

And on she went, her cart rattling softly. Maxie was her name. Her hair was white, but luxuriant still. She wore its shag like a plumed battle-casque hooding her brow, head and neck. It tendrilled like tree-roots on her gaunt denimed shoulders. Her ancient whippet though, Ramses, was aged beyond all vigor. She bent her face to him as she pushed, and Ramses, a living skeleton, raised, in palsied dabs, his tiny muzzle towards her, sniffed too, now and again, the early autumn air.

In the front of the cart were a kitchen-box of goods and utensils, and next to it the bedding-and-clothes box. Last night they had shared their sleeping bag among the trees below the Legion of Honor. Had a twig fire in her firecan—invisible from twenty feet away. Had soup and tea for them both, and then some blazing stars to look at above the Golden Gate. Ramses had gone to sleep. Maxie had reread and relished Mitchell Smith's *Due North* by her tiny reading light.

Here they were back at their building. Maxie's home, Butler Street County Housing, was sited in the hills above the Panhandle, the neighborhood at least a nice one. The building had its own little parking lot, and well-kept plantings all around. She had a niche in these where she always tucked her cart. She took the knapsack of her and Ramses' dirty laundry, put her two days' dirty dishes and cooking pan into its side pockets, and slipped it on. Had already slipped on the child-carrier pouch frontwards, and tenderly hoisted Ramses, holstering him against her chest.

Her apartment was on the third floor, and there was a lot of hallway-life on the third floor, hang-around kids and young men with drugs to sell each other, and attitude to maintain in front of each other. Everybody poor and desperate enough to make violence always an uneasy possibility. Inside the entry she turned hard right for the stairs. The tough element always claimed the elevators. The stairs were faster anyway, and better exercise.

She emerged in the hall of her wing, and found her local, mainly Hispanic, crew on duty. Their lead rapster, in a sideways-billed cap, was a guy she thought of as Dog. That's what he called Maxie because of her always carrying Ramses, and what he called her now:

"Hey Dawg! Dawg back! Wassit gonna be? You need to pay you police services fee. Now iss twenny aweek, Dog, why you don't pay up? You gotta pay the vig, Dog! You gotta pay the vig!"

This was the way it was supposed to go: Maxie would reply *I'm not payin anything! Get outta my way!* She would say this, but not try to get past them. Then Dog would push his bullying little riff again, and then Maxie would refuse again—all while his audience just sort of idly enjoyed the show of Dog putting Maxie through her paces. And then, at last, they'd let her pass.

But this afternoon Maxie was wrung out. That crazy woman had ticked her off, reminded her that truly, Ramses was near death. Scared, weary and pissed, she snapped, "Leave me alone! Get your lazy candyass outta my way! You moron! Vig is interest on a loan! You're trying to extort Protection from me, you ignorant asshole!"

That stopped Mr. Dog hard for a moment, took him like a punch, her steely contempt where he'd thought himself comfortably feared.

If Dog hadn't had his whole crew with him, if it had been just him and another one he particularly hung with, a guy they called Carne who had sick dreamy eyes, then he would have hit her, certainly cracked her jaw, or some part of her body.

As it was, he shoved her, the heels of his hands to her shoulders, and she stumbled backwards, fighting to keep her feet under her, and Ramses safe in his carrier. Back she came, marched past them to her doorway, got inside.

As she ran the tub full, Maxie faced it: a line had been crossed. They'd laid hands on her, and it might come readier next time. These kids had nothing, possessed not even the barest information about their world. They would cling to whatever sad debris life brought their way. Would seize and cultivate any contest that got started in their hallway world.

It was on the chilly side in the bathroom. She put Ramses in the electric blanket while she bathed and washed her hair. Bathed him next, while their tomato-soup-with-cheese-melted-in was cooling—Ramses' vitamins mixed in his, Maxie's in hers. After they ate, there were all the utensils to be scoured and re-packed in the pockets of the knapsack. She cleaned and flossed her teeth, and then hung Ramses in a clean carrier on her chest and took up the knapsack of wash. Time to check out the laundry room.

She cracked her door open. The corridor was empty. She made quick time to the stairwell and slipped inside it. Stood listening.

Ten flights of metal stairs and scarred pipe-railing above her, a zigzag of six flights below her. From the laundry room door would well the echoes of any activity. Nothing.

She always listened before descending. People partied down there, dealt, OD'd occasionally, and Maxie always stood ready to turn on a dime and truck on out to a laundromat in the neighborhood—more expensive but hassle-free.

She started down quietly. Got down four of the six flights, the laundry room and the maze of storage lockers that surrounded it sounding perfectly empty . . . and then there came one very soft little resonance of metal.

So minor a sound, like the slightest tap against the hollowness of one of the big washers or driers down there. Listening, listening she heard nothing more.

It could have been the stir of someone hiding down there.

She peered into Ramses' face, checking as she'd done through the years for his reading of a risky vicinity. He looked up at her, feebly alert, but inscrutable. Ah, how her little sidekick's life had waned.

A flare of anger started Maxie down again. She was sick of dodging around this gloomy, risky place. But old persons, well, the whole world was bigger and scarier for them all. If she was tired of ducking and maneuvering in the world's brutal bigness, Maxie should just give up, right? The fact was, she would save two bucks using these machines. That was an extra cocktail at Pete's tonight. So. Was she getting so chicken-shit that she didn't dare go down there and win herself a bit of luxury?

The stairwell door hung open, and the laundry room beyond it was deserted. She walked down both aisles to be sure, and checked the bank of driers. The long-defunct machine back in the corner still stood with its door open, though the band of yellow plastic tape across it had been broken.

She approached it down the damp concrete aisle, where suds lay on the floor by the bank of washers opposite. A faint, ragged noise rose from the pouch. Ramses was growling a warning and there was something big inside the drier's black drum.

A person. A woman? Yes. A little Latin woman, curled up as if asleep. Was she asleep? And as Maxie leaned her head inside, Ramses' little growl grew echosome.

Asleep. She breathed softly, the little brown moon of her face childish and candid, seeming to dream.

On drugs? Drunk? Whatever, leave her be. You stick tight to your own business in this place. She backed quietly from the drier, and something squishy crackled under the heel of her Nike. She turned around.

One of the big washers behind her had shut down mid-cycle, had a load of unmoving suds in it, while the door of the one beside it hung open, thick suds dripping from the door's glass eye. She'd trod in the mess of foam it had shed on the floor. There was her shoe-print in the suds, and something small and dark crushed in its midst.

A slug? It always smelled so earthy down here, and right now more than ever. The dense dirt the whole building was rooted in, you could feel it right outside these concrete walls.

She went into the other aisle, got all their wash into one load, and set it going. She put Ramses down on the floor, and was folding his pouch into a little mat for him, when he got up and tottered off. Maxie smiled. Sometimes the earthen aura down here persuaded the old Ramses that he was outside where he could take a dump. Let him. It would be small and dry and easily scooped. She watched his trembly progress.

Damn that self-righteous old bitch, but it was true: her poor friend was on his way out. Maxie had gotten him for Jack in those last two years Jack was dying. Jack had named him, for his habit of ramming blindly into things as an impetuous pup. Fifteen years dead, the dear man. How she missed him still! And now old Ramses here, the last piece of life they'd shared, was passing out of the world.

Maxie opened *The Guns of August*, and fell right into it, re-entered that vast machine of long-ago armies locked in stasis, locked in butchery.

She would allow herself an extra cigarette today—six, not five. Her regimen iron-fast these last ten years, her six-smoke days were an indulgence earned by their rarity. She lit one up, and gorged on the satiny entrails of a Marlboro's smoke as she read.

Going to dry her load, she saw Ramses down at the end of the aisle, sitting before the little Latina's odd dormitory, his gaze alternating between it and the lush suds still undecayed on the floor. When Maxie started her own dryer, it roused no stir from the sleeper. How strange to have a little dreaming neighbor like this. What kind of life would the girl step back into when she woke? What dangers, disorders, unmet needs? How many years did she have left? Far more than Maxie had, no doubt.

Maureen had one of those decent-sized little backyards some houses have out in the Avenues, and she and Muffin were out in it, watering their flowerbeds. The dog two yards over, King, that dreadful big mastiff of Wyatt and Eve's, was barking again. His relentless barking had long ago worn a blister on Maureen's patience, and then the blister had become more like a callus, though sometimes it was more like a blister again.

Meanwhile little Muffin, also vocal, was yipping incessantly at the hose. Maureen thumbed the water into a fan and moistened the trilliums, finding Muffy's puppy-relentlessness a little trying after all. Maureen had been younger when she'd broken in her beloved Buddy. But if you loved small dogs, you had to handle that hyperness that goes with them, especially at first.

No one could replace Buddy of course. The grief for Buddy, whom she'd had to put to sleep, came to her again, as Maureen had long ago accepted it would. She gazed down upon Muffin, trying to see in him the dear companion he would become in future years. As she was musing in this way, the hose she held gave a kind of lurch in her inattentive grip, twitched sideways, and sent a stronger stream down on Muffin, drenching his head in mid-bark. The dog shook himself, and then began to lick his chops, while Maureen looked closer at what seemed to be a thicker kind of water now coming our of her garden hose. It fel slicker to her thumb and fingers, and it splattered rather than splashed on the soil.

And against the background of the soil, into which it quickly soaked, it was hard to tell but weren't there, like, little black clots in the water? They soaked in too fast to be sure.

Then the water ran normal again. Some bit of debris in the line.

"I don't drink that much Maxie," Vera said, stabbing the bar with her forefinger, "and I saw what I saw. You enjoying that drink?" Vera had a sharp nose for a black lady, and little tufted, alarmed-looking eyebrows that made her eyes seem on the brink of outrage.

"I am enjoying it, and I am listening."

"What number is that?" Referring to the cigarette Maxie was unlimbering.

"Two. I get six today. I might smoke two in a row, sitting on this very stool." Maxie waved another round from Pete. She had Ramses in the sling—would have wanted to bring in his box and put it on the stool next to hers, but Pete drew the line. "The dog can come in, but not in his bed for Chrissake! I already let you park your goddamn bag-lady cart outback, Maxie! This is a bar! Jack would have said the same!"

"Jack loved Ramses!"

"This is a bar, all right," put in Vera, "but this is a Neighborhood Bar. It celebrates Neighborhood Diversity; including the whackadoo practices of the local seniors." Elbowing Maxie's ribs here. They had been neighbors for seven years, and then Vera had protested against the decline of the Butler Street Housing. She had agitated and done the red tape till she was re-lodged in a better building. And now, that building was already as bad as Butler, if not worse.

"So. What do you think, girl? About what I saw? Look at me. Do you think I'm drunk?"

"No."

"Well this is exactly how it was last night crossing the Panhandle. So you going to just dismiss what I told you?"

Crossing the Panhandle at about two a.m., Vera had seen a man lying on a bench under one of the pathway lamps. He was passed out, it seemed, as she approached, still a block away, but then the man suddenly appeared to be struck by seizure. His legs started violently kicking out as he lay there

Vera hurried forward, the path curving and some trees blocking her view for several long moments as she limpingly picked up speed, striding as fast as her bad left hip would let her.

When she came back into view just yards from the bench, the man lay quiet again, totally still, his eyelids shut, his face slack, his left arm hanging off the bench—and one of the legs of his trousers flat and empty on the slats of the bench.

"I like to've wet myself," were Vera's words. She had seen both legs kicking in the dim lamplight and now this empty fabric tube.

And just then, she heard a scraping, as of rough skin wrestling through undergrowth. She caught a blur of movement off in the grass to her right.'

"And it reached some bushes, and right where it left the grass and pushed in between 'em, I saw something big and thick worm itself across, with like pebbly skin!"

Vera pursued, too astonished to do otherwise, and the grass, uncut for some time, snagged her jerky gait. There was a curious tearing sound and then a vigorous, receding slither. She groped into the bushes, and threaded her way into the clear again. Between the trees along the Panhandle's border she glimpsed, across Fell Street, something big moving low to the ground, reaching the far curb just ahead of an oncoming truck, and diving into the darkness beneath a parked van.

And Vera, in the weeds near where she stood, found a shoe, its laces still tied but the whole shoe ruptured, a bouquet of tatters attached to a sole. Dazed, she unwillingly returned to the bench. There was no sign of the man. In a cluster of bushes not too distant, she heard a muffled thrashing. "I thought it over, but then I headed home. No way was I messin' around in them bushes."

Vera glared at Maxie, awaiting her response.

"Well," said Maxie. "I can only say that's strange. And I have to add that last night was obviously one of those occasional nights when you get a little drunker than you think you are."

Vera looked at her gloomily. She didn't seem to want to challenge this, but didn't seem able to believe it either.

Maxie cruised down the pleasant asphalted lanes of Golden Gate Park, trending down seawards. The sun, while still an hour high, sank into a rising layer of mist, and dimmed to a Martian wafer, brick-red. A sharp wind came up and started driving the mist inland through the park, draping streamers of fog through the towering cypresses, and tangling it in the eucalypti's blown cascades of gray-black foliage. Shreds of mist licked her face and she tucked Ramses more warmly in his box. The weather-shift stirred her. In the white-out of driving mist, the great trees rippled like coral reefs in a streaming sea of air.

Wind always excited Maxie, though it bit her harder in her lean old age. Ramses seemed stirred too, looked livelier up at her from his thick swaddling, relishing the silver rush of the air. "Put you to sleep?" she scoffed. "Crazy bitch! Isn't this an amazing evening?" She crossed the Great Highway, and walked along the seaside promenade, pushing their cart's rattling prow into the wind. A surprisingly thick foam churned on the surf, the caked yellow froth of hard-lashed seas. Copious fragments of it came tumbling and winging across the broad beach. They climbed the embankment, to fly in chunks and tatters across the promenade, scud out into the Great Highway, and plaster the passing traffic here and there with rags of dirty bubbles.

The cold spray licking Maxie's cheekbones felt dense and glutinous. And, through all this wind and the sharp sea-smell, there was a haunting swamp scent, a fetor that belonged to dark murk and deep jungle, not at all to windblown coasts. Yet here it was, eddying inside the cowl of Maxie's parka, probing her nostrils with the smell of putrefaction.

She trudged up past the Cliff House, past the guano-bleached crags just offshore in the surfs crash. Even this high above the sea the dirty blizzard still blew past her, crossing the pavements. Tonight she'd go into those trees again, up beyond the pits of the old Sutro Baths.

Soon it was falling dark, but by that time they were snug in the lee of two close-growing trees, lying back half-propped on a mattress of dry needles and fern fronds, she and Ramses snug in their waterproof fiber-filled mountain bag. Plenty of hot-burning cypress twigs lay broken and stockpiled, while the tiny trail stove housed a hot little blaze at their side, and heated her cocoa in an enameled tin cup. They lay back looking through the gaps in the trees down on the narrowing waters of the Golden Gate, the Bridge ankle deep in the steel-gray sea. The vista grew dimmer, as the headlights rivering atop the Bridge grew brighter. Beyond the Bridge, mist filled the Bay, and muted the glints of the city lights along its eastern shore.

Maxie lit her fourth cigarette of the day—two more still to come!—and congratulated herself, not for the first time, on her long-ago inspiration to take to the streets, to spend two thirds of her days and nights outdoors. How much better the night sky was than any ceiling! And how much better to be moving around! Where in the world was there a more beautiful city than San Francisco? Why lie in any box in the time you've got left, eh old girl?

Her shopping cart had been an inspired idea—a declaration of poverty, a protection against thieves. She'd found the perfect way to go abroad in the world. She took a deep drag, and streamed it up towards the first shyly appearing stars. Sipped her cocoa. It would be sweet to have Jack beside her now. They could describe to each other how grand and impossible the Bridge looked, bestriding the sea.

"I miss you, my love," she said quietly. It always hurt her to say it aloud, and always had a sweetness too, as if Jack just might hear it.

Within the murmur of the wind in the trees, within that restless commotion, she felt wrapped in the conversation, the hum of the forest's green life was that a trickling sound she heard?

There was a moon well up in the misty night, and when Maxie peered into the trees for the sound's source, her eye caught a glinting *something* in the ferns a few yards to her left.

A little seepage from the loam? Maybe something a little more profuse than seepage—she saw a silvery little braid of movement there. It was months since any rain.

She finished her cocoa and got out her second-to-last smog. Snapped it alight, and blew the satin smoke from her nostrils. The sound of the night had changed around her. The hillside seemed restive in a new way, not just with the wind's passage, but stirred by little secretive movements everywhere, a host of small half-hidden lives all working in the earth and in the leaf mold and among the roots of the trees, the roots right under her.

She consumed the cigarette, cupping the coal between drags so the wind wouldn't accelerate its burn-down. And by the time she'd finished it, had decided that, when she'd gathered ferns and needles for her mattress, there had been no seepage over there, where now she saw it. She weighed her comfort against her curiosity.

In the end, the restlessness in the earth goaded her to action. She extracted herself carefully from the bag, resettling it closely around Ramses. Stepped into her jeans and her Nikes.

Only a glow of embers came from the square mouth of her tin-can stove. She stepped across springy earth into deepening shadow.

Here was a shallow cleft in the sloping soil, and a leakage, not of water, but of a loose viscous fluid, bubbly with strong curdlike bubbles that put her in mind, somehow, of the suds dripping from that open washer door this afternoon.

"You oughta watch out for that stuff."

The voice was calm but so unexpectedly nearby that Maxie had a neural meltdown.

"You sonofabitch! Don't you have the manners to greet someone? What're you doing, sneaking up to me?"

"I been standing here ten minutes. I thought you saw me." But there was a sour humor in the old man's eyes that confessed he'd enjoyed making her jump. He was small and lean in dark sweatshirt and jeans, helmeted in a black wool cap with a tiny brim and earflaps, his face all gaunt. But he had a major handlebar mustache that was remarkably thick for a man this old. The mustache made Maxie think of a ragged white alley cat draped over a fence.

"So why are you standing here! There's plenty of room on this hill. We want our goddamn privacy!"

"You shouldn't be lyin' here! That's what I'm tellin' ya! You gotta watch out for this stuff, for anything comes from the water table."

"For anything that comes from the water table?"

"You speak English, doncha?"

"Better than you."

This made the handlebar man mad. "Maybe so, but you don't know shit. Just do yourself and everyone else a favor and don't step in it, if that's not too complicated for ya."

And he walked off into the trees—pretty quiet and quick in his movements too, and soon gone from sight and hearing.

Maxie crouched down over the seepage, stirred around in it a little with a twig. It was clotted, with little shadows in the clots. She'd grown up in the Central Valley. "Frogspawn," she said. Or toadspawn, up on these moist hillsides. That's all it was. The mustache man was an urban whack, freaked out by unfamiliar Nature. She sighed, and went back to her sleeping bag.

Snuggling down and cradling Ramses, she told him, "That guy seemed almost sane at first, didn't he?"

But, deeper in the night, Ramses' movement woke her. He had climbed her shoulder, and stayed there with his muzzle aimed at the seepage. And remained so, after she had fallen back into sleep.

Maureen had fallen asleep in her Barcalounger, snug in quilts with the clicker at hand and Muffin curled on her lap. It was Muffin's sleeping there that had put

Maureen under, and now it was his gentle movements in her lap that awakened her. She had a vague sensation of small, light forms dispersing across her thighs.

Her wakening was hazy and slow, for she'd had one of her nice pills before she and Muffin settled down. She raised her head, so comfy and heavy. Yes, there he was in her lap, his adorable little muzzle thrust up inquiringly towards Maureen's face, and his little fawn-colored flanks so fluffy. But.

Maureen hoisted herself a little higher. Muffin blinked calmly back at her. But Muffy had no legs. No legs at all. Muffin was only his head, his fat fluffy little torso, and his tail. He looked perfectly sleek, like he'd never had legs!

Maureen was utterly, albeit groggily, astonished.

And just then she felt a delicate movement across the slipper on her right foot.

The shock of it gave her the hydraulic lift to sit all the way up. A slender little jointed shape jackknifed off her slipper, and vanished.

Scooping up Muffin, Maureen surged to her feet in astonished terror. Here was her dog! As smooth as a little guinea pig, but without even a guinea pig's tiny legs! He was just a plump, furry tube! His tail wagged in response to Maureen's hands, but lackadaisically. His jaws were slightly parted, and he seemed very lightly to pant.

Maureen set him on the couch, rushed, whimpering softly, to the phone, and punched out her vet's number from memory. Soon she was in a frantic altercation with the vet's answering service, Maureen crying banshee-like that an ambulance must come for Muffin and herself and that Dr. Groner had to come in to meet them at the pet hospital at once! Maureen encountered, within a suede glove of courtesy, an iron fist of refusal—and then was galvanized to discover, in her pacings, that Muffin had disappeared from his nest of cushions. But how could the poor dog move?

In a panic she dropped the phone, and searched under the sofa. Down the hall behind her, came the little clap of the backdoor pet-door. It was only Tasha, Maureen's cranky old portly little Persian, waddling dourly toward her. Still in shock, Maureen responded by rote, went to the kitchen to be sure Tasha's dish was full. The kitchen was dark but a slant of light from the Barcalounger lamp showed the shadow of food in the dish. Wasting no energy on greeting, Tasha padded a beeline to her supper.

Trembling with determination, Maureen took up the phone again. If it had to be 911, so be it.

A thump and a slithery scrabbling and the rattle of spilt kibble brought her head round. Tasha lay—half in shadow—thrashing mightily, and what looked like long tapery fish with froggy skin, three of them, were eating her legs! Three of her legs as the cat kicked and thrashed them in the air, and clawed at them with her one free paw, but the fish—muscular, powerful—swallowed her legs into their froggy tubes with great gulps, lurching closer to her torso, four of them now! For Tasha's tail was also taken, by yet another of the little monsters that lurched suddenly from the darkness! Oh dear God in Heaven what was Happening?

A commotion rose from the back of the couch and she whirled. Around from the back and over the top poured another one of these toad-skinned fish, much bigger than the other four. Maureen screamed and leaped backwards, stumbled and fell back into her Barcalounger. And saw that atop this bigger monster's toadlike skull, there were two little tufted peaks, and instantly recognized those dear little saliences: they were the tips of Muffin's ears. But already they were no longer like ears. They were melting, sinking to a tarry substance that seemed to weave itself into the toad-skin hemisphere, melting to a dark resin that was already merging with the monster's amphibious skin. This had been Muffin! This hideous fish! It launched itself, and the creature—big as a cat itself—seemed to have only Tasha in its sights. It launched to the floor and thrashed across it, pushing itself along by—Maureen saw them now—the thrusts of four little legs that looked almost like fins with little clawed feet.

A strange calm fell upon Maureen. All of this was so impossible that it was fascinating. Maureen's religion had a dimension of true feeling in her heart. The world's dazzling multiplicity often moved her deeply with reverence and awe. And often she inwardly exclaimed, *Behold the wonders of God's creation, for how can man conceive any end to their variety?*

For look! The lesser fish had fled to the shadows already, and now Tasha had only one leg, and no tail. Gamely, Tasha hoisted her head to encounter the big toad-fish's advance, its glossy parabolic jaws gaping wider, wider, as it thrashed its way across the floor, and leapt, and engulfed Tasha right up to her remaining leg. Then it reared up its toadlike gullet, and bolted Tasha's leg down too.

Maureen watched in awe. And terror too, of course, but encompassing the fear was a bemused sense of privilege for being honored with a revelation. She was being shown a miracle. She was not the futile, undistinguished woman she had, unknown to herself, feared that she was! She was being shown a miracle, and it filled her with gratitude.

Or perhaps this terror simply had made her insane?

But she did not feel insane. She felt tingly. Her thumb itched, and from it a kind of heat seemed to flow out and into all the rest of her body. She lay back watching Tasha's devourer calmly. The creature seemed slightly to swell, to change—its tail a bit shorter, its legs a bit bigger and more clearly jointed. It waddled its way down the hall, out of her view. There was a clatter of the pet door. And Maureen felt herself alone in the house.

Her body was quite comfortable really. And this was just exactly what she should be doing. After such a revelation, she should be lying here comfortably, meditating upon the wonder of it, and raising hosannas in her heart to a beneficent God capable of such wonders, and loving her enough to share them with her.

At sunrise Maxie rose and broke camp. Went upslope to the cluster of trees where she'd hidden her cart, and then down to the coffee shop just above the Cliff House. Here they accepted her with Ramses in his sling. She had a couple eggs and a cup of coffee. Went to the restroom. One thing about walking around all day was, you were regular as clockwork.

She had a second cup (having laid out her money with a dollar tip—as always) and savored it as she looked from the window. Watched the waves rolling in below the bare foundations of the vanished Sutro Baths. There was still a lot of foam on the waters.

It drew her attention. No gale now to froth it up, but big yellowish mats and ridges of this lather mantled the waves. And still, on this morning's milder breeze, it blew ashore, even way up here. Little rags of it tufted the dead water of the two square tarns that had been the Baths.

Outside, she got Ramses into his box-bed, and rolled him on down to the paths that networked the site.

When she was closer to the pools, she saw that the froth lay unmelting. Odd. Come to that, it was odd there was so much water in those pits. What was the norm for October, after months without rain?

She pushed to the path beyond the site, and out a ways around the shoulder of the bluffs. The foam lay in a shore-hugging band, not that wide, really, and seeming to narrow as it wrapped around the headland, towards the Golden Gate. Like a great decorative scarf flung round the cliffs' base.

"It's me. Over here."

Again calmly spoken but this time the Handlebar Man stood fifteen feet up slope from her.

"That's much better," Maxie said. "I hate being snuck up on. So, you talk about the water table you know about water in general? Like all that foam down there? There's no wind to whip it up . . . "

"Ocean's part of the water table. You don't think it honeycombs the whole damn peninsula here?"

He let a silence follow.

"Okay," she said. "So?"

"I'm not good at explaining. I hafta show you. You'll hafta park the cart and bag the dog."

"Have you been spying on me? How do you know I carry him in a sling?"

"Hey, I know every walker in this city. I get around. I keep my eyes open. So do you wanna believe, or do you wanna bury your head?"

"In the sand?"

"In the sand."

"Lead on. I've got a knife," [true] "and I've got a gun," [untrue] "and I know how to use them both." [untrue—neither one].

He led them back up into the trees. She parked her cart under cover, slung Ramses on her chest. Ramses looked alert and eager, as if today an added amperage coursed through him. The little whippet had always been her warning system, and he was telling her to follow this man.

"I'm Maxie."

"I'm Leon." He didn't look back at her, leading them upslope through the trees, rounding the shoulder of the headland. As they advanced northeasterly, the northern pylon of the Golden Gate just peeked into view, until the woods got thicker and the ground got steeper and she had to give all her attention to the trail.

Leon's route, scarcely a proper path itself, crossed many a clearer path descending steeply to the beach below. This crooked deer trail moved only gradually down the bluffs as it arced round them.

Now the bluff got quite steep, and the hillside in-folded deeply. And within this seam, a sharper, deeper gully lay. It was bare dirt, running perhaps a hundred yards down the bluff, heavily overgrown along its crests to either side, but in its depth just bare rock and the reddish clay of the cliffside's flesh.

"Step here," said Leon quietly, stopping, turning to her. "You up to it? We gotta go down to that outcrop by the lower angle—see it?"

"I'm up to it," Maxie snapped.

Still, it was steep, and the earth had to be worked with the heel to furnish footholds, and the shrubs used for steadying handholds. Ramses stirred in his pouch, and his muzzle probed the cold blue morning air.

The rim shelved a little. Leon called a halt, and they looked down into the gully. A damp breath welled from it. He pointed towards its apex, upslope of them. "Looka there. You see the stream creeping out of this thing?"

The earth seemed moister round a seam in the clay up there, and yes, she could now see that a thin sheen threaded its way all the way down along the gully's floor, and into the shrubbery below it.

"I don't see any flow."

"Look at that slickness. It's transparent but it's like thick, right?"

"Okay, there's some moisture I guess. So what?"

"This gully right here is where all that foam along the beach is coming from."

"Hey, Leon. You've gotta be kidding."

"No. But since you don't know shit, of course you'd say that."

"Hey, I don't like your mouth. I don't like your mustache either. It looks like the whiskers on a walrus's ass."

"You've seen the whiskers on a walrus's ass?"

"A white walrus's ass."

"Okay. Okay. Why should you trust me? But I'll tell you what. Come back here just before dark tonight, and get into some cover, and stay hidden, and watch this ravine. You won't watch long, before you see exactly what I'm talkin' about."

The morning sun slanted through the kitchen windows. From her Barcalounger, Maureen gazed dreamily at Tasha's dish, the scattered kibble on the linoleum, and not even a whisker of Tasha herself. Tasha had been eaten by what Muffin had turned into!

Amazing as this was, it was just a beginning. Maureen had lain for hours perfectly calm, except that her calm wasn't exactly calm, it was richer than that, more powerful. She felt a golden wholeness, a physical sense of completeness and purpose. Felt utterly relaxed, and utterly vibrant.

And, stranger than this, she felt *multiple*. More than having thoughts now, she seemed to be having a chorus of them. It dawned on Maureen for the first time in her long life that her mind was not really inside her body, not exactly, but that rather it was bombarding her body with constant queries and tests from more or less outside it.

And this dawned on her precisely because, for the first time, she felt that her mind was inside her body, or was multiply inside three separate parts of it. There was first her upper body, and she knew it from within. She was inside her ribcage. She didn't picture her ribcage—she was in it, enveloped in its blood-slick membranes, in the blood-swollen loaves of her lungs.

And her wonder at this was echoed, for she was also inside her legs, separately inside each one, her knowledge tendriled round their long bones like a ghostly ivy; marveling at the architecture of muscle and tendon and vein.

Never had Maureen felt so complete unto herself—felt herself to be such an exotic construction of bone and meat and soul! A wonderful coolth flushed through her tripart self, as if she had been dipped in a tarn of the blackest, deepest, purest water.

So within herself—within her three selves!—did she feel, that she did not at first realize that her eyes were closed and she lay in a sun-shot darkness. She willed her eyes to open, and it was revealed to her that she had no eyelids, nothing answered the movement of her will. At the same time, this seemed to matter not at all, so gorgeous was the architecture of tissue and vein she lay bathed in, wrapped in.

She tried to touch herself, to learn how she was changing, and it was revealed to her she had no arms while it seemed her feet were bulging, swelling (with a distant noise of ruptured slippers) and her legs' junctures with her waist were thinning, twisting, and her waist itself was doing likewise. And at the end of this vigorous unbraiding, it seemed three linked tails disengaged.

Maureen's legs thrust muscularly forth, and they (and her other selves in them) departed, surging reptilically down the hall and bursting—first one, then the other—with a slick whispery sound of passage out through the pet door.

While she who remained in the Barcalounger lay with tail thrashing to a metabolic rhythm, lay enthralled by the great strength blossoming in her newly potent shape.

Transfiguration! Accelerating now. Her flesh became whip-taut and cool. In smooth convulsions, her head and jaws usurped all the mass of her erstwhile body from the ribs up. And her eyes came back! My God, how they came back! Maureen could see all the way around her, her great orbs swiveling like greased ball bearings, eyes big enough to hold the world, catch every least movement in it.

Then, huge-jawed, her skin a glossy armor tough as leather, she wrenched free of her robe. She leapt, in a cavorting dolphins arc, from the Barcalounger, and hit the floor with the four surprises of little legs and clawed feet to break her impact. She scrabbled and slithered toward the front door.

By God in Heaven, Maureen was hungry! It was a raging void in her, a cyclone of need. But her head was too huge for the pet door, and her forefoot too crude for the knob. She rammed the door, cracking it lengthwise, but also hurting her head. She mustn't use her head as a ram yet. Her instinct told her that food was strength, and she would grow mightier with eating. The kitchen window should be easier than the door. She craved something large to eat, and the thought of the backyard—even as she toiled swiftly back down the hall—brought instantly to mind what she wanted to eat. It was when she was out back gardening, that she was most tormented by King's barking.

She leapt up onto the kitchen table. Perched on the table, her legs seeming to grow with every passing second, she gathered herself for a mightier leap—straight at the double panes above the kitchen sink.

Erupting into morning sun, in a sparkling spray of glass, Maureen dropped splay-legged—*whumph*—onto her deep, lush lawn.

King lived two yards over. Even now he was barking, with deep, baying deliberation.

She regarded her sturdy plank fence. She sensed that a moment was coming, not too distant, when she would have hind legs that could launch her right over it. But for the present, she began to ram and claw her way into the soft earth at the base of the fence.

She made rapid progress into the soil. As she worked, she heard the strains of Barry Manilow. That was why King was so vocal—his people, Wyatt and Eve—were out in their Jacuzzi on the back deck, enjoying the day with him.

With her cart stashed, knapsack packed, and Ramses in his sling, Maxie headed down one of the steep trails to the beach. Ramses was lively, head up out of the pouch, turning the little wand of his muzzle left and right. And there was a scent of something. A cool October day, a shred or two of cloud across the blue, but it didn't smell as fresh as it looked. There was a rankness that flirted with her mind.

Ramses got even livelier. Had to be put down. Tottered to a tree and peed on it. He seemed conscious of some adversary here, one he meant to meet. She put him in the sling the rest of the way down, but when they reached the narrow beach, he insisted on getting down again and tottered, zig and zag, ahead of her.

Maxie climbed the rocks a little way, and saw the yellow curdled foam mantling the sea for a hundred yards offshore, an unbroken collar arcing eastwards, curving round back towards the Golden Gate. In that direction the creamy expanse narrowed. Would it taper finally to a point of origin?

Ramses was already well ahead of her. She hurried after. Look at the life and purpose in him today! Put him to sleep? The idiocy of that woman.

They picked their way across rock shelf and gravel bar. Maxie found Ramses' unflagging energy as astonishing as she did the foam, which was indeed tapering, narrowing, till they came to a sharp invagination of the bluffs' wall.

Rounding this, they confronted a vertical cleft that vanished into the vegetation overhead. It was reminiscent of the much higher one Leon had taken her to, but its cleft was moister, and faintly foamy, and from its juncture with the barnacled rocks, a thin, milky threadwork branched out into the sea. The whole great stream of foam rose here!

Her clawed feet seemed to grow in strength with use—they gave Maureen a surprising amount of leverage in the earth. But it was her massive muscled head, and sinewy fish-like thrust, that enabled her momentum through the loam.

Surfacing in a spray of marigolds (Miss Saunders' largest bed of them) she charged to the next fence, and dove again against the earth, the dense soil a medium almost as yielding as water to her miraculous new shape.

She erupted in front of King's sizeable little house, which was in the corner of the yard the dog most loved—for from here he could bark at houses on every side of him. Maxie rose like a geyser of hunger, a craving void that must obliterate this beast. King had spirit. He yelped, he snarled, he lunged—into Maureen's widening, up-rushing jaws, which possessed his forelegs, head and chest, and lifted his struggling hindquarters skywards.

The game brute was chewing ferociously on Maureen's tongue, a massy organ which felt not pain, but tingling imminence, and then that tongue swelled and thrust more deeply into King's throat, a thick, expanding root that exploded King's skull within her mouth. She heaved him back, and yet again back, bagging the dog—near inert now, just tremoring—all the way down her gullet.

For an indeterminate time she crouched there, hidden by King's house from Wyatt and Eve in their Jacuzzi. Crouched there while Barry Manilow swelled suavely overhead. Crouched there discovering that King within her, though the architecture of him was dissolving in her corrosive stomach acids, though the brain and the bone shell that had held his heartbeats, his thoughts, were dissolving in her hunger, King himself was not dissolving, the animal's spirit emerged intact within her as his fleshly structure crumbled away. She felt, in the darkness of her digestion, the barking brute's horror and dismay, to find himself existing within the black sphere of her belly.

And as if this doleful incarcerated life in her were some kind of dynamo, an imperative deep in her new body, Maureen's bones branched creaking to life, and the muscles of her legs bulged along these bones. Almighty God in Heaven! I behold your wonders and I cry hallelujah unto you! Behold I open like a blossom under your radiance!

Swelled—in moments!—to half again her size, Maureen could just overlook the roof of the doghouse. In her almost spherical gaze, how shapely did Wyatt and Eve look, waist-deep in their Jacuzzi, drinks at their elbows! And how she hungered for them! Their fleshiness. In them lay her own more lordly stature! Behold the greatness the Lord declared that she had earned! To snatch them into her need's whirlwind would be to tower like a colossus when the meal was done. Still her hind legs grew, her steel-spring knees jutting higher to her sides, the muscles swelling like melons. And now, low though she squatted, Wyatt saw her.

She met his gaze. Such a square, fleshy young man, very intimidating whenever she'd gone to him with her faint, courteous complaints about King's barking. At present he didn't look threatening, looked astonished and suddenly Maureen absolutely knew that she could splash down into that hot tub with a single leap—

And as she thought it, launched it, thrust old bony mother earth so powerfully beneath her that she hung on air, a weightless bubble sailing the blue sky, and hit the water swallowing, Wyatt already socketed in her vast mouth, so that she reared his legs high in a crown of spray, and got him all down with a gulp.

She sat in the water with Eve, pinning her against the tub's rim. Maureen and Eve both sat astonished—Eve at Wyatt's vanishing, and Maureen at Wyatt's arrival within her, for as her cauldron belly's acids licked him swiftly to bone, his mind, his memories coalesced within her own. She knew him inhabiting her, and he, thus pent, knew her.

Loving Lord! You show me, unworthy, your wonders! Your glory is as a feast you set before me!

She was saddened to find that she could not communicate this gratitude to Eve, and tell Eve how she was not going to be annihilated, but was to live again within Maureen. Her attempt at explanation produced only a long sticky amphibious hiss, at which poor frightened Eve cried out, and peed in the tub water. Maureen gripped Eve with her forefeet, and thrust the young woman headfirst into her jaws. Soon, once she was dissolved, Eve would understand, would know it was all right.

For almost an hour longer, her globed eyes dreaming, her body sunk in metabolic meditation, she squatted in the foaming water. It seemed her mind half dozed, while her body grew so vast that stars were coming out inside her, winking on here and there, a visceral swarm of tiny suns.

Then Maureen came more awake. These stars she felt inside her. These myriad points of light. they were her eggs. She had to find her way to water—big water, in the dark earth. She had to meet someone.

· · ·

Ramses squirmed to be put in his bed-box in the cart's prow. Not to curl up, but to sit propped on his rickety forelegs, sniffing the air, his attention drawn everywhere. Her little protector was back, but what kind of danger could waken him so? She walked along California, up Arguello to its end, crossed the park, thence along Waller (Haight itself, though she liked to scope all the people and what they were wearing, took too much steering of her cart), and then down along Divisadero to the Castro. Went into the Gin and Beer It, which had a back alley where Yves let her park her cart between his dumpsters.

"How's our little man?" Yves leaned his beaky nose down to Ramses, who dabbed his answering muzzle from the sling. To Maxie, setting up her gimlet, he said, "Why didn't you tell me you had a new friend?"

"I don't have a new friend."

"Well, Leon said to tell you, if you showed up, to stick around a little and he'd be back."

"A scrawny whacko with a white mustache?"

"So you do know him. I've known him for years. He's a walker, like you. And here he is! Well howdy, Miss Dee." This to Leon's companion. A gray-haired woman with a handsome face-gray eyes and gaunt cheeks. She carried an old fashioned walking stick with a brass head.

Leon said, "Maxie, this is Dee. Let's take a table—you gotta talk to Dee, Maxie."

"Don't be so abrupt." Dee poked his shoulder. "I'm very pleased to meet you, Maxie. I've seen you around. The thing is, I do have to talk to you. Would you please? Can I buy you another gimlet?"

"Well, sure. Yes you can, dear." It was fun using the old-ladyism "dear." She had the right, had maybe fifteen years on Dee, and liked her too, liked her eyes, both kind and tough. It occurred to her Jack had been just around this woman's age when he died.

At the table Leon sat opposite Maxie, and while Dee got some books from her little backpack, Maxie asked him, "What are you staring at?"

"I'm just keepin' my mouth shut till you've heard her and gone through all the usual changes."

A comeback died in Maxie's throat. For some reason, his sarcastic conviction called sharply back to her Vera's two a.m. vision in the Panhandle. Vera was not the hallucinating type. A cold, cottony sensation moved delicately down Maxie's spine, recalling white rags of sourceless sea foam, tumbling before the wind.

"There's no way to ease into this," Dee told her. "Please. Just listen. And after a while, I'll tell you what I've seen with my own eyes." And she began to read from a battered gray book.

"Our little Earth is beset by Titans. In the infinitude of space and time, the Great Old Ones swim like krakens through the deep. Time and again they find us, in worlds that have been, and worlds that have yet to be anywhere and anywhen they find, have found, will find us, time without end, but in this present time, in the cosmic deep they navigate, there hangs one particular window of light and color that draws them. Like a stained-glass pane high above, it tempts the titans' appetites with a flash of rainbow radiance. And that is the window on our twenty-first century.

"For now, in our age, it is this Queen of Cities, skirted by her seas, it is this jewel among metropoloi, crowned with towers, limbed with mighty bridges, robed in lushly architected stone—it is San Francisco that beguiles the Titans' mossy megalithic eyes, as they drift through the cosmic benthos.

"In our present time, it is towards San Francisco they converge, hither they swim! Hither they glide, drawn to this radiant window on the rest of our world.

"Of the Great Old Ones, the mightiest, dread Chthulu, is among us already. He appropriates our souls, possesses our wills. Legions of his minions, his devout Ganymedes, already infest our corporate boardrooms, our governments, our churches.

"Dagon too is among us already. He feeds more frankly on our flesh. His benthic zombies come dripping ashore to harvest our bodies in the night, while offshore his vast hands can seize the greatest vessel and crack it for the nutmeats of its crews.

"Tsathoggua too is among us already."

Here Leon laid an interrupting hand on Dee's arm. He leaned toward Maxie and told her, "Tsathoggua. That's the one you can meet for yourself, right where I showed you. You can meet him tonight. Then you'll know some shit!"

Maureen moved through the foliage of Golden Gate Park in the dusk. She went by leaps and lurks, vaulting through the dense cover, and crouching with rubbery resilience through more open ground—and freezing, seizing, and feeding wherever sudden occasion presented itself. She consumed a jogger, a small, quick woman in black spandex. She launched the elastic shroud of her tongue and snatched a wildly kicking cop off his motorbike and down her throat.

And went on, seeking water. Her body knew the touch of water all around her. Each wart on her great surface (she was big as a Volkswagen bug now) sensed every molecule of water in a radius of miles. Just west, of course, the mighty Pacific foamed on the beach, but no, this water was too turbulent to receive her tender spawn.

She sensed already the smaller, stiller pool she sought. Sensed too that she would soon meet her mate-to-be. He drew even now towards the selfsame spot. The eggs within her seethed to be born, and thus it was, just as the first few stars were coming out, that she muscled through the foliage around the rim of Stow Lake.

The paths, the little plaza, the parking lot were deserted, but out on the oil-black lens of the lake there was movement, and a muted, hilarious commotion. A couple kids had broken the lock on a paddleboat and ridden it from its corral out to the open water. Bottles glinted, and hoarse guffaws broke out, imperfectly muffled. The little scamps! Maureen hungered fiercely for them!

But even as she advanced, a glittery black hugeness erupted near the boat, and overturned it. Two human shapes thrashed spray and foam and were engulfed as one by wide, inhuman jaws.

It was He, and his feeding was her own—she felt it in her own bowels, and her unborn young rejoiced in the feast. Maureen and He were already one, were two halves of a host on the very threshold of being born. Maureen slid down into the lake.

In the silken dark, buoyant as bubbles, they met. They clasped fore claws and spun and tumbled and spiraled in the satiny deep. For the first time in her life, Maureen knew Love, and knew its consummation was at hand. She broke their grip and swam towards the lake rim. A muddy cove she found, curtained by leafy vines, and into this she climbed, leaving only her hindquarters in the water, and waited His advent.

His great smooth underbelly surged onto her back. He locked his forelegs round her throat, his hindlegs round her mighty thighs. His cloacum hung just atop her own, still shallowly submerged.

In a delirium of fulfillment, Maureen unpent her eggs, and felt them bubble unendingly from her cloacum.

Each bubble was an atom of her own raging hunger, and that hunger in herself was not diminished by its ejection, its diffusion over the black lake. With this birthing her own hunger was vastly magnified, enlarged into this spreading fan of spawn.

For as she spawned, her mate's sperm joined its stream to hers, the sperm like a gelatinous explosive, a viscous dynamite that individually detonated each little globe of her greed, and woke it to life.

Long was their transport! Long their embrace! Long and long the sweet effusion of their kindled brood upon the waters!

Until, at length, they lay spent, lay piggybacked as one in a curious, tingly hiatus that became a growing expectancy of something else, something more awaiting them, something vastly larger than the miracle they had just performed.

Maureen knew they had just begun, not ended, something grand and glorious. Of course her tadpoles even now a-forming, would within this very night sprout limbs and disperse into the surrounding greenery, would radiate from the park in all directions and find their way into storm drains and sewers and backyards and gardens all over San Francisco. But none of this now seemed half as important as what lay before her.

She and her mate crouched, cold to the wonder they'd worked. A greater marvel beckoned them now, a radiant immensity drew them to itself, commanded their nearness as a shining planet commands its moons.

Her mate unclenched her, and slid crunching away through the foliage. Maureen followed him.

Leon led them along the path he had shown Maxie this morning. They talked low, and interruptedly, for by moonlight the path was even trickier. "The thing to hold onto," Dee said, "is to know they can be hurt. Can be fought."

"I have to be honest," said Maxie. "I don't think I quite believe what you've told me." Back in the Gin and Beer It, Dee had told her a very great deal indeed, as night fell outside, and the time drew on to come here.

Ahead, Leon growled, "No problem. You will."

They smelled it just before they reached the gully's edge: a coldly yeasty breath of swamp. He brought them to a place where the rim of the gully shelved slightly. There was crouching room here where the scrub grew more sparsely. The seam was a darkness below them, save at its upper end where the moon angled in and glinted on the seepage from the cleft clay there.

Too old to crouch, Maxie sat on the coarse grass, and set Ramses down between her legs on a pad made from his folded pouch, for he whined to be set free. He sat there alertly, still galvanized by that vitality he'd shown all day.

"Just remember," Leon growled. "Don't do anything. We're just here to see. So you'll know."

Maureen had seen a print of a wonderful religious painting somewhere, where all these souls were rising up a shadowy shaft, rising into a circle of glorious radiance above, their faces and arms lifted in love and acclaim towards the eternal light that drew them up to Itself.

That image had stayed with her for years, sometimes made her eyes misty; just thinking of that moment when God lifted his chosen ones straight up to His everlasting bosom.

And this was happening to her. The shadowy shaft was a dense night-black undergrowth she climbed through, and her mate, some ways upslope, climbed before her. She toiled her bulk up through the lightless tangle of this World Below, and there was a great light, a sun above her that she climbed to. Its radiance had not yet burst forth, but it was near, so near! Just ahead up this steep bluff at whose foot they had emerged from the sea.

Tears welled from Maureen's huge globular eyes. She had always known this was coming to her! Yes she had! Not out of pride, but because she had always taken the teachings of her church to heart, had always done the right thing, had walked steadfastly on the higher path.

Now the foliage yielded to a deep bare gully, an incision up the flank of the bluff. Ahead there in its blade-shaped pool of shadow, was her mate: a mottled, muscled sheen toiling toward the apex of the fissure. The gibbous moon peeked in up there to show his goal: a muddy seam in the clay not unlike her own cloacum.

There lay her re-birth. Her life unending! She climbed in awe. Her mate thrust himself into the fissure, his great bulk smoothly, incredibly received by the dense earth, till shortly only his herculean hind legs were visible. They pistoned once, twice—and he had vanished into the cliff side.

Maureen's heart took wing. She leapt forward, but was still some thirty yards short of her own apotheosis, when something small and snarling hurtled down upon her from the gully's rim. Agony collided with her left eye, and tiny teeth tore at it. This dwarfish but excruciating assault severely trauma-ed her ecstatic soul. She seized the attacker in her foreclaws—a tiny dog!—and crushed its life out, even as she thrashed and rolled side to side, battering the walls of the gully in her pain.

It caused a kind of rapture, to see the Impossible so plainly. As Maxie watched the huge amphibian claw its way into the earth, something stirred far away inside her, a primitive jubilation in her soul. It was true! The life in her exulted to know for a fact that the universe was a miracle in progress.

And then she realized there was another monster, following the first one up the gorge. In her rapture she rose to her feet—all three of them were standing, as if they were invisible, looking on from another world. There was a commotion in the grass at Maxie's feet, and suddenly there was Ramses, a stripe of moonlight across the last glimpse of him Maxie ever saw, diving into the dark, his little fangs bared. The dauntless whippet plunged straight down upon one of the second monster's eyes!

The brute thrashed explosively, down there in its darkness, its glossy hide flashing in its throes. "Ramses," Maxie whispered, seeing her little friend killed then, stepping to the gully's extreme brink.

Up where the first brute had penetrated, the moonlit earth moved. The clay tremored, and the seam in it spread, and from this aperture, a geyser of glittering flesh erupted into the moonlight. An immense tongue leapt ninety feet down the gorge and snatched back from it, and into the moonlight, the titan toad that seemed titanic no longer: the brute Ramses had died defending her from was mummied in tongue up to its eyes. The moonlight flashed on the trail of blood that glittered from its wounded eye, and then it was snatched peremptorily into the cliffside.

In a dim green light, in an immense cavern within the cliff, Maureen—so silkenly bandaged in tongue, like a fetus undelivered!—was lifted higher, higher, to hang above an alien planet, a single cyclopean Eye. Its pupil was a tarn of absolute black, ringed with a thin golden iris. The black void fractionally contracted as it studied her, making the pupil seem like an unearthly maw taking tiny bites of her.

And perhaps this was the mouth that spoke to her, for its words murmured stickily in the very center of her mind:

All you've seen and done is mine. All you know I will forever know.

And then Maureen was snatched into a different cavern, a Carlsbad of unearthly flesh, where a sunless sea of acids foamed.

There followed a dreadful passage for Maureen, a purgatory really. Wherein she swam in acid in perfect darkness. Wherein her meat and her blood and her bones turned to smoke, and drifted away from her thrashing and astonished soul.

But then she was whole and calm. She was cleansed. Was purely and only her own immortal soul! In fact, she was Reborn, as her pastor had always promised! And all her memories, all her feelings, were still minutely, eternally hers, delivered out of the body's griefs and woes.

For an immeasurable time she lay in this blissful revelation. But gradually, a tiny question kindled. Why was Eternity so dark?

But no. No, it was not dark exactly. Dimly intricate visions swarmed round her, dizzying glimpses that her reaching thought could touch in all directions. Dear God! There was a multitude around her. No darkness this, but a matrix of other souls. Wherever she turned, she met a streaming traffic, a mob of other minds.

Wonder filled her, followed by the remotest little tingle of unease. This wasn't exactly like paradise. Wasn't it a bit more like being stored in a tank? Maureen struggled to understand the Benign Intent here.

Perhaps the fault was hers. Yes. She was supposed to reach out completely, to participate in her apotheosis. She must really look about her. Really commune with her angelic company.

And when she really reached, dear God, she found a wealth indeed! She entered an astonishingly detailed landscape, sunsets on planets unknown, wars fought in alien bodies, unspeakable grapplings of these indescribable bodies. Entered grieving reminiscences, entered the beloved winds of a carven ice world where wolvish beings skated on paws of polished bone and exultingly drank moonlight forever gone, entered amoebic manta-rays winging like gossamer through maroon oceans of methane, balletically copulating within a gas-giant home world forever gone, entered long- fingered saurians, graceful as butterflies on water wings like great ribbed fans, farming the continental shelves of amber seas forever gone.

And suddenly she heard, understood the ghostly tumult of remembered voices arising from this multitude. It was a stentorian chorus of woe everlasting.

As this understanding dawned, an alteration moved through this whole mosaic of pent minds. An impalpable wave arose, and its front was sweeping towards her and seized her. She was lifted, was hung in an acid bath of searing light, and every instant of her sixty-five years flashed through her, was lived again in one unending moment. And with her own life, all the lives she had collected were also evoked within that searching illumination—King, Wyatt, Eve, the little jogger, the kicking cop—each intricate detail of their being flowered in her devourer's possessive gaze.

And then Maureen subsided again into that vast anonymity of captured lives, that universal hubbub of unsleeping memories.

Now she understood. Now Maureen knew it all. Oh, how they had lied in that church of hers! How blackly and solemnly and piously her Pastor had lied! This was not an eternity in glory! This was not a Beneficent God!

The sun was well up. They sat on a slope below the Legion of Honor, backs leaning against different sides of a cedar's trunk. They had fallen asleep in these postures some time near dawn, and now awake, they still sat silent for a long time, gazing into space. At length Dee sighed, and took out her battered gray book. "Margold says some things about Tsathoggua." She turned pages. "Yes. Here, right after this passage about Dagon. I told you I've seen Dagon myself, or part of him." She read aloud. " 'Dagon has cruised our world before, came up into the Sunless Sea beneath the Mountains of Madness and fed upon the Elder Race, and in another eon he dived from the skies upon Earth in the ancient Deluge that drowned it, and swam in those storm-tormented waters, snatching into his jaws the flood-doomed nations clawing at the surface, clinging to their rafts and spars and shards.' "

Silence fell. Dee's eyes were somewhere else.

Maxie prompted, "That's Dagon."

"Yes."

"And Tsathoggua?"

Dee blinked. Again she read aloud. " 'But of these Titans, Tsathoggua's is the deepest, most chthonic hunger. His meal is meat and minds. The populations he's plundered seethe in his belly, time without end, their spirits intact, a mighty choir of woeful souls, each life a self-knowing cell of the toad-god's entrails, wherein the greedy movement of their devourer's mind sweeps through them, as Tsathoggua, again and again, relishes each life individually, like a miser gloating on his hoard.' "

They sat propped against the tree as on an axis of sanity, remembering the night just past. A very old tomcat stepped out of the bushes: tattered ears, shabby white fur with tabby patches, he came up slowly but purposefully, mere locomotion clearly enough work for him that he wasted no energy on cautious approaches. Came up to Maxie and stood looking at her.

"I wonder if he likes cheese," she said, dubious. Cats weren't her animal. She peeled open a cheese-and-cracker packet from her knapsack.

"Cats love it," Leon said.

This one seemed to. And it turned out he didn't mind Ramses' bed-box either, nor the rattle of the cart, once he realized he could lie safely at ease in it and look around. He had very scrutinizing yellow eyes. Maxie, looking back into them, was thinking, Why not? He needs a friend.

It was a long walk to Pete's, but no one objected to it as a destination. None of them thought of separating, of being alone with what they had seen.

The bar was empty, and Pete agreed to let her park her cart in the back corridor to the restrooms, so the cat wouldn't be startled into running off. Not a word was said of Ramses—Pete appeared to understand.

They took a table, three doubles, and a pitcher of beer. They drank in sips, looking into one another's eyes from time to time, wordlessly, just confirming what they had seen last night, what they sat there still seeing, again and again.

In walked Vera, purposeful, climbed a stool and pointed at the bar in front of her with a look at Pete. Swiveled the stool and sat looking thoughtfully at Maxie and her two new friends. Maxie gestured her over, but Vera stayed on her perch.

"I was just over at Butler looking for you," Vera said. "Big to-do. Copcars in the parking lot. Down in the laundry room this morning? Still dark? That Dawg and his twin, that Carne creep. They were clocking smack down there— Community Market night down in the laundry, right? You know that Ramon asshole from up on four? Well he said he was goin' down to do laundry, but of course he was goin' down to cop was what it was. He told the cops when he went in, he saw some big animal eating Dawg! Eating him whole! And Carne nowhere in sight—just one of his kicked-off shoes!"

No one said anything, though behind the bar, Pete's hands froze for a moment on the glass he was polishing. Vera gazed with dawning surprise at the unsurprised gazes of the three tired old folks staring at her from the table.

Leon said, "You ought to come over, sit here with us, miss. Set here by me why doncha?" Maxie and Dee looked at him. In the bony terrain visible behind his great shaggy mustaches and eyebrows, they were amazed to discern an attempt at suavity on Leon's part.

The four of them talked for a considerable while, during which Pete gave up on the glasses and just leaned there on his bar, listening to them. A short silence followed.

"I think I'll have to move out," Maxie mused.

"Move in with me," Dee said. "A room to yourself, though you might share sometimes with my young friend Scat. We should all be drawing together anyway. All of us who know."

Never was a sane man more dangerously close to the arcana of basic entity—
never was an organic brain nearer to utter annihilation in the chaos that
transcends form and force and symmetry. I learned whence Cthulhu first came,
and why half the great temporary stars of history had flared forth . . . and I
was told the essence (though not the source) of the Hounds of Tindalos.
"The Whisperer in Darkness" · H.P. Lovecraft (1930)

The motto of all the mongoose family is "Run and find out" . . .
"Rikki-tikki-tavi" · Rudyard Kipling (1894)

· MONGOOSE ·
Elizabeth Bear & Sarah Monette

Izrael Irizarry stepped through a bright-scarred airlock onto Kadath Station, lurching a little as he adjusted to station gravity. On his shoulder, Mongoose extended her neck, her barbels flaring, flicked her tongue out to taste the air, and colored a question. Another few steps, and he smelled what Mongoose smelled, the sharp stink of toves, ammoniac and bitter.

He touched the tentacle coiled around his throat with the quick double tap that meant *soon*. Mongoose colored displeasure, and Irizarry stroked the slick velvet wedge of her head in consolation and restraint. Her four compound and twelve simple eyes glittered and her color softened, but did not change, as she leaned into the caress. She was eager to hunt and he didn't blame her. The boojum *Manfred von Richthofen* took care of its own vermin. Mongoose had had to make do with a share of Irizarry's rations, and she hated eating dead things.

If Irizarry could smell toves, it was more than the "minor infestation" the message from the station master had led him to expect. Of course, that message had reached Irizarry third or fourth or fifteenth hand, and he had no idea how long it had taken. Perhaps when the station master had sent for him, it had been minor.

But he knew the ways of bureaucrats, and he wondered.

People did double-takes as he passed, even the heavily-modded Christian cultists with their telescoping limbs and biolin eyes. You found them on every station and steelships too, though mostly they wouldn't work the boojums. Nobody liked Christians much, but they could work in situations that would kill an unmodded human or a even a gilly, so captains and station masters tolerated them.

There were a lot of gillies in Kadath's hallways, and they all stopped to blink at Mongoose. One, an indenturee, stopped and made an elaborate hand-flapping bow. Irizarry felt one of Mongoose's tendrils work itself through two of his earrings. Although she didn't understand staring exactly—her compound eyes made the idea alien to her—she felt the attention and was made shy by it.

Unlike the boojum-ships they serviced, the stations—Providence, Kadath, Leng, Dunwich, and the others—were man-made. Their radial symmetry was predictable, and to find the station master, Irizarry only had to work his way inward from the *Manfred von Richthofen*'s dock to the hub. There he found one of the inevitable safety maps (you are here; in case of decompression, proceed in an orderly manner to the life vaults located here, here, or here) and leaned close to squint at the tiny lettering. Mongoose copied him, tilting her head first one way, then another, though flat representations meant nothing to her. He made out STATION MASTER'S OFFICE finally, on a oval bubble, the door of which was actually in sight.

"Here we go, girl," he said to Mongoose (who, stone-deaf though she was, pressed against him in response to the vibration of his voice). He hated this part of the job, hated dealing with apparatchiks and functionaries, and of course the Station Master's office was full of them, a receptionist, and then a secretary, and then someone who was maybe the *other* kind of secretary, and then finally— Mongoose by now halfway down the back of his shirt and entirely hidden by his hair and Irizarry himself half stifled by memories of someone he didn't want to remember being—he was ushered into an inner room where Station Master Lee, her arms crossed and her round face set in a scowl, was waiting.

"Mr. Irizarry," she said, unfolding her arms long enough to stick one hand out in a facsimile of a congenial greeting.

He held up a hand in response, relieved to see no sign of recognition in her face. It was Irizarry's experience that dead lives were best left lie where they fell. "Sorry, Station Master," he said. "I can't."

He thought of asking her about the reek of toves on the air, if she understood just how bad the situation had become. People could convince themselves of a lot of bullshit, given half a chance.

Instead, he decided to talk about his partner. "Mongoose hates it when I touch other people. She gets jealous, like a parrot."

"The cheshire's here?" She let her hand drop to her side, the expression on her face a mixture of respect and alarm. "Is it out of phase?"

Well, at least Station Master Lee knew a little more about cheshire-cats than most people. "No," Irizarry said. "She's down my shirt."

Half a standard hour later, wading through the damp bowels of a ventilation pore, Irizarry tapped his rebreather to try to clear some of the tove-stench from his nostrils and mouth. It didn't help much; he was getting close.

Here, Mongoose wasn't shy at all. She slithered up on top of his head, barbels and graspers extended to full length, pulsing slowly in predatory greens and reds. Her tendrils slithered through his hair and coiled about his throat, fading in and out of phase. He placed his fingertips on her slick-resilient hide to restrain her. The last thing he needed was for Mongoose to go spectral and charge off down the corridor after the tove colony.

It wasn't that she wouldn't come back, because she would—but that was only if she didn't get herself into more trouble than she could get out of without his help. "Steady," he said, though of course she couldn't hear him. A creature adapted to vacuum had no ears. But she could feel his voice vibrate in his throat, and a tendril brushed his lips, feeling the puff of air and the shape of the word. He tapped her tendril twice again—*soon*—and felt it contract. She flashed hungry orange in his peripheral vision. She was experimenting with jaguar rosettes—they had had long discussions of jaguars and tigers after their nightly reading of Pooh on the *Manfred von Richthofen*, as Mongoose had wanted to know what jagulars and tiggers were. Irizarry had already taught her about mongooses, and he'd read *Alice in Wonderland* so she would know what a Cheshire Cat was. Two days later—he still remembered it vividly—she had disappeared quite slowly, starting with the tips of the long coils of her tail and tendrils and ending with the needle-sharp crystalline array of her teeth. And then she'd phased back in, all excited aquamarine and pink, almost bouncing, and he'd praised her and stroked her and reminded himself not to think of her as a cat. Or a mongoose.

She had readily grasped the distinction between jaguars and jagulars, and had almost as quickly decided that she was a jagular; Irizarry had almost started to argue, but then thought better of it. She was, after all, a Very Good Dropper. And nobody ever saw her coming unless she wanted them to.

When the faint glow of the toves came into view at the bottom of the pore, he felt her shiver all over, luxuriantly, before she shimmered dark and folded herself tight against his scalp. Irizarry doused his own lights as well, flipping the passive infrared goggles down over his eyes. Toves were as blind as Mongoose was deaf, but an infestation this bad could mean the cracks were growing large enough for bigger things to wiggle through, and if there were raths, no sense in letting the monsters know he was coming.

He tapped the tendril curled around his throat three times, and whispered "Go." She didn't need him to tell her twice; really, he thought wryly, she didn't need him to tell her at all. He barely felt her featherweight disengage before she was gone down the corridor as silently as a hunting owl. She was invisible to his goggles, her body at ambient temperature, but he knew from experience that her barbels and vanes would be spread wide, and he'd hear the shrieks when she came in among the toves.

The toves covered the corridor ceiling, arm-long carapaces adhered by a foul-smelling secretion that oozed from between the sections of their exoskeletons. The upper third of each tove's body bent down like a dangling bough, bringing the glowing, sticky lure and flesh-ripping pincers into play. Irizarry had no idea what they fed on in their own phase, or dimension, or whatever.

Here, though, he knew what they ate. Anything they could get.

He kept his shock probe ready, splashing after, to assist her if it turned out necessary. That was sure a lot of toves, and even a cheshire-cat could get in trouble if she was outnumbered. Ahead of him, a tove warbled and went suddenly dark; Mongoose had made her first kill.

Within moments, the tove colony was in full warble, the harmonics making Irizarry's head ache. He moved forward carefully, alert now for signs of raths. The largest tove colony he'd ever seen was on the derelict steelship *Jenny Lind*, which he and Mongoose had explored when they were working salvage on the boojum *Harriet Tubman*. The hulk had been covered inside and out with toves; the colony was so vast that, having eaten everything else, it had started cannibalizing itself, toves eating their neighbors and being eaten in turn. Mongoose had glutted herself before the Harriet Tubman ate the wreckage, and in the refuse she left behind, Irizarry had found the strange starlike bones of an adult rath, consumed by its own prey. The bandersnatch that had killed the humans on the *Jenny Lind* had died with her reactor core and her captain. A handful of passengers and crew had escaped to tell the tale.

He refocused. This colony wasn't as large as those heaving masses on the *Jenny Lind*, but it was the largest he'd ever encountered not in a quarantine situation, and if there weren't raths somewhere on Kadath Station, he'd eat his infrared goggles.

A dead tove landed at his feet, its eyeless head neatly separated from its segmented body, and a heartbeat later Mongoose phased in on his shoulder and made her deep clicking noise that meant, *Irizarry! Pay attention!*

He held his hand out, raised to shoulder level, and Mongoose flowed between the two, keeping her bulk on his shoulder, with tendrils resting against his lips and larynx, but her tentacles wrapping around his hand to communicate. He pushed his goggles up with his free hand and switched on his belt light so he could read her colors.

She was anxious, strobing yellow and green. *Many,* she shaped against his palm, and then emphatically, *R.*

"R" was bad—it meant *rath*—but it was better than "B." If a bandersnatch had come through, all of them were walking dead, and Kadath Station was already as doomed as the *Jenny Lind.* "Do you smell it?" he asked under the warbling of the toves.

Taste, said Mongoose, and because Irizarry had been her partner for almost five Solar, he understood: the toves tasted of rath, meaning that they had recently been feeding on rath guano, and given the swiftness of toves' digestive systems, that meant a rath was patrolling territory on the station.

Mongoose's grip tightened on his shoulder. *R,* she said again. *R. R. R.*

Irizarry's heart lurched and sank. More than one rath. The cracks were widening.

A bandersnatch was only a matter of time.

Station Master Lee didn't want to hear it. It was all there in the way she stood, the way she pretended distraction to avoid eye-contact. He knew the rules of this game, probably better than she did. He stepped into her personal space. Mongoose shivered against the nape of his neck, her tendrils threading his hair. Even without being able to see her, he knew she was a deep, anxious emerald.

"A rath?" said Station Master Lee, with a toss of her head that might have looked flirtatious on a younger or less hostile woman, and moved away again. "Don't be ridiculous. There hasn't been a rath on Kadath Station since my grandfather's time."

"Doesn't mean there isn't an infestation now," Irizarry said quietly. If she was going to be dramatic, that was his cue to stay still and calm. "And I said raths. Plural."

"That's even more ridiculous. Mr. Irizarry, if this is some ill-conceived attempt to drive up your price—"

"It isn't." He was careful to say it flatly, not indignantly. "Station Master, I understand that this isn't what you want to hear, but you have to quarantine Kadath."

"Can't be done," she said, her tone brisk and flat, as if he'd asked her to pilot Kadath through the rings of Saturn.

"Of course it can!" Irizarry said, and she finally turned to look at him, outraged that he dared to contradict her. Against his neck, Mongoose flexed one set of claws. She didn't like it when he was angry.

Mostly, that wasn't a problem. Mostly, Irizarry knew anger was a waste of time and energy. It didn't solve anything. It didn't fix anything. It couldn't bring back anything that was lost. People, lives. The sorts of things that got washed away in the tides of time. Or were purged, whether you wanted them gone or not.

But this was . . . "You do know what a colony of adult raths can do, don't you? With a contained population of prey? Tell me, Station Master, have you started noticing fewer indigents in the shelters?"

She turned away again, dismissing his existence from her cosmology. "The matter is not open for discussion, Mr. Irizarry. I hired you to deal with an alleged infestation. I expect you to do so. If you feel you can't, you are of course welcome to leave the station with whatever ship takes your fancy. I believe the *Arthur Gordon Pym* is headed in-system, or perhaps you'd prefer the Jupiter run?"

He didn't have to win this fight, he reminded himself. He could walk away, try to warn somebody else, get himself and Mongoose the hell off Kadath Station. "All right, Station Master. But remember that I warned you, when your secretaries start disappearing."

He was at the door when she cried, "Irizarry!"

He stopped, but didn't turn.

"I can't," she said, low and rushed, as if she was afraid of being overheard. "I can't quarantine the station. Our numbers are already in the red this quarter, and the new political officer . . . it's my head on the block, don't you understand?"

He didn't understand. Didn't want to. It was one of the reasons he was a wayfarer, because he never wanted to let himself be like her again.

"If Sanderson finds out about the quarantine, she finds out about you. Will your papers stand up to a close inspection, Mr. Irizarry?"

He wheeled, mouth open to tell her what he thought of her and her clumsy attempts at blackmail, and she said, "I'll double your fee."

At the same time, Mongoose tugged on several strands of his hair, and he realized he could feel her heart beating, hard and rapid, against his spine. It was her distress he answered, not the Station Master's bribe. "All right," he said. "I'll do the best I can."

· · ·

Toves and raths colonized like an epidemic, outward from a single originating point, Patient Zero in this case being the tear in spacetime that the first tove had wriggled through. More tears would develop as the toves multiplied, but it was that first one that would become large enough for a rath. While toves were simply lazy—energy efficient, the Arkhamers said primly—and never crawled farther than was necessary to find a useable anchoring point, raths were cautious. Their marauding was centered on the original tear because they kept their escape route open. And tore it wider and wider.

Toves weren't the problem, although they were a nuisance, with their tendency to use up valuable oxygen, clog ductwork, eat pets, drip goo from ceilings, and crunch wetly when you stepped on them. Raths were worse; raths were vicious predators. Their natural prey might be toves, but they didn't draw the line at disappearing weakened humans or small gillies, either.

But even they weren't the danger that had made it hard for Irizarry to sleep the past two rest shifts. What toves tore and raths widened was an access for the apex predator of this alien food chain.

The bandersnatch: *Pseudocanis tindalosi*. The old records and the indigent Arkhamers called them hounds, but of course they weren't, any more than Mongoose was a cat. Irizarry had seen archive video from derelict stations and ships, the bandersnatch's flickering angular limbs appearing like spiked mantis arms from the corners of sealed rooms, the carnage that ensued. He'd never heard of anyone left alive on a station where a bandersnatch manifested, unless they made it to a panic pod damned fast. More importantly, even the Arkhamers in their archive-ships, breeders of Mongoose and all her kind, admitted they had no records of anyone *surviving* a bandersnatch rather than *escaping* it.

And what he had to do, loosely put, was find the core of the infestation before the bandersnatches did, so that he could eradicate the toves and raths and the stress they were putting on this little corner of the universe. Find the core—somewhere in the miles upon miles of Kadath's infrastructure. Which was why he was in this little-used service corridor, letting Mongoose commune with every ventilation duct they found.

Anywhere near the access shafts infested by the colony, Kadath Station's passages reeked of tove—ammoniac, sulfurous. The stench infiltrated the edges of Irizarry's mask as he lifted his face to a ventilation duct. Wincing in anticipation, he broke the seal on the rebreather and pulled it away from his face on the stiff elastic straps, careful not to lose his grip. A broken nose would not improve his day.

A cultist engineer skittered past on sucker-tipped limbs, her four snake-arms coiled tight beside her for the narrow corridor. She had a pretty smile, for a Christian.

Mongoose was too intent on her prey to be shy. The size of the tove colony might make her nervous, but Mongoose loved the smell—like a good dinner heating, Irizarry imagined. She unfolded herself around his head like a tendriled hood, tentacles outreached, body flaring as she stretched towards the ventilation fan. He felt her lean, her barbels shivering, and turned to face the way her wedge-shaped head twisted.

He almost tipped backwards when he found himself face to face with someone he hadn't even known was there. A woman, average height, average weight, brown hair drawn back in a smooth club; her skin was space-pale and faintly reddened across the cheeks, as if the IR filters on a suit hadn't quite protected her. She wore a sleek space-black uniform with dull silver epaulets and four pewter-colored bands at each wrist. An insignia with a stylized sun and Earth-Moon dyad clung over her heart.

The political officer, who was obviously unconcerned by Mongoose's ostentatious display of sensory equipment.

Mongoose absorbed her tendrils in like a startled anemone, pressing the warm underside of her head to Irizarry's scalp where the hair was thinning. He was surprised she didn't vanish down his shirt, because he felt her trembling against his neck.

The political officer didn't extend her hand. "Mr. Irizarry? You're a hard man to find. I'm Intelligence Colonel Sadhi Sanderson. I'd like to ask you a few quick questions, please."

"I'm, uh, a little busy right now," Irizarry said, and added uneasily, "Ma'am." The *last* thing he wanted to do was to offend her.

Sanderson looked up at Mongoose. "Yes, you would appear to be hunting," she said, her voice dry as scouring powder. "That's one of the things I want to talk about."

Oh *shit*. He had kept out of the political officer's way for a day and a half, and really that was a pretty good run, given the obvious tensions between Lee and Sanderson, and the things he'd heard in the Transient Barracks: the gillies were all terrified of Sanderson, and nobody seemed to have a good word for Lee. Even the Christians, mouths thinned primly, could say of Lee only that she didn't actively persecute them. Irizarry had been stuck on a steelship with a Christian congregation for nearly half a year once, and he knew their eagerness to speak well of everyone; he didn't know whether that was actually part of their faith, or just a survival tactic, but when Elder Dawson said, "She does not trouble us," he understood quite precisely what that meant.

Of Sanderson, they said even less, but Irizarry understood that, too. There was no love lost between the extremist cults and the government. But he'd heard plenty from the ice miners and dock workers and particularly from the crew of an impounded steelship who were profanely eloquent on the subject. Upshot: Colonel Sanderson was new in town, cleaning house, and profoundly not a woman you wanted to fuck with.

"I'd be happy to come to your office in an hour, maybe two?" he said. "It's just that—"

Mongoose's grip on his scalp tightened, sudden and sharp enough that he yelped; he realized that her head had moved back toward the duct while he fenced weakly with Colonel Sanderson, and now it was nearly *in* the duct, at the end of a foot and a half of iridescent neck.

"Mr. Irizarry?"

He held a hand up, because really this wasn't a good time, and yelped again when Mongoose reached down and grabbed it. He knew better than to forget how fluid her body was, that it was really no more than a compromise with the dimension he could sense her in, but sometimes it surprised him anyway.

And then Mongoose said, *Nagina*, and if Colonel Sanderson hadn't been standing right there, her eyebrows indicating that he was already at the very end of the slack she was willing to cut, he would have cursed aloud. Short of a bandersnatch—and that could still be along any time now, don't forget, Irizarry—a breeding rath was the worst news they could have.

"Your cheshire seems unsettled," Sanderson said, not sounding in the least alarmed. "Is there a problem?"

"She's eager to eat. And, er. She doesn't like strangers." It was as true as anything you could say about Mongoose, and the violent colors cycling down her tendrils gave him an idea what her chromatophores were doing behind his head.

"I can see that," Sanderson said. "Cobalt and yellow, in that stippled pattern—and flickering in and out of phase—she's acting aggressive, but that's fear, isn't it?"

Whatever Irizarry had been about to say, her observation stopped him short. He blinked at her—*like a gilly*, he thought uncharitably—and only realized he'd taken yet another step back when the warmth of the bulkhead pressed his coveralls to his spine.

"You know," Sanderson said mock-confidentially, "this entire corridor *reeks* of toves. So let me guess: it's not just toves anymore."

Irizarry was still stuck at her being able to read Mongoose's colors. "What do you know about cheshires?" he said.

She smiled at him as if at a slow student. "Rather a lot. I was on the *Jenny Lind* as an ensign—there was a cheshire on board, and I saw . . . It's not the sort of thing you forget, Mr. Irizarry, having been there once." Something complicated crossed her face—there for a flash and then gone. "The cheshire that died on the *Jenny Lind* was called Demon," Irizarry said, carefully. "Her partner was Long Mike Spider. You knew them?"

"Spider John," Sanderson said, looking down at the backs of her hands. She picked a cuticle with the opposite thumbnail. "He went by Spider John. You have the cheshire's name right, though."

When she looked back up, the arch of her carefully shaped brow told him he hadn't been fooling anyone.

"Right," Irizarry said. "Spider John."

"They were friends of mine." She shook her head. "I was just a pup. First billet, and I was assigned as Demon's liaison. Spider John liked to say he and I had the same job. But I couldn't make the captain believe him when he tried to tell her how bad it was."

"How'd you make it off after the bandersnatch got through?" Irizarry asked. He wasn't foolish enough to think that her confidences were anything other than a means of demonstrating to him why he could trust her, but the frustration and tired sadness sounded sincere.

"It went for Spider John first—it must have known he was a threat. And Demon—she threw herself at it, never mind it was five times her size. She bought us time to get to the panic pod and Captain Golovnina time to get to the core overrides."

She paused. "I saw it, you know. Just a glimpse. Wriggling through this . . . this *rip* in the air, like a big gaunt hound ripping through a hole in a blanket with knotty paws. I spent years wondering if it got my scent. Once they scent prey, you know, they never stop. . . . "

She trailed off, raising her gaze to meet his. He couldn't decide if the furrow between her eyes was embarrassment at having revealed so much, or the calculated cataloguing of his response.

"So you recognize the smell, is what you're saying."

She had a way of answering questions with other questions. "Am I right about the raths?"

He nodded. "A breeder."

She winced.

He took a deep breath and stepped away from the bulkhead. "Colonel Sanderson—I have to get it *now* if I'm going to get it at all."

She touched the microwave pulse pistol at her hip. "Want some company?"

He didn't. Really, truly didn't. And if he had, he wouldn't have chosen Kadath Station's political officer. But he couldn't afford to offend her . . . and he wasn't licensed to carry a weapon.

"All right," he said and hoped he didn't sound as grudging as he felt. "But don't get in Mongoose's way."

Colonel Sanderson offered him a tight, feral smile. "Wouldn't dream of it."

The only thing that stank more than a pile of live toves was a bunch of half-eaten ones.

"Going to have to vacuum-scrub the whole sector," Sanderson said, her breath hissing through her filters.

If we live long enough to need to, Irizarry, thought, but had the sense to keep his mouth shut. You didn't talk defeat around a politico. And if you were unfortunate enough to come to the attention of one, you certainly didn't let her see you thinking it.

Mongoose forged on ahead, but Irizarry noticed she was careful to stay within the range of his lights, and at least one of her tendrils stayed focused back on him and Sanderson at all times. If this were a normal infestation, Mongoose would be scampering along the corridor ceilings, leaving scattered bits of half-consumed tove and streaks of bioluminescent ichor in her wake. But this time, she edged along, testing each surface before her with quivering barbels so that Irizarry was reminded of a tentative spider or an exploratory octopus.

He edged along behind her, watching her colors go dim and cautious. She paused at each intersection, testing the air in every direction, and waited for her escort to catch up.

The service tubes of Kadath Station were mostly large enough for Irizarry and Sanderson to walk single-file through, though sometimes they were obliged to crouch, and once or twice Irizarry found himself slithering on his stomach through tacky half-dried tove slime. He imagined—he hoped it was imagining—that he could sense the thinning and stretch of reality all around them, see it in the warp of the tunnels and the bend of deck plates. He imagined that he glimpsed faint shapes from the corners of his eyes, caught a whisper of sound, a hint of scent, as of something almost there.

Hypochondria, he told himself firmly, aware that that was the wrong word and not really caring. But as he dropped down onto his belly again, to squeeze through a tiny access point—this one clogged with the fresh corpses of newly-slaughtered toves—he needed all the comfort he could invent.

He almost ran into Mongoose when he'd cleared the hole. She scuttled back to him and huddled under his chest, tendrils writhing, so close to out of phase that she was barely a warm shadow. When he saw what was on the other side, he wished he'd invented a little more.

This must be one of Kadath Station's recycling and reclamation centers, a bowl ten meters across sweeping down to a pile of rubbish in the middle. These were the sorts of places you always found minor tove infestations. Ships and stations might be supposed to be kept clear of vermin, but in practice, the dimensional stresses of sharing the spacelanes with boojums meant that just wasn't possible. And in Kadath, somebody hadn't been doing their job.

Sanderson touched his ankle, and Irizarry hastily drew himself aside so she could come through after. He was suddenly grateful for her company.

He really didn't want to be here alone.

Irizarry had never seen a tove infestation like this, not even on the *Jenny Lind*. The entire roof of the chamber was thick with their sluglike bodies, long lure-tongues dangling as much as half a meter down. Small flitting things—young raths, near-transparent in their phase shift—filled the space before him. As Irizarry watched, one blundered into the lure of a tove, and the tove contracted with sudden convulsive force. The rath never stood a chance.

Nagina, Mongoose said. *Nagina, Nagina, Nagina.*

Indeed, down among the junk in the pit, something big was stirring. But that wasn't all. That pressure Irizarry had sensed earlier, the feeling that many eyes were watching him, gaunt bodies stretching against whatever frail fabric held them back—here, it was redoubled, until he almost felt the brush of not-quite-in-phase whiskers along the nape of his neck.

Sanderson crawled up beside him, her pistol in one hand. Mongoose didn't seem to mind her there.

"What's down there?" she asked, her voice hissing on constrained breaths.

"The breeding pit," Irizarry said. "You feel that? Kind of funny, stretchy feeling in the universe?"

Sanderson nodded behind her mask. "It's not going to make you any happier, is it, if I tell you I've felt it before?"

Irizarry was wearily, grimly unsurprised. But then Sanderson said, "What do we do?"

He was taken aback and it must have shown, even behind the rebreather, because she said sharply, "*You're* the expert. Which I assume is why you're on

Kadath Station to begin with and why Station Master Lee has been so anxious that I not know it. Though with an infestation of this size, I don't know how she thought she was going to hide it much longer anyway."

"Call it sabotage," Irizarry said absently. "Blame the Christians. Or the gillies. Or disgruntled spacers, like the crew off the *Caruso*. It happens a lot, Colonel. Somebody like me and Mongoose comes in and cleans up the toves, the station authorities get to crack down on whoever's being the worst pain in the ass, and life keeps on turning over. But she waited too long."

Down in the pit, the breeder heaved again. Breeding raths were slow—much slower than the juveniles, or the sexually dormant adult rovers—but that was because they were armored like titanium armadillos. When threatened, one of two things happened. Babies flocked to mama, mama rolled herself in a ball, and it would take a tactical nuke to kill them. Or mama went on the warpath. Irizarry had seen a pissed-off breeder take out a bulkhead on a steelship once; it was pure dumb luck that it hadn't breached the hull.

And, of course, once they started spawning, as this one had, they could produce between ten and twenty babies a day for anywhere from a week to a month, depending on the food supply. And the more babies they produced, the weaker the walls of the world got, and the closer the bandersnatches would come.

"The first thing we have to do," he said to Colonel Sanderson, "as in, *right now*, is kill the breeder. Then you quarantine the station and get parties of volunteers to hunt down the rovers, before they can bring another breeder through, or turn into breeders, or however the fuck it works, which frankly I don't know. It'll take fire to clear this nest of toves, but Mongoose and I can probably get the rest. And *fire*, Colonel Sanderson. Toves don't give a shit about vacuum."

She could have reproved him for his language; she didn't. She just nodded and said, "How do we kill the breeder?"

"Yeah," Irizarry said. "That's the question."

Mongoose clicked sharply, her *Irizarry!* noise.

"No," Irizarry said. "Mongoose, don't—"

But she wasn't paying attention. She had only a limited amount of patience for his weird interactions with other members of his species and his insistence on *waiting*, and he'd clearly used it all up. She was Rikki Tikki Tavi, and the breeder was Nagina, and Mongoose knew what had to happen. She launched off Irizarry's shoulders, shifting phase as she went, and without contact between them, there was nothing he could do to call her back. In less than a second, he didn't even know where she was.

"You any good with that thing?" he said to Colonel Sanderson, pointing at her pistol.

"Yes," she said, but her eyebrows were going up again. "But, forgive me, isn't this what cheshires are for?"

"Against rovers, sure. But—Colonel, have you ever seen a breeder?"

Across the bowl, a tove warbled, the chorus immediately taken up by its neighbors. Mongoose had started.

"No," Sanderson said, looking down at where the breeder humped and wallowed and finally stood up, shaking off ethereal babies and half-eaten toves. "Oh. *Gods*."

You couldn't describe a rath. You couldn't even look at one for more than a few seconds before you started getting a migraine aura. Rovers were just blots of shadow. The breeder was massive, armored, and had no recognizable features, save for its hideous, drooling, ragged edged maw. Irizarry didn't know if it had eyes, or even needed them.

"She can kill it," he said, "but only if she can get at its underside. Otherwise, all it has to do is wait until it has a clear swing, and she's . . . " He shuddered. "I'll be lucky to find enough of her for a funeral. So what *we* have to do now, Colonel, is piss it off enough to give her a chance. Or"—he had to be fair; this was not Colonel Sanderson's job—"if you'll lend me your pistol, you don't have to stay."

She looked at him, her dark eyes very bright, and then she turned to look at the breeder, which was swinging its shapeless head in slow arcs, trying, no doubt, to track Mongoose. "Fuck that, Mr. Irizarry," she said crisply. "Tell me where to aim."

"You won't hurt it," he'd warned her, and she'd nodded, but he was pretty sure she hadn't really understood until she fired her first shot and the breeder didn't even *notice*. But Sanderson hadn't given up; her mouth had thinned, and she'd settled into her stance, and she'd fired again, at the breeder's feet as Irizarry had told her. A breeding rath's feet weren't vulnerable as such, but they were sensitive, much more sensitive than the human-logical target of its head. Even so, it was concentrating hard on Mongoose, who was making toves scream at various random points around the circumference of the breeding pit, and it took another three shots aimed at that same near front foot before the breeder's head swung in their direction.

It made a noise, a sort of "wooaaurgh" sound, and Irizarry and Sanderson were promptly swarmed by juvenile raths.

"Ah, fuck," said Irizarry. "Try not to kill them."

"I'm sorry, try *not* to kill them?"

"If we kill too many of them, it'll decide we're a threat rather than an annoyance. And then it rolls up in a ball, and we have no chance of killing it until it unrolls again. And by then, there will be a lot more raths here."

"And quite possibly a bandersnatch," Sanderson finished. "But—" She batted away a half-corporeal rath that was trying to wrap itself around the warmth of her pistol.

"If we stood perfectly still for long enough," Irizarry said, "they could probably leech out enough of our body heat to send us into hypothermia. But they can't bite when they're this young. I knew a cheshire-man once who swore they ate by crawling down into the breeder's stomach to lap up what it'd digested. I'm still hoping that's not true. Just keep aiming at that foot."

"You got it."

Irizarry had to admit, Sanderson was steady as a rock. He shooed juvenile raths away from both of them, Mongoose continued her depredations out there in the dark, and Sanderson, having found her target, fired at it in a nice steady rhythm. She didn't miss; she didn't try to get fancy. Only, after a while, she said out of the corner of her mouth, "You know, my battery won't last forever."

"I know," Irizarry said. "But this is good. It's working."

"How can you *tell*?"

"It's getting mad."

"How can you tell?"

"The vocalizing." The rath had gone from its "wooaaurgh" sound to a series of guttural huffing noises, interspersed with high-pitched yips. "It's warning us off. Keep firing."

"All right," Sanderson said. Irizarry cleared another couple of juveniles off her head. He was trying not to think about what it meant that no adult raths had come to the pit—just how much of Kadath Station had they claimed?

"*Have* there been any disappearances lately?" he asked Sanderson.

She didn't look at him, but there was a long silence before she said, "None that *seemed* like disappearances. Our population is by necessity transient, and none too fond of authority. And, frankly, I've had so much trouble with the station master's office that I'm not sure my information is reliable."

It had to hurt for a political officer to admit that. Irizarry said, "We're very likely to find human bones down there. And in their caches."

Sanderson started to answer him, but the breeder decided it had had enough. It wheeled toward them, its maw gaping wider, and started through the mounds of garbage and corpses in their direction.

"What now?" said Sanderson.

"Keep firing," said Irizarry. *Mongoose, wherever you are, please be ready.*

He'd been about seventy-five percent sure that the rath would stand up on its hind legs when it reached them. Raths weren't sapient, not like cheshires, but they were smart. They knew that the quickest way to kill a human was to take its head off, and the second quickest was to disembowel it, neither of which they could do on all fours. And humans weren't any threat to a breeder's vulnerable abdomen; Sanderson's pistol might give the breeder a hot foot, but there was no way it could penetrate the breeder's skin.

It was a terrible plan—there was that whole twenty-five percent where he and Sanderson died screaming while the breeder ate them from the feet up— but it worked. The breeder heaved itself upright, massive, indistinct paw going back for a blow that would shear Sanderson's head off her neck and probably bounce it off the nearest bulkhead, and with no warning of any kind, not for the humans, not for the rath, Mongoose phased viciously in, claws and teeth and sharp edged tentacles all less than two inches from the rath's belly and moving fast.

The rath screamed and curled in on itself, but it was too late. Mongoose had already caught the lips of its—oh gods and fishes, Irizarry didn't know the word. Vagina? Cloaca? Ovipositor? The place where little baby raths came into the world. The only vulnerability a breeder had. Into which Mongoose shoved the narrow wedge of her head, and her clawed front feet, and began to rip.

Before the rath could even reach for her, her malleable body was already entirely inside it, and it—screaming, scrabbling—was doomed.

Irizarry caught Sanderson's elbow and said, "Now would be a good time, *very slowly*, to back away. Let the lady do her job."

Irizarry almost made it off of Kadath clean.

He'd had no difficulty in getting a berth for himself and Mongoose—after a party or two of volunteers had seen her in action, after the stories started spreading about the breeder, he'd nearly come to the point of beating off the steelship captains with a stick. And in the end, he'd chosen the offer of the captain of the *Erich Zann*, a boojum; Captain Alvarez had a long-term salvage contract in the Kuiper belt—"cleaning up after the ice miners," she'd said with a wry smile—and Irizarry felt like salvage was maybe where he wanted to be for a while. There'd be plenty for Mongoose to hunt, and nobody's life in danger. Even a bandersnatch wasn't much more than a case of indigestion for a boojum.

He'd got his money out of the station master's office—hadn't even had to talk to Station Master Lee, who maybe, from the things he was hearing, wasn't going to be station master much longer. You could either be ineffectual *or* you could piss off your political officer. Not both at once. And her secretary so very obviously didn't want to bother her that it was easy to say, "We had a contract," and to plant his feet and smile. It wasn't the doubled fee she'd promised him, but he didn't even want that. Just the money he was owed.

So his business was taken care of. He'd brought Mongoose out to the *Erich Zann*, and insofar as he and Captain Alvarez could tell, the boojum and the cheshire liked each other. He'd bought himself new underwear and let Mongoose pick out a new pair of earrings for him. And he'd gone ahead and splurged, since he was, after all, *on* Kadath Station and might as well make the most of it, and bought a selection of books for his reader, including *The Wind in the Willows*. He was looking forward, in an odd, quiet way, to the long nights out beyond Neptune: reading to Mongoose, finding out what she thought about Rat and Mole and Toad and Badger.

Peace—or as close to it as Izrael Irizarry was ever likely to get.

He'd cleaned out his cubby in the Transient Barracks, slung his bag over one shoulder with Mongoose riding on the other, and was actually in sight of the *Erich Zann*'s dock when a voice behind him called his name.

Colonel Sanderson.

He froze in the middle of a stride, torn between turning around to greet her and bolting like a rabbit, and then she'd caught up to him. "Mr. Irizarry," she said. "I hoped I could buy you a drink before you go."

He couldn't help the deeply suspicious look he gave her. She spread her hands, showing them empty. "Truly. No threats, no tricks. Just a drink. To say thank you." Her smile was lopsided; she knew how unlikely those words sounded in the mouth of a political officer.

And any other political officer, Irizarry wouldn't have believed them. But he'd seen her stand her ground in front of a breeder rath, and he'd seen her turn and puke her guts out when she got a good look at what Mongoose did to it. If she wanted to thank him, he owed it to her to sit still for it.

"All right," he said, and added awkwardly, "Thank you."

They went to one of Kadath's tourist bars: bright and quaint and cheerful and completely unlike the spacer bars Irizarry was used to. On the other hand, he could see why Sanderson picked this one. No one here, except maybe the bartender, had the least idea who she was, and the bartender's wide-eyed double take meant that they got excellent service: prompt and very quiet.

Irizarry ordered a pink lady—he liked them, and Mongoose, in delight, turned the same color pink, with rosettes matched to the maraschino "cherry." Sanderson ordered whisky, neat, which had very little resemblance to the whisky Irizarry remembered from planetside. She took a long swallow of it, then set the glass down and said, "I never got a chance to ask Spider John this: how did you get your cheshire?"

It was clever of her to invoke Spider John and Demon like that, but Irizarry still wasn't sure she'd earned the story. After the silence had gone on a little too long, Sanderson picked her glass up, took another swallow, and said, "I know who you are."

"I'm *nobody*," Irizarry said. He didn't let himself tense up, because Mongoose wouldn't miss that cue, and she was touchy enough, what with all the steelship captains, that he wasn't sure what she might think the proper response was. And he wasn't sure, if she decided the proper response was to rip Sanderson's face off, that he would be able to make himself disagree with her in time.

"I promised," Sanderson said. "No threats. I'm not trying to trace you, I'm not asking any questions about the lady you used to work for. And, truly, I'm only *asking* how you met *this* lady. You don't have to tell me."

"No," Irizarry said mildly. "I don't." But Mongoose, still pink, was coiling down his arm to investigate the glass—not its contents, since the interest of the egg-whites would be more than outweighed by the sharp sting to her nose of the alcohol, but the upside-down cone on a stem of a martini glass. She liked geometry. And this wasn't a story that could hurt anyone.

He said, "I was working my way across Jupiter's moons, oh, five years ago now. Ironically enough, I got trapped in a quarantine. Not for vermin, but for the black rot. It was a long time, and things got . . . ugly."

He glanced at her and saw he didn't need to elaborate.

"There were Arkhamers trapped there, too, in their huge old scow of a ship. And when the water rationing got tight, there were people that said the Arkhamers shouldn't have any—said that if it was the other way 'round, they wouldn't give us any. And so when the Arkhamers sent one of their daughters for their share . . . " He still remembered her scream, a grown woman's terror in a child's voice, and so he shrugged and said, "I did the only thing I could. After that, it was safer for me on their ship than it was on the station, so I spent some time with them. Their Professors let me stay.

"They're not bad people," he added, suddenly urgent. "I don't say I understand what they believe, or why, but they were good to me, and they did share their water with the crew of the ship in the next berth. And of course, they had cheshires.

Cheshires all over the place, cleanest steelship you've ever seen. There was a litter born right about the time the quarantine finally lifted. Jemima—the little girl I helped—she insisted they give me pick of the litter, and that was Mongoose."

Mongoose, knowing the shape of her own name on Irizarry's lips, began to purr, and rubbed her head gently against his fingers. He petted her, feeling his tension ease, and said, "And I wanted to be a biologist before things got complicated."

"Huh," said Sanderson. "Do you know what they are?"

"Sorry?" He was still mostly thinking about the Arkhamers, and braced himself for the usual round of superstitious nonsense: demons or necromancers or what-not.

But Sanderson said, "Cheshires. Do you know what they are?"

"What do you mean, 'What they are'? They're cheshires."

"After Demon and Spider John . . . I did some reading and I found a professor or two—Arkhamers, yes—to ask." She smiled, very thinly. "I've found, in this job, that people are often remarkably willing to answer my questions. And I found out. They're bandersnatches."

"Colonel Sanderson, not to be disrespectful—"

"Sub-adult bandersnatches," Sanderson said. "Trained and bred and intentionally stunted so that they never mature fully."

Mongoose, he realized, had been watching, because she caught his hand and said emphatically, *Not*.

"Mongoose disagrees with you," he said and found himself smiling. "And really, I think she would know."

Sanderson's eyebrows went up. "And what does Mongoose think she is?"

He asked, and Mongoose answered promptly, pink dissolving into champagne and gold: *Jagular*. But there was a thrill of uncertainty behind it, as if she wasn't quite sure of what she stated so emphatically. And then, with a sharp toss of her head at Colonel Sanderson, like any teenage girl: *Mongoose*.

Sanderson was still watching him sharply. "Well?"

"She says she's Mongoose."

And Sanderson really wasn't trying to threaten him, or playing some elaborate political game, because her face softened in a real smile, and she said, "Of course she is."

Irizarry swished a sweet mouthful between his teeth. He thought of what Sanderson has said, of the bandersnatch on the *Jenny Lind* wriggling through stretched rips in reality like a spiny, deathly puppy tearing a blanket. "How would you domesticate a bandersnatch?"

She shrugged. "If I knew that, I'd be an Arkhamer, wouldn't I?" Gently, she extended the back of her hand for Mongoose to sniff. Mongoose, surprising Irizarry, extended one tentative tendril and let it hover just over the back of Sanderson's wrist.

Sanderson tipped her head, smiling affectionately, and didn't move her hand. "But if I had to guess, I'd say you do it by making friends."

· A COLDER WAR ·
Charles Stross

Analyst

Roger Jourgensen tilts back in his chair, reading.

He's a fair-haired man, in his mid-thirties: hair razor-cropped, skin pallid from too much time spent under artificial lights. Spectacles, short-sleeved white shirt and tie, photographic ID badge on a chain round his neck. He works in an air-conditioned office with no windows.

The file he is reading frightens him.

Once, when Roger was a young boy, his father took him to an open day at Nellis AFB, out in the California desert. Sunlight glared brilliantly from the polished silverplate flanks of the big bombers, sitting in their concrete-lined dispersal bays behind barriers and blinking radiation monitors. The brightly colored streamers flying from their pitot tubes lent them a strange, almost festive appearance. But they were sleeping nightmares: once awakened, nobody—except the flight crew— could come within a mile of the nuclear-powered bombers and live.

Looking at the gleaming, bulging pods slung under their wingtip pylons, Roger had a premature inkling of the fires that waited within, a frigid terror that echoed the siren wail of the air raid warnings. He'd sucked nervously on his ice cream and gripped his father's hand tightly while the band ripped through a cheerful Sousa march, and only forgot his fear when a flock of Thunderchiefs sliced by overhead and rattled the car windows for miles around.

He has the same feeling now, as an adult reading this intelligence assessment, that he had as a child, watching the nuclear powered bombers sleeping in their concrete beds.

There's a blurry photograph of a concrete box inside the file, snapped from above by a high-flying U-2 during the autumn of '61. Three coffin-shaped lakes, bulking dark and gloomy beneath the arctic sun; a canal heading west, deep in the Soviet heartland, surrounded by warning trefoils and armed guards. Deep waters saturated with calcium salts, concrete coffer-dams lined with gold and lead. A sleeping giant pointed at NATO, more terrifying than any nuclear weapon.

Project Koschei.

Red Square Redux

Warning

The following briefing film is classified SECRET GOLD JULY BOOJUM. If you do not have SECRET GOLD JULY BOOJUM clearance, leave the auditorium now and report to your unit security officer for debriefing. Failing to observe this notice is an imprisonable offense.

You have sixty seconds to comply.

Video clip

Red Square in springtime. The sky overhead is clear and blue; there's a little wispy cirrus at high altitude. It forms a brilliant backdrop for flight after flight of five four-engined bombers that thunder across the horizon and drop behind the Kremlin's high walls.

Voice-over

Red Square, the May Day parade, 1962. This is the first time that the Soviet Union has publicly displayed weapons classified GOLD JULY BOOJUM. Here they are:

Video clip

Later in the same day. A seemingly endless stream of armor and soldiers marches across the square, turning the air gray with diesel fumes. The trucks roll in line eight abreast, with soldiers sitting erect in the back. Behind them rumble a battalion of T-56s, their commanders standing at attention in their cupolas, saluting the stand. Jets race low and loud overhead, formations of MiG-17 fighters.

Behind the tanks sprawl a formation of four low-loaders: huge tractors towing low-sling trailers, their load beds strapped down under olive-drab tarpaulins. Whatever is under them is uneven, a bit like a loaf of bread the size of a small house. The trucks have an escort of jeep-like vehicles on each side, armed soldiers sitting at attention in their backs.

There are big five-pointed stars painted in silver on each tarpaulin,

494 · A Colder War

like outlines of stars. Each star is surrounded by a stylized silver circle; a unit insignia, perhaps, but not in the standard format for Red Army units. There's lettering around the circles, in a strangely stylized script.

Voice-over

These are live servitors under transient control. The vehicles towing them bear the insignia of the second Guards Engineering Brigade, a penal construction unit based in Bokhara and used for structural engineering assignments relating to nuclear installations in the Ukraine and Azerbaijan. This is the first time that any Dresden Agreement party openly demonstrated ownership of this technology: in this instance, the conclusion we are intended to draw is that the sixty-seventh Guard Engineering Brigade operates four units. Given existing figures for the Soviet ORBAT we can then extrapolate a total task strength of two hundred and eighty eight servitors, if this unit is unexceptional.

Video clip

Five huge Tu-95 Bear bombers thunder across the Moscow skies.

Voice-over

This conclusion is questionable. For example, in 1964 a total of two hundred and forty Bear bomber passes were made over the reviewing stand in front of the Lenin mausoleum. However, at that time technical reconnaissance assets verified that the Soviet air force has hard stand parking for only one hundred and sixty of these aircraft, and estimates of airframe production based on photographs of the extent of the Tupolev bureau's works indicate that total production to that date was between sixty and one hundred and eighty bombers.

Further analysis of photographic evidence from the 1964 parade suggests that a single group of twenty aircraft in four formations of five made repeated passes through the same airspace, the main arc of their circuit lying outside visual observation range of Moscow. This gave rise to the erroneous capacity report of 1964 in which the first strike delivery capability of the Soviet Union was over-estimated by as much as three hundred percent.

We must therefore take anything that they show us in Red Square with a pinch of salt when preparing force estimates. Quite possibly these four servitors are all they've got. Then again, the actual battalion strength may be considerably higher.

Still photographic sequence

From very high altitude—possibly in orbit—an eagle's eye view of a remote village in mountainous country. Small huts huddle together beneath a craggy outcrop; goats graze nearby.

In the second photograph, something has rolled through the village leaving a trail of devastation. The path is quite unlike the trail of damage left by an artillery bombardment: something roughly four meters wide has shaved the rocky plateau smooth, wearing it down as if with a terrible heat. A corner of a shack leans drunkenly, the other half sliced away cleanly. White bones gleam faintly in the track; no vultures descend to stab at the remains.

Voice-over

These images were taken very recently, on successive orbital passes of a KH-11 satellite. They were timed precisely eighty-nine minutes apart. This village was the home of a noted Mujahedin leader. Note the similar footprint to the payloads on the load beds of the trucks seen at the 1962 parade.

These indicators were present, denoting the presence of servitor units in use by Soviet forces in Afghanistan: the four meter wide gauge of the assimilation track. The total molecular breakdown of organic matter in the track. The speed of destruction—the event took less than five thousand seconds to completion, no survivors were visible, and the causative agent had already been uplifted by the time of the second orbital pass. This, despite the residents of the community being armed with DShK heavy machine guns, rocket propelled grenade launchers, and AK-47s. Lastly: there is no sign of the causative agent even deviating from its course, but the entire area is depopulated. Except for excarnated residue there is no sign of human habitation.

In the presence of such unique indicators, we have no alternative but to conclude that the Soviet Union has violated the Dresden Agreement by deploying GOLD JULY BOOJUM in a combat mode in the Khyber pass. There are no grounds to believe that a NATO armoured division would have fared any better than these mujahedin without nuclear support . . .

Puzzle Palace

Roger isn't a soldier. He's not much of a patriot, either: he signed up with the CIA after college, in the aftermath of the Church Commission hearings in the early seventies. The Company was out of the assassination business, just a bureaucratic engine rolling out National Security assessments: that's fine by Roger. Only now, five years later, he's no longer able to roll along, casually disengaged, like a car in neutral bowling down a shallow incline towards his retirement, pension and a gold watch. He puts the file down on his desk and, with a shaking hand, pulls an illicit cigarette from the pack he keeps in his drawer. He lights it and leans back for a moment to draw breath, force relaxation, staring at smoke rolling in the air beneath the merciless light until his hand stops shaking.

Most people think spies are afraid of guns, or KGB guards, or barbed wire, but in point of fact the most dangerous thing they face is paper. Papers carry secrets. Papers can carry death warrants. Papers like this one, this folio with its blurry eighteen year old faked missile photographs and estimates of time/survivor curves and pervasive psychosis ratios, can give you nightmares, dragging you awake screaming in the middle of the night. It's one of a series of highly classified pieces of paper that he is summarizing for the eyes of the National Security Council and the President Elect—if his head of department and the DDCIA approve it—and here he is, having to calm his nerves with a cigarette before he turns the next page.

After a few minutes, Roger's hand is still. He leaves his cigarette in the eagle-headed ash tray and picks up the intelligence report again. It's a summary, itself the distillation of thousands of pages and hundreds of photographs. It's barely twenty pages long: as of 1963, its date of preparation, the CIA knew very little about Project Koschei. Just the bare skeleton, and rumors from a highly-placed spy. And their own equivalent project, of course. Lacking the Soviet lead in that particular field, the USAF fielded the silver-plated white elephants of the NB-39 project: twelve atomic-powered bombers armed with XK-PLUTO, ready to tackle Project Koschei should the Soviets show signs of unsealing the bunker. Three hundred megatons of H-bombs pointed at a single target, and nobody was certain it would be enough to do the job.

And then there was the hard-to-conceal fiasco in Antarctica. Egg on face: a subterranean nuclear test program in international territory! If nothing else, it had been enough to stop JFK running for a second term. The test program was a bad excuse: but it was far better than confessing what had really happened to the 501st Airborne Division on the cold plateau beyond Mount Erebus. The plateau that the public didn't know about, that didn't show up on the maps issued by the geological survey departments of those governments party to the Dresden Agreement of 1931—an arrangement that even Hitler had stuck to.

The plateau that had swallowed more U-2 spy planes than the Soviet Union, more surface expeditions than darkest Africa.

Shit. How the hell am I going to put this together for him?

Roger's spent the past five hours staring at this twenty page report, trying to think of a way of summarizing their drily quantifiable terror in words that will give the reader power over them, the power to think the unthinkable: but it's proving difficult. The new man in the White House is straight-talking, demands straight answers. He's pious enough not to believe in the supernatural, confident enough that just listening to one of his speeches is an uplifting experience if you can close your eyes and believe in morning in America. There is probably no way of explaining Project Koschei, or XK-PLUTO, or MK-NIGHTMARE, or the gates, without watering them down into just another weapons system—which they are not. Weapons may have deadly or hideous effects, but they acquire moral character from the actions of those who use them. Whereas these projects are indelibly stained by a patina of ancient evil . . .

He hopes that if the balloon ever does go up, if the sirens wail, he and Andrea and Jason will be left behind to face the nuclear fire. It'll be a merciful death compared with what he suspect lurks out there, in the unexplored vastness beyond the gates. The vastness that made Nixon cancel the manned space program, leaving just the standing joke of a white-elephant shuttle, when he realized just how hideously dangerous the space race might become. The darkness that broke Jimmy Carter's faith and turned Lyndon B. Johnson into an alcoholic.

He stands up, nervously shifts from one foot to the other. Looks round at the walls of his cubicle. For a moment the cigarette smoldering on the edge of his ash tray catches his attention: wisps of blue-gray smoke coil like lazy dragons in the air above it, writhing in a strange cuneiform text. He blinks and they're gone, and the skin in the small of his back prickles as if someone had pissed on his grave.

"Shit." Finally, a spoken word in the silence. His hand is shaking as he stubs the cigarette out. *Mustn't let this get to me.* He glances at the wall. It's nineteen hundred hours; too late, too late. He should go home, Andy will be worrying herself sick.

In the end it's all too much. He slides the thin folder into the safe behind his chair, turns the locking handle and spins the dial, then signs himself out of the reading room and goes through the usual exit search.

During the thirty-mile drive home, he spits out of the window, trying to rid his mouth of the taste of Auschwitz ashes.

· · ·

Late Night in the White House

The colonel is febrile, jittering about the room with gung-ho enthusiasm. "That was a mighty fine report you pulled together, Jourgensen!" He paces over to the niche between the office filing cabinet and the wall, turns on the spot, paces back to the far side of his desk. "You understand the fundamentals. I like that. A few more guys like you running the company and we wouldn't have this fuckup in Tehran." He grins, contagiously. The colonel is a firestorm of enthusiasm, burning out of control like a forties comic-book hero. He has Roger on the edge of his chair, almost sitting at attention. Roger has to bite his tongue to remind himself not to call the colonel "sir"—he's a civilian, not in the chain of command. "That's why I've asked Deputy Director McMurdo to reassign you to this office, to work on my team as company liaison. And I'm pleased to say that he's agreed."

Roger can't stop himself: "To work here, sir?" *Here* is in the basement of the Executive Office Building, an extension hanging off the White House. Whoever the colonel is he's got *pull*, in positively magical quantities. "What will I be doing, sir? You said, your team—"

"Relax a bit. Drink your coffee." The colonel paces back behind his desk, sits down. Roger sips cautiously at the brown sludge in the mug with the Marine Corps crest. "The president told me to organize a team," says the colonel, so casually that Roger nearly chokes on his coffee, "to handle contingencies. October surprises. Those asshole commies down in Nicaragua. 'We're eyeball to eyeball with an Evil Empire, Ozzie, and we can't afford to blink'—those were his exact words. The Evil Empire uses dirty tricks. But nowadays we're better than they are: buncha hicks, like some third-world dictatorship—Upper Volta with shoggoths. My job is to pin them down and cut them up. Don't give them a chance to whack the shoe on the UN table, demand concessions. If they want to bluff I'll call 'em on it. If they want to go toe-to-toe I'll dance with 'em." He's up and pacing again. "The company used to do that, and do it okay, back in the fifties and sixties. But too many bleeding hearts—it makes me sick. If you guys went back to wet ops today you'd have journalists following you every time you went to the john in case it was newsworthy.

"Well, we aren't going to do it that way this time. It's a small team and the buck stops here." The colonel pauses, then glances at the ceiling. "Well, maybe up there. But you get the picture. I need someone who knows the company, an insider who has clearance up the wazoo who can go in and get the dope before it goes through a fucking committee of ass-watching bureaucrats. I'm also getting someone from the Puzzle Palace, and some words to give me pull with Big Black." He glances at Roger sharply, and Roger nods: he's cleared for National Security Agency—Puzzle Palace—intelligence, and knows about Big Black, the National Reconnaissance Office, which is so secret that even its existence is still classified.

Roger is impressed by this colonel, despite his better judgment. Within the Byzantine world of the US intelligence services, he is talking about building his very own pocket battleship and sailing it under the jolly roger with letters of marque and reprise signed by the president. But Roger still has some questions to ask, to scope out the limits of what Colonel North is capable of. "What about FEVER DREAM, sir?"

The colonel puts his coffee-cup down. "I own it," he says, bluntly. "And NIGHTMARE. And PLUTO. *Any means necessary* he said, and I have an executive order with the ink still damp to prove it. Those projects aren't part of the national command structure any more. Officially they've been stood down from active status and are being considered for inclusion in the next round of arms reduction talks. They're not part of the deterrent ORBAT any more; we're standardizing on just nuclear weapons. Unofficially, they're part of my group, and I will use them as necessary to contain and reduce the Evil Empire's warmaking abilities."

Roger's skin crawls with an echo of that childhood terror. "And the Dresden Agreement . . . ?"

"Don't worry. Nothing short of *them* breaking it would lead me to do so." The colonel grins, toothily. "Which is where you come in . . . "

The Moonlit Shores of Lake Vostok

The metal pier is dry and cold, the temperature hovering close to zero degrees Fahrenheit. It's oppressively dark in the cavern under the ice, and Roger shivers inside his multiple layers of insulation, shifts from foot to foot to keep warm. He has to swallow to keep his ears clear and he feels slightly dizzy from the pressure in the artificial bubble of air, pumped under the icy ceiling to allow humans to exist here, under the Ross Ice Shelf; they'll all spend more than a day sitting in depressurization chambers on the way back up to the surface.

There is no sound from the waters lapping just below the edge of the pier. The floodlights vanish into the surface and keep going—the water in the sub-surface Antarctic lake is incredibly clear—but are swallowed up rapidly, giving an impression of infinite, inky depths.

Roger is here as the colonel's representative, to observe the arrival of the probe, receive the consignment they're carrying, and report back that everything is running smoothly. The others try to ignore him, jittery at the presence of the man from DC. There're a gaggle of engineers and artificers, flown out via McMurdo base to handle the midget sub's operations. A nervous lieutenant supervises a squad of marines with complicated-looking weapons, half gun and half video camera, stationed at the corners of the raft. And there's the usual platform crew, deep-sea rig maintenance types—but subdued and nervous looking. They're afloat in a bubble of pressurized air wedged against the underside of the Antarctic ice sheet: below them stretch the still, supercooled waters of Lake Vostok.

They're waiting for a rendezvous.

"Five hundred yards," reports one of the techs. "Rising on ten." His companion nods. They're waiting for the men in the midget sub drilling quietly through three miles of frigid water, intruders in a long-drowned tomb. "Have 'em back on board in no time." The sub has been away for nearly a day; it set out with enough battery juice for the journey, and enough air to keep the crew breathing for a long time if there's a system failure, but they've learned the hard way that fail-safe systems aren't. Not out here, at the edge of the human world.

Roger shuffles some more. "I was afraid the battery load on that cell you replaced would trip an undervoltage isolator and we'd be here till Hell freezes over," the sub driver jokes to his neighbor.

Looking round, Roger sees one of the marines cross himself. "Have you heard anything from Gorman or Suslowicz?" he asks quietly.

The lieutenant checks his clipboard. "Not since departure, sir," he says. "We don't have comms with the sub while it's submerged: too small for ELF, and we don't want to alert anybody who might be, uh, listening."

"Indeed." The yellow hunchback shape of the midget submarine appears at the edge of the radiance shed by the floodlights. Surface waters undulate, oily, as the sub rises.

"Crew transfer vehicle sighted," the driver mutters into his mike. He's suddenly very busy adjusting trim settings, blowing bottled air into ballast tanks, discussing ullage levels and blade count with his number two. The crane crew are busy too, running their long boom out over the lake.

The sub's hatch is visible now, bobbing along the top of the water: the lieutenant is suddenly active. "Jones! Civatti! Stake it out, left and center!" The crane is already swinging the huge lifting hook over the sub, waiting to bring it aboard. "I want eyeballs on the portholes before you crack this thing!" It's the tenth run—seventh manned—through the eye of the needle on the lake bed, the drowned structure so like an ancient temple, and Roger has a bad feeling about it. *We can't get away with this forever*, he reasons. *Sooner or later . . .*

The sub comes out of the water like a gigantic yellow bath toy, a cyborg whale designed by a god with a sense of humor. It takes tense minutes to winch it in and maneuver it safely onto the platform. Marines take up position, shining torches in through two of the portholes that bulge myopically from the smooth curve of the sub's nose. Up on top someone is talking into a handset plugged into the stubby conning tower; the hatch locking wheel begins to turn.

"Gorman, sir," It's the lieutenant. In the light of the sodium floods everything looks sallow and washed-out; the soldier's face is the color of damp cardboard, slack with relief.

Roger waits while the submariner—Gorman—clambers unsteadily down from the top deck. He's a tall, emaciated-looking man, wearing a red thermal suit three sizes too big for him: salt-and-pepper stubble textures his jaw with sandpaper. Right now, he looks like a cholera victim; sallow skin, smell of acrid ketones as his body eats its own protein reserves, a more revolting miasma hovering over him. There's a slim aluminum briefcase chained to his left wrist, a bracelet of bruises darkening the skin above it. Roger steps forward.

"Sir?" Gorman straightens up for a moment: almost a shadow of military attention. He's unable to sustain it. "We made the pickup. Here's the QA sample; the rest is down below. You have the unlocking code?" he asks wearily.

Jourgensen nods. "One. Five. Eight. One. Two. Two. Nine."

Gorman slowly dials it into a combination lock on the briefcase, lets it fall open and unthreads the chain from his wrist. Floodlights glisten on polythene bags stuffed with white powder, five kilos of high-grade heroin from the hills of Afghanistan; there's another quarter of a ton packed in boxes in the crew compartment. The lieutenant inspects it, closes the case and passes it to Jourgensen. "Delivery successful, sir." From the ruins on the high plateau of the Taklamakan desert to American territory in Antarctica, by way of a detour through gates linking alien worlds: gates that nobody knows how to create or destroy except the Predecessors—and they aren't talking.

"What's it like through there?" Roger demands, shoulders tense. "*What did you see?*"

Up on top, Suslowicz is sitting in the sub's hatch, half slumping against the crane's attachment post. There's obviously something very wrong with him. Gorman shakes his head and looks away: the wan light makes the razor-sharp creases on his face stand out, like the crackled and shattered surface of a Jovian moon. Crow's feet. Wrinkles. Signs of age. Hair the color of moonlight. "It took so long," he says, almost complaining. Sinks to his knees. "All that *time* we've been gone . . . " He leans against the side of the sub, a pale shadow, aged beyond his years. "The sun was so *bright*. And our radiation detectors. Must have been a solar flare or something." He doubles over and retches at the edge of the platform.

Roger looks at him for a long, thoughtful minute: Gorman is twenty-five and a fixer for Big Black, early history in the Green Berets. He was in rude good health two days ago, when he set off through the gate to make the pick-up. Roger glances at the lieutenant. "I'd better go and tell the colonel," he says. A pause. "Get these two back to Recovery and see they're looked after. I don't expect we'll be sending any more crews through Victor-Tango for a while."

He turns and walks towards the lift shaft, hands clasped behind his back to keep them from shaking. Behind him, alien moonlight glimmers across the floor of Lake Vostok, three miles and untold light years from home.

General LeMay Would Be Proud

Warning

The following briefing film is classified SECRET INDIGO MARCH SNIPE. If you do not have SECRET INDIGO MARCH SNIPE clearance, leave the auditorium now and report to your unit security officer for debriefing. Failing to observe this notice is an imprisonable offense.

   You have sixty seconds to comply.

Video clip

Shot of huge bomber, rounded gun turrets sprouting like mushrooms from the decaying log of its fuselage, weirdly bulbous engine pods slung too far out towards each wingtip, four turbine tubes clumped around each atomic kernel.

Voice-over

"The Convair B-39 Peacemaker is the most formidable weapon in our Strategic Air Command's arsenal for peace. Powered by eight nuclear-heated Pratt and Whitney NP-4051 turbojets, it circles endlessly above the Arctic ice cap, waiting for the call. This is Item One, the flight training and test bird: twelve other birds await criticality on the ground, for once launched a B-39 can only be landed at two airfields in Alaska that are equipped to handle them. This one's been airborne for nine months so far, and shows no signs of age."

Cut to:

A shark the size of a Boeing 727 falls away from the open bomb bay of the monster. Stubby delta wings slice through the air, propelled by a rocket-bright glare.

Voice-over

"A modified Navajo missile—test article for an XK-PLUTO payload—dives away from a carrier plane. Unlike the real thing, this one carries no hydrogen bombs, no direct-cycle fission ramjet to bring retaliatory destruction to the enemy. Traveling at Mach 3 the XK-PLUTO will overfly enemy territory, dropping megaton-range bombs until, its payload exhausted, it seeks out and circles a final enemy. Once over the target it will eject its reactor core and rain molten plutonium on the heads of the enemy. XK-PLUTO is a total weapon: every aspect of its design, from the shockwave it creates as it hurtles along at treetop height to the structure of its atomic reactor, is designed to inflict damage."

Cut to:

Belsen postcards, Auschwitz movies: a holiday in Hell.

Voice-over

"This is why we need such a weapon. This is what it deters. The abominations first raised by the Third Reich's *Organisation Todt*, now removed to the Ukraine and deployed in the service of New Soviet Man as our enemy calls himself."

Cut to:

A sinister gray concrete slab, the upper surface of a Mayan step pyramid built with East German cement. Barbed wire, guns. A drained canal slashes north from the base of the pyramid towards the Baltic coastline, relic of the installation process: this is where it came from. The slave barracks squat beside the pyramid like a horrible memorial to its black-uniformed builders.

Cut to:

The new resting place: a big concrete monolith surrounded by three concrete lined lakes and a canal. It sits in the midst of a Ukraine landscape, flat as a pancake, stretching out forever in all directions.

Voice-over

"This is Project Koschei. The Kremlin's key to the gates of Hell . . . "

• • •

Technology Taster

"We know they first came here during the Precambrian age."

Professor Gould is busy with his viewgraphs, eyes down, trying not to pay too much attention to his audience. "We have samples of macrofauna, discovered by palaeontologist Charles D. Walcott on his pioneering expeditions into the Canadian Rockies, near the eastern border of British Columbia—" a hand-drawing of something indescribably weird fetches up on the screen "—like this *opabina*, which died there six hundred and forty million years ago. Fossils of soft-bodied animals that old are rare; the Burgess shale deposits are the best record of the Precambrian fauna anyone has found to date."

A skinny woman with big hair and bigger shoulder-pads sniffs loudly; she has no truck with these antediluvian dates. Roger winces sympathy for the academic. He'd rather she wasn't here, but somehow she got wind of the famous paleontologist's visit—and she's the colonel's administrative assistant. Telling her to leave would be a career-limiting move.

"The important item to note—" photograph of a mangled piece of rock, visual echoes of the *opabina*—"is the tooth marks. We find them also—their exact cognates—on the ring segments of the Z-series specimens returned by the Pabodie Antarctic expedition of 1926. The world of the Precambrian was laid out differently from our own; most of the land masses that today are separate continents were joined into one huge structure. Indeed, these samples were originally separated by only two thousand miles or thereabouts. Suggesting that they brought their own parasites with them."

"What do tooth-marks tell us about them, that we need to know?" asks the colonel.

The doctor looks up. His eyes gleam: "That something liked to eat them when they were fresh." There's a brief rattle of laughter. "Something with jaws that open and close like the iris in your camera. Something we thought was extinct."

Another viewgraph, this time with a blurry underwater photograph on it. The thing looks a bit like a weird fish—a turbocharged, armored hagfish with side-skirts and spoilers, or maybe a squid with not enough tentacles. The upper head is a flattened disk, fronted by two bizarre fern-like tentacles drooping over the weird sucker-mouth on its underside. "This snapshot was taken in Lake Vostok last year. It should be dead: there's nothing there for it to eat. This, ladies and gentlemen, is *Anomalocaris*, our toothy chewer." He pauses for a moment. "I'm very grateful to you for showing it to me," he adds, "even though it's going to make a lot of my colleagues very angry."

Is that a shy grin? The professor moves on rapidly, not giving Roger a chance to fathom his real reaction. "Now *this* is interesting in the extreme," Gould comments. Whatever it is, it looks like a cauliflower head, or maybe a brain: fractally branching stalks continuously diminishing in length and diameter, until they turn into an iridescent fuzzy manifold wrapped around a central stem. The base of the stem is rooted to a barrel-shaped structure that stands on four stubby tentacles.

"We had somehow managed to cram *Anomalocaris* into our taxonomy, but this is something that has no precedent. It bears a striking resemblance to an enlarged body segment of *Hallucigena*—" here he shows another viewgraph, something like a stiletto-heeled centipede wearing a war-bonnet of tentacles— "but a year ago we worked out that we had poor *Hallucigena* upside down and it was actually just a spiny worm. And the high levels of iridium and diamond in the head here . . . this isn't a living creature, at least not within the animal kingdom I've been studying for the past thirty years. There's no cellular structure at all. I asked one of my colleagues for help and they were completely unable to isolate any DNA or RNA from it at all. It's more like a machine that displays biological levels of complexity."

"Can you put a date to it?" asks the colonel.

"Yup." The professor grins. "It predates the wave of atmospheric atomic testing that began in 1945; that's about all. We think it's from some time in the first half of this century, last half of last century. It's been dead for years, but there are older people still walking this earth. In contrast—" he flips to the picture of *Anomalocaris* "—this specimen we found in rocks that are roughly six hundred and ten million years old." He whips up another shot: similar structure, much clearer. "Note how similar it is to the dead but not decomposed one. They're obviously still alive somewhere."

He looks at the colonel, suddenly bashful and tongue-tied: "Can I talk about the, uh, thing we were, like, earlier . . . ?"

"Sure. Go ahead. Everyone here is cleared for it." The colonel's casual wave takes in the big-haired secretary, and Roger, and the two guys from Big Black who are taking notes, and the very serious woman from the Secret Service, and even the balding, worried-looking admiral with the double chin and coke-bottle glasses.

"Oh. Alright." Bashfulness falls away. "Well, we've done some preliminary dissections on the *Anomalocaris* tissues you supplied us with. And we've sent some samples for laboratory analysis—nothing anyone could deduce much from," he adds hastily. He straightens up. "What we discovered is quite simple: these samples didn't originate in Earth's ecosystem. Cladistic analysis of their intracellular characteristics and what we've been able to work out of their biochemistry indicates, not a point of divergence from our own ancestry, but the absence of common ancestry. A *cabbage* is more human, has more in common with us, than that creature. You can't tell by looking at the fossils, six hundred million years after it died, but live tissue samples are something else.

"Item: it's a multicellular organism, but each cell appears to have multiple structures like nuclei—a thing called a syncitium. No DNA, it uses RNA with a couple of base pairs that aren't used by terrestrial biology. We haven't been able to figure out what most of its organelles do, what their terrestrial cognates would be, and it builds proteins using a couple of amino acids that we don't. That *nothing* does. Either it's descended from an ancestry that diverged from ours before the *archaeobacteria*, or—more probably—it is no relative at all." He isn't smiling any more. "The gateways, colonel?"

"Yeah, that's about the size of it. The critter you've got there was retrieved by one of our, uh, missions. On the other side of a gate."

Gould nods. "I don't suppose you could get me some more?" he asks hopefully.

"All missions are suspended pending an investigation into an accident we had earlier this year," the colonel says, with a significant glance at Roger. Suslowicz died two weeks ago; Gorman is still disastrously sick, connective tissue rotting in his body, massive radiation exposure the probable cause. Normal service will not be resumed; the pipeline will remain empty until someone can figure out a way to make the deliveries without losing the crew. Roger inclines his head minutely.

"Oh well." The professor shrugs. "Let me know if you do. By the way, do you have anything approximating a fix on the other end of the gate?"

"No," says the colonel, and this time Roger knows he's lying. Mission four, before the colonel diverted their payload capacity to another purpose, planted a compact radio telescope in an empty courtyard in the city on the far side of the gate. XK-Masada, where the air's too thin to breathe without oxygen; where the sky is indigo, and the buildings cast razor-sharp shadows across a rocky plain baked to the consistency of pottery under a blood-red sun. Subsequent analysis of pulsar signals recorded by the station confirmed that it was nearly six hundred light years closer to the galactic core, inward along the same spiral arm. There are glyphs on the alien buildings that resemble symbols seen in grainy black-and-white Minox photos of the doors of the bunker in the Ukraine. Symbols behind which the subject of Project Koschei lies undead and sleeping:

something evil, scraped from a nest in the drowned wreckage of a city on the Baltic floor. "Why do you want to know where they came from?"

"Well. We know so little about the context in which life evolves." For a moment the professor looks wistful. "We have—had—only one datum point: Earth, this world. Now we have a second, a fragment of a second. If we get a third, we can begin to ask deep questions like, not, 'is there life out there?'— because we know the answer to that one, now—but questions like 'what sort of life is out there?' and 'is there a place for us?'"

Roger shudders: *Idiot*, he thinks. *If only you knew you wouldn't be so happy*— He restrains the urge to speak up. Doing so would be another career-limiting move. More to the point, it might be a life-expectancy-limiting move for the professor, who certainly didn't deserve any such drastic punishment for his cooperation. Besides, Harvard professors visiting the Executive Office Building in DC are harder to disappear than comm-symp teachers in some fly-blown jungle village in Nicaragua. Somebody might notice. The colonel would be annoyed.

Roger realizes that Professor Gould is staring at him. "Do you have a question for me?" asks the distinguished paleontologist.

"Uh—in a moment." Roger shakes himself. Remembering time-survivor curves, the captured Nazi medical atrocity records mapping the ability of a human brain to survive in close proximity to the Baltic Singularity. Mengele's insanity. The SS's final attempt to liquidate the survivors, the witnesses. Koschei, primed and pointed at the American heartland like a darkly evil gun. The "world-eating mind" adrift in brilliant dreams of madness, estivating in the absence of its prey: dreaming of the minds of sapient beings, be they barrel-bodied wing-flying tentacular things, or their human inheritors. "Do you think they could have been intelligent, professor? Conscious, like us?"

"I'd say so." Gould's eyes glitter. "This one—" he points to a viewgraph— "isn't alive as we know it. And this one—" he's found a Predecessor, god help him, barrel-bodied and bat-winged—"had what looks like a lot of very complex ganglia, not a brain as we know it, but at least as massive as our own. And some specialized grasping adaptations that might be interpreted as facilitating tool use. Put the two together and you have a high level technological civilization. Gateways between planets orbiting different stars. Alien flora, fauna, or whatever. I'd say an interstellar civilization isn't out of the picture. One that has been extinct for deep geological time—ten times as long as the dinosaurs— but that has left relics that work." His voice is trembling with emotion. "We humans, we've barely scratched the surface! The longest lasting of our relics?

All our buildings will be dust in twenty thousand years, even the pyramids. Neil Armstrong's footprints in the Sea of Tranquility will crumble under micrometeoroid bombardment in a mere half million years or so. The emptied oil fields will refill over ten million years, methane percolating up through the mantle: continental drift will erase everything. But these people . . . ! They built to last. There's so much to learn from them. I wonder if we're worthy pretenders to their technological crown?"

"I'm sure we are, professor," the colonel's secretary says brassily. "Isn't that right, Ollie?"

The colonel nods, grinning. "You betcha, Fawn. You betcha!"

The Great Satan

Roger sits in the bar in the King David hotel, drinking from a tall glass of second-rate lemonade and sweating in spite of the air conditioning. He's dizzy and disoriented from jet-lag, the gut-cramps have only let him come down from his room in the past hour, and he has another two hours to go before he can try to place a call to Andrea. They had another blazing row before he flew out here; she doesn't understand why he keeps having to visit odd corners of the globe. She only knows that his son is growing up thinking a father is a voice that phones at odd times of day.

Roger is mildly depressed, despite the buzz of doing business at this level. He spends a lot of time worrying about what will happen if they're found out—what Andrea will do, or Jason for that matter, Jason whose father is a phone call away all the time—if Roger is led away in handcuffs beneath the glare of flash bulbs. If the colonel sings, if the shy bald admiral is browbeaten into spilling the beans to Congress, who will look after them then?

Roger has no illusions about what kills black operations: there are too many people in the loop, too many elaborate front corporations and numbered bank accounts and shady Middle Eastern arms dealers. Sooner or later someone will find a reason to talk, and Roger is in too deep. He isn't just the company liaison officer any more: he's become the colonel's bag-man, his shadow, the guy with the diplomatic passport and the bulging briefcase full of heroin and end-user certificates.

At least the ship will sink from the top down, he thinks. There are people very high up who want the colonel to succeed. When the shit hits the fan and is sprayed across the front page of the *Washington Post*, it will likely take down cabinet members and secretaries of state: the President himself will have to take the witness stand and deny everything. The republic will question itself.

A hand descends on his shoulder, sharply cutting off his reverie. "Howdy, Roger! Whatcha worrying about now?"

Jourgensen looks up wearily. "Stuff," he says gloomily. "Have a seat." The redneck from the embassy—Mike Hamilton, some kind of junior attaché for embassy protocol by cover—pulls out a chair and crashes down on it like a friendly car wreck. He's not really a redneck, Roger knows—rednecks don't come with doctorates in foreign relations from Yale—but he likes people to think he's a bumpkin when he wants to get something from them.

"He's early," says Hamilton, looking past Roger's ear, voice suddenly all business. "Play the agenda, I'm your dim but friendly good cop. Got the background? Deniables ready?"

Roger nods, then glances round and sees Mehmet (family name unknown) approaching from the other side of the room. Mehmet is impeccably manicured and tailored, wearing a suit from Jermyn Street that costs more than Roger earns in a month. He has a neatly trimmed beard and mustache and talks with a pronounced English accent. Mehmet is a Turkish name, not a Persian one: pseudonym, of course. To look at him you would think he was a westernized Turkish businessman—certainly not an Iranian revolutionary with heavy links to Hezbollah and (whisper this), Old Man Ruholla himself, the hermit of Qom. Never, ever, in a thousand years, the unofficial Iranian ambassador to the Little Satan in Tel Aviv.

Mehmet strides over. A brief exchange of pleasantries masks the essential formality of their meeting: he's early, a deliberate move to put them off-balance. He's outnumbered, too, and that's also a move to put them on the defensive, because the first rule of diplomacy is never to put yourself in a negotiating situation where the other side can assert any kind of moral authority, and sheer weight of numbers is a powerful psychological tool.

"Roger, my dear fellow." He smiles at Jourgensen. "And the charming Dr. Hamilton, I see." The smile broadens. "I take it the good colonel is desirous of news of his friends?"

Jourgensen nods. "That is indeed the case."

Mehmet stops smiling. For a moment he looks ten years older. "I visited them," he says shortly. "No, I was *taken* to see them. It is indeed grave, my friends. They are in the hands of very dangerous men, men who have nothing to lose and are filled with hatred."

Roger speaks: "There is a debt between us—"

Mehmet holds up a hand. "Peace, my friend. We will come to that. These are men of violence, men who have seen their homes destroyed and families subjected to indignities, and their hearts are full of anger. It will take a large display of repentance, a high blood-price, to buy their acquiescence. That is part of our law, you understand? The family of the bereaved may demand blood-price of the transgressor, and how else might the world be? They see it in these terms: that you must repent of your evils and assist them in waging holy war against those who would defile the will of Allah."

Roger sighs. "We do what we can," he says. "We're shipping them arms. We're fighting the Soviets every way we can without provoking the big one. What more do they want? The hostages—that's not playing well in DC. There's got to be some give and take. If Hezbollah don't release them soon they'll just convince everyone what they're not serious about negotiating. And that'll be an end to it. The colonel *wants* to help you, but he's got to have something to show the man at the top, right?"

Mehmet nods. "You and I are men of the world and understand that this keeping of hostages is not rational, but they look to you for defense against the Great Satan that assails them, and their blood burns with anger that your nation, for all its fine words, takes no action. The Great Satan rampages in Afghanistan, taking whole villages by night, and what is done? The United States turns its back. And they are not the only ones who feel betrayed. Our Ba'athist foes from Iraq . . . in Basra the unholy brotherhood of Takrit and their servants the Mukhabarat hold nightly sacrifice upon the altar of Yair-Suthot; the fountains of blood in Tehran testify to their effect. If the richest, most powerful nation on earth refuses to fight, these men of violence from the Bekaa think, how may we unstopper the ears of that nation? And they are not sophisticates like you or I."

He looks at Roger, who hunches his shoulders uneasily. "We *can't* move against the Soviets openly! They must understand that it would be the end of far more than their little war. If the Taliban want American help against the Russians, it cannot be delivered openly."

"It is not the Russians that we quarrel with," Mehmet says quietly, "but their choice in allies. They believe themselves to be infidel atheists, but by their deeds they shall be known; the icy spoor of Leng is upon them, their tools are those described in the *Kitab al Azif*. We have proof that they have violated the terms of the Dresden Agreement. The accursed and unhallowed stalk the frozen passes of the Himalayas by night, taking all whose path they cross. And will you stopper your ears even as the Russians grow in misplaced confidence, sure that their dominance of these forces of evil is complete? The gates are opening everywhere, as it was prophesied. Last week we flew an F-14C with a camera relay pod through one of them. The pilot and weapons operator are in paradise now, but we have glanced into Hell and have the film and radar plots to prove it."

The Iranian ambassador fixes the redneck from the embassy with an icy gaze. "Tell your ambassador that we have opened preliminary discussions with Mossad, with a view to purchasing the produce of a factory at Dimona, in the Negev desert. Past insults may be set aside, for the present danger imperils all of us. They are receptive to our arguments, even if you are not: his holiness the Ayatollah has declared in private that any warrior who carries a nuclear device into the abode of the eater of souls will certainly achieve paradise. There will be an end to the followers of the ancient abominations on this Earth, Dr. Hamilton, even if we have to push the nuclear bombs down their throats with our own hands!"

Swimming Pool

"Mr. Jourgensen, at what point did you become aware that the Iranian government was threatening to violate UN Resolution 216 and the Non-Proliferation Protocol to the 1956 Geneva accords?"

Roger sweats under the hot lights: his heartbeat accelerates. "I'm not sure I understand the question, sir."

"I asked you a direct question. Which part don't you understand? I'm going to repeat myself slowly: when did you realize that the Iranian Government was threatening to violate Resolution 216 and the 1956 Geneva Accords on nuclear proliferation?"

Roger shakes his head. It's like a bad dream, unseen insects buzzing furiously around him. "Sir, I had no direct dealings with the Iranian government. All I know is that I was asked to carry messages to and from a guy called Mehmet who I was told knew something about our hostages in Beirut. My understanding is that the colonel has been conducting secret negotiations with this gentleman or his backers for some time—a couple of years—now. Mehmet made allusions to parties in the Iranian administration but I have no way of knowing if he was telling the truth, and I never saw any diplomatic credentials."

There's an inquisition of dark-suited congressmen opposite him, like a jury of teachers sitting in judgment over an errant pupil. The trouble is, these teachers can put him in front of a judge and send him to prison for many years, so that Jason really *will* grow up with a father who's a voice on the telephone, a father who isn't around to take him to air shows or ball games or any of the other rituals of growing up. They're talking to each other quietly, deciding on another line of questioning: Roger shifts uneasily in his chair. This is a closed hearing, the television camera a gesture in the direction of the Congressional Archives: a pack of hungry Democrats have scented Republican blood in the water.

The congressman in the middle looks towards Roger. "Stop right there. Where did you know about this guy Mehmet from? Who told you to go see him and who told you what he was?"

Roger swallows. "I got a memo from Fawn, like always. Admiral Poindexter wanted a man on the spot to talk to this guy, a messenger, basically, who was already in the loop. Colonel North signed off on it and told me to charge the trip to his discretionary fund." That must have been the wrong thing to say, because two of the congressmen are leaning together and whispering in each other's ears, and an aide obligingly sidles up to accept a note, then dashes away. "I was told that Mehmet was a mediator," Roger adds. "In trying to resolve the Beirut hostage thing."

"A mediator." The guy asking the questions looks at him in disbelief.

The man to his left—who looks as old as the moon, thin white hair, liver spots on his hooked nose, eyelids like sacks—chuckles appreciatively. "Yeah. Like Hitler was a *diplomat*. 'One more territorial demand'—" he glances round. "Nobody else remember that?" he asks plaintively.

"No sir," Roger says very seriously.

The prime interrogator snorts. "What did Mehmet tell you Iran was going to do, exactly?"

Roger thinks for a moment. "He said they were going to buy something from a factory at Dimona. I understood this to be the Israeli Defense Ministry's nuclear weapons research institute, and the only logical item—in the context of our discussion—was a nuclear weapon. Or weapons. He said the Ayatollah had decreed that a suicide bomber who took out the temple of Yog-Sothoth in Basra would achieve paradise, and that they also had hard evidence that the Soviets have deployed certain illegal weapons systems in Afghanistan. This was in the context of discussing illegal weapons proliferation; he was very insistent about the Iraq thing."

"What exactly are these weapons systems?" demands the third inquisitor, a quiet, hawk-faced man sitting on the left of the panel.

"The *shoggot'im*, they're called: *servitors*. There are several kinds of advanced robotic systems made out of molecular components: they can change shape, restructure material at the atomic level—act like corrosive acid, or secrete diamonds. Some of them are like a tenuous mist—what Dr. Drexler at MIT calls a utility fog—while others are more like an oily globule. Apparently they may be able to manufacture more of themselves, but they're not really alive in any meaning of the term we're familiar with. They're programmable, like robots, using a command language deduced from recovered records of the forerunners who left them here. The Molotov Raid of 1930 brought back a large consignment of them; all we have to go on are the scraps they missed, and reports by the Antarctic Survey. Professor Liebkunst's files in particular are most frustrating—"

"Stop. So you're saying the Russians have these, uh, Shoggoths, but we don't have any. And even those dumb Arab bastards in Baghdad are working on them. So you're saying we've got a, a Shoggoth gap? A strategic chink in our armor? And now the Iranians say the Russians are using them in Afghanistan?"

Roger speaks rapidly: "That is minimally correct, sir, although countervailing weapons have been developed to reduce the risk of a unilateral preemption escalating to an exchange of weakly godlike agencies." The congressman in the middle nods encouragingly. "For the past three decades, the B-39 Peacemaker force has been tasked by SIOP with maintaining an XK-PLUTO capability directed at ablating the ability of the Russians to activate Project Koschei, the dormant alien entity they captured from the Nazis at the end of the last war. We have twelve PLUTO-class atomic-powered cruise missiles pointed at that thing, day and night, as many megatons as the entire Minuteman force. In principle, we will be able to blast it to pieces before it can be brought to full wakefulness and eat the minds of everyone within two hundred miles."

He warms to his subject. "Secondly, we believe the Soviet control of Shoggoth technology is rudimentary at best. They know how to tell them to roll over an Afghan hill-farmer village, but they can't manufacture more of them. Their utility as weapons is limited—but terrifying—but they're not much of a problem. A greater issue is the temple in Basra. This contains an operational gateway, and according to Mehmet the Iraqi political secret police, the Mukhabarat, are trying to figure out how to manipulate it; they're trying to summon something through it. He seemed to be mostly afraid that they—and the Russians—would lose control of whatever it was; presumably another weakly godlike creature like the K-Thulu entity at the core of Project Koschei."

The old guy speaks: "This foo-loo thing, boy—you can drop those stupid K prefixes around me—is it one of a kind?"

Roger shakes his head. "I don't know, sir. We know the gateways link to at least three other planets. There may be many that we don't know of. We don't know how to create them or close them; all we can do is send people through, or pile bricks in the opening." He nearly bites his tongue, because there are more than three worlds out there, and he's been to at least one of them: the bolt-hole on XK-Masada, built by the NRO from their secret budget. He's seen the mile-high dome Buckminster Fuller spent his last decade designing for them, the rings of Patriot air defense missiles. A squadron of black diamond-shaped fighters from the Skunk works, said to be invisible to radar, patrols the empty skies of XK-Masada. Hydroponic farms and empty barracks and apartment blocks await the senators and congressmen and their families and thousands of support personnel. In event of war they'll be evacuated through the small gate that has been moved to the Executive Office Building basement, in a room beneath the swimming pool where Jack used to go skinny-dipping with Marilyn.

"Off the record now." The old congressman waves his hand in a chopping gesture: "I say *off*, boy." The cameraman switches off his machine and leaves. He leans forward, towards Roger. "What you're telling me is, we've been waging a secret war since, when? The end of the second world war? Earlier, the Pabodie Antarctic expedition in the twenties, whose survivors brought back the first of these alien relics? And now the Eye-ranians have gotten into the game and figure it's part of their fight with Saddam?"

"Sir." Roger barely trusts himself to do more than nod.

"Well." The congressman eyes his neighbor sharply. "Let me put it to you that you have heard the phrase, 'the great filter.' What does it mean to you?"

"The great—?" Roger stops. *Professor Gould*, he thinks. "We had a professor of paleontology lecture us," he explains. "I think he mentioned it. Something about why there aren't any aliens in flying saucers buzzing us the whole time."

The congressman snorts. His neighbor starts and sits up. "Thanks to Pabodie and his followers, Liebkunst and the like, we know there's a lot of life in the universe. The great filter, boy, is whatever force stops most of it developing intelligence and coming to visit. Something, somehow, kills intelligent species before they develop this kind of technology for themselves. How about meddling with relics of the Elder Ones? What do you think of that?"

Roger licks his lips nervously. "That sounds like a good possibility, sir," he says. His unease is building.

The congressman's expression is intense: "These weapons your colonel is dicking around with make all our nukes look like a toy bow and arrow, and all you can say is *it's a good possibility, sir?* Seems to me like someone in the Oval Office has been asleep at the switch."

"Sir, Executive Order 2047, issued January 1980, directed the armed forces to standardize on nuclear weapons to fill the mass destruction role. All other items were to be developmentally suspended, with surplus stocks allocated to the supervision of Admiral Poindexter's joint munitions expenditure committee. Which Colonel North was detached to by the USMC high command, with the full cognizance of the White House—"

The door opens. The congressman looks round angrily: "I thought I said we weren't to be disturbed!"

The aide standing there looks uncertain. "Sir, there's been an, uh, major security incident, and we need to evacuate—"

"Where? What happened?" demands the congressman. But Roger, with a sinking feeling, realizes that the aide isn't watching the house committee members: and the guy behind him is Secret Service.

"Basra. There's been an attack, sir." A furtive glance at Roger, as his brain freezes in denial: "If you'd all please come this way . . . "

Bombing in Fifteen Minutes

Heads down, through a corridor where congressional staffers hurry about carrying papers, urgently calling one another. A cadre of dark-suited Secret Service agents close in, hustling Roger along in the wake of the committee members. A wailing like tinnitus fills his ears. "What's happening?" he asks, but nobody answers.

Down into the basement. Another corridor, where two marine guards are waiting with drawn weapons. The Secret Service guys are exchanging terse reports by radio. The committee men are hustled away along a narrow service tunnel: Roger is stalled by the entrance. "What's going on?" he asks his minder.

"Just a moment, sir." More listening: these guys cock their heads to one side as they take instruction, birds of prey scanning the horizon for prey. "Delta four coming in. Over. You're clear to go along the tunnel now, sir. This way."

"What's *happening?*" Roger demands as he lets himself be hustled into the corridor, along to the end and round a sharp corner. Numb shock takes hold: he keeps putting one foot in front of the other.

"We're now at Defcon One, sir. You're down on the special list as part of the house staff. Next door on the left, sir."

The queue in the dim-lit basement room is moving fast, white-gloved guards with clipboards checking off men and a few women in suits as they step through a steel blast door one by one and disappear from view. Roger looks round in bewilderment: he sees a familiar face. "Fawn! What's going on?"

The secretary looks puzzled. "I don't know. Roger? I thought you were testifying today."

"So did I." They're at the door. "What else?"

"Ronnie was making a big speech in Helsinki; the colonel had me record it in his office. Something about not coexisting with the Empire of Evil. He cracked some kinda joke about how we start bombing in fifteen minutes, then this—"

They're at the door. It opens on a steel-walled airlock and the marine guard is taking their badges and hustling them inside. Two staff types and a middle-aged brigadier join them and the door thumps shut. The background noise vanishes, Roger's ears pop, then the inner door opens and another marine guard waves them through into the receiving hall.

"Where are we?" asks the big-haired secretary, staring around.

"Welcome to XK-Masada," says Roger. Then his childhood horrors catch up with him and he goes in search of a toilet to throw up in.

We Need You Back

Roger spends the next week in a state of numbed shock. His apartment here is like a small hotel room—a hotel with security, air conditioning, and windows that only open onto an interior atrium. He pays little attention to his surroundings. It's not as if he has a home to return to.

Roger stops shaving. Stops changing his socks. Stops looking in mirrors or combing his hair. He smokes a lot, orders cheap bourbon from the commissary, and drinks himself into an amnesic stupor each night. He is, frankly, a mess. Self-destructive. Everything disintegrated under him at once: his job, the people he held in high regard, his family, his life. All the time he can't get one thing out of his head: the expression on Gorman's face as he stands there, in front of the submarine, rotting from the inside out with radiation sickness, dead and not yet knowing it. It's why he's stopped looking in mirrors.

On the fourth day he's slumped in a chair watching taped *I Love Lucy* reruns on the boob tube when the door to his suite opens quietly. Someone comes in. He doesn't look round until the colonel walks across the screen and unplugs the TV set at the wall, then sits down in the chair next to him. The colonel has bags of dark skin under his eyes; his jacket is rumpled and his collar is unbuttoned.

"You've got to stop this, Roger," he says quietly. "You look like shit."

"Yeah, well. You too."

The colonel passes him a slim manila folder. Without wanting to, Roger slides out the single sheet of paper within.

"So it was them."

"Yeah." A moment's silence. "For what it's worth, we haven't lost yet. We may yet pull your wife and son out alive. Or be able to go back home."

"Your family too, I suppose." Roger's touched by the colonel's consideration, the pious hope that Andrea and Jason will be all right, even through his shell of misery. He realizes his glass is empty. Instead of refilling it he puts it down on the carpet beside his feet. "*Why?*"

The colonel removes the sheet of paper from his numb fingers. "Probably someone spotted you in the King David and traced you back to us. The Mukhabarat had agents everywhere, and if they were in league with the KGB . . . " he shrugs. "Things escalated rapidly. Then the president cracked that joke over a hot mike that was supposed to be switched off . . . Have you been checking in with the desk summaries this week?"

Roger looks at him blankly. "Should I?"

"Oh, things are still happening." The colonel leans back and stretches his feet out. "From what we can tell of the situation on the other side, not everyone's dead yet. Ligachev's screaming blue murder over the hotline, accusing us of genocide: but he's still talking. Europe is a mess and nobody knows what's going on in the Middle East—even the Blackbirds aren't making it back out again."

"The thing at Takrit."

"Yeah. It's bad news, Roger. We need you back."

"Bad news?"

"The worst." The colonel jams his hands between his knees, stares at the floor like a bashful child. "Saddam Hussein al-Takriti spent years trying to get his hands on Elder technology. It looks like he finally succeeded in stabilizing the gate into Sothoth. Whole villages disappeared, Marsh Arabs, wiped out in the swamps of Eastern Iraq. Reports of yellow rain, people's skin melting right off their bones. The Iranians got itchy and finally went nuclear. Trouble is, they did so two hours before that speech. Some asshole in Plotsk launched half the Uralskoye SS-20 grid—they went to launch on warning eight months ago—burning south, praise Jesus. Scratch the Middle East, period—everything from the Nile to the Khyber Pass is toast. We're still waiting for the callback on Moscow, but SAC has put the whole Peacemaker force on airborne alert. So far we've lost the eastern seaboard as far south as North Virginia and they've lost the Donbass basin and Vladivostok. Things are a mess; nobody can even agree whether we're fighting the commies or something else. But the box at Chernobyl—Project Koschei—the doors are open, Roger. We orbited a Keyhole-eleven over it and there are tracks, leading west. The PLUTO strike didn't stop it—and nobody knows what the fuck is going on in WarPac country. Or France, or Germany, or Japan, or England."

The colonel makes a grab for Roger's Wild Turkey, rubs the neck clean and swallows from the bottle. He looks at Roger with a wild expression on his face. "Koschei is loose, Roger. They fucking woke the thing. And now they can't control it. Can you believe that?"

"I can believe that."

"I want you back behind a desk tomorrow morning, Roger. We need to know what this Thulu creature is capable of. We need to know what to do to stop it. Forget Iraq; Iraq is a smoking hole in the map. But K-Thulu is heading towards the Atlantic Coast. What are we going to do if it doesn't stop?"

Masada

The city of XK-Masada sprouts like a vast mushroom, a mile-wide dome emerging from the top of a cold plateau on a dry planet that orbits a dying star. The jagged black shapes of F-117s howl across the empty skies outside it at dusk and dawn, patrolling the threatening emptiness that stretches as far as the mind can imagine.

Shadows move in the streets of the city, hollowed out human shells in uniform. They rustle around the feet of the towering concrete blocks like the dry leaves of autumn, obsessively focused on the tasks that lend structure to their remaining days. Above them tower masts of steel, propping up the huge geodesic dome that arches across the sky: blocking out the hostile, alien constellations, protecting frail humanity from the dust storms that periodically scour the bones of the ancient world. The gravity here is a little lighter, the night sky whorled and marbled by the diaphanous sheets of gas blasted off the dying star that lights their days. During the long winter nights, a flurry of carbon dioxide snow dusts the surface of the dome: but the air is bone-dry, the city slaking its thirst on subterranean aquifers.

This planet was once alive—there is still a scummy sea of algae near the equator that feeds oxygen into the atmosphere, and there is a range of volcanoes near the North Pole that speaks of plate tectonics in motion—but it is visibly dying. There is a lot of history here, but no future.

Sometimes, in the early hours when he cannot sleep, Roger walks outside the city, along the edge of the dry plateau. Machines labor on behind him, keeping the city tenuously intact: he pays them little attention. There is talk of mounting an expedition to Earth one of these years, to salvage whatever is left before the searing winds of time erase them forever. Roger doesn't like to think about that. He tries to avoid thinking about Earth as much as possible: except when he cannot sleep but walks along the cliff top, prodding at memories of Andrea and Jason and his parents and sister and relatives and friends, each of them as painful as the socket of a missing tooth. He has a mouthful of emptiness, bitter and aching, out here on the edge of the plateau.

Sometimes Roger thinks he's the last human being alive. He works in an office, feverishly trying to sort out what went wrong: and bodies move around him, talking, eating in the canteen, sometimes talking *to* him and waiting as if they expect a dialogue. There are bodies here, men and some women chatting, civilian and some military—but no people. One of the bodies, an army surgeon, told him he's suffering from a common stress disorder, survivor's guilt. This may be so, Roger admits, but it doesn't change anything. Soulless days follow sleepless nights into oblivion, dust trickling over the side of the cliff like sand into the un-dug graves of his family.

A narrow path runs along the side of the plateau, just downhill from the foundations of the city power plant where huge apertures belch air warmed by the radiators of the nuclear reactor. Roger follows the path, gravel and sandy rock crunching under his worn shoes. Foreign stars twinkle overhead, forming unrecognizable patterns that tell him he's far from home. The trail drops away from the top of the plateau, until the city is an unseen shadow looming above and behind his shoulder. To his right is a dizzying panorama, the huge rift valley with its ancient city of the dead stretched out before him. Beyond it rise alien mountains, their peaks as high and airless as the dead volcanoes of Mars.

About half a mile away from the dome, the trail circles an outcrop of rock and takes a downhill switchback turn. Roger stops at the bend and looks out across the desert at his feet. He sits down, leans against the rough cliff face and stretches his legs out across the path, so that his feet dangle over nothingness. Far below him, the dead valley is furrowed with rectangular depressions; once, millions of years ago, they might have been fields, but nothing like that survives to this date. They're just dead, like everyone else on this world. Like Roger.

In his shirt pocket, a crumpled, precious pack of cigarettes. He pulls a white cylinder out with shaking fingers, sniffs at it, then flicks his lighter under it. Scarcity has forced him to cut back: he coughs at the first lungful of stale smoke, a harsh, racking croak. The irony of being saved from lung cancer by a world war is not lost on him.

He blows smoke out, a tenuous trail streaming across the cliff. "Why me?" he asks quietly.

The emptiness takes its time answering. When it does, it speaks with the colonel's voice. "You know the reason."

"I didn't want to do it," he hears himself saying. "I didn't want to leave them behind."

The void laughs at him. There are miles of empty air beneath his dangling feet. "You had no choice."

"Yes I did! I didn't have to come here." He pauses. "I didn't have to do anything," he says quietly, and inhales another lungful of death. "It was all automatic. Maybe it was inevitable."

"—Evitable," echoes the distant horizon. Something dark and angular skims across the stars, like an echo of extinct pterosaurs. Turbofans whirring within its belly, the F117 hunts on: patrolling to keep at bay the ancient evil, unaware that the battle is already lost. "Your family could still be alive, you know."

He looks up. "They could?" Andrea? Jason? "Alive?"

The void laughs again, unfriendly: "There is life eternal within the eater of souls. Nobody is ever forgotten or allowed to rest in peace. They populate the simulation spaces of its mind, exploring all the possible alternative endings to their life. There is a fate worse than death, you know."

Roger looks at his cigarette disbelievingly: throws it far out into the night sky above the plain. He watches it fall until its ember is no longer visible. Then he gets up. For a long moment he stands poised on the edge of the cliff nerving himself, and thinking. Then he takes a step back, turns, and slowly makes his way back up the trail towards the redoubt on the plateau. If his analysis of the situation is wrong, at least he is still alive. And if he is right, dying would be no escape.

He wonders why Hell is so cold at this time of year.

• ABOUT THE AUTHORS •

Dale Bailey lives in North Carolina with his family and has published three novels, *The Fallen, House of Bones*, and *Sleeping Policemen* (with Jack Slay, Jr.). A fourth novel, *The Clearing*, is in the works. His short fiction, available in *The Resurrection Man's Legacy and Other Stories*, won the International Horror Guild Award, and has been twice nominated for the Nebula Award.

Nathan Ballingrud lives with his daughter in Asheville, NC. His stories have appeared in several places, including *Inferno: New Tales of Terror and the Supernatural, The Del Rey Book of Science Fiction and Fantasy*, and a number of year's best anthologies. He won the Shirley Jackson Award for his short story "The Monsters of Heaven."

Laird Barron's most recent story collection, *Occultation*, and novella *Mysterium Tremendum* both received Shirley Jackson Awards in 2011. An earlier collection, *The Imago Sequence*, was also a Jackson award winner. His fiction has appeared in *Sci Fiction, The Magazine of Fantasy & Science Fiction*, and numerous anthologies and is frequently reprinted in various "year's best" anthologies. He is now at work on his first novel, *The Croning*.

Elizabeth Bear was born on the same day as Frodo and Bilbo Baggins, but in a different year. She is the Hugo and Sturgeon Award-winning author of over a dozen novels and fifty short stories. She lives in Connecticut with a ridiculous dog and a cat who is an internet celebrity.

Steve Duffy's third collection of short supernatural fiction, *Tragic Life Stories*, was published in 2010. A fourth collection, *The Moment of Panic*, is due out soon, and will include the International Horror Guild award-winning short story, "The Rag-and-Bone Men." Duffy lives in North Wales.

Neil Gaiman is the *New York Times* bestselling author of novels *Neverwhere, Stardust, American Gods, Coraline, Anansi Boys, The Graveyard Book*, and (with Terry Pratchett) *Good Omens*; the Sandman series of graphic novels; and the story collections *Smoke and Mirrors* and *Fragile Things*. He has won numerous literary awards including the Hugo, the Nebula, the World Fantasy, and the Stoker Awards, as well as the Newbery medal.

Cody Goodfellow is the author of the Lovecraftian novels *Radiant Dawn* and *Ravenous Dusk*, as well as novel *Perfect Union*. He co-wrote novels *Jake's Wake* and *The Day Before* with John Skipp. His best short fiction is collected in *Silent Weapons for Quiet Wars*.

Caitlín R. Kiernan is the author of several novels, including *Low Red Moon*, *Daughter of Hounds*, and *The Red Tree*, which was nominated for both the Shirley Jackson and World Fantasy awards. Her next novel, *The Drowning Girl: A Memoir*, will be released in 2012. Since 2000, her shorter tales of the weird, fantastic, and macabre have been collected in several volumes, including *Tales of Pain and Wonder*; *From Weird and Distant Shores*; *To Charles Fort, With Love*; *Alabaster*; *A is for Alien*; and *The Ammonite Violin & Others*. A retrospective of her early writing, *Two Worlds and In Between: The Best of Caitlín R. Kiernan (Volume One)* will be published in 2012. She lives in H.P. Lovecraft's beloved Providence, RI, with her partner Kathryn.

David Barr Kirtley's short fiction appears in books such as *New Voices in Science Fiction*, *Fantasy: The Best of the Year*, and *The Living Dead*; in magazines such as *Realms of Fantasy*, *Weird Tales*, *Intergalactic Medicine Show*, and *Lightspeed*; and on podcasts such as Escape Pod and Pseudopod. He's also the co-host, along with John Joseph Adams, of the *Geek's Guide to the Galaxy* podcast on io9.com, an interview and talk show devoted to science fiction and related topics.

Marc Laidlaw is the author of six novels, including the International Horror Guild Award winner, *The 37th Mandala*. His short stories have appeared in numerous magazines and anthologies since the 1970s. In 1997, he joined Valve Software as a writer and creator of *Half-Life*, which has become one of the most popular videogame series of all time. He lives in Washington State with his wife and two daughters, and continues to writes occasional short fiction between playing too many videogames.

John Langan is the author of a novel, *House of Windows*, and a collection of stories, *Mr. Gaunt and Other Uneasy Encounters*. He recently co-edited *Creatures: Thirty Years of Monsters* with Paul Tremblay. Langan lives in upstate New York with his wife, son, dog, and a trio of mutually-suspicious cats.

Before becoming a full-time writer, **Paul McAuley** earned a Ph.D. in botany, worked as a researcher in biology in various universities (including Oxford and UCLA) and as a lecturer in botany at St. Andrews University. His first novel, *Four Hundred Billion Stars*, won the Philip K. Dick Memorial Award; *Fairyland* won Arthur C. Clarke and John W. Campbell Awards. Novel *Pasquale's Angel* was honored with the Sidewise Award, and short story "The Temptation of Dr Stein" earned the British Fantasy Award. He lives in London most of the time.

Nick Mamatas is the author of a few Lovecraftian pieces, including the novels *Move Under Ground* and, with Brian Keene, *The Damned Highway*. His Lovecraftian short pieces have appeared in *Lovecraft Unbound, Dark Wings II*, and *Shotguns vs Cthulhu*. With Ellen Datlow, Nick co-edited an anthology of "true" regional ghost stories, *Haunted Legends,* and currently he edits an imprint of Japanese science fiction and fantasy in translation, Haikasoru. His fiction and editorial work have been nominated for the Bram Stoker award four times, the Hugo award twice, and the World Fantasy, International Horror Guild, and Shirley Jackson awards.

China Miéville is the author of *King Rat; Perdido Street Station,* winner of the Arthur C. Clarke Award and the British Fantasy Award; *The Scar,* winner of the Locus and British Fantasy Awards; *Iron Council,* winner of the Locus and Arthur C. Clarke Awards; *Looking for Jake,* a collection of short stories; *Un Lun Dun,* his *New York Times* bestselling book for younger readers; *The City & The City,* winner of Arthur C. Clarke, Hugo, BSFA, and World Fantasy Awards; his most recent novel is *Kraken. Railsea,* another novel for younger readers, is slated for 2012. He lives and works in London. He wrote the introduction to Lovecraft's *At the Mountains of Madness: The Definitive Edition.*

Sarah Monette lives in a 105-year-old house in the Upper Midwest with a great many books, two cats, and one husband. Her Ph.D. diploma in English Literature hangs in the kitchen. Her first four novels constituted The Doctrine of Labyrinths series. Themed short story collection *The Bone Key,* first published in 2007, was recently republished in a new edition. The newly published *Somewhere Beneath Those Waves* collects other short fiction. She has written two novels (*A Companion to Wolves* and *The Tempering of Men*) and three short stories with Elizabeth Bear. Her novel, *The Goblin Emperor,* will come out under the name Katherine Addison. Visit her online at sarahmonette.com.

Kim Newman is a novelist, critic and broadcaster. His fiction includes *The Night Mayor, Bad Dreams, Jago, The Quorum, The Original Dr Shade and Other Stories, Life's Lottery, Back in the USSA* (with Eugene Byrne) and *The Man From the Diogenes Club* under his own name and *The Vampire Genevieve* and *Orgy of the Blood Parasites* as Jack Yeovil. His nonfiction books include *Ghastly Beyond Belief* (with Neil Gaiman), *Horror: 100 Best Books* (with Stephen Jones), *Wild West Movies, The BFI Companion to Horror, Millennium Movies,* and BFI Classics studies of *Cat People* and *Doctor Who*. Newman's current publications are expanded reissues of the Anno Dracula series and *The Hound of the d'Urbervilles* and a much-expanded edition of *Nightmare Movies*. His website is johnnyalucard.com.

Norman Partridge's fiction includes horror, suspense, and the fantastic— "sometimes all in one story" according to Joe Lansdale. Partridge's novel *Dark Harvest* was chosen by *Publishers Weekly* as one of the 100 Best Books of 2006, and two short story collections were published in 2010—*Lesser Demons* and *Johnny Halloween*. Other work includes the Jack Baddalach mysteries *Saguaro Riptide* and *The Ten-Ounce Siesta*, plus *The Crow: Wicked Prayer*, which was adapted for film. Partridge's work has received multiple Bram Stoker awards. He can be found online at NormanPartridge.com and americanfrankenstein. blogspot.com.

Holly Phillips lives in a small city on a large island off the west coast of Canada. She is the author of the award-winning collection *In the Palace of Repose* and novels *The Burning Girl* and *The Engine's Child*. You can visit her website site at hollyphillips.com.

Lon Prater is a retired Navy officer by day, writer of odd little tales by night. His short fiction has appeared in the Stoker-winning anthology *Borderlands 5, Writers of the Future XXI*, and Origins Award finalist *Frontier Cthulhu*. Prater has written two novels. He is an avid Texas Hold'em player, occasional stunt kite flyer, and connoisseur of history, theme parks and haunted hayrides. To find out more, see lonprater.com.

Tim Pratt's fiction has appeared in *The Best American Short Stories, The Mammoth Book of Best New Horror,* and other nice places. His most recent collection is *Hart & Boot & Other Stories*. His work has won a Hugo Award and been nominated for World Fantasy, Sturgeon, Stoker, Mythopoeic, and

Nebula Awards. He blogs intermittently at timpratt.org, where you can also find links to many of his stories. Pratt is a senior editor at *Locus*, the magazine of the science fiction and fantasy field, and he lives in Berkeley CA with his wife—writer Heather Shaw—and their son.

Cherie Priest is the author of ten novels including *Ganymeade*, *Dreadnought*, and *Boneshaker*—which was nominated for a Nebula Award and a Hugo Award, and won the Locus Award for Best Science Fiction Novel—plus *Bloodshot*, the Eden Moore series, *Clementine*, and *Fathom*.

W.H. Pugmire has been writing Lovecraftian weird fiction since the 1970s, striving to write tales that echo the golden age of *Weird Tales*, yet also revealing his neoteric decadence as outrageous punk rock queer. His books include *The Tangled Muse*, *Some Unknown Gulf of Night*, *The Strange Dark One: Tales of Nyarlathotep*, and *Sesqua Valley and Other Haunts*. He is the Queen of Eldritch Horror.

Michael Shea learned to love the "genres" from the great Jack Vance's *Eyes of the Overworld*, chance-discovered in a flophouse in Juneau when Shea was twenty-one. He tilled the field of sword-and-sorcery for more than a decade (*Quest for Simbilis*, *In Yana the Touch of Undyine*, *Nifft the Lean*). Concurrently he wallowed in the delights of supernatural/extraterrestrial horror, primarily in the novella form, and this remains his genre of choice (as can be seen in the collections *Polyphemus* and *The Autopsy and Other Tales*). In the last decade or so he has added *hommages* to H.P. Lovecraft to his novella work (as in collection *Copping Squid.*) Currently he is writing a trilogy of near-future thrillers. The first, *The Extra* was published last year; its sequel, *Assault on Sunrise* is slated for 2012.

John Shirley's influential novel *Wetbones* blended Lovecraftian supernatural horror with razor-sharp, outlaw street savvy; novel *City Come A-Walkin'* and the A Song Called Youth trilogy (*Eclipse*, *Eclipse Corona*, *Eclipse Penumbra*) were seminal to cyberpunk. Among his many novels are *Demons*, *Bleak History*, and the forthcoming *Everything Is Broken*. His numerous short stories have been collected in eight volumes including the Stoker and International Horror Guild Award-winning *Black Butterflies* and *In Extremis: The Most Extreme Short Stories* of John Shirley. He was co-screenwriter of the film *The Crow*, and has written lyrics for Blue Öyster Cult. His website is john-shirley.com.

Smith is a novelist and screenwriter. As **Michael Marshall Smith** he has published over seventy short stories and three novels—*Only Forward, Spares,* and *One of Us*—winning the Philip K. Dick, International Horror Guild, and August Derleth Awards as well as France's Prix Bob Morane. He has won the British Fantasy Award for Best Short Fiction four times, more than any other author. Writing as Michael Marshall, he has published six best-selling thrillers, including *The Straw Men, The Intruders,* and *Bad Things. The Servants* was published under the name M.M. Smith. His latest Michael Marshall novel is *Killer Move.* He lives in North London with his wife, son, and two cats. His website is michaelmarshallsmith.com

William Browning Spencer is the author of novel *Résumé with Monsters*—which blends soul-destroying Lovecraftian horrors with soul-destroying lousy jobs—as well as the novels *Maybe I'll Call Anna, Zod Wallop,* and *Irrational Fears.* His two short story collections are *The Return of Count Electric and Other Stories* and *The Ocean and All Its Devices.*

Charles Stross is a full-time science fiction writer and resident of Edinburgh, Scotland. The winner of two Locus Reader Awards and two Hugo Awards, Stross has written eighteen novels and two short story collections. His works have been translated into over twelve languages. His Laundry Files novels and novellas have been termed "Lovecraftian near-future techno-SF thrillers."

Don Webb is the author of fifteen novels including *The Double, Essential Saltes,* and *Endless Honeymoon.* He has written over three hundred short stories that have been published in *Year's Best Science Fiction, Year's Best Horror,* and *Year's Best Fantasy,* among others. His story "The Great White Bed" earned an International Horror Guild Award nomination and his "anti-novel," *Uncle Ovid's Exercise Book,* won the Fiction Collective Award. Webb has been writing Lovecraftian fiction for twenty-five years.

About the Editor

Paula Guran is Senior Editor for Prime Books and edits the annual Year's Best Dark Fantasy and Horror series. She edited the Juno fantasy imprint for six years both in its small press incarnation as well as for Pocket Books. Guran has received two Bram Stoker Awards, two International Horror Guild Award Awards, and two World Fantasy Award nominations. She lives in Akron, Ohio.

• ACKNOWLEDGEMENTS •

"The Crevasse" © 2009 by Dale Bailey & Nathan Ballingrud. First Publication: *Lovecraft Unbound*, ed. Ellen Datlow (Dark Horse).

"Old Virginia" © 2003 by Laird Barron. First publication: *The Magazine of Fantasy & Science Fiction*, February 2003.

"Shoggoths in Bloom" © 2008 by Elizabeth Bear. First publication: *Asimov's*, March 2008.

"Mongoose" © 2009 by Elizabeth Bear & Sarah Monette. First Publication: *Lovecraft Unbound*, ed. Ellen Datlow (Dark Horse).

"The Oram County Whoosit" © 2008 by Steve Duffy. First publication: *Shades of Darkness*, eds. Barbara & Christopher Roden (Ash-Tree Press).

"Study in Emerald" © 2003 by Neil Gaiman. First publication: *Shadows Over Baker Street*, ed. Michael Reaves (Del Rey).

"Grinding Rock" © 2003 by Cody Goodfellow. First publication: *Book of Dark Wisdom #5* (January 2005).

"Pickman's Other Model (1929)" © 2008 by Caitlín R. Kiernan. First publication: *Sirenia Digest #28*, March 2008.

"The Disciple" © 2002 by David Barr Kirtley. First publication: *Weird Tales #328* (Summer 2002).

"The Vicar of R'lyeh" © 2007 by Marc Laidlaw. First publication: *Flurb #4*, Fall 2007.

"Mr. Gaunt" © 2002 by John Langan. First publication: *The Magazine of Fantasy & Science Fiction*, September 2002.

"Take Me to the River" © 2005 by Paul McAuley. First publication: *Weird Shadows Over Innsmouth*, ed. Stephen Jones (Fedogan & Bremer).

"The Dude Who Collected Lovecraft" © 2008 by Nick Mamatas & Tim Pratt. First Publication: *ChiZine*, April 2008.